THERAPY

* A NOVEL *

David Lodge

Secker & Warburg
London

First published in England 1995
by Martin Secker & Warburg Limited
Michelin House, 81 Fulham Road, London SW3 6RB

Reprinted 1995 (twice)

Copyright © David Lodge 1995

The author has asserted his moral rights

A CIP catalogue record for this book
is available from the British Library
Hardback ISBN 0 436 20334 0
Paperback ISBN 0 436 20255 7

"Mr Bleaney" from Philip Larkin's *The Whitsun Weddings* is quoted by permission of
Faber & Faber Ltd. "Too Young" (Lippman/Dee) is quoted by permission
Copyright © 1951 Jefferson Music Inc USA Copyright renewed 1979 Aria
Music Company, USA Campbell Connolly & Co Ltd, 8–9 Frith Street London W1
All rights Reserved. International Copyright Secured.

Typeset in 11 point Plantin
by Deltatype Ltd, Ellesmere Port, Cheshire
Printed in Great Britain
by Clays Ltd, St. Ives plc

To Dad, with love

Many people have kindly helped me with the research for and composition of this novel, by answering my questions and/or by reading and commenting on the text. I am especially indebted to Marie Andrews, Bernard and Anne Bergonzi, Izak Winkel Holm, Michael Paul and Martin Shardlow.

The locations of events in this novel are the usual mixture of the real and the imaginary, but the characters and their actions are entirely fictitious, with the possible exception of the writer-presenter of a television documentary briefly mentioned in Part Four.

D.L.

Therapy. The treatment of physical, mental or social disorders or disease.

– Collins English Dictionary

"You know what, Søren? There's nothing the matter with you but your silly habit of holding yourself round-shouldered. Just straighten your back and stand up and your sickness will be over."

– Christian Lund,
uncle of Søren Kierkegaard.

"Writing is a form of therapy."

– Graham Greene

* * ONE * *

RIGHT, here goes.

Monday morning, 15th Feb., 1993. A mild February day has brought the squirrels out of hibernation. The leafless trees in the garden make a kind of adventure playground for them. I watched two playing tag in the chestnuts just outside my study window: spiralling up a trunk, dodging and feinting among the branches, then scampering along a bough and leaping to the next tree, then zooming down the side of its trunk headfirst, freezing halfway, claws sticking like Velcro to the corrugated bark, then streaking across the grass, one trying to shake off the other by jinking and swerving and turning on a sixpence till he reached the bole of a Canadian poplar and they both rocketed up its side into the thin elastic branches and balanced there, swaying gently and blinking contentedly at each other. Pure play – no question. They were just larking about, exercising their agility for the sheer fun of it. If there's such a thing as reincarnation, I wouldn't mind coming back as a squirrel. They must have knee-joints like tempered steel.

The first time I felt the pain was about a year ago. I was leaving the London flat, hurrying to catch the 18.10 from Euston, scuttling backwards and forwards between the four rooms, stuffing scripts and dirty socks into my briefcase, shutting windows, switching off lights, re-setting the central-heating timer, emptying milk cartons down the sink, sloshing Sanilav round the toilet bowl – in short, going through the Before You Leave The Flat hit-list that Sally had written out and stuck on the fridge door with magnetic yellow Smileys, when I felt it: a sharp, piercing pain, like a red-hot needle thrust into the inside of the right knee and then withdrawn, leaving a quickly fading afterburn. I uttered a sharp, surprised cry and keeled over on to the bed (I was in the bedroom at the time). "Christ!" I said, aloud, although I was alone. "What the fuck was that?"

Gingerly I got to my feet. (Should that be "gingerlyly"? No, I've just looked it up, adjective and adverb both have the same form.) Gingerly I got to my feet and tested my weight on the knee, took a few paces forward (funny word actually, nothing to do with ginger, I always thought it meant the way you taste ground ginger, very carefully, dipping a moistened finger into it, and then trying it on the tip of your tongue, but no, it's thought to come from Old French *genson*, dainty, or *gent*, of noble birth, neither of which applies to me). I took a few paces forward without any ill-effects, shrugged, and put it down to some freakish twitch of a nerve, like the sudden excruciating crick you can get in your neck sometimes, twisting round to get something from the back seat of a car. I left the flat, caught my train, and thought no more about it.

About a week later, when I was working in my study, I crossed my legs underneath the desk, and I felt it again, the sudden stab of pain on the inside of the right knee, which made me gasp, sucking in a lungful of air and then expelling it with a resounding "*Fuuuuckinell!*" From then onwards, I began to get the pain with increasing frequency, though there was nothing predictable about it. It rarely happened when I might have expected it, like when I was playing golf or tennis, but it could happen just *after* a game, in the club-house bar, or while driving home, or when I was sitting perfectly still in my study, or lying in bed. It would make me cry out in the middle of the night, so that Sally thought I was having a nightmare. In fact nightmares are about the only thing I don't have, in that line. I have depression, anxiety, panic attacks, night sweats, insomnia, but not nightmares. I never did dream much. Which simply means, I understand, that I don't remember my dreams, because we dream all the time we're asleep, so they say. It's as if there's an unwatched telly flickering all night long inside my head. The Dream Channel. I wish I could make a video recording of it. Maybe I would get a clue then to what's the

4

matter with me. I don't mean my knee. I mean my head. My mind. My soul.

I felt it was a bit hard that I should get a mysterious pain in the knee on top of all my other problems. Admittedly, there are worse things that can happen to you, physically. For instance: cancer, multiple sclerosis, motor neurone disease, emphysema, Alzheimer's and AIDS. Not to mention the things you can be born with, like muscular dystrophy, cerebral palsy, haemophilia and epilepsy. Not to mention war, pestilence and famine. Funny how knowing that doesn't make the pain in your knee any easier to bear.

Perhaps it's what they call "compassion fatigue", the idea that we get so much human suffering thrust in our faces every day from the media that we've become sort of numbed, we've used up all our reserves of pity, anger, outrage, and can only think of the pain in our own knee. I haven't got to that stage yet, not quite, but I know what they mean. I get a lot of charity appeals through the mail. I think they pass names and addresses to each other: you only have to make a donation to one organization and, before you know where you are, the envelopes are falling through the letterbox faster than you can pick them up. OXFAM, CAFOD, UNICEF, Save the Children, Royal Institute for the Blind, Red Cross, Imperial Cancer, Muscular Dystrophy, Shelter, etc. etc., all containing form letters and leaflets printed on recycled paper with smudgy b/w pictures of starving black babies with limbs like twigs and heads like old men, or young kids in wheelchairs, or stunned-looking refugees, or amputees on crutches. How is one supposed to stem this tide of human misery? Well, I'll tell you what I do. I subscribe a thousand pounds a year to an organization that gives you a special cheque book to make donations to the charities of your choice. They also recover the tax you've paid on the money, which bumps it up to £1400 in my case. So every year I dispense fourteen hundred quid in little parcels: £50 for the starving babies of Somalia, £30 for the rape victims in Bosnia, £45 towards a water pump in Bangladesh, £25 to a drug-abuse rehabilitation unit in Basildon, £30 for AIDS research, and so on, until the account is empty. It's rather like trying to mop up the oceans of the world with a box of Kleenex, but it keeps compassion fatigue at bay.

Of course, I could afford to give much more. I could afford *ten* thousand a year from my present income, without too much pain. I could give it all away, for that matter, it still wouldn't be more than a box of Kleenex. So I keep most of it and spend it on, among other things, private medical treatment for my knee.

I went to my GP first. He recommended physiotherapy. After a while, the physiotherapist recommended that I see a consultant. The consultant recommended an arthroscopy. That's a new kind of hi-tech microsurgery, all done by television and fibre-optics. The surgeon pumps water into your leg to create a kind of studio in there, and then sticks three needle-thin instruments into it. One has a camera on the end, another is a cutting tool and the third is a pump for sucking out the debris. They're so fine you can hardly tell the difference between them with the naked eye and the surgeon doesn't even have to put a stitch in the perforations afterwards. He sees what's wrong with your knee-joint by wiggling it about and watching it on a TV monitor, and then cuts away the torn cartilage or tissue or rough bit of bone or whatever it is that's causing the trouble. I'd heard that some patients have just a local anaesthetic and watch the whole operation on the monitor as it's being done, but I didn't fancy that, and said so. Nizar smiled reassuringly. (That's the name of my orthopaedic consultant, Mr Nizar. I call him Knees 'R Us. Not to his face, of course. He's from the Near East, Lebanon or Syria or one of those places, and well out of it from what I hear.) He said I would have a general anaesthetic, but he would give me a videotape of the op to take home. He wasn't joking, either. I knew people had their weddings and christenings and holidays videotaped nowadays instead of photographed, but I didn't know it had got as far as operations. I suppose you could make up a little compilation and invite your friends round to view it over wine and cheese. "*That's my appendectomy, had it done in 1984, or was it '85 . . . neat, eh? . . . And this is my open heart surgery, oops, a little bit of camera-jog there . . . Dorothy's womb-scrape is coming up next . . .*" [Memo: idea for *The People Next*

Door in this?] I said to Nizar, "You could probably run a little video-rental business on the side for folk who haven't had any operations of their own." He laughed. He was very confident about the arthroscopy. He claimed that there was a ninety-five per cent success rate. I suppose somebody's got to be in the unlucky five per cent.

I had the operation done at Rummidge General. Being a private patient I would normally have gone into the Abbey, the BUPA hospital near the cricket ground, but they had a bit of a bottleneck there at the time – they were refurbishing one of their operating theatres or something – and Nizar said he could fit me in quicker if I came into the General, where he works one day a week for the NHS. He promised I would have a room to myself, and as the op entailed staying in for only one night, I agreed. I wanted to get it over and done with as soon as possible.

As soon as I arrived at the General by taxi, at nine o'clock one winter morning, I began to wish I'd waited for a bed at the Abbey. The General is a huge, gloomy Victorian pile, blackened redbrick on the outside, slimy green and cream paint on the inside. The main reception area was already full of rows of people slumped in moulded plastic chairs, with that air of abandoned hope I always associate with NHS hospitals. One man had blood seeping through a bandage wrapped round his forehead. A baby was screaming its head off.

Nizar had given me a scrap of graph paper with his name scrawled on it, and the date and time of my appointment – a ludicrously inadequate document for admission to a hospital, I thought, but the receptionist seemed to recognize it, and directed me to a ward on the third floor. I took the lift and was told off by a sharp-faced nursing sister who stepped in at the first floor and pointed out that it was for the use of hospital staff only. "Where are you going?" she demanded. "Ward 3J," I said. "I'm having a minor operation. Mr Nizar." "Oh," she said with a slight sneer, "You're one of his private patients, are you?" I got the impression she disapproved of private patients being treated in NHS hospitals. "I'm only in for one night," I said, in mitigation. She gave a brief, barking laugh, which unsettled me. It turned out that she was in charge of Ward 3J. I wonder sometimes if she didn't deliberately engineer the harrowing ordeal of the next hour and a half.

There was a row of black plastic chairs up against the wall outside the ward where I sat for about twenty minutes before a thin, drawn-looking young Asian woman, in a house-doctor's white coat, came and wrote down my particulars. She asked me if I had any allergies and tied a dogtag with my name on it to my wrist. Then she led me to a small, two-bed room. There was a man in striped pyjamas lying on one of the beds, with his face to the wall. I was about to protest that I had been promised a private room, when he turned over to look at us and I saw that he was black, probably Caribbean. Not wishing to appear racist, I swallowed my complaint. The house-doctor ordered me to take off all my clothes and to put on one of those hospital nightgowns that open down the back, which was lying folded on top of the vacant bed. She told me to remove any false teeth, glass eyes, artificial limbs or other such accessories I might be secreting on my person, and then left me. I undressed and put on the gown, watched enviously by the Caribbean. He told me he had been admitted three days ago, for a hernia operation, and nobody had come near him since. He seemed to have dropped into some kind of black hole in the system.

I sat on the edge of the bed in my gown, feeling the draught up my legs. The Caribbean turned his face to the wall again and seemed to fall into a light sleep, groaning and whimpering to himself occasionally. The young Asian house-doctor came back into the room and checked the name on my dogtag against her notes as if she had never met me before. She asked me again if I had any allergies. I was rapidly losing faith in this hospital. "That man says he has been here three days and nobody has taken any notice of him," I said. "Well, at least he's had some sleep," said the house-doctor, "which is more than I've had for the last thirty-six hours." She left the room again. Time passed very slowly. A low winter sun shone through the dusty window. I watched the shadow of the window-frame inch its way across the linotiled floor. Then a nurse and a porter pushing a stretcher on wheels came to fetch me to the operating theatre. The porter was a young local man with a poker-player's pallid, impassive face, and the nurse a buxom Irish girl whose starched uniform seemed a size too small for her, giving her a slightly tarty look. The porter tossed me the usual local greeting – "A'right?" – and told me to hop on to the stretcher. I said, "I could walk, you know, in a dressing-gown. I'm not in any actual pain." In fact I hadn't felt a single twinge in the knee for over a week, which is pretty typical of all such ailments: as soon as you decide to have treatment, the symptoms disappear. "No, you've got to be wheeled," he said. "Regulations." Carefully holding the flaps of my gown together like an Edwardian lady adjusting her bustle, I mounted the stretcher and lay down. The nurse asked me if I was nervous. "Should I be?" I asked. She giggled but made no comment. The porter checked the name on my dogtag. "Passmore, yes. Right leg amputation, ennit?" "No!" I exclaimed, sitting up in alarm. "Just a minor knee operation." "He's only having you on," said the nurse. "Stop it, Tom." "Just pulling your leg," said Tom, deadpan. They covered me with a blanket and tucked it in, pinning my arms to my sides. "Stops you getting knocked as we go through the swing doors," Tom explained. The Caribbean woke up and raised himself on one elbow to watch me go. "So long," I said. I never saw him again.

You feel curiously helpless when you're lying on your back on a stretcher without a pillow under your head. You can't tell where you are or where you're going. All you can see is ceilings, and the ceilings of the General Hospital weren't a pretty sight: cracked plaster, flaking emulsion, cobwebs in corners and dead flies in the lighting fixtures. We seemed to be travelling through miles and miles of corridors. "Got to take the scenic route today," Tom remarked from behind my head. "Theatre lift's broke, ennit? Have to take you down to the basement by the utilities lift and then across to the other wing, then up the other lift and back over again." The utilities lift was industrial-size: cavernous, dimly lit and smelling faintly of boiled cabbage and laundry. As I was pushed over the threshold the wheels caught on something and I found myself staring up into the space between the lift and the shaft at the black greasy cables and grooved wheels of the ancient-looking machinery. It was like being in one of those arty-farty movies where everything is shot from unnatural angles.

Tom clashed the folding gate shut, the nurse pressed a button and the lift began to descend very slowly with much creaking and groaning. Its ceiling was even more depressing than the ceilings of the corridors. My companions conducted a desultory conversation out of my sight. "Got a smoke on you?" said the nurse. "No," said Tom, "I've given it up. Gave it up last Tuesday." "Why?" "Health." "What d'you do instead?" "Lots and lots of sex," said Tom levelly. The nurse giggled. "I'll tell you a secret, though," said Tom. "I hid cigarettes all over the hospital when I gave up, in case I get desperate. There's one in the basement." "What kind is it?" "Benson's. You can have it if you like." "Alright," said the nurse, "thanks." The lift stopped with a jolt.

The air in the basement was hot and dry from the central-heating plant, and I began to perspire under the blanket as Tom pushed me between walls of cartons and boxes and bins of hospital supplies. Cobwebs hung thickly from the vaulted ceiling like batshit. The wheels jolted over the stone-flagged floor, jarring my spine. Tom stopped for a minute to ferret for one of his hidden cigarettes. He and the nurse disappeared behind a mountainous bale of laundry, and I heard a little squeal and scuffle which suggested he had exacted a favour in return for the Benson and Hedges. I couldn't believe what was happening to me. How could a private patient be subjected to such indignities? It was as if I'd paid for Club Class and found myself in a broken seat at the back of the plane next to the toilet with smokers coughing in my face (metaphorically speaking – the nurse didn't have the nerve to actually light up). What made it worse was knowing that I'd get no sympathy from Sally when I told her the story: she disapproves of private medicine on principle and refused to join BUPA when I did.

We moved on again, twisting and turning through the labyrinth of stores, until we reached another, similar lift on the far side of the enormous basement, and rose slowly back into daylight. There was another long journey through more corridors – then suddenly everything changed. I passed through swing doors from the nineteenth century to the twentieth, from Victorian Gothic to hi-tech modern. It was like stepping on to a brightly lit, elegant studio set after stumbling about in the dark, cable-encumbered space at the back of a sound stage. Everything was white and silver, stainless and gleaming in the diffused light, and the medical staff welcomed me with kind smiles and soft, cultured voices. I was deftly lifted off the stretcher and onto another, more sophisticated mobile bed, on which I was wheeled into an anteroom where the anaesthetist was waiting. He asked me to flex my left hand, and warned me in soothing tones to expect a slight prick as he inserted a kind of plastic valve into a vein in my arm. Nizar sauntered into the room, swathed in pale blue theatre overalls and wearing a snood over his hair, looking like a plump pyjama-clad housewife who had just risen from her bed and hadn't taken her curlers out yet. " 'Morning, old bean," he greeted me. "Everything tickety-boo?" Nizar speaks immaculate English, but I think he must have read a lot of P. G. Wodehouse once. I was about to say, no, it hadn't been at all tickety-boo so far, but this didn't seem the right moment to complain about my reception. Besides, a warm drowsy feeling of well-being was beginning to come over me. Nizar was looking at X-rays of my knee, holding them up before a lighted screen. "Ah yes," he murmured to himself, as if vaguely recognizing a snapshot of some fleeting acquaintance from the past. He came over and stood at the side of the bed opposite the anaesthetist. They smiled down at me. "A hand-joiner," the anaesthetist commented. What was he implying, I wondered. My blanket had been removed, and not knowing what else to with my hands I had clasped them on my stomach. The anaesthetist patted my hands. "That's good, very good," he said reassuringly. "Some people clench their fists, bite their nails." Nizar lifted the hem of my gown and squeezed my knee. I sniggered and was about to make a joke about sexual harassment when I passed out.

When I came round, I was back in the two-bedded room but the Caribbean man had gone, nobody could tell me where. My right leg, swaddled in bandages, was as big as an elephant's. Sally, who visited me on her way home from work, thought it looked very funny. As I anticipated, I got no sympathy when I described my morning. "Serves you right for queue-jumping," she said. "My Auntie Emily has been waiting two years for a hip operation." Nizar came in later and asked me to lift my leg gently a few inches off the bed. I did it very gently – gingerly, you might say – without adverse effect, and he seemed satisfied. "Jolly good," he said, "spiffing."

After a few days on crutches, waiting for the swelling to subside, and several weeks of physiotherapy and controlled exercise to get the quadriceps back to strength, I started to get the same intermittent pain as before. *Fuuuuuuckinell!* I couldn't believe it. Nizar couldn't believe it either. He reckoned he'd identified the trouble – a bit of tissue called plica that was getting nipped in the knee joint – and cut it away. We watched the video of my operation together on the TV in his office. I hadn't been able to bring myself to watch it before. It was a brightly lit, coloured, circular image, like looking through the porthole of a submarine with a powerful searchlight. "There it is, you see!" cried Nizar. All I could see was what looked like a slim silvery eel biting chunks out of the soft underside of a shellfish. The little steel jaws snapped viciously and fragments of my knee floated off to be sucked out by the aspirator. I couldn't watch for long. I always was squeamish about violence on television.

"Well?" I said, when Nizar switched off the video. "Well, frankly old bean, I'm baffled," he said. "You saw for yourself the plica that was causing the trouble, and you saw me cut it away. There's no evidence of torn meniscus or arthritic degeneration of the joint. There's no bally reason why the knee should be giving you any more pain."

"But it is," I said.

"Yes, quite so. It's jolly annoying."

"Particularly for me," I said.

"It must be idiopathic patella chondromalacia," said Nizar. When I asked him to explain he said, "Patella chondromalacia means pain in the knee, and idiopathic means it's peculiar to you, old boy." He smiled as if awarding me a prize.

I asked him what could be done about it, and he said, rather less confidently than before, that he could do another arthroscopy, to see if he had by any chance missed something in the first one, or I could try aspirins and physiotherapy. I said I would try aspirins and physiotherapy.

"Of course, I'd do it in the BUPA hospital next time," he said. He was aware that I had been less than enchanted with the standard of care at the General.

"Even so," I said. "I'm not rushing into another operation."

When I told Roland – that's the name of my physiotherapist – when I told Roland the substance of this consultation, he gave his sardonic lopsided smile and said, "You've got Internal Derangement of the Knee. That's what the orthopaedic surgeons call it amongst themselves. Internal Derangement of the Knee. I.D.K. I Don't Know."

Roland is blind, by the way. That's another thing that can happen to you that's worse than a pain in the knee. Blindness.

Tuesday afternoon, 16th Feb. Immediately after writing that last bit yesterday I thought I would try shutting my eyes for a bit, to give myself an idea of what it would be like to be blind, and remind myself how lucky I am compared to poor old Roland. I actually went so far as to blindfold myself, with a sleeping mask British Airways gave me once on a flight from Los Angeles. I thought I would see what it was like to do something quite simple and ordinary, like making a cup of tea, without being able to see. The experiment didn't last long. Trying to get out of the study and into the kitchen I cracked my knee, the right one needless to say, against the open drawer of a filing cabinet. I tore off the blindfold and hopped round the room cursing and blaspheming so terribly I finally shocked myself into silence. I was sure I'd done my knee in for good. But after a while the pain wore off, and this morning the joint doesn't seem to be any worse than it was before. No better, either, of course.

There's one advantage of having Internal Derangement of the Knee, and that is, when people ring you up, and ask you how you are, and you don't want to say, "terminally depressed," but don't feel like pretending that you're brimming over with happiness either, you can always complain about your knee. My agent, Jake Endicott, just called to confirm our lunch appointment tomorrow, and I gave him an earful about the knee first. He's having a meeting with the people at Heartland this afternoon to discuss whether they're going to commission another series of *The People Next Door*. I delivered the last script of the present series only a few weeks ago, but these things have to be decided long in advance, because the actors' contracts will be coming up for renewal soon. Jake is confident that Heartland will commission at least one more series, and probably two. "With audience figures like you're getting, they'd be crazy not to." He said he would tell me the upshot of his meeting at lunch tomorrow. He's taking me to Groucho's. He always does.

It's a year since my arthroscopy, and I'm still getting pain. Should I risk another operation? I Don't Know. I can't decide. I can't make a decision about anything these days. I couldn't decide what tie to wear this morning. If I can't make a decision about a little thing like a tie, how can I make my mind up about an operation? I hesitated so long over my tie-rack that I was in danger of being late for my appointment with Alexandra. I couldn't decide between a dark, conservative tie or a bright, splashy one. Eventually I narrowed the choice down to a plain navy knitted job from Marks and Sparks and an Italian silk number hand-painted in orange, brown and red. But then neither of them seemed to go with the shirt I was wearing, so I had to change that. Time was running out: I put the silk tie round my neck and stuffed the woollen one into my jacket pocket in case I had second thoughts on my way over to Alexandra's office. I did, too – changed over to the knitted tie at a red light. Alexandra is my shrink, my current shrink. Dr Alexandra Marbles. No, her real name is Marples. I call her Marbles for a joke. If she ever moves or retires, I'll be able to say I've lost my Marbles. She doesn't know I call her that, but she wouldn't mind if she did. She *would* mind if she knew I referred to her as my shrink, though. She doesn't describe herself as a psychiatrist, you see, but as a cognitive behaviour therapist.

I have a lot of therapy. On Mondays I see Roland for Physiotherapy, on Tuesdays I see Alexandra for Cognitive Behaviour Therapy, and on Fridays I have either aromatherapy or acupuncture. Wednesdays and Thursdays I'm usually in London, but then I see Amy, which is a sort of therapy too, I suppose.

What's the difference between a psychiatrist and a cognitive behaviour therapist? Well, as I understand it, a psychiatrist tries to uncover the hidden cause of your neurosis, whereas the cognitive behaviour therapist treats the symptoms that are making you miserable. For instance, you might suffer from claustrophobia in buses and trains, and a psychiatrist would try to discover some traumatic experience in your previous life that caused it. Say you were sexually assaulted as a child in a train when it went through a tunnel or something like that, by a man who was sitting next to you – say he interfered with you while it was dark in the compartment because of the tunnel and you were terrified and ashamed and didn't dare accuse the man when the train came out of the tunnel and never even told your parents or anyone about it afterwards but suppressed the memory completely. Then if the psychiatrist could get you to remember that experience and see that it wasn't your fault, you wouldn't suffer from the claustrophobia any more. That's the theory, anyway. The trouble is, as cognitive behaviour therapists point out, it can take for ever to discover the suppressed traumatic experience, even supposing there was one. Take Amy, for instance. She's been in analysis for three years, and she sees her shrink *every day*, Monday to Friday, nine to nine-fifty every morning on her way to work. Imagine how much it's costing her. I asked her once how she would know when she was cured. She said, "When I don't feel the need to see Karl any more." Karl is her shrink, Dr Karl Kiss. If you ask me, Karl is on to a good thing.

So a cognitive behaviour therapist would probably give you a programme for conditioning yourself to travelling by public transport, like going round the Inner Circle on the Tube, travelling for just one stop the first time, then two, then three, and so on, in the off-peak time for starters, then in the rush hour, rewarding yourself each time you increased the length of your journey with some kind of treat, a drink or a meal or a new tie, whatever turns you on – and you're so pleased with your own achievements and these little presents to yourself that you forget to be frightened and finally wake up to the fact that there is nothing to be frightened *of*. That's the theory, anyway. Amy wasn't impressed when I tried to explain it to her. She said, "But supposing one day you got raped on the Inner Circle?" She's rather literal-minded, Amy.

Mind you, people do get raped on the Inner Circle, these days. Even men.

It was my GP who referred me to Alexandra. "She's very good," he assured me. "She's very practical. Doesn't waste time poking around in your unconscious, asking you about potty training, or whether you saw your parents having it off together, that sort of thing." I was relieved to hear that. And Alexandra has certainly been a help. I mean the breathing exercises are quite effective, for about five minutes after I've done them. And I always feel calmer after I've seen her, for at least a couple of hours. She specializes in something called rational-emotive therapy, RET for short. The idea is to get the patient to see that his fears or phobias are based on an incorrect or unwarranted interpretation of the facts. In a way I know that already, but it helps to have Alexandra spell it out. There are times, though, when I hanker after a bit of old-fashioned Viennese analysis, when I almost envy Amy her daily Kiss. (The guy's name is actually pronounced "Kish", he's Hungarian, but I prefer to call him "Kiss".) The thing is, I wasn't always unhappy. I can remember a time when I was happy. Reasonably content anyway. Or at least, a time when I didn't think I was *un*happy, which is perhaps the same thing as being happy. Or reasonably content. But somewhere, sometime, I lost it, the knack of just living, without being anxious and depressed. How? I Don't Know.

"So how are you today?" Alexandra said, as she always does at the beginning of our sessions. We sit facing each other across ten feet of deep-pile pale grey carpet in two easy chairs, in her handsome, high-ceilinged office, which, apart from the antique desk by the window, and a tall functional filing cabinet in one corner, is furnished more like a drawing-room. The chairs are placed each side of a fireplace, where a gas fire made of imitation coals burns cheerfully throughout the winter months, and a vase of freshly cut flowers stands in the summer. Alexandra is tall and slim, and wears graceful, flowing clothes: silk shirts and pleated skirts of fine wool long enough to cover her knees demurely when she sits down. She has a narrow, fine-boned face on top of a very long, slender neck, and her hair is drawn back in a tight bun, or is it chignon? Imagine a rather beautiful, long-lashed female giraffe drawn by Walt Disney.

I began by telling her of my pathological indecision over the ties. "Pathological?" she said. "What makes you use that word?" She's always picking me up on negative words I use about myself.

"Well, I mean, a *tie*, for God's sake! I wasted half an hour of my life anguishing about . . . I mean, how trivial can you get?"

Alexandra asked me why I had found it so difficult to decide between the two ties.

"I thought, if I wore the plain dark blue one you would take it as a sign that I was depressed, or rather as a sign that I was *giving in* to my depression, instead of fighting it. But when I put on the bright one, I thought you would take it as a sign that I'd got over my depression, but I haven't. It seemed to me that whichever tie I wore would be a kind of lie." Alexandra smiled, and I experienced that deceptive lift of the spirits that often comes in therapy when you give a neat answer, like a clever kid in school.

"You could have dispensed with a tie altogether."

"I considered that. But I always wear a tie to these sessions. It's an old habit. It's how I was brought up: always dress properly when you're going to the doctor's. If I suddenly stopped wearing a tie you might think it signified something – disrespect, dissatisfaction – and I'm not dissatisfied. Well, only with myself."

A few weeks ago Alexandra got me to write a short description of myself. I found it quite an interesting exercise. I suppose it was what got me going on the idea of writing this . . . whatever it is. Journal. Diary. Confession. Up till now, I've always written exclusively in dramatic form – sketches, scripts, screenplays. Of course, there's a bit of description in every TV script – stage directions, notes on characters for the casting director ("*JUDY is a good-looking bottle-blonde in her twenties*"), but nothing detailed, nothing analytical, apart from the lines. That's what TV is – all lines. The lines people speak and the lines of the cathode-ray tube that make up the picture. Everything's either in the picture, which tells you where you are, or in the dialogue, which tells you what the characters are thinking and feeling, and often you don't even need words for *that* – a shrug of the shoulders, a widening of the eyes will do it. Whereas if you're writing a book, you've got nothing but words for everything: behaviour, looks, thoughts, feelings, the whole boiling. I take my hat off to book writers, I do honestly.

✳ Laurence Passmore ✳

A SELF-DESCRIPTION

I AM FIFTY-EIGHT YEARS OLD, five feet nine-and-a-half inches tall and thirteen stone eight pounds in weight – which is two stone more than it should be according to the table in our dog-eared copy of *The Family Book of Health*. I didn't acquire the nickname "Tubby" until I was a National Serviceman in the Army, after which it stuck. But I was always a bit on the heavy side for my height, even when I played football as a youth, with a barrel-shaped torso that curved gently outwards from the chest to the point where shirt met shorts. My stomach was all muscle in those days, and useful for bustling opposing players off the ball, but as I got older, in spite of regular exercise, the muscle turned to flab and then spread to my hips and bum, so now I'm more pear-shaped than barrel-shaped. They say that inside every fat man there's a thin man struggling to get out, and I hear his stifled groans every time I look into the bathroom mirror. It's not just the shape of my torso that bothers me, either, and it's not just the torso, come to that. My chest is covered with what looks like a doormat-sized Brillo pad that grows right up to my Adam's apple: if I wear an open-necked shirt, wiry tendrils sprout from the top like some kind of fast-growing fungus from outer space in an old Nigel Kneale serial. And by a cruel twist of genetic fate I have practically no hair *above* the Adam's apple. My pate is as bald as an electric light bulb, like my father's, apart from a little fringe around the ears, and at the nape, which I wear very long, hanging down over my collar. It looks a bit tramp-like, but I can hardly bear to have it cut, each strand is so precious. I hate to see it falling on to the barber-shop floor – I feel they should put it in a paper bag for me to take home. I tried to grow a moustache once, but it turned out rather funny-looking, grey on one side and a sort of gingery-brown on the other, so I shaved it off quick. I considered growing a beard, but I was afraid it would look like a continuation of my chest. So there's nothing to disguise the ordinariness of my face: a pink, puffy oval, creased and wrinkled like a slowly deflating balloon, with pouchy cheeks, a fleshy, slightly bulbous nose and two rather sad-looking watery-blue eyes. My teeth are nothing to write home about, either, but they are my own, the ones you can see anyway (I have a bridge on the lower right-hand side where a few molars are missing). My neck is as thick as a tree-trunk, but my arms are rather short, making it difficult to buy shirts that fit. For most of my life I put up with shirts with cuffs that fell down over my hands as far as the knuckle unless restrained by a long-sleeved sweater or elastic bands round the elbows. Then I went to America where they have discovered that some men have arms shorter than average (in Britain for some reason you are only allowed to have arms that are longer than average) and bought a dozen shirts at Brooks Brothers with 32″ sleeves. I top up my wardrobe from an American mail-order firm that started trading in England a few years ago. Of course, I could afford to have my shirts made to measure nowadays, but the snobby-looking shops around Picadilly where they do it put me off and the striped poplins in the windows are too prim for my taste. In any case, I can't stand shopping. I'm an impatient bloke. At least, I am now. I used not to be. Queuing, for instance. When I was young, queuing was a way of life, I thought nothing of it. Queuing for buses, queuing for the pictures, queuing in shops. Nowadays I hardly ever ride on a bus, I watch most movies at home on video, and if I go into a shop and there are more than two people waiting to be served, more likely than not I'll turn round and walk straight out. I'd rather do without whatever I came for. I especially hate banks and post offices where they have those cordoned-off lanes like Airport Immigration where you have to shuffle slowly forward in line and when you get to the head of the queue you have to keep swivelling your head to see which counter is the first to be free, and more likely than not you don't spot it and some clever dick behind you nudges you in the kidneys and says, "Your turn, mate." I do as much of my banking as possible by a computerized phoneline system nowadays, and I send most of my letters by fax, or have Datapost call at the house if I have a script to mail, but occasionally I need some stamps and have to go and stand in one of those long Post Office queues with a lot of old biddies and single parents with snuffling infants in pushchairs waiting to collect their pensions and income support, and I can hardly restrain myself from shouting, "Isn't it about time we had a counter for people who just want to buy stamps? Who want to *post* things? After all, this *is* a Post Office, isn't it?" That's just a figure of speech, of course, I can restrain myself very easily, I wouldn't dream of shouting anything at all in a public place, but that's the way I feel. I never show my feelings much. Most people who know me would be surprised if I told them I was impatient. I have a reputation in the TV world for being rather placid, unflappable, for keeping my cool when all around are losing theirs. They'd be surprised to learn that I was unhappy with my physique, too. They think I like being called Tubby. I tried dropping a hint once or twice that I wouldn't mind being called Laz instead, but it didn't catch on. The only parts of my body that I'm reasonably pleased with are the extremities, the hands and feet. My feet are quite small, size seven, and narrow, with a high instep. They look good in the Italian shoes I buy more frequently than is strictly necessary. I was always light on my feet, considering the bulk they have to support, a nifty dribbler of a football and not a bad ballroom dancer. I move about the house very quietly, sometimes making my wife jump when she turns round and finds me right behind her. My hands are quite small too, but with long, shapely fingers like a pianist's, not that I can play any keyboard except an IBM one.

✳ ✳ ✳ ✳ ✳ ✳ ✳ ✳ ✳ ✳ ✳ ✳ ✳ ✳ ✳ ✳ ✳ ✳

I gave this self-description to Alexandra and she glanced at it and said, "Is this all?" I said it was the longest piece of continuous prose I'd written in years. She said, "It hasn't any paragraphs, why is that?" and I explained that I was out of practice in writing paragraphs, I was used to writing lines, speeches, so my self-description had come out as a kind of monologue. I said: "I can only write as if I'm speaking to someone." (It's true. Take this journal for example – I've no intention of letting anybody else read it, but I can only write it as if it's addressed to a "you". I've no idea who "you" is. Just an imaginary, sympathetic ear.) Alexandra put my self-description away in a drawer to read later. At our next meeting she said it was interesting but very negative. "It's mostly about what's wrong with your body, or what you think is wrong with it, and even the two good points you mention, your hands and your feet, are undercut by the references to buying too many shoes and not being able to play the piano." Alexandra thinks I'm suffering from lack of self-esteem. She's probably right, though I read in the paper that there's a lot of it about. There's something like an epidemic of lack of self-esteem in Britain at the moment. Maybe it has something to do with the recession. Not in my case, though. I'm not in recession. I'm doing fine. I'm well-off. I'm almost rich. *The People Next Door*, which has been running for five years, is watched by thirteen million people every week, and there's an American adaptation which is just as successful, and other foreign-language versions all round the globe. Money from these sub-licences pours into my bank account like water from a running tap. So what's the matter with me? Why aren't I satisfied? I don't know.

Alexandra says it's because I'm a perfectionist. I demand impossibly high standards from myself, so I'm bound to be disappointed. There may be some truth in that. Most people in show business are perfectionists. They may be producing crap, acting in crap, writing crap, but they try and make it *perfect* crap. That's the essential difference between us and other people. If you go into the Post Office to buy stamps, the clerk doesn't aim to give you perfect service. Efficient, maybe, if you're lucky, but perfect – no. Why should he try? What's the point? There's no difference between one first-class stamp and another, and there's a very limited number of ways in which you can tear them off the sheets and shove them across the counter. He does the same transactions, day in, day out, year in, year out, he's trapped on a treadmill of repetition. But there's something special about every single episode of a sitcom, however trite and formulaic it may be, and that's for two reasons. The first is that nobody *needs* a sitcom, like they sooner or later need postage stamps, so its only justification for existing is that it gives pleasure, and it won't do that if it's exactly the same as last week's. The second reason is that everyone involved is aware of the first reason, and knows that they'd better make it as good as it possibly can be, or they'll be out of a job. You'd be surprised how much collective effort and thought goes into every line, every gesture, every reaction shot. In rehearsals, right up to recording, everybody's thinking: how can we sharpen this, improve that, get an extra laugh there . . . Then the critics slag you off with a couple of snide sentences. That's the one drawback of television as a medium: television critics. You see, although I'm lacking in self-esteem, that doesn't mean to say that I don't want to be esteemed by others. In fact I get pretty depressed if they don't esteem me. But I get depressed anyway, because I don't esteem myself. I want everybody to think I'm perfect, while not believing it myself. Why? I don't know. I.D.K.

Early on in my treatment, Alexandra told me to take a sheet of paper and write down a list of all the good things about my life in one column and all the bad things in another. Under the "Good" column I wrote:

1. Professionally successful
2. Well-off
3. Good health
4. Stable marriage
5. Kids successfully launched in adult life
6. Nice house
7. Great car
8. As many holidays as I want.

Under the "Bad" column I wrote just one thing:

1. Feel unhappy most of the time.

A few weeks later I added another item:

2. Pain in knee.

It's not so much the pain itself that gets me down as the way it limits my scope for physical exercise. Sport used to be my chief form of therapy, though I didn't call it that. I just enjoyed hitting and kicking and chasing balls about – always did, ever since I was a kid playing in a London backstreet. I suppose I got a charge from showing that I was better at it than people expected me to be – that my thick, ungainly body was capable of a surprising agility, and even grace, when it had a ball to play with. (There has to be a ball: without one I'm about as graceful as a hippopotamus.) Of course it's common knowledge that sport is a harmless way of discharging tension, sluicing adrenalin through the system. But best of all, it helps you sleep. I don't know anything like that glowing, aching tiredness you feel after a keen game of squash or eighteen holes of golf or five sets of tennis, the luxury of stretching out your limbs between the sheets when you go to bed, knowing you're just about to slide effortlessly into a long, deep sleep. Sex is nowhere near as effective. It will send you off for a couple of hours, but that's about all. Sally and I made love last night (at her suggestion, it usually is these days) and I fell asleep immediately afterwards, as if I'd been sandbagged, with her naked in my arms. But I woke at 2.30 feeling chilly and wide awake, with Sally breathing quietly beside me in one of the oversized T-shirts she uses for nighties, and although I went for a pee and put on my pyjamas, I couldn't get back to sleep. I just lay there with my mind spinning – spiralling, I should say, down and down into the dark. Bad thoughts. Gloomy thoughts. My knee was throbbing – I suppose the sex had set it off – and I began to wonder whether it wasn't the first sign of bone cancer and how I'd cope with having my leg amputated if this was how I coped with a mere Internal Derangement of the Knee.

That's the sort of thought that comes to you in the middle of the night. I hate these involuntary vigils, lying awake in the dark with Sally calmly asleep beside me, wondering whether I should turn on the bedside lamp and read for a while, or go downstairs and make a hot drink, or take a sleeping pill, buying a few hours' oblivion at the cost of feeling next day as if my bone marrow has been siphoned off in the night and replaced with lead. Alexandra says I should read till I'm sleepy again, but I don't like to turn on my bedside lamp in case it disturbs Sally and in any case Alexandra says you should get up and read in another room, but I can't face going downstairs into the silent, empty living space of the house, like an intruder in my own home. So usually I just lie there, as I did last night, hoping to drop off, twisting and turning in the effort to find a comfortable position. I snuggled up to Sally for a while, but she got too hot and pushed me away in her sleep. So then I tried hugging myself, with my arms crossed tightly over my chest, each hand grasping the opposite shoulder, like a man in a strait-jacket. That's what I ought to wear instead of pyjamas, if you ask me.

✳ ✳ ✳ ✳ ✳ ✳ ✳ ✳ ✳ ✳ ✳ ✳ ✳ ✳ ✳ ✳ ✳ ✳

Wednesday 17th Feb. 2.05 a.m. Tonight we didn't have sex and I woke even earlier: 1.40. I stared appalled at the red figures on the LCD of my alarm clock, which cast a hellish glow on the polished surface of the bedside cabinet. I decided to try getting up this time, and swung my feet to the floor and felt for my slippers before I had a chance to change my mind. Downstairs I pulled a jogging-suit over my pyjamas and made a pot of tea which I carried into my study. And here I am, sitting in front of the computer, tapping out this. Where was I yesterday? Oh, yes. Sport.

Roland says I shouldn't do any sport until the symptoms have disappeared, with or without another operation. I'm allowed to work out on some of the machines in the Club's multi-gym, the ones that don't involve the knee, and I can swim as long as I don't do the breast-stroke – the frog kick is bad for the knee-joint, apparently. But I never did like working out – it bears the same relation to real sport as masturbation does to real sex, if you ask me; and as for swimming, the breast-stroke happens to be the only one I can do properly. Squash is right out, for obvious reasons. Golf too, unfortunately: the lateral twist on the right knee at the follow-through of the swing is lethal. But I do play a bit of tennis still, wearing a kind of brace on the knee which keeps it more or less rigid. I have to sort of drag the right leg like Long John Silver when I hop around the court, but it's better than nothing.

They have indoor courts at the Club, and anyway you can play outdoors nearly all the year round with these mild winters we've been having – it seems to be one of the few beneficial effects of global warming.

I play with three other middle-aged cripples at the Club. There's Joe, he's got serious back trouble, wears a corset all the time and can barely manage to serve overarm; Rupert, who was in a bad car crash a few years ago and limps with both legs, if that's possible; and Humphrey, who has arthritis in his feet and a plastic hip-joint. We exploit each other's handicaps mercilessly. For instance, if Joe is playing against me up at the net I'll return high because I know he can't lift his racket above his head, and if I'm defending the baseline he'll keep switching the direction of his returns from one side of the court to the other because he knows I can't move very fast with my brace. It would bring tears to your eyes to watch us, of either laughter or pity.

Naturally I can't partner Sally in mixed doubles any more, which is a great shame because we used to do rather well in the Club veterans' tournaments. Sometimes she'll knock up with me, but she won't play a singles game because she says I'd do my knee in trying to win, and she's probably right. I usually beat her when I was fit, but now she's improving her game while I languish. I was down at the Club the other day with my physically-challenged peer group when she turned up, having come straight from work for a spot of coaching. It gave me quite a surprise, actually, when she walked along the back of the indoor court with Brett Sutton, the Club coach, because I wasn't expecting to see her there. I didn't know that she'd arranged the lesson, or more likely she'd told me and I hadn't taken in it. That's become a worrying habit of mine lately: people talk to me and I go through the motions of listening and responding, but when they finish I realize I haven't taken in a single word, because I've been following some train of thought of my own. It's another type of Internal Derangement. Sally gets pissed off when she twigs it – understandably – so when she waved casually to me through the netting, I waved back casually in case I was supposed to know that she had arranged to have coaching that afternoon. In fact there was a second or two when I didn't recognize her – just registered her as a tall, attractive-looking blonde. She was wearing a shocking-pink and white shell suit I hadn't seen before, and I'm still not used to her new hair. One day just before Christmas she went out in the morning grey and came back in the afternoon gold. When I asked her why she hadn't warned me, she said she wanted to see my unrehearsed reaction. I said it looked terrific. If I didn't sound over the moon, it was sheer envy. (I've tried several treatments for baldness without success. The last one consisted of hanging upside down for minutes on end to make the blood rush to your head. It was called Inversion Therapy.) When I sussed it was her down at the tennis club, I felt a little glow of proprietorial pride in her lissome figure and bouncing golden locks. The other guys noticed her too.

"You want to watch your missus, Tubby," said Joe, as we changed ends between games. "By the time you're fit again, she'll be running rings round you."

"You reckon?" I said.

"Yeah, he's a good coach. Good at other things too, I've heard." Joe winked at the other two, and of course Humphrey backed him up.

"He's certainly got the tackle. I saw him in the showers the other day. It must be a ten-incher."

"How d'you measure up to that, Tubby?"

"You'll have to raise your game."

"You'll get yourself arrested one day, Humphrey," I said. "Ogling blokes in the showers." The others hooted with laughter.

This kind of joshing is standard between us four. No harm in it. Humphrey's a bachelor, lives with his mother and doesn't have a girlfriend, but nobody supposes for a moment that he's gay. If we did, we wouldn't wind him up about it. Likewise with the innuendo about Brett Sutton and Sally. It's a stock joke that all the women in the club wet their knickers at the sight of him – he's tall, dark, and handsome enough to wear his hair in a ponytail without looking like a ponce – but nobody believes any real hanky-panky goes on.

For some reason I remembered this conversation as we were going to bed tonight, and relayed it to Sally. She sniffed and said, "Isn't it a bit late in the day for you lot to be worrying about the size of your willies?"

I said that for a really dedicated worrier it was never too late.

One thing I've never worried about, though, is Sally's fidelity. We've had our ups and downs, of course, in nearly thirty years of marriage, but we've always been faithful to each other. Not for lack of opportunity, I may say, at least on my side, the entertainment world being what it is, and I daresay on hers too, though I can't believe that she's exposed to the same occupational temptations. Her colleagues at the Poly, or rather University as I must learn to call it now, don't look much of an erotic turn-on to me. But that's not the point. We've always been faithful to each other. How can I be sure? I just am. Sally was a virgin when I met her, nice girls usually were in those days, and I wasn't all that experienced myself. My sexual history was a very slim volume, consisting of isolated, opportunistic couplings with garrison slags in the Army, with drunken girls at drama-school parties, and with lonely landladies in seedy theatrical digs. I don't think I had sex with any of them more than twice, and it was always fairly quick and in the missionary position. To enjoy sex you need comfort – clean sheets, firm mattresses, warm bedrooms – and continuity. Sally and I learned about making love together, more or less from scratch. If she were to go with anyone else, something new in her behaviour, some unfamiliar adjustment of her limbs, some variation in her caresses, would tell me, I'm certain. I always have trouble with adultery stories, especially those where one partner has been betraying the other for years. How could you not know? Of course, Sally doesn't know about Amy. But then I'm not having an affair with Amy. What am I having with her? I don't know.

I met Amy six years ago when she was hired to help cast the first series of *The People Next Door*. Needless to say, she did a brilliant job. Some people in the business reckon that ninety per cent of the success of a sitcom is in the casting. As a writer I would question that, naturally, but it's true that the best script in the world won't work if the actors are all wrong. And the right ones are not always everybody's obvious

28

fiirst choice. It was Amy's idea, for instance, to cast Deborah Radcliffe as Priscilla, the middle-class mother – a classical actress who'd just been let go by the Royal Shakespeare, and had never done sitcom before in her life. Nobody except Amy would have thought of her for Priscilla, but she took to the part like a duck to water. Now she's a household name and can earn five grand for a thirty-second commercial.

It's a funny business, casting. It's a gift, like fortune-telling or water-divining, but you also need a trained memory. Amy has a mind like a Rolodex: when you ask her advice about casting a part she goes into a kind of trance, her eyes turn up to the ceiling, and you can almost hear the *fllick-flick-flick* inside her head as she spools through that mental card-index where the essence of every actor and actress she has ever seen is inscribed. When Amy goes to see a show, she's not just watching the actors perform their given roles, she's imagining them all the time in other roles, so that by the end of the evening she's assimilated not only their performance on the night, but also their potential for quite other performances. You might go with Amy to see *Macbeth* at the RSC and say to her on the way home, "Wasn't Deborah Radcliffe a great Lady Macbeth?" and she'd say, "Mmm, I'd love to see her do Judith Bliss in *Hay Fever*." I wonder sometimes whether this habit of mind doesn't prevent her from enjoying what's going on in front of her. Perhaps that's what we have in common – neither of us being able to live in the present, always hankering after some phantom of perfection elsewhere.

I put this to her once. "Balls, darling," she said. "With the greatest respect, complete *cojones*. You forget that every now and again I pull it off. I achieve the perfect fit between actor and role. *Then* I enjoy the show and nothing but the show. I live for those moments. So do you, for that matter. I mean when everything in an episode goes exactly right. You sit in front of the telly holding your breath thinking, they can't possibly keep this up, it's going to dip in a moment, but they do, and it doesn't – that's what it's all about, *n'est ce pas*?"

"I can't remember when I thought an episode was that good," I said.

"What about the fumigation one?"

"Yes, the fumigation one was good."

"It was bloody brilliant."

That's what I like about Amy – she's always pumping up my self-esteem. Sally's style is more bracing: stop moping and get on with your life. In fact in every way they're antithetical. Sally is a blonde, blue-eyed English rose, tall, supple, athletic. Amy is the Mediterranean type (her father was a Greek Cypriot): dark, short and buxom, with a head of frizzy black curls and eyes like raisins. She smokes, wears a lot of make-up, and never walks anywhere, let alone runs, if she can possibly avoid it. We had to run for a train once at Euston: I shot ahead and held the door open for her as she came waddling down the ramp on her high heels like a panicked duck, all her necklaces and earrings and scarves and bags and other female paraphernalia atremble, and I burst out laughing. I just couldn't help myself. Amy asked me what was so funny as she scrambled breathlessly aboard, and when I told her she refused to speak to me for the rest of the journey. (Incidentally, I just looked up "paraphernalia" in the dictionary because I wasn't sure I'd spelled it right, and discovered it comes from the Latin *paraphema*, meaning "a woman's personal property apart from her dowry." Interesting.)

It was one of our very few tiffs. We get on very well together as a rule, exchanging industry gossip, trading personal moans and reassurances, comparing therapies. Amy is divorced, with custody of her fourteen-year-old daughter, Zelda, who is just discovering boys and giving Amy a hard time about clothes, staying out late, going to dubious discos, etc. etc. Amy is terrified that Zelda's going to get into sex and drugs any minute now, and distrusts her ex-husband, Saul, a theatre manager who has the kid to stay one weekend every month and who, Amy says, has no morals, or, to quote her exactly, "wouldn't recognize a moral if it bit him on the nose." Nevertheless she feels riven with guilt about the break-up of the marriage, fearing that Zelda will go off the rails for lack of a father-figure in the home. Amy started analysis primarily to discover what went wrong between herself and Saul. In a sense she knew that already: it was sex. Saul wanted to do things that she didn't want to do, so eventually he found someone else to do them with. But she's still trying to work out whether this was his fault or hers, and doesn't seem to be any nearer a conclusion. Analysis has a way of unravelling the self: the longer you pull on the thread, the more flaws you find.

I see Amy nearly every week, when I go to London. Sometimes we go to a show, but more often than not we just spend a quiet evening together, at the flat, and/or have a bite to eat at one of the local restaurants. There's never been any question of sex in our relationship, because Amy doesn't really want it and I don't really need it. I get plenty of sex at home. Sally seems full of erotic appetite these days – I think it must be the hormone replacement therapy she's having for the menopause. Sometimes, to stimulate my own sluggish libido, I suggest something Saul wanted to do with Amy, and Sally hasn't turned me down yet. When she asks me where I get these ideas from, I tell her magazines and books, and she's quite satisfied. If it ever got back to Sally that I was seen out in London with Amy, it wouldn't bother her because I don't conceal the fact that we meet occasionally. Sally thinks it's for professional reasons, which in part it is.

So really you would say that I've got it made, wouldn't you? I've solved the monogamy problem, which is to say the monotony problem, without the guilt of infidelity. I have a sexy wife at home and a platonic mistress in London. What have I got to complain about? I don't know.

It's three-thirty. I think I'll go back to bed and see if I can get a few hours' kip before sparrowfart.

Wednesday 11 a.m. I did sleep for a few hours, but it wasn't a refreshing sleep. I woke feeling knackered, like I used to be after guard duty in National Service: two hours on, four hours off, all through the night, and all through the day too, if it was a weekend. Christ, just writing that down brings it all back: snatching sleep lying on a bunk fully dressed in ankle-bruising boots and neck-chafing battledress under the glare of a naked electric light bulb, and then being roughly woken to gulp down sweetened lukewarm tea, and maybe some cold congealed eggs and baked beans, before stumbling

31

out yawning and shivering into the night, to loiter for two hours by the barrack gates, or circle the silent shuttered huts and stores, listening to your own footsteps, watching your own shadow lengthen and shorten under the arc-lamps. Let me just concentrate for a moment on that memory, close my eyes and try and squeeze the misery out of it, so that I will appreciate my present comforts.

Tried it. No good. Doesn't work.

I'm writing this on my laptop on the train to London. First class, naturally. Definition of a well-off man: somebody who pays for a first-class ticket out of his own pocket. It's tax-deductible of course, but still . . . Most of my fellow passengers in this carriage are on expenses. Businessmen with digital-lock briefcases and mobile phones, and businesswomen with wide-shouldered jackets and bulging filofaxes. The odd retired county type in tweeds. I'm wearing a suit myself today in honour of the Groucho, but sometimes, when I'm in jeans and leather jacket, with my tramp's haircut falling over the back of the collar, people glance suspiciously at me as if they think I'm in the wrong part of the train. Not the conductors, though – they know me. I travel up and down a lot on this line.

Don't get the idea that I'm an enthusiast for British Rail's Inter-City service to London. *Au contraire*, as Amy would say (she likes to pepper her conversation with foreign phrases). There are a lot of things I don't like about it. For instance: I don't like the smell of the bacon and tomato rolls that pollute the air of the carriage every time somebody brings one back from the buffet car and opens the little polystyrene box they micro-wave them in. I don't like the brake linings on the wheels of the Pullman rolling stock which when warm emit sulphurous-smelling fumes, allegedly harmless to health, that creep into the carriages and mingle with the smell of bacon and tomato rolls. I don't like the taste of the bacon and tomato rolls when I am foolish enough to buy one for myself, somehow suppressing the memory of how naff it was last time. I don't like the fact that if you ask at the buffet for a cup of coffee you will be given a giant-sized plastic beaker of the stuff unless you ask for a small (i.e., normal) size. I don't like the way the train rocks from side to side when it picks up any kind of speed, causing the coffee to slop over the sides of the plastic beaker as you raise it to your lips, scalding your fingers and dripping onto your lap. I don't like the fact that if the air-conditioning fails, as it not infrequently does, you can't ventilate the carriage because the windows are sealed. I don't like the way that, not infrequently, but never when the air-conditioning has failed, the automatic sliding doors at each end of the coach jam in the open position, and cannot be closed manually, or if they can be closed, slowly open again of their own accord, or are opened by passing passengers who leave them open assuming that they will close automatically, obliging you either to leap up every few minutes to close the doors or sit in a permanent draught. I don't like the catches in the WC compartments designed to hold the toilet seats in an upright position, which are spring-loaded, but often loose or broken, so that when you are in mid-pee, holding on to a grab handle with one hand and aiming your todger with the other, the seat, dislodged from the upright position by the violent motion of the train, will suddenly fall forwards, breaking the stream of urine and causing it to spatter your trousers. I don't like the way the train always races at top speed along the section of the track that runs beside the M1, overtaking all the cars and lorries in order to advertise the superiority of rail travel, and then a few minutes later comes to a halt in a field near Rugby because of a signalling failure.

Ow! Ouch! Yaroo! Sudden stab of pain in the knee, for no discernible reason.

Sally said the other day that it was my thorn in the flesh. I wondered where the phrase came from and went to look it up. (I do a lot of looking up – it's how I compensate for my lousy education. My study is full of reference books, I buy them compulsively.) I discovered that it was from Saint Paul's Second Epistle to the Corinthians: "*And lest I should be exalted above measure through the abundance of revelations, there was given to me a thorn in the flesh, the messenger of Satan to buffet me . . .*" I came back into the kitchen with the Bible, rather pleased with myself, and read the verse out to Sally. She stared at me and said, "But that's what I just told you," and I realized I'd had one of my absent-minded spells, and while I was wondering where the phrase came from she had been telling me. "Oh, yes, I know you said it was St Paul," I lied. "But what's the application to my knee? The text seems a bit obscure." "That's the point," she said. "Nobody knows what Paul's thorn in the flesh was. It's a mystery. Like your knee." She knows a lot about religion, does Sally, much more than I do. Her father was a vicar.

True to form, the train has stopped, for no apparent reason, amid empty fields. In the sudden hush the remarks of a man in shirtsleeves across the aisle speaking into his cellphone about a contract for warehouse shelving are annoyingly intrusive. I would really prefer to drive to London, but the traffic is impossible once you get off the M1, not to mention *on* the M1, and parking in the West End is such a hassle that it's really not worth the effort. So I drive the car to Rummidge Expo station, which is only fifteen minutes from home, and leave it in the car park there. I'm always a little bit apprehensive on the return journey in case I find somebody has scratched it, or even nicked it, though it has all the latest alarms and security systems. It's a wonderful vehicle, with a 24-valve three-litre V6 engine, automatic transmission, power steering, cruise control, air-conditioning, ABS brakes, six-speaker audio system, electric tilt-and-slide sunroof and every other gadget you can imagine. It goes like the wind, smooth and incredibly quiet. It's the silent effortless power that intoxicates me. I never was one for noisy *brrrm brmmm* sports cars, and I never did understand the British obsession with manual gear-changing. Is it a substitute for sex, I wonder, that endless fondling of the knob on the end of the gear lever, that perpetual pumping of the clutch pedal? They say that you don't get the same acceleration in the middle range with an automatic, but there's quite enough if your engine is as powerful as the one in my car. It's also incredibly, heartstoppingly beautiful.

I fell in love with it at first sight, parked outside the showroom, low and streamlined, sculpted out of what looked like mist with the sun shining through it, a very very pale silvery grey, with a pearly lustre. I kept finding reasons to drive past the showroom so that I could look at it again, and each time I felt a pang of desire. I daresay a lot of other people driving past felt the same way, but unlike them I knew I could walk into the showroom and buy the car without even having to think if I could afford it. But I hesitated and hung back. Why? Because, when I couldn't afford a car like that, I disapproved of cars like that: fast, flash, energy-wasteful – and Japanese. I always said I'd never buy a Japanese car, not so much out of economic patriotism (I used to drive Fords which usually turned out to have been made in Belgium or Germany) as for emotional reasons. I'm old enough to remember World War Two, and I had an uncle who died as a POW working on the Siamese railway. I thought something bad would happen to me if I bought this car, or that at the very least I would feel guilty and miserable driving it. And yet I coveted it. It became one of my "things" – things I can't decide, can't forget, can't leave alone. Things I wake up in the middle of the night worrying about.

I bought all the motoring magazines hoping that I would find some damning criticism of the car that would enable me to decide against it. No go. Some of the road-test reports were a bit condescending – "bland", "docile", even "inscrutable", were some of the epithets they used – but you could tell that nobody could find anything wrong with it. I hardly slept at all for a week, stewing it over. Can you believe it? While war raged in Yugoslavia, thousands died daily of AIDS in Africa, bombs exploded in Northern Ireland and the unemployment figures rose inexorably in Britain, I could think of nothing except whether or not to buy this car.

I began to get on Sally's nerves. "For God's sake, go and have a test drive, and if you like the car, buy it," she said. (She drives an Escort herself, changes it every three years after a two-minute telephone conversation with her dealer, and never gives another thought to the matter.) So I had a test-drive. And of course I liked the car. I loved the car. I was utterly seduced and enraptured by the car. But I told the salesman I would think about it. "What is there to think about?" Sally demanded, when I came home. "You like the car, you can afford the car, why not buy the car?" I said I would sleep on it. Which meant, of course, that I lay awake all night worrying about it. In the morning at breakfast I announced that I had reached a decision. "Oh yes?" said Sally, without raising her eyes from the newspaper. "What is it?"

"I've decided against," I said. "However irrational my scruples may be, I'll never be free from them, so I'd better not buy it." "OK," said Sally. "What will you buy instead?" "I don't really need to buy anything," I said. "My present car is good for another year or two." "Fine," said Sally. But she sounded disappointed. I began to worry again whether I'd made the right decision.

A couple of days later, I drove past the showroom and the car was missing. I went in and buttonholed the salesman. I practically dragged him from his seat by the lapels, like people do in movies. Someone else had bought my car! I couldn't believe it. I felt as if my bride had been abducted on our wedding eve. I said I wanted the car. *I had to have the car.* The salesman said he could get me another one in two or three weeks, but when he checked on his computer there wasn't an exactly similar model in the same colour in the country. It's not one of those Japanese manufacturers that have set up factories in Britain – they import from Japan under the quota system. He said there was one in a container ship somewhere on the high seas, but delivery would take a couple of months. To cut a long story short, I ended up paying £1000 over the list price to gazump the chap who had just bought my car.

I've never regretted it. The car is a joy to drive. I'm only sorry that Mum and Dad aren't around any more, so I can't give them a spin in it. I feel the need for someone to reflect back to me my pride of ownership. Sally's no use for that – to her a car is just a functional machine. Amy has never even seen the vehicle, because I don't drive to London. My children, on their occasional visits, regard it with a mixture of mockery and disapproval – Jane refers to it as the "Richmobile" and Adam says it's a compensation for hair-loss. What I need is an appreciative passenger. Like Maureen Kavanagh, for instance, my first girlfriend. Neither of our families could afford to run a car in those far-off days. A ride in any kind of car was a rare treat, intensely packed with novel sensations. I remember Maureen going into kinks when my Uncle Bert took us to Brighton one bank holiday in his old pre-war Singer that smelled of petrol and leather and swayed on its springs like a pram. I imagine driving up to her house in my present streamlined supercar and glimpsing her face at the

36

window all wonder; and then she bursts out of the front door and bounds down the steps and jumps in and wriggles about in her seat with excitement, trying all the gadgets, laughing and wrinkling up her nose in that way she had, and looking adoringly at me as I drive off. That's what Maureen used to do: look adoringly at me. Nobody ever did it since, not Sally, not Amy, not Louise or any of the other women who've occasionally made a pass at me. I haven't seen Maureen for nearly forty years – God knows where she is, or what she's doing, or what she looks like now. Sitting beside me in the car she's still sweet sixteen, dressed in her best summer frock, white with pink roses on it, though I'm as I am now, fat and bald and fifty-eight. It makes no kind of sense, but that's what fantasies are for, I suppose.

The train is approaching Euston. The conductor has apologized over the PA system for its late arrival, "which was due to a signalling failure near Tring". I used to be a closet supporter of privatizing British Rail, before the Transport Minister announced his plans to separate the company that maintains the track from the companies that run the trains. You can imagine how well that will work, and what wonderful alibis it will provide for late-running trains. Are they mad? Is this Internal Derangement of the Government?

Actually, I read somewhere that John Major has a dodgy knee. Had to give up cricket, apparently. Explains a lot, that.

❊   ❊   ❊   ❊   ❊   ❊   ❊   ❊   ❊   ❊   ❊   ❊   ❊   ❊   ❊   ❊   ❊

Wednesday 10.15 p.m. Amy has just left. We came back to the flat from Gabrielli's to watch "News at Ten" on my little Sony, to keep abreast of the global gloom (atrocities in Bosnia, floods in Bangladesh, drought in Zimbabwe, imminent collapse of Russian economy, British trade deficit worst ever recorded), and then I put her in a cab back to St John's Wood. She doesn't like to be out late if she can help it, on account of Zelda, though her lodger, Miriam, a speech therapist with a conveniently quiet social life, keeps an eye on the girl when Amy is out in the evenings.

Now I'm alone in the flat, and possibly in the whole building. The other owners, like me, are only occasionally in residence – there's a long-haul air hostess, a Swiss businessman whose job requires him to shuttle between London and Zürich, accompanied by his secretary and/or mistress, and a gay American couple, academics of some kind, who only come here in university vacations. Two flats are still unsold, because of the recession. I haven't seen anybody in the lift or hall today, but I never feel lonely here, as I sometimes do at home during the day, when Sally is at work. It's so quiet in those suburban streets. Whereas here it is never quiet, even at night. The growl and throb of buses and taxis inching up the Charing Cross Road in low gear carry faintly through the double glazing, punctuated occasionally by the shrill ululation of a police car or ambulance. If I go to the window, I look down on pavements still thronged with people coming out of theatres, cinemas, restaurants and pubs, or standing about munching takeaway junk food or swigging beer and coke from the can, their breath condensing in the cold night air. Very rarely does anyone raise their eyes from the ground level of the building, which is occupied by a pizza & pasta restaurant, and notice that there are six luxury flats above it, with a man standing at one of the windows, pulling the curtain aside, looking down at them. It isn't a place where you would expect anybody to *live*, and indeed it wouldn't be much fun to do so three hundred and sixty-five days a year. It's too noisy and dirty. Noise not just from the traffic, but also from the high-pitched whine of restaurant ventilator fans at the back of the building that never seem to be turned off, and dirt not just in the air, which leaves a fine sediment of black dust on every surface though I keep the windows shut most of the time, but also on the ground, the pavement permanently covered with a slimy patina of mud and spittle and spilt milk and beer dregs and vomit, and scattered over with crushed burger boxes, crumpled drinks cans, discarded plastic wrappers and paper bags, soiled tissues and used bus tickets. The efforts of the Westminster Borough street-cleaners are simply swamped by the sheer numbers of litter-producing pedestrians in this bit of London. And the human detritus is just as visible: drunks, bums, loonies and criminal-looking types abound. Beggars accost you all the time, and by 10 p.m. every shop doorway has its sleeping occupant. "*Louche*" was Amy's verdict on the ambience (or, as she would say, *ambiance*) when I first brought her here, but I'm not sure that's the right word. (I looked it up, it means shifty and disreputable, from the French word for squint.) The porn and peepshow district is half a mile away. Here second-hand bookshops and famous theatres jostle with fastfood outlets and multicinemas. It's certainly not your conventional des. res. area, but as a metropolitan base for an out-of-towner like me, the situation is hard to beat. London is a midden anyway. If you have to live here you're better off perched on the steaming, gleaming pinnacle of the dunghill, instead of burrowing your way up and down through all the strata of compacted old shit every morning and evening. I know: I've been a London commuter in my time.

When we moved to Rummidge from London twelve years ago, because of Sally's job, all my friends regarded me with ill-concealed pity, as if I was being exiled to Siberia. I was a bit apprehensive myself, to be honest, never having lived north of Palmer's Green in my life (apart from Army Basic Training in Yorkshire, and touring when I was a young actor, neither of which really counts as "living") but I reckoned that it was only fair to let Sally take the chance of a career move from schoolteaching to higher education. She'd worked bloody hard, doing an M.Ed. part-time while being Deputy Head of a Junior School in Stoke Newington, and the advertisement for the lecture-ship in the Education Department at Rummidge Poly was bang on the nose of her research field, psycholinguistics and language acquisition (don't ask me to explain it). So she applied and got the job. Now she's Principal Lecturer. Maybe she'll be a Professor one day, now that the Poly has become a University. Professor Sally Passmore: it has a ring to it. Pity about the name of the University. They couldn't call it the University of Rummidge because there was one already, so they called it James Watt University, after the great local inventor. You can bet your life that this rather cumbersome title will soon be shortened to "Watt University", and imagine the conversational confusion *that* will cause. "What university did you go

to?" "Watt University." "Yes, what university?" "*Watt* University."
And so on.

Anyway, I was a bit apprehensive about the move at the time, we all
were, the kids too, having always lived in the South-East. But the first
thing we discovered was that the price we got for our scruffy inter-war
semi in Palmer's Green would buy us a spacious five-bedroomed
detached Edwardian villa in a pleasant part of Rummidge, so that I
could have a study of my own for the first time in our married life,
looking out on to a lawn screened by mature trees, instead of the bay
window of our lounge with a view of an identical scruffy semi across
the street; and the second thing we discovered was that Sally and the
kids could get to their college and schools with half the hassle and in
half the time they were used to in London; and the third thing we
discovered was that people were still civil to each other outside
London, that shop assistants said "lovely" when you gave them the
right change, and that taxi-drivers looked pleasantly surprised when
you tipped them, and that the workmen who came to repair your
washing-machine or decorate your house or repair your roof were
courteous and efficient and reliable. The superior quality of life in
Britain outside London was still a well-kept secret in those days, and
Sally and I could hardly contain our mirth at the thought of all our
friends back in the capital pitying us as they sat in their traffic jams or
hung from straps in crowded commuter trains or tried in vain to get a
plumber to answer the phone at the weekend. Our luck changed in
more ways than one with the move to Rummidge. Who knows
whether *The People Next Door* would have ever seen the light of studio
if I hadn't met Ollie Silver at a civic reception Sally had been invited
to, just when Heartland were looking for a new idea for a sitcom . . .

When Jane and Adam left home to go to University we moved out
to Hollywell, a semi-rural suburb on the southern outskirts of the city
– the stockbroker belt I suppose it would be called in the South-East,
only stockbrokers are rather thin on the ground in the Midlands. Our
neighbours are mostly senior managers in industry, or accountants,
doctors and lawyers. The houses are all modern detached, in
different styles, set well back from the road and bristling with burglar
alarms. It's green and leafy and quiet. On a weekday the loudest noise

40

is the whine of the milk float delivering semi-skimmed milk and organic yoghurt and free-range eggs door-to-door. At the weekend you sometimes hear the hollow clop of ponies' hoofs or the rasp of Range-Rover tyres on the tarmac. The Country Club, with its eighteen-hole golf course, tennis courts, indoor and outdoor pools and spa, is just ten minutes away. That's the main reason we moved to Hollywell – that and the fact that it's conveniently close to Rummidge Expo station.

The station was built fairly recently to serve the International Exhibition Centre and the Airport. It's all very modern and hi-tech, apart from the main Gents. For some reason they seem to have lovingly reconstructed a vintage British Rail loo in the heart of all the marble and glass and chromium plate, complete with pee-up-against-the-wall zinc urinals, chipped white tiles, and even a rich pong of blocked drains. Apart from that, it's a great improvement on the City Centre station, and is twelve minutes nearer London for me. Because, of course, if you're in any branch of show business, you can't keep away from London entirely. Heartland record in their Rummidge studios as a condition of their franchise – bringing employment to the region and all that – but they have offices in London and rehearse most of their shows there because that's where most actors and directors live. So I'm always up and down to Euston on good old BR. I bought the flat three years ago, partly as an investment (though property prices have fallen since) but mainly to save myself the fatigue of a return journey in one day, or the alternative hassle of checking in and out of hotels. I suppose at the back of my mind also was the thought that it would be a private place to meet Amy.

Lately I've come to value the privacy, the anonymity of the place even more. Nobody on the pavement knows I'm up here in my cosy, centrally-heated, double-glazed eyrie. And if I go down into the street to get a newspaper or pick up a pint of milk from the 24-hour Asian grocery store on the corner, and mingle with the tourists and the bums and the young runaways and the kids up from the suburbs for an evening out and the office workers who stopped for a drink on the way home and decided to make a night of it, and the actors and catering workers and buskers and policemen and beggars and newspaper vendors – their gaze will slide over me without clicking into focus, nobody will recognize me, nobody will greet me or ask how I am, and I don't have to pretend to anyone that I'm happy.

Amy came to the flat straight from work and we had a couple of g & t's before going round the corner to Gabrielli's for a bite to eat. Sometimes, if she comes here from home, she brings one of her own dishes from her deep-freeze, *moussaka*, or beef with olives or *coq au vin*, and heats it up in my microwave, but usually we eat out. Very occasionally she invites me to dinner at her house and lays on a super spread, but it's always a dinner *party*, with other people present. Amy doesn't want Zelda to get the idea that there's anything special about her relationship with me, though I can't believe the kid doesn't suspect something, seeing her mother sometimes going out in the evening dressed to kill and carrying a container of home-made frozen food in one of her smartly gloved hands. "Because I hide it in my handbag, *stupido*," Amy said, when I raised this question once. And it's true that she carries an exceptionally large handbag, one of those soft Italian leather scrips, full of female paraphernalia (or should I just say paraphernalia?) – lipsticks and eyeliner, face-powder and per-fume, cigarettes and lighters, pens and pencils, notebooks and diaries, aspirin and Elastoplast, Tampax and panti-liners, a veritable life-support system, in which a plastic container of frozen *moussaka* could be concealed without much difficulty.

I was replacing a phutted lightbulb when Amy buzzed the entryphone, so I was slow to push the button that brought her comically distorted face, all mouth and nose and eyes, swimming into view on the videoscreen in my microscopic hall. "Hurry up, Lorenzo," she said, "I'm dying for a pee and a drink, in that order." One of the things I like about Amy is that she never calls me Tubby. She calls me by a lot of other familiar names, but never that one. I pushed the button to open the front door, and moments later admitted her to the flat. Her cheek was cold against mine as we embraced, and I inhaled a heady whiff of her favourite perfume, Givenchy, eddying round her throat and ears. I hung up her coat and fiixed drinks while she went to the bathroom. She emerged a few minutes later, lips gleaming with freshly applied lipstick, sank into an armchair, crossed her fat little legs, lit a cigarette, took her drink and said, "Cheers, darling. How's the knee?"

I told her it had given me one bad twinge today, in the train.

"And how's the *Angst*?"

"What's that?"

"Oh, come, sweetheart! Don't pretend you don't know what *Angst* is. German for anxiety. Or is it anguish?"

"Don't ask me," I said. "You know I'm hopeless at languages."

"Well anyway, how have you been? Apart from the knee."

"Pretty bad." I described my state of mind over the last few days in some detail.

"It's because you're not writing." She meant script-writing.

"But I am writing," I said. "I'm writing a journal."

Amy's black eyes blinked with surprise. "What on earth for?"

I shrugged. "I don't know. It started with something I did for Alexandra."

"You should write something that will take you out of yourself, not deeper in. Is there going to be another series?"

"I'll tell you later," I said. "I had lunch about it with Jake. How was your day?"

"Oh awful, awful," she said grimacing. Amy's days are invariably awful. I don't think she'd be really happy if they weren't. "I had a row with Zelda at breakfast about the pigsty state of her room. Well, *c'est normal*. But then Karl's secretary called to say he couldn't see me today because of a sore throat, though why he should cancel just because of a sore throat I don't know, because sometimes he doesn't say anything by choice, but his secretary said he had a temperature too. So of course I've been on edge all day like a junkie needing a fix. And Michael Hinchcliffe, whose agent told me he was 'technically available' for that BBC spy serial, and would have been wonderful in the part, has taken a film offer instead, the sod. Not to mention Harriet's latest clanger." Harriet is Amy's partner in the casting agency. Her long-standing relationship with a man called Norman has just broken up and she is consequently unable to think straight and is apt to weep uncontrollably when speaking to clients on the phone. Amy said she would tell me about Harriet's latest clanger when I had told her about my lunch with Jake, so we went out and settled ourselves at our usual table in Gabrielli's first.

Jake Endicott is the only agent I ever had. He wrote to me when he heard a sketch of mine on the radio, yonks ago, and offered to take me on. For years nothing much happened, but then I struck oil with *The People Next Door* and I wouldn't be surprised if I was his number one client now. He had booked a table in the back room at Groucho's, under the glass roof. It's his kind of place. Everybody is there to see and be seen without letting on that that's what they're there for. There's a special kind of glance that habitués have perfected I call the Groucho Fast Pan, which consists of sweeping the room with your eyes very rapidly under half-lowered lids, checking for the presence of celebrities, while laughing like a drain at something your companion has just said, whether it's funny or not. I had imagined it was just going to be a social lunch, a bit of gossip, a bit of mutual congratulation, but it turned out that Jake had something significant to report.

When we had ordered (I chose smoked duck's breast on a warm salad of rocket and lollo rosso, followed by sausage and mash at a price that would have given my poor old Mum and Dad a heart-attack apiece) Jake said, "Well, the good news is, Heartland want to commission another two series."

"And what's the bad news?" I asked.

"The bad news is that Debbie wants out." Jake looked anxiously at me, waiting for my reaction.

It wasn't exactly a bombshell. I knew that the present series was the last Debbie Radcliffe had contracted for, and I could well believe that she was getting tired of spending more than half of every year making *The People Next Door*. Sitcom is hard work for actors. It's the weekly rep of TV. The schedule for *The People Next Door* is: readthrough on Tuesday and rehearse Wednesday to Friday in London, travel up to Rummidge on Saturday, dress-rehearse and record there on Sunday, day off on Monday, and start again with the next script on Tuesday. It wipes out the actors' weekends, and if filming on location is required that sometimes takes up their day off. They're well paid, but it's a gruelling routine and they dare not get ill. More to the point: for an actress like Deborah Radcliffe, the character of Priscilla Springfield must have ceased to be a challenge some time ago. True, she's free to do live theatre for about four months a year, between series, but that's not quite long enough for a West End production and anyway Sod's Law would ensure that the parts she wanted didn't come up when she was available. So I wasn't surprised to learn that she wanted her freedom. Jake, needless to say, didn't see it that way. "The ingratitude of people in this profession . . ." he sighed, shaking his head and twisting a sliver of gravadlax on the end of his fork in a puddle of dill sauce. "Who ever heard of Deborah Radcliffe before *The People Next Door*, apart from a few people on the RSC mailing list? We made her a star, and now she's just turning her back on us. Whatever happened to loyalty?"

"Come off it, Jake," I said. "We're lucky that we've had her this long."

"Thank me for that, my boy," said Jake. (He's actually ten years younger than me, but he likes to play the father in our relationship.) "*I* pressured Heartland into writing a four-year retainer into her renewal contract, after the first series. They would have settled for three."

"I know, Jake, you did well," I said. "I suppose this isn't just a ploy by her agent to up her fee?"

"That was my first thought, naturally, but she says she wouldn't do it for double."

"How can we have another series without Debbie?" I said. "We can't cast another actress. The audience wouldn't accept it. Debbie *is* Priscilla, as far as they're concerned."

Jake allowed the waiter to refill our wine glasses, then leaned forward and lowered his voice. "I spoke to the people at Heartland about that David Treece, Mel Spacks and Ollie. Incidentally, this is *completely* confidential, Tubby. Are you going to rehearsal tomorrow? Then don't breathe a *word*. The rest of the cast know nothing about

Debbie leaving. Heartland want you to do a rewrite on the last script."

"What's wrong with it?"

"There's nothing wrong with it. But you're going to have to write Debbie out of the series."

"You mean, kill off Priscilla?"

"Good God, no. This is a *comedy* series, for Chrissake, not drama. No, Priscilla's got to leave Edward."

"Leave him? Why?"

"Well, that's your department, old son. Perhaps she meets another fella."

"Don't be daft, Jake. Priscilla would never desert Edward. It's just not in her nature."

"Well, women do funny things. Look at Margaret. She left me."

"That's because you were having an affair with Rhoda."

"Well, maybe Edward could have an affair with someone to provoke Priscilla into divorcing him. There's your new character!"

"It's not in Edward's nature either. He and Priscilla are the archetypal monogamous couple. They're about as likely to split up as Sally and me."

We argued for a while. I pointed out that the Springfields, in spite of their trendy liberal opinions and cultural sophistication, are really deeply conventional at heart, whereas the next-door Davises, for all their vulgarity and philistinism, are much more tolerant and liberated. Jake knew this already, of course.

"All right," he said at last. "What do you suggest?"

"Perhaps we should call it a day," I said, without premeditation. Jake nearly choked on his sautéd sweetbreads and polenta.

"You mean, kill the show at the end of this series?"

"Perhaps it's reached the end of its natural life." I wasn't sure whether I believed this, but I discovered to my surprise that I wasn't unduly bothered by the prospect.

Jake, though, was very bothered. He dabbed his mouth with his napkin. "Tubby, don't do this to me. Tell me you're joking. *The People Next Door* could run for another three series. There are a lot of

46

golden eggs still to come out of that goose. You'd be cutting your own throat."

"He's right, you know," Amy said, when I related this conversation to her over supper (in the light of the Groucho lunch, I confined myself virtuously to one dish, spinach canelloni, but poached from Amy's dessert, a voluptuous tiramisu). "Unless you've got an idea for another series?"

"I haven't," I admitted. "But I could live quite comfortably on the money I've already earned from *The People Next Door*."

"You mean, *retire*? You'd go mad."

"I'm going mad anyway," I said.

"No, you're not," said Amy. "You don't know what mad means."

When we had thoroughly discussed the ins and outs and pros and cons of trying to go on with *The People Next Door* without Deborah Radcliffe, it was Amy's turn to tell me about her day in more detail. But I'm ashamed to say that now I come to try and record that part of our conversation, I can't remember much about it. I know that Harriet's latest clanger was sending the wrong actress to an interview at the BBC, causing great offence and embarrassment all round, but I'm afraid my mind wandered fairly early on in the relation of this story, and I failed to register the surname of the actress, so that when I came to again, and Amy was saying how furious Joanna had been, I didn't know which Joanna she was talking about and it was too late to ask without revealing that I hadn't been listening. So I had to confine myself to nodding and shaking my head knowingly and making sympathetic noises and uttering vague generalizations, but Amy didn't seem to notice, or if she noticed, not to mind. Then she talked about Zelda, and I don't remember a word of that, though I could make it up fairly confidently, since Amy's complaints about Zelda are always much the same.

I didn't tell Amy the whole of my conversation with Jake. At the end of the meal, while we were waiting for the waiter to come back with the receipted bill and Jake's platinum credit card, he said casually, fast-panning round the room and waving discreetly to Stephen Fry, who was just leaving, "Any chance of borrowing your flat next week,

Tubby?" I assumed he had some foreign client arriving whom he wanted to put up, until he added, "Just for an afternoon. Any day that suits you." He caught my eye and grinned slyly. "We'll bring our own sheets."

I was shocked. It's less than two years since Jake's marriage to Margaret ended in an acrimonious divorce and he married his then secretary, Rhoda. Margaret had become a kind of friend, or at least a familiar fixture, over the years, and I've only recently got used to Jake going to functions or staying for the occasional weekend accompanied by Rhoda instead. He could see from my expression that I was disturbed.

"Of course, if it's inconvenient, just say so . . ."

"It's not a matter of convenience or inconvenience, Jake," I said. "It's just that I'd never be able to look Rhoda straight in the eye again."

"This doesn't affect Rhoda, believe me," he said earnestly. "It's not an affair. We're both happily married. We just have a common interest in recreational sex."

"I'd rather not be involved," I said.

"No problem," he said, with a dismissive wave of his hand. "Forget I ever asked." He added, with a trace of anxiety, "You won't mention it to Sally?"

"No, I won't. But isn't it about time you packed it in, this lark?"

"It keeps me feeling young," he said complacently. He does look young, too, for his age, not to say immature. He's got one of those faces sometimes described as "boyish": chubby cheeks, slightly protuberant eyes, snub nose, a mischievous grin. You wouldn't call him good-looking. It's hard to understand how he manages to pull the birds. Perhaps it's the eager, puppyish, tail-wagging energy he seems to have such endless reserves of. "You should try it, Tubby," he said. "You've been looking peaky lately."

When we sat on the sofa together to watch *News at Ten*, I put my arm round Amy's back and she leaned her head against my shoulder. It's the furthest we ever go in physical intimacy, except that our goodbye kiss is always on the lips; it seems safe to go that far when we're parting. We don't neck while we're sitting on the sofa, nor have I ever attempted any squeezing or stroking below the neckline. I admit that I sometimes wonder what Amy would look like naked. The image that comes into my mind is a slightly overweight version of that famous nude by whatsisname, the Spanish bloke, old master, he did two paintings of the same woman reclining on a couch, one clothed, one naked, I must look it up. Amy is always so *dressed*, so thoroughly buttoned and zipped and sheathed in her layers of carefully co-ordinated clothing that it's hard to imagine her ever being completely naked except in the bath, and even then I bet she covers herself with foam. Divesting Amy of her clothes would be a slow and exciting business, like unpacking an expensively and intricately wrapped parcel, rustling with layers of fragrant tissue paper, in the dark. (It would have to be in the dark – she told me one of her problems with Saul was his insistence on making love with the lights on.) Whereas Sally's clothes are loose and casual, and so few and functional that she can strip in about ten seconds flat, which she frequently does after coming home from work, walking around upstairs stark naked while doing humdrum domestic tasks like changing the sheets or sorting the laundry.

This train of thought is proving rather arousing, but unprofitably so, since Sally is not here to slake my lust and Amy wouldn't even if she were. Why do I only seem to get horny these days in London, where my girlfriend is contentedly chaste, and almost never at home in Rummidge, where I have a partner of tireless sexual appetite? I don't know.

"You should try it, Tubby." How does Jake know I haven't tried it? It must show in my body language, somehow. Or my face, my eyes. Jake's eyes light up like an infra-red security scanner every time a pretty girl comes within range.

I suppose the nearest I came to trying it in recent memory was with Louise, in L.A., three or four years ago, when I went out for a month to advise on the American version of *The People Next Door*. She was a "creative executive" in the American production company, a Vice-President in fact, which isn't quite as impressive as it sounds to a

British ear, but pretty good all the same for a woman in her early thirties. She was my minder and intermediary with the scriptwriting team. There were eight writers working on the pilot. Eight. They sat round a long table drinking coffee and Diet Coke, anxiously trying out gags on each other. As the company had bought the rights they could do anything they liked with my scripts, and they did, throwing out most of the original storylines and dialogue and retaining only the basic concept of incompatible neighbours. It seemed to me that I was being paid thousands of dollars for almost nothing, but I wasn't complaining. At first I used to attend the script conferences and brainstorming sessions dutifully, but after a while I begin to think my presence was only an embarrassment and a distraction to these people, who seemed engaged in some desperately competitive contest from which I was happily excluded, and my participation became more and more a matter of stretching out on a lounger beside the pool of the Beverly Wilshire and reading the draft scripts which Louise Lightfoot brought to me in her smart, leather-trimmed canvas script satchel. She used to come back at the end of the day in her little Japanese sports coupé to collect my notes, and drink a cocktail, and more often than not we would eat together. She had recently split up with a partner and "wasn't seeing anybody" and I, marooned in Beverly Hills, was very glad of her company. She took me to the "in" Hollywood restaurants and pointed out the important producers and agents. She took me to movie previews and premières. She took me to art galleries and little theatres and, on the grounds that it would help me understand American television, to more plebeian places of resort: drive-in Burger Kings and Donut Delites, ten-pin bowling alleys, and on one occasion a baseball game.

Louise was small but shapely in build. Straight bobbed brown hair which always shone and swung as if it had been freshly washed, which it invariably had been. Perfect teeth. Is there anybody in Hollywood who hasn't got perfect teeth? But Louise needed them, because she laughed a lot. It was a resonant, full-bodied laugh, rather a surprise given her petite figure and general style of poised professional career woman; and when she laughed she threw back her head and shook it from side to side, making her hair fan out. I seemed to be able to produce this effect very easily. My wry little British digs at Hollywood manners and Californiaspeak tickled Louise. Naturally, for a script-writer there is nothing more gratifying than having an attractive and intelligent young woman helpless with laughter at your jokes.

One warm evening towards the end of my stay, we drove down to Venice to eat at one of the shoreside fish places they have there. We ate outside on the restaurant's deck to watch the sun set on the Pacific in a vulgar blaze of Technicolor glory, and sat on in the gloaming over coffee and a second bottle of Napa Valley Chardonnay, with just a small oil-lamp flickering between us on the table. For once I wasn't trying to make her laugh, but talking seriously about my writing career, and the thrill of making the breakthrough with *The People Next Door*. I paused to ask if I should order some more coffee and she smiled and said, "No, what I'd like to do now is take you back to my place and fuck your brains out."

"Would you really?" I stalled, grateful for the semi-darkness as I struggled to arrange my thoughts.

"Yep, how does that grab you, Mr Passmore?" The "Mr Passmore" was a joke, of course – we had been on first-name terms since Day One. But that was how she always referred to me when speaking to other people in the company. I had heard her doing it on the phone. "*Mr Passmore thinks it's a mistake to make the Davises a Latino family, but he will defer to our judgement. Mr Passmore thinks the scene beginning page thirty-two of the twelfth draft is overly sentimental.*" Louise said it was a mark of respect in the industry.

"It's very sweet of you, Louise," I said, "and don't think that I wouldn't like to go to bed with you, because I would. But, to coin a phrase, I love my wife."

"She would never know," said Louise. "How could it hurt her?"

"I'd feel so guilty it would probably show," I said. "Or I'd blurt it out one day." I sighed miserably. "I'm sorry."

"Hey, it's no big deal, Tubby, I'm not in love with you or anything. Why don't you get the check?"

Driving me back to my hotel she said suddenly, "Am I the only girl you've had these scruples about?" and I said I'd always had them, and she said, "Well, that makes me feel better."

I didn't sleep much that night, tossing and turning in my vast bed at the Beverly Wilshire, wondering whether to call Louise and ask if I could have second thoughts, but I didn't; and although we saw each other again on several occasions it was never quite the same, she was gradually backing away instead of coming closer. She drove me to the airport at the end of my stay and kissed me on the cheek and said, " 'Bye, Tubby, it's been great." I agreed enthusiastically, but I spent most of the flight home wondering what I'd missed.

Time to go to bed. I wonder what they'll be showing on the Dream Channel tonight. Blue movies, I shouldn't wonder.

* * * * * * * * * * * * * * * * *

Thursday morning, 18th Feb. The video entryphone in the flat is connected to a camera in the porch which gives you a choice of two shots: a close-up of the face of the person ringing your bell, and a wide shot of the porch, with the street in the background. Sometimes in idle moments I press the button for the wide shot to have a look at the people passing or pausing on the pavement. It gives me ideas for characters – you see all types – and I suppose there's a certain childish, voyeuristic pleasure in using the gadget. It's like an inverted periscope. From my cosy cabin high above the ground I scan life on the scruffy surface: tourists frowning over their street-maps, young girls too vain to cover their skimpy going-out gear with topcoats clutching themselves against the cold, young bucks in leather jackets scuffling and nudging each other, infatuated couples stopping in mid-stride to kiss, bumped by impatient men with briefcases hurrying to catch a train at Charing Cross.

Last night, for no particular reason, I pressed the button as I was going to bed, and blow me if there wasn't someone kipping down for the night in the porch. I suppose it's surprising it hasn't happened before, but it's a very small square space not big enough for a grown man to lie down in without his feet sticking out onto the pavement. This bloke was sitting up inside his sleeping-bag, with his back against one wall and his feet against the other, and his head sunk on his chest. He looked young, with a pointed, foxy face and long, lank hair falling down over his eyes.

I felt quite shocked to see him there, then angry. What a nerve! He was taking up the whole porch. It would be impossible to go in or out without stepping over him. Not that I wanted to go in or out any more that night, but one of the other residents might turn up, and in any case it lowered the tone of the property to have him camped there. I thought about going downstairs and telling him to push off, but I was already in pyjamas and I didn't fancy confronting him in dressing-gown and slippers or alternatively going to the trouble of dressing myself again. I thought of phoning the police and asking them to move him on, but there's so much serious crime in this part of London that I doubted whether they would be bothered to respond, and anyway they would want to know if I had already requested him to move on myself. I stood there, staring at the fuzzy black and white image, wishing that sound as well as vision could be activated from inside the flat on the entryphone, so that I could bark, *"Hey, you! Piss off!"* through the loudspeaker, and watch his reaction on the video screen. I smiled at the thought, then felt a bit of a bastard for smiling.

These young people who beg and sleep rough on the streets of London, they bother me. They're not like the tramps and winos who have always been with us, filthy and smelly and dressed in rags. The new vagrants are usually quite nicely clothed, in new-looking anoraks and jeans and Doc Martens, and they have thickly quilted sleeping bags that wouldn't disgrace an Outward Bound course. And whereas the tramps skulk like insects in dark neglected places like under railway arches or beside rubbish tips, these youngsters choose shop doorways in brightly lit West End streets, or the staircases and passages of the Underground, so that you can't avoid them. Their presence is like an accusation – but what are they accusing us of? Did we drive them onto the streets? They look so normal, so presentable, they ask you so politely if you have any change, that it's hard to believe they couldn't find shelter, and even work, if they really tried. Not in the West End, perhaps, but who says they have a right to a home in the West End? I have one, but I had to work for it.

Thus and so went my self-justificatory interior monologue, as I went to bed and, eventually, to sleep. I woke at four and went for a pee. On my way back to bed I pressed the video button on the entryphone, and he was still there, curled up inside his sleeping-bag on the tiled floor of the porch, like a dog in its basket. A police car flashed past in the background, and I heard the strident blare of its siren through the double-glazed windows of the living-room, but the youth didn't stir. When I looked again at half past seven this morning, he had gone.

✳ ✳ ✳ ✳ ✳ ✳ ✳ ✳ ✳ ✳ ✳ ✳ ✳ ✳ ✳ ✳ ✳

Thursday afternoon. I'm writing this on the 5.10 from Euston. I meant to catch the 4.40, but my taxi got trapped in a huge traffic jam caused by a bomb alert in Centre Point. The police had cordoned off the intersection of Tottenham Court Road and Oxford Street, and the traffic was backed up in all directions. I said to the cab-driver, "Who's trying to blow up the building – the IRA or Prince Charles?" But he didn't get the joke – or, more likely, he wasn't amused. These bomb scares keep the tourists away and hurt his business.

I dropped in on a rehearsal this morning, as is my usual practice on Thursdays. When *The People Next Door* was new and still finding its feet I used to attend rehearsals practically every day, but now it runs like a train (or like a train *should* run – this one has suddenly slowed to a crawl for some reason, and we haven't even got to Watford Junction) and I just put in an appearance once a week to check that everything's going smoothly, and maybe do a little fine-tuning on the script. Rehearsals are held in a converted church hall near Pimlico tube station, its floor marked out with lines corresponding to the studio set in Rummidge. Walking in there on a winter's day would disabuse you of any illusion that television light entertainment is a glamorous profession. (I think that's the first time I've ever used the word "disabuse". I like it – it has a touch of class.) The brick walls are painted an institutional slime green and curdled cream, like Rummidge General Hospital, and the windows are barred and glazed with grimy frosted glass. There's the usual job-lot of miscellaneous furniture pushed against the walls or arranged in the various "rooms": splay-legged Formica-topped tables, plastic stacking chairs, collapsing three-piece suites, and beds with unsavoury-looking mattresses. Apart from the trestle table in one corner with a coffee machine, soft drinks, fruit and snacks laid out on it, the place could be a Salvation Army refuge or a depository for second-hand furniture. The actors wear old, comfortable clothes – all except Debbie, who always looks as if she's on her way to be photographed for *Vogue* – and when they aren't required for a scene they sit slumped in the broken-down chairs, reading newspapers and paperback novels, doing crosswords, knitting or, in Debbie's case, embroidering.

But they all look up and give me a cheerful smile and greeting as I come in. *"Hi, Tubby! How're you? How goes it?"* Actors are always very punctilious that way. Most producers and directors secretly despise writers, regarding them as mere drudges whose job it is to provide the raw material for the exercise of their own creativity, necessary evils who must be kept firmly in their place. Actors, however, regard writers with respect, even a certain awe. They know that the Writer is the ultimate source of the lines without which they themselves are impotent; and they know that, in the case of a long-running series, it is in his power to enhance or reduce the importance of their roles in episodes as yet unwritten. So they usually go out of their way to be nice to him.

This week they're doing Episode Seven of the present series, due to be transmitted in five weeks' time. Do they, I wonder, have any inkling that this may be the last series? No, I detect no signs of anxiety in their eyes or body language as we exchange greetings. Only between Debbie and myself does a message flash briefly, as I stoop to kiss her cheek where she sits in an old armchair, doing her eternal embroidery, and our eyes meet: she knows that I know that she wants out. Otherwise the secret seems to be safe for the time being. Not even Hal Lipkin, the director, knows yet. He bustles over to me as soon as I come in, frowning and biting his ballpen, but it's a query about the script that's on his mind.

Sitcom is pure television, a combination of continuity and novelty. The continuity comes from the basic "situation" – in our case, two families with radically different lifestyles living next door to each other: the happy-go-lucky, welfare-sponging Davises, having unexpectedly inherited a house in a gentrified inner-city street, decide to move into it instead of selling it, to the ill-concealed dismay of their next-door neighbours, the cultured, middle-class, *Guardian*-reading Springfields. The viewers quickly become familiar with the characters and look forward to watching them behave in exactly the same way, every week, like their own relatives. The novelty comes from the story each episode tells. The art of sitcom is finding new stories to tell, week after week, within the familiar framework. It can't be a very complicated story, because you've only got twenty-five minutes to tell it in and, for both budgetary and technical reasons, most of the action must take place in the same studio set.

I was looking forward to seeing this week's episode in production, because it's one of those cases where we approach the territory of serious drama. Basically sitcom is light, family entertainment, which aims to amuse and divert the viewers, not to disturb and upset them. But if it doesn't occasionally touch on the deeper, darker side of life, however glancingly, then the audience won't believe in the characters and will lose interest in their fortunes. This week's episode centres on the Springfields' teenage daughter, Alice, who's about sixteen. When the series started five years ago, she was about fifteen. Phoebe Osborne, who plays her, was fourteen when she started and is now nineteen, but fortunately she hasn't grown much in that time and it's amazing what make-up and hairstyling can do. Adult characters in long-running sitcoms lead enchanted lives, they never age, but with the juveniles you have to allow for a certain amount of growth in the actors, and build it into the script. When young Mark Harrington's voice broke, for instance (he plays the Springfields' youngest, Robert) I made it a running joke for a whole series.

Anyway, this week's episode centres on Edward and Priscilla's fear that Alice may be pregnant, because she keeps throwing up. Cindy Davis next door is a teenage unmarried mother, her Mum looks after the baby while she's at school, and the dramatic point of the episode is that while the Springfields have been terribly liberal-minded about Cindy, they're horrorstruck at the thought of the same thing happening to their own daughter, especially as the likely father is young Terry Davis, whom Alice has been dating with their teeth-gritting consent. Needless to say, Alice isn't pregnant or even at risk since she won't allow Terry any liberties at all. She keeps throwing up because the sexually frustrated Terry is spiking the goats' milk which is delivered exclusively for Alice's use (she's allergic to cows' milk) with an alleged aphrodisiac (in fact a mild emetic) with the collusion of his mate, Rodge, the milkman's assistant. This is eventually revealed when Priscilla accidentally helps herself to Alice's special milk and is violently sick. ("EDWARD (*aghast*): Don't tell me you're pregnant too?") But before that a good deal of comedy is generated by the elaborately circuitous ways in which Edward and Priscilla try to check out their dreadful suspicion, and the contrast between their public tolerance and private disapproval of single-parent families.

"It's running a bit long, Tubby," Hal said, indistinctly because he was gripping a ballpen between his teeth as he riffled through his copy of the script. Another ballpen protruded from his wiry thatch of hair just above his right ear – parked there some time earlier and forgotten. (*I* should be so lucky.) "I was wondering if we could cut a few lines here," he mumbled. I knew exactly which lines he was going to point to before he found the page:

> EDWARD: Well, if she *is* pregnant, she'll have to have a termination.
>
> PRISCILLA (*angrily*): I suppose you think that will solve everything?
>
> EDWARD: Hang on! I thought you were all in favour of a woman's right to choose?
>
> PRISCILLA: She's not a woman, she's a child. Anyway, suppose she chooses to have the baby?
>
> PAUSE, AS EDWARD FACES UP TO THIS POSSIBILITY.
>
> EDWARD (*quietly but firmly*): Then of course we shall support her.
>
> PRISCILLA (*softening*): Yes, of course.
>
> PRISCILLA *REACHES OUT AND SQUEEZES* EDWARD'S *HAND*.

I'd already had a run-in about these lines with Ollie Silvers, my producer, when I first delivered the script. Actually he's much more than my producer nowadays, he's Head of Series and Serials at Heartland, no less; but since *The People Next Door* was in a sense his baby, and still gets better ratings than anything else Heartland does, he couldn't bear to hand it over to a line producer when he was promoted, and still finds time somehow to poke his nose into the detail of every episode. He said you couldn't have references to abortion in a sitcom, even one that goes out after the nine-o'clock watershed when young viewers are supposed to be tucked up in bed, because it's too controversial, and too upsetting. I said it was unrealistic to suppose that an educated middle-class couple would discuss the possible pregnancy of their schoolgirl daughter without mentioning the subject. Ollie said that audiences accepted the conventions of sitcom, that some things simply weren't mentioned, and they liked it that way. I said that all kinds of things that used to be taboo in sitcom were acceptable now. Ollie said, not abortion. I said, there's always a first time. He said, why on our show? I said, why not? He gave in, or so I thought. I might have known he'd find a way to get rid of the lines.

When I asked Hal if the cut was Ollie's idea, Hal looked a bit embarrassed. "Ollie was in yesterday," he admitted. "He did suggest the lines aren't absolutely essential to the story."

"Not absolutely essential," I said. "Just a little moment of truth."

Hal looked unhappy and said we could discuss the matter further with Ollie, who was coming in after lunch, but I said it was too late in the day to have a knock-down-drag-out argument on a matter of principle. The cast would pick up the vibrations and get anxious and uptight about the scene. Hal looked relieved, and hurried off to tell Suzie, his production assistant, to amend the script. I left before Ollie arrived. Now I wonder why I didn't put up more of a fight.

The senior conductor has just announced that we are approaching Rugby. "Rugby will be the next station stop." BR has taken to using this cumbersome phrase, "station stop" lately, presumably to distinguish scheduled stops at stations from unscheduled ones in the middle of fields, concerned perhaps that passengers disoriented by the fumes of bacon and tomato rolls and overheated brake linings in carriages with defective air-conditioning might otherwise stumble out on to the track by mistake and get killed.

Thursday evening. I got home at about 7.30. The train was only twelve minutes late in the end, and I found my car, unscathed by thieves or vandals, waiting for me where I had left it, like a faithful pet. I roused it with the remote button on my keyring as I approached and it blinked its indicator lights at me and cheeped three times, as the doorlocks clicked open. These remote-control gadgets give me an inexhaustible childish pleasure. Our garage door is operated by one, and it amuses me to start it opening as I turn the corner at the end of the road so that I can drive straight in without pausing. As the door yawned open this evening I saw that Sally's car wasn't parked inside, and when I let myself into the house I found a note in the kitchen to say that she'd gone down to the Club for a swim and sauna. I felt unreasonably disappointed, because I was all primed to tell her about the crisis over Debbie Radcliffe and the argument about the cut in this week's episode. Not that she would be dying to hear about either topic. *Au contraire.*

In my experience there are two kinds of writers' wives. One kind is a combination of nanny, secretary and fan-club president. She reads the writer's work in progress and always praises it; she watches his programmes at transmission and laughs at every joke; she winces at a bad review and rejoices at a good one as feelingly as he does; she keeps an anxious eye on his mood and workrate, brings him cups of tea and coffee at regular intervals, tiptoeing in and out of his study without disturbing his concentration; she answers the telephone and replies to letters, protecting him from tiresome and unprofitable invitations, requests and propositions; she keeps a note of his appointments and reminds him of them in good time, drives him to the station or airport and meets him again when he returns, and gives cocktail parties and dinner parties for his professional friends and patrons. The other kind is like Sally, who does none of these things, and has a career of her own which she considers just as important as her spouse's, if not more so.

Actually, Sally is the only writer's wife of this kind that I've met, though I suppose there must be others.

So it wasn't that I was hoping for sympathetic advice and knowledgeable counsel when I got home, just an opportunity to get some oppressive thoughts off my chest. Driving from the station, I felt a growing conviction that I had made a mistake in giving in so easily to cutting the reference to abortion in this week's script, and began to torment myself by wondering whether or not to re-open discussion of the matter by phoning Ollie and Hal at their respective homes – knowing that I would be in a very weak position, having agreed to the cut this morning, and that I would create bad feeling all round by trying to revoke that decision, without actually achieving anything in the end anyway because it was probably too late to change the script again. Probably, but not *necessarily*. The actors rehearsed the cut version this afternoon, but could if required restore the missing lines at tomorrow's rehearsal.

I paced restlessly around the empty house, picked up the telephone a couple of times, and put it down again without dialling. I made myself a ham sandwich, but the meat was too cold from the fridge to have any flavour, and drank a can of beer that filled my stomach with gas. I turned on the telly at random and found myself watching a rival sitcom on BBC1 which seemed much wittier and sharper than *The People Next Door*, and switched it off again after ten minutes. I went into my study and sat down at the computer.

I feel self-esteem leaking out of me like water from an old bucket. I despise myself both for my weakness in accepting the cut and for my vacillation over whether to do anything about it. My knee has begun to throb, like a rheumatic joint sensitive to the approach of bad weather. I sense a storm of depression flickering on the horizon, and a tidal wave of despair gathering itself to swamp me.

Thank God. Sally has just come in. I just heard the door slam behind her, and her cheerful call from the front hall.

✳ ✳ ✳ ✳ ✳ ✳ ✳ ✳ ✳ ✳ ✳ ✳ ✳ ✳ ✳ ✳ ✳

Friday morning 19th Feb. There was appeal from MIND in my mail this morning. First time I've had one from them, I think. They must have got my address from one of the other charities. Inside the envelope was a letter and a blue balloon. There was an instruction at the top of the letter: *"Please blow up the balloon before you read any further, but don't tie a knot in it."* So I blew up the balloon, and on it, drawn in white lines, appeared the profile of a man's head, looking a bit like me actually, with a thick neck and no visible hair; and packed inside the cranium, one on top of the other, like thoughts, were the words: BEREAVED, UNEMPLOYED, MONEY, SEPARATED, MORTGAGE, DIVORCED, HEALTH. *"To you,"* said the letter, *"the words on the balloon may seem just that – words. But the events they describe are at the heart of someone's nervous breakdown."*

Just then, the doorbell rang. Sally had left for work, so I went to the front door, still holding the balloon by its tail, pinched between thumb and index finger to stop the air from escaping. I felt a vaguely superstitious compulsion to obey the instructions in the letter, like a character in a fairy tale.

It was the milkman, wanting to be paid. He looked at the balloon and grinned. "Having a party?" he said. It was half past nine in the morning. "Your birthday, is it?" he said. "Many happy returns."

"It just came in the post," I said, gesturing lamely with the balloon. "How much do we owe you?" I fiddled a ten-pound note out of my wallet one-handed.

"Cracking programme the other night," said the milkman as he gave me my change. "When Pop Davis hid all those cigarettes around the house before he gave up smoking . . . very funny."

"Thanks, glad you enjoyed it," I said. All the local tradesmen know I write the scripts for *The People Next Door*. I can do instant audience research on my own doorstep.

I took the balloon back into my study and picked up the letter from MIND. *"Just as the words grow larger with the balloon, so somebody's problems can seem greater as the pressure on them increases,"* it said.

61

I looked again at the words packed inside the head. I'm not bereaved (or not very recently – Mum died four years ago, and Dad seven), I'm not unemployed, I have plenty of money, I'm not separated or divorced, and I could pay off my mortgage tomorrow if I wanted to, but my accountant advised me against because of the tax relief. The only way I qualify for a nervous breakdown is under Health, though I suspect MIND was thinking of something more life-threatening than Internal Derangement of the Knee.

I skimmed through the rest of the letter: *"Suicide . . . psychosis . . . halfway house . . . helpline . . ."* After the final appeal for money, there was a PS: *"You can let the air out of the balloon now. And as you do so, please think about how quickly the pressure of someone's problems can be released with the time, care, and special understanding your gift will give today."* I let the balloon go and it rocketed round the room like a madly farting bluebottle for a few seconds before hitting a window pane and collapsing to the floor. I got out my charity chequebook and sent MIND £36 to provide somebody with a specially trained mental health nurse for a morning.

I could do with one myself today.

Last night, after Sally came in, we talked in the kitchen as she made herself a cup of hot chocolate, and I had a scotch. Or rather I talked, and she listened, rather abstractedly. She was feeling languorously euphoric from her sauna and seemed to have more than usual difficulty in focusing on my professional problems. When I announced that the lines about abortion had been cut from this week's script, she said, "Oh, good," and although she saw from my expression that this was the wrong response, she typically proceeded to defend it, saying that *The People Next Door* was too light-hearted a show to accommodate such a heavy subject – exactly Ollie's argument. Then, when I told her that the future of the show was threatened by Debbie's intention of leaving at the end of the present series, Sally said, "Well, that will suit you, won't it? You can do something new with another producer prepared to take more risks than Ollie." Which was quite logical, but not particularly helpful, since I don't have an idea for a new show, and am unlikely to get one in my present state.

Sally ran her finger round the inside of her cup and licked it. "When are you going to bed?" she said, which is her usual way of suggesting that we have sex, so we did, and I couldn't come. I had an erection, but no climax. Perhaps it was the scotch, on top of the beer, I don't know, but it was worrying, like working a pump handle and getting nothing out of the spout. Sally came – at least I think she did. I saw a programme on television the other night in which a lot of women were sitting round talking about sex and every one of them had faked orgasm on occasion, either to reassure their partners or to bring an unsatisfactory experience to a conclusion. Perhaps Sally does too. I don't know. She went off to sleep happily enough. I heard her breathing settle into a deep, slow rhythm before I dropped off myself. I woke again at 2.35 with the collar of my pyjama jacket damp with sweat. I felt a great sense of foreboding, as if there was something unpleasant I had forgotten and had to remember. Then I remembered: now I had Internal Derangement of the Gonads on top of all my other problems. I contemplated a life without sex, without tennis, without a TV show. I felt myself spiralling down into the dark. I always think of despair as a downward spiral movement – like an aeroplane that loses a wing and falls through the air like a leaf, twisting and turning as the pilot struggles helplessly with the controls, the engine note rising to a high-pitched scream, the altimeter needle spinning round and round the dial towards zero.

Reading through that last entry reminded me of Amy's odd question, "How's your *Angst*?" and I looked the word up. I was slightly surprised to find it in my English dictionary: "**1.** *An acute but unspecific sense of anxiety or remorse.* **2.** *(In Existentialist philosophy) the dread caused by man's awareness that his future is not determined, but must be freely chosen.*" I didn't fully understand the second definition – philosophy is one of the bigger blank spots in my education. But I felt a little shiver of recognition at the word "dread". It sounds more like what I suffer than "anxiety". Anxiety sounds trivial, somehow. You can feel anxious about catching a train, or missing the post. I suppose that's why we've borrowed the German word. *Angst* has a sombre resonance to it, and you make a kind of grimace of pain as you pronounce it. But "Dread" is good. Dread is what I feel when I wake in the small hours in a cold sweat. Acute but unspecific Dread. Of course I soon think of specific things to attach it to. Impotence, for instance.

It has to happen sometime, of course, to every man. Fifty-eight seems a bit premature, but I suppose it's not impossible. Sooner or later, anyway, there has to be a last time. The trouble is, you'll only know when you discover that you can't do it any more. It's not like your last cigarette before you quit smoking, or your last game of football before you hang up your boots. You can't make a special occasion of your last fuck because you won't know it is your last one while you're having it; and by the time you find out you probably won't be able to remember what it was like.

I just looked up Existentialism in a paperback dictionary of modern thought. *"A body of philosophical doctrine that dramatically emphasizes the contrast between human existence and the kind of existence possessed by natural objects. Men, endowed with will and consciousness, find themselves in an alien world of objects which have neither."* That didn't seem much of a discovery to me. I thought I knew that already. *"Existentialism was inaugurated by Kierkegaard in a violent reaction against the all-encompassing absolute Idealism of Hegel."* Oh, it was, was it? I looked up Kierkegaard. *"Kierkegaard, Søren. Danish philosopher, 1813–55. See under EXISTENTIALISM."*

I looked up Kierkegaard in another book, a biographical dictionary. He was the son of a self-made merchant and inherited a considerable fortune from his father. He spent it all on studying philosophy and religion. He was engaged to a girl called Regine but broke it off because he decided he wasn't suited to marriage. He trained to be a minister but never took orders and at the end of his life wrote some controversial essays attacking conventional Christianity. Apart from a couple of spells in Berlin, he never left Copenhagen. His life sounded as dull as it was short. But the article listed some of his books at the end. I can't describe how I felt as I read the titles. If the hairs on the back of my neck were shorter, they would have lifted.

Fear and Trembling, The Sickness Unto Death, The Concept of Dread –
they didn't sound like titles of philosophy books, they seemed to
name my condition like arrows thudding into a target. Even the ones I
couldn't understand, or guess at the contents of, like *Either/Or* and
Repetition, seemed pregnant with hidden meaning designed especially for me. And, what do you know, Kierkegaard wrote a Journal. I
must get hold of it, and some of the other books.

✶ ✶ ✶ ✶ ✶ ✶ ✶ ✶ ✶ ✶ ✶ ✶ ✶ ✶ ✶ ✶ ✶

Friday evening. Acupuncture at the Wellbeing Clinic this afternoon.
Miss Wu began, as she always does, by taking my pulse, holding my
wrist between her cool damp fingers as delicately as if it were the stem
of a fragile and precious flower, and asked me how I was. I was
tempted to tell her about my ejaculation problem last night, but
chickened out. Miss Wu, who was born in Hong Kong but brought
up in Rummidge, is very shy and demure. She always leaves the room
while I strip to my underpants and climb on to the high padded couch
and cover myself with a cellular blanket; and she always knocks on the
door to check that I'm ready before she comes back in. I thought she
might be embarrassed if I mentioned my seminal no-show, and to tell
you the truth I didn't fancy the idea of needles being stuck in my
scrotum. Not that she normally puts the needles where you might
expect, but you never know. So I just mentioned my usual symptoms
and she put the needles in my hands and feet, as she usually does.
They look a bit like the pins with coloured plastic heads that are used
on wall-maps and notice-boards. You feel a kind of tingling jolt when
she hits the right spot, sometimes it can be as powerful as a low-
voltage electric shock. There's definitely something to this acupuncture business, though whether it does you any lasting good, I don't
know. I went to Miss Wu originally for my Internal Derangement of
the Knee, but she told me frankly that she didn't think she could do
much about it except to assist the healing process by improving my
general physical and mental health, so I settled for that. I feel better
afterwards for the rest of the day, and maybe the next morning, but
after that the effect seems to wear off. There's a slightly penitential

aspect to it – the needles do hurt a little, and you're not allowed to drink alcohol on the day of the treatment, which is probably why I feel better for it – but I find Miss Wu's infinitely gentle manner comforting. She always apologizes if a particularly strong reaction to the needle makes me jump; and when (very rarely) she can't find the spot, and has to have several tries, she gets quite distressed. When she accidentally drew blood one day, I thought she would die of shame.

While the treatment is going on we chat, usually about my family. She takes a keen interest in the lives of Adam and Jane. Her questions, and my occasional difficulty in answering them, make me guiltily aware how little thought I give to my children these days, but they have their own lives now, independent and self-sufficient, and they know that if they are in serious need of money they only have to ask. Adam works for a computer software company in Cambridge, and his wife Rachel teaches Art History part-time at the University of Suffolk. They have a young baby so they're completely taken up with the complex logistics of their domestic and professional lives. Jane, who did a degree in archaeology, was lucky enough to get a job at the museum in Dorchester, and lives in Swanage with her boyfriend Gus, a stonemason. They lead a quiet, unambitious, vegetarian life in that dull little resort and seem happy enough in a New Age sort of way. We see them all together these days only at Christmas, when we have them to stay in Hollywell. A tiny shadow of a frown passed across Miss Wu's face when she realized from my remarks that Jane and Gus are not married – I guess that this would not be acceptable in her community. Well, I hope Jane will get married one day, preferably not to Gus, though she could probably do worse. Today I boldly asked Miss Wu if she expected to marry herself and she smiled and blushed and lowered her eyes, and said, "Marriage is a very serious responsibility." She took my pulse again and pronounced that it was much improved and wrote down something in her book. Then she left the room for me to get dressed.

I left her cheque in a plain brown envelope on the little table where she keeps her needles and other stuff. The first time she treated me I made the mistake of taking out my wallet and crassly thrusting banknotes into her hand. She was very embarrassed, and so was I when I perceived my *faux pas*. Paying therapists is always a bit tricky. Alexandra prefers to do it all by mail. Amy told me that on the last Friday of every month when she goes into Karl Kiss's consulting room there's a little envelope on the couch with her bill in it. She picks it up and silently secretes it in her handbag. It is never referred to by either of them. It's not surprising, really, this reticence. Healing shouldn't be a financial transaction – Jesus didn't charge for miracles. But therapists have to live. Miss Wu only charges fifteen quid for a one-hour session. I wrote her out a cheque for twenty, once, but this only caused more embarrassment because she ran after me in the car park and said I'd made a mistake.

When I was dressed she came back into the room and we made an appointment for two weeks' time. Next Friday I have aromatherapy. Miss Wu doesn't know that, though.

I'm game for almost any kind of therapy except chemotherapy. I mean tranquillizers, antidepressants, that sort of stuff. I tried it once. It was quite a long time ago, 1979. My first very own sitcom was in development with Estuary – *Role Over*, the one about a house-husband with a newly liberated, careerist wife. I was working on the pilot when Jake called me with an offer from BBC Light Entertainment to join the script-writing team for a new comedy series. It was a typical twist in the life of a freelance writer: after struggling for years to get my work produced, suddenly I was in demand from two different channels at once, I decided that I couldn't do both jobs in tandem. (Jake thought I could, but then all *he* had to do was draw up two contracts and hold out two hands for his commission.) So I turned down the Beeb, since *Role Over* was obviously the more important project. Instead of just telephoning Jake, I wrote him a long letter setting out my reasons in minutely argued detail, more for my own sake than for his (I doubt if he even bothered to read it through to the end). But the pilot was a disaster, so bad that Estuary wouldn't even expose it to the light of cathode tube, and it looked as if the series would never happen. Naturally I began to regret my decision about the BBC offer. Indeed "regret" is a ridiculously inadequate description of my state of mind. I was convinced that I had totally destroyed my career, committed professional suicide, passed up the best opportunity of my life etc. etc. I suppose, looking back, it was my first really bad attack of Internal Derangement. I couldn't think about anything else but my fateful decision. I couldn't work, I couldn't relax, I couldn't read, couldn't watch TV, couldn't converse with anybody on anything for more than a few minutes before my thought process, like the stylus arm of a haunted record deck, returned inexorably to the groove of futile brooding on The Decision. I developed Irritable Bowel Syndrome, and went about drained of energy by the peristaltic commotion in my gut, fell exhausted into bed at ten-thirty and woke two hours later soaked in sweat, to spend the rest of the night mentally rewriting my letter to Jake demonstrating with impeccable logic why I could perfectly well work for the BBC and Estuary at the same time, and constructing other scenarios which turned back the clock and allowed me to escape in fantasy the consequences of my decision: my letter to Jake was lost, or returned to me unopened because wrongly addressed, or the BBC came back pleading with me to have second thoughts, and so on. After a week of this, Sally made me go and see my GP, a taciturn Scot called Patterson, not the one I have now. I told him about my restless bowels and sleeplessness, and guardedly admitted to being under stress (I wasn't yet prepared to open the door on the raving madhouse of my mind to another person). Patterson listened, grunted, and wrote me out a prescription for Valium.

I was a Valium virgin – I suppose that was why the effect of the drug was so powerful. I couldn't believe it, the extraordinary peace and relaxation that enveloped me like a warm blanket within minutes. My fears and anxieties shrank and receded and disappeared, like gibbering ghosts in the light of day. That night I slept like a baby, for ten hours. The next morning I felt torpid and mildly depressed in an unfocused sort of way. I dimly sensed bad thoughts mustering below the horizon of consciousness, getting ready to return, but another little pale green tablet zapped that threat, and cocooned me in tranquillity again. I was all right – not exactly in scintillating form either creatively or socially, but perfectly all right – as long as I was taking the pills. But when I finished the course, my obsession returned like a rabid Rottweiler freed from the leash. I was in an infinitely worse state than I had been before.

The addictive nature of Valium wasn't fully appreciated in those days, and of course I hadn't been taking it long enough to become addicted anyway, but I went through a kind of cold turkey as I struggled against the temptation to go back to Patterson and ask for another prescription. I knew that if I did so, I would become totally dependent. Not just that, but I was sure that I would never be able to write as long as I was on Valium. Of course I couldn't write while I was *off* it, either, at the time, but I had a kind of intuition that eventually the nightmare would pass of its own accord. And of course it did, ten seconds after Jake called me to say Estuary were going to re-cast and do another pilot. It got an encouraging response, and they commissioned a whole series, which was a modest success, my first, while the BBC show bombed. A year later I could hardly remember why I had ever doubted the wisdom of my original decision. But I remembered the withdrawal symptoms after the last Valium and vowed never to expose myself to that again.

Two spasms in the knee while I was writing this, one sharp enough to make me cry out.

❋ ❋ ❋ ❋ ❋ ❋ ❋ ❋ ❋ ❋ ❋ ❋ ❋ ❋ ❋ ❋ ❋

Saturday evening, 20th Feb. I heard a surprising and rather disturbing story from Rupert at the Club today. Sally and I went there after an early lunch to play tennis, outdoors. It was a lovely winter's day, dry and sunny, the air crisp but still. Sally played doubles with three other women, I with my crippled cronies. It takes us blokes a long time to get into our kit, we have to put on so many bandages, splints, supports, trusses and prostheses first – it's like mediaeval knights getting into their armour before a battle. So Sally and her pals were well into their first set as we walked, or rather limped, past their court on our way to ours. Rupert's wife Betty was partnering Sally, and just at that moment she played a particularly good backhand volley to win a point, and we all applauded. "Betty's been having some coaching too, has she, Rupert?" Joe remarked, with a grin. "Yes," said Rupert, rather abruptly. "Well, our Mr Sutton certainly does something for the ladies," said Joe. "I don't know what exactly, but . . ." "Oh, knock it off, Joe," said Rupert irritably, striding on ahead. Joe pulled a face and waggled his eyebrows at Humphrey and me, but said nothing more until we reached the court and picked partners.

I played with Humphrey, and we beat the other two in five sets, 6–2, 5–7, 6–4, 3–6, 7–5. It was a keenly contested match, even if to an observer it might have looked from the speed of our movements as if we were playing underwater. My backhand was working well for once, and I played a couple of cracking returns of service, low over the net, that took Rupert quite by surprise. There's nothing quite so satisfying as a sweetly hit backhand, it seems so effortless. I actually won the match with a mistimed volley off the frame of my racquet, which was more characteristic of our normal play. However, it was all very enjoyable. Joe wanted to switch partners and play the best of three sets, but my knee had tightened up ominously, and Rupert said his painkillers were beginning to wear off (he always takes a couple of tablets before a game), so we left the other two to play singles and went for a drink after we'd showered. We carried our pints to a nice quiet corner of the Club bar. In spite of the occasional twinge of pain in my knee, I felt good, glowing from the exercise, almost like the old days, and relished the cool bitter, but Rupert frowned into his jar as if there was something nasty at the bottom of it. "I wish Joe wouldn't keep on about Brett Sutton," he said. "It's embarrassing. It's worse than embarrassing, it's unpleasant. It's like watching somebody picking at a scab." I asked him what he meant. He said, lowering his voice, "Didn't you know about Jean?" "Jean who?" I said stupidly. "Oh, you weren't there, were you," Rupert said. "Joe's Jean. She had it off with young Ritchie at the New Year's Eve do."

Young Ritchie is Alistair, son of Sam Ritchie, the Club's golf pro. He looks after the shop when his father is out giving lessons, and does a bit of beginners' tuition himself. He can't be more than twenty-five. "You're not serious?" I said. "Cross my heart," Rupert said. "Jean got tight, and started complaining because Joe wouldn't dance, then she got young Ritchie to dance with her, giggling and hanging round his neck she was, then some time later they both disappeared. Joe went looking for her, and found them together in the First Aid room, in a compromising position. It's not the first time it's been used for that purpose, I believe. They'd locked the door, but Joe had a key, being on the Committee." I asked Rupert how he knew all this. "Jean told Betty, and Betty told me." I shook my head incredulously. I wondered why Joe was making all these cracks about Brett Sutton being the club gigolo, if he himself had just been cuckolded by young Ritchie. "Diversionary tactics, I suppose," Rupert said. "He's trying to draw attention away from Ritchie and Jean." "What possessed young Ritchie?" I said. "Jean is old enough to be his mother." "Perhaps it was pity," Rupert suggested. "Jean told him she hadn't had it since Joe had his back operation." "Had what?" "*It,*" said Rupert. "Sex. You're a bit slow on the uptake today, Tubby." "Sorry, I'm gobsmacked," I said. I was thinking of our conversation in the indoor courts last week: it was disturbing to realize that what I took to be Joe's harmless teasing had had this painful subtext. I recalled now that Rupert hadn't joined in the banter, though Humphrey had. "Does Humphrey know about this?" I asked. "I dunno. I don't think so. He hasn't got a wife to pass on the gossip, has he? I'm surprised Sally hasn't picked it up." Perhaps she has, I thought, and hasn't told me.

But when I asked her later if she'd heard any scandal about Jean Wellington, she said, no. "But then I wouldn't," she said. "It's a trade-off, that sort of gossip. You don't get any dirt if you don't dish some yourself." I thought she would ask me for more details, but she didn't. Sally has extraordinary self-control in that way. Or perhaps she just isn't curious about other people's private lives. She's very wrapped up in her work at the moment – not only her teaching and research, but admin. There's a lot of reorganization going on as a result of the change of status from Poly to University. They can make up their own degree programmes now, and Sally is chairing a new inter-Faculty postgraduate degree course in Applied Linguistics shared between Education and Humanities, as well as sitting on numerous committees, internal and external, with names like F-QUAC (Faculty Quality Assurance Committee) and C-CUE

(Council for College and University English), and organizing the in-service training of local junior-school teachers to implement the new National Curriculum. I think she's being exploited by her Head of Department, who gives her all the trickiest jobs because he knows she'll do them better than anyone else, but when I tell her this she just shrugs and says that it shows he's a good manager. She brings home piles of boring agendas and reports to work through in the evenings and at the weekends. We sit in silence on opposite sides of the fireplace, she with her committee papers, I connected to the muted television by the umbilical cord of my headphones.

Severe twinge in the knee while I was watching the news tonight. I suddenly shouted "Fuck!" Sally looked up from her papers enquiringly. I took off the headphones momentarily and said, "Knee." Sally nodded and went back to her reading. I went back to the news. The main story was a development in the James Bulger murder case, which has been dominating the media for days. Last week the little boy, only two years old, was enticed away from a butcher's shop in a shopping mall in Bootle by two older boys, while his mother's attention was distracted. Later he was found dead, with appalling injuries, beside a railway line. The abduction was recorded by a security video camera, and every newspaper and TV news pro-gramme has carried the almost unbearably poignant blurred still of the toddler being led away by the two older boys, trustingly holding the hand of one of them, like an advertisement for Startrite shoes. It appears that several adults saw the trio after that, and noticed that the little boy was crying and looking distressed, but nobody intervened. Tonight it was announced that two ten-year-old boys have been charged with murder. "The question is being asked," the TV reporter said, standing against the backdrop of the Bootle shopping mall, "What kind of society do we live in, in which such things can happen?" A pretty sick one, is the answer.

✳ ✳ ✳ ✳ ✳ ✳ ✳ ✳ ✳ ✳ ✳ ✳ ✳ ✳ ✳ ✳ ✳ ✳

Sunday 21st Feb. 6.30 p.m. I'm writing this on my laptop in the break between the dress rehearsal and the recording of *The People Next Door*, sitting at a Formica table in the Heartland Studios canteen, surrounded by soiled plates and cups and glasses left over from an early dinner shared with the cast and production team, and not yet cleared away by the somewhat lackadaisical catering staff. Recording begins at 7.30, after a half-hour warm-up session for the audience. The actors have gone off to Make-Up for repairs, or are resting in their dressing-rooms. Hal is doing a last check on the camera script with his PA and vision mixer, Ollie is having a drink with David Treece, Heartland's Controller of Comedy (I love that title), and I have just managed to shake off the attentions of Mark Harrington's chaperone, Samantha, who lingered after the others had gone, so I have an hour to myself. Samantha Handy has a degree in Drama from Exeter University and is doing the job *faute de mieux*, as Amy would say. Looking after a twelve-year-old boy whose chief topic of conversation is computer games, and making sure he does his homework, is obviously not her natural vocation. She really wants to write for television and seems to think I can help her get a commission. She's a good-looking redhead, with amazing boobs, and I suppose another man, Jake Endicott for instance, might be tempted to encourage her in this illusion, but I told her frankly that she would do better to try and persuade Ollie to give her some scripts to report on as a first step. She pouted a little and said, "It's just that I have this fabulous idea for an offbeat soap, a kind of English *Twin Peaks*. Sooner or later somebody else is going to think of it, and I couldn't bear that." "What is it?" I said, averting my eyes from her own twin peaks; and then added hastily, "No, don't tell me. Tell Ollie. I don't want to be accused of pinching it one day." She smiled and said it wasn't my sort of thing, it was too kinky. "What's kinky?" said Mark, who was working his way through a second helping of Mississippi Mud Pie. "None of your business," said Samantha, flicking him lightly on the ear with a long, tapered fingernail. She asked me if I thought she should get an agent, and I said I thought that would be a good idea, but I didn't offer to introduce her to Jake Endicott. This was entirely for her own good, but naturally she didn't appreciate my

73

chivalrous motives, and took her young charge off to Make-Up slightly miffed.

I never miss these Sunday recording sessions if I can help it. It's not that I can contribute much at this late stage, but there's always a kind of First Night excitement about the occasion, because of the studio audience. You never know who they're going to be or how they're going to react. The ones who write in for tickets are usually fans and can be relied upon to laugh in the right places, but there's always a risk that because the tickets are free people won't show up on the night. To be sure of filling the seats Heartland relies mostly on organized groups, like social clubs and staff associations looking for a cheap night out – bussing them in and out so they can't escape. Sometimes you get a party from an old people's home who are too gaga to follow the plot, or too deaf to hear the dialogue, or too short-sighted to see the monitors, and once we had a group of Japanese who didn't have a word of English between them and sat in baffled silence throughout, smiling politely. Other nights you get a crowd who really enjoy themselves, and the cast surf through the show on continuous waves of laughter. The unpredictability of the studio audience makes sitcom the nearest thing on television to live theatre, which is probably why I get such a buzz out of the recording sessions.

Heartland TV's Rummidge studios occupy a huge new building that looks a bit like an airport terminal from the outside, all cantilevered glass and tubular steel flying buttresses, erected three years ago on reclaimed derelict industrial land about a mile from the city centre, between a canal and a railway line. It was intended to be the hub of a vast Media Park, full of studios, galleries, printshops and advertising agencies, which never materialized because of the recession. There's nothing on the site except the gleaming Heartland monolith and its enormous landscaped car park. *The People Next Door* is recorded in Studio C, the biggest one, big enough to house an airship, with raked seating for three hundred and sixty running its entire length. On the floor, facing the seats, the permanent set is laid out – a particularly large and complex one, since there are two of everything: two living

74

rooms, two kitchens, two hallways and staircases, all separated by a party wall. *Party Wall* was my original working title, in fact, and the split-screen we use for some scenes, with action going on simultaneously in both households, is the visual trademark of the show, and frankly the only innovative thing about it. About a million lights sprout from the ceiling on metal stalks, like an inverted field of sunflowers, and the air-conditioning, designed to cope with all of them at once, is too cool for comfort. I always wear a thick sweater to dress rehearsals, even in summer. Hal Lipkin and most of the other production staff sport *The People Next Door* sweatshirts, navy blue with the title sloping in yellow cursive writing across the chest.

This is a long hard day for everyone, but especially for Hal. He's totally in command, totally responsible. When I arrived in the late morning he was down on the set talking to Ron Deakin, who was standing on top of a stepladder with a Black and Decker power tool. It's a "party wall" kitchen scene. Pop Davis is in the process of putting up some shelves under the sarcastic goading of Dolly Davis, while Priscilla and Edward next door are having a worried conversation about Alice, distracted by the whine of the drill. At the climax of the scene Pop Davis pushes his drill right through the wall, dislodging a saucepan that nearly falls on Edward's head – a tricky bit of business, which depends on pin-sharp timing. They've rehearsed it of course, but now they're having to do it for the first time with real props. The lead on Ron's Black and Decker is not long enough to reach the powerpoint, and there's a hiatus while the electrician goes to fetch an extension cord. The cameramen yawn and look at their watches to see how long it is to the next coffee-break. The actors stretch and pace about the set. Phoebe Osborne practises ballet steps in front of a mirror. Making television programmes consists very largely of waiting around.

The day's routine is slow and methodical. First Hal directs a scene from the edge of the set, stopping and starting to re-block the moves if necessary, until he's satisfied. Then he retires to the control room to see what it looks like from there. Five cameras are positioned at different angles to the set, focused on different characters or groups of characters, and each one is sending its pictures to a black-and-white monitor in the control room. A colour monitor in the middle of the bank of screens shows what will be recorded tonight on the master tape: a selection made by the production assistant, following a camera script prepared by Hal, in which every shot is numbered and allocated to a particular camera. She chants out the numbers to the vision mixer at her side as the action proceeds, and he presses the appropriate buttons. If you're sitting in the studio audience you can tell which camera is actually recording at any given moment because a little red bulb on the camera body lights up. From the gallery Hal speaks to his floor manager Isabel through her headset, and she relays his instructions to the cast. Sometimes he decides he needs to change a shot, or insert a new one, but it's striking how seldom he has to do this. He's already "seen" the entire show in his head, shot by shot.

Multicamera, as this technique is known in the trade, is peculiar to television. In the early days of the medium everything was done this way, even serious drama – and done *live* (imagine the tension and stress, with actors running round the back of the set to get into position for their next scene). Nowadays most drama and a good deal of sitcom is done on film or single-camera video. In other words, they're made like movies, every scene being shot several times from various angles and focal distances, in take after take, on location rather than in a studio, and then edited at the director's leisure. Directors prefer this method because it makes them feel like genuine *auteurs*. The younger ones sneer at multicamera and call it "joined-up television", but the fact is that most of them couldn't handle it, and would have their limitations cruelly exposed if they tried. With post-production editing you can always cover up your mistakes, but multicamera requires everything to be pretty well perfect on the night. It's a dying art, and Hal is one of the few masters of it still around.

Ollie came into the studio later and sat down beside me. He was wearing one of his Boss suits – he must own a wardrobeful. I think he buys them because of the name. As he sat down the wide shoulders of the jacket rode up and nudged his big red ears. Bracketing his broken nose, these make him look like an ex-boxer, and indeed it's rumoured that he started his career promoting fights in the East End of London.

"We must talk," he said. "About Debbie?" I asked. He looked alarmed and raised his finger to his lips. "Not so loud, walls have ears," he said, though we were alone in the raked seating and the nearest wall was fifty feet away. "Lunch? Dinner?" I suggested. "No, I want to involve Hal, and the cast will think it's funny if we get into a huddle on our own. Can you stay for a drink after the recording?" I said I could. At that moment I was surprised to hear Lewis Parker saying from the set, "*Well, if she is pregnant she'll have to have a termination,*" and Debbie replying, "*I suppose you think that will solve everything.*" I turned to Ollie. "I thought those lines had been cut." "We decided to respect your artistic integrity, Tubby," Ollie said, with a wolfish grin. When I asked Hal about it in a coffee break, he explained that they had saved some time by cutting a bit of business in a later scene so there had been no need to lose the lines after all. But I wonder if this isn't part of some plot to soften me up for the more serious matter of Priscilla's role.

It's five to seven. Time for me to take my seat in the studio. Wonder what kind of an audience we've got.

✣ ✣ ✣ ✣ ✣ ✣ ✣ ✣ ✣ ✣ ✣ ✣ ✣ ✣ ✣ ✣ ✣

Monday morning, 22nd Feb. The audience turned out to be bloody awful. For starters we had a Moronic Laugher among them. That's always bad news: some idiot with a very loud, inane laugh, who goes on baying or cackling or shrieking at something long after everybody else has stopped, or starts up when nobody else is laughing, in the lull between two gags. It distracts the audience – after a while they start laughing at the Moronic Laugher instead of at the show – and it plays havoc with the actors' timing. Billy Barlow, our warm-up man, spotted the danger right away and tried to subdue the woman (for some reason, it's invariably a woman) with a few sarcastic asides, but Moronic Laughers are impervious to irony. "Did I say something funny?" he enquired as she cackled suddenly (she was a cackler) in the middle of his perfectly straight explanation of some technical term. "I think it must be in your mind, madam. This is a family show – no innuendos. You know what an innuendo is, don't you? Italian

77

for suppository." There was enough laughter to drown the cackler temporarily, though I've known Billy get a lot more with that joke on other occasions.

The warm-up man is essential to a successful recording. Not only does he have to get the audience in a receptive mood beforehand, he also has to bridge the gaps between scenes, as the cameras are moved from one part of the set to another, and fill in the pauses while the technicians check the tape after each take; and if a retake or pick-up is required he has to soothe the audience's impatience and appeal for their co-operation in laughing at the same lines the second time round. Billy is the best in the business, but there are limits to what even he can do. This audience was really sticky. They merely tittered at what should have been big laughs, and were silent when they should have tittered. As line after line fell flat the cast got anxious, and began to make mistakes or dry, requiring frequent re-takes, which made the audience still more unresponsive. Billy began to perspire, pacing up and down in front of the seats with his radio mike, frantically cracking jokes, his capped teeth exposed in a strained smile. I laughed like a drain, though I'd heard them all before, to encourage the people around me. I even forced a laugh at some of my own lines, something I never normally do. I began to think that it couldn't just be the audience's fault, there must be something wrong with the script. It had obviously been a bad idea to centre the plot on Alice's suspected pregnancy. Ollie and Sally had been right. The subject was making the audience uneasy. Then of course, when it came to the lines about termination, in the dramatic pause that followed Priscilla's question, *"Suppose she chooses to have the baby?"* the Moronic Laugher broke the silence with all the sensitive understanding of a mynah bird. I covered my face with my hands.

They wrapped the programme at five past nine, after more retakes than I could ever remember. Billy hypocritically thanked the audience for their support, and we all dispersed. The actors scurried from the set, giving me tired little waves and wan smiles of farewell. They're always in a hurry to get off on Sunday nights, to drive or catch the last train to London, and there was no temptation to linger tonight. I would have been glad to slope off home myself, if I hadn't

78

had the confab with Ollie and Hal pending. I went to the control room, where Hal was running both hands through his birds' nest of wiry hair. "Jesus Christ, Tubby, who were those zombies out there tonight?" I shrugged my bafflement. "Maybe it was the script," I said miserably. Ollie came steaming into the room in time to hear this. "It wouldn't have made any difference if you were Shakespeare, Oscar Wilde and Groucho Marx rolled into one," he said, "those fuckers would have killed anybody's script. Where did we get them from – the local morgue?" Suzie the PA said she thought the largest contingent was a local factory's social club. "Well, the first thing I'm going to do tomorrow morning is find out who the hell they were and who invited them, and make sure they never come to a recording again. Let's go and have a drink. We need it."

Ollie is notoriously tight-fisted, and always wriggles out of standing his round if he possibly can. He's always the last to say, "Anybody for another one?" – by which time anyone who's driving has switched to fruit juice or stopped drinking altogether. When we go to the bar with him, Hal and I usually have a bit of fun trying to trick him into buying the first round – for instance, Hal will pretend to remember he's left something in the control room, and double back, shouting his order over his shoulder, and I'll suddenly veer into the Gents, doing the same. But yesterday evening neither of us had the heart for it, and Hal bought the first round without putting up any kind of fight. "Cheers," he said gloomily. We drank and sat in silence for a moment. "I've put Hal in the picture about Debbie," Ollie said. Hal nodded gravely. "It's a bitch," he said. But I knew I couldn't count on any real support from him. When push came to shove, he would side with Ollie. "Jake told you what we're suggesting, Tubby?" Ollie said.

At this moment Suzie came into the bar, and looked around until she spotted us. "Not a word about the Debbie thing," Ollie warned in a low voice, as she approached our table. I offered her a seat, but she shook her head. "I won't stop, thanks," she said. "I went outside and mingled with the audience while they were waiting for their buses. Most of them are from an electrical component factory in West Wallsbury. They heard on Friday that it's going to shut down at the end of next month. They all got redundancy notices with their payslips." We looked at each other. "Well, that explains a lot," I said. "Just our luck," said Hal. "Sodding management might have waited till tomorrow," said Ollie.

I was sorry for the workers, but the explanation couldn't have come at a better time as far as I was concerned. I'd been so demoralized by the way that evening's show had bombed that I would probably have agreed to anything Ollie and Hal proposed. Now, I no longer blamed myself. I was a bloody good scriptwriter after all – always had been and always would be. I was ready to do battle for my principles. "Jake gave me a rough idea of what you have in mind," I said to Ollie. "You want me to write Priscilla out of the story, is that it?" "What we have in mind," said Ollie, "is an amicable separation which removes Priscilla from the scene at the end of the current series, and sets up a new female interest in Edward's life for the next one." "*Amicable?*" I exploded. "They would be completely traumatized." "There would be a certain amount of pain, of course," said Ollie, "but Edward and Priscilla are mature modern people. They know that one in three marriages ends in divorce. So does our audience. You're always saying sitcom should deal with the serious things in life occasionally, Tubby." "As long as it's consistent with character," I said. "Why should Priscilla want to leave Edward?"

They had various bizarre suggestions: e.g., Priscilla decides she's a lesbian and goes off with a girlfriend; she gets oriental religion and goes off to an ashram to learn meditation; she is offered a wonderful job in California; or she just falls for a handsome foreigner. I asked them if they seriously thought any of these developments were (*a*) credible or (*b*) manageable in just one episode. "You might have to rewrite the last two or three, to prepare the ground," Ollie conceded, avoiding the first question. "I have an idea for the final episode," said Hal. "Let me run it by you." "This is a great idea, Tubby," Ollie assured me. Hal leaned forward. "After Priscilla walks out, Edward advertises for a housekeeper, and this stunning bird arrives at the door for an interview. Edward suddenly sees there may be a silver lining to his troubles. It's the very last shot of the series. Leaves the punters feeling better about the split, and interested in what will

80

happen in the next series. What do you think?" "I think it stinks," I said. "Naturally you'd be paid handsomely for the extra work," said Ollie. "To be frank, you and Jake have us over a barrel on this one." He glanced slyly at me from under his hooded eyelids to see if he had awakened my greed by this admission. I said it wasn't money I was concerned about, but character and motivation. Hal asked me if I had any better ideas. I said: "The only plausible way to remove Priscilla from the show is to kill her." Ollie and Hal exchanged startled looks. "You mean, like have her murdered?" Hal faltered. I said, of course not, maybe a car crash or a swift fatal disease. Or a minor operation that goes wrong. "Tubby, I don't believe I'm hearing this," said Ollie. "We're talking sitcom here, not soap. You can't have one of your principal characters *die*. It's a no-no." I said there was always a first time. "That's what you said about tonight's episode," said Ollie, "and look what happened." "That was the audience's fault," I protested, "you said so yourself." "The best audience in the world is going to be stymied if they turn up expecting a comedy show and find that it's all about the mother of a family dying in the prime of life," said Ollie, and Hal sagely nodded his agreement. Then Ollie said something that really made me angry. "We appreciate how hard this is for you, Tubby. Perhaps we should think about getting another writer to work on it." "No way, José," I said. "It's commonplace in America," Ollie said. "They have whole teams of writers working on shows like ours." I know," I said, "that's why the shows sound like a string of gags written by a committee. I'll tell you another thing about America. In New York they have street signs saying, 'Don't even think of parking here.' That's how I feel about *The People Next Door*." I glowered at Ollie. "It's been a long day," said Hal nervously. "We're all tired." "Yeah, we'll talk again," said Ollie. "Not about other writers," I said. "I'd rather scuttle the ship than hand it over to somebody else." It seemed a good exit line, so I got to my feet and bade them both goodnight.

I just opened the dictionary to check the spelling of "glowered", and as I flipped the pages the headword "Dover's Powder" caught my eye. The definition said: *"a preparation of opium and ipecac, formerly used to relieve pain and check spasms. Named after Thomas Dover (1660–1742) English physician.''* I wonder if you can still get it. Might be good for my knee.

It's amazing what you can learn from dictionaries by accident. That's one reason why I never use the Spellchecker on my computer. The other reason is that it has such a pathetically small vocabulary. If it doesn't recognize a word it suggests another one it thinks you might have meant to write. This can be quite funny sometimes. Like once I wrote "Freud" and the computer came back with the suggestion, "Fraud?" I told Amy, but she wasn't amused.

I called Jake this morning and reported my conversation with Ollie and Hal. He was sympathetic but not exactly supportive. "I think you should be as flexible as you can," he said. "Heartland are desperately keen for the series to continue. It's their comedy flagship." "Whose side are you on, Jake?" I asked him. "Yours, of course, Tubby." Of course. But at heart Jake believes in Ollie Silver's adage, "Art for art's sake but money for Christ's sake." I arranged to call in at his office on Thursday.

Had a restless night last night. Sally was already in bed and asleep when I got back from the recording. I snuggled up to her spoonwise and went off quite quickly, but was jerked awake at two thirty by internal derangement of the knee. I lay awake for hours, replaying the events of yesterday in my head, and waiting for the next twinge. This morning I noticed a touch of tennis elbow, too, when I was shaving. Be great, wouldn't it, if I had another operation on my knee, only to find I had to give up tennis because of the elbow? Good job it's my day for physiotherapy.

Monday evening. I asked Roland if he'd ever heard of Dover's Powder, but he said it didn't ring a bell. He's a connoisseur of anti-inflammatory gels with names like Movelat and Traxam and Ibuleve (reminds me of the song, *"Ibuleve for every drop of rain that falls, a flower grows . . ."*) which he rubs into my knee after ultrasonic treatment. (*"Ibuleve for every stab of pain that galls, new tissue grows . . .*") Physiotherapy these days is largely automated. When I'm stripped down and ready on the couch, Roland wheels a big box of electronic tricks into the room and wires me up to it, or aims a dish or a lamp or a laser at the affected part. It's amazing how deftly he handles the equipment. There's just one gadget I have to operate myself. It gives electric shocks which stimulate the quadriceps, and I have to turn up the voltage to the maximum I can bear. It's like self-inflicted torture. Funny how much the pursuit of fitness has in common with the infliction of pain. From my couch, shackled with wires and electrodes, I gaze through the window and across a small courtyard at the glass wall of a gymnasium where men, grimacing with effort and glistening with sweat, are exercising on machines that, apart from their hi-tech finish, could be engines of torture straight out of a mediaeval dungeon: racks, pulleys, weights, and treadmills.

Roland asked me if I had heard about the trans-sexual trout. No, I said, tell me about the trans-sexual trout. He's a mine of information, is Roland. His wife reads interesting snippets out of the newspaper to him, and he remembers everything. Apparently male trout are suffering sex-changes because of the high level of female hormones getting into the sewage outfall from contraceptive pills and hormone replacement therapy. It's feared that all the male fish in the affected rivers will become hermaphrodites, and cease to reproduce. "Makes you think, doesn't it?" said Roland. "After all, we drink the same water eventually. Next thing you know, men will be growing breasts." I wondered if Roland was winding me up. I have a lot of fatty tissue on my chest, under the hair. Roland might have felt it one day, when he was giving me a massage.

Perhaps I couldn't come the other night because I'm turning into a hermaphrodite. Internal Derangement of the Hormones.

✳ ✳ ✳ ✳ ✳ ✳ ✳ ✳ ✳ ✳ ✳ ✳ ✳ ✳ ✳ ✳ ✳

Tuesday evening, 23rd Feb. I asked for Dover's Powder in the biggest Boots in Rummidge today, but the pharmacist said he'd never heard of it, and he couldn't find it in his book of patent medicines. I said, "I expect it was banned because of the opium," and he gave me a funny look. I left the shop before he could call the Drug Squad.

I went into the City Centre primarily to buy some books by Kierkegaard, but didn't have much joy. Waterstone's only had the Penguin edition of *Fear and Trembling*, so I bought that and went along to Dillons. When Dillons proved to have the same book and nothing else, I began to feel my usual symptoms of shopping syndrome, i.e. unreasonable rage and impatience. Low Frustration Tolerance, LFT, it's called, according to Alexandra. I'm afraid I was very scathing to a harmless assistant who thought "Kierkegaard" was two words and started searching on her microfiche under "Gaard." Fortunately the Central Library was better supplied. I was able to borrow *The Concept of Dread*, and a couple of the other titles that had intrigued me, *Either/Or* and *Repetition*. The *Journals* were out.

It's quite a while since I used the Library, and I hardly recognized it from the outside. It's a typical piece of sixties civic architecture, a brutalist construction in untreated concrete, said by the Prince of Wales to resemble a municipal incinerating plant. It's built in a hollow square around a central courtyard in which there was once a shallow pond and a seldom-functioning fountain, the repository for much unseemly garbage. This gloomy and draughty space was a public thoroughfare, though most people avoided it, especially at night. Recently, however, it's been converted into a glazed and tiled atrium, festooned with hanging greenery, adorned with neoclassical fibreglass statues, and designated "The Rialto" in pink neon lettering. The floor area is dedicated to a variety of boutiques, stalls and catering outlets of a vaguely Italianate character. Operatic muzak and Neapolitan pop songs ooze from hidden speakers. I sat down at a table "outside" Giuseppe's café-bar (outside still being indoors in this studio-like setting) and ordered a *cappuccino*, which seemed designed to be inhaled through the nose rather than drunk, since it consisted mostly of foam.

Much of the city centre has been given the same kind of face-lift, in a brave attempt to make it attractive to tourists and visiting businessmen. Resigned to the erosion of the region's traditional industrial base, the city fathers looked to service industries as an alternative source of employment. A vast conference centre and a state-of-the-art concert hall now face the Library from the other end of a tessellated piazza. Hotels, wine bars, nightclubs and restaurants have sprung up in the neighbourhood, almost overnight. The surrounding canals have been cleaned up and their towpaths paved for the exploration of industrial archeology. It was a typical project of the later Thatcher years, that brief flare of prosperity and optimism between the recession of the early eighties and the recession of the early nineties. Now the new buildings, with their stainless steel escalators and glass lifts and piped music, stand expectant and almost empty, like a theme park before opening day, or like some utopian capital city of a third-world country, built for ideological reasons in the middle of the jungle, an object of wonder to the natives but seldom visited by foreigners. The principal patrons of the Rialto in the daytime are unemployed youths, truanting schoolkids, and mothers with infant children, who are grateful for a warm and cheerful place in which to while away the winter afternoons. Plus the occasional privileged wanker like me.

I don't recall hearing the word "recession" until a few years ago. Where did it come from, and what does it mean exactly? For once the dictionary is not much help: *"a temporary depression in economic activity or prosperity."* How long does a recession have to last before it's called a depression? Even the Slump of the Thirties was "temporary", in the long run. Perhaps there's so much psychological depression about that somebody decided we needed a new word for the economic sort. Recession-depression, recession-depression. The words echo in my head, like the rhythm of a steam engine. They're connected, of course. People get depressed because they can't get a job, or their businesses collapse or their houses are repossessed. They lose hope. A Gallup poll published today said that nearly half the people in the country would like to emigrate if they could. Walking about the city centre this afternoon you'd have thought they already had.

My young brother Ken emigrated to Australia in the early seventies, when it was easier than it is now, and never made a better

85

decision in his life. He's an electrician by trade. In London he worked for one of the big stores in the West End and never made enough money to buy a decent car or a house big enough for his growing family. Now he has his own contracting business in Adelaide, and a ranch-style house in the suburbs with a two-car garage and a swimming pool. Until *The People Next Door* took off, he was doing considerably better than me. Mind you, he was always happier than me, even when he was hard up. He has a naturally cheerful temperament. Funny how some people have, and some people haven't, even when their genes were dealt from the same deck.

I went to my appointment with Alexandra straight from the Rialto, and, as I was describing the scene to her, I let slip the phrase "privileged wanker". "Why do you call yourself that?" she demanded. "Wanker because I was sitting about drinking coffee in the middle of the day," I replied, "and privileged because it was a free choice, not because I had nothing better to do." "If I remember rightly," she said, "you told me that you work extremely hard when you're writing a television series, often up to twelve hours a day." I nodded. "Are you not entitled to relax at other times?" "Yes, of course," I said, "I meant I was struck by the contrast between my life and the lives of the no-hopers in the Rialto." "How do you know they have no hope?" I didn't, of course. "Did they look hopeless?" I had to admit they hadn't. In fact they probably looked more cheerful than me to an observing eye, swapping jokes and cigarettes, tapping their feet in time to the muzak. "But with the recession the way it is," I said, "I have this sense that I'm getting richer while everybody else around me is getting poorer. It makes me feel guilty." "Do you feel personally responsible for the recession?" "No, of course not." "In fact, I think you told me that your earnings from abroad are quite considerable?" "Yes." "So you're actually making a positive contribution to the nation's trading balance?" "You could look at it that way, I suppose." "Who *is* responsible for the recession, would you say?" I thought for a moment. "No individual, of course. It's a complex of factors, mostly outside anyone's control. But I think the Government could do more to alleviate its effects." "Did you vote for this Government?" "No,

I've always voted Labour," I said. "But . . ." I hesitated. Suddenly the stakes had become very high. "But what?" "But I felt secretly relieved when the Tories won."

I had never admitted this to anybody before, not even to myself. I was flooded with a mixture of shame and relief at having finally uncovered a genuine reason for my lack of self-esteem. I felt as I imagine Freud's patients felt when they broke down and admitted that they had always wanted to have sex with their mummies and daddies. "Why was that?" Alexandra enquired calmly. "Because it meant I wouldn't have to pay higher taxes," I said. "As I understand it," said Alexandra, "the Labour Party proposed to the electorate a rise in income tax, the electorate rejected it, and now the Labour Party has dropped it. Is that your understanding?" "Yes," I said. "So what are you feeling guilty about?" Alexandra said. "I don't know," I said.

I think Alexandra's talents are wasted on me. She should be working in the City of London convincing people that Greed is good.

I had a go at *The Concept of Dread* this evening – thought I'd start with the title that seemed most obviously relevant to me – but it was a great disappointment. The table of contents alone was enough to put me off:

Chap. I   *Dread as the presupposition of original sin and as explaining it retrogressively by going back to its origin.*

Chap. II   *Dread as original sin progressively.*

Chap. III *Dread as the consequence of that sin which is the default of the consciousness of sin.*

Chap. IV   *The dread in sin, or dread as the consequence of sin in the particular individual.*

Chap. V   *Dread as saving experience by means of faith.*

I've never regarded myself as a religious person. I believe in God, I suppose. I mean I believe there's Something (rather than Somebody) beyond the horizons of our understanding, which explains, or would explain if we could interrogate it, why we're here and what it's all about. And I have a sort of faith that we survive after death to find out

87

the answer to those questions, simply because it's intolerable to think that we never will, that our consciousness goes out at death like an electric light being switched off. Not much of a reason for believing, I admit, but there you are. I respect Jesus as an ethical thinker, not casting the first stone and turning the other cheek and so on, but I wouldn't call myself a Christian. My Mum and Dad sent me to Sunday school when I was a nipper – don't ask me why, because they never went to church themselves except for weddings and funerals. I liked going at first because we had a very pretty teacher called Miss Willow, with yellow curls and blue eyes and a lovely dimpled smile, who got us to act out stories from the Bible – I suppose that was my first experience of drama. But then she left and instead we had a severe-looking middle-aged lady called Mrs Turner, with hairs growing out of a big spot on her chin, who told us our souls were stained black with sin and had to be washed in the Blood of the Lamb. I had nightmares about being dunked in a bath full of blood by Mrs Turner, and after that my parents didn't make me go to Sunday School any more.

Much later, when I was a teenager, I used to attend a Catholic Youth Club, because Maureen Kavanagh was a Catholic and belonged to it; and occasionally I would get trapped or dragged in to some kind of service on Sunday evenings, a recitation of the rosary in the parish hall, or something they called Benediction in the church next door, a funny business with a lot of hymn-singing in Latin and clouds of incense and the priest on the altar holding up something like a gold football trophy. I always felt awkward and embarrassed on these occasions, not knowing what I was supposed to do next, sit or stand or kneel. I was never tempted to become a Catholic, though Maureen used to throw out the occasional wistful hint. There seemed to be far too much about sin in her religion, too. Most of the things I wanted to do with Maureen (and she wanted to do with me) turned out to be sins.

So all this stuff about sin in the chapter headings of *The Concept of Dread* was discouraging, and the actual book confirmed my misgivings. It was dead boring and very difficult to follow. He defines dread, for instance, as *"freedom's appearance before itself in possibility."* What the fuck does that mean? To tell you the truth I skimmed though the book, dipping here and there and hardly understanding a word. There was just one interesting bit at the very end:

> I would say that learning to know dread is an adventure which every man has to affront if he would not go to perdition either by not having known dread or by sinking under it. He therefore who has learned rightly to be in dread has learned the most important thing.

But what is learning rightly to be in dread, and how is it different from sinking under it? That's what I'd like to know.

Three spasms in the knee today, one while driving, two while sitting at my desk.

✳ ✳ ✳ ✳ ✳ ✳ ✳ ✳ ✳ ✳ ✳ ✳ ✳ ✳ ✳ ✳ ✳

Wednesday 24th Feb, 11.30 p.m. Bobby Moore died today, of cancer. He was only fifty-one. People in the media must have known he was ill, because the BBC had a tribute all ready to slot into *Sportsnight* tonight. It included an interview with Bobby Charlton that must have been live, though, or recorded today, because he was crying. I was nearly crying myself, as a matter of fact.

The first I knew of it was when Amy and I came out of a cinema in Leicester Square at about eight. We'd been to an early-evening showing of *Reservoir Dogs*. A brilliant, horrible film. The scene where one of the gangsters tortures a helpless cop is the most sickening thing I've ever seen. Everybody in the film dies violently. I honestly believe that every character you see is shot to death – the police who shoot the Harvey Keitel character at the end are just voices off camera. Amy didn't seem disturbed by the mayhem. She was more bothered by the fact that she couldn't recall what she had seen one of the actors in before, and kept muttering to me, "Was it *House of Games*? No. Was it *Taxi-driver*? No. What was it?" until I had to beg her to shut up. As we came out of the cinema, she said triumphantly, "I remember now, it wasn't a movie at all, it was an episode of *Miami Vice*." Just at that moment I clocked a newspaper billboard, "BOBBY MOORE DIES." Suddenly the deaths in *Reservoir Dogs* seemed cartoon-thin. I hurried Amy through her supper so that I could get back to the flat to watch the telly, and she decided to go home straight from Gabrielli's. "I can see you want to be alone with your grief," she said sardonically, and she wasn't far wrong.

There were lots of clips of Bobby Moore in his prime as a player in *Sportsnight*, with of course a special emphasis on the World Cup Final of 1966, and that unforgettable image of Moore receiving the cup from the Queen, carefully wiping his hands on his shirt first, and then turning to face the crowd, holding the trophy high in the air for the whole of Wembley, and the whole country, to worship. What a day that was. England 4, Germany 2, after extra time. A story straight out of a boys' comic. Who believed at the start of the tournament that, after years of humiliation by South Americans and Slavs, we'd at last be world champions in the game we'd invented? What heroes they were, that team. I can still recite the names from memory. Banks, Wilson, Cohen, Moore (*capt.*), Stiles, Jack Charlton, Ball, Hurst, Hunt, Peters and Bobby Charlton. He cried on that occasion, too, I seem to remember. But not Bobby Moore, always the model captain, calm, confident, poised. He had immaculate timing as a player – it made up for his slowness on the turn. Seeing the clips brought it all back: the way his long leg would stretch out at the last possible moment and take the ball off an opponent's toe without fouling him. And then the way he would bring the ball out of defence and into attack, head up, back straight, like a captain leading a cavalry charge. He looked like a Greek god, with his clean-cut limbs and short golden curls. Bobby Moore. They don't make them like that any more. They make overpaid lager louts plastered with advertising logos, who spit all over the pitch and swear so much that lip-reading deaf viewers write to the BBC to complain.

(I make an exception of Ryan Giggs, the young Manchester United winger. He's a lovely player, thrilling to watch when he's running at a defence with the ball apparently tied to his feet, scattering them like sheep. And he still has his innocence, if you know what I mean. He hasn't yet been kicked into caution and cynicism, he hasn't been worn down by playing too many games too close together, he hasn't had his head turned by stardom. He still plays as if he enjoys the game, like a kid. I tell you what I like about him most: when he's done something really good, scored a goal, or dribbled past three players, or made a perfect cross, and he's trotting back towards the centre circle, and the crowd are going wild, he *frowns*. He looks terribly serious, like a little boy who's trying to seem ever so grown-up, as if it's the only way he can stop himself from turning cartwheels or beating his chest or screaming with excitement. I love that, the way he frowns when he's done something really brilliant.)

But back to Bobby Moore and that glorious June day of the 1966 World Cup Final. Even Sally, who was never a great soccer fan, got caught up in the excitement, put Jane to sleep in her pram and sat down to watch the telly with me and Adam – who was too young to really understand what it was all about, but sensed intuitively that it was important and sat patiently through the whole match with his thumb in his mouth and his blanket-comforter pressed to his cheek, watching me all the time instead of the screen. It was our first colour set. England wore red shirts instead of the usual all-white strip, strawberry-jam red. I suppose we tossed up with Germany for the privilege of wearing white, and lost, but we should have stuck with red ever after, it seemed to bring us luck. We were lucky to be awarded that third goal, which was why getting the fourth one was so deliriously satisfying. When the ball went in the net you could hear the cheering coming out of the neighbours' open windows; and when it was all over people went into their back gardens, or out into the street, grinning all over their faces, to babble about it to other people they'd never said more than "Good morning" to in their lives before.

It was a time of hope, a time when it was possible to feel patriotic without being typecast as a Tory blimp. The shame of Suez was behind us, and now we were beating the world in the things that really mattered to ordinary people, sport and pop music and fashion and television. Britain was the Beatles and mini-skirts and *That Was The Week That Was* and the victorious England team. I wonder if the Queen was watcing the telly tonight, and what she felt seeing herself presenting the World Cup to Bobby Moore. A pang or two of nostalgia, I should think. *"Those were the days, Philip, eh?"* Those were the days when she could wake up in the morning confident of not having to read detailed accounts of the sexual misbehaviour of her family in the newspapers: Dianagate, Camillagate, Squidgey tapes, Charles's tampon fantasies, Fergie's toe-sucking. Internal Derangement of the Monarchy. I was never a great one for the Royal Family, but you can't help feeling sorry for the poor old Queen.

Which reminds me of an oddly disturbing experience I had this morning on my way to London. As I waited for the train at Rummidge Expo, I spotted Nizar further up the platform. I was just going up to greet him, my face already arranged into a suitable smile, when I saw that he was with a young woman. She wasn't young enough to be his daughter, and I knew she wasn't his wife, because I'd seen a silver-framed photo of the wife on his desk, a plump, rather severe-looking matron in a floral dress, flanked by three children, and she bore no resemblance to this tall slim young woman with glistening black hair falling to the shoulders of a smartly cut black woollen coat. Nizar was standing very close to her, talking animatedly and touching her, his surgeon's fingers fluttering over the collar of her coat and adjusting her hair and plucking at her sleeves, in a manner which was at once possessive and deferential, like a star's dresser. She was smiling complacently at whatever Nizar was murmuring into her ear, with her head bent because he was several inches shorter than herself, but she happened to look up just as I clocked what was going on. Fortunately she didn't know me from Adam. I wheeled round and retreated rapidly to the waiting room, where I sat down and hid my face behind the *Guardian* until the train arrived.

There seems to be an adultery epidemic going on: Jake, Jean Wellington, the Royal Family, and now Nizar. What I want to know is, why should *I* feel embarrassed, even guilty, at having surprised Nizar with his bimbo? Why did *I* run away? Why did *I* hide? I don't know.

Sally and I haven't made love since last Thursday. I've been going to bed at different times from her, or complaining of indigestion or of feeling a cold coming on, etc., to discourage the idea. I'm scared of fiinding that I can't come again. I suppose I could try masturbating, just to check there's nothing mechanically wrong.

* * * * * * * * * * * * * * * * *

Thursday morning, 25th Feb. After I wrote that last bit, I undressed and lay on the bed with a towel handy and tried to jerk myself off. It's a long time since I did this, getting on for thirty-five years in fact, and I was out of practice. I couldn't find any Vaseline in the bathroom cabinet, and it so happened that I'd just run out of olive oil in the kitchen, so I lubricated my cock with Paul Newman's Own Salad Dressing, which was a mistake. First of all it was freezing cold from the fridge and had a shrivelling rather than a stimulating effect at first, secondly the vinegar and lemon juice in it stung like hell, and thirdly I began to smell like Gabrielli's *pollo alla cacciatora* as the herbs warmed up with the friction. But the main problem was that I couldn't summon up the appropriate thoughts. Instead of erotic imagery I kept thinking of Bobby Moore triumphantly holding aloft the Jules Rimet trophy, or Tim Roth lying in a pool of his own blood in *Reservoir Dogs*, with the red stain spreading up his shirt front till he looked as if he was wearing the England strip.

I thought of trying one of the telephone sex lines I'd heard so much about lately – but where would I get a number from? The Yellow Pages weren't any use, and I hardly thought I could consult Directory Enquiries. Then I remembered that there was an old listings magazine in the magazine rack, and sure enough I found columns of ads for phone sex in the back pages. I chose a number that promised *"Fast Instant Sex Relief, Hard Smutty Sex Talk"* with a footnote explaining that *"due to new EEC regulations we can now bring you European-strength action."* I listened for about ten minutes to a girl describing with much sighing and groaning the process of peeling and swallowing a banana, and began to wonder whether it was EEC agricultural regulations that were being invoked. It was a total con, and so were the other two lines I tried.

It occurred to me that I was only a few minutes' walk from the largest concentration of pornographic bookshops in the country, and although it was now well past midnight, some of them might still be open. It was a bind having to get dressed again to go out, but I was determined to bring my experiment to a conclusion. Then, just as I was about to leave the flat, it crossed my mind to check the front porch on the entryphone video screen – and, sure enough, there was my squatter of last week, curled up cosily inside his sleeping bag. I recognized his pointed nose and chin peeping out of the top of the bag, and the hank of hair over his eyes. I stared at the picture until the camera cut out automatically and I was left with my own faint grey reflection in the screen. I imagined myself going downstairs and opening the front door. Either I would have to wake him up and have an argument, or I would have to step over him as if he wasn't there – and not just once, but twice, since I would be returning after a short interval with a bundle of girlie magazines under my arm. Neither of these alternatives appealed to me. I undressed again and went back to bed, suffering acutely from Low Frustration Tolerance. It was as if this vagrant was holding me a moral prisoner in my own home.

Eventually I managed to produce a spurt of jism by sheer physical effort, so I know the plumbing is basically sound, but my cock is quite sore and it hasn't done my tennis elbow any good either.

✳ ✳ ✳ ✳ ✳ ✳ ✳ ✳ ✳ ✳ ✳ ✳ ✳ ✳ ✳ ✳ ✳

Thursday afternoon. I'm sitting in the Pullman lounge, Euston station, waiting for the 5.10. I meant to catch the 4.40, but just missed it. The ticket-collector saw me running down the ramp and shut the barrier when I was ten yards short, at 4.39 precisely. The station is plastered with notices saying that platforms will be closed one minute before the advertised departure times of trains *"in the interests of punctuality and customer safety"*, but he could have let me through without endangering either. I had no luggage except the briefcase containing my laptop. The last coach of the train was only twenty yards away, with the guard standing at ease beside it, looking up the deserted platform, waiting for the OFF signal. I could have made it easily, as I vehemently pointed out, but the guy at the barrier, an officious, determined little Asian, wouldn't let me. I tried to push past him, but he pushed me back. We actually wrestled for a full minute, until the train finally pulled out, and I turned on my heel and walked furiously back up the ramp, uttering empty threats about making a complaint. He has better grounds for complaint than me (should that be "I"?) – indeed, he could probably have me for assault.

I'm still trembling a bit from the adrenalin rush, and I think I've pulled a small muscle in my back in the struggle. Pretty stupid behaviour, really, when you come to think about it, as I shall do very shortly. Low Frustration Tolerance will give way to Low Self-Esteem, and another wave of depression will move in to cover the Passmore psyche with low cloud and outbreaks of drizzle. Quite unnecessary. After all, it's only half an hour till the next train, and the Pullman Lounge is a very civilized place to wait in. It's rather like a brothel, or how I imagine brothels to be, but without the sex. You go up the stairs that lead to the table-service restaurant and the Superloo, and halfway along the passage to the latter there's a discreetly inconspicuous door with a bell-push and speaker grille in the wall beside it. When you press the bell-push, a female voice asks you if you have a first-class ticket, and if you say "Yes" the door springs open with a click and a buzz, and you're in. There's a nice-looking girl at the desk who smiles as you show your ticket and sign the Visitors' Book, and offers you complimentary coffee or tea. It's calm and hushed inside, air-conditioned, carpeted and comfortably furnished with armchairs and banquettes upholstered in soothing tones of blue and grey. There are newspapers, and telephones, and a photocopier. Down below, the hoi polloi waiting for trains must sit on their luggage, or on the floor (since there are no seats in the vast marbled concourse) or else patronize one of the fast-food outlets – Upper Crust, Casey Jones, The Hot Croissant, Pizza Hut, etc. – that cluster together in a junk-food theme park at one end of

I got so carried away by that bit of description that I discovered I'd missed the 5.10 as well. Or rather I discovered I'd left myself only two minutes in which to catch it, and I couldn't bear the thought of running down the ramp towards the same ticket-collector and having him shut the barrier in my face again, like some kind of dream

95

repetition of the original trauma. So I may as well, while I wait for the 5.40, record why I was on such a short fuse in the first place.

I called in at Jake's office on my way to Euston. It's a small set of rooms over a tatty tee-shirt and souvenir shop in Carnaby Street. There was a new girl in the tiny reception office at the top of the stairs, tall and slim, in a very tight, very short black dress that barely covered her bum when she stood up. She introduced herself as Linda. After she'd shown me into Jake's room and shut the door, he said, "I know what you're thinking, and no, she isn't the one. Not," he added, with his cheeky chappie grin, "that I could swear she won't be, one day. Did you get a look at those legs?" "I could hardly avoid it, could I?" I said. "Given the dimensions of your office and her skirt." Jake laughed. "What's the news from Heartland?" I said. He stopped laughing. "Tubby," he said, leaning forward earnestly in his swivel chair, "you're going to have to find some acceptable way of writing Priscilla out of the series. Acceptable to everyone, I mean. I know you can, if you set your mind to it." "And if I can't?" I said. Jake spread his hands. "Then they'll get somebody else to do it." I felt a small, premonitory spasm of anxiety. "They can't do that without my agreement, can they?" "I'm afraid they can," said Jake, swivelling his chair to pull open a drawer, and avoiding my eye in the process. "I looked up the original contract." He took a file from the drawer and passed it to me across the desk. "Clause fourteen is the relevant one."

The contract for the first series had been drawn up a long time ago, when I was just another scriptwriter, with no particular clout. Clause fourteen said that if they asked me to write further series based on the same characters, and I declined, they could employ other writers to do the job, paying me a token royalty for the original concept. I can't recall giving this clause any special thought at the time, but I'm not surprised that I agreed to it. Getting the programme extended for another series was then my dearest ambition, and the idea that I might not want to write it myself would have seemed absurd. But the clause referred not just to a second series, but to "series", in the indefinite plural. Effectively I had signed away my copyright in the story and characters. I reproached Jake for not having spotted the danger and re-negotiated the clause in subsequent contracts. He said he didn't think Heartland would have played ball anyway. I don't agree. I think we could have twisted their arm between the second and the third series, they were so keen. Even now I can't believe that they would turn the whole show over to another writer, or writers. It's my baby. It's me. Nobody else could make it work as well.

Could they?

This is a dangerous train of thought, fraught with new possibilities for loss of self-esteem. Anyway, I'd better stop, or I'll miss the 5.40 as well.

* * * * * * * * * * * * * * * * * *

Friday 26th Feb., 8 p.m. Jake called this morning to say he'd received a note from Ollie Silvers, *"just summarizing the main points of our conversation with Tubby last Sunday, to avoid any misunderstanding."* This brings clause fourteen into operation, and means that I have twelve weeks in which to make up my mind whether to write Priscilla out of the script myself, or let someone else do the deed.

Aromatherapy with Dudley this afternoon. Dudley Neil-Hutchinson, to give his name both barrels. He looks a bit like a hippie Lytton Strachey – tall, spindly, with a long woolly beard that you'd think was attached to his granny glasses. He wears jeans and deck shoes and ethnic print shirts and waistcoats from the Oxfam shop. He tucks his beard into the waistcoats so that it doesn't tickle when he massages you. He practises at home in a modern three-bedroomed semi near the airport, triple-glazed to exclude the sound of aircraft taking off and landing. Sometimes, lying prone on the massage table, you feel a shadow pass over you and if you look up quickly enough you catch a glimpse of a huge plane swooping silently over the rooftops, so close you can pick out the white faces of passengers at the portholes. It's quite alarming at first. Dudley does two mornings a week at the Wellbeing, but I prefer to go to his house for treatment because I don't want Miss Wu to know I'm resorting to aromatherapy as well as acupuncture. She's so sensitive, she might take it as a personal vote of no confidence in her skills. I can just imagine bumping into her as I came out of a session with Dudley, and the silent, hurt look of reproach in her dark brown eyes. Miss Wu doesn't know about Alexandra, either. Alexandra knows about Miss Wu, but not about Dudley. I haven't told her, not because she'd feel threatened, but because she might be disappointed in me. She respects acupuncture, but I don't think she would have much time for aromatherapy.

It was June Mayfield who put me onto it. She works in Make-Up at Heartland, and sits in the wings during recordings of *The People Next Door*, ready to dart forward and titivate Debbie's hair when required, or powder the actors' noses if they get shiny under the lights. I was chatting to her in the canteen one day and she told me aromatherapy had changed her life, curing her of the migraines that had been the bane of her existence for years. She gave me Dudley's card, and I thought I'd give it a try. I'd just given up yoga, on account of my Internal Derangement of the Knee, so I had a vacant slot in my therapy schedule. I used to go once a fortnight to Miss Flynn, a seventy-five-year-old lady with elastic joints who teaches Pranayama yoga. It's not the sort where you stand on your head for hours or tie yourself in knots that have to be unravelled in Casualty. It's mostly about breathing and relaxation, but it does entail attempting the lotus position or at least the half-lotus, which Miss Flynn didn't think would be a good idea while I was having trouble with my knee, so I packed it in. To tell you the truth, I was never much good at yoga anyway. I could never manage the "slipped second" which is a vital part of it, when you're supposed to empty your mind and not think of anything at all. Miss Flynn tried to teach me a mental routine according to which you empty your mind first of thoughts about work, then of thoughts about family and friends, then of thoughts about yourself. Well, I could never get past first base. As soon as I silently pronounced the word "work" to myself, thoughts about script revisions and casting problems and audience figures would start swarming in my head. I would develop worries about work that I never had before.

Aromatherapy is easier. You just lie there and let the therapist massage you with what are called essential oils. The theory behind it is quite simple – perhaps too simple. Dudley explained it to me at my first session. "If you hurt yourself, what's your instinctive reaction? You rub the affected part, right?" I asked how you rub your mind. He said, "Ah, that's where the essential oils come in." Aromatherapists think that, through absorption into the skin, the oils enter the bloodstream and thus affect the brain. Also that the inhalation of the oils' distinctive aromas has a stimulating or calming effect on the nervous system, depending on which ones you use. There are uppers and downers in aromatherapy, or "high notes" and "bass notes" as they call them. According to Dudley, it's a very ancient form of medicine which was practised in China and Egypt yonks ago. But, like everything else, nowadays it's computerized. When I go to see Dudley I tell him my symptoms, and he writes them into his personally devised aromatherapy programme, called PHEW (no, I made that up, the filename is ATP), presses a key, and the computer comes up with a list of suggested essential oils – juniper, jasmine, peppermint or whatever. Then Dudley lets me sniff them and makes up a cocktail of the ones I like best, using a vegetable "carrier oil" as a base.

I didn't feel the same inhibition about discussing sexual matters with Dudley as I did last week with Miss Wu, so when he asked me how I'd been since the last treatment, I mentioned the non-ejaculation incident. He said that the ability to have sexual congress without ejaculating was highly prized by oriental mystics. I said they were welcome to it. He tapped away at his Apple Mac for a few moments and it came up with bergamot, ylang-ylang and rose otto. "Didn't you give me rose for depression, last time?" I said, with a hint of suspicion in my voice. "It's a very versatile oil," said Dudley suavely. "It's used against impotence and frigidity as well as depression. Also grief and the menopause." I asked him if that included the male menopause, and he laughed without answering.

✳ ✳ ✳ ✳ ✳ ✳ ✳ ✳ ✳ ✳ ✳ ✳ ✳ ✳ ✳ ✳ ✳

Saturday, 27th Feb. Well, it worked, up to a point. We made love last night and I came. I don't think Sally did, but she wasn't really in the mood, and seemed surprised when I suggested it. I can't say the earth moved for me, either, but at least I had an ejaculation. So the old essential oil of rose did the trick, as far as impotence is concerned. But not as far as depression, grief and the male menopause are concerned. I woke at 3.05 with my brain churning like a cement-mixer, anxieties like sharp pebbles in a general grey sludge of Dread, and spent the next few hours in a shallow dozing state, dropping off and waking again with the fleeting sensation of having been in a dream without being able to remember what it was. My dreams are like silvery fish: I grab at their tails, but they wriggle from my grasp, and shimmy down into the dark depths. I wake gasping for breath, my heart pounding, like a diver surfacing. Eventually I dropped a sleeping tablet and lapsed into a dreamless coma from which I woke, in an empty bed, at nine-thirty, sullen and dry-mouthed.

Sally had left a note to say she'd gone to Sainsbury's. I had some errands to do myself, so walked to the High Street. I was standing impatiently in line at the Post Office when I heard a woman's voice say at my shoulder, "Are you desperate?" I swivelled round, thinking she was addressing me, but it was a mother talking to her little boy. "Can't you wait till we get home?" she said. The little boy shook his head miserably and pressed his knees closer together.

Later. I was desperate enough to give old Kierkegaard another go, and had better luck this time. I dipped into *Either/Or*, because the title intrigued me. A socking great book, in two volumes, and very confusingly written, a dog's breakfast of essays, stories, letters etc., written by two fictitious characters called A and B, and edited by a third called Victor Eremitus, all aliases for Kierkegaard I presume. What particularly caught my eye was a short piece in the first volume called "The Unhappiest Man". As I read it, I felt like I did when I first saw the list of Kierkegaard's book titles, that he was speaking directly to my condition.

According to K., the unhappy man is "always absent to himself, never present to himself." My first reaction was: no, wrong, Søren old son – I never stop thinking about myself, that's the trouble. But then I thought, thinking about yourself isn't the same as being present to yourself. Sally is present to herself, because she takes herself for granted, she never doubts herself – or at least not for long. She *coincides* with herself. Whereas I'm like one of those cartoon characters in a cheap comic, the kind where the colour doesn't quite fit the outline of the drawing: there's a gap or overlap between the two, a kind of blur. That's me: Desperate Dan with his blue chin sticking out but not quite coinciding with his jawline.

Kierkegaard explains that the unhappy man is never present to himself because he's always living in the past or the future. He's always either hoping or remembering. Either he thinks things were better in the past or he hopes they'll be better in the future, but they're always bad *now*. That's ordinary common-or-garden unhappiness. But the unhappy man "in a stricter sense" isn't even present to himself in his remembering or his hoping. Kierkegaard gives the example of a man who looks back wistfully to the joys of childhood which in fact he never himself experienced (perhaps he was thinking of his own case). Likewise the "unhappy hoper" is never present to himself in his hoping, for reasons which were obscure to me until I came to this passage: "Unhappy individuals who hope never have the same pain as those who remember. Hoping individuals always have a more gratifying disappointment."

I know exactly what he means by "gratifying disappointment". I worry about making decisions because I'm trying to guard against things turning out badly. I *hope* they'll turn out well, but if they do turn out well I hardly notice it because I've made myself miserable imagining how they could turn out badly; and if they turn out badly in some unforeseen way (like clause fourteen in the Heartland contract) that only confirms my underlying belief that the worst misfortunes are unexpected. If you're an unhappy hoper you don't really believe things will get better in the future (because if you did you wouldn't be unhappy). Which means that when they *don't* get better it proves you were right all along. That's why your disappointment is gratifying. Neat, eh?

I also have a persistent feeling that things were better in the past – that I must have been happy once, otherwise I wouldn't know I was unhappy now, and somewhere along the way I lost it, I blew it, I let it go, though I can only recall that "it" in fleeting fragments, like watching the 1966 World Cup Final. It's possible, however, that I'm kidding myself, that really I was always miserable because I was always an unhappy hoper. Which paradoxically would make me an unhappy rememberer too.

How can you be both? Easy-peasy! That's precisely the definition of the unhappiest man:

> This is what it amounts to: on the one hand, he constantly hopes for something he should be remembering . . . On the other hand he constantly remembers something he should be hoping for . . . Consequently what he hopes for lies behind him and what he remembers lies before him . . . He is forever quite close to the goal and at the same moment at a distance from it; he now discovers that what it is that makes him unhappy, because now he has it, or because he is this way, is precisely what a few years ago would have made him happy if he had had it then, whereas then he was unhappy because he did not have it.

Oh yes, this guy has my number alright. The unhappiest man. Why then am I grinning all over my face as I read?

✳   ✳   ✳   ✳   ✳   ✳   ✳   ✳   ✳   ✳   ✳   ✳   ✳   ✳   ✳   ✳

Sunday afternoon, 28th Feb. I didn't go to the studio today. I thought I would show Heartland that I resent the way they're treating me. Sally approved. I left a message on the office answerphone early this morning to say I wouldn't be coming in. I didn't give a reason, but Ollie and Hal will figure it out. It's the first time I've missed a recording since last April, when I had a stomach bug. Needless to say, I'm punishing myself more than I'm punishing them. Hal will be too busy to brood on my absence, and Ollie is not the brooding type. Whereas I have nothing to do except brood. The day has passed with excruciating slowness. I keep looking at the clock and working out what stage of rehearsal they will have reached. It's five past four now, and dark already. It's bitterly cold outside, with a thin coating of snow. Blizzards expected in other parts of the country, the papers say.

The posh Sundays are full of handwringing and breastbeating. The country seems to be going through some huge crisis of confidence, Internal Derangement of the National Psyche. The Gallup poll published last week showed eighty per cent of the electorate were dissatisfied with the Government's performance. According to another poll, more than forty per cent of young people think that Britain will become a worse country to live in over the next decade. Which means, presumably, they think that either Labour won't win the next election, or it won't make any difference if they do. We've become a nation of unhappy hopers.

And unhappy rememberers: I wasn't the only one, it seems, to feel that the death of Bobby Moore measured the extent of our decline. There are lots of nostalgic articles in the papers about him and the 1966 World Cup. Our losing the third Test in succession to India this week hasn't helped national morale, either. *India!* When I was a boy a Test series against India was always a dead boring prospect because it was bound to be a walkover for England.

It's half past five. Rehearsals will be over by now, and the cast will be tucking into their meal in the canteen before going off to Make-Up. Ron Deakin always has sausage, egg and chips. He swears he never eats fry-ups at home, but says that sausage, egg and chips go with the character of Pop Davis. He's quite superstitious about it – got into quite a panic one day, when they ran out of sausages in the kitchen. I wonder if he will be put off by my not being there as usual tonight. The actors like me to be around on recording day, they find it reassuring. I'm afraid I'm punishing them, as well as myself, by staying away.

The more I think about it, and I can think of nothing else, the worse I feel. I'm trying to resist deciding that I have made the wrong decision, but I can feel myself being drawn inexorably towards that conclusion as if by the gravitational force of a black hole. In short, I can feel myself getting into one of my "states". The state, *c'est moi*, as Amy might say. How am I going to get through the rest of the evening? I stare at the key marked HELP on my keyboard. If only it could.

* * * * * * * * * * * * * * * * *

Monday morning, 1st March. At about 6.45 yesterday evening, just as Sally was laying the table for our evening meal, my nerve broke. I rushed out of the house, shouting an explanation to Sally without giving her time to tell me I was a fool, backed the Richmobile out of the garage, slithering and sliding all over the drive – I damn near dented the offside wing on the gatepost – and drove at imprudent speed into Rummidge, arriving at the studio just in time to take my seat for the recording.

It went brilliantly. A wonderful audience – sharp, appreciative, together. And the script wasn't bad, either, though I says it myself. The story-line is that the Springfields decide to put their house up for sale in order to get away from the Davises, but without telling the Davises because they feel guilty about it, and the Davises keep unknowingly sabotaging the plan by turning up or doing something outrageous just when the Springfields are showing potential buyers round the house. The audience loved it. I expect a lot of them want to move house themselves and can't because they have negative equity. Negative equity is when your mortgage is more than your house is worth. There's a lot of it about. It's a kind of internal derangement of the property market. Not funny, if you've got it, but it might make you see the funny side of Edward and Priscilla's dilemma. Or, to put it another way, watching their farcical trials and tribulations might make you feel better about your negative equity, especially as the episode ends with the Springfields reconciled to staying where they are. I often feel that sitcom has that kind of therapeutic social effect.

The cast felt the good vibrations coming from the audience and were in cracking form. There were hardly any re-takes. We wrapped at eight-thirty. Everybody was smiling afterwards. "Hallo, Tubby," said Ron Deakin, "we missed you at rehearsal today." I mumbled something about being tied up. Hal gave me a quizzical look, but said nothing. Isabel, the floor manager, told me I'd been well out of it, that the rehearsal had been full of snags and cock-ups. "But that's always the way," she said. "If the rehearsal runs like a train, you can be sure the recording will be a disaster." (Isabel is an unhappy hoper.) Ollie wasn't there: he'd phoned in to say the roads were too dodgy in his part of the world. Several members of the cast decided to stay overnight in Rummidge in view of the weather, so we all went to the bar. There was a genial, relaxed atmosphere, everybody basking in the sense of a job well done, cracking jokes, buying rounds. I felt a huge affection for them all. It's like an extended family, and in a way I'm the father of it. Without my scripts, they would never have come together.

Samantha Handy came into the bar, having tucked young Mark up in bed for the night at a nearby hotel, just as I was leaving. She gave me a nice smile, so I smiled back, pleased that she evidently didn't bear me a grudge from last week's conversation. "Oh, are you going already?" she said. "Breaking up the party?" "Got to," I said. "How's the script-writing going?" "I'm going to discuss my idea with an agent," she said. "I've got an appointment with Jake Endicott next week. He's *your* agent, isn't he? I mentioned that I knew you, I hope you don't mind." "No, of course not," I said, thinking to myself, *Cheeky bitch!* "Be careful what you wear," I said. She looked anxious. "Why? Has he got a thing about clothes?" "He's got a thing about good-looking young women," I said. "I'd advise a nice, long, baggy bin-liner." She laughed. Well, she can't say I didn't warn her. Jake will go ape when he sees those knockers. She has a pretty face, too, round and freckled, with a hint of a double chin that's like a trailer for the opulent curves straining at her blouse-front. She took my advice about asking Ollie if she could read some scripts and apparently he's given her a bundle to report on. A young woman to watch, in more ways than one.

I drove home slowly and deliberately on the icy, deserted roads. Sally was already asleep when I got in. Something about her posture in the bed, flat on her back, and the set of her mouth, told me that she had gone to bed displeased with me – whether for breaking my resolution to stay away from the recording, or for fastforwarding out of the house just as she was serving up supper, or for driving in dangerous conditions, or for all these things, I couldn't tell. I found out this morning it was something else. Apparently, after I told her I wouldn't be going to the studio as usual yesterday, she'd invited a couple of neighbours round for a drink in the evening. She swears she told me, so I suppose she must have done, though I haven't the faintest memory of it. Worrying. She had to phone the Websters again and cancel. Embarrassing, undoubtedly. They're Tory-voting zombies, but they ask us every year to their Christmas Eve drinks party, and we never ask them back. (On the rare occasions when we give a party I pore over the guest list for hours, agonizing over the choice of names, trying to arrive at a perfectly balanced crowd of scintillating and mutually compatible conversationalists. The Websters are not even considered for such gatherings, though excluding them doesn't of course prevent me from being in a state of anxiety bordering on hysteria as the party approaches, or from anaesthetizing myself with drink as soon as possible after it starts.) So yesterday evening would have been an opportunity to level up the scores a bit. Sally says now we'll have to ask them to dinner to make up. I hope that's just a threat. Anyway, I'm in the doghouse. All the euphoria of last night has evaporated. My knee is playing up this morning, and I've definitely pulled a muscle in my back.

✳ ✳ ✳ ✳ ✳ ✳ ✳ ✳ ✳ ✳ ✳ ✳ ✳ ✳ ✳ ✳ ✳

Monday afternoon. Just back from physiotherapy. I told Roland about the back muscle, but not that I pulled it fighting with a bantam-weight Pakistani ticket-puncher. He assumed it was another tennis injury. In fact I haven't played this past week, partly because of the weather and partly because I haven't felt like getting together with my usual partners after what Rupert had told me about Joe and Jean. Roland gave me an old-fashioned back massage as well as Ultrasound on the knee. It's what physiotherapy was all about when he trained – he's good at it and he enjoys it. His hands are his eyes, he feels his way into the deepest core of your aches and pains, and gently but firmly eases away the inflammation. Dudley isn't a patch on him.

Roland's wife had read him something out of the paper over breakfast this morning, about new extracts from the Diana Squidgey tapes being published in Australia. I said I found it hard to believe these conversations were overheard accidentally. Roland didn't. It came out that he spends a lot of time at night listening to police messages on the VHF waveband of his Sony portable. "I listen for hours, sometimes," he said. "In bed, with the earphones on. There was a drug bust in Angleside last night. Quite exciting it was." So Roland suffers from insomnia too. It must be particularly horrible if you're blind, lying awake in the night, dark on dark.

One of the depressing things about depression is knowing that there are lots of people in the world with far more reason to feel depressed than you have, and finding that, so far from making you snap out of your depression, it only makes you despise yourself more and thus feel more depressed. The purest form of depression is when you can give absolutely no reason why you're depressed. As B says, in *Either/Or*, "A person in sorrow or distress knows why he sorrows or is distressed. If you ask a melancholic what it is that weighs down on him, he will reply, 'I don't know what it is, I can't explain it.' Therein lies melancholy's infinitude."

I'm beginning to get the hang of this peculiar book. The first part consists of the papers of A – jottings, essays like "The Unhappiest Man", and a journal called *The Seducer's Diary*, which is supposed to have been edited by A, but written by someone else called Johannes. A is a young intellectual layabout who suffers from depression, only he calls it melancholy, and makes a cult of it. In the *Diary* Johannes describes how he seduces a beautiful innocent girl called Cordelia, just to see if he can pull it off against all the odds, and then callously discards her when he succeeds:

> now it is over and I want never to see her again . . . Now all resistance is impossible, and only when it is there is it beautiful to love; once it is gone, love is only weakness and habit.

It's not clear whether we're supposed to think *The Seducer's Diary* is something A found, or that he made it up, or that it's really a disguised confession. It's riveting stuff, anyway, though there's no sex in it – no bonking, I mean. There's a lot about sexual feelings. This, for example:

Today my eyes have rested upon her for the first time. It is said that sleep can make an eyelid so heavy that it closes of its own accord; perhaps this glance of mine has a similar effect. Her eyes close, and yet obscure forces stir within her. She does not see that I am looking at her, she feels it, feels it through her whole body. Her eyes close and it is night, but inside her it is broad daylight.

Perhaps that's how Jake pulls the birds.

The second part of *Either/Or* consists of some inordinately long letters from B to A, attacking A's philosophy of life, and urging him to give up melancholy and get his act together. B seems to be a lawyer or a judge, and is happily married. He's a bit of a prig, actually, but a shrewd one. The bit I quoted just now about melancholy's infinitude is from his second letter, entitled "The Equilibrium between the Aesthetic and the Ethical in the Development of the Personality," but the book as a whole is about the *opposition* of the aesthetic and the ethical. A is the aesthete, B is the ethicist, if that's a word. (Yes, it is. Just looked it up.) A says: either/or, it doesn't matter what you choose, you will regret your choice whatever it is. "If you marry, you will regret it, if you do not marry you will regret it; if you marry or do not marry, you will regret both," and so on. That's why A is so interested in seduction (whether the seduction of Cordelia was real or imagined, A is clearly fascinated by the idea, which means so was old Søren), because to him marriage entails choice (which he would inevitably regret) whereas seduction makes someone else choose and leaves him free. By having Cordelia, Johannes proved to himself that she wasn't worth having, and is free to discard her and go back to his melancholy. "My melancholy is the most faithful mistress I have known," he says. "What wonder then that I love her in return?"

B says you must choose. To choose is to be ethical. He defends marriage. He attacks melancholy. "Melancholy is sin, really it is a sin as great as any, for it is the sin of not willing deeply and sincerely, and this is the mother to all sins." He is kind enough to add: "I gladly admit that melancholy is in a sense not a bad sign, for as a rule only the most gifted natures are afflicted with it." But B is in no doubt that the ethical life is superior to the aesthetic. "The person who lives ethically has seen himself, knows himself, permeates his whole concretion with his consciousness, does not allow vague thoughts to fuss around in

him, nor tempting possibilities to distract him with their legerdemain
. . . He knows himself." Or herself. Sally is the ethical type, whereas
I'm the aesthetic type – except that I believe in marriage, so the cap
doesn't quite fit. And where does Kierkegaard himself stand? Is he A
or B, or both, or neither? Is he saying that you must choose between
A's philosophy and B's, or that whichever you choose you will regret
it?

Reading Kierkegaard is like flying through heavy cloud. Every now
and again there's a break and you get a brief, brilliantly lit view of the
ground, and then you're back in the swirling grey mist again, with not
a fucking clue where you are.

Monday evening. According to an encylopaedia I've just looked up,
Kierkegaard came to think that the aesthetic and the ethical are only
stages on the way to full enlightenment, which is "religious". The
ethical seems to be superior to the aesthetic, but in the end proves to
be founded on nothing more substantial. Then you have to throw
yourself on God's mercy. I don't much like the sound of that. But in
making that "leap", man "finally chooses himself". A haunting,
tantalizing phrase: how can you choose yourself when you already are
yourself? It sounds like nonsense, yet I have an inkling of what it
might mean.

Sally signalled that she is still pissed off with me by declining to watch
The People Next Door tonight, claiming she was too busy. It's a
Monday night ritual, when the show is on the box, that we sit down at
nine o'clock and watch it together. It's a funny thing, but however
familiar you are with a TV programme before it's transmitted, having
written the script, attended rehearsals, watched the recording and
seen a VHS tape of the final edited version, it's always different when
you watch it being actually transmitted. Knowing that millions of
other people are watching it at the same time, and *for the first time*,
changes it somehow. It's too late to alter it or stop it, and that imparts
an edge to the experience. It's a faint replica of what happens in the
theatre when you do your show in front of an audience for the first
time. Every Monday evening as the last commercial before the

programme freezes and fades on the screen, and the familiar theme tune strikes up over the title sequence, I feel my pulse quickening. And absurdly I find myself willing the cast on as if they were performing live, mentally urging them to get the most out of their lines and sight gags, though rationally I know that everything, every syllable and pause, every nuance of voice and gesture, and the responses of the studio audience, are already fixed and unalterable.

Sally gave up reading my scripts in draft years ago – or perhaps I gave up showing them to her: it was six of one and half a dozen of the other. She never much liked the basic concept of *The People Next Door*, and didn't think it would catch on. When it was a runaway success she was pleased of course, for my sake, and for the sake of the lolly that started gushing through the letterbox as if we'd struck oil in the back garden. But, typically, it didn't shake her faith in her judgement in the least. Then she started to work so hard at her own job that she really had no time or energy to spare for reading scripts, so I stopped bothering her with them. In fact it's more useful to me to have her watch the programmes not knowing what's coming next. It gives me an idea of how the other 12,999,999 viewers are reacting, if I multiply her appreciation by a factor of about eight. When Sally gives a chuckle, you can bet they're falling off their chairs and wetting themselves all over the country. But tonight I had to sit through the show in glum silence, on my own.

✳ ✳ ✳ ✳ ✳ ✳ ✳ ✳ ✳ ✳ ✳ ✳ ✳ ✳ ✳ ✳ ✳

Tuesday afternoon, 2nd March. To Alexandra today. She had a cold, and a stuffed-up nose which she kept blowing ineffectually like somebody learning to play the cornet. "Excuse me for mentioning it," I said, "but you'll give yourself sinus trouble if you blow your nose like that. I had a yoga teacher once who showed me how to clear my nose, one nostril at a time." I demonstrated, by pressing a finger against one side of my schnozzle, then against the other. Alexandra smiled weakly and thanked me for the advice. It's the one thing about yoga that's really stayed with me. How to blow your nose.

Alexandra asked me how I'd been in the last week. I told her about the kerfuffle over the future of *The People Next Door*. She asked me what I was going to do. "I don't know," I said. "All I know is that whatever I do, I'll regret it. If I write Priscilla out of the script, I'll regret it, if I let someone else do it, I'll regret it. I've been reading Kierkegaard," I added, thinking Alexandra would be impressed, but she didn't respond. Perhaps she didn't hear: she blew her nose just as I said "Kierkegaard."

"You're prejudging the issue," she said. "You're setting yourself up for failure."

"I'm just facing facts," I said. "My indecision is final, as the man said. Take last weekend." I told her about my vacillation over attending the recording session.

"But you did stick to a decision in the end," Alexandra observed. "You went to the studio. Do you regret it?"

"Yes, because it put me in the wrong with Sally."

"You didn't know at the time that she had invited those neighbours round."

"No, but I should have listened when she told me. And anyway I knew she would disapprove of my going to the studio for other reasons, like the road conditions – that's why I rushed out of the house before she had the chance to talk me out of it. If I *had* given her the chance, I would have finally got the message that the Websters were coming round."

"And in that case you would have stayed in?"

"Of course."

"And is that what you wish had happened?"

I thought for a moment. "No," I said.

We both laughed, rather despairingly.

Am I really in despair? No, nothing as dramatic as that. More like what B calls doubt. He makes a distinction between doubt and despair. Despair is better because at least it entails choice. "So then choose despair, since despair is itself a choice, for one can doubt without choosing to, but despair one cannot without choosing to do so. And when one despairs one chooses again, and what does one choose? One chooses oneself, not in one's immediacy, not as this contingent individual, one chooses oneself in one's eternal validity." Sounds impressive, but is it possible to choose despair and not want to top yourself? Could you just accept despair, live in it, be proud of it, rejoice in it?

B says there's one thing he agrees with A about: that if you're a poet you're bound to be miserable, because "poet-existence as such lies in the obscurity that results from despair's not being carried through, from the soul's constantly shivering in despair and the spirit's being unable to gain its true transparency." So it seems you can be shivering in despair without actually choosing it. Is this my state? Does it apply to script-writer-existence as well as poet-existence?

Philip Larkin knew all about this sort of despair. I just looked up "Mr Bleaney":

> But if he stood and watched the frigid wind
> Tousling the clouds, lay on the fusty bed
> Telling himself that this was home, and grinned,
> And shivered, without shaking off the dread
>
> That how we live measures our own nature,
> And at his age having no more to show
> Than one hired box should make him pretty sure
> He warranted no better, I don't know.

It's all there: "Shivered . . . dread . . . I don't know."

What made me think of Larkin was a report in the paper today that Andrew Motion's forthcoming biography will reveal him in an even worse light than the recent edition of his letters. I haven't read the *Letters* and I don't want to. I don't want to read the new biography, either. Larkin is my favourite modern poet (about the only one I can understand, actually) and I don't want to have the pleasure of reading him ruined. Apparently he used to end telephone conversations to Kingsley Amis by saying, "Fuck Oxfam." Admittedly, there are worse things than saying "Fuck Oxfam", for instance actually doing it, like the gunmen in Somalia who steal the aid intended for starving women and children, but still, what did he want to say a stupid thing like that for? I took out my charity cheque book and sent off fifty quid to OXFAM. I did it for Philip Larkin. Like Maureen used to collect indulgences and credit them to her dead granddad. She explained it to me one day, all about Purgatory and temporary punishment –

daftest stuff you ever heard in your life. Maureen Kavanagh. I wonder what happened to her. I wonder where she is now.

✳ ✳ ✳ ✳ ✳ ✳ ✳ ✳ ✳ ✳ ✳ ✳ ✳ ✳ ✳ ✳

Wednesday 3rd March, late. I met the squatter in the entryway tonight. This is how it happened.

Amy and I went to see *An Inspector Calls* at the National. Brilliant production on a stunning surrealist set, played without a break, like a perfectly remembered dream. I never rated Priestley before, but tonight he seemed as good as bloody Sophocles. Even Amy was swept away – she didn't attempt to recast the play once over supper. We ate in Ovations, a selection of starters – they're always better than the main courses. Amy had two and I had three. And a bottle of Sancerre between us. We had a lot to talk about besides the play: my trouble with Heartland and Amy's latest crisis over Zelda. Amy found a pill in Zelda's school blouse pocket when she was doing the laundry, and she was afraid it was either Ecstasy or a contraceptive. She couldn't decide which would be worse, but she didn't dare to ask the girl about it for fear of being accused of spying on her. She fished the pill, sealed inside an airmail envelope, out of her great swollen bladder of a handbag, and tipped it on to my side-plate for inspection. I said it looked like an Amplex tablet to me, and offered to suck it and see. I did, and it was. Amy was hugely relieved at first. Then she said, with a frown, "Why is she worried about bad breath? She must be kissing boys." I said, "Weren't you at her age?" She said, "Yes, but not with our tongues down each other's throats like they do now." "We used to," I said, "it was called French kissing." "Well, you can get AIDS from it nowadays," said Amy. I said I didn't think you could, though I don't really know.

Then I told her about clause fourteen. She said it was outrageous and I should sack Jake and get the Writers' Guild to challenge the contract. I said that changing my agent wouldn't solve the problem and that Jake's lawyer had already checked the contract and it was impregnable. Amy said, "*Merde.*" We kicked around various ideas for writing Priscilla out of the series, which became more and more facetious as the level of the wine fell in the bottle: Priscilla is reclaimed by a former husband whom she supposed to be dead, and whom she omitted to mention to Edward when they married; Priscilla has a sex-change operation; Priscilla is kidnapped by aliens from outer space . . . I still think the best solution is for Priscilla to die in the last episode of the present series, but Amy wasn't surprised that Ollie and Hal gave it the thumbs-down. "Not death, darling, *anything* but death." I said that was a rather strong reaction. "Oh God, you sound just like Karl," she said.

The remark gave me a rare glimpse of what passes between Amy and her analyst. She's usually rather secretive about their relationship. All I know is that she goes to his office every weekday morning at nine sharp, and he comes into the waiting room and says good morning, and she precedes him into the consulting room and lies down on the couch and he sits behind her and she talks for fifty minutes. You're not supposed to come with a prepared topic, but to say whatever comes into your head. I asked Amy once what happened if nothing worth saying came into your head, and she said you would be silent. Apparently she could in theory be completely silent for the whole fifty minutes and Karl would still collect his fee; though Amy being Amy, this has never actually happened.

It was about eleven when we came out of the theatre. I put Amy in a cab, and walked home to exercise the old knee joint. Roland says I should walk at least half an hour every day. I always enjoy crossing Waterloo Bridge, especially at night, with the buildings all floodlit: Big Ben and the Houses of Parliament to the west, the dome of St Paul's and the knife-sharp spires of other Wren churches to the east, with the red light on top of Canary Wharf winking on the horizon. London still feels like a great city, seen from Waterloo Bridge. Disillusionment sets in when you turn into the Strand and find that all the shop doorways have their quilted occupants, like mummies in a museum.

It didn't occur to me that my own chap would be in residence, perhaps because I'd only ever seen him from inside the flat, on the video screen, well after midnight. He was sitting against the wall of the entryway, with his legs and lower trunk inside his sleeping-bag, smoking a roll-up. I said, "Hey, out of it, you can't sleep here." He looked up at me, brushing a long forelock of lank ginger hair from his eyes. I should say he's about seventeen. Hard to tell. He had a faint smear of gingery bristle on his chin. "I wasn't asleep," he said.

"I've seen you sleeping here before," I said. "Hop it."

"Why?" he said. "I'm not doin' any harm." He drew his knees up inside the sleeping-bag, as if to let me pass without stepping over him.

"It's private property," I said.

"Property is theft," he said, with a sly sort of grin, as if he was trying me out.

"Oh ho," I said, covering my surprise with sarcasm, "a Marxist vagrant. What next?"

"It weren't Marx," he said, "it was proud one." Or that's what it sounded like.

"What proud one?" I said.

His eyes seemed to go out of focus momentarily, and he shook his head in a dogged sort of way. "I dunno, but it weren't Marx. I looked it up once."

"Anything wrong, sir?"

I turned round. Blow me if there weren't a couple of coppers standing there. They'd materialized as if in answer to an unspoken prayer. Except that I didn't want them now. Or not yet. Not at that precise moment. I surprised in myself a strange reluctance to hand the youth over to the power of the law. I don't suppose they would have done anything worse than move him on, but I didn't have time to work that out. It was a split-second decision. "It's alright, officer," I said, to the one who had spoken to me. "I know this young man." The young man himself had meanwhile scrambled to his feet and was busily rolling up his sleeping-bag.

"You live here, do you, sir?" said the policeman. I produced my keys in an over-eager demonstration of ownership. The two-way cell radio clipped to the chest of the other policeman began to squawk and crackle with some message about a burglar alarm in Lisle Street, and after a few more words with me the two of them walked away in step.

"Thanks," said the youth.

I looked at him, already regretting my decision. ("If you shop him you will regret it, if you don't shop him you will regret it, shop him or don't shop him, you will regret both . . .") I was strongly tempted to tell him to bugger off, sharpish, but, glancing up the street, I saw the two coppers eyeing me from the next corner. "I suppose you'd better come in for a few minutes," I said.

He looked at me suspiciously from under his hank of hair. "Yer not queer, are yer?" he said.

"Good God, no," I said. As we silently ascended in the lift, I realized why I hadn't taken advantage of the miraculous appearance of the two policemen to get rid of him. It was that little phrase, "*I looked it up*," that had thrown me momentarily off balance, and on to his side. Another looker-upper. It was as if I had encountered on my doorstep a younger, less privileged image of myself.

"Nice," he said approvingly, as I let him into the flat and switched on the lights. He went over to the window and looked down into the street. "Cor," he said. "You can hardly hear the traffic."

"It's double-glazed," I said. "Look, I only invited you here to stop the police hassling you. I'll give you a cup of tea, if you like –"

"Ta," he said, sitting down promptly on the sofa.

"– I'll give you a cup of tea, but that's it, understand? Then you're on your way, and I don't want to see you here again, ever. All right?" He nodded, rather less emphatically than I could have wished, and took a tin of rolling tobacco out of his pocket. "And I'd rather you didn't smoke, if you don't mind," I said.

He sighed, and shrugged, and put the tin back in the pocket of his anorak. He was wearing the regulation kit of the young West End vagrant: quilted anorak, blue jeans, Doc Martens, plus a grubby fawn knitted scarf so long it dangled to his ankles. "Mind if I take this off?" he said, shrugging off the anorak without waiting for my permission. "It's a bit warmer than I'm used to." Without the artificial padding of the anorak, he looked thin and frail in a threadbare jersey out at the elbows. "Don't use this place much, do yer?" he said. "Wherejer live the rest of the week?" I told him. "Oh, yeah, up north, ennit?" he said vaguely. "Wodjer need two places for?"

His inquisitiveness made me uneasy. To stem the flow of questions, I asked him some myself. His name is Grahame – with an "e", he informed me, as if this mute suffix was a rare and aristocratic distinction. He comes from Dagenham, and has the kind of background you might expect: broken home, absentee father, mother a boozer, truancy from school, in trouble with the law when he was twelve, taken into care, placed with foster parents, ran away, was put in a home, ran away from that, came Up West, as he calls the West End, drawn by the bright lights. Lives by begging, and the occasional casual job, handing out fliers in Leicester Square, washing cars in a Soho garage. I asked him why he didn't try and get a regular job, and he said solemnly, "I value my freedom." He's a queer mixture of naivety and streetwise sophistication, only half-educated, but with some surprising nuggets of information buried in that half. He saw a copy of Kierkegaard's *Repetition* that I bought second-hand in Charing Cross Road today, and picked it up, frowning at the spine. "Kierkegaard," he said, "the first existentialist." I laughed aloud in sheer astonishment. "What d'you know about existentialism?" I said. "Existence precedes essence," he said, as if reciting the beginning of a nursery rhyme. He wasn't reading from the dust jacket, because the book didn't have one. I think he's one of these people with a photographic memory. He'd seen the phrases somewhere and memorized them without having a clue what they mean. But it was astonishing that his eye had fallen on them in the first place. I asked him where he'd come across Kierkegaard's name before, and he said, in the Library. "I noticed it," he said, " 'cos of the funny spelling. The two 'a's'. Like '*Aarghhh!*' in a comic." He spends a lot of time in the Westminster Reference Library, just off Leicester Square, browsing through encyclopaedias. "If you just go in for the warm, they chuck you out after a while," he said. "But they can't if you're reading the books."

The longer the conversation went on, the more difficult it became to bring it to a close and turn him out into the cold street again. "Where will you sleep tonight?" I asked him. "I dunno," he said. "Can't I sleep downstairs?" "No," I said firmly. He sighed. "Pity, it's a nice little porch. Clean. No draughts to speak of. I 'spect I'll find somewhere."

"How much does the cheapest bed cost round here?" I asked.

He gave me a quick appraising glance. "Fifteen quid."

"I don't believe you."

"I'm not talking doss-houses," he said, with a certain indignation, "I'm not talking Sally Army. I'd rather sleep on the pavement than in one of them places, filthy old men coughing and farting all night and interfering with you in the toilets."

In the end I gave him the fifteen pounds, and escorted him out of the building. In the porch he thanked me nonchalantly, turned up his collar, and sloped off in the direction of Trafalgar Square. I very much doubt whether he will blow his windfall on a room for the night – it would keep him in food and tobacco for two or three days – but my conscience is salved. Or is it?

As I was going to bed, it occurred to me to try and solve the mystery of "proud one" by consulting the dictionary I keep in the flat. It has names of famous people in it, as well as words, and sure enough, there he was, though I'd never heard of him before: "*Proudhon, Pierre Joseph. 1809–65, French socialist, whose pamphlet* What is Property? *(1840) declared that property is theft.*" How about that?

QUAINT TALES OF BRITISH RAIL NO. 167
(By "Intercitizen")

For some months past the escalator between the taxi drop underneath Euston station and the main concourse has been out of action. Before that, it was intermittently under repair. Large plywood screens were erected round it for weeks at a time, and passengers, or "customers" as British Rail calls us nowadays, struggling up the emergency staircase with our luggage, babies, pushchairs, elderly and infirm relatives etc., would hear from behind this barricade the banging and clattering of fitters wrestling with the machine's constipated intestines. Then the screen would be removed, the moving staircase would move again for a few days, and then it would break down again. Lately it has been left in this state, stricken in mid-cycle, no apparent effort being made to repair it. With typical British stoicism passengers have got accustomed to using it as if it were an ordinary solid staircase, though the steps are uncomfortably high for this purpose. There is a lift somewhere, but to use it you have to have a porter, and there are no porters to be found at the taxi drop.

Recently a printed notice appeared at the foot of this paralysed machine:

WELCOME NEWS
A New Escalator for Euston

We are sorry this escalator is out of use. It is life expired [*sic*]. An order has been placed for the manufacture and installation of a new escalator. It will be finished and ready for use by August 1993.

Intercity Retail Manager

Thursday evening, 4th March.
I had lunch with Jake today, at Groucho's. We saw off two bottles of Beaujolais Villages between us, which I enjoyed at the time but regretted later. I went straight to Euston by taxi and, having some time in hand, copied out the notice at the bottom of the broken escalator, swaying slightly on my feet and giggling to myself, attracting curious glances from passengers as they hurried past and hurled themselves at the steel assault course. "*It is life expired.*" I like it. It could be a new slogan for British Rail as privatization approaches, instead of "*We're Getting There.*"

I fell asleep in the train and woke feeling like shit just as it was pulling out of Rummidge Expo station. I could pick out the Richmobile in the car park, its pearly paintwork blanched by the arclights. I had to wait half an hour at Rummidge Central for a train back, and mooched about for a while in the shopping precinct above the station. Most of the plateglass windows were plastered with SALE notices, or exposed bare and dusty interiors, the shells of liquidated businesses. I bought an evening newspaper. "MAJOR TAKES SWING AT DOOM-MONGERS," said one headline. "900,000 WHITE-COLLAR WORKERS UNEMPLOYED," said another. Muzak piped soothingly from hidden speakers.

I descend to the subterranean gloom of the platforms to catch my train. It is reported running late. Waiting passengers sit hunched with hands in pockets on the wooden benches, their breath condensing in the chill damp air, gazing wistfully along the track to the mouth of a tunnel where a red signal light glows. An adenoidal voice apologizes for the delay, "which is due to operating difficulties." It is life expired.

Jake saw Samantha on Tuesday. "Smart kid," he said. "Thanks for pointing her in my direction." "I didn't," I said. "I only warned her about your deplorable morals." He laughed. "Don't worry, my boy, she's not my type. She has no ankles, have you noticed?" "Can't say I have," I said. "I never got that far down." "Legs are very important to me," Jake said. "Take the lovely Linda, for example." He was eloquent for some minutes on the subject of his new secretary's legs, hissing and flashing like scissor-blades in black nylon tights under her hanky-sized skirt as she walks in and out of his office. "I've got to have her," he said. "It's only a matter of time." We were well into the second bottle at this stage. I asked him if he didn't sometimes feel a qualm of guilt about his philandering.

JAKE: But of course. That's the point. That's the attraction. The attraction of the forbidden. Listen, I'll tell you a story. (JAKE *refills* TUBBY'S *glass and then his own.*) It happened last summer. I was sitting in the garden one Sunday afternoon browsing through the papers – Rhoda was indoors doing something in the kitchen – and the kids next door were playing in their garden in one of those inflatable paddling pools. It was a hot day. They had some friends or relatives visiting, so there were two boys and two girls of about the same age, four to six years old, I suppose. I couldn't see because of the hedge, but I could hear them alright. You know how water seems to excite kids – makes them even noisier than usual. There was a lot of shouting and shrieking and splashing from next door. I got a bit peeved about it, actually. We didn't have many weekends last summer when it was warm enough to sit out in the garden, and here was my precious sabbath being ruined. So I levered myself off the lounger and went over to the hedge intending to ask if they could lower the volume a bit. As I approached, I heard one of the little girls say, obviously to one of the little boys, "You're not allowed to pull our knickers down." She spoke in a very clear, posh voice, like a juvenile Samantha describing a rule in croquet. "You're not allowed to pull our knickers down." Well, I just curled up. I had to stuff a knuckle in my mouth to stop myself laughing aloud. The kid's remark was completely innocent of sexual meaning, of course. But for me it summed up the whole business. The world is full of desirable women and you're not allowed to pull their knickers down – unless you're married to them, and then there's no fun in it. But sometimes we get lucky and they let us. It's always the same, under the knickers, of course. The same old hole, I mean. But it's always different, too, because of the knickers. "You're not allowed to pull our knickers down." Says it all. (JAKE *drains glass*.)

Friday evening 5th March. To the Wellbeing this afternoon for acupuncture. (Sings, to the opening bars of "Jealousy": *"Therapy! Nothing but therapy! It's never-ending, Not to mention what I'm spending . . ."*) Actually I feel more positive this evening than I have lately, but I don't know whether this is because of the acupuncture or because I haven't had anything to drink. Miss Wu did her stuff with heat today instead of the usual needles. She puts little granules of what looks like incense on my skin at the pressure points, and applies a lighted taper to them, one at a time. They glow red-hot like cinders, and give off wisps of faintly perfumed smoke. I feel like a human joss-stick. The idea is that as the granules burn down, the heat increases and produces an effect like the stimulus of a needle, but she has to whip them off with a pair of tweezers before they actually burn me. I have to tell her precisely when the sensation of heat becomes painful, otherwise the smell of singed flesh mingles with the smell of incense. It's quite exciting.

Miss Wu asked me about the family. I was slightly abashed to discover that I had nothing new to report since my last visit. I have a vague memory that Sally spoke to Jane on the phone a few days ago, and relayed some news to me, but I didn't take it in at the time, and I was too embarrassed to ask Sally later what it was, because she's still pissed off with me for letting her down over the Websters. I'm afraid I've been a bit preoccupied lately. I've been reading a lot of Kierkegaard, and a biography of him by Walter Lowrie. Writing this journal takes up a lot of time, too. I don't know how long I'll be able to keep it going at this rate – I'm amazed by how much printout I've got already. Kierkegaard's journals in their complete, unedited form run to 10,000 pages apparently. I picked up a paperback selection of them in Charing Cross Road. There's a passage early on about him going to see his doctor which made me sit up. Kierkegaard asked the doctor if he thought his melancholy could be overcome by willpower. The doctor said he doubted it, and that it might be dangerous even to try. Kierkegaard resigned himself to living with his depression:

> From that instant my choice was made. That grievous malforma-
> tion with its attendant sufferings (which undoubtedly would have
> caused most others to commit suicide, if they had enough spirit left
> to grasp the utter misery of that torture) is what I have regarded as
> the thorn in the flesh, my limitation, my cross . . .

The thorn in the flesh! How about that?

Søren Kierkegaard. Just the name on the title page has a peculiar, arresting effect. It's so strange, so extravagantly foreign-looking to an English eye – almost extra-terrestrial. That weird *o* with the slash through it, like the zero sign on a computer screen – it might belong to some synthetic language invented by a sci-fi writer. And the double *aa* in the surname is almost as exotic. There are no native English words with two consecutive a's, I think, and not many loan-words either. I've always been irritated by the nerds who put small ads in newspapers beginning with a meaningless row of *A*'s, just to be sure of getting pole position in the column, like: "*AAAA Escort for sale, D Reg., 50,000 miles, £3000 o.n.o.*" It's cheating. There ought to be a rule against it, then people would have to use a bit of ingenuity. I just looked at the first page in the dictionary: *aa, aardvark, Aarhus*, . . . *Aa* is a Hawaiian word for a certain kind of volcanic rock, and an *aardvark* is a nocturnal mammal that eats termites – the name comes from obsolete Afrikaans, it says. *"Aardvark-grey Escort for sale"* would make an eye-catching ad. (I presume by night all aardvarks are grey.)

Once you start browsing in dictionaries, you never know where it will lead you. I noticed that *Aarhus*, the name of a port in Denmark, was given the alternative spelling of *Århus*. Further research revealed that this is the usual way the double *aa* is written in modern Danish, a single *a* with a little circle on top. So if Kierkegaard were alive today he would write his name as Kierkegård. More unsettling still was the discovery that all this time I've been pronouncing his name incorrectly. I thought it was something like Sor'n Key-erk-er-guard. Not at all. Apparently the *o* is pronounced like *eu* in the French *deux*, the *Kierk* is pronounced as *Kirg* with a hard *g*, the *aa* sounds like *awe* in English, and the *d* is mute. So the name sounds something like Seuren Kirgegor. I think I'll stick with the English pronunciation.

The *a* with the little circle on top reminds me of something, but I can't for the life of me remember what. Frustrating. It'll come back to me one day, when I'm not trying.

I've also been reading *Repetition*, subtitled *An Essay in Experimental Psychology*. A rum book. Well, they're all rum books. Each one is different, but the same themes and obsessions keep cropping up: courtship, seduction, indecision, guilt, depression, despair. *Repetition* has another pretend-author, Constantine Constantius, who is the friend and confidant of a nameless young man, and *he's* a bit like A in *Either/Or*. The young man falls in love with a girl who reciprocates his feelings and they become engaged. But instead of being made happy by this situation, the guy is immediately plunged into the deepest depression (Constantius calls it "melancholy", like Kierkegaard in his *Journals*). What triggers this reaction is a fragment of verse (the young man has ambitions to be a poet himself) which he finds himself repeating again and again:

> To my arm-chair there comes a dream
> From the springtime of youth
> A longing intense
> For thee, thou sun amongst women.

The young man is a classic case of the unhappiest man. Instead of living in the present, enjoying his engagement, he remembers the future; that is to say, he imagines himself looking back on his youthful love from the vantage point of disillusioned old age, like the speaker of the poem, and then there seems to be no point in getting married. "He was in love, deeply and sincerely in love, that was evident – and yet all at once, in one of the first days of his engagement, he was capable of recollecting his love. Substantially he was through with the whole relationship. Before he begins he has taken such a terrible stride that he has leapt over the whole of life." It's a wonderfully barmy and yet entirely plausible way of cheating yourself of happiness. Constantius sums it up: "He longs for the girl, he has to restrain himself by force from hanging around her the whole day, and yet at the very first instant he has become an old man with respect to the whole relationship . . . That he would become unhappy was clear enough, and that the girl would become unhappy was no less clear." He decides that for the girl's own good he must break off the engagement. But how can he do this without making her feel rejected?

Constantius advises him to pretend to have a mistress – to set up a shop-girl in an apartment and go through the motions of visiting her – so that his fiancée will despise him and break off the engagement herself. The young man accepts this advice, but at the last moment lacks the nerve to carry it out, and simply disappears from Copenhagen. After an interval he starts writing letters to Constantius, analysing his conduct and his feelings in relation to the girl. He's still completely obsessed with her, of course. He's become an unhappy rememberer. "What am I doing now? I begin all over again from the beginning, and from the wrong end. I shun every outward reminder of the whole thing, yet my soul, day and night, waking and sleeping, is incessantly employed with it." He identifies himself with Job. (I looked up Job in the Bible. I'd never actually read the Book of Job before. It's surprisingly readable – bloody brilliant, actually.) Like Job, the young man bewails his miserable condition ("My life has been brought to an impasse, I loathe existence, it is without savour, lacking salt and sense"), but whereas Job blames God, the young man doesn't believe in God, so he isn't sure whose fault it is: "How did I obtain an interest in this enterprise they call reality? Why should I have an interest in it? Is it not a voluntary concern? And if I am to be compelled to take part in it, where is the director?" The young man longs for some sudden transforming event or revelation, a "tempest" like the one that comes at the end of the Book of Job, when God really sticks it to Job and says in effect, "Can you do what I can do? If not, belt up," and Job submits and God rewards him by giving him twice as many sheep and camels and she-asses as he had before. "Job is blessed and has received everything double," says the young man. "This is what is called a repetition." Then he reads in a newspaper that the girl has married somebody else, and he writes to Constantius that the news has liberated him from his obsession: "I am again myself . . . The discord in my nature is resolved, I am again unified . . . is this not then a repetition? Did I not get everything doubly restored? Did I not get myself again, precisely in such a way that I must doubly feel its significance?" His last letter ends with a rapturous thankyou to the girl, and an ecstatic dedication of himself to the life of the mind:

> . . . first a libation to her who saved a soul which sat in the solitude
> of despair. Hail to feminine magnanimity! Long life to the high
> flight of thought, to moral danger in the service of the idea! Hail to
> the danger of battle! Hail to the solemn exultation of victory! Hail
> to the dance in the vortex of the infinite! Hail to the breaking wave
> which covers me in the abyss! Hail to the breaking wave which hurls
> me up above the stars!

Now if you know anything about Kierkegaard's life, and I know a bit by now, you don't need to be told that this story was very close to his own experience. Soon after he got engaged to Regine he started to have doubts about whether they could ever be happy together, because of his own temperament. So he broke off the engagement, even though he was still in love with the girl, and she was still in love with him and begged him not to break it off, as did her father. Kierkegaard went away to live in Berlin for a while, where he wrote *Either/Or*, which was a long, roundabout apology and explanation for his conduct towards Regine. He said later that it was written for her and that the "Seducer's Diary" in particular was meant to "help her push her boat from the shore", i.e., to sever her emotional attachment to him, by making her think that anyone capable of creating the character of Johannes must be something of a cold-blooded selfish bastard himself. You could say that Kierkegaard's writing "The Seducer's Diary" was like the young man in *Repetition* pretending to have a mistress. In fact, when he finished *Either/Or*, Kierkegaard immediately started work on *Repetition*, going over the same ground in a story that was much closer to his own experience. But when he came back to Copenhagen and discovered that Regine was already engaged to somebody else, was he overjoyed? Did he feel liberated and unified like the hero of *Repetition*? Did he hell. He was devastated. There's an entry in the Journals at this time which obviously describes his feelings:

> The most dreadful thing that can happen to a man is to become ridiculous in his own eyes in a matter of essential importance, to discover, for example, that the sum and substance of his sentiment is rubbish.

Obviously he'd been secretly hoping that his decision to break off the engagement would be miraculously reversed without his own volition, and that he would marry Regine after all. Even when he was sailing to Germany, on his way to Berlin, he noted in his journal: "Notwithstanding it is imprudent for my peace of mind, I cannot leave off thinking of the indescribable moment when I might return to her." *That* was the repetition he had in mind: he would get Regine twice. Like Job he would be blessed and receive everything double. He actually heard about her new engagement when he was working on *Repetition*, and scrapped the original ending of the story, in which the hero commits suicide because he cannot bear to think of the suffering he has caused his beloved.

So all that high-falutin' stuff about feminine magnanimity and the vortex of the infinite was an attempt to get over his disappointment at Regine's transference of her affections to someone else, an effort to see this as a triumph and vindication of his conduct, not an exposure of his folly. It didn't work. He never ceased to love her, or think of her, or write about her (directly or indirectly) for the rest of his life; and he left everything he owned to her in his will (there wasn't much left when he died, but it's the thought that counts, and in this case reveals). What a fool! But what an endearing, entirely human fool.

Repetition is a typically teasing, haunting Kierkegaard title. We normally think of repetition as inherently boring, something to be avoided if possible, as in "repetitive job". But in this book it's seen as something fantastically precious and desirable. One meaning of it is the restoration of what seems to be lost (e.g. Job's prosperity, the young man's faith in himself). But another sense is the enjoyment of what you have. It's the same as living-in-the-present, "it has the blessed certainty of the instant." It means being set free from the curse of unhappy hoping and unhappy remembering. "Hope is a charming maiden that slips through the fingers, recollection is a beautiful old woman but of no use at the instant, repetition is a beloved wife of whom one never tires."

It occurs to me that you could turn that last metaphor around: not repetition is a beloved wife, but a beloved wife (or beloved husband) is repetition. To appreciate the real value of marriage you have to discard the superficial idea of repetition as something boring and negative, and see it as, on the contrary, something liberating and positive – the secret of happiness, no less. That's why B, in *Either/Or*, begins his attack on A's aesthetic philosophy of life (and the melancholia which goes with it) by defending marriage, and urging A to marry (This is getting quite exciting: I haven't thought as hard as this for years, if ever.)

Take sex, for instance. Married sex is the repetition of an act. The element of repetition outweighs any variation there may be between one occasion and another. However many postures you experiment with, however many erotic techniques and sex-toys and games and visual aids you might employ, the fact that you have the same partner means that every act is essentially (or do I mean existentially?) the same. And if our experience is anything to go by (mine and Sally's, I mean) most couples eventually settle on a certain pattern of love-making which suits them both, and repeat it over and over. How many sex acts are there in a long-lasting marriage? Thousands. Some will be more satisfying than others, but does anybody remember them all distinctly? No, they merge and blend in the memory. That's why philanderers like Jake think married sex is inherently boring. They insist upon variety in sex, and after a while the means of obtaining variety become more important than the act itself. For them the essence of sex is in the anticipation, the plotting, the planning, the desiring, the wooing, the secrecy, the deceptions, the assignations. You don't make assignations with your spouse. There's no need. Sex is just there, to enjoy when you want it; and if your partner doesn't feel like it for some reason, because they're tired or have a cold or want to stop up and watch something on the telly, well, that's no big deal, because there will be plenty of other opportunities. What's so wonderful about married sex (and especially middle-aged, post-menopausal sex, when the birth-control business is over and done with) is that you don't have to be thinking about it all the time. I suspect that Jake is thinking about it even while he's phoning clients and drawing up contracts; probably the only time he *isn't* thinking about sex is when he's actually having it (because orgasm is a kind of slipped second, it empties the mind of thought for an instant) but I bet as soon as he comes he's thinking about it again.

What applies to sex applies to everything else in marriage: work, recreation, meals, whatever. It's all repetition. The longer you live together, the less you change, and the more repetition there is in daily life. You know each other's minds, thoughts, habits: who sleeps on which side of the bed, who gets up first in the morning, who takes coffee and who takes tea at breakfast, who likes to read the news section of the paper first and who the review section, and so on. You need to speak to each other less and less. To an outsider it looks like boredom and alienation. It's a commonplace that you can always tell which couples in a restaurant are married to each other because they're eating in silence. But does this mean that they're unhappy with each other's company? Not at all. They're merely behaving as they do at home, as they do all the time. It's not that they have nothing to say to each other, but that it doesn't have to be said. Being happily married means that you don't have to *perform* marriage, you just live in it, like a fish lives in the sea. It's remarkable Kierkegaard intuitively understood that, even though he was never married himself, and threw away his best chance of having the experience.

Sally just came into my study to tell me she wants a separation. She says she told me earlier this evening, over supper, but I wasn't listening. I listened this time, but I still can't take it in.

※ ※ TWO ※ ※

✳ ✳ Brett Sutton ✳ ✳

Statement of .... Michael Brett SUTTON
Age of Witness .... Over 21
Occupation of witness .... Tennis Coach
Address .... 41 Upton Road, RUMMIDGE R27 9LP.

*This statement, consisting of 5 pages, each signed by me, is true to the best of
my knowledge and belief and I make it knowing that, if it is tendered in
evidence, I shall be liable to prosecution if I have wilfully stated anything
which I know to be false or do not believe to be true.*
Dated the: 21st March 1993.

I first noticed Mr Passmore behaving strangely towards me about two
weeks ago. I've been coaching his wife for some months, but I know
him only slightly, as someone I would say hello to if we passed each
other at the Club, nothing more. I've never coached him. Mrs
Passmore told me he had a chronic knee injury which hadn't
responded to surgery, and it handicaps him considerably as regards
tennis. I've seen him playing occasionally, wearing a rigid brace, and I
thought he managed pretty well, considering, but I imagine he finds it
very frustrating not being able to move around the court properly. I
think perhaps that's why he got this crazy idea into his head. If you're
keen on sport, there's nothing worse than long-term injury. I know –
I've been through it myself: cartilage problems, tendinitis, I've had
them all. It really gets you down. The whole world looks grey,
everything seems against you. You only have to get some crisis in your
personal life and you flip. Mr Passmore doesn't look the athletic type,
but I gather sport matters to him. Mrs Passmore told me that before

his injury they used to play each other a lot, but now she doesn't like to because he can't bear her to win, but he complains if she doesn't try to. Actually I think she could beat him now even if he was fully fit: she's come on a lot, lately. I've been coaching her twice a week all through this winter.

The first time Mr Passmore behaved oddly towards me was in the Men's locker room at the Club, about two weeks ago, though I hardly registered it at the time. It's only in retrospect that it seems significant. I was stripping off my tennis gear before taking a shower, and I happened to look up and saw Mr Passmore, staring at me. He was fully dressed. As soon as he caught my eye, he looked away, and started fiddling with the key of his locker. I wouldn't have thought anything of it except that before he caught my eye he was fairly obviously staring at my private parts. I won't say it's never happened to me before, but it surprised me coming from Mr Passmore. I actually wondered whether I'd imagined it, it was all over so fast. Anyway, I soon forgot all about it.

A few days later I was coaching Mrs Passmore on one of the indoor courts, in the evening, and Mr Passmore turned up and sat watching us from behind the netting at the end of the hall. I presumed that he'd made an appointment to meet his wife at the Club, and was early. I smiled at him, but he didn't smile back. His being there seemed to bother Mrs Passmore. She started making mistakes in her play, mis-hitting the ball. Eventually she went over to Mr Passmore and spoke to him through the netting. I gathered that she was asking him to leave, but he just shook his head and smiled in a sneery sort of way. She came over to me then and said that she was sorry, but she'd have to stop the coaching session. She looked angry and upset. She insisted on paying me for the full session though she'd only had half-an-hour. She walked out of the court without a glance at Mr Passmore, who remained seated on the bench, hunched inside his overcoat, with his hands in the pockets. I felt a bit embarrassed, walking past him on my way out. I assumed they were having some kind of row. I didn't dream for a moment that it had anything to do with me.

A few days after that, the phone calls started. The phone would ring, I'd pick it up and say "Hallo?" and no one would reply. After a while there would be a click, as the caller put the receiver down. The calls came at all hours, sometimes in the middle of the night. I reported them to BT, but they said there was nothing they could do. They advised me to disconnect my bedside phone at night, so I did, and left the answerphone on downstairs. Next morning, there were two calls recorded, but no messages. One evening about nine o'clock I answered the phone and a high falsetto voice said, "Can I speak to Sally, please? This is her mother." I said I thought she must have the wrong number. She didn't seem to hear me, and asked again to speak to Sally, saying it was urgent. I said there was nobody called Sally at my address. I didn't make the connection with Mrs Passmore, even though we are on first-name terms. And although the voice sounded rather strange, it never crossed my mind that it was an impersonation.

A few nights after that I was woken in the middle of the night by a noise. You know what it's like when that happens: by the time you're fully awake, the noise has stopped and you have no idea where it came from, or whether the whole thing was a dream. I put on a tracksuit, because I always sleep in the nude, and went downstairs to check, but there was no sign of anyone trying to break in. I heard a car starting up in the street outside and went to the front door just in time to see a white car turning the corner at the end of the street. Well, it looked white under the street-lighting, but it could have been silver. I didn't have a good enough view to identify the make. The next morning I discovered that someone had been in the back garden. They'd got in by the side way and knocked over some panes of glass that were leaning up against the tool-shed – I'm in the middle of building a cold-frame. Three of the panes were broken. That must have been the noise I heard.

Two days later I got up in the morning and found my ladder leaning up against the wall of the house under my bedroom window. Someone had taken it from the space between the garage and the garden fence where I keep it. There was no sign of any attempt to break in, but I was alarmed. That was when I first reported the incidents to your station. Police Constable Roberts came round. He advised me to have a burglar-alarm system fitted. I was in the process of getting quotes when I lost my house keys. I keep them in my tennis bag usually during the day, because they're rather heavy in the pocket of my tracksuit, but last Friday they disappeared. I was beginning to get seriously worried, by now, that someone was trying to burgle my house. I thought I knew who it was too – a member of the Club's groundstaff. I'd rather not say who. I have a number of trophies at home, you see, and this person once asked me about them, and what they were worth. I made an arrangement with a locksmith to have the locks changed the next day.

That night – it was about three o'clock – I was woken by Nigel squeezing my arm and whispering in my ear, "I think there's someone in the room." He was shaking with fear. I turned on the bedside lamp, and there was Mr Passmore standing on the rug on my side of the bed, with a torch in one hand and a large pair of scissors in the other. I didn't like the look of the scissors – they were big, dangerous-looking things, like drapers' shears. As I said, I always sleep naked, and so does Nigel, and there was nothing within reach I could have used to defend us with. I tried to keep calm. I asked Mr Passmore what he thought he was doing. He didn't answer. He was staring at Nigel, completely gobsmacked. Nigel, who was nearest the door, jumped out of bed and ran downstairs to phone 999. Mr Passmore looked round the room in a dazed sort of way and said, "I seem to have made a mistake." I said, "I think you have." He said, "I was looking for my wife." I said, "Well, she's not here. She's never been here." Suddenly it all fell into place, and I realized what had been going on, in his head I mean. I couldn't help laughing, partly in relief, partly because he looked such a fool standing there with the scissors in his hand. I said, "What were you going to do with those, castrate me?" He said, "I was going to cut your ponytail off."

I don't want to press charges. To be perfectly honest I'd rather not have to give evidence in court which might be reported in the local press. It could have a damaging effect on my work. Some of the members of the Club are prejudiced, I'm afraid. I'm not ashamed of being gay, but I'm discreet about it. I live a fair distance from the Club, and nobody there knows anything about my private life. I don't think Mr Passmore will cause me any more trouble, and he's offered to pay for the broken panes of glass.

❋ ❋ Amy ❋ ❋

WELL, THE MOST AWFUL THING has happened. Laurence's wife wants a separation. He called me last night to tell me. I knew at once it must be something *catastrophique* because I've told him not to phone me at home unless it's terribly important. I have to go upstairs to my bedroom extension, and Zelda always wants to know afterwards who called and what it was about, and I wouldn't put it past her to listen in on the downstairs phone. We have a routine that Laurence phones me at the office in the lunch hour or I call him when he's at his flat. I know you think I should be more upfront with Zelda about my relationship with Laurence, but – No, I know you haven't *said* as much, Karl, but I can tell. Well, of course, if you insist, I must take your word, but I suppose it's possible that *subconsciously* you disapprove. I mean, if *I* can suppress things, I suppose it's possible you can, too, isn't it? Or are you sure you're absolutely completely totally superhumanly rational? Sorry, sorry. I'm very upset, I hardly slept a wink last night. No, he had no idea. He's utterly devastated. Apparently she just marched into his study on Friday evening and announced that she wanted a separation. Just like that. Said she just couldn't stand living with him any more, he was like a zombie, that was the word she used, a zombie. Well, he is often a little *distrait*, I have to admit, but writers often are, in my experience. I should have thought she'd be used to it by now, but evidently not. She said they didn't communicate, and they didn't have anything in common any more, and now that the children were grown up and had left home there was no point their going on living together.

Lorenzo spent the whole weekend trying to talk her out of it, but to no avail. Well, I think first he tried to argue that there was nothing wrong with the marriage, that it was like any other marriage, something to do with repetition and Kierkegaard, I couldn't quite follow it, he was hardly coherent, poor dear. Yes, he's developed a thing about Kierkegaard lately, for some reason. Anyway, when that didn't work he changed tack and said he would turn over a new leaf and talk to her at meals and take an interest in her work and go away with her on Weekend Breaks and that sort of thing, but she said it was too late.

Sally. Her name's Sally. I've only met her a few times, mostly at parties given by Heartland, and she always struck me as rather guarded and self-contained. She likes to make one drink last the whole evening and stay cold sober while all around her are getting smashed. I think it confirms her sense of what a worthless load of layabouts we television folk are. Goodlooking in a rather *noli me tangere* way. High cheekbones, a strong chin. A bit like Patricia Hodge, but more athletic, more windbeaten. Oh. I keep forgetting that you never go to the theatre or watch television. What on earth *do* you do in your spare time? Oh, I might have guessed. Do you read Kierkegaard? He doesn't sound my cup of tea. Or Laurence's either, come to that. I wonder what he sees in him. No, Laurence asked her if there was anyone else, and she says there isn't. I asked him if it was conceivable that Sally suspected there was something between him and me, something more than what there actually is I mean, which is entirely innocent, as you know, but he said absolutely not. Well, she knows that we're good friends but I don't think she has any idea how often we see each other outside work and I wondered if someone had been gossiping or sending poison-pen letters, but Laurence said she didn't mention my name or accuse him of anything like that. Oh dear. *Quel cauchemar!*

I should have thought it was obvious. Laurence is my dearest friend, my dearest male friend anyway. I don't like to see him wretched. I know you're smiling cynically. Anyway, I don't mind admitting that my reasons for feeling upset are partly selfish. I was very happy with our relationship. It suited me. It was intimate without being . . . I don't know. All right, without being sexual. But no, I don't mean sexual, or not just sexual, I mean possessive or demanding or something. After all, our relationship was never sex*less*. There's always been an element of . . . of gallantry in Laurence's treatment of me. Yes, gallantry. But the fact that he's happily married – was happily married – and that that was understood by both of us, took all the potential tension out of the relationship. We could enjoy each other's company without wondering whether we wanted to go to bed together or whether we expected each other to want to, if you follow me. I enjoyed dressing up to go out with Laurence – dressing up to go out with a girlfriend is never quite the same – but I didn't have to think about *un*dressing for him afterwards. If you're a single woman and you go out with a man you've either got to insist tediously on going Dutch or you have an uneasy feeling that you're incurring some kind of erotic debt which may be called in at any moment.

No, I've no idea what his sex life was like with Sally. We never discussed it. Yes, I told him all about my experiences with Saul, but he never told me anything about him and Sally. I didn't ask. A kind of *pudeur* restrained me. *Pudeur*. After all, they were still married, it would have been an intrusion . . . Oh, all right, perhaps I didn't want to hear about it in case she turned out to be one of those women who have multiple orgasms as easy as shelling peas and can do the whole Kama Sutra standing on their heads. What's so funny about that? They do stand on their heads in the Kama Sutra? Oh well, you know what I mean. I've never pretended I don't feel inadequate about sex. I mean, why else am I here? But I was never jealous of Sally. She was welcome to that part of Laurence's life, and to that part of Laurence for that matter. I just didn't want to hear about it. Oh, am I using the past tense? Yes I am, aren't I. Well, I certainly don't think that our relationship is over, but I suppose I'm afraid it will change, in ways I can't predict. Unless they get back together, of course. I suggested to Laurence that they should see a marriage counsellor, but he just groaned and said, "They'll only say I need psychotherapy, and I'm having that already." I asked him how he knew that's what they would say, and he said, "From experience." It seems this isn't the first time Sally has been seriously pissed off with the marriage. Once she walked out of the house for a whole weekend, he didn't know where she'd gone, and came back just as he was phoning the police.

She didn't say a word for days because she'd got laryngitis, she'd been tramping all over the Malverns in pouring rain, but when she got her voice back she insisted on their going to marriage guidance. That's how Laurence started on psychotherapy. He never told me that before. I suppose there was no reason why he should, but it was a little disturbing to have it sprung on me now. I suppose one never does tell anybody *everything* about oneself. Except one's analyst of course . . .

Well, I saw Laurence yesterday evening, at his flat. He rang me at work to say he was coming up to town but he didn't want to eat out, so I knew I was in for a long, harrowing *tête à tête*. I stopped off at Fortnum's after work to pick up some quiche and salad. Laurence didn't eat much of it, but he drank quite a lot. He's very depressed. I mean, he was depressed before, but now he's really got something to be depressed about. Yes, I think he's quite conscious of the irony.

Things haven't improved *chez* Passmore. Sally has moved into the guest bedroom. She goes to work early in the morning and comes back late in the evening, so she doesn't have to talk to Laurence. She says she'll talk at the weekend, but she can't cope with his problems and do her own job at the same time. I think it's rather ominous that she says "*his* problems", not "their problems", don't you? Mind you, I understand how she feels about talking to Laurence in his present state. After four hours of it last night I was completely *fiinito*. I felt like a sponge that had been saturated and squeezed so often it had lost all its spring. And then, when I said I had to go home, he asked me to stay the night. He said it wasn't for sex, but just so he could hold me. He hasn't had any proper sleep since last Friday, and he does look quite hollow-eyed, poor sweet. He said, "I think it would help me to sleep if I could just hold you."

Well, of course it was out of the question. I mean, leaving aside whether I wanted to be held, and the risk of its developing into something else, I couldn't possibly stay out all night without warning. Zelda would've been worried sick, and if I'd phoned her with some improvised story she would have seen through it immediately, she always knows when I'm lying, it's one of her most irritating habits. Incidentally, it was Bad Breast time again this morning. Yes. We had a bitter row at breakfast, about muesli. Not *just* about muesli, of course. They didn't have her usual brand at Safeways the last time I went shopping so I bought another kind and this morning the old packet had run out so I put this other one on the table and she refused to touch it because it had added sugar. A *minuscule* quantity, and brown sugar too, the healthy sort, as I pointed out, but she refused to eat any of it, and as it's the only thing she ever has for breakfast, apart from coffee, she went off to school on an empty stomach, leaving me feeling incredibly guilty, exactly as she had intended, of course. Her parting shot was to say that I was trying to make her eat sugar because she's slim and I'm fat, "disgustingly fat" was the phrase she used, do you think that's true? No, I don't mean about my being disgustingly fat, I don't consider myself fat at all, even though I would like to lose a few pounds. I mean is it possible that I'm subconsciously jealous of Zelda's figure? Oh you always bat these questions back at me. I don't know. Perhaps I am a little bit. But I honestly didn't know there was any sugar in the bloody muesli.

Where was I? Oh yes, Laurence. Well, I had to say no, though I did feel badly about it, he looked so woeful, so pleading, like a dog that wants to come in out of the rain. I said, couldn't he take a sleeping pill, and he said he didn't want to because they made him so depressed when he woke up, and if he got any more depressed than he was already he was afraid he'd top himself. He smiled when he said that to show it was a joke, but it worried me. He did go and see his psychotherapist on Monday, but she doesn't seem to have been much help. That may be Laurence's fault, because when I asked him he couldn't remember anything she'd said. I'm not sure he took in anything *I* said last night, either. All he wants to do is pour out his version of things, not listen to any constructive advice. I nearly said to him, you should try analysis, darling, that's all I do, five days a week: pour out my version of things without getting any constructive advice. Just my little joke, Karl. Yes, of course I know that jokes are disguised forms of aggression . . .

Well, things have gone from bad to worse. Sally's moved out of the house, and Laurence is all on his own there. It's a five-bedroomed detached, in an upmarket residential area on the outskirts of Rummidge. I've never been there, but he showed me some photographs. It's what the estate agents call a modern house of character. I couldn't say what character. French farmhouse crossed with golf club, perhaps. Not my taste, but comfortable and substantial. Set well back from the road, at the end of a longish drive, with a lot of trees and shrubs round it. He said to me once, "It's so quiet there I could hear my hair growing, if I had any hair." Yes, he's bald. Didn't I ever mention it? He jokes about it, but I think it bothers him. Anyway, I don't like to think of him all on his own in that house, like a bead in a rattle.

I gathered that last weekend was rather fraught. Sally told him she was prepared to talk, but there had to be a time limit on their discussions, not more than two hours at a time, and only one session a day. It sounded like quite a sensible idea to me, but Laurence couldn't accept it. He says her college sent her on a management course recently and she's trying to treat their marital crisis as if it were an industrial dispute, with agendas and adjournments. He agreed to the condition, but when it came to the crunch, and the two hours were up, he wouldn't stop. Eventually she said that if he didn't stop harassing her she would move out of the house until he came to his senses. And he rather foolishly said, "All right, move out, see if I care," or words to that effect, so she did. She wouldn't tell him where she was going and she hasn't told him since.

Laurence is convinced that there is another man after all and that she staged this row so she could be with him. He thinks he knows who it is, too: the tennis coach at their sports club. It doesn't sound like Sally to me, but you can never tell. You remember I told you Saul swore blind there was nobody else when he asked me for a divorce, and then I discovered he'd been screwing Janine for months. Laurence says Sally started taking tennis lessons a few months ago and shortly afterwards she decided to colour her hair. No, it doesn't sound much to go on, but he's quite convinced and in his present mood there's no arguing with him. He isn't coming to London this week because he says he's too busy. I think he means too busy stalking the tennis coach. I don't like the sound of it at all, but I can't help feeling a guilty kind of relief that I won't have to do another four-hour counselling session tonight.

Laurence is taking up more and more of our time, isn't he? Can't you say something to get me off the subject? What about some free association? I used to enjoy that, we never seem to do it any more.

All right. Mother. My mother. In the kitchen at Highgate. The afternoon sun is shining through the frosted kitchen window, throwing a mottled pattern on the table, and over her arms and hands. She's wearing one of those old-fashioned floral print pinafores that crossed at the back and tied at the front. We're chopping vegetables together for a stew, or soup. I'm about thirteen, fourteen. I've just started my periods. She's telling me about the facts of life. About how easy it is to get pregnant, and how wary I must be of men and boys. Chopping up carrots as she speaks, as if she would like to cut off their willies . . . I wonder why I should think of that? I suppose it's because I'm worried about Zelda. Of course I've told her all about the facts of life, but should I make sure she's fixed up with contraception or will she take that as an encouragement to promiscuity? You don't think that's it? What then? Oh, go on, Karl, let yourself go for once, give me an interpretation. No, don't – I know, it's really about me and Laurence, isn't it? Oh God . . .

Well, Sally has got herself a lawyer now. Yes, Laurence had a letter from him asking if he'll instruct his own solicitor to enter into discussions about a separation settlement. Also with a proposal from Sally that they should agree to go to their sports club on alternate days, to avoid embarrassing encounters. Apparently Laurence has been going down there and watching Sally practising with the tennis coach. She says it puts her off her game. I should think it would. Of course this has only convinced him all the more that she has something to hide *re* the tennis coach. Laurence told his solicitor to tell Sally's that if she wanted to live apart from him she would have to do it on her own salary plus she could have back whatever she had contributed to their savings, which isn't very much of course compared to what Laurence has earned in recent years. I think it's a bad sign that they're quarrelling about money already, and using lawyers, that was when things became really nasty between Saul and me. Oh dear, I have a dreadful feeling of *déjà vu* about all this . . .

Well, things have gone from bad to worse. Laurence has had an injunction served on him to stop him going into the college where Sally works, or university I think it's called now, Volt University or Watt University – something electrical anyway. Her lawyer wrote back to say that she considered herself entitled to half their savings because she supported him for years by her teaching when he was trying to make it as a scriptwriter. Laurence went to the University in a towering rage and ambushed her outside her office and made a public scene. She told him that he was out of his mind. Well, I think perhaps he is, poor sweet. So Sally took out an injunction against him, and if he goes there again he could be arrested. In fact he's not even allowed to go within a one-mile radius of the place. That particularly annoys him because it means he can't try and follow her when she leaves work to find out where she's living. He's been keeping watch on the tennis coach's house, but so far no luck. He says it's only a matter of time before he catches them. I think he means *in flagrante*. Heaven knows what he thinks he's going to do if he does catch them. Laurence would hardly be a match for a tennis coach if it came to blows . . .

Well, it seems that Sally wasn't having an affair after all, not with the tennis coach anyway. Apparently he's gay. Yes. Well, I must admit I had a job not to laugh myself, when Laurence told me. I don't know exactly how he found out, he was a bit evasive on the phone, but he seemed quite certain. He sounded very low, too, poor sweet. As long as he suspected the tennis coach he had a target for his anger and resentment. You can't hate someone if you don't know who they are. Anyway, I suspect he's beginning to think that Sally may have been telling the truth after all, about why she wanted a separation – that she just couldn't bear living with him any more. It hasn't done anything for his self-esteem. I remember when I found out about Janine, I was a tiny bit secretly relieved as well as absolutely furious, because it meant that I needn't blame myself for the failure of the marriage. Or not entirely.

Another depressing development for Laurence is that his children know about the split now. I think that's a kind of Rubicon as far as he's concerned. As long as they didn't know, there was always the possibility that he and Sally might get back together again with no serious damage done, no embarrassment, no loss of face. When Sally walked out the last thing he said to her – he told me he ran down the drive after her car and banged on her window to make her wind it down – the last thing he said was, "Don't tell Jane and Adam." Of course they had to know sooner or later. Sally probably told them almost immediately, but Laurence has only just found out that they know. He's had phone calls from both of them. They're being very careful not to take sides, but the main thing that's struck him is that they don't seem to be terribly upset or even terribly surprised. It's obvious to me that Sally must have been confiding in them for some time and preparing them for what's happened. I think this is beginning to dawn on Laurence, too. "I feel as if I've been living in a dream," he said, "and I've just woken up. But what I've woken up to is a nightmare." Poor Lorenzo. Speaking of dreams, I had a very peculiar one last night . . .

Well, it's happened, I knew it would, I could see it coming: Laurence wants to sleep with me. Not just to hold me. For sex. The beast with two backs. It was one of Saul's expressions, don't pretend you've never heard it before, Karl. It's in Shakespeare somewhere. I can't remember which play, but I'm sure it's in Shakespeare. Well, it's no odder than most of the other available phrases. "Sleep with," for instance. I knew a girl once, called Muriel, who used to say she was sleeping with her boss when she meant that she had it off with him in the back of his Jaguar in Epping Forest during their lunch hour. I shouldn't think they got much sleep.

Laurence raised the subject over dinner last night. I suppose I should have been forewarned when he took me to Rules instead of our usual *trattoria*. And encouraged me to order the lobster. It was just as well we were eating early and the restaurant was half-empty, otherwise people would have been falling off their chairs trying to listen in. He said the only reason he hadn't tried to make love to me before was because he believed in fidelity in marriage, and I chipped in *tout de suite* to say that I quite understood and respected him for it. He said it was very generous of me to take that view but he felt he had been exploiting me in a way, enjoying my company without any commitment, and that now Sally had walked out on him there was no reason why we should inhibit ourselves any longer. I said that I didn't feel at all exploited, or inhibited for that matter. Not quite as bluntly as that, of course. I tried to explain that I valued our relationship precisely because there were no sexual strings to it, hence no tension, no anxiety, no jealousy. He looked very dejected and said, "Are you saying you don't love me?" and I said, "Darling, I haven't *allowed* myself to love you in that way." He said, "Well, now you can." And I said, "Supposing I allow myself to, and then Sally and you get together again, what then?" He said very gloomily that he couldn't imagine that could ever happen. Relations between them are getting worse. She's talking about a divorce now, because Laurence refuses to discuss financial arrangements for a voluntary separation, which is very silly of him. His solicitor told him Sally would get half their joint assets and up to a third of their joint income as maintenance in a divorce settlement. Laurence thinks that she shouldn't get anything at all, because she deserted him. The letters are flying back and forth between the lawyers. And now he wants to sleep with me.

So what should I do? Oh, I know you won't tell me, it's just a rhetorical question. Except a rhetorical question is when the answer is implied, isn't it? And I don't know the answer to this one. I told Laurence I would think about it, and I have, I've thought of little else since last night, but I don't know what to do, I really don't. I'm very fond of Laurence, and I'd like to help him through this crisis. I realize that he just wants to be comforted and I wish I was like one of those earth-motherly, heart-of-gold women in movies who give their bodies generously to nice men at the drop of a hat, but I'm not. Fortunately Laurence remains wonderfully *galant*. We went back to his flat after Rules began to fill up with the post-theatre crowd and talked some more, but there was no hanky-panky or any attempt at it. A strange

146

thing happened when he saw me out, though. He always comes down in the lift with me and puts me in a taxi to go home. When we opened the street door of the building, there in the entryway was one of those young vagrants you see everywhere nowadays, in a sleeping- bag. We had to practically step over him to get into the street. Well, I just ignored him, it seemed the safest thing to do, but Laurence said *hallo* to him, as if there were nothing untoward about his being there, as if the man, or boy rather, was somebody he knew. While we stood on the pavement looking out for a taxi, I hissed at Laurence, "Who is that?" and he replied, "Grahame." As if he was a neighbour or something. Then a taxi came and I didn't have a chance to ask him anything more. I think I had a dream about it last night . . .

Well, I suppose the fact that I used that expression of Saul's, the beast with two backs, last time, and applied it to Laurence, could be significant – is that what you were getting at? That I'm afraid of having sex with Laurence because sex with Saul was such a disaster? But is that cowardice or good sense?

I know you think it's unnatural that I've never had sex with anyone since the divorce. No, I know you haven't said so explicitly – when did you ever say anything explicitly? But I can read between the lines. Well, for instance you referred to my relationship with Laurence as a sort of *mariage blanc*. Well, I'm virtually certain it was you who said it, not me. Anyway, I distinctly remember your suggesting that I was using my relationship with Laurence as a kind of alibi. And I said that we've become so close that having sex with anyone else would have seemed like infidelity. Which is true.

Zelda comes into it too, of course. If I decide to go to bed with Laurence, will she find out? Can I keep it from her? Should I keep it from her? Would knowing about it drive her into the arms of some lecherous spotty youth? You hinted once that I hadn't come to terms with the fact that sooner or later she's going to have sex. That as long as she was under-age I could rationalize my defence of her virginity as responsible parenthood, but that eventually she would become a young adult and decide to have sex with somebody and that there would be nothing I could do to prevent it and so I'd better accept it,

147

but that I wouldn't be able to if I didn't have a satisfying sexual relationship of my own. So maybe this is a heaven-sent opportunity for me to become what you would consider a whole woman again, would you say?

Then at the back of my mind there's another consideration. The possibility of marriage. If Sally and Laurence divorce, it would be sort of logical for *us* to get hitched. No, I don't think so, otherwise he would have mentioned it when he was trying to seduce me the other night. That may be why he took me to Rules, actually, because the *padrona* at the Italian restaurant we usually go to is always singing the praises of matrimony, casting hints that Lorenzo ought to make an honest woman of me – she doesn't know he's married already. I think that secretly, or unconsciously, he still yearns to be reconciled with Sally. He complains bitterly about her behaviour, but I think if she agreed to give the marriage another try he'd scurry back to her with his tail wagging. I'm under no illusions about that. But if she's serious, if she really goes through with it, then I'm pretty sure he would want to marry again. I understand the way his mind works better than he does himself. He's the marrying type. And who would he marry but me?

I've been trying to imagine what it would be like. There might be some resistance from Zelda at first, but I think she would accept him eventually. It would be good for her to have an adult male in the house, good for both of us. A slightly rosy, soft-focus picture keeps coming into my mind of the three of us together in the kitchen, Laurence helping Zelda with her homework at the kitchen table, and me smiling benevolently from the Aga. We don't have an Aga, so I suppose that implies that I would want to move house. Whatever Sally got in a divorce settlement, Laurence would still be pretty well off. You know how it is once you start daydreaming, you think vaguely about the possibility of getting married again, and before you know where you are you're choosing the curtain material for your summer cottage in the Dordogne. But it has occurred to me that if Laurence were to pop the question one day, it would be as well to know already if we were, you know, physically compatible, don't you think? Or don't you?

I'm sure it wouldn't be a really bad experience, anyway. Laurence is very sweet and gentle. Saul was always so overbearing in bed. Do this, do that, do this faster, do that slower. He directed us as if we were making a porn movie. It wouldn't be like that with Laurence. He wouldn't expect me to do anything kinky – at least, I don't think he would. Yes, Karl, I know it's a subjective concept . . .

Well, did you see the story in *Public Interest?* The latest issue, it came out yesterday. No, I don't suppose you do, but everybody else I know reads it avidly. While pretending to despise it of course. It has a media gossip column called "O.C." It's short for "Off Camera." Somehow they got hold of the story of Laurence and the tennis coach. Yes. It seems that Laurence actually broke into the man's house in the middle of the night, hoping to surprise him in bed with Sally, and found him in bed with another man. Can you imagine? No, I had no idea until I read the rag myself. Harriet came into the office yesterday morning with the latest issue and laid it on the desk in front of me without a word, open at the "O.C." page. I practically *died* when I read it. Then I phoned Laurence but his agent had already told him. He says the story is essentially accurate, except that it has him holding a jemmy in his hand when in fact it was a pair of scissors. You may well ask. Apparently he was going to cut off the man's ponytail. Just as well the rag didn't get hold of *that* detail. The whole piece was cruelly mocking, needless to say. "Tubby Passmore, follically-challenged scribe of the Heartland sitcom 'The People Next Door', found himself recently in a situation funnier than anything he has invented . . ." That sort of thing. And there was a cartoon of him as Whatsisname, the Greek god who was married to Venus and found her in bed with Mars – Vulcan, that's the one. It was done in the style of an old painting, "after Titian", or Tintoretto, or somebody, it said underneath. With poor Lorenzo very fat and bald in a tunic and the tennis coach and his friend very naked, intertwined on the bed, and all of them looking very embarrassed. It was quite witty, actually, if you weren't personally involved. Laurence doesn't know how they got hold of the story. The tennis coach didn't press charges because he wants to keep his private life under wraps, so he obviously wasn't the source. Fortunately for him the piece doesn't give his name. But the police were involved, so probably one of them sold the story to *P.I.* Laurence is devastated. He feels the whole world is laughing at him. He daren't show his face in the Groucho or his tennis club or anywhere people know him. The cartoon seemed to cut particularly deep. He went off and looked up the story of Venus and Mars and Vulcan and discovered that Vulcan had a gammy leg. He seemed to think that was a diabolically clever touch, though I think it's just coincidence myself. Yes, Laurence has a bad knee, didn't I tell you before? He gets sudden piercing pains in the knee joint for no apparent reason. He's had surgery but it came back. I'm sure it's psychosomatic. I've asked him if he can remember any childhood trauma associated with his knee, but he says not. Which reminds me, the other day I remembered an accident that happened to me when I was a little girl . . .

Well, I've told Laurence I will. Sleep with him, of course. Yes. He's been in such depths of depression about the *Public Interest* story that I felt I must do something to cheer him up. No, of course it isn't my only motive. Yes, I probably had made my mind up already. Well, almost. The *P.I.* business just tipped the balance. So I'm taking two days off from work and we're making a long weekend of it. The weekend after next. Leaving Thursday evening, returning Monday afternoon. So I'll have to miss my sessions on the Friday and the Monday. Yes, I know I'll have to pay for them, Karl, I remember that little speech you made when I started. Well, if you detect an underlying note of hostility I daresay there is one. Considering I've hardly missed a session in three years, I should have thought you might have waived the fees on this occasion, after all it's a kind of emergency. To save Laurence's sanity. I expect he would pay the fees himself if I asked him, but you probably wouldn't approve of that, would you?

I don't know yet, Laurence is making the arrangements. I said anywhere, as long as it's abroad, and preferably warm. I felt we had to go away somewhere. *My* house is out of the question, of course, and it wouldn't feel right in his flat either, not the first time, anyway,. It's very small, and sometimes you feel the whole sordid West End is pressing against the walls and windows trying to get in: the restaurant smells, the traffic noise, the tourists and the dossers . . . Yes, I did ask him about that young vagrant. It seems he started camping out in Laurence's porch a few weeks ago. Laurence tried to get rid of him, but in a very Laurentian way ended up inviting him in for a cup of tea. Bad move. Then he gave him some money to find a bed for the night. *Very* bad move. Of course the youth came back soon afterwards, hoping for more *largesse*. Laurence claims he hasn't given him any, but he's certainly abandoned any attempt to get rid of him. I told him to get the police to move him on, but he wouldn't. "He isn't doing any harm," he said. "And he keeps the burglars away." Which I suppose is true, in a way. The flats are unoccupied most of the time. But I suspect Laurence lets him stay there because he's lonely. Laurence is lonely. I think he likes having somebody to greet as he goes in and out, somebody who doesn't read *Public Interest*. I had a dream last night about that cartoon, by the way. I was Venus, Saul was Mars and Laurence was Vulcan. What do you make of that?

Well, we're going to Tenerife, I'm afraid. Laurence went to a travel agent and said he wanted somewhere warm abroad but not long-haul and that's what they came up with. I wish I'd made the arrangements myself now. Laurence is not really up to it. Sally always used to book their holidays. The Canary Islands *sound* nice, the name I mean, but I've never heard a good word about them from anybody who's actually been there. Have you? *Been* there. No, I don't suppose you would. Harriet went to Gran Canaria once and said it was ghastly though she tried to deny it yesterday not to depress me. Perhaps Tenerife is nicer. Well, it's only a few days after all, and at least it will be warm.

I've told Zelda that I'm going on business – that Laurence is setting an episode of *TPND* in the Canaries, a story about a package holiday, and that we've got to cast some local people for it. It's a rather implausible alibi, actually. Not the idea of the Canaries as such, because they do film the occasional episode on location, and in fact Laurence is rather taken with the package holiday idea, imagining the

Springfields waking up in their hotel room on their first day, delighted at having escaped from the Davises for a fortnight, only to find them having breakfast on the next balcony, maybe he'll actually write it if there's another series – but that I would have to go there to cast it, especially at this stage, is unlikely, if you know anything about the business. Zelda accepted it with a suspicious lack of suspicion. I can't help feeling that she knows there's more to this trip than television, but I must say she's been as sweet as pie about it. She's been very helpful about advising me what clothes to take. It seems a queer reversal of roles, as if she's helping me plan my *trousseau*. I've arranged for Zelda to spend the weekend with her friend Serena, so that's put her in a good mood. And Serena's mother is a sensible woman so I don't have to worry about them getting up to mischief. All in all, I'm rather looking forward to the trip. I can do with a few days of *la dolce vita* in the sun.

Well, as a dirty weekend it was a disaster, to put it bluntly. It wasn't up to much as a holiday, either, at first. Have you ever been to Tenerife? No, you said, I remember. Well, given a choice between the Siberian salt mines and a four-star hotel in Playa de las Americas, I'd choose Siberia any day. Playa de las Americas is the name of the resort where we stayed. Laurence chose it from the travel agent's brochure because it's near the airport, and we were due to arrive late at night. Well, that seemed to make sense, but it turned out to be the most ghastly place you can imagine. *Playa* is the Spanish for beach, of course, but it doesn't have a beach, not what I'd call a beach. Just a strip of black mud. All the beaches in Tenerife are black, they look like photographic negatives. The whole island is essentially an enormous lump of coke, and the beaches are made of powdered coke. It's volcanic, you see. There's actually a huge great volcano in the middle of the island. Unfortunately it's not active, otherwise it might erupt and raze Playa de las Americas to the ground. Then it might be worth visiting, like Pompeii. Picturesque concrete ruins with tourists carbonized in the act of parading in wet tee-shirts and pouring *sangria*

down their throats.

Apparently only a few years ago it was just a tract of rocky barren shoreline, then some developers decided to build a resort there, and now it's Blackpool beside the Atlantic. There's a gaudy mainstreet called the Avenida Litoral that's always choked with traffic and lined with the most vulgar bars and cafés and discos you ever saw, emitting deafening music and flashing lights and greasy cooking smells all round the clock, and apart from that there's nothing except block after block of high-rise hotels and timeshare apartments. It's a concrete nightmare, with hardly any trees or grass.

We didn't realize how horrible it was immediately, because it was dark when we arrived, and the taxi from the airport took us by what seemed a suspiciously roundabout route to me, but on reflection perhaps the driver was trying to spare us the full impact of the Avenida Litoral on our very first evening. We didn't speak much during the drive, except to remark on how warm and humid the air was. There wasn't much else to talk about because we couldn't see anything until we reached the outskirts of Playa de las Americas, and then what we saw didn't excite comment: deserted building sites and immobile cranes and blank cliffs of apartment buildings with just a few windows lit up and *De Venta* signs outside, and then a long arterial road lined with hotels. Everything was made of ferro-concrete, bathed in a sickly low-wattage yellow light from the streetlamps, and everything looked as if it had been built, very cheaply, the week before last. I could sense Laurence slumping lower and lower in his corner of the back of the car. Both of us already knew we'd come to Pitsville, but we couldn't bring ourselves to admit it. A dreadful constraint had come over us since we landed: the conscious-ness of what we had come here to DO, and our anxiety that it should be a success, made us fearful of breathing a word of disappointment about the venue.

At least, I consoled myself, the hotel is bound to be all right. Four stars, Laurence had assured me. But four stars in Tenerife doesn't mean what it means in England. Four stars in Tenerife is your just-slightly-above-average package holiday hotel. I dread to think what a one-star hotel in Tenerife is like. My heart sank – and it was already somewhere near my knees – when we walked into the lobby and took in the vinyl-tiled floor and the plastic-covered sofas and the dusty rubber plants wilting under the fluorescent ceiling lights. Laurence checked in and we followed the porter up in the lift in silence. Our room was bare and functional, clean enough, but smelling strongly of disinfectant. There were twin beds. Laurence looked at them with dismay and told the porter he had ordered a double room. The porter said all the rooms in the hotel had twin beds. Laurence's shoulders slumped a few degrees lower. When the porter had gone he apologized dolefully and vowed vengeance on the travel agent when he got home. I said gamely that it didn't matter and opened the sliding windows to step out on to the little balcony. The swimming pool was spread out below – a random shape, like a blot in a Rorschach test, set among artificial rocks and palm trees. It was lit from under the water, and glowed a brilliant blue in the night. The pool was the only thing we had seen so far that was remotely romantic, but the effect was spoiled by the powerful public-baths odour of chlorine that rose from the water, and the thump of the bass notes from a disco still in deafening progress on the far side. I closed the shutters against the noise and the smell and turned on the air-conditioning. Laurence was dragging the beds together, making a frightful noise as the bed-legs squeaked on the tiled floor and revealing that the room wasn't quite as clean as it had first looked because there was dust behind and underneath the bedside cabinets, and discovering that the leads on the bedside lamps weren't long enough to stretch to the new positions, so we ended up putting the beds back where they were. I was secretly relieved because it made it easier to suggest that we went straight off to sleep. It was late and I was exhausted and I felt about as sexy as a sack of Brussels sprouts. I think Laurence felt much the same, because he agreed readily enough. We used the bathroom decorously, one after the other, and then kissed chastely and got into our respective beds. Immediately I could feel through the thin sheets that my mattress was plastic-covered. Can you believe it? I thought only babies and elderly incontinents were given plastic-covered mattresses. Not so – package tourists too. I can tell you're fidgeting, Karl – you want to know whether we DID IT in the end, or not, don't you? Well, you'll just have to be patient. This is my story and I'm going to tell it in my own way. Oh, is it? Already? Well, till tomorrow, then.

Well, what do you think has happened? You'll never guess. Sally has moved back into their house in Rummidge and announced that she's going to stay, living separate lives. Yes, that's what it's called, "separate lives", it's a recognized legal term. It means you share the marital home while divorce proceedings are going on, but you don't live together. Don't cohabit. Laurence got back home yesterday – he spent the night in his London flat – to find Sally waiting for him with a typewritten sheet of proposals about how they should share the house, who should have which bedroom, and what hours they should each have the use of the kitchen and what days use of the washing machine. Sally was very explicit about not doing Laurence's laundry. She'd already bagged the master bedroom with the *en suite* bathroom, and had a new lock fitted on the bedroom door. He found all his suits and shirts and things had been very carefully moved and neatly put away in the guestroom. He's absolutely furious, but his lawyer says there's nothing he can do about it. Sally chose her moment well. She'd asked if she could collect some clothes from the house last weekend, and he said yes, any time, because he'd be away, and she had her own keys to the house of course. But instead of taking her clothes away she moved back in, when he wasn't there to try and stop her. No, she doesn't know that he was in Tenerife with me. In fact, she *mustn't* know.

Oh yes, where was I? Well, nothing happened the first night, as I said, except that we slept in our separate beds – till quite late, in spite of the incontinents' mattresses, because we were both so tired. We ordered breakfast in our room. It wasn't encouraging: canned orange juice, limp cardboard-flavoured croissants, jam and marmalade in little plastic containers – the continuation of airline food by other means. We tried eating out on our little balcony, but were driven inside by the sun, which was already surprisingly hot. The balcony faced east and didn't have an awning or an umbrella. So we ate in the room with the shutters closed. Laurence re-read the *Evening*

Standard which he'd bought the day before in London. He offered to share it with me, but I felt his reading over breakfast at all was not quite *comme il faut*, in the circs. When I made a little joke about it, he frowned in a puzzled sort of way and said, "But I always read the paper over breakfast," as if it were a fundamental law of the universe. It's extraordinary how as soon as you have to share space with somebody, you begin to see them in a completely different light, and things about them irritate you which you never expected. It reminded me of my first months of married life. I remember how appalled I was by the way Saul used to leave the toilet, with streaks of shit in the bowl, as if nobody had ever explained to him what a toilet-brush was for, but of course it was years before I could bring myself to mention it. Sharing the toilet in Tenerife was a bit of a nightmare, too, as a matter of fact, but the less said about that the better.

We decided to spend our first morning lazing beside the – Oh, yes, you *would* want to know about that, wouldn't you? Well, the bathroom was windowless, as they usually are in modern hotels, and the extractor fan didn't seem to be working, at least it wasn't making any kind of noise, so I made sure I used the bathroom first after breakfast. It won't surprise you in the light of our previous discussions about toilet training that, how shall I put this, that when I manage to do number twos the stools are rather small, hard, dense little things. Are you sure you want me to go on? Well, the fact is that this Tenerife toilet simply couldn't cope with them. When I pulled the chain they danced about merrily in the water like little brown rubber balls, and refused to disappear. I kept pulling the chain and they just kept bobbing back to the surface. Talk about the return of the repressed. I got quite frantic. I just couldn't leave the bathroom until I got rid of them. I mean, it's not very pleasant to find someone else's turds floating in the toilet just as you're going to use it, and it certainly puts a damper on romance, wouldn't you say? I couldn't bring myself to apologize or explain to Laurence, or make a joke of it. You have to be married to somebody for at least five years to do that. What I really needed was a good bucket of water to slosh into the toilet bowl, but the only container in the bathroom was a waste-paper bin made of plastic latticework. Eventually I got rid of my little pellets by pushing them round the U-bend one by one with the toilet brush, but it's not an experience I would care to repeat.

Well, as I say, we decided to spend our first morning lazing beside the pool. But when we got down there, every lounger and every parasol was taken. People were sprawled all over the place, soaking up the skin cancer. Laurence is very fair-skinned and he has an extraordinary amount of hair on his torso which soaks up suntan lotion like blotting-paper but lets all the harmful rays through. I tan easily, but I've read so many bloodcurdling articles in women's magazines lately about the effect on your skin that now I'm terrified of exposing a single inch. The only bit of shade was a scruffy patch of grass right up against the wall of the hotel and miles from the poolside. We sat there uncomfortably on our towels for a while and I began to work up a grudge against the people who had claimed loungers by dumping their belongings on them and then buggered off for a late breakfast. I suggested to Laurence that we should requisition a pair of these unoccupied loungers, but he wouldn't. Men are such cowards about things like that. So I did it on my own. There were two loungers side by side under a palm tree with folded towels on them, so I just moved a towel from one lounger to the other and made myself comfortable. After about twenty minutes a woman came up and glared at me, but I pretended to be asleep and after a while she picked up both towels and went away, and Laurence came over rather sheepishly and took the other lounger.

This small victory put me in a good mood for a while, but it soon wore off. I'm not much of a swimmer and Laurence has to be careful because of his knee, and the pool which looked all right from the balcony was actually rather unpleasant to swim in, the wrong shape and overcrowded with boisterous children and reeking of chlorine. I read somewhere that it's not the chlorine itself that makes the smell but the chemical reaction with urine, so those kids must have been peeing in the water for all they were worth, and kept going back to the Coke machine to refuel. After we'd had our dip, there wasn't anything to do except read, and the loungers weren't really designed for reading, they were that cheap sort that you just can't adjust. The tubular steel frame bends upwards a bit at the end, but not enough to

157

support your head at a comfortable reading height, so that you have to hold the book up in the air and after about five minutes your arms feel as if they're going to drop off. I'd brought A. S. Byatt's *Possession* with me, and Lorenzo had something by Kierkegaard, *Fear and Trembling* I think it was called, which didn't sound very appropriate to the occasion. You could tell what kind of people the other guests in the hotel were by what they were reading: Danielle Steel and Jeffrey Archer and the English tabloids which had arrived in the middle of the morning. Most of them looked to me like car workers from Luton but I didn't say so because Laurence has a thing about metropolitan snobbery.

Neither of us had brought swimming-towels from home, thinking that a four-star hotel would provide them, but this one didn't, and there was only one smallish bathtowel per person in the room, so we decided to go for a walk and do a little shopping. We needed sunhats, too, and rubber flip-flops, because the concrete round the pool was hot as hell by this time. So we got dressed again and out we went into the noonday sun, which was beating off the pavement and bouncing off the walls of the timeshare apartment buildings like laser beams. According to the hotel's streetplan we were only a couple of blocks from the sea, so we thought we'd walk in that direction and look for a beach shop, but there was no beach and no shop, just a low wall at the end of a cul-de-sac, and below it a narrow strip of what looked like wet cinders being churned by the sea. We turned round and walked back to the main road where there was a little shopping centre, built underground for some reason, a dismal tunnel of shops selling souvenir tat and tourist requisites. It seemed impossible to buy anything that hadn't got the word "Tenerife" blazoned on it, or a map of the island printed on it. Something in me rebelled against buying a towel I wouldn't be seen dead with once I got home, so we followed the main road into the centre of the town to see if we could find a wider selection. It turned out to be a walk of well over a mile, almost completely devoid of shade. At first it was boring, and then it got horrible. There was an especially horrible bit on the Avenida Litoral called the Veronicas, densely packed with bars and clubs and restaurants offering "*Paella* and chips" and "Beans on the toast".

Most of these places had disco music blaring into the street from the loudspeakers to attract customers, or else they were showing at maximum volume videos of old British sitcoms on wall-mounted television sets. It seemed to sum up the total vacuousness of Playa de las Americas as a holiday resort. Here were all these Brits, sitting on an extinct volcano in the middle of the sea two thousand miles from home, buying drinks so they could watch old episodes of *Porridge* and *Only Fools and Horses* and *It Ain't Half Hot, Mum*. "Did you ever see anything so pathetic?" I said to Laurence, and just then we came up to a café that was showing *The People Next Door*. It wasn't getting a very good audience rating, I'm afraid. In fact there were only four people in the place, a middle-aged couple looking like scalded giant crabs, and a pair of sulky young women with punk hairstyles. Of course, Laurence had to go in. I never knew a writer yet who could avert his eyes from a television screen when his own work is being shown. Laurence ordered a beer for himself and a g & t for me, and sat there mesmerized, with a fond smile on his face, like an infatuated parent watching a home movie of his infant son's first steps. I mean, nobody is more of a fan of Laurence's work than me, but I hadn't come all this way to sit in a bar and watch golden oldies from *The People Next Door*. There seemed to be only one thing to do, so I did it. I tossed back my g & t and ordered another one, a double. Laurence had another beer, and we shared a microwaved pizza, and then we had a brandy each with our coffee. Laurence suggested that we go back to the hotel for a *siesta*. In the taxi on the way back he put his arm round my shoulder, so I guessed what kind of a *siesta* he had in mind. Oh, is it time already? Till tomorrow then. Yes, of course I've heard of Scheherazade, what about her . . . ?

Well, it was lucky I was half-pissed, otherwise it would have been just too embarrassing for words. I mean, one either had to laugh or cry, and having a few drinks inside me, I laughed. I got the giggles as soon as I saw Laurence putting on his knee-support when we were preparing for our *siesta*. It's made of some spongy stretch fabric, like they use to make wet-suits, and it's bright red, with a hole in it for his kneecap to poke through. It looked particularly funny when he had nothing else on. He seemed rather surprised by my reaction. Apparently he always wears it when he and Sally have sex. When he put on an elasticated elbow bandage as well I nearly had hysterics. He explained that he'd had a recurrence of tennis elbow lately and didn't want to take any chances. I wondered if he was going to put on anything else, a pair of shin-pads perhaps, or a cycling helmet. Actually that wouldn't have been a bad idea, because the bed was so narrow he was in some danger of falling on the floor during foreplay. This involved a lot of licking and nuzzling on his part. I just closed my eyes and let him browse. It was quite nice, though ticklish, and I kept giggling when I think I was supposed to moan. Then it appeared he wanted me to straddle him while he lay on his back, because of his knee, and that he expected me to handle the trickiest bit of the proceedings myself, so to speak. I knew an actress once who told me that she had a recurrent dream of being on stage without knowing the play she was in, having to guess her lines and moves from what the other actors were saying and doing. I felt as if I was understudying Sally under a similar handicap. I don't know what she makes of the part, but I felt like a cross between a hooker and an orthopaedic nurse. However, I went through with it gamely, and jigged up and down a bit on top of him until he gave a groan and I rolled off. But it turned out that he was groaning because he couldn't come. "Perhaps you had a little too much to drink at lunch, darling," I said. "Perhaps," he said gloomily. "Was it all right for you?" Of course I said it was wonderful, though to be honest I've had more pleasure from a nice hot bath at the end of a long day, or a really top-class Belgian chocolate with a cup of freshly-ground Colombian coffee. Frankly.

Well, we slept for an hour or so after that, and then we showered and had a cup of tea on our balcony, which was in the shade by now, and read our books until it was time to go down and have a drink in the bar before dinner. We weren't talking to each other much because everything that came into our heads, my head anyway, was something we dared not say, about how awful the place was and what a disaster the whole trip was turning out to be, knowing there were three days still to go. We were on *demi-pension* terms at the hotel. They gave us little coupons when we checked in that you had to surrender as you went into the dining-room, a vast barrack of a place with about four hundred people shovelling food into themselves for all they were worth as if they were eating against the clock in some kind of TV gameshow. You helped yourself to *hors d'oeuvres* and desserts and they brought the main course to your table. There was a choice of chicken *chasseur* and fish fried in breadcrumbs. It was about BBC canteen standard, edible but dull. We had a bottle of red wine but I drank most of it because Laurence was girding himself to perform later. It didn't make for a very relaxing evening. We went out for a stroll and walked down to the shore again to watch the waves churning the wet cinders. Then there seemed nothing else to do except go to bed. It was either that or go back into town and what the Veronicas was like at night was all too easy to imagine. So we made love again and the same thing happened. He had an erection, but he couldn't, what's the word, emit, no matter how hard I jigged up and down. He was frightfully upset about it, though I said it didn't matter, in fact I was delighted, I never did like the sensation of slowly leaking into one's nightie afterwards. He said, "There must be something wrong with me." I said, "It's not you, it's this ghastly hotel and the dreadful place it's in, it's enough to make anyone impotent."

It was the first time I'd expressed my real feelings since we got there. He took it like a slap in the face. "I'm sorry," he said stiffly. "I did my best." "Of course you did, *chéri*," I said. "I'm not blaming you, it was the stupid travel agent. But why don't we move somewhere nicer?" "We can't," he said. "I paid in advance." He seemed to think we were under a contractual obligation to stay the full four nights. It took me quite a while to get him to see that we could well afford – at least *he* could – to forfeit the cost of the remaining two. It was as if the ghosts of his parents had risen up to forbid such a scandalous waste of money. "Anyway," he said, "there's only one five-star hotel in Playa de las Americas, and it's full. The travel agent tried it." "I should think it *is* full," I said. "Anybody who booked into a five-star hotel in Playa de las Americas would probably barricade themselves in their room and never come out. But I suppose there are five-star hotels in other places in Tenerife?" "How would we get there?" Laurence said. "Hire a car, my sweet," I said, thinking to myself, this is like talking to a child.

Well, by taking command of the arrangements, I got us out of that hellhole immediately after breakfast next morning. Laurence would have liked to sneak out of the hotel without telling them, but we had to check out to pay for some extras so I had the satisfaction of telling the reception staff why we were going, not that they cared. We hired an air-conditioned car from Avis and drove up the coast to the capital, Santa Cruz. You never saw such a barren, boring landscape in your life, like the surface of the moon in a heatwave. But Santa Cruz is quite a nice little town, slightly scruffy but civilized. There's one really classy hotel, with a pool in a beautiful shady garden, and a decent restaurant. Robert Maxwell had his last meal there, actually, before he threw himself off his yacht. If he had been in Playa de las Americas there wouldn't have been all that speculation about why he did it.

Well, we had a very pleasant weekend in Santa Cruz. The hotel gave us a huge high-ceilinged suite, with a marble bathroom with a window that opened, and a vast double bed in which we cuddled and slept like babies. We didn't do anything else in it. I said to Laurence, don't let's risk another *débâcle*, my dear, now that things are going so nicely, and he seemed happy to agree. The truth is that I had decided I wasn't going to marry Laurence even if he asked me, and that I didn't want a sexual relationship with him, or indeed anyone else. I decided I could do without sex, thankyou very much, for the rest of my life. I realized what a fool I'd been, going on and on analysing my relationship with Saul, wondering what went wrong, why I didn't satisfy him, when it was what satisfied *me* that was important, and putting my body at the disposal of another man after all these years wasn't going to do that. I hope Laurence and I can go back to our chaste, companionable relationship, but if we can't, *tant pis*.

So really, it wasn't such a disaster after all, my dirty weekend. I really think I see things more clearly than ever before, as a result of it. I see that there's nothing *wrong* with me. I can accept myself for what I am. I don't *need* sex. I don't *need* a man. And I don't need *you*, Karl, not any more. Yes. This is the end of the analysis. You told me I'd know. And I do. This is our last session, Karl. Yes. This is the big goodbye. I'm cured.

✳ ✳ Louise ✳ ✳

STELLA? . . . IT´S LOUISE . . . Hi! . . . Oh fine. How about you? . . . Oh. I *thought* you sounded depressed on the answerphone . . . Yeah, look I'm sorry I didn't get back to you before, but I've been so busy you wouldn't believe . . . Meetings meetings meetings . . . Yeah, it's the same movie, only now it's called *Switchback*. You know what they say about Hollywood, everything takes either five minutes or five years, and this baby looks like it's gonna be a five-year pain in the ass. Anyway, why are you in the pits? . . . Uh huh . . . Uh huh . . . I kinda guessed . . . Listen, sweetheart, you won't thank me for saying this right now, but honestly you're better off without him . . . Sure I never liked him, but was I right or was I right? Didn't I say, never trust a man who wears a gold cross round his neck? . . . He exploited you, honey . . . As soon as you'd like paid for his root-canal work, and the acting lessons, he dumped you . . . Well, of course you feel that way now, but you'll get over it, trust me, I've been there. Wait a minute, I got another call. Don't go away . . .

Hi. That was Nick, calling from New York, just to say hallo . . . Yeah, just for a few days. He's got this client who's opening a play off-Broadway. Say, Stella, you want me to take your mind off your troubles with this really weird thing that happened to me yesterday? . . . OK, kick off your shoes and put your feet up and lend me your ears . . .

It was about six o'clock yesterday evening. I'd just come in from a meeting at Global Artists, and showered and changed and was wondering whether to fix myself something to eat or call Sushi Express, when the phone rings and I hear this British voice saying, "Hallo, Louise, this is Laurence Passmore." Laurence Passmore?

Like the name means nothing to me, and I don't recognize the voice. So I say, "Oh yes?" in a neutral kinda way, and the guy gives a nervous little giggle and says, "I suppose this is what disc-jockeys call a blast from the past." "Do I know you?" I say, and there's like a pained silence for about a minute and then he says, "The people next door? Four years ago?" and the penny drops. This is the guy who created the original British version of *Who's Next Door?* Yeah. It's called *The People Next Door* over there. When I was working for Mediamax they bought the rights, and he came over from England as like a consultant on the pilot, and I was assigned to look after him. But like the name "Laurence" hadn't rung a bell. "Didn't you have a different name, then?" I asked him. "Tubby," he said. "Tubby Passmore, of course," I said. He came into sharper focus at once: fiftyish, balding, stocky build. He was a nice guy. Kinda shy, but nice. "I never liked that nickname, to tell you the truth," he said, "but I seem to be stuck with it." "Hey," I said, "Nice of you to call. What business brings you to L.A.?" "Well, I'm not here on business, actually," he said. Brits say "actually" an awful lot, have you noticed? "Vacation?" I said, thinking he must be on his way to Hawaii or somewhere. "A sort of vacation," he said, and then: "I was wondering whether you would be free for dinner this evening."

Well, ninety-nine times out of a hundred, it would have been outta the question. Nick and I were out every night last week. *Every night.* But as it happened Nick was away and I had nothing planned and I thought, what the hell, why not? I knew there would be nothing below the line on this date . . . Because once, when he was here before, I made a play for him and he backed off . . . Yeah . . . Well, I'd just split up with Jed and I was kinda lonely. So was he. But he turned me down, in the nicest possible way, because he loved his wife . . . Yeah, there are such men, Stella. In England there are anyway . . . Well, when I said yes to dinner he was like ecstatic. He said he was staying at the Beverly Wilshire and I thought to myself, anybody who is paying for himself at the Beverly Wilshire is my kind of date, and I was just wondering whether I had enough pull with the maître d' at Morton's to get us a table at short notice when he said, "I'd like to go to that fish restaurant down by the beach at Venice where we went before." Well,

I couldn't remember what restaurant he was talking about, and he couldn't remember the name, but he said he would recognize it if he saw it, so I did the decent thing and offered to drive us down there. Venice isn't my favourite place, but I figured maybe it was just as well I wasn't seen at Morton's with an obscure English TV writer – I mean it's not like this guy is Tom Stoppard or Christopher Hampton or anything.

So I put on something casual and drove down to Beverly Hills to pick up Tubby Passmore at the appointed time. He was hovering by the doors, so I didn't get out of the car, just honked and waved. It took him about ten minutes to notice me. He looked just as I remembered him, perhaps a few pounds heavier, with a big potato-shaped face and a fringe of baby-fine hair hanging down over the collar of his jacket. Nice smile. But I couldn't imagine why I'd ever wanted to get in the sack with him. He got into the car and I said "Welcome back to L.A." and stuck out my hand just as he made a lunge at my cheek, so there was a little confusion but we laughed it off. He said, almost accusingly, "You've changed your car," and I laughed and said, "I should think so. I must have had at least five cars since you were here . . ." No, it's a Mercedes. I traded in the BMW for a white Mercedes with red leather interior. It looks great. Just a minute, I got another call . . .

Fuckit fuckit fuckit . . . Sorry, just thinking aloud. That was Lou Renwick at Global Artists. Our star won't sign unless his buddy directs, and the buddy's last picture was a crock of shit. These people are such assholes. Never mind, I'm gonna hang in there. I have points in this one . . . Yeah, I optioned the book . . . Where was I? Oh, yeah, well, we drive out to Venice, and walk up and down by the beach, weaving between the joggers and surfers and roller-skaters and frisbee-throwers and dog-walkers, looking for this restaurant, and eventually he thinks he's found it, but it has the wrong name and it isn't even a regular fish restaurant but a Thai place. However when we ask inside they say they've only been in business for about a year, so we figure it probably is the right one. In fact the look of it stirs a faint memory in me too.

Tubby wanted to eat outside, though it was kinda cool and I was underdressed for *al fresco* dining . . . Oh, a sleeveless top, and that black cotton skirt I bought in your shop last year. With the gold buttons? That's the one. Tubby said there'd been a wonderful sunset when we ate in Venice before, but yesterday was overcast you remember, so there was no particular reason to sit outside, but he more or less insisted. The waiter asked if we'd like anything to drink and Tubby looked at me and said, "Whiskey sour, yes?" and I laughed and said I didn't drink cocktails any more, I'd just have a mineral water, and he looked strangely put out. "You *will* drink some wine?" he said anxiously, and I said maybe a glass. He ordered a bottle of Napa Valley Chardonnay, which struck me as a tad economical for a guy who was shacked up at the Beverly Wilshire, but I didn't say anything.

All the way out to Venice I'd been jabbering away about *Switchback* because my head was full of it and I guess I was like showing off a bit, letting him know I'm a pukka movie producer now, not just a TV executive. So when we'd ordered our food I figured it was time to let him have his turn. "So what's been happening to you, lately?" I said. Well, it was like the moment in a disaster movie when somebody casually opens a door in a ship and a million tons of seawater knocks them off their feet. He gave a sigh that was like almost a groan, and proceeded to pour out a tale of unrelieved woe. He said his wife wanted to divorce him and his TV company wanted to take his show away from him and he had a chronic knee injury that wouldn't heal. Seems his wife walked out without warning, and then walked right back in again two weeks later to share the house under some special arrangement called "separate lives". Like they not only have separate bedrooms but they have to take turns to use the kitchen and the washing machine. Apparently the British divorce courts are very strict on laundry. Yeah. If she knowingly washed his socks it could screw up her petition, he says. Not that there's any risk of that. They don't even speak to each other when they meet on the stairs. They send each other notes, like North and South Korea. No. He suspects there's somebody, but she says not, she just doesn't want to be married to him any more. Their kids are grown up . . . She's some kind of college professor. He said it just blew him away when she told him . . . Nearly

166

thirty years – can you believe it? I didn't know there was anybody left in the entire world, outside of a Sunset Home, who'd been married to the same person for thirty years. What seemed to bug him more than anything was that all that time he'd never cheated on her once. "Not that I haven't been tempted," he said. "Well, you know that, Louise." And then he gave me this long, soulful look out of his pale blue, bloodshot eyes.

I tell you, I broke out in goosebumps all over, and it wasn't because of the breeze coming off the ocean. I suddenly realized what this date was all *about*. I realized that it was in this very restaurant that I had tried to seduce him all those years ago . . . Yeah! The whole thing came flooding back into my head, like a flashback sequence in an old *film noir*. We'd had a nice dinner and a bottle of wine and I'd snuck out to the Ladies' room between courses to do some blow . . . Yeah, I was doing drugs in those days . . . Always carried a stash in my handbag, Colombia's favourite cash crop . . . But Tubby wasn't into that sorta stuff. He thought when people offered him coke at a party they meant a drink. He thought being loaded meant having a lotta money. Even the idea of smoking pot freaked him out, so I never let on I was snorting the hard stuff. I wonder he never guessed, the way I used to laugh at his little English quips. Anyway, there I was, feeling high and horny, and there was this nice clean Englishman sitting opposite who obviously fancied me but was too decent or too timid to take the initiative, so I took it myself. Apparently I said I'd like to take him home and fuck his brains out . . . Yeah. He quoted the exact words to me. They were engraved on his memory. You see what I mean? This whole date was like a reprise of the one all those years ago. The Venice restaurant, the table outside, the Napa Valley Chardonnay . . . That was why he was so upset that I'd changed my car and the fish restaurant had turned into a Thai restaurant and I didn't drink whiskey sours any more. That was why he made us sit outside. He was trying to recreate the exact circumstances of that evening four years ago as far as possible in every detail. Every detail except one . . . Exactly! Now that his wife had walked out on him he wanted to take me up on my offer to fuck him. He'd flown all the way from England specifically for that purpose. It didn't seem to have occurred to him

167

that my circumstances might have changed in the meantime, not to mention my mood. I guess in his head I was forever sitting at that table beside the ocean, gazing wistfully out to sea and waiting for him to reappear, released from his matrimonial vows, to sweep me into his arms. Wait a minute, I got another call . . .

Hi. How did we exist before Call Waiting? That was Gloria Fawn's agent. She passed on *Switchback*. So what's new, I don't suppose he even showed her the script. Well, fuck 'em . . . Oh yeah, so like I was saying, it really freaked me out to think that this guy had flown six thousand miles to change his mind about a proposition that was four years old. It was like you said to someone, pass the salt, and four years later he shows up with a salt cellar. Well, I figured I'd better set him straight as soon as possible, so when he tried to top up my wine glass I put my hand over it and said I was cutting down because I was trying to conceive and if I succeeded I'd have to give up completely . . . Yeah. I thought I'd better go for it. The old biological clock is ticking away. Nick is keen . . . Well, thanks, Stella. I'm relying on you for some chic maternity wear . . . Anyway, this announcement stopped Tubby Passmore in his tracks, but he still didn't get it. I think for a moment he thought I wanted to have a child by *him* . . . Well, you can laugh, but this guy is unreal, I'm telling you. So then I explained I was with Nick and he like crumpled in front of my eyes. I thought he was going to start crying into his shrimp and lemon-grass soup. I said to him, "What's the matter?" though I knew very well what was the matter, and he quoted Kierkegaard at me . . . Yeah, Kierkegaard the philosopher. Not Kierkegaard the smorgasbord. Heh heh. He said, "The most dreadful thing that can happen to a man is to become ridiculous in his own eyes in a matter of essential importance." Yeah. That was it. I wrote it down afterwards.

Well, as you can imagine, the evening never recovered. I ate all the food and he drank all the wine, and I did all the talking. I couldn't help feeling sorry for the guy, so I told him about Prozac. Believe it or not, he'd never heard of it. He shook his head and said he never took tranquillizers. "I had a bad experience with Valium, once," he said. Valium! I mean this guy is pharmaceutically in the Stone Age. I explained to him that Prozac wasn't a tranquillizer, or an ordinary anti-depressant, but an entirely new wonder-drug. I gave him a real sales pitch . . . Sure, honey, don't you? Doesn't everybody in Hollywood? . . . Well, Nick and I swear by it. Sure. We have a chart thumbtacked to the kitchen wall telling us when to take our little green and white capsules . . . Well, it changed my life . . . No, I wasn't depressed, you don't have to be depressed to take it. It does wonders for your self-confidence. Like I'd never have had the courage to resign from Mediamax without Prozac . . . Oh, yeah, I read that story in *Time* magazine but I never experienced anything like that . . . You should try it, really, Stella . . . Well, there is one side effect, I have to admit: it makes it harder to have an orgasm. But as you haven't got a lover at the moment, honey, what have you got to lose? No, of course not, Stella, but Prozac could tide you over . . . Well, fine, honey, we all have our own ways of coping with adversity . . . Oh, I drove him back to the Beverly Wilshire and he fell asleep in the car, either from booze or jet-lag or disappointment or a combination of all of them. The bell captain opened the door of the car, and I gave Tubby a kiss on the cheek, and pushed him out and watched him stumble into the lobby. I felt kinda sorry for him, but what could I do? . . . I don't know, I suppose he'll go back to London . . . Would you really? . . . Well, I don't know. I could ask him, if you like . . . Are you sure this is a good idea, Stella? . . . Well, if you say so. You realize he's not exactly England's answer to Warren Beatty, don't you? . . . Oh he's clean all right, you don't have to worry about that. I'll call him right now and tell him I've got this gorgeous unattached girlfriend who's dying to meet him . . . Speak to you soon.

✳ ✳ Ollie ✳ ✳

OH, HALLO GEORGE, how goes it in Current Affairs? Good good. Oh, surviving, just about. Thanks, I need one. Draught Bass, please. Oh, make it a pint. Ta. Yeah, one of those mornings. My secretary is off sick, our fax machine is on the blink, the BBC have snapped up a Canadian soap I had my eye on, and some cunt of a solicitor is suing us because he has the same name as the bent lawyer in that episode of *Motorway Patrol* – did you see it? No, the week before last. Ah, thank you, Gracie. And a packet of crisps, smoky bacon flavour. No, no, George, let me pay for the crisps. Well, if you insist. Thanks, Gracie. Cheers, George. Ah. I needed that. What? Oh, I suppose we'll buy him off with a few grand, it's cheaper in the long run. Shall we sit down? Over there, in the corner. I like to have my back to the wall in this place, less chance of being overheard. Yeah, but it doesn't mean they're not out to get you. Ha ha. Here we are. Have a crisp. If I could open the bloody packet. They should make something to open these plastic packets with, something like a cigar-cutter you could carry in your pocket, I've a good mind to patent it, you could make a fortune. Oops! See what I mean? Either it won't open at all or it splits down the middle and spills the whole shoot in your lap. Have one, anyway. I saw a bloke in a pub the other day, I swear to God he went ten rounds with a packet of Walton's Crisps. Broke a fingernail trying to tear the packet open, damn near broke a tooth trying to bite through it, finished up in desperation setting fire to it with his cigarette-lighter. I kid you not. I think he was trying to melt the corner of the packet but it went up in flames, whoosh, singed the bloke's eyebrows and stank the place out with the smell of burning chip fat. Honest. Now if we put that on television we wouldn't dare say Walton's Crisps, they'd be down on us like a ton of bricks, well fair enough I suppose, but it's coming to something if you have to check the name of every bloody solicitor in the country before a script can be cleared. Nice drop of beer, this.

Yeah, it's been one of those mornings all right. To top it all, I had a meeting with Tubby Passmore. A basket case if ever there was one. Well, he's giving me a lot of grief at the moment. I suppose you know about Debbie Radcliffe? Oh, I thought Dave Treece would've put you in the picture. Well, keep it under your hat, but she wants to leave *The People Next Door*. Yeah. You bet it's serious. Her contract runs out at the end of the current series, and she won't renew at any price, the stupid cow. I dunno, she says she wants to go back on the stage. Is she? Well, I wouldn't know, I never go to the theatre if I can help it. Can't stand it. It's like being strapped to your seat in front of a telly with only one channel. And you can't talk, you can't eat, you can't drink, you can't go out for a piss, you can't even cross your legs because there's no room. And they charge you twenty quid for the privilege. Anyway, she's adamant, so we've got to write her part out of the show. It's still getting great ratings, as you know. Absolutely. At least one more series, probably two or three. So we asked Tubby to rewrite the last episode or two of the present series so as to get rid of Priscilla, you know, Debbie's part, to make way for a new woman in Edward's life in the next series, see? We gave Tubby some ideas, but he wouldn't buy any of 'em. He said the only way was to literally kill her off. In a car accident or on the operating table or something. Yeah, unbelievable, isn't it? We'd have the whole fucking country crying its eyes out. Debbie's got to go in a way that leaves the viewers feeling good, stands to reason. I mean, nobody's pretending it's easy. But if there's one thing I've learned from twenty-seven years in television, it's that *there's always a solution*. I don't care what the problem is, whether it's scripts or casting or locations or budget, there's always a solution – if you think hard enough. The trouble is most people are too fucking idle to make the effort. Only they call it integrity. Tubby said he'd rather see the show come to an end than compromise the integrity of his characters. Did you ever hear such bullshit? This is sitcom we're talking about, not fucking Ibsen. I'm afraid he's getting delusions of grandeur, the latest is he wants to write a – Oh, well, fortunately we discovered that under our contract we can hire another writer to take over if Tubby declines to write another series. Yeah. Of course, we don't *want* to. We'd prefer Tubby to do the job himself. Oh, fuck his moral rights, George! The point is that he could do the job better than anybody else, if he would only make the effort. Well, it's a standoff at the moment. He has five weeks to come up with an acceptable idea to ease Debbie out of the show, or else we get another writer. I dunno, I'm not very hopeful. He doesn't seem to be living in the real world these days. His private life is in deep shit. You know his wife's left him? Yeah. First I knew about it was when he called me up one night, at home, very late. He sounded a bit pissed – you know, breathing heavily and long pauses between words. He said he had an idea for writing Debbie out of the show. "Suppose," he said, "suppose Priscilla just walks out on Edward without warning? Suppose she just tells him in the last episode that she doesn't want to stay married to him? There isn't any other man. She just doesn't love him any more. She doesn't even like him any more. She says living with him is like living with a zombie. So she's decided to leave him." I said to him, "Don't be ridiculous, Tubby. There has to be more motivation than that. Nobody will believe it." He said, "Won't they?" and put the phone down. Next thing I hear is that his wife has walked out on him. You saw that piece in *Public Interest*? Well, that was the point, wasn't it? There was no other man. The bloke was gay. Looks as if Tubby's wife walked out because, like he said, she just didn't want to be married to him any more. He's taken it very hard. Of course, anybody would. Will you have another? Same again? What was it, the Club red? Oh, the Saint Emilion, right. You think it's worth the extra, do you? No, no, you shall have the Saint Emilion, George. I don't know anything about wine, never pretended to. Small or large? I think I'll just have a half myself, work to do this afternoon. Oh, right. I'm going to get myself a pie, what about you? Chicken and mushroom, right.

There we are. One large glass of Saint Emilion. They'll call out when the pies are ready. We're nineteen. I was in a pub the other day where they give you playing-cards instead of these cloakroom tickets.

The girl at the bar calls out "Queen of Hearts" or "Ten of Spades" or whatever. Clever idea, I thought. I'm always losing these fiddly little things and forgetting my number. Your pie was one twenty-five by the way. Oh, ta. That's all the change I've got, I'll have to owe you the ten pee, alright? Cheers. Yes, well, he made an appointment to see me this morning. I thought perhaps he'd had a brilliant new idea about how to get rid of Debbie's part, but no such luck. Instead it turns out that he wants to try his hand at straight drama. Yeah. You won't believe this, George. He wants to do a series about a geezer called Kikkiguard. Oh, is that how you pronounce it? You've heard of him, then? Yeah, that's right, a Danish philosopher. What else do you know about him? Well, I didn't even know that much, till Tubby told me. I was gobsmacked, (*a*), that he was interested in the subject, and (*b*), that he thought we would be. I said to him, very slowly, "You want to write a drama series for Heartland Television about a Danish philosopher?" I mean, if he'd said it was about a Danish pastry it wouldn't have sounded any dafter. He just nodded his head. I managed not to laugh in his face. I've been through this before with comedy writers. They all get ideas above their station eventually. They want to do without a studio audience, or write about social problems. The other week Tubby had a reference to abortion in his script. I ask you – abortion in a sitcom! You have to either humour them or tell 'em to get stuffed. I still have hopes Tubby may see sense about *The People Next Door*, so I humoured him. I said, "OK, Tubby, pitch it to me. What's the story?"

Well, there was no story, to speak of. This, whatsisname, Kierkegaard bloke, was the son of a wealthy merchant in Copenhagen, we're in what, the Victorian period, early Victorian. The old man was a gloomy, guilt-ridden old bugger, who brought his children up accordingly. They were very strict Protestants. When he was a young man Kierkegaard kicked against the traces a bit. "They think he may have gone to a brothel once," Tubby said. "Just once?" I said. "He felt very guilty about it," Tubby said. "It was probably his only sexual experience. He got engaged to a girl called Regine later, but he broke it off." "Why?" I said. "He didn't think they'd be happy," he said. "He suffered a lot from depression, like his father." "I can see this isn't going to be a comedy series, Tubby," I said. "No," he said, without cracking a smile. "It's a very sad story. After he broke off the engagement, nobody could understand why, he went off to Berlin for a while and wrote a book called *Either/Or*. He came back to Copenhagen, secretly hoping for a reconciliation with Regine, but found she'd got engaged to another man." He stopped and looked at me soulfully, as if this was the biggest tragedy in the history of the world. "I see," I said, after a while. "And what did he do then?" "He wrote a lot of books," Tubby said. "He was qualified to be a minister, but he didn't agree with making religion a kind of career. Luckily he'd inherited a substantial fortune from his father." "It sounds like the only bit of luck he did have," I said. Oh, did she say nineteen, George? Over here, my love, we're nineteen. One steak and kidney and one chicken and mushroom, that's it. Lovely. Thanks. That was quick. Microwaved of course. You want to be careful with your first bite, they can burn your bloody tongue these pies. They're hotter inside than they look. Mm, not bad. What's yours like? Good. So. Tubby Passmore, yes. I asked him if Kierkegaard was famous in his lifetime. "No," said Tubby. "His books were considered peculiar and obscure. He was ahead of his time. He was the founder of existentialism. He reacted against the all-encompassing idealism of Hegel." "This doesn't sound like the stuff of prime-time commercial television, Tubby," I said. "I would only glance at the books," he said. "The main emphasis would be on Kierkegaard's love for Regine. He was never able to forget her, even after she got married." "What happened?" I said. "Did they have an affair?" He looked quite shocked at the suggestion. "No, no," he said. "He saw her around Copenhagen – it was a small place in those days – but they never spoke. Once they came face to face in church and he thought she was going to say something, but she didn't, and neither did he. It would make a great scene," he said. "Tremendous emotion, without a word spoken. Just close-ups. And music, of course." Apparently that was the nearest they ever came to getting together again. When Kierke-gaard asked the husband's permission to write to her, he refused. "But he always loved her," Tubby said. "He left her everything in his will, though there wasn't much left when he died." I asked him what

174

he died of. "An infection of the lungs," he said. "But in my opinion it was really a broken heart. He had lost the will to live. Nobody really understood his suffering. When he was on his deathbed, his uncle said that there was nothing wrong with him that couldn't be cured by straightening his shoulders. He was only forty-eight when he died." I asked what else this geezer did apart from writing books. The answer was, nothing very much, except take carriage drives in the country. I said, "Where's your jeopardy, Tubby? Where's your suspense?" He looked rather taken aback. "This isn't a thriller," he said. "But you've got to have some kind of threat to your hero," I said. "Well," he said, "there was a time when a satirical magazine started to attack him. That caused him a lot of pain. They made fun of his trousers." "His trousers?" I said. I tell you George, I had a struggle to keep a straight face through all this. "Yes, they printed caricatures of him with one leg of his trousers shorter than the other." Well, as soon as he said "caricature" I remembered that cartoon in *Public Interest*, and it all clicked into place. Yeah, you got it in one. The guy's developed some sort of strange identification with this Kierkegaard bloke. It's all connected with his marital problems. But I didn't let on. I just recapped the story as he'd pitched it to me. "OK, Tubby, let me see if I've got this right," I said. "There's this Danish philosopher, nineteenth century, who gets engaged to a bird called Regine, breaks off the engagement for reasons nobody understands, she marries another guy, they never speak to each other again, he lives for another twenty-odd years writing books nobody understands, then he dies, and a hundred years later he's hailed as the father of existentialism. Do you really think there's a TV drama series there?" He thought for a moment, and then he said, "Perhaps it would be better as a one-off." "Much better," I said. "But of course, that's not my territory. You'd have to talk to Alec Woosnam about it." I thought that was a rather clever move, sending him off to bend Alec's ear about Kierkegaard. No, of course Alec won't buy it, do me a favour! But he'll string Tubby along if I ask him to. Get him to write a treatment, talk to people at Channel Four, go through the motions. If we indulge him on Kierkegaard, he just might play ball over Debbie's part in *The People Next Door*. No, he doesn't have a script editor. We had one on the first series, but we never felt the need after that. Tubby turns in his scripts direct to me and Hal, and we work on them together. I don't think he'd take kindly to having a script editor again. But it's a thought, George, definitely a thought. Another one? Well I shouldn't really, but this pie's given me a terrible thirst, must be oversalted. Oh, you might as well make it a pint. Ta.

✳ ✳ Samantha ✳ ✳

HETTY, DARLING, HOW ARE YOU? Omigod, I don't need to ask, do I? Poor you. Your jaw is swollen out like a pumpkin. I expect you're surprised to see me, but I phoned and your flatmate told me you were here, and as I was passing I thought I'd pop in even though it's not a proper visiting hour. I don't think they really mind, do they? Can't you talk at all? Oh dear, what a shame. I was looking forward to a nice chat. Well, you'll just have to nod and shake your head and use your eyes, darling, like a good television actress. I bought you some grapes, where shall I put them – on here? They've been washed, so you can help yourself. No? Can't eat *anything*? What a curse wisdom teeth are. Badly impacted was it? *Two* of them? No wonder you look so poorly. Mmm . . . these are rather delicious. No pips. You're sure that if I peeled one for you, you wouldn't . . . ? No? Oh well, all right. Does it hurt terribly? I suppose they pumped you full of painkillers. You *must* demand more as soon as they wear off. Hospitals are terribly mean about that, they think pain is improving. Well, I'm going to have to make all the conversational running, aren't I? Fortunately I've got lots to talk about. The fact is I just had the most bizarre weekend and I'm dying to tell somebody all about it who isn't connected with work. I've got a new job at Heartland, you see, a proper job. Script editor. I started last week. Basically it means you read the writer's first drafts and make comments and suggestions and generally act as a buffer between him and the producer or director. It's the first stepping-stone to writing or producing oneself. You know I've been chaperoning that little brat Mark Harrington in *The People Next Door*? Well now I'm working with the writer, Tubby Passmore. Well, you may pull a face, Hetty, but thirteen million people can't be wrong, not in television they can't. Tubby asked for me himself. I got to know him through the chaperoning – we would meet at rehearsals, in the canteen and so on. He was always perfectly pleasant, but rather shy. I had him down as a herbivore. I always say there are two kinds of men, the herbivores and the carnivores. It's something about the way they look at you. Because I've got these tits I get a lot of looks. I know you used to say at school that you'd kill for them, Hetty, but frankly I'd give anything for a figure like yours. No, honestly. Clothes hang so much better on a flat-chested figure. Not that you're *completely* flat, darling, but you know what I mean. Anyway, some men just run their eyes appreciatively over you as if you were a statue or something, those are the herbivores, they just want to browse, and others look at you as if they would like to tear your clothes off and sink their teeth into you, those are the carnivores. Jake Endicott is a carnivore. He's my agent. Tubby's agent too, as it happens. And Ollie Silvers, the producer of *The People Next Door* – he's another carnivore. When I talked to Tubby one day about my writing ambitions, he suggested I asked Ollie to give me some scripts to read and report on, you know, unsolicited ones, the slush-pile. So I went to see him wearing my cream linen suit without a blouse and all through the interview I could see he was trying to look down my front to see what I was wearing under the jacket, if anything. I walked out of his office with a pile of scripts. I can see you disapprove, Hetty, but I'm completely postfeminist about this, I'm afraid. I think it's a great mistake for women to make all this fuss about sexual harassment. It's like unilateral disarmament. In a man's world we've got to use all the wiles and weapons we've got. I don't think you should shake your head as hard as that, darling, your stitches might come undone. It may be different in the Civil Service, for all I know. Anyway, as I say, I thought Tubby was a confirmed herbivore. If we were sitting at the same table in the canteen or the bar, he would chat to me in a fatherly sort of way, but he never made a pass or anything approaching one. He's old enough to *be* my father, actually. On the corpulent side, as the name implies. Balding. A big egg-shaped head. He always reminds me of the pictures of Humpty Dumpty in a copy of *Alice in Wonderland* I had as a child. I cultivated him purely out of self-interest, I don't mind admitting. Goodness I must stop eating your grapes. Just one more then.

Well, as I was saying, Tubby always seemed completely immune to my feminine charms, in fact I was slightly piqued by his lack of interest, but then his attitude suddenly changed. It was after his marriage broke up – oh, I forgot to mention, his wife left him a month or two ago. There were lots of rumours – that she'd come out as a lesbian or gone to live in an ashram or that she found him in bed with her tennis coach. All wildly off the mark, as I found out later. We didn't see much of him for some weeks. But then he turned up at rehearsals one day, in London, a grotty place in Pimlico that Heartland use, and immediately made a set at me. Without any warning. I remember seeing him push through the swing doors and stand at the threshold looking round the room until he spotted me, and then he came straight over and plonked himself down beside me, hardly bothering to say hallo to Hal Lipkin, that's the director, or any of the cast. Deborah Radcliffe smiled at him but he walked straight past her without a glance, which didn't please her very much. I could see her looking daggers at us out of the corner of my eye. Tubby looked wrecked. Bloodshot eyes. Unshaven. Crumpled clothes. It turned out that he'd just flown in from L.A., and come straight to the rehearsal rooms from Heathrow. I said that it showed great devotion to duty and he stared at me as if he didn't understand what I was talking about, so I said, "I mean, attending rehearsals when you must be exhausted." He said, "Oh, bugger the rehearsals," and in the next breath asked me out to dinner that very evening. Well, I was supposed to be going to see a film with James, but I didn't let that stop me. I mean if a famous, well, famous in television terms, writer asks a nobody like me out to dinner, you go. If you don't want to stay a nobody all your life, you go. That's the way it works, darling, believe me. Incidentally, James thinks I spent this last weekend visiting my grandmother in Torquay, just remember that if you should happen to see him, won't you?

So Tubby took me to this little Italian restaurant in Soho, Gabrielli's. I'd never been there before, but he was obviously a regular. They received him with open arms as if he was a long-lost son

– all except the owner's wife, who was giving me the evil eye for some reason. Tubby was basking in all the attention until the woman came over to put some breadsticks on the table and said, looking at me, "Is this your daughter, then, Signor Passmore?" and Tubby went very red and said, no I wasn't, and then this woman said, "And 'ow is Signora Amy?" and Tubby went even redder and said he didn't know, he hadn't seen her for a while, and this interfering old bitch gave a smug sort of smile and disappeared into the kitchen. Tubby looked like Humpty Dumpty after he'd fallen off the wall. He muttered that he sometimes ate there with Amy Porteus, the casting director for *The People Next Door*. I've met her a couple of times. She's a dumpy little brunette, in her forties I should say, always slightly overdressed and reeking of perfume. I said in a bantering tone that he obviously wasn't in the habit of bringing young women there anyway, and he said dourly no, he wasn't, and asked if I would like a drink. I had a Campari and soda and he had just a mineral water. I told him about my idea for a soap, and he nodded his head and said it sounded interesting, but he didn't really seem to be attending. What darling, what don't you understand? Mime it. Oh! Not a soup, darling, a *soap*, you know like *Eastenders*, only what I have in mind is more like *Westenders*. I asked him if he'd been to L.A. on business, and he said, "Partly," but he didn't explain what the other part was. They served us quite a decent meal and we had a bottle of Chianti that was supposed to be very special but he drank hardly any of it, he said because of his jet-lag, he was afraid he might fall asleep. Over the dessert he steered the conversation rather clumsily towards sex. "You've no idea," he said, "how repressed we were about sex when I was young. Nice girls simply didn't. So nice boys couldn't, most of the time. The country was full of twenty-five-year-old virgins, many of them male. I suppose you find that difficult to credit. I suppose you wouldn't think twice about having sex with someone you liked, would you?" So I said – what? Oh, right, I'll speak more quietly. These beds are rather close together, aren't they? What's she in for? Mime it. Appendix? No. Hysterectomy? Really? Well mimed, darling. You know, there's the makings of a rather good parlour game here.

So I said it would depend on whether I really liked the person, and he looked at me soulfully and said, "Do you really like *me*, Samantha?" Well, I was a bit taken aback at the speed with which we'd reached this point. It was like being taken for a ride in one of those GTi's that look like sedate family saloons and do nought to sixty in about three seconds flat. So I laughed my tinkle-of-tiny-bells laugh and said it sounded like a leading question. He looked very despondent and said, "So you don't, then?" I said on the contrary I liked him very much but I thought he was exhausted and jet-lagged and didn't quite know what he was doing or saying and I didn't want to take advantage of him. Well he pondered that for a moment, frowning to himself, and I thought, you've blown it, Samantha, but to my relief his Humpty-Dumpty face broke into a smile, and he said, "You're absolutely right. What about some dessert? They do a rather good tiramisu here." He poured himself a full glass of wine, knocked it back as if making up for lost time, and ordered another bottle. He talked about football for the rest of the meal, which I can't say is my favourite conversational topic, but fortunately we'd nearly finished. He put me in a cab outside the restaurant, gave the driver a tenner for the fare, and kissed me on the cheek like an uncle. Ah, here comes the tea-trolley. Can you drink from a cup? Oh good. I was going to say that if you couldn't, I'd drink it for you. Shall I take your biscuits, then? Pity to waste them. Mmm, custard creams, my favourite. What a shame you can't have any.

So where was I? Oh yes, well a few days later I got a message to go and see Ollie Silvers at Heartland's London office. I spent a whole morning agonizing over what to wear, and what to leave off, but in the event it turned out to be quite unnecessary because he offered me the job straightaway. Hal Lipkin was with him. They sat at each end of a long sofa, and took turns to shoot remarks at me. "You may have noticed that Mr Passmore's been acting rather strangely lately," Ollie said. "His marriage is on the rocks," Hal said. "He's taken it very hard," said Ollie. "We're concerned about him," said Hal. "We're also concerned about the show," said Ollie. "We'd like to do another series," said Hal. "But a snag has cropped up," said Ollie. I can't tell you what the snag is, darling, because they swore me to secrecy. I know you don't mix with media journalists, but nevertheless. I shouldn't even have told you there *is* a problem. It's all terribly hush-hush. Basically they want Tubby to rewrite the last scripts of the present series to open the way for a new development of the story in the next series. Putting a new sit in the sitcom, you might say. "But Tubby doesn't seem to be able to concentrate his mind on the problem," said Hal. "So we think he needs a script editor," said Ollie. "A kind of minder-cum-dramaturge," said Hal. "Somebody to keep his nose to the grindstone and his arse to the typing chair," said Ollie. "We put it to Tubby," said Hal. "And he asked for you," said Ollie. They hadn't given me a chance to say a word all this time – I was just looking from one to the other like a spectator at Wimbledon. But now they paused as if inviting a response. I said I was flattered. "You should be," Ollie said. "We would have preferred somebody with more experience," said Hal. "But those reports you wrote for me were very sharp," said Ollie. "And you must know the show inside-out by now, watching rehearsals all this time," said Hal. I said, "Yes. I expect that's why Mr Passmore suggested me for the job." Ollie gave me a carnivorous leer and said, "Yes, I expect it is." He didn't know, of course, that Tubby had taken me out to dinner and propositioned me just a few days before.

Naturally I assumed that this new development was a rather more subtle second attempt at seduction on Tubby's part. So I wasn't surprised when almost the first thing he did when I started work was invite me to go away with him for a weekend. I called him from my new office, or rather from my new desk in the office I share with two other girls. We're all script editors – for some reason script editors nearly always *are* women. Like midwives. I said, "Hallo, this is Samantha, I suppose you know I'm your new script editor," and he said, "Yes, I'm very pleased you took the job." I didn't let on that I knew he'd asked for me. I said, "When shall we meet?" and he said, "Come to Copenhagen with me next weekend." I said, "What for?" and he said, "I've got to do some research." I said, "What has Copenhagen got to do with *The People Next Door*?" and he said, "Nothing. I'm writing a film about Kierkegaard, didn't Ollie tell you?" I said that no, Ollie hadn't made that entirely clear, but I was of course happy to help him in any way I could. He said he would book flights and hotel rooms and get back to me about the details. I noticed the plural "rooms" with approval. I mean, I understood what I was letting myself in for, but a girl has her pride. You needn't look at me like that, Hetty.

As soon as he was off the phone, I called Ollie and told him Tubby seemed to think I had been assigned to help him develop a film about Kierkegaard, not *The People Next Door*. You do know who Kierkegaard is, don't you darling, or rather was? Of course you do, you did PPE at Oxford. Sorry. I have to admit he was just a name to me before the weekend, but now I know more about him than I really want to. Not the most obvious subject for a TV film, you must agree. By the way, in case you think I've got his name wrong, that's the way they pronounce it in Danish, Kierke*gawd*, as in "Oh my Gawd," which is what Ollie said when I told him Tubby wanted to take me to Copenhagen and why. I heard him sighing and muttering to himself, and the click of a lighter as he lit a cigar, and then he said, "Look, Samantha my love, go along with it, humour him, do the Kierkegaard bit, go through the motions, but just keep reminding him at every opportunity about *The People Next Door*, OK?" I said, OK.

Have you ever been to Copenhagen? Neither had I till this weekend. It's very nice, but just a little dull. Very clean, very quiet – hardly any traffic at all compared to London. Apparently they had the very first pedestrianized shopping precinct in Europe. It seems to sum the Danes up, somehow. They're terribly green and energy-conscious. We stayed at a luxury hotel but the heat was turned down to a point that was almost uncomfortable, and in the room there was a little card asking you to help conserve the earth's resources by cutting down on unnecessary laundry. The card is red on one side and green on the other, and if you leave it green side up they only change your sheets every third day, and they don't change the towels at all unless you leave them on the bathroom floor. Which is all very sensible and responsible but just a teeny bit of a downer. I mean, I'm as green as the next woman at home, for instance I always buy my shampoo in biodegradable bottles, but one of the pleasures of staying in a luxury hotel is sleeping in crisp new sheets every night and using a fresh towel every time you take a shower. I'm afraid I left my card red side up all through the weekend and avoided the chambermaid's eye if I met her in the corridor.

We flew from Heathrow on Friday evening – Club Class, nothing but the best my dear, a hot meal with real knives and forks and as much booze as you could down in the two hours. I drank rather a lot of champagne and probably talked too much in consequence, at least the woman in the row in front kept turning round to glare at me, but Tubby seemed quite amused. By the time we got to the hotel, though, I was beginning to feel rather tired and I asked if he'd mind if I went straight to bed. He looked a bit disappointed, but then said gallantly, no, not at all, it was a good idea, he'd do the same and then we'd be fresh for the morning. So we parted very decorously in the corridor outside my room, under the eyes of the porter. I fell into bed and passed out.

The next day was bright and sunny, ideal for exploring Copenhagen on foot. Tubby had never been there before either. He wanted to get the feel of the place, and also look for possible locations. There's no shortage of well-preserved eighteenth- and early-nineteenth-century buildings, but the problem is modern traffic signs and street furniture. And there's a picturesque dock called Nyhavn, with genuine old ships moored in it, but the genuine old buildings overlooking it have been converted into trendy restaurants and a tourist hotel. "We'll probably end up shooting the film somewhere else entirely," Tubby said, "somewhere on the Baltic or the Black Sea." We had a smorgasbord lunch at a place on the Nyhavn and then went to the City Museum where they have a Kierkegaard room.

Tubby was very excited about this in anticipation, but it turned out to be a bit of an anticlimax, at least I thought so. A smallish room for a museum, about thirty feet by fifteen, with a few sticks of furniture and half a dozen glass cases displaying bits and pieces connected with Kierkegaard – his pipes, his magnifying glass, some pictures and old books. You wouldn't have given them a second glance in an antique shop, but Tubby pored over them as if they were sacred relics. He was especially interested in a portrait of Kierkegaard's fiancée, Regine. He was engaged to her for about a year and then broke it off, but regretted it ever after according to Tubby. The portrait was a small oil painting of a young woman in a low-cut green dress with a dark green shawl round her shoulders. He stared at the picture for about five minutes without blinking. "She looks like you," he said eventually. "Do you think so?" I said. She had dark brown eyes and hair to match, so I suppose he meant she had big tits. Actually, to be fair, there was something about the mouth and chin that was not unlike me. She also looked as if she was quite fun – there was a suspicion of a smile on her lips and a twinkle in her eye. Which was more than you could say for Kierkegaard, to judge from the drawing of him that was in the same case: a skinny, crooked, long-nosed old fogey in a stovepipe hat and carrying a furled umbrella like a gun under his arm. Tubby said it was a caricature done for a newspaper when Kierkegaard was in his forties, and pointed out another drawing done by a friend when he was a young man where he looked quite handsome, but somehow you didn't believe in it as much as in the caricature. The crooked back was because he suffered from curvature of the spine. He used to prefer to write standing up at a high desk, which was one of the pieces of furniture in the room. Tubby stood at it himself for a moment, making some notes in a reporter's notebook he'd brought with him, and a little German girl who had come into the room with her parents stared at him as he was writing and said to her father, *"Ist das Herr Kierkegaard?"* I laughed, because anyone who looked less like Kierkegaard would be hard to imagine. Tubby heard me laugh and looked round. "What is it?" he asked. When I explained, he blushed with pleasure. He's absolutely obsessed with Kierkegaard, especially his relationship with this girl Regine. There was another piece of furniture in the room, at the opposite end to the desk, a sort of cupboard about five feet high. Tubby found out from the museum brochure that Kierkegaard had it made especially to keep his mementos of Regine in. Apparently she pleaded with him not to break off their engagement, and said she would be glad to be allowed to spend the rest of her life with him even if she had to live in a little cupboard, the silly cow. "That's why it hasn't got any shelves inside," Tubby said. "So she would just fit inside." I swear his eyes filled with tears as he read it out of the brochure.

We had dinner that evening in the hotel restaurant: plain cuisine but excellent ingredients, mostly fish, beautifully cooked. I had baked turbot. Am I boring you, darling? Oh, good, I just thought I saw your eyes close for a moment. Well all through the meal I kept trying to turn the conversation on to the topic of *The People Next Door* and he kept dragging it back to Kierkegaard and Regine. I really began to get thoroughly sick of the subject. I was also hankering to see a bit of Copenhagen nightlife after dinner. I mean it has the reputation of being a very liberated city, with lots of sex shops and video parlours and live sex shows and suchlike. I hadn't seen a trace of anything like that so far, but I presumed they must be somewhere. I wanted to do a little research of my own, for my *Westenders* project. But when I threw out some hints to this effect, Tubby seemed strangely slow on the uptake, almost as if he didn't *want* to understand me. I thought perhaps he had plans for a private live sex show with just the two of us, but no. At about ten-fifteen he yawned and said it had been a long day and perhaps it was time to turn in. Well I was astonished – and, I have to admit, a little piqued. I mean it wasn't that I positively fancied him, but I expected him to show a little more evidence of fancying me. I couldn't believe that he had brought me all the way to Copenhagen just to talk about Kierkegaard.

The next morning was Sunday, and Tubby insisted we went to church, because that was what Kierkegaard would have done. He was very religious apparently, in an eccentric sort of way. So we went to this incredibly dreary Lutheran service, all in Danish of course, which made it even more boring than chapel at school, if you can believe that. And after lunch we went to see Kierkegaard's tomb. He's buried in a cemetery about two miles from the city centre. His name actually means "churchyard" in Danish, so as Tubby observed we were visiting Kierkegaard in the *kierkegaard*, which was about the only joke of the afternoon. It was quite a nice place, with flower beds and trees planted to make avenues, and according to the guidebook the Copenhagen people use it like a park in fine weather and have picnics there and everything, but the afternoon we were there it was raining. We had some trouble locating the grave, and when we did find it it was a bit of a let-down, like the room in the museum. It's a little patch of ground enclosed by an iron railing, with a monument to Kierkegaard's father in the middle and two stone tablets propped up against it with the names of his wife and children including Søren carved on them. That's Kierkegaard's first name, Søren, with one of those funny crossed-out Danish os. But you probably knew that already, didn't you? Sorry, darling. We stood in the rain for a few minutes in respectful silence. Tubby took his hat off, and the rain ran off his bald pate and down his face and off the end of his nose and chin. We didn't have an umbrella, and I soon began to feel rather damp and uncomfortable, but Tubby insisted on looking for Regine's grave. He'd read somewhere that she was buried in the same churchyard. There was a kind of index to all the graves on a noticeboard near the entrance, but Tubby couldn't remember Regine's married name so he had to look through columns and columns until he came to a Regine Schlegel. "That's her!" he cried, and charged off to look for the plot – 58D or whatever it was – only he couldn't find it. The plots are not very well marked, and there was nobody around to ask because it was Sunday and pouring with rain, and I was getting more and more fed up squelching about in sopping wet clothes and shoes with water dripping off the trees and running down the back of my neck and I said I wanted to go back to the hotel, and he said rather crossly, all right, go, and gave me some money to take a taxi, so I did. I had a long hot bath and used *two* clean towels and threw them both on the floor and had tea from room service and a miniature bottle of cherry brandy from the minibar, and began to feel in a better humour. Tubby came back about two hours later, soaked to the skin. And despondent because he hadn't managed to find Regine's grave and there wouldn't be time to go back the next morning and ask somebody because we had to catch an early plane.

The evening followed the same pattern as before: dinner in the hotel restaurant followed by a proposal from Tubby that we retire early – to our own rooms. I couldn't believe it. I began to wonder if there was something wrong with me, like bad breath, but I checked as I was getting ready for bed and it was sweet and fresh. Then I took off all my clothes and looked at myself in the mirror and I couldn't see anything wrong there either, in fact I thought to myself that if I were a man I wouldn't be able to keep my hands off me, if you follow. I was beginning to feel rather randy, to be honest, out of sheer frustration, and not a *bit* sleepy, so I decided to watch an adult movie on the hotel's in-house video channel. I got a half-bottle of champagne out of the minibar and sat me down in front of the telly in my dressing-gown and tuned in. *Well*, my dear, what a surprise I got! I don't know if you've ever watched one of those movies in a British hotel. No? Well, you haven't missed anything, believe me. I used to watch them occasionally when I stayed at the Rummidge Post House on the chaperoning job, just for a giggle. One of my duties was to make sure the little Harrington brat couldn't watch them. The hotel reception used to put a bar on the set in his room, much to his disgust. In fact, those films have nothing more explicit in them than many pro-grammes you see on network television, indeed less so, the only difference being that the so-called adult movies consist *entirely* of sex scenes, and look incredibly cheap, and are incredibly badly acted and have incredibly silly story lines. And they're extremely short and full of clumsy jump-cuts because all the really raunchy bits have been censored for hotel distribution. Well I was hoping that the Danish ones might be a bit more daring, but I wasn't prepared for hard-core pornography, which was what I got. I switched on in the middle of the film and there were two men and a girl naked on a bed together. Both the men had absolutely enormous erections and one was being sucked off voraciously by the girl, as if her life depended on it, while the other one was doing her from behind, you know, doggy-fashion. I couldn't believe my –

What? Oh. I'm sorry, but I wasn't talking to you. Well, I can't help it if your hearing is unusually good. If you don't want to eavesdrop on other people's private conversations, why don't you put those earphones on and listen to the radio?

Hmmph! What a cheek. I mean, I'm sorry about her hysterectomy and everything, but she didn't have to be so stroppy. I wasn't talking all that loud, was I? Oh, all right, Hetty, I'll move my chair nearer to the bed and murmur in your ear, is that better? So there were these three people in the film sucking and fucking away like mad and after about ten minutes they all had the most tremendous orgasms – no really, they did, Hetty, honestly. At least the men did, because they pulled their willies out to show the semen squirting all over the place. The girl rubbed it into her cheeks as if it was skincare lotion. Are you feeling all right, darling? You're looking a little pale. The time? It's . . . good heavens, half past three. I must go soon, but I'll just finish the story. Well the film went on in the same style. The next scene showed two naked girls, one black and one white, taking turns to lick each other, but they weren't real lesbians because the two men from the previous scene peeped through the window at them and came in and it turned into another orgy. Well, I don't mind telling you that by this time I was quite wet with excitement and one big hot flush from head to toe. I've never felt so randy in my entire life. I was *beside* myself. I would have fucked *anybody* at that moment, never mind the nice clean English scriptwriter in the next room who had, I thought, brought me to Copenhagen specifically for that purpose. It could only be shyness, I decided, that was holding him back. I should phone him up and tell him about the amazing video I had found on the hotel telly and invite him to come and watch it with me. I reckoned that a few minutes' exposure to the movie, sitting next to me in my dressing-gown with not a stitch on underneath, would soon see off his shyness. I should perhaps explain that I had polished off the half-bottle of champers by this time and was feeling pretty reckless as well as randy. He took quite a time to answer the phone, so I said I hoped I hadn't woken him up. He said, no, he had been watching television and had just turned down the volume before picking up the phone. Only he hadn't turned it down quite enough. I recognized the tinkly disco music and faint moaning and groaning in the background. There's not very much dialogue in these films. Not much work for a script editor, I should think. I giggled and said, "I think you must be watching the same movie as me." He mumbled something, sounding terribly embarrassed, and I said, "Wouldn't it be more fun if we watched it together? Why don't you come along to my room?" There was a silence and then he said, "I don't think that would be a good idea," and I said, "Why not?" and he said, "I just don't." Well, we sparred like that for a while, and then I got impatient and said, "For God's sake, what's the matter with you? Last week in that Italian restaurant you made it very obvious that you fancied me, and now that I'm practically throwing myself at you, you hang back. What did you bring me here for if you don't want to sleep with me?" There was another pause and then he said, "You're quite right, that was why I asked you to come, but when I got here I found I couldn't do it." I asked him why not. He said, "Because of Kierkegaard." I thought this was terribly funny and said, "We won't tell him." He said, "No, I'm serious. Perhaps on Friday evening, if you hadn't been so tired . . ." "You mean pissed," I said, "Well, whatever," he said. "But as I started to explore Copenhagen and think about Kierke-gaard, and especially when we went to the room in the museum, it was as if I felt his presence, like a spirit or a good angel, saying, 'Don't exploit this young girl.' He had a thing about young girls, you see." "But I'm dying to be exploited," I said. "Come and exploit me, in any position you like. Look at the screen, now. Would you like that? I'll do it with you." I won't tell you what it was, darling, you might be shocked. "You don't know what you're saying," he said. "You'd regret it in the morning." "No I wouldn't," I said. "Anyway, why are you watching this filthy movie if you're so virtuous? Would Kierke-gaard approve of that?" "Probably not," he said, "but I'm not doing any harm to anyone else." "Tubby," I said, putting on my most seductive voice, "I want you. I need you. Now. Come. Take me." He gave a sort of groan and said, "I can't. I've just taken a towel from the bathroom." It was a second or two before the penny dropped. I said, "Well, I hope you leave it on the floor so the next guest doesn't get it," and slammed the phone down in a temper. I turned off the telly, swallowed a sleeping tablet and a miniature of scotch and passed out. When I woke up the next morning I saw the funny side of it, but Tubby couldn't face me. He left a message at Reception with my air ticket, saying that he'd gone back to the cemetery to look for Regine's grave and would be returning by a later plane. So what do you think of that for a story? Oh, I forgot, you can't speak. Never mind, I've got to dash anyway. Oh, dear, I've eaten all your grapes. Listen, I'll come back tomorrow and bring you some more. No? You think you'll be out by then? Really? Well, I'll give you a ring at home, then. Goodbye, darling. I *have* enjoyed our chat.

* * Sally * *

BEFORE WE START, Dr Marples, I'd like to establish the agenda of this meeting, so there's no misunderstanding. I agreed to see you because I want Tubby to accept that our marriage is over. I'd like to help you to help him to come to terms with that fact. I'm not interested in trying to negotiate a reconciliation. I hope that's quite clear. That's why I said in my letter that I would only meet you on my own. We're beyond marriage counselling now, well beyond it. Quite sure. Yes, we tried it before – didn't Tubby tell you? About four or five years ago. I can't remember her name. It was somebody in Relate. After a few weeks with both of us, she recommended that Tubby should have psychotherapy for his depression. He told you about *that*, I presume? Yes, Dr Wilson. Well, he saw him for about six months, and he seemed better for a while. Our relationship improved, we didn't bother to go back to Relate. But within a year he was worse than ever. I decided that he would never be any different, and that I'd better organize my life so that I was less affected by his moods. I threw myself into work. God knows there was no shortage of things to do. Teaching, research, administration – committees, working parties, syllabus design and suchlike. My colleagues complain about the paperwork in higher education these days, but I rather enjoy mastering it. I have to face the fact that I'm never going to do earth-shaking research, I started too late, but I'm good at admin. My field is psycholinguistics, language acquisition in young children. I have published the odd paper. Oh does he? Well, he doesn't understand a word of it, so he's easily impressed. He's not really an intellectual, Tubby. I mean, he has a wonderful ear for speech, obviously, but he can't think abstractly about it. It's all intuitive with him.

So I threw myself into work. I didn't consider divorce at that stage. I was brought up very conventionally, my father was a C of E vicar, and for me there's always been a certain stigma attached to divorce. It's an admission of failure in a way, and I don't like to fail at anything I set out to do. I knew that to other people – friends, relatives, even our children – our marriage must have seemed very successful. It had lasted so long without any visible upsets, and our standard of living soared with Tubby's success. We had the big house in Hollywell, the flat in London, the two cars, holidays in luxury hotels, and so on. The children were through university and happily settled in adult life. I think most people we knew envied us. It would have been galling – it *has* been galling these last few weeks – to admit that the outward appearance was an illusion. I suppose too I shrank from the bitterness and anger that seem inseparable from divorce. We'd seen a fair amount of it among our friends. I thought, if I occupied myself fully at work, I could put up with Tubby's moodiness at home. I used to bring work home as well, as extra protection. It was a wall I could retreat behind. I thought that as long as we enjoyed doing *some* things together, like tennis, and golf, and were still having sex regularly, that would be enough to sustain the marriage. Yes, I read an article once that made a great impression on me, saying that marriage breakdown in the fifties – I mean between couples in their fifties, not the nineteen-fifties – was nearly always associated with one partner's loss of interest in sex. So I worked hard at that. Well, if he didn't initiate it, I did. After sport was always a good time, when we were both feeling good from the exercise. I thought that sport and sex and a comfortable lifestyle would be enough to get us through the Difficult Fifties – that's what the article was called, it comes back to me now, "The Difficult Fifties."

Well, I was wrong. It wasn't enough. Tubby's knee injury didn't help, of course. It separated us as regards sport – he couldn't compete with me any more – and it put a damper on sex. He wouldn't risk it for weeks, months, after the operation, and even then he always seemed more concerned about protecting his knee than having a good time. Then when it became apparent that the operation hadn't been a success, he fell into a deeper depression than ever. This past year he's been impossible to live with, completely wrapped up in himself, not listening to a word anybody says to him. Well, I suppose he must listen to his agent and his producer and so on, he could hardly function otherwise, but he didn't listen to what *I* was saying to him. You've no idea how infuriating it is when you've been talking to someone for minutes on end, and they've been nodding and making phatic noises, and then you realize they haven't taken in a single word you've said. You feel such a fool. It's as if you were teaching a class while writing on the blackboard and then you turn round to find that they've all quietly left the room and you've been talking to yourself for you don't know how long. The last straw was when I told him Jane had rung up to tell us she was pregnant – Jane's our daughter – and that she and her partner were going to get married, and he just grunted, "Oh yes? Good," and went on reading bloody Kierkegaard. And, you'd hardly credit this, even when I keyed myself up to tell him that I'd had enough and wanted to separate he didn't listen to what I was saying at first.

Oh, I'm afraid I can't take this Kierkegaard thing seriously. I told you, Tubby's not an intellectual. It's just a fad, something to impress other people with. Perhaps me. Perhaps himself. A device to dignify his petty little depressions as existentialist *Angst*. No, I've not read any myself, but I know roughly what he's about. My father used to quote him occasionally in his sermons. Not any more, but of course we had to when we were children, every Sunday, morning and evening. I think that's why I find Tubby's obsession with Kierkegaard rather absurd. Tubby had a totally secular upbringing, knows absolutely nothing about religion, whereas I've been all through it and out the other side. It was painful, I can tell you. For years I concealed it from my father, that I no longer believed. I think it broke his heart when I finally came clean. Perhaps I waited too long to tell him what I really felt, as I did with Tubby about our marriage.

Well, I could say that it was none of your business, couldn't I? But no, there isn't anyone else. I suppose Tubby's been unloading his paranoid fantasies on you. You know about his ridiculous suspicion of my tennis coach? Poor man, I haven't been able to look him in the eye since, let alone have any lessons. I really don't know why Tubby

193

went berserk with jealousy. Well, yes I do, it was because he just couldn't accept that the problem in our marriage was himself. It had to be somebody else's fault, mine, or some phantom lover of mine. It would have been so much better for all concerned if he could have faced facts calmly. All I wanted was an amicable separation and a reasonable financial settlement. It was all his fault that it's escalated into a battle, with lawyers and injunctions and separate lives in the house and so on. He could still avoid a lot of unnecessary pain and expense by simply agreeing to the divorce, and making a fair settlement. No, he's not. He's at his London flat, I suppose. I don't know, I haven't seen him in the last few weeks. The bills keep coming in for the house, for gas and electricity and so on, and I forward them to him but he doesn't pay them, so I've had to pay some myself to avoid having the services turned off, which isn't fair. He very meanly drew out most of the money in our joint bank account the day after I left the house, and all the deposit accounts are in his name only, so I'm having to meet all my expenses out of my monthly salary, including lawyers' fees. I'm really having a struggle to make ends meet.

No, I don't hate him, in spite of the way he's behaved. I feel sorry for him. But there's nothing I can do for him any more. He must work out his own salvation. I have to study my own needs. I'm not a hard-hearted woman. Tubby pretends that I am, but I'm not. It hasn't been easy for me, all this stuff with lawyers and so on. But having screwed myself up to take this step, I've got to see it through. This is my last chance to forge an independent life for myself. I'm just young enough to do it, I think. A few years younger than Tubby, yes.

It was such a long time ago. We were two different people, really. I was doing teaching practice in a Junior School in Leeds and he turned up there one day with a theatre group that toured schools. Five young people, would-be actors who couldn't get Equity cards, had formed a company on a shoestring and were going around the country in an old Dormobile, towing a trailer full of props. They did stripped-down versions of Shakespeare for secondary schools and dramatized fairy-tales for juniors. They weren't very good, to be honest, but they made up in enthusiasm for what they lacked in technique. After they'd done their show in the school hall and the kids had gone home, we invited them into the staff-room for tea and biscuits. I thought they were terribly bohemian and adventurous. My own life had been so respectable and sheltered in comparison. I did English at Royal Holloway, a women's college of London University marooned in the Surrey stockbroker belt. My parents insisted on my going to a single-sex college if I wasn't going to live at home, and I failed my Oxbridge entrance exams, so it was Royal Holloway or Leeds University. I was determined to get away from home, but I came back to do my PGCE in Leeds, to save money. I chose junior-school teaching – not many graduates did – because I didn't fancy trying to control the roughs and toughs in the state comprehensives that were replacing the kind of grammar school I had gone to myself. In those days I wore pastel twin-sets and pleated skirts to mid-calf and sensible shoes and hardly any make-up. These young actors wore scruffy dark sweaters with holes in them, and had long greasy hair and smoked a lot. There were three boys and two girls and they all slept together in the Dormobile most of the time, Tubby told me, to save money. One night he parked it on top of a hill and didn't put the handbrake on properly, and it slowly trundled down the hill until it ran up against a police station. He told the story in such a droll way, he made me laugh aloud. That's what first attracted me to him, I think – the way he could make me laugh spontaneously, joyously. Laughing at home tended to be politely restrained or – amongst us children – mocking and sarcastic. With Tubby, I laughed before I realized I was laughing. If I were to try and put into a nutshell what has been wrong with our marriage for the last few years – why I didn't get anything out of it, any happiness, any glad-to-be-alive feeling – I'd say it was because he didn't make me laugh any more. Ironic, really, isn't it, when you think that every week he makes millions of people laugh at his television show. Not me, I'm afraid. I find it totally unfunny.

Anyway, that first day, he rather cheekily asked for my phone number and I rather recklessly gave it to him. I met him several times while he and his friends were in the Leeds area, in the evenings in pubs. Pubs! I had hardly ever been in a pub before I met Tubby. I didn't invite him home. I knew my parents wouldn't approve of him,

195

though they would never admit why – because he was unkempt and under-educated and had a Cockney accent. I suppose you know he left school at sixteen? Well he did, with just a couple of O-Levels. He went to grammar school after the Eleven-Plus but never fitted in, was always bottom of the class. I don't know – a combination of temperament, bad teaching and lack of support at home, I suppose. His parents were working-class – very decent, but not very education-conscious. Anyway, Tubby left school as soon as he could, and went to work as an office-boy for a theatrical impresario, that's how he got interested in the stage. After National Service he went to drama school and tried to make it as an actor. That was when I met him. He played all the comic parts in the Dormobile troupe's repertory, and wrote the scripts for their fairy-tale adaptations. He discovered in due course that he was better at writing than acting. We kept in touch after the troupe left Yorkshire. That summer I went up to Edinburgh, where they were doing a show in the Festival – the Fringe, of course – and distributed fliers and programmes, without telling my parents what I was up to. Then, much against their wishes, I applied for my first teaching job in London, knowing Tubby was based there. The Dormobile company had gone bust, and he was scraping a living as a temporary office worker, writing jokes for stand-up comedians in his spare time. We started to go steady. Eventually I had to bring him home one weekend to meet the family. I knew it would be sticky, and it was.

My father had a living in an inner suburb of Leeds which had been going down in the world for decades. The church was huge, neo-gothic, blackened redbrick. I can't remember it ever being full. It had been built on the top of a hill by the wealthy manufacturers and merchants who originally lived in the big stone villas that surrounded it, overlooking their factories and warehouses and the streets of terraced workers' cottages at the bottom of the hill. There were still a few professional middle-class owner-occupiers when my father took over the parish, but most of the big houses were converted into flats or occupied by extended Asian families in the nineteen-fifties. My father was an earnest, well-meaning man, who read the *Guardian* when it was still called the *Manchester Guardian*, and did his best to make the

Church responsive to the needs of the inner city, but the inner city never seemed to be very interested apart from weddings and christenings and funerals. My mother supported him loyally, scrimping and saving to bring up her children in a respectable middle-class style on my father's inadequate stipend. There were four of us, two boys and two girls. I was the second oldest. We all went to local single-sex grammar schools, but we grew up in a kind of cultural bubble, insulated from the lives of our peers. We had no television, partly because Father disapproved of it, but also because we couldn't afford it. Going to the cinema was such a rare treat that the intensity of the experience used to upset me, and I rather dreaded the prospect as a child. We had a gramophone, but only classical records. We all learned to play musical instruments, though none of us had any real talent, and sometimes the whole family would sit down together and stumble through a piece of chamber music, making a noise that started the neighbourhood dogs howling. We were teetotal – again, as much from economy as principle. And we were very argumentative. The main family recreation was scoring points off each other in conversation, especially at meals.

Tubby was completely flummoxed by this. He wasn't used to family meals in any case. He very rarely sat down at the same table with his mother and father and brother, except for Sunday lunch and other high days and holidays. When he lived at home, he and his father and his brother would eat separately, at different times from each other, and from Mrs Passmore. When they came in in the evening, from work or school, she would ask them what they wanted, and then she would cook it and wait on them at table, as if she was running a café, while they ate with a newspaper or a book propped up against the salt cellar. I couldn't believe it when I first visited his home.

He found our domestic life equally bizarre, "as archaic as the *Forsyte Saga*," he said to me once: sitting down *en famille* two or three times a day, with grace before and after meals, cloth napkins which you had to replace in your own special napkin-ring at the end of each meal so as to save laundry, and proper cutlery, however worn and tarnished, soup spoons for soup and fish knives and forks for fish, and so on. Our food was pretty horrible, and there was never enough of it when it was nice, but it was served with due ceremony and decorum. Poor Tubby was completely adrift that first weekend. He started eating before everyone else was served, he used his dessert spoon for his soup and his soup spoon for dessert and committed all kinds of other *faux pas* that had my younger brother and sister sniggering up their sleeves. But what really stunned him was the cut-and-thrust of mealtime conversation. It wasn't that there was any real debate. Father thought he was encouraging us to think for ourselves, but in fact there were very strict limits to what it was permissible to say. You couldn't have argued against the existence of God, for instance, or the truth of Christianity or the indissolubility of marriage. We children very soon cottoned on to these constraints, and domestic conversation became more of a point-scoring game, the aim being to discredit one of your siblings in the eyes of the rest of the family. If you misused a word, for instance, or made some error of fact, the others would be down on you at once like a ton of bricks. Tubby couldn't cope with this at all. Of course, he used it much later in *The People Next Door*. The Springfields and the Davises are based essentially on my family and his, *mutatis mutandis*. The Springfields are totally secular, but that mixture of highmindedness and disputatiousness, their un-acknowledged snobbery and prejudice, all go back to Tubby's first impression of my family, while the Davises are a more rumbustious, somewhat sentimentalized version of his own, with bits of his Uncle Bert and Aunt Molly added. I suppose that's why I never cared for the programme. It stirs too many painful memories. Our wedding was particularly gruesome, with the two sets of totally incompatible relatives grinding and grating against each other.

Why did I marry him? I thought I was in love with him. Well, perhaps I was. What is love, except thinking you're in it? I was longing to rebel against my parents without knowing how to do it. Marrying Tubby was a way of asserting my independence. And we were both desperate for sex – I mean just the normal appetites of youth – but I wasn't rebellious enough to think of having it outside marriage. And then Tubby did have an undeniable charm in those days. He had faith in himself, in his gift, and he made me share that faith. But most of all, he was fun to be with. He made me laugh.

✳ ✳ THREE ✳ ✳

TUESDAY, 25th May. The plane trees outside my window are in leaf: rather listless, anaemic leaf, with no visible blossom, not like the creamy phallic candles of the chestnuts outside my study in Hollywell. There aren't any squirrels scampering about in these branches, either, but that's hardly surprising. I should be grateful – I *am* grateful – that trees grow here at all, considering the pollution in central London. There's a narrow, featureless short cut between Brewer Street and Regent Street called Air Street that always makes me smile when I clock the nameplate. Smile rather than laugh because it's invariably choked with traffic pumping carcinogenic exhaust fumes into the atmosphere, and you wouldn't want to open your mouth if you could help it. Air Street. I don't know how it got the name, but you could make a fortune selling bottled air round here.

Now that I'm living permanently in the flat I find it claustrophobic. I miss the clean-smelling air of Hollywell, I miss the squirrels playing tag in the garden, I miss the daytime hush of those suburban streets where the loudest noise at this time of year is the burr of a distant lawnmower, or the *pock pock* of a game of tennis. But I couldn't stand the strain of sharing the house with Sally any longer. Passing her in stony-faced silence on the stairs or in the hall; exchanging curt accusing little notes ("*If you must leave the laundry to soak, please remove it before it is my turn to use the utility room.*" "*As I bought the last bottle of Rinse-Aid for the dishwasher perhaps you would like to replace it next time*"); hiding when she opened the front door to a neighbour or tradesman so that we wouldn't be obliged to speak to each other in front of them; picking up the phone to make a call and dropping it like a hot brick because Sally was already using it, and then being tempted to press the monitor button and listen in . . . Whoever dreamed up that "separate lives" lark had a sadistic streak – or a warped sense of humour. When I described it to Jake he said, "You know, there's a great idea for a sitcom there." I haven't spoken to him since.

It feels strange, writing this journal again. There's quite a gap in it. After Sally dropped her bombshell that evening (what exactly is, or was, a bombshell, incidentally? And how do you drop one without blowing yourself up? Is it a grenade, or a mortar shell, or was it a primitive kind of aerial bomb that they lobbed out of the open cockpits of the old biplanes? The dictionary isn't much help) – after Sally burst into my study that Friday evening, and announced that she wanted a separation, I was too upset to be able to write anything, even a journal, for weeks. I was beside myself with jealousy and rage and self-pity. (Now *there*'s a good cliché for you, "beside myself ": as if you're so full of negative feelings that you shake your mind loose from your body, severing the connections between them, and the one is unable to voice the pain of the other.) All I could think of was how to get even with Sally: by being obstructive over money; by trying to track down and expose the lover I was sure she must have; and by having an affair with somebody myself. Why did I think that this last would bother her, I wonder? In any case, even if I'd succeeded I wouldn't have been able to let Sally know, because then she could have sued for a quick divorce on the grounds of adultery. If I try and untwist the tangled and frazzled wires of my motivation at that time, I would have to say that I was trying to make up for lost philandering.

What was most painful about Sally's UDI was of course her rejection of me as a person, and the implied judgement that our thirty years together, or a good many of them, had been worthless, meaningless, as far as she was concerned. After she walked out of the house I sat on the floor of the living-room with all our family photograph albums, which I hadn't looked at for years, spread out around me, and turned the pages with tears streaming down my cheeks. The unbearable poignancy of those snaps! Sally and the children grinning into the lens from deckchairs, pushchairs, swings, sandcastles, paddling pools, swimming pools, bicycle saddles, pony saddles, the decks of cross-Channel ferries and the patios of French *gîtes*. The kids gradually getting taller and stronger from year to year, Sally getting a little thinner in the face and greyer in the hair, but always looking healthy and happy. Yes, happy. Surely the camera couldn't lie? I snivelled and wiped away my tears and blew my nose, peering intently at the brightly coloured Kodak prints to see if I could discern in Sally's face any sign of the disaffection to come. But her eyes were too small, I couldn't see into the eyes, which is the only place where a person can't disguise what they're thinking. Perhaps it had all been an illusion, our "happy marriage", a smile for the camera.

Once you begin to doubt your marriage, you begin to doubt your grasp of reality. I thought I knew Sally – suddenly I found I didn't. So perhaps I didn't know myself. Perhaps I didn't know anything. This was such a vertiginous conclusion that I sheered away from it, and took refuge in anger. I demonized Sally. The breakup of our marriage was all her fault. Whatever truth there might be in her complaints about my self-centredness, moodiness, abstractedness, etc. etc. (and admittedly my inattention to the news about Jane's pregnancy was an embarrassing lapse) they didn't amount to grounds for leaving me. There had to be another reason, viz., another man. There were plenty of examples of adultery in our circle of acquaintance to support the hypothesis. And our lifestyle since the children left home would have made it very easy for Sally to maintain another relationship, with me being in London for two days a week, and her professional life a closed book as far as I was concerned. What particularly angered me was that I hadn't taken advantage of the situation myself. "Anger" isn't quite the word, though. Chagrin, or as Amy would say, *chagrin*, is better – it has the teeth-grinding, bottled-up, you'll-be-sorry-for-this quality of resentment that had me in its grip. I was chagrined at the thought of all the women I might so easily have had in the course of my professional life, especially in recent years, if I hadn't resolved to be faithful to Sally: actresses and production assistants and publicity girls and secretaries – all susceptible to the *mana* of a successful writer. Freud said, so Amy told me once, that all writers are driven by three ambitions: fame, money and the love of women (or men, I presume, as the case might be, though I don't think Freud took much account of women writers, or gay ones). I admit to pursuing the first two ambitions, but scrupulously abstained from the third on principle. And what was my reward? To be put out to grass when I had served my turn, when my sexual powers were on the wane.

That last thought threw me into a panic. How many years did I have left to make up for lost opportunities in the past? I recalled what I had written in my journal a few weeks earlier: *"You won't know it is your last fuck while you're having it, and by the time you find out you probably won't be able to remember what it was like."* I tried to remember when Sally and I last made love, and couldn't. I looked back through the journal and found it logged under Saturday, 27th February. There wasn't any detail, except that Sally had seemed surprised when I took the initiative, and complied rather listlessly. Reading that fuelled my suspicions. I leafed back further to the conversation with the boys at the tennis club: *"You want to watch your Missus, Tubby . . . Good at other games, too, I'm told . . . He's certainly got the tackle . . ."* The solution to the mystery burst inside my head like a flare. Brett Sutton, of course! The tennis lessons, the new sports clothes, the sudden decision to dye her hair . . . It all fitted together. My head became a blue-movie house, flickering with lurid images of Sally naked on the couch in the Club's First Aid room, throwing back her head in ecstasy as Brett Sutton shafted her with his enormous cock.

I discovered I was mistaken about Brett Sutton. But the need to have sex myself, as soon as possible – for revenge, for compensation, for reassurance – became an all-consuming preoccupation. Naturally I thought first of Amy. For some years our relationship had had all the marks of an affair – the secrecy and regularity of our meetings, the discreet restaurant meals, the covert telephone calls, the exchange of confidences – everything except the act of intercourse. I had refrained from crossing that threshold out of misplaced loyalty to Sally. Now there was no moral reason to hold back. So I argued to myself at the time, the immediate post-bombshell time. What I didn't consider was (*a*) whether I really desired Amy and (*b*) whether she desired me. We discovered in Tenerife that the answer to both questions was "no".

❊ ❊ ❊ ❊ ❊ ❊ ❊ ❊ ❊ ❊ ❊ ❊ ❊ ❊ ❊ ❊ ❊

Wednesday 26th May. Letters from Jane and Adam this morning. I didn't feel like opening them – just recognizing the handwriting on the envelopes turned my stomach over – but I couldn't settle to anything until I did. Both were short notes asking how I am and inviting me to visit. I suspect some kindly collusion: the coincidence of receiving them on the same day is too blatant.

I saw each of them separately after Sally walked out of the house, but before she moved back. Adam and I had lunch in London one day, and then I went down to spend a weekend in Swanage with Jane and Gus. Both were uncomfortable occasions. For the lunch with Adam I chose a restaurant I'd never been to before, so I wouldn't be recognized. It turned out to be full, with tables much too close together, so Adam and I couldn't speak freely even if we'd wanted to, and had to communicate in a kind of elliptical code. If anyone *was* eavesdropping they probably thought we were discussing a rather unsuccessful dinner party rather than the break-up of a thirty-year-old marriage. I preferred that, though, to the weekend in Swanage, when Gus kept tactfully leaving Jane and me on our own to have the kind of heart-to-heart conversation neither of us really wanted, because we'd never had one before and didn't know how to do it. Jane's relationship to me has always been a humorously scolding one, getting at me for environmentally unsound forms of consumption, like bottled mineral water, coloured paperclips, and hardwood bookshelves, or for sexist jokes in *The People Next Door*. It was a game we played, partly for the entertainment of others. We didn't seem to have a routine for talking intimately.

On the Sunday afternoon Jane and I took their dog for a walk along the crescent-shaped beach, exchanging desultory observations about the weather, the tide, the windsurfers in the bay. The baby is due in October, apparently. I asked her how she was feeling as regards the pregnancy, and she said she was over the morning-sickness period thank God; but that topic fizzled out too, perhaps because it was uncomfortably connected in both our minds with the terminal row between Sally and me. Then on the way back, when we were nearly at the cottage, Jane said abruptly, "Why don't you just give Mummy what she wants? You'd still have plenty to live on, wouldn't you?" I said it was a matter of principle. I didn't accept that Sally could walk out on me just because she found me difficult to live with, and still expect me to support her in the style of life to which she'd become accustomed. Jane said, "You mean, she was being paid to put up with your moods?" I said, "No, of course not." But in a way I suppose Jane was right, though I wouldn't have put it quite like that. She's a shrewd girl, Jane. She said, "I think your making all that money from *The People Next Door* had a bad effect on both of you. You seemed to worry more than when you were hard up. And Mummy became jealous." I had never thought before that Sally might be jealous of my success.

Although both Jane and Adam tried to be impartial, I felt that privately they were both on Sally's "side", so I didn't seek them out again after those two meetings. Also I was plotting to take Amy to Tenerife and afraid they might find out and tell Sally.

Tenerife was certainly a disastrous choice, but really the whole enterprise was doomed before it began. While I had kept Amy under wraps, as it were, never attempting any contact more intimate than a friendly kiss or cuddle, I invested her with a certain glamour, the glamour of the forbidden, the self-denied. Once I had her naked on a bed she was just a plump little lady with rather hairy legs which I hadn't noticed before because she always wore stockings or tights. She also had a body distinctly lacking in muscle tone. I couldn't help comparing her physique unfavourably with Sally's, and reflecting that something seemed to have gone seriously wrong with my strategy. What on earth was I doing in this shitty hotel room in this godawful resort with a woman considerably less desirable than the estranged wife I was trying to get even with? It was hardly surprising that Tenerife was an erotic disaster. As soon as I got back – indeed, even before – I began to thumb through my mental backlist of female acquaintance in search of a likely partner younger and more attractive than Amy. I came up with Louise.

Within days I was airborne again, en route for Los Angeles. Another fiasco. Indeed, a double fiasco, if you count the blind date with Stella which Louise fixed up for me after she shattered my hopes. Some hopes. I knew, really, even as I booked my flight to L.A. (open ticket, Business Class; it cost the earth but I wanted to arrive in good shape) that the likelihood of Louise still being unattached and available after all those years was remote in the extreme, and simply suppressed the knowledge because I couldn't bear the thought of failure. It was like Kierkegaard going back to Copenhagen a year after breaking off his engagement, fondly imagining Regine would still be unattached and grieving for him, and then discovering that she was engaged to Schlegel. The attraction of Louise was precisely that she was someone I could have had in the past, and had foolishly, perversely, denied myself. It was the lure of Repetition, the idea of having Louise offer herself to me again, making possession doubly sweet, that impelled me to travel all those thousands of miles.

Stella, on the other hand, was just a potential one-night stand as far as I was concerned. I had a day and a night to kill before the next available flight back to London, so when Louise called me the morning after our outing to Venice to say that she had a friend who was dying to meet me, I agreed. I met her in the lobby of the Beverly Wilshire and took her to dinner in the hotel's ludicrously expensive restaurant. She seemed quite attractive at first sight, blonde and slim and groomed to a high polish. I blinked in the glitter and dazzle of her teeth, hair-lacquer, nail-varnish and costume jewellery. But her smiles lasted just a fraction of a second longer than seemed quite natural, and her facial skin had a tightness under the pancake make-up that suggested it had been lifted. She didn't beat about the bush, saying over our pre-dinner Margaritas, "Louise tells me we have a lot in common: we've both been betrayed and we both want to get laid, right?" I laughed uneasily, and asked her what she did for a living. It turned out that she owns a boutique on Rodeo Drive where Louise shops sometimes. When we were seated she startled me by asking if I had been tested for HIV. I said no, it hadn't seemed necessary, because I had always been faithful to my wife. "So Louise told me," Stella said. "What about your wife? Has she been faithful to you?" I said I now believed that she had been, and asked her what she would like to eat. "I'll have a Caesar salad and *fiilet mignon*, very rare. You don't mind my asking you these questions, Tubby?" "Oh no," I said politely. "Only in my experience it's best to get these things outa the way at the beginning. Then we can both relax. How about since your wife walked out? You been with anybody else?" "Just once," I said. "A very old friend." "You used a condom, of course?" "Oh yes, of course," I lied. Actually Amy had used a diaphragm. I think Stella could tell I was lying. "You have some with you?" she said, when they had brought us the Caesar salad. "Well, not *on* me," I said. "I meant, in your room." "Well, there may be some in the minibar," I quipped, "it seems to have everything else." "It doesn't matter, I have some in my purse," Stella said without cracking a smile. When she started talking about latex gloves and dental dams over the *fiilet mignon*, I panicked. If she was so concerned about safe sex, I thought to myself, she must have reason to be. For the first time in my life I simulated acute internal derangement of the knee, writhing about in my seat in, though I says it myself, a very convincing impression of unbearable pain. The guests at neighbouring tables were quite concerned. The maître d' flashed a signal to the waiters and two of them carried me out into the lobby. I apologized to Stella, excused myself and retired to bed alone. Stella asked me to call her the next day, but the next day I was on the first plane out of LAX to Heathrow.

It was somewhere over the polar icecap that Samantha rose before my inward eye like a vision of sexual promise. Why hadn't I thought of her before? She was young, desirable, and had gone out of her way to cultivate my acquaintance. Furthermore she exuded health and hygiene, and was extremely smart. You couldn't imagine Samantha taking any risks with unsafe sex. Yes, she was obviously my best chance of proving to myself I was still a man. I could hardly wait to land in Heathrow. Red-eyed, soiled and unshaven, I jumped into a cab and went straight to the studio, where I knew I would find Samantha at rehearsal.

It wasn't surprising that my first clumsy attempt at seduction failed, especially with Signora Gabrielli doing her best to fuck it up. But when, a few days later, Ollie suggested assigning a script editor to work with me I saw my opportunity and insisted on Samantha. She understood very well what a favour I had done her, and was clearly prepared to pay for it in time-honoured showbiz style. My fatal mistake, fatal from the philandering point of view I mean, was to stage the seduction in Copenhagen, trying to kill two birds with one stone: combining a little Kierkegaard research with the long-desired, long-frustrated illicit fuck, in a luxury hotel far, but not inconveniently far, from anywhere we were likely to be recognized. I should have known that the two missions wouldn't mix. I should have reckoned with the effect of walking the pavements that Kierkegaard walked a century and a half ago, seeing the actual streets, squares and buildings that were just names in print before, Nytorv, Nørregade, the Borgerdyd-skole, and examining the poignant, homely mementos of S.K. in the Bymuseum: his pipes, his purse, his magnifying glass and the case Regine made for it; the cruel caricature in the *Corsair*; and the portrait of Regine, bonny, buxom and with a smile just about to part her full lips, obviously painted in her happy days before Kierkegaard broke off their engagement. And then to stand at Kierkegaard's very desk and write on it! I had the most extraordinary feeling that he was present somehow in the room, hovering at my shoulder.

In consequence I found myself curiously and embarrassingly reluctant to pursue the amorous objective of the trip, and when the beautiful Samantha shamelessly offered me all the delights of her sumptuous body, I couldn't take advantage of it. Something held me back, and it wasn't the fear of impotence, or of aggravating my knee injury. Call it conscience. Call it Kierkegaard. They have become one and the same thing. I think Kierkegaard is the thin man inside me that has been struggling to get out, and in Copenhagen he finally did.

Kierkegaard says somewhere in the *Journals* that when he discovered that Regine was engaged to Schlegel, and realized that he had lost her irrevocably, "my feeling was this: either you throw yourself into wild dissipation, or into religiousness absolute." My frantic, idiotic sexual odyssey after Sally walked out, trying desperately to get laid in turn by Amy, Louise, Stella and Samantha, was my attempt at wild dissipation. But when it failed, religion wasn't a viable alternative for me. All I could do by way of relief was wank, and write. Actually, it was all Kierkegaard could do for quite a time – write. (Perhaps he wanked too, it wouldn't entirely surprise me.) It's only the late books, the ones he published under his own name, that can be described as "absolutely religious", and frankly I find them a turn-off. The titles alone are a turn-off: most of them are called *Edifying Discourses*. The so-called pseudonymous works, especially the ones he wrote immediately after the break-up with Regine, under the names of Victor Eremitus, Constantine Constantius, Johannes de Silentio and other quaint aliases, are very different, and much more interesting: a kind of effort to come to terms with his experience, to accept the consequences of his own choices, by approaching the material obliquely, indirectly, though fictions, concealed behind masks. It was the same impulse that made me write the monologues, I suppose. Dramatic monologues, I think they're called, because they're addressed to somebody whose lines are just implied. I remember that much from Fifth-Form English. We had to learn one by Browning, off by heart. "My Last Duchess":

> That's my last duchess, painted on the wall
> Looking as if she were alive. I call
> That piece a wonder now . . .

The Duke is a crazy jealous husband who, it turns out, has murdered his wife. I would never have murdered Sally, of course, but there were times when I came close to hitting her.

It was Alexandra's idea, in a way, though she had no notion of the torrent of words her suggestion would release, or the form they would take. I went to see her in a state of dull despair about a week after I got back from Copenhagen. I had renounced dissipation, but I still felt depressed. It was like the economy. The day I returned from Denmark (on the last plane – it took me hours to find Regine's grave, a flat tombstone rather pathetically overgrown with vegetation, but after all her true monument is Kierkegaard's works) the Government announced that the recession was officially over, but nobody could tell the difference. Production might be rising at the rate of 0.2 per cent, but there were still millions of people unemployed and hundreds of thousands trapped in negative equity.

I holed up in my flat. I didn't want to go out in case I was recognized. I lived in terror of meeting someone I knew. (Anyone except Grahame, of course. When I feel unbearably lonely I invite him in for a cup of tea or cocoa and a chat. He's always there in the evenings from about nine o'clock onwards, and sometimes during the day too. He's become a kind of sitting tenant.) I felt sure that all my friends and acquaintances were thinking and talking about me all the time, laughing and sniggering over the cartoon in *Public Interest*. When I went up to Rummidge to see Alexandra I travelled standard class and wore my Ray-Bans, hoping the ticket collectors wouldn't recognize me. I was sure they read *Public Interest* too.

I asked Alexandra about Prozac. She looked surprised. "I thought you were opposed to drug therapy," she said. "This is supposed to be something entirely new," I said. "Non-addictive. No side-effects. In the States even people who aren't depressed take it, because it makes them feel so good." Alexandra knew all about Prozac, of course, and gave me a technical explanation of how it's supposed to work, all about neurotransmitters and serotonin re-uptake inhibitors. I couldn't really follow it. I said I was already a bit slow on the re-uptake, and hardly needed any more inhibiting in that line, but apparently that wasn't what it meant at all. Alexandra views Prozac with some suspicion. "It's not true that there are no side-effects," she said. "Even advocates admit that it inhibits the patient's capacity to achieve orgasm." "Well, I'm already suffering the side-effect," I said, "so I might as well take the drug." Alexandra laughed, baring her big teeth in the widest grin I have ever drawn from her. She hastily straightened her features. "There are unconfirmed reports of more serious side-effects," she said. "Patients hallucinating, trying to mutilate themselves. There's even a murderer who's claiming that he killed under the influence of Prozac." "My friend didn't mention anything like that," I said. "She told me it makes you feel better than well." Alexandra looked at me in silence for a moment with her big brown gentle eyes. "I'll put you on Prozac if you really want me to," she said. "But you must understand what's entailed. I'm not talking about side-effects, now, I'm talking about *effects*. These new SRI drugs change people's personalities. They act on the mind like plastic surgery acts on the body. Prozac may give you back your self-esteem, but it won't be the same self." I thought for a moment. "What else do you suggest?" I said.

Alexandra suggested that I should write down exactly what I thought other people were saying and thinking about me, privately or to each other. I recognized the strategy, of course. She believed that it was not the *actuality* of other people's opinions, but my *fear* of what these opinions might be, that was making me wretched. Once I focused on the question – *what do other people really think of me?* – and made myself answer it explicitly, then instead of projecting my lack of self-esteem onto others, and allowing it to rebound upon myself, I would be forced to acknowledge that other people didn't really loathe and despise me, but respected and sympathized with and even liked me. It didn't quite work out like that, though.

Being the sort of writer I am, I couldn't just summarize other people's views of me, I had to let them speak their thoughts in their own voices. And what they said wasn't very flattering. "You've been very hard on yourself," Alexandra said, when she finally saw what I'd written. It took me some weeks – I got a bit carried away – and I only sent the stuff to her last week, quite a bulky package. I went up to Rummidge yesterday for her verdict. "They're very funny, very acute," she said, leafing through the sheaves of A4 with a reminiscent smile playing over her pale, unpainted lips, "but you've been very hard on yourself." I shrugged and said I had tried to see myself truthfully from other people's points of view. "But you must have made up a lot of these things." Not all that much, I said.

I had to use my imagination a bit, of course. I never saw Brett Sutton's statement to the police, for instance, but I had to make one myself, and they gave me a copy to take home, so I knew what the format was like, and it wasn't hard to guess what Brett Sutton's version of events would have been. And although Amy was always very secretive about her sessions with Karl Kiss, I knew she would have been giving him daily bulletins about developments in our relationship following Sally's bombshell, and I've had plenty of opportunity to study the way she thinks and talks. Most of the things she says to Karl in the monologue she said to me at one time or another, like remembering her mother slicing carrots in the kitchen while telling her the facts of life, or dreaming of the cartoon in *Public Interest* with me as Vulcan and Saul as Mars. The bit about her sewage-disposal problems in the Playa de las Americas hotel was an extrapolation from listening to her endlessly cranking the handle of the toilet when she was in the bathroom. The ending is a little too neat, perhaps, but I couldn't resist it. Amy did return to England in a bouncy, self-assertive mood, saying that she was going to give Karl his "*congé*", but the last I heard she was back in analysis again. I don't see much of Amy, actually, these days. We tried meeting again for a meal once or twice, but we couldn't seem to get back onto the old friendly footing. Embarrassing memories of Tenerife kept getting in the way.

Whether Louise actually described our reunion to Stella in such detail, I have no idea, but whatever she told her would have been on the phone. Louise may have given up smoking and drinking and drugs (apart from Prozac), but she's completely addicted to the telephone. She had her dinky Japanese portable beside her plate at the Venice restaurant all through our meal, and kept interrupting my heartbroken confidences to take and make calls about her movie Ollie wasn't difficult. I must have been trapped with him in a bar a hundred times. I did take a few liberties with Samantha. She mentioned – I can't remember the context now – that she had a friend who was suffering from impacted wisdom teeth, but the hospital visit was all my invention. I just liked the idea of this helpless, speechless captive auditor unable to stem the flow of Samantha's loud recapitulation of our would-be dirty weekend in Copenhagen. She's a smart babe, Samantha, but sensitivity is not her strong point.

The hardest one to write was Sally's. I didn't show it to Alexandra because she might have thought I was taking a liberty, writing her into it. I know she invited Sally to come and see her, because she asked if I had any objection (I said no). And I believe Sally agreed, but Alexandra never told me what she said, so I assumed it was discouraging. It was almost physically painful, reliving the bust-up through Sally's eyes. That's why the monologue changes halfway from being one side of a conversation with Alexandra to being a stream of reminiscence about our courtship. But that was painful too, reliving those days of hope and promise and laughter. The most chilling thing that Sally said to me in the course of that long hellish weekend of argument and pleading and recrimination before she walked out, the moment when I knew, really knew, in my heart, that I'd lost her, was when she said: "You don't make me laugh any more."

✳ ✳ ✳ ✳ ✳ ✳ ✳ ✳ ✳ ✳ ✳ ✳ ✳ ✳ ✳ ✳ ✳ ✳

Thursday 27th May, 10 a.m. It took me all day to write yesterday's entry. I worked without a break, except for five minutes when I nipped out to Pret A Manger for a prawn and avocado sandwich, which I ate at the table as I went on writing. There was a lot to catch up on.

I finished at about seven, feeling tired, hungry and thirsty. My knee was giving me gyp too: sitting in one position for long periods is bad for it. (What is "gyp", I wonder? Dictionary says "*probably a contraction of* gee up", which doesn't sound very probable to me. More likely something to do with Egypt, as in "gyppy tummy", a bit of army slang from the days of the Empire.) I went out to stretch my legs and refuel. It was a fine warm evening. The young swarmed round Leicester Square tube station as they always do at that time of day, whatever the season. They bubble up from the subway like some irrepressible underground spring, spill out on to the pavement, and stand around outside the Hippodrome in their flimsy casual clothes looking eager and expectant. What are they hoping for? I don't think most of them could tell you if you asked them. Some adventure, some encounter, some miraculous transformation of their ordinary lives. A few, of course, are waiting for a date. I see their faces light up as they spot their boyfriend or girlfriend approaching. They embrace, oblivious to the fat baldy in the leather jacket sauntering past with his hands in his pockets, and move off, arms round each other's waists, to some restaurant or cinema or bar throbbing with amplified rock music. I used to meet Sally on this corner when we were courting. Now I buy a *Standard* to read over my Chinese meal in Lisle Street.

The trouble with eating alone, well one of the troubles anyway, is that you tend to order too much and eat too fast. When I came back from the restaurant, bloated and belching, it was only 8.30, and still light. But Grahame was already settling himself down for the night on the porch. I invited him in to watch the second half of the European Cup Final between AC Milan and Marseille. Marseille won 1–0. A good game, though it's hard to work up much passion about a match with no British club involved. I remember when Manchester United won the European Cup with George Best in the side. Delirious. I asked Grahame if he remembered, but of course he wasn't even born then.

Grahame is lucky to still be occupying the porch. Herr Bohl, the Swiss businessman who owns flat number 5 and resides there occasionally, took exception to his presence and proposed to call the police and have him ejected. I appealed to Bohl to let him stay on the grounds that he keeps the porch beautifully clean and deters passers-by from tossing their rubbish into it and drunks from using it as a nocturnal urinal, which they used to do frequently and copiously. This cunning appeal to the Swiss obsession with hygiene paid off. Herr Bohl had to admit that the porch smelled considerably sweeter since Grahame's occupancy, and withdrew his threat to call the police.

It helped my case that Grahame himself always looks clean and doesn't smell at all. This puzzled me for a long time until one day I ventured to ask him how he managed it. He smiled slyly and told me he would let me into a secret. The next day he led me to a place on Trafalgar Square, just a door in the wall with an electronic lock on it that I must have passed scores of times without noticing it. Grahame tapped out a sequence of numbers on the keypad and the lock buzzed and opened. Inside was an underground labyrinth of rooms providing food, games, showers and a launderette. It's a kind of refuge for homeless young people. There are even dressing-gowns provided so that if you've only got one set of clothes you can sit and wait while they're being washed and dried. It reminded me a bit of the Pullman Lounge at Euston Station. I sent a donation to the charity that runs it the other day. Knowing it's there makes me feel slightly less guilty about knowing that Grahame is sleeping in the porch. The rich man in his castle, the poor man at his gate . . .

Actually, there's no reason why I should feel guilty at all. Grahame has chosen to live on the street. Out of a pretty lousy set of options, admittedly, but it's probably the best life he's ever had – certainly the most independent. "I am the master of my fate," he said to me solemnly one day. It was one of these phrases he had seen somewhere and memorized, without knowing who said it. I looked it up in my dictionary of quotations. It comes from a poem by W. E. Henley:

> It matters not how strait the gate,
> How charged with punishments the scroll,
> I am the master of my fate:
> I am the captain of my soul.

I wish I was.

11.15. Jake just rang. I listened to him leave a message on the answerphone without picking up the receiver or returning his call. He was trying to lure me to lunch at Groucho's. He's getting jittery because we're approaching the deadline after which Heartland can exercise their right to employ another writer. Well, let them. I'm much more interested in Søren and Regine than in Priscilla and Edward these days, but I know Ollie Silvers has no intention of making a programme about Kierkegaard, however much work I do on *The People Next Door*, so why should I bother?

Grahame was quite impressed when he found out I was a TV scriptwriter, but when I mentioned the name of the show he said, "Oh, that," in a distinctly sniffy tone. I thought this was a bit cheeky, especially as he was swigging my tea and stuffing himself with carrot cake from Pret A Manger at the time. "It's all right, I suppose," he said, "if you like that sort of thing." I pressed him to explain why he obviously didn't like it himself. "Well, it ain't real, is it?" he said. "I mean, every week there's some great row in one of the houses, but it's always sorted out by the end of the programme, and everybody's sweet as pie again. Nothing ever changes. Nobody ever gets really hurt. Nobody hits anybody. None of the kids ever run away." "Alice ran away once," I pointed out. "Yeah, for about ten minutes," he said. He meant ten minutes of screen time, but I didn't quibble. I took his point.

2.15 p.m. I went out for a pub lunch and when I came back there was a message from Samantha on the answerphone: she's had an idea for solving the Debbie–Priscilla problem that she wants to discuss with me. She said she would be back at her desk by three, which seems to imply a rather leisurely lunch, but gave me time to leave a message on *her* answerphone, asking her to put the idea on paper and mail it to me. I only communicate by answerphone or letter nowadays. This allows me to control the agenda of all discussions and avoid the dreaded question, *"How are you?"* Sometimes if I'm feeling particularly lonely I call my bank's Phoneline service and check the balances in my various accounts with the girl whose recorded voice guides you through the digitally coded procedure. She sounds rather nice, and she doesn't ask how you are. Though if you make a mistake she says, *"I'm sorry, there appears to be a problem."* Too true, darling, I tell her.

"Only when I write do I feel well. Then I forget all of life's vexations, all its sufferings, then I am wrapped in thought and am happy." – Kierkegaard's journal, 1847. While I was writing the monologues I was – not happy exactly, but occupied, absorbed, interested. It was like working on a script. I had a task to perform, and I got some satisfaction in performing it. Now that I've finished the task, and brought my journal more or less up to date, I feel restless, nervous, ill-at-ease, unable to settle to anything. I have no aim or objective, apart from making it as difficult as possible for Sally to get her hands on my money, and my heart isn't really in that any more. I've got to go up to Rummidge to see my lawyer tomorrow. I could instruct him to throw in the towel, settle the divorce as quickly as possible and give Sally what she wants. But would that make me feel any better? No. It's another either/or situation. It doesn't matter what I do, I'm bound to regret it. *If you divorce you'll regret it, if you don't divorce you'll regret it. Divorce or don't divorce, you'll regret both.*

Perhaps I still hope that Sally and I will get together again, that I can have my old life back, that everything will be as it used to be. Perhaps, in spite of all my tantrums and tears and plots for revenge – or because of them – I haven't truly despaired of our marriage. B says to A: "In order truly to despair one must really want to, but when one truly wills despair one is truly beyond it; when one has truly chosen despair one has truly chosen what despair chooses, namely oneself in one's eternal validity." I suppose you could say I chose myself when I declined Alexandra's offer to put me on Prozac, but it didn't feel like an act of existential self-affirmation at the time. More like a captured criminal holding out his wrists for the handcuffs.

5.30. I suddenly thought that as I'm going up to Rummidge tomorrow, I might as well try to fit some therapy in. I made a couple of phone calls. Roland was fully booked, but Dudley was able to give me an appointment in the afternoon. I didn't try Miss Wu. I haven't seen her since that Friday when Sally dropped her bombshell. I haven't felt like it. Nothing to do with Miss Wu. Association of ideas: acupuncture and my life falling apart.

9.30. I ate at an Indian restaurant this evening and came home at about nine, spicing the metropolitan pollution with explosive, aromatic farts. Grahame said a man had rung my doorbell. From his description I guessed it was Jake. "Friend of yours, is he?" Grahame enquired. "Sort of," I said. "He asked me if I'd seen you lately. Didn't give a very flattering description." Naturally I asked what it was. "Fattish, bald, round-shouldered." The last epithet shook me a bit. I've never thought of myself as particularly round-shouldered. It must be the effect of depression. How you feel is how you look. I don't think it was only his childhood accident that made Kierkegaard's spine curve. "What did you tell him?" I asked. "I didn't tell him nothing," said Grahame. "Good," I said. "You did well."

✳ ✳ ✳ ✳ ✳ ✳ ✳ ✳ ✳ ✳ ✳ ✳ ✳ ✳ ✳ ✳ ✳

Friday 28th May. 7.45 p.m. Just returned from Rummidge. I drove, simply to give the Richmobile a run: I keep it in a lock-up garage near King's Cross, and hardly ever use it these days. Not that there was much pleasure to be had on the M1 today. It had broken out in a rash of cones, like scarlet fever, and contraflow between Junctions 9 and 11 was causing a five-mile tailback. Apparently a car towing a caravan had contraflowed into a lorry. So I was late for my appointment with Dennis Shorthouse. He specializes in divorce and family litigation for my solicitors, Dobson McKitterick. I never had any dealings with him until the bust-up with Sally. He's tall, grey-haired, with a spare frame and a lined, beaky face, and rarely moves from behind his large, eerily tidy desk. Just as some doctors keep themselves preternaturally clean and neat as if to ward off infection, so Shorthouse seems to use his desk as some kind of *cordon sanitaire* to keep his clients' misery at a safe distance. It has an in-tray and an out-tray, both always empty, a spotless blotter and a digital clock, subtly angled towards the client's chair like a taxi-meter, so you can see how much his advice is costing you.

He'd had a letter from Sally's solicitors, threatening to sue for divorce on the grounds of unreasonable behaviour. "As you know, adultery and unreasonable behaviour are the only grounds for an immediate divorce," he said. I asked him what constituted unreasonable behaviour. "A very good question," he said, joining his fingertips and leaning forward across the desk. He launched into a long disquisition, but I'm afraid my mind wandered and I suddenly became aware that he had fallen silent and was looking expectantly at me. "I'm sorry, would you just repeat that, please?" I said. His smile became a trifle forced. "Repeat how much?" he said. "Just the last bit," I said, not having a clue how long he had been speaking. "I asked you, what kind of unreasonable behaviour Mrs Passmore was likely to complain of, if she were under oath." I thought for a moment.

219

"Would my not listening when she was talking to me count?" I said. "It might," he said. "It would depend on the judge." I got the impression that if Shorthouse were judging me himself, I wouldn't stand much chance. "Have you ever physically assaulted your wife?" he said. "Good God, no," I said. "What about drunkenness, verbal abuse, jealous rages, false accusations, that sort of thing?" "Only since she walked out on me," I said. "I didn't hear you say that," he said. He paused for a moment before summing up: "I don't think Mrs Passmore will risk lodging an unreasonable behaviour petition. She won't qualify for legal aid, and if she were to lose the costs could be considerable. Also she would be back to square one as regards the divorce. She's threatening this to bring pressure on you to co-operate. I don't think you need worry." Shorthouse smirked, obviously pleased with his analysis. "You mean she won't get a divorce?" I said. "Oh, she'll get it eventually, of course, on grounds of irretrievable breakdown of the marriage. It's a question of how long you want to make her wait." "And how much I want to pay you to delay things?" I said. "Quite so," he said, glancing at the clock. I told him to carry on delaying.

Then I went to see Dudley. Drawing up outside his house I thought wistfully of all the previous occasions on which I had visited him with nothing more serious to complain of than a general, ill-defined malaise. A wide-bodied jet thundered overhead as I rang the doorbell, making me cringe and cover my ears. Dudley told me it was a new scheduled service to New York. "Be useful to you, won't it, in your line of work?" he remarked, "You won't have to go from Heathrow any more." Dudley has a rather exaggerated notion of the glamour of a TV scriptwriter's life. I told him I was living in London now, anyway, and the reason. "I don't suppose you have an essential oil for marital breakdown, do you?" I said. "I can give you something for stress," he offered. I asked him if he could do anything about my knee, which had been playing up badly on the M1. He tapped away on his computer and said he would try lavender, which was allegedly good for aches and pains *and* stress. He took a little phial out of his big, brass-bound case of essential oils, and invited me to smell it.

I don't think Dudley can have ever used lavender on me before, because sniffing it triggered the most extraordinarily vivid memory – of Maureen Kavanagh, my first girlfriend. She's been flitting in and out of my consciousness ever since I started this journal, like a figure glimpsed indistinctly at the edge of a distant wood, moving between the trees, gliding in and out of the shadows. The smell of lavender drew her out into the open – the lavender and Kierkegaard. I made a note some weeks ago that the symbol for the double *aa* in modern Danish, the single *a* with a little circle on top, reminded me of something I couldn't pin down at the time. Well, it was Maureen's handwriting. She used to dot her *i*s that way, with a little circle instead of a point, like a trail of bubbles above the lines of her big round handwriting. I don't know where she got the idea from. We used to write to each other even though we saw each other every morning at the tram stop, just for the thrill of having private letters. I used to write her rather passionate love-letters and she would send back shy little notes of disappointing banality: "I did homework after tea, then I helped Mum with her ironing. Did you listen in to Tony Hancock? We were in fits." She used mauve stationery from Woolworths that was scented with lavender. That whiff from Dudley's phial brought it all back – not just her handwriting, but Maureen in all her specificity. Maureen. My first love. My first breast.

There was a letter from Samantha in the mailbox when I got in, with her idea for writing Debbie's part out of *The People Next Door* : in the last episode Priscilla is knocked off her bike by a lorry and killed instantly, but returns as a ghost, which only Edward can see, and urges him to find another partner. Not exactly original, but it has possibilities. You have to admit, the girl is smart. In another mood, I might have tinkered with it. But all I can think about at the moment is Maureen. I feel an irresistible urge coming over me to write about her.

✳ Maureen ✳

A MEMOIR

I FIRST BECAME AWARE of Maureen Kavanagh's existence when I was fifteen, though nearly a year passed before I managed to speak to her and discover her name. I used to see her every weekday morning, as I waited for the tram which took me on the first stage of my tedious three-leg journey to school. That was Lambeth Merchants', a direct-grant grammar school to which, pushed by a well-intentioned junior-school head, I unluckily gained admission at the Eleven-Plus. I say unluckily because I believe now that I would have been happier, and therefore have learned more, at some less prestigious and pretentious establishment. I had the innate intelligence, but not the social and cultural back-up, to benefit from the education on offer at Lambeth Merchants'. It was an ancient foundation that took obsessive pride in its history and tradition. It accepted fee-paying pupils as well as the cream of the 11-Plus, and modelled itself on the classic English public school, with "Houses" (though there were no boarders), a chapel, a school song with words in Latin, and numerous arcane rituals and privileges. The buildings were sooty neo-gothic redbrick, turreted and crenellated, with stained-glass windows in the chapel and the main assembly hall. The teachers wore gowns. I never fitted in and never did well academically, languishing at the bottom of my class for most of my school career. My Mum and Dad were unable to help me with my homework, and indulged my tendency to skimp it. I spent most evenings listening to comedy shows on the radio (my classics are *ITMA, Much Binding in the Marsh, Take It From Here*, and *The Goon Show*, not the *Aeneid* and *David Copperfield*) or playing football and cricket in the street with my mates from the local secondary modern. Sport was encouraged at Lambeth Merchants' – they even gave "caps" for representing the school – but the winter game was rugby, which I loathed, and school cricket was played with a pomp and circumstance that I found tedious. The only success I enjoyed at school was as a comic actor in the annual play. Otherwise I was made to feel stupid and uncouth. I became the class clown, and perennial butt of the masters' sarcasm. I was caned frequently. I looked forward to leaving school as soon as I had taken the O-Level examinations I did not expect to pass.

Maureen went to the Sacred Heart convent school in Greenwich, also courtesy of the Eleven-Plus. She had an equally awkward journey from Hatchford where we both lived, but in the opposite direction. Hatchford was, I suppose, a desirable outer suburb of London when it was first built at the end of the nineteenth century, just where the Thames plain meets the first Surrey hills, but was almost part of the decaying inner city by the time we were born. Maureen lived at the top of one of the hills, in the lower half of a huge Victorian villa that had been divided into flats. Her family inhabited the basement and ground floor. We lived in a little terraced house in Albert Street, one of the streets off the main road at the bottom of the hill, where the trams ran. My dad was a tram-driver.

It was a hard job. He had to stand for eight hours or more at the controls, on a platform open to the elements on one side, and a certain amount of brute force was needed to apply the brakes. In the winter he came home from work chilled and haggard, and crouched over the coal fire in the living-room, hardly able to speak till he had thawed out. There was a more modern type of tram, streamlined and fully enclosed, which I saw occasionally in other parts of London, but my Dad always worked on the old clapped-out pre-war trams, open at each end, that screeched and rattled and groaned as they lurched from stop to stop. Those red, double-decker trams, with a single headlamp that glowed in the fog like a bleary eye, with their clanging bells, their brass fittings and wooden seats polished by the friction of innumerable hands and bums, their top decks reeking of cigarette-smoke and sick, their muffled grey-faced drivers and chirpy, mittened clippies, are inseparably linked with my memories of childhood and adolescence.

Every weekday I caught my first tram at Hatchford Five Ways on my way to school. I used to wait not at the stop itself but on the corner just before it, outside a flower shop, from which I could sight my tram as soon as it appeared around a distant curve in the main road, swaying on the rails like a galleon at sea. By moving my angle of vision about thirty degrees I could also look up the long straight incline of Beecher's Road. Maureen always appeared at the top at the same time, at five minutes to eight, and took three minutes to reach the bottom. She passed me, crossed the road, and walked a few yards to wait for a tram going in the opposite direction to mine. I watched her boldly when she was distant, covertly as she approached me, while ostensibly looking out for my tram. After she had passed, I would saunter to my stop, and watch her as she waited, with her back turned to me, on the other side of the road. Sometimes, just as she came up to the corner, I would risk turning my head in feigned boredom or impatience at the non-appearance of the tram, and glance at her as if by accident. Usually she had her eyes lowered, but on one occasion she was looking straight at me and our eyes met. She blushed crimson and looked quickly down at the pavement as she passed. I don't think I breathed for five minutes afterwards.

This went on for months. Perhaps a year. I didn't know who she was, or anything about her, except that I was in love with her. She was beautiful. I suppose a less impressionable, or more blasé, observer might have described her as "pretty" or "nice-looking" rather than beautiful, judging her to be a little too short in the neck, or a little too thick in the waist, to qualify for the highest accolade, but to me she was beautiful. Even in her school uniform – a pudding-bowl hat, a gaberdine raincoat and pleated pinafore dress, all in a dead, depressing shade of navy blue – she was beautiful. She wore the hat at a jaunty angle, or perhaps it was the natural springiness of her auburn hair that pushed it to the back of her head, the rim framing her heart-shaped, heart-stopping face: big, dark brown eyes, a small, neat nose, generous mouth, dimpled chin. How can you describe beauty in words? It's hopeless, like shuffling bits of an Identikit picture around. Her hair was long and wavy, drawn over her ears and gathered by a clasp at the back of her neck into a kind of loose mane that fell halfway down her back. She wore her raincoat unbuttoned, flapping open at the front, with the sleeves turned back to expose the cuffs of her white blouse, and the belt knotted behind. I discovered later that she and her schoolfriends spent endless hours contriving such tiny modifications of the uniform, trying to outwit the nuns' repressive regulations. She carried her books in a kind of shopping-bag, which gave her a womanly, grown-up look, and made my big leather satchel seem childish in comparison.

I thought of her last thing at night, before I fell asleep, and when I woke in the morning. If, as very rarely happened, she was late appearing at the top of Beecher's Road, I would let my tram go by without boarding it, and take the consequences of being late for school (two strokes of the cane) rather than forfeit my daily sight of her. It was the purest, most selfless romantic devotion. It was Dante and Beatrice in a suburban key. Nobody knew my secret, and torture wouldn't have dragged it from me. I was going through the usual hormonal storm of adolescence at the time, swamped and buffeted by bodily changes and sensations I could neither control nor put a name to – erections and nocturnal emissions and sprouting body hair and the rest of it. There was no sex education at Lambeth Merchants', and my Mum and Dad, with the deep repressive puritanism of the respectable working class, never discussed the subject. Of course the usual smutty jokes and boasts circulated in the school playground and were illustrated on the walls of the school bogs, but it was difficult to elicit basic information from those who appeared to know without betraying a humiliating ignorance. One day a boy I trusted told me the facts of life as we walked back from an illicit lunchtime visit to the local chip-shop – "when your dick gets stiff you poke it in the girl's slit and come off in her" – but this act, though inflaming to contemplate, seemed ugly and unclean, not something I wanted to associate with the angel who descended daily from the top of Beecher's Road to receive my dumb adoration.

Of course I longed to speak to her, and thought continually about possible ways of getting into conversation with her. The simplest method, I told myself, would be to smile and say hallo one morning, as she passed. After all, we were not total strangers – it was a quite

225

normal thing to do to somebody you met regularly in the street, even if you didn't know their name. The worst that could happen was that she would ignore me, and walk straight past without responding to my greeting. Ah, but that worst was chilling to contemplate. What would I do the *next* morning? And every morning after that? As long as I didn't accost her, she couldn't rebuff me, and my love was safe even if unrequited. I spent many hours fantasizing about more dramatic and irresistible ways of making her acquaintance – for example, pulling her back from certain death as she was about to step under the wheels of a tram, or defending her from attack by some ruffian bent on robbery or rape. But she always showed admirable caution and common sense when crossing the road, and the pavements of Hatchford at eight o'clock in the morning were rather short of ruffians (this, after all, was 1951, when the word "mugging" was unknown, and even at night unaccompanied women felt safe in well-lit London streets).

The event that finally brought us together was less heroic than these imaginary scenarios, but it seemed almost miraculous to me at the time, as if some sympathetic deity, aware of my tongue-tied longing to make the girl's acquaintance, had finally lost patience, plucked her into the air and flung her to the ground at my feet. She was late appearing at the top of Beecher's Road that day, and I could see that she was hurrying down the hill. Every now and then she would break into a run – that rather endearing kind of running that girls do, moving their legs mainly from the knees, throwing out their heels at an angle behind them – and then, encumbered by her heavy bag of books, she would slow to a brisk walking pace for an interval. In this flustered and flurried state she seemed more than usually beautiful. Her hat was off her head, retained by the narrow elastic strap round her throat, her long mane swung to and fro, and the energy of her stride made her bosom move about thrillingly beneath her white blouse and pinafore dress. I kept her in my direct line of vision longer than usual, as long as I dared; but eventually, to avoid giving the impression of staring rudely, I had to avert my eyes and go through the pretence of looking along the main road for my tram – which was in fact, by this time, quite near.

I heard a cry and suddenly there she was, sprawled at my feet, her books scattered all over the pavement. Breaking into a run again, she had caught the toe of her shoe on the edge of an uneven paving-stone, tripped, and fallen, dropping her bag as she broke her fall. She was up on her feet in an instant, before I could lend her a supporting hand, but I was able to help her pick up her books, and to speak to her. "Are you alright?" "Mmm," she mumbled, sucking a grazed knuckle. "Stupid." This last epithet was clearly addressed to herself, or possibly to the paving-stone, not to me. She was blushing furiously. My tram passed, its wheels grating and squealing in the grooved tracks as it took the corner. "That's your tram," she said. "It doesn't matter," I replied, filled with rapture at the implication of this remark – that she had been observing my movements as closely as I had been observing hers over the past months. I carefully gathered up a number of foolscap sheets that had fallen out of a folder, covered with large round handwriting, the *is* topped with little circles instead of dots, and handed them to her. "Thanks," she muttered, stuffing them into her bag, and hurried away, limping slightly.

She was just in time to catch her usual tram – I saw her emerge from the top of the stairs on to the upper deck as it passed me moments later. My own tram had gone without me, but I didn't care. *I had actually spoken to her!* I had almost touched her. I kicked myself for not having been quick enough to help her get up from the ground – but never mind: a contact had been made, words had been exchanged, and I had done her a small service by picking up her books and papers. From now on I would be able to smile and say hallo every morning when she passed me. As I contemplated this exciting prospect, something shiny caught my eye in the gutter: it was the clip on a Biro pen, which had obviously fallen out of her bag. I pounced on it exultantly and stowed it away in an inside pocket, next to my heart.

Ballpoint pens were still something of a novelty in those days, and absurdly expensive, so I knew the girl would be pleased to have it restored to her. I slept with it under my pillow that night (it leaked and left blue stains on the sheet and pillowcase, for which I was bitterly berated by my mother, and clipped round the ear by my father) and took up my usual position outside the florist's shop the next morning five minutes earlier than usual, to be sure of not missing the pen's owner. She was indeed a little early herself in making her appearance at the top of Beecher's Road, and descended the incline slowly, with a kind of self-conscious deliberation, carefully placing each foot in front of the other, looking down at the pavement – not, I was sure, just to avoid tripping up again, but because she knew I was observing her, waiting for her. They were tense, highly charged minutes that ticked by as she walked down the hill towards me. It was like that wonderful shot at the end of *The Third Man*, when Harry Lime's girlfriend walks towards Holly Martins along the avenue in the frozen cemetery, except that she walks right past him without a glance, and this girl was not going to, because I had a flawless pretext to stop her and talk to her.

As she approached me she affected interest in a flight of starlings wheeling and swooping in the sky above the Co-op bakery, but when she was a few yards away she glanced at me and gave me a shy smile of recognition. "Erm, I think you dropped this yesterday," I blurted out, whipping the Biro from my pocket and holding it out to her. Her face lit up with pleasure. "Oh, thanks ever so much," she said, stopping and taking the pen. "I thought I'd lost it. I came back here yesterday afternoon and looked, but I couldn't find it." "No, well, I had it," I said, and we both laughed inanely. When she laughed, the tip of her nose twitched and wrinkled up like a rabbit's. "Well, thanks again," she said, moving on. "If I'd known where you lived, I'd have brought it round," I said, desperately trying to detain her. "That's alright," she said, walking backwards, "As long as I've got it back. I daren't tell my Mum I'd lost it." She treated me to another delicious nose-wrinkling smile, turned her back on me and disappeared round the corner. I still didn't know her name.

It wasn't long before I found out, though. Every morning after her providential dive at my feet I smiled and said hallo as she passed, and she blushed and smiled and said hallo back. Soon I added to my greeting some carefully rehearsed remark about the weather or enquiry about the functioning of the ballpoint pen or complaint about the lateness of my tram which invited a reply on her part, and one day she lingered at the corner outside the florist's for a few moments' proper conversation. I asked her what her name was. "Maureen." "Mine's Laurence." "Turn me over," she said, and giggled at my blank look. "Don't you know the story of Saint Laurence?" I shook my head. "He was martyred by being slowly roasted on a gridiron," she said. "He said, 'Turn me over, this side is done.'" "When was that?" I asked, wincing sympathetically. "I dunno exactly," she said. "Roman times, I think."

This grotesque and slightly sick anecdote, related as if there was nothing the least disturbing about it, was the first indication I had that Maureen was a Catholic, confirmed the following day when she told me the name of her school. I had noticed the heart embroidered with red and gold thread on her blazer badge, but without realizing its religious significance. "It means the Sacred Heart of Jesus," she said, making a little reflex inclination of her head as she pronounced the Holy Name. These pious allusions to gridirons and hearts, with their incongruous associations of kitchens and offal, made me slightly uneasy, reminding me of Mrs Turner's threats to wash me in the Blood of the Lamb in infancy, but didn't deter me from seeking to make Maureen my girlfriend.

I had never had a girlfriend before, and was uncertain of how to start, but I knew that courting couples often went to the cinema together, because I had queued with them outside the local Odeon, and observed them necking in the back rows. One day, as Maureen lingered outside the florist's, I summoned up the courage to ask her if she would go to the pictures with me the following weekend. She blushed and looked at once excited and apprehensive. "I dunno. I'd have to ask my Mum and Dad," she said.

The next morning she appeared at the top of Beecher's Road accompanied by an enormous man, at least six foot tall and, it seemed to me, as wide as our house. I knew it must be Maureen's father, who she had told me was foreman at a local building firm, and viewed his approach with alarm. I was afraid not so much of physical assault as of a humiliating public scene. So, obviously, was Maureen, for I could see she was dragging her feet and hanging her head sulkily. As they drew nearer, I fixed my gaze on the long perspective of the main road, with its shining tram-tracks receding to infinity, and hoped against hope that Mr Kavanagh was just escorting Maureen, and would ignore me if I made no attempt to greet her. No such luck. A huge shape in a navy-blue donkey-jacket loomed over me.

"Are you the young blackguard who's been pesterin' my daughter?" he demanded in a thick Irish accent.

"Eh?" I said, stalling. I glanced at Maureen, but she avoided my eye. She was red in the face and looked as if she had been crying. "Dad!" she murmured plaintively. The young overalled assistant arranging flowers in buckets outside the florist's paused in her labours to enjoy the drama.

Mr Kavanagh poked me in the chest with a huge forefinger, horny and calloused and hard as a policeman's truncheon. "My daughter's a respectable girl. I won't have her talkin' to strange fellas on street corners, understand?"

I nodded.

"Mind you do, then. Off you go to school." This last remark was addressed to Maureen, who slouched off with one despairing, apologetic glance at me. Mr Kavanagh's attention seemed caught by my school blazer, a gaudy crimson garment with silver buttons, which I loathed, and he screwed up his eyes at the elaborate coat of arms with its Latin motto on the breast pocket. "What's this school that you go to?" I told him, and he seemed impressed in spite of himself. "Mind you behave yourself, or I'll report you to your headmaster," he said. He turned on his heel and walked back up the hill. I stayed where I was, looking along the main road until my tram came in sight, and my pulse rate returned to normal.

Of course this incident only drew Maureen and me closer together. We became a pair of star-crossed lovers, defying her father's ban on further contact. We continued to exchange a few words every morning, though I now prudently stationed myself just round the corner, out of sight of anyone surveying the Five Ways from the top of Beecher's Road. In due course Maureen persuaded her mother to let me call at their house one Saturday afternoon when her father was out, working overtime, so that she could see for herself I wasn't the kind of street-corner lout they had imagined when she first asked if she could go to the pictures with me. "Wear your school blazer," Maureen advised, shrewdly. So, to the astonishment of my own parents and disgust of my mates, I missed a home game at Charlton and put on the blazer I never normally wore at weekends and walked up the long hill to Maureen's house. Mrs Kavanagh gave me a cup of tea and a slice of home-made soda bread in her big, dark, chaotic basement kitchen, and burped a baby over her shoulder as she assessed me. She was a handsome woman in her forties grown stout from childbearing. She had her daughter's long hair, but it was going grey, and piled up in an untidy knot at the back of her head. Like her husband she spoke with an Irish brogue, though Maureen and her siblings had the same South London accent as myself. Maureen was the eldest child, and the apple of her parents' eye. Her scholarship to the Sacred Heart convent was the subject of particular pride, and the fact that I was a grammar-school boy was obviously a mark in my favour. Against me was the fact that I was a *boy*, and non-Catholic, therefore an inherent threat to Maureen's virtue. "You look like a decent sort of lad," said Mrs Kavanagh, "but her father thinks Maureen is too young to be gallivanting about with boys, and so do I. She has her homework to do." "Not every night, Mum," Maureen protested. "You already have the Youth Club on Sundays," said Mrs Kavanagh, "That's quite enough socializing at your age."

I asked if I could join the youth club.

"It's the parish youth club," said Mrs Kavanagh. "You have to be a Catholic."

"No you don't, Mum," Maureen said. "Father Jerome said non-Catholics can join if they're interested in the Church." Maureen looked at me and blushed.

"I'm very interested," I said, quickly.

"Is that so?" Mrs Kavanagh looked at me sceptically, but she knew she had been out-manoeuvred. "Well, if Father Jerome says it's alright, I suppose it's alright."

Needless to say, I had no genuine interest in Catholicism, or indeed in religion of any kind. My parents were not churchgoers, and observed the Sabbath only to the extent of forbidding me and my brother to play in the street on Sundays. Lambeth Merchants' was nominally C of E, but the prayers and hymns at morning assembly, and occasional services in the chapel, seemed part of the school's ceaseless celebration of its own heritage rather than the expression of any moral or theological idea. That some people, like Maureen and her family, should voluntarily submit themselves to such boredom every Sunday morning, when they could be enjoying a long lie-in instead, was incomprehensible to me. Nevertheless I was prepared to feign a polite interest in her religion, if that was the price of being allowed to keep Maureen company.

The following Sunday evening I turned up, by arrangement with Maureen, outside the local Roman Catholic church, a squat redbrick building with a larger-than-lifesize statue of the Virgin Mary outside. She had her arms extended, and a carved inscription on the plinth said: "I AM THE IMMACULATE CONCEPTION." A service was going on inside, and I lurked in the porch, listening to the unfamiliar hymns and droning prayers, my nostrils tickled by a strong sweet smell which I guessed must be incense. Suddenly there was a clamour of high-pitched bells, and I peeped through the doorway, looking down the aisle to the altar. It was quite a sight, ablaze with dozens of tall, thin lighted candles. The priest, dressed in a heavy embroidered robe of white and gold, was holding up something that flashed and glinted with reflected light, a white disc in a glass case, with golden rays sticking out all round it like a sunburst. He held the base of the thing wrapped in an embroidered scarf he had round his shoulders, as if it was too hot to touch, or radioactive. All the people, and there were a surprising number of them, were kneeling with their heads bowed. Maureen explained to me in due course that the white disc was a consecrated host, and that they believed it was the real body and blood of Jesus, but to me the whole business seemed more pagan than Christian. The singing sounded queer too. Instead of the rousing hymns I was used to at school ("To be a Pilgrim" was my favourite) they were singing slow, dirge-like anthems that I couldn't comprehend because they were in Latin, never my best subject. I had to admit, though, that there was a kind of atmosphere about the service that you didn't get in the school chapel.

What I liked about Catholics from the beginning was that there was nothing holier-than-thou about them. When the congregation came pouring out of the church, they might have been coming out of the pictures, or even a pub, the way they greeted each other and joked and chatted and offered each other cigarettes. Maureen came out accompanied by her mother, their heads covered with scarves. Mrs Kavanagh began talking to another woman in a hat. Maureen spotted me, and came over, smiling. "You found the way, then?" she greeted me. "What if your Dad sees us talking?" I asked nervously. "Oh, he never comes to Benediction," she said, untying her headscarf and shaking out her hair. "Thank the Lord." The paradoxical nature of this remark didn't strike me, and in any case my attention was fully absorbed by her hair. I had never seen it unrestrained before, fanned out in shining waves over her shoulders. She seemed more beautiful than ever. Conscious of my gaze, she blushed, and said she must introduce me to Father Jerome. Mrs Kavanagh seemed to have disappeared.

Father Jerome was the younger of the two priests who ran the parish, though he wasn't exactly young. He didn't look at all like our school chaplain or any other clergyman I had encountered. He didn't even resemble himself on the altar – for it was he who had presided over the service just finished. He was a gaunt, grizzled Dubliner, with nicotine-stained fingers and a shaving cut on his chin which he seemed to have staunched with a fragment of toilet-paper. He wore a long black cassock that reached to his scuffed shoes, with deep pockets in which he kept the materials for rolling his own cigarettes. One of these he lit with a pyrotechnic display of flame and sparks. "So you want to join our youth club, do you, young fella?" he said, brushing glowing wisps of tobacco from his cassock. "Yes please, sir," I said. "Then you'd better learn to call me Father instead of sir." "Yes, sir – Father, I mean," I stammered. Father Jerome grinned, revealing a disconcerting gap in his stained and uneven teeth. He asked me a few more questions about where I lived and where I went to school. The name of Lambeth Merchants' had its usual effect, and I became a probationary member of the Immaculate Conception parish youth club.

One of the first things Maureen had to do was to explain the name of her church. I presumed that it referred to Mary's being a virgin when she had Jesus, but no, apparently it meant that Mary herself was conceived "without the stain of original sin." I found the language of Catholicism very strange, especially the way they used words in their devotions, like "virgin", "conceived", "womb", that would have been regarded as bordering on the indecent in ordinary conversation, certainly in my home. I could hardly believe my ears when Maureen told me that she had to go to Mass on New Year's Day because it was the Feast of the Circumcision. "The feast of *what*?" "The Circumcision." "Whose circumcision?" "Our Lord's, of course. When he was a baby. Our Lady and Saint Joseph took him to the Temple and he was circumcised. It was like the Jewish baptism." I laughed incredulously. "D'you know what circumcision *is*?" Maureen blushed and giggled, wrinkling up her nose. " 'Course." "What is it, then?" "I'm not going to say." "You don't really know." "Yes I do." "I bet you don't." I persisted in my prurient interrogation until she blurted out that it meant "snipping off a bit of skin from the end of the baby's widdler," by which time my own widdler was standing up inside my grey flannel trousers like a relay-runner's baton. We were walking home from the youth club Sunday social at the time, and fortunately I was wearing a raincoat.

The youth club met twice a week in the Infants' School attached to the church: on Wednesdays for games, mainly ping-pong, and on Sundays for a "social". This consisted of dancing to gramophone records and partaking of sandwiches and orange squash or tea prepared by teams of girls working to a roster. The boys were required to stack the infants' desks at the sides of the room at the beginning of the evening, and replace them in rows at the end. We had the use of two classrooms normally divided by a folding partition wall. The floor was made of worn, unpolished wood blocks, the walls were covered with infantile paintings and educational charts, and the lighting was bleakly utilitarian. The gramophone was a single-speaker portable, and the records a collection of scratchy 78s. But to me, just emerging from the chrysalis of boyhood, the youth club was a site of exciting and sophisticated pleasures.

I learned to dance from a matronly lady of the parish who came in on games nights (when Maureen was seldom allowed out by her parents) and gave free lessons. I discovered that I was surprisingly good at it. "Hold your partner firmly!" was Mrs Gaynor's constant injunction, one I was glad to follow, especially when Maureen was my partner on Sunday nights. I danced mostly with her, needless to say, but club protocol forbade exclusive pairing, and I was a rather popular choice in "ladies' invitation" sets because of my nifty footwork. It was of course ballroom dancing – quickstep, foxtrot and waltz – with a few old-time dances thrown in for variety. We danced to strict-tempo music by Victor Sylvester, diversified with popular hits by Nat King Cole, Frankie Laine, Guy Mitchell and other vocalists of the day. Pee Wee Hunt's "Twelfth Street Rag" was a great favourite, but jiving was not allowed – it was expressly forbidden by Father Jerome – and the solo twisting, ducking and swaying that passes for dancing nowadays was still in the womb of time, awaiting its birth in the sixties. When, nowadays, I put my head inside a discothèque or nightclub patronized by young people, I'm struck by the contrast between the eroticism of the ambience – the dim, lurid lighting, the orgasmic throb of the music, the tight-fitting, provocative clothes – and the tactile impoverishment of the actual dancing. I suppose they have so much physical contact afterwards that they don't miss it on the dance floor, but for us it was the other way round. Dancing meant that, even in a church youth club, you were actually allowed to hold a girl in your arms in public, perhaps a girl you'd never even met before you asked her to dance, feel her thighs brush against yours under her rustling petticoats, sense the warmth of her bosom against your chest, inhale the scent behind her ears or the smell of shampoo from her freshly washed hair as it tickled your cheek. Of course you had to pretend that this wasn't the point of it, you had to chat about the weather or the music or whatever while you steered your partner around the floor, but the licence for physical sensation was considerable. Imagine a cocktail party where all the guests are masturbating while ostensibly preoccupied with sipping white wine and discussing the latest books and plays, and you have some idea what dancing was like for adolescents in the early nineteen-fifties.

Admittedly, Father Jerome did his best to damp down the fires of lust, insisting on opening the evening's proceedings with a tedious recitation of the "Hail Mary" ten times in succession, something he referred to as "a mystery of the holy rosary" – it was certainly a mystery to me what anybody got out of the droning gabble of words. And he hung about afterwards, eyeing the dancing couples to make sure everything was decent and above board. There was actually a clause in the club rules – it was known as Rule Five, and was the subject of mildly risqué humour among the members – that there must always be light visible between dancing couples; but it was not rigidly enforced or observed. Anyway, Father Jerome usually left (it was rumoured to drink whisky and play whist with some cronies in the presbytery) well before the last waltz, when we would turn out some of the lights, and the bolder spirits would dance cheek-to-cheek, or at least chest-to-chest. Naturally I always ensured that Maureen was my partner then. She was not an exceptionally good dancer, and when I saw her partnered by other boys she sometimes looked positively clumsy, which I didn't mind at all. She was responsive to my firm lead, and laughed with delight when I whirled her round and round at the end of a record, making her skirts swirl. She had two outfits for the Sunday-night socials: a black taffeta skirt worn with various blouses, and a white frock covered with pink roses that fitted her tightly round her bosom, which was shapely and well-developed for her age.

I was soon accepted by the other members of the club, especially after I joined its football team, which played on Sunday afternoons against other South London parishes, some with similarly bizarre names to ours, so you would get scorelines like, "Immaculate Conception 2, Precious Blood 1" or "Perpetual Succour 3, Forty Martyrs nil." I played at inside right, to such good effect that we won the league championship that season. I was top scorer, with twenty-six goals. The manager of a rival team found out that I wasn't a Catholic and made an official complaint that I shouldn't have been allowed to play in the league. For a while it looked as if the trophy might be taken away from us, but after we threatened to pull out of the league we were allowed to keep it.

We played on bumpy, sloping pitches in public parks, travelling by tram or bus, and changing in damp cheerless huts with a toilet and cold-water handbasin if we were lucky, but never baths or showers. The mud caked on my knees on the way home, and sitting in the bath later I would slowly straighten my legs in the water and pretend my knees were two volcanic islands sinking into the sea. When they had disappeared my engorged penis would rear up from the steaming, murky water like a wicked sea-serpent, as I thought about Maureen who would be washing her hair at the same time in preparation for the Sunday-evening social. She had told me she usually did this while taking a bath, because it was difficult to rinse her long hair while bending over a sink. I imagined her sitting in the warm, sudsy water, filling an enamel jug from the tap, pouring it over her head and making the long tresses stick to the curve of her breasts, like a picture of a mermaid I had seen once.

Maureen and some of the other girls from the youth club used to come to the Sunday-afternoon football matches to support us. When I scored a goal, I would look for her on the sidelines as I trotted back to the centre circle with the modest, self-contained demeanour I imitated from Charlie Vaughan, the Charlton Athletic centre-forward, and receive her adoring smile. I remember one goal in particular I scored with a spectacular flying header, I think it was a match against Our Lady of Perpetual Succour, Brickley, the neigh-bouring parish, and therefore something of a local derby. The goal was a pure fluke, actually, because I was never a great header of the ball. It was two-all in the last minutes of the game when I collected the ball from a clearance by our goalkeeper, beat a couple of opposing players and passed the ball out to our right-winger. His name was Jenkins – Jenksy, we called him: a small, prematurely wizened, stooped-shouldered boy, who smoked a Woodbine not only before and after every match, but also at half-time, and had been known to beg a drag of a spectator's cigarette during a lull in the game itself. In spite of appearances, he was surprisingly fast, especially going downhill, as he was on this occasion. He scuttled down the wing towards the corner-flag and crossed the ball, as he usually did, without looking, anxious to get rid of it before the opposing left-back caught up and crunched into him. I came pounding into the penalty area just as the ball came across in front of me at about waist height. I launched myself into the air and by lucky chance caught it smack in the middle of my forehead. It went into the net like a rocket before the goalie could move. The fact that the goal *had* a net (not many pitches we played on ran to such refinements) made it all the more satisfying. The opposing players gaped at me. My team-mates pulled me to my feet and clapped me on the back. Maureen and the other girls from Immaculate Conception were jumping up and down on the sidelines, cheering like mad. I don't think I have ever experienced a moment of such pure exultation in my life since. It was that night, after walking Maureen home from the youth club social, that I touched her breast for the first time, outside her blouse.

That would have been about a year after I first spoke to her. We advanced in physical intimacy slowly, and by infinitesimal degrees, for several reasons: my inexperience, Maureen's innocence, her parents' suspicious surveillance. Mr and Mrs Kavanagh were very strict, even by the standards of those days. They couldn't stop us meeting at the youth club, and they could hardly object to my escorting her home afterwards, but they forbade her to go out with me alone, to the pictures or anywhere else. On Saturday evenings she was required to babysit while they went to an Irish Club in Peckham, but she wasn't allowed to have me in the house while they were out, and she wasn't allowed to visit me at home. We continued to meet every morning at the tram stop, of course (except that it was a bus stop, now: the London trams were being phased out, and the tracks ripped up and tarmacked over – my Dad was given a desk job in the depot, and didn't complain) and we left our respective houses early to have more time to chat. I used to hand Maureen love letters to read on her way to school – she told me never to post them because her parents would have been sure to intercept one sooner or later. I asked her to post hers to me because it seemed grown-up to be receiving private correspondence, especially in mauve envelopes smelling of lavender, driving my young brother frantic with frustrated curiosity. There was little danger that my parents would pry into their contents, which were in any case totally innocuous. The letters were written on mauve lavender-scented notepaper in a big round hand, with the little circles over the *is*. On reflection, I think she got the idea from the advertisements for Biro pens. She used to get told off for it at school. Apart from the brief morning encounters at the tram stop, we could only meet in the context of youth-club activities – the socials, the games nights, the football matches, and occasional rambles in the Kent and Surrey green belt in the summer months.

Perhaps these restrictions helped to keep us devoted to each other for so long. We never had time to become bored with each other's company, and in defying Maureen's parents' disapproval we felt as if we were enacting some deeply romantic drama. Nat King Cole said it all for us in "Too Young", rolling the vowels round in his mouth like boiled sweets, to a background of syrupy strings and plangent piano chords:

> They try to tell us we're too young,
> Too young to really be in love.
> They say that love's a word,
> A word we've only heard
> But can't begin to know the meaning of.
> And yet we're not too young to know,
> This love will last though years may go . . .

It was our favourite tune, and I would always make sure that Maureen was my partner when somebody put it on the turntable.

Almost the only time we had alone together was when I walked her home from the youth-club socials on Sunday nights. At first, awkward and unsure of how to comport myself in this novel situation, I used to slouch along with my hands in my pockets, a yard apart from Maureen. But one cold night, to my intense delight, she drew close to me as if for warmth, and slipped her arm through mine. I swelled with the pride of possession. Now she was truly my girlfriend. She chattered on my arm like a canary in a cage – about the people at the youth club, about her schoolfriends and teachers, about her family, with its huge network of relations in Ireland and even America.

Maureen was always brimming over with news, gossip, anecdotes, whenever we met. It was trivial stuff, but enchanting to me. I tried to forget about my own school when I was out of it, and my family seemed less interesting than Maureen's, so I was content to let her make most of the conversational running. But occasionally she would question me about my parents and my early life, and she loved me to tell her how for so long I used to look out for her every morning at the corner of Hatchford Five Ways without ever daring to speak to her.

Even after she took my arm on the way home from the youth club, weeks passed before I ventured to kiss her goodnight outside her house. It was a clumsy, botched kiss, half on her mouth, half on her cheek, which took her by surprise, but it was returned with warmth. She broke away immediately with a murmured "Goodnight," and ran up the steps to her front door; but the next morning at the tram stop there was a dazed glow in her eyes, a new softness in her smile, and I knew that the kiss had been as momentous for her as for me.

I had to learn to kiss as I had learned to dance. In our male-dominated household there was almost a taboo on touching of any kind, whereas in Maureen's family, she told me, it was customary for all the children, even the boys, to kiss their parents goodnight. That was a very different matter from kissing me, of course, but it explained how naturally Maureen lifted her face to mine, how comfortable and relaxed she felt in my arms. Oh the rapture of those first embraces! What is it about kissing in adolescence? I suppose it gives you an intuitive sense of what sex will be like, the girl's lips and mouth being like the secret inside flesh of her body: pink, wet, tender. Certainly what we used to call French kissing, pushing your tongues into each other's mouths, is a kind of mimic intercourse. But it was a long time before Maureen and I went as far as that. For many months it seemed quite intoxicating enough to simply kiss, clasped in each other's arms, lips to lips, eyes closed, holding our breath for minutes at a time.

We used to do it in the shadows of the basement area of Maureen's house, putting up with the smell from the nearby dustbins for the sake of privacy. We stood there in all weathers. If it was raining, Maureen would hold her umbrella over both of us as we embraced. In cold weather I would undo the toggles of my duffelcoat (a proud new acquisition for weekend wear) and open the front of her raincoat to create a kind of tent in which to draw her close. One night I found the rose-patterned dress had a button missing at the back and slid my hand through the gap and felt her bare skin between her shoulder-blades. She shuddered and opened her lips a little more as she pressed them against mine. Weeks later I found my way through the front of her blouse, and caressed her stomach over a slippery satin slip. So it went on. Inch by inch I extended my exploration of her body, virgin territory in every sense of the word. Maureen was tender and yielding in my arms, wanting to be loved, loving to be caressed, but quite without sexual self-consciousness. She must have often felt my erect penis through our clothing as we embraced, but she never remarked on it, nor gave any sign of being embarrassed by it. Perhaps she thought mature widdlers were permanently hard as bones. Erections were more of a problem for me. When we had to part (it was dangerous to linger in the area for more than ten or fifteen minutes, for Mr Kavanagh knew when the youth-club socials ended and would sometimes come out on to the front porch to look down the road, while we cowered, half-frightened, half-amused, just underneath him) I would wait till Maureen had run up the steps and let herself into the house before walking off stiffly and bent slightly forward, like a man on stilts.

I suppose Maureen must have experienced her own symptoms of sexual arousal, but I doubt whether she recognized them as such. She had a naturally pure mind, pure without being prudish. Dirty jokes left her looking genuinely blank. She talked about wanting to get married and have children when she grew up, but she didn't seem to connect this with sexuality. Yet she loved to be kissed and cuddled. She purred in my arms like a kitten. Such sensuality and innocence could hardly co-exist nowadays, I believe, when teenagers are exposed to so much sexual information and imagery. Never mind the soft-porn videos and magazines available from any High Street video store or newsagent – your average 15-certificate movie contains scenes and language that would have had half the audience ejaculating into their trousers forty years ago, and have sent the makers and distributors to gaol. No wonder kids today want to have sex as soon as they're able. I wonder if they even bother with kissing at all, now, before they get their kit off and jump into bed.

I was less pure-minded than Maureen, but not much more knowing. Though I indulged in vague fantasies of having sex with her, especially just before falling asleep, and had frequent wet dreams in consequence, I had no intention of seducing her, and would certainly have made a terrible hash of it if I had tried. I set my sights no higher than getting to feel her naked breasts. But that was a kind of seduction when I accomplished it.

I had got as far as cupping one breast gently, inside her blouse, as we kissed, feeling the stitching of her brassière like Braille on my fingertips, when her Catholic conscience kicked in. In retrospect, it's surprising that it hadn't done so before. The trigger was a "retreat" at her school – a funny name, it seemed for me, for the event as she described it, three days of sermons, devotions and periods of compulsory silence, though the military associations were appropriate enough to its immediate effect on our relationship. It was a Dunkirk of the flesh. The visiting priest running the retreat (Maureen described him as big and grey-bearded, like pictures of God the Father, with piercing eyes that seemed to look right into your soul) had addressed the Fifth-Form girls in the presence of a grimly nodding Mother Superior on the subject of Holy Purity, and frightened them all silly with the awful consequences of desecrating their Temples of the Holy Ghost, as he designated their bodies. "If any girl here," he thundered, and Maureen claimed that he looked especially at her as he spoke, "should cause a boy to commit a sin of impurity in thought, word or deed, by the way she dresses or behaves, she is as guilty of that sin as he. More guilty, because the male of our species is less able to control licentious desires than the female." Afterwards the girls had to go to confession to him, and he winkled out of them the details of such liberties as they had allowed boys to take with their Temples of the Holy Ghost. It seems very obvious to me now that he was a dirty old man who got his kicks out of prying into the sexual feelings and experiences of vulnerable adolescent girls, and making them cry. He certainly made Maureen cry. So did I, when she told me I mustn't touch her "there" any more.

If there was one element of the Catholic religion above all others that made me determined to remain a Protestant, or an atheist (I wasn't quite sure what I really believed), it was Confession. From time to time Maureen made efforts to interest me in her faith, and I knew without having to be told that her dearest wish was to be the agent of my conversion. I thought it prudent to put in the occasional appearance at Benediction on Sunday evenings, to keep her happy and justify my membership of the youth club, but I steered clear of Mass after giving it a couple of tries. It was mostly in Latin (a subject that made my life particularly miserable at school until I was allowed to drop it and substitute Art) mumbled inaudibly by a priest with his back turned, and seemed to bore the rest of the congregation almost as much as it bored me, since many of them were saying their rosaries while it went on – though, God knows, the Rosary was even more boring, and unfortunately was an official part of Benediction. No wonder Catholics burst out of the church in such high spirits after these services, talking and laughing and breaking out packets of cigarettes: it was sheer relief from the almost unendurable boredom inside. The only exception was the Midnight Mass at Christmas, which was jollied up by carol-singing and the excitement of staying out late. Other aspects of the Catholic religion, like the startlingly realistic paintings and sculptures of the Crucifixion inside the church, the terraces of guttering votive candles, not eating meat on Fridays, giving up sweets for Lent, praying to Saint Anthony if you lost something, and acquiring "indulgences" as a kind of insurance policy for the afterlife, seemed merely quaintly superstitious. But Confession was in a different class.

One day when we were in the church on our own for some reason – I think Maureen was lighting a candle for some "intention" or other, perhaps my conversion – I peeped into one of the cupboard-like confessionals built against the side of the church. On one side was a door with the priest's name on it; on the other side a curtain. I drew back the curtain and saw the padded kneeler and the small square of wire mesh, like a flattened meat-cover, through which you whispered your sins to the priest. The mere idea made my flesh creep. Ironic, really, considering how dependent I became on psychotherapy later in life, but in adolescence nothing is more repugnant than the idea of sharing your most secret and shaming thoughts with a grown-up.

Maureen tried to rid me of my prejudice. Religious Instruction was her best subject at school. She had got to the convent and held her own there by conscientious hard work rather than natural brilliance, and the rote-learning of R.I. suited her abilities. "It's not the priest you're telling, it's God." "Why not just tell God, then, in a prayer?" "Because it wouldn't be a sacrament." Out of my theological depth, I grunted sceptically. "Anyway," Maureen went on, "the priest doesn't know who you are. It's dark." "Suppose he recognizes your voice?" I said. Maureen conceded that she usually avoided going to Father Jerome for that very reason, but insisted that even if the priest did recognize your voice he wasn't allowed to let on, and he would never under any circumstances reveal what you confessed to anybody else, because of the seal of confession. "Even if you'd committed murder?" Even then, she assured me, though there was a catch: "He wouldn't give you absolution unless you promised to give yourself up." And what was absolution, I enquired, pronouncing it "ablution" by mistake and making Maureen giggle, before she launched into a long rigmarole about forgiveness and grace and penance and purgatory and temporal punishment, that made about as much sense to me as if she had recited the rules of contract bridge. I asked her once, early in our relationship, what sins she confessed herself and not surprisingly she wouldn't tell me. But she did tell me about her Confession on the school retreat, and how the priest had said it was a sin for me to touch her as I had been doing and that I mustn't do it any more and that to avoid "the occasion of sin" we mustn't go down into the area and cuddle when I saw her home but just shake hands or perhaps exchange a single chaste kiss.

Dismayed by this turn of events, I concentrated all my resources on reversing it. I protested, I argued, I wheedled; I was eloquent, I was pathetic, I was cunning. And of course, in the end, I won. The boy always does win such struggles, if the girl can't bear to risk losing him, and Maureen couldn't. No doubt she had given me her heart because I was the first to ask for it. But I was also quite good-looking at that stage of my life. I hadn't yet acquired the nickname Tubby, and I still had my hair – rather gorgeous blond hair, as a matter of fact, which I combed back in a billowing wave petrified with Brylcreem. Also I was the best dancer in the youth club and star of the football team. Such things matter to young girls more than exam results and career prospects. We both took our O-Level exams that year. Maureen achieved five lowish passes, enough to proceed to the sixth form; I failed everything except English Literature and Art, and left school to work in the office of a big theatrical impresario in the West End, having responded to an advertisement in the *Evening Standard*. I was only a glorified office-boy, to tell the truth, franking mail, taking it to the Post Office, fetching sandwiches for the staff, and so on, but something of the glamour of the business rubbed off on me. Famous actors and actresses passed through our dingy office above a Shaftesbury Avenue theatre on the way to the boss's inner sanctum, and they would smile and say a word to me as I took their coats or fetched them cups of coffee. I quickly picked up the language of show business and responded to its febrile excitements, the highs and lows of hits and flops. I suppose Maureen recognized that I was maturing rapidly in this sophisticated milieu, and in danger of growing away from her. I was sometimes given complimentary tickets to shows, but there was no hope that Mr and Mrs Kavanagh would let her go to them with me. We no longer met every morning at the tram stop, because I now took a Southern Electric train from Hatchford Station to Charing Cross. Our meetings on Sundays and our walks home from the youth-club socials therefore became all the more precious. She could not deny me her kisses for long. I coaxed her into the shadows at the bottom of the area steps and slowly I inched my way back to the state of intimacy that had existed before.

I don't know what compact she made with God or her conscience – I thought it prudent not to enquire. I knew that she went to confession once a month, and to communion every week, and that her parents would get suspicious if she deviated from this routine; and I knew, because she had explained it to me once, that you couldn't get absolution for a sin unless you promised not to do it again, and that to swallow the consecrated host in a state of sin was another sin, worse than the first. There was some kind of distinction between big sins and little sins she may have used as a loophole. Big sins were called mortal sins. I can't remember what the little ones were called, but you could go to communion without being absolved of them. I'm very much afraid, though, that the poor girl thought breast-touching was a mortal sin, and believed she was in serious danger of going to hell if she should die without warning.

Her air and expression subtly altered in that period, though I was probably the only one to register the change. She lost some of her usual exuberance. There was a kind of abstractedness in her eyes, a wanness about her smile. Even her complexion suffered: her skin lost its glow, a rash of pimples occasionally broke out round her mouth. But most significant of all, she allowed me more freedoms than before, as if she had abandoned all hope of being good, or as she would have put it, in a state of grace, and further defence of her modesty was therefore pointless. When, one warm September night, I unbuttoned her blouse, and unfastened, with infinite care and delicacy, like a burglar picking a lock, the hook and eye that fastened her brassière, I encountered no resistance, nor did she utter a word of protest. She just stood there in the dark, beside the dustbins, passive and trembling very slightly, like a lamb brought to the sacrifice. She wasn't wearing a slip. Holding my breath I gently released a breast, the left one, from its cup. It rolled into my palm like a ripe fruit. God! I've never felt a sensation like it, before or since, like the first feel of Maureen's young breast – so soft, so smooth, so tender, so firm, so elastic, so mysteriously gravity-defying. I lifted the breast a centi-metre, and weighed it in my cupped palm, then gently lowered my hand again until it just fitted the shape without supporting it. That her breast should still hang there, proud and firm, seemed as miraculous a phenomenon as the Earth itself floating in space. I took the weight again and gently squeezed the breast as it lolled in my palm like a naked cherub. I don't know how long we stood there in the dark, not speaking, hardly breathing, until she murmured, "I must go," put her hands behind her back to do up the fastener of her brassière, and vanished up the steps.

From that night onwards our kissing sessions invariably incorporated my touching her breasts under her clothing. It was the climax of the ritual, like the priest raising the glittering monstrance aloft at Benediction. I learned the contours of her breasts so well that I could have moulded them in plaster blindfolded. They were almost perfect hemispheres, tipped with small pointed nipples that hardened under my touch like tiny erections. How I longed to see them as well as touch them, and to suck and nuzzle them and bury my head in the warm valley between them! I was also beginning to harbour designs on the lower half of her anatomy, and to dwell licentiously on the possibility of getting my hands inside her knickers. Obviously none of this could be decently accomplished standing up in the dank basement area. Somehow or other I must contrive to be alone with her indoors somewhere. I was racking my brains for some such stratagem, when I suffered a sudden and unexpected setback. As I was seeing her home one night, she came to a halt under a lamp-post at some distance from her house and said, looking at me earnestly and twisting her hair in her fingers, that the kissing, and everything that went with it, had to stop. It was all because of the youth-club Nativity play.

The idea of the play had come from Bede Harrington, the chairman of the club committee. I had never heard of anyone called Bede before, and when I first met him I asked him in all innocence if his name was spelled B-e-a-d, as in rosary. He obviously thought I was taking the piss and informed me stiffly that Bede was the name of an ancient British saint, a monk known as the Venerable Bede. Bede Harrington himself enjoyed a fair amount of veneration in the parish, especially from the adult members. He was a year or two older than me and Maureen, and had had a brilliant academic career at St Aloysius's, the local Catholic grammar school. At the time of which I write he was Head Boy, in the third-year Sixth, and had just obtained a place at Oxford to study – or, as he liked to say, showing off his inside knowledge, "read" – English the following year. He was tall, with a long, thin, white face, its pallor heightened by his heavy horn-rimmed glasses, and by the coarse black hair that seemed to part in the wrong place, since it was always sticking up in the air or falling over his eyes. In spite of his intellectual achievements, Bede Harrington lacked the accomplishments most highly valued in the youth club. He didn't dance and he didn't play football, or indeed do any other sport. He had always been excused games at school because of his shortsightedness, and he claimed simply not to be interested in dancing. I believe he was in fact very interested in the opportunities it offered to get into physical contact with girls, but knew that, with his gangly, ill-co-ordinated limbs and enormous feet, he probably wouldn't be much good at it, and couldn't bear to look ridiculous while he was learning. Bede Harrington had to excel at whatever he did. So he made his mark on the youth club by getting himself elected as chairman of the committee and bossing everybody else around. He edited a club Newsletter, a smudgy, cyclostyled document written largely by himself, and forced upon the reluctant membership occasional events of an intellectual nature, like debates and quizzes, at which he could shine. During the Sunday-night socials he was to be seen in deep conference with Father Jerome, or frowning over the club's catering accounts, or sitting alone on a tilted chair, with his hands in his pockets and his long legs stretched out, surveying the shuffling, rotating throng with a faint, superior smile, like a school-master indulging the childish pastimes of his charges. There was a wistful longing in his eyes, though, and it sometimes seemed to me that they lingered with particular covetousness on Maureen, as she swayed in my arms to the music.

The Nativity play was a typical piece of Bede Harrington self-promotion. Not only did he write the script himself; he directed it, acted in it, designed it, selected the recorded music for it, and did almost everything else to do with it except sew the costumes, a task delegated to his adoring mother and hapless sisters. The play was to be performed in the Infants' school on three evenings in the week before Christmas, and again at a local old people's home run by nuns, for one night only, on January 6th, the feast of the Epiphany –

"Twelfth Night", as he pedantically informed us at the first auditions.

These took place on a Wednesday club night early in November. I went along to keep a proprietorial eye on Maureen. Bede Harrington had taken her aside the previous Sunday evening while I was dancing with somebody else, and extracted a promise from her to read for the part of the Virgin Mary. She was flattered and excited at the prospect, and since I was unable to persuade her to withdraw, I thought I had better join her. Bede looked surprised and not very pleased to see me at the auditions. "I didn't think this was your sort of thing," he said. "And, to be perfectly honest, I'm not sure it would be quite right to have a non-Catholic in the parish Nativity play. I'd have to ask Father Jerome."

It came as no surprise that Bede had reserved the part of Joseph for himself. I daresay he would have doubled as the Angel Gabriel, and played all three Kings as well, if it had been practicable. Maureen was quickly confirmed in the part of Mary. I flipped through a copy of the cyclostyled script in search of a suitable part for myself. "What about Herod?" I said. "Surely you don't have to be a Catholic to play him?"

"You can have a go if you like," Bede said grudgingly.

I did the scene where Herod realizes that the Three Kings are not going to return to tell him where they found the infant Messiah, as he had hypocritically asked them to do, pretending he wanted to pay homage himself, and ruthlessly orders the massacre of every male child under two in the region of Bethlehem. As I mentioned earlier, acting was about the only thing I was any good at, at school. I gave a terrific audition. I out-Heroded Herod, to coin a phrase. When I finished the other aspirant actors spontaneously applauded, and Bede could hardly avoid giving me the part. Maureen looked at me adoringly: not only was I the best dancer and top scorer in the club, I was also obviously the star actor too. She herself was not, to be honest, much of an actress. Her voice was too small, her body-language too timid, to communicate across the footlights. (A figure of speech, of course: we had no footlights. All we had in the way of stage lighting was a battery of desk lamps with coloured bulbs.) But her part mainly required her to look meek and serenely beautiful, which she was able to do without speaking or moving about much.

I quite enjoyed the first weeks of rehearsals. I particularly enjoyed teasing Bede Harrington and undermining his authority. I quarrelled with his direction, offered suggestions for improving his script, continually improvised new business, and blinded him with theatrical science, throwing around technical terms I had picked up from work, and with which he was unfamiliar, like "block", "dry" and "up-stage". I said the title of his play, *The Fruit of the Womb* (an allusion to the "Hail Mary") reminded me of "Fruit of the Loom" on the label inside my vests, provoking such mirth that he was obliged to change it to *The Story of Christmas*. I clowned outrageously, reading the part of Herod in a variety of funny voices, impersonations of Tony Hancock and Bluebottle and Father Jerome, and causing the rest of the cast to collapse in hysterics. Bede, needless to say, responded to these antics with ill grace, and threatened to expel me at one point, but I backed down and apologized. I didn't want to be fired from the show. Not only was it rather fun, but it afforded me many extra opportunities to meet Maureen, and see her home, which Mr and Mrs Kavanagh could not possibly veto. And I certainly didn't want to leave her unprotected in Bede Harrington's directorial power. I had noticed that, in his role as Joseph, he took every opportunity to put a supporting arm round Mary's shoulder on the journey to Bethlehem and during the Flight into Egypt. By watching his performance very intently, with a faint, sardonic smile on my face, I was confident that I deprived him of any thrill from these physical contacts; and afterwards, when I walked Maureen home, I enjoyed my own sensual pleasures all the more.

Then Bede succumbed, rather late in life, to chicken pox, and was off sick for two weeks. He sent a message that we should carry on rehearsing under the direction of a boy called Peter Marello, who was playing the Chief Shepherd. But Peter was also captain of the football team and a good mate of mine. He deferred readily to my judgement in matters theatrical, as did the other members of the cast, and I became in effect the acting director. I thought I improved the show no end, but Bede wasn't best pleased when he returned, spotted with fading pustules and pockmarks, to see the result.

I had cut out the tedious recitation of the whole of T.S. Eliot's "The Journey of the Magi" which Bede had put into the mouth of one of the Three Kings, and written two big new scenes for Herod, based on memories of Sunday-School bible stories and Scripture lessons at school. One had Herod dying horribly, eaten up by worms – this promised to be a wonderful Grand-Guignol spectacle, involving the use of Heinz tinned spaghetti in tomato sauce as a prop. The other was a kind of flash-forward to the beheading of John the Baptist by Herod at the behest of Salomé. I had persuaded a girl called Josie, in principle, to do the dance of the seven veils in a body-stocking; she was a cheerful peroxide-assisted blonde who worked in Woolworths, wore bright red lipstick, and had a reputation for being a good sport, or rather vulgar, according to your point of view. Unfortunately it appeared that I had muddled up three different Herods in the New Testament, so Bede deleted these "excrescences", as he called them, without my being able to put up much of a fight. Even so, I think it is safe to say that the character of Herod figured more prominently in our nativity play than in any version since the Wakefield cycle.

We were now well into December, and Father Jerome, who had left us very much to our own devices up till then, requested to see a run-through. It was perhaps just as well that Salomé's dance of the seven veils had been cut, because even without it our play was insufficiently reverent for Father Jerome's taste. To do Bede Harrington justice, he had tried to get away from the usual series of pious tableaux, and to write something more modern, or as we would learn to say in another decade, "relevant". After the Annunciation, for example, Mary suffered from her Nazarene neighbours something of the prejudice experienced by unmarried mothers in modern Britain, and the difficulty of finding room in the inn at Bethlehem was obliquely linked to the contemporary housing shortage. Father Jerome insisted on the removal of all such unscriptural material. But it was the spirit of the whole production which really disturbed him. It was too profane. "It's more like a pantomime than a Nativity play," he said, baring his fangs in a mirthless grin. "Herod, for instance, puts the Holy Family in the shade entirely." Bede looked at me reproachfully, but his long face lengthened even more as Father Jerome went on: "That's not Laurence's fault. He's a fine actor, giving his best. The trouble is with the rest of youse. There's not half enough spirituality. Just consider what this play is *about*. The Word made Flesh. God Himself come down from heaven as a helpless babby, to dwell amongst men. Tink of what it meant to Mary to be singled out to be the Mother of God – " here he looked searchingly at Maureen, who blushed deeply and lowered her eyes. "Tink what it meant to Saint Joseph, responsible for the safety of the Mother of God, and her infant Son. Tink what it meant to the shepherds, poor hopeless fellas whose lives were little better than the beasts they looked after, when the Angel of the Lord appeared to them saying, 'I bring you tidings of great joy, that shall be to all people, for this day is born to you a saviour, which is Christ the Lord.' You have got to *become* those people. It's not enough to *play* your parts. You've got to *pray* your parts. You should begin every rehearsal with a prayer."

Father Jerome went on for some time in this vein. It was in its way a remarkable speech, worthy of Stanislavsky. He completely trans-formed the atmosphere of our rehearsals, which he regularly attended from that day on. The cast approached their parts with a new seriousness and dedication. Father Jerome had convinced them that they must draw on their own spiritual life for inspiration, and if they didn't have a spiritual life they had better acquire one. This of course was very bad news for me, as regards my relationship with Maureen. After his public homily, I noticed that the priest drew her aside and engaged her in earnest conversation. There was something omi-nously suggestive of a penitent in her posture as she sat beside him, her eyes lowered, hands joined in her lap, nodding silently as she listened. Sure enough, on our way home that evening, she stopped me at the corner of her street and said, "It's late, Laurence. I'd better go straight in. Let's say goodnight." "But we can't kiss properly here," I said. She was silent for a moment, twisting and untwisting a strand of hair round her finger. "I don't think we should kiss any more," she said. "Not like we usually do. Not while I'm Our Lady."

Perhaps Father Jerome had observed that Maureen and I were very close. Maybe he suspected that I was leading her astray in the Temple of the Holy Ghost department. I don't know, but he certainly did the business on her conscience that evening. He told her what an extraordinary privilege it was for any young girl to portray the Mother of God. He reminded her that her own name was an Irish form of "Mary". He said how pleased and proud her parents must be that she had been chosen for the part, and how she must strive to be worthy of it, in thought, word and deed. As Maureen relayed his words in a mumbled paraphrase I tried to laugh off their effect, without success. Then I attempted rational persuasion, holding her hands and looking earnestly into her eyes, also in vain. Then I tried sulking. "Good-night, then," I said, plunging my hands into my raincoat pockets. "You can kiss me once," said Maureen miserably, her lifted face blue under the streetlamp. "Just once? Under Rule Five?" I sneered. "Don't," she said, her lip trembling, her eyes filling with tears. "Oh, grow up, Maureen," I said, and turned on my heel and walked away.

I spent a miserable, restless night, and next morning I was late for work because instead of catching my usual train I stood at the corner of Hatchford Five Ways and waited for Maureen. I could see her figure stiffen with sudden self-consciousness, even a hundred yards away, as she recognized me. Of course she had spent a wretched night too – her face was pale and her eyelids swollen. We were reconciled almost before my words of apology were out, and she went off to school with a buoyant step and a smile on her face.

I was confident that, as before, I would gradually overcome her scruples. I was wrong. It was no longer just a private matter of conscience for Maureen. She was convinced that to go on necking with me while portraying the Virgin Mary would be a kind of sacrilege, which might bring the wrath of God down not only upon herself but upon the play itself and everyone concerned in it. She still loved me, it caused her real anguish to deny me her embraces, but she was determined to remain pure for the duration of the production. Indeed, she made a kind of vow to that effect, after going to Confession (to old Father Malachi, the parish priest) and Communion, the weekend after Father Jerome's intervention.

If I'd had any sense or tact, I would have resigned myself to the situation, and bided my time. But I was young, and arrogant and selfish. I didn't relish the prospect of a chaste Christmas and New Year, a season when it seemed to me one was entitled to expect a greater, not a lesser, degree of sensual licence. The 6th of January seemed a long way off. I suggested a compromise: no necking until after the first run of the play was over, but a relaxation of the rule between Christmas Eve and New Year's Eve, inclusive. Maureen shook her head. "Don't," she murmured, "Please don't bargain with me." "Well, when then?" I insisted brutally. "How soon after the last performance are we going to get back to normal?" "I don't know," she said, "I'm not sure it *was* normal." "Are you trying to tell me we're never going to?" I demanded. Then she burst into tears, and I sighed and apologized and we made it up, for a while, until I couldn't resist nagging her again.

All this time the play was in the throes of final rehearsals, so we were forced constantly into each other's company. But tempers were short and nerves frayed all round, so I don't think anyone in the cast noticed that Maureen and I were going through a sticky patch except perhaps Josie, who had a small part as the Innkeeper's wife. I had long been aware that Josie fancied me from the regularity with which she asked me to dance in Ladies' Invitations, and I was aware, too, that she was jealous of Maureen's starring role in *The Story of Christmas*. Apart from Herod, Josie's was the only really unsympathetic character in the play; we were drawn together in rehearsals by this circumstance, and by a shared indifference to the religiosity which had overtaken the production, and deprived it of most of its fun. When the rest of the cast solemnly recited the rosary at the beginning of every rehearsal, led by Father Jerome or Bede Harrington, I would catch her eye and try to make her giggle. I flattered her performance at rehearsals and coached her in her lines. At the Sunday-night socials I asked her to dance more frequently than before.

Maureen observed all this, of course. The dumb pain I saw in her eyes gave me an occasional pang of remorse, but didn't alter my cruel design, to bring pressure on her virtue by arousing her jealousy. Perhaps subconsciously I wanted our relationship to end. I was trying to crush something in myself as well as in her. I called it childishness, stupidity, naivety, in my own mind, but I might have called it innocence. The world of the parish youth club, which had seemed so enchanting when Maureen first introduced me to it, now seemed . . . well, parochial, especially in comparison with the world I encountered at work. From office gossip about affairs between actors and actresses, casting-couches and theatrical parties, I picked up a lurid and exciting notion of adult sexual behaviour against which Maureen's convent-girl scruples about letting me fondle her tits (as they were coarsely referred to in the office) seemed simply absurd. I ached to lose my virginity, and it obviously wasn't going to be with Maureen, unless and until I married her, a possibility as remote as flying to the moon. In any case, I had observed what married life on a low income was like in my own home, and it didn't appeal to me. I aspired to a freer, more expansive lifestyle, though I had no idea what form it might take.

The crisis came on the night of the last performance of the Nativity play before Christmas. It was a full house. The show had enjoyed great word-of-mouth in the parish, and there had even been a review, short but favourable, in the local newspaper. The review was unsigned and I would have suspected Bede Harrington of having written it himself if the writer hadn't been particularly complimentary about my own performance. I think the backstage struggle of wills between myself and Maureen actually imparted a special intensity to our performances. My Herod was more muted than in the early days of rehearsals, but more authentically cruel. I felt a thrilling *frisson*, a kind of collective shudder, run through the audience as I gave orders for the Massacre of the Innocents. And there was a tragic quality in Maureen's Virgin Mary, even in the Annunciation scene – "as if," said the anonymous reviewer, "she saw prophetically the Seven Swords of Sorrow that would pierce her heart in the years to come." (Come to think of it, perhaps Father Jerome wrote that review.)

We didn't have a cast party, exactly, at the end of the three-night run, but there was a sort of celebration with cocoa and chocolate biscuits and crisps organized by Peter Marello's girlfriend Anne, our stage manager, when we had taken off our costumes and washed off our make-up and dismantled the set and stored it away for the final performance at Epiphany. Father Jerome blessed and congratulated us and departed. We were exhausted, but jubilant, and reluctant to break up the collective euphoria by going home. Even Maureen was happy. Her parents and her brothers and sisters had come back to see the show a second time, and she had heard her father shouting "Bravo!" from the back of the hall when we took our curtain call. I had discouraged my own parents from coming, but my Mum had attended the first night and pronounced it "very nice though a bit loud" (she meant the music, especially the "Ride of the Valkyries" which accompanied the Flight into Egypt) and my brother, who had accompanied her, looked at me the next morning almost with respect. Bede Harrington, his head quite turned by success, was full of grandiose plans to write a Passion Play for the following Easter. It was to be in blank verse, I seem to remember, with speaking parts for the various instruments of the Crucifixion – the Cross, the Nails, the Crown of Thorns, etc. In magnanimous mood, he offered me the part of Scourge without the formality of an audition. I said I would think about it.

The conversation turned to our various plans for Christmas, and I chose this moment to announce that my boss had given me four complimentary tickets for his production of *The Babes in the Wood* at the Prince of Wales on Boxing Day. These were really intended for me to take my family, but some imp put it into my head to impress the company with a casually generous gesture, and to put Maureen to the test at the same time. I asked Peter and Anne if they would like to go with Maureen and me. They accepted readily, but Maureen, as I had anticipated, said that her parents wouldn't let her. "What, not even at Christmas?" I said. She looked at me, pleading with her eyes not to be publicly humiliated. "You know what they're like," she said. "Pity," I said, aware that Josie was listening intently. "Anyone else interes- ted?" "Ooh, I'll go, I love pantos," Josie said promptly. She added, "You don't mind, do you, Maureen?" "No, I don't mind," Maureen whispered. Her expression was stricken. I might as well have taken the dagger I wore on my belt as Herod, and plunged it into her heart.

There was an awkward pause for a moment, which I covered by recalling a near-disaster with a sagging backcloth in the crib scene of our play, and we were soon engaged in a noisy and hilarious recapitulation of the entire performance. Maureen didn't contribute, and when I looked round for her, she had disappeared. She had left without saying goodnight to anyone. I walked home alone, moodily kicking an empty tobacco tin ahead of me. I did not feel very pleased with myself, but I managed somehow to blame Maureen for "spoiling Christmas". I didn't join her at Midnight Mass as I had intended. Christmas Day at home passed in the usual claustrophobic stupor. I went through with the Boxing Day excursion to the pantomime, pretending to my parents that I only had a single ticket, and meeting Josie, Peter and Anne at Charing Cross station. Josie was dressed like a tart and had drenched herself in cheap scent. She daringly asked for gin and orange at the interval, nearly bankrupting me in the process, and laughed raucously at all the blue jokes in the show, much to the embarrassment of Peter and Anne. Afterwards I saw Josie home to her family's council flat, and embraced her in a dark space under the communal stairs to which she led me without preliminaries. She thrust her tongue halfway down my throat and clamped one of my hands firmly onto one of her breasts, which was encased in a wired, sharply pointed brassière. I had little doubt that she would have allowed me to go further, but had no inclination to do so. Her perfume did not entirely mask the smell of stale perspiration from her armpits, and I was already tired of her vacuous chatter and strident laugh.

The next day I received a letter from Maureen, posted on Christmas Eve, saying she thought it would be best if we didn't see each other for a while, apart from the last performance of the play. It was written in her round, girlish hand on the usual mauve notepaper smelling of lavender, but the *i*s were all dotted normally, not with the little bubbly circles. I didn't reply to the letter, but I sent one to Bede Harrington saying I couldn't make the last performance of the play, and recommending that he ask Peter Marello to double as Herod. I never went to the youth club again, and I dropped out of the football team. I missed the exercise, and it was probably from that time that my waistline began to expand, especially as I was acquiring a taste for beer. I became friendly with a young man called Nigel who worked in the box-office of the theatre over which our office was located, and he introduced me to a number of Soho pubs. We spent a lot of time together, and it was months before I realised that he was homosexually inclined. The girls in the office assumed that I must be too, so I made little headway with them. I didn't lose my virginity, in fact, until I was in the Army, doing National Service, and that was a quick and sordid business with a tipsy WRAC, up against the wall of a lorry park.

I saw Maureen occasionally in the months that followed the production of the Nativity play, in the street, or getting on and off a bus, but I didn't speak to her. If she saw me, she didn't show it. She looked increasingly girlish and unsophisticated to my eyes, in her eternal navy-blue raincoat and her unchanging hairstyle. Once, just after I received my National Service papers, we came face to face in a chemist's shop – I was going in as she was going out. We exchanged a few awkward words. I asked her about school. She said she was thinking of going in for nursing. She asked me about work. I told her I had just been called up, and that I hoped to be sent abroad and to see a bit of life.

In the event I was trained as a clerk and posted to a part of North Germany where beetroot fields stretched to the horizon and it was so cold in winter that I cried once on guard duty and the tears froze on my cheeks. The only escape I found from terminal boredom was through acting in and writing scripts for revues, pantomimes, drag shows and other home-made entertainments on the base. When I got back to civvy street I was determined to make my career in some branch of show business. I got a place in one of the less prestigious London drama schools, with a small scholarship which I supplemented by working in a pub at nights. I didn't see Maureen around Hatchford when I went back to visit Mum and Dad. I ran into Peter Marello once and he told me that she had left home to train as a nurse. That was about thirty-five years ago. I haven't seen or heard of her since.

Sunday 6th June. It took me a whole week to write that, doing practically nothing else. I printed off the last few pages at ten o'clock last night, and went out to stretch my legs and buy the Sunday papers. Men were unloading them from a van onto the pavement outside Leicester Square tube station, like fishermen selling their catch on the quayside, ripping open the bales of different sections – news, sport, business, arts – and hastily assembling the papers on the spot as the punters thrust out their money. It always gives me a kick to buy tomorrow's papers today, the illusion of getting a peep at the future. In fact, what I've been doing is catching up on the news of the past week. Nothing much has changed in the big wide world. Eleven people were killed when the Bosnian Serbs lobbed mortar shells into a football stadium in Sarajevo. Twenty-five UN soldiers were killed in an ambush by General Aidid's troops in Somalia. John Major has the lowest popularity rating of any British Prime Minister since polling began. I'm beginning to feel almost sorry for him. I wonder whether it isn't a cunning Tory plot to capture the low self-esteem vote.

I didn't buy any papers last week because I didn't want to be distracted from the task in hand. I hardly listened to the radio or watched television, either. I made an exception of the England – Norway match last Wednesday, and regretted it. What humiliation. Beaten 2–0 by a bunch of part-timers, and probably knocked out of the World Cup in consequence. They should declare a day of national mourning and send Graham Taylor to the salt mines. (He'd probably organize his chain-gang into a 3–5–2 formation, and have them all banging into each other like the England team.) It spoiled my concentration on the memoir for at least half a day, that result.

I don't think I've ever done anything quite like it before. Perhaps I'm turning into a book writer. There's no "you" in it, I notice. Instead of telling the story as I might to a friend or somebody in a pub, my usual way, I was trying to recover the truth of the original experience for myself, struggling to find the words that would do maximum justice to it. I revised it a lot. I'm used to that, of course – scriptwriting is mostly rewriting – but in response to the input of other people. This time I was the only reader, the only critic, and I revised as I went along. And I did something I haven't done since I bought my first electric typewriter – wrote the first drafts of each section in longhand. Somehow it seems more natural to try and recover the past with a pen in your hand than with your fingers poised over a keyboard. The pen is like a tool, a cutting or digging tool, slicing down through the roots, probing the rockbed of memory. Of course I used a bit of licence in the dialogue. It all happened forty years ago and I didn't take any notes. But I'm pretty sure that I've been true to the emotions, and that's the important thing. I can't leave the piece alone, though: I keep picking up the printed-out sheets, re-reading them, tinkering and revising, when what I should be doing is tidying up the flat.

The kitchen looks like a tip, heaped with soiled plates and empty takeaway food containers, there's a pile of unopened mail on the coffee table, and the answerphone has stopped receiving messages because the tape is full. Grahame was quite disgusted by the state of the place when he came in to watch the England match. He has higher standards of housekeeping than me – sometimes he borrows my dustpan and brush to sweep his little square of marbled floor in the porch. I fear his days of occupation may be numbered, though. The two American academics in number 4 are over for the summer vacation, and they entertain a lot. Understandably they object to having a resident bum in the entryway over whom their arriving and departing guests must step. They told me in the lift yesterday that they were going to complain to the police. I tried to persuade them that Grahame was no ordinary bum, but without making much impression. He doesn't help his cause by referring to them contempt-uously as "them yank poofters".

What reading and re-reading the memoir leaves me with is an overwhelming sense of loss. Not just the loss of Maureen's love, but the loss of innocence – hers and my own. In the past, whenever I thought of her – and it wasn't very often – it was with a kind of fond, wry, inner smile: nice kid, first girlfriend, how naive we both were, water under the bridge, that sort of thing. Going back over the history of our relationship in detail, I realized *for the first time* what an appalling thing I had done all those years ago. I broke a young girl's heart, callously, selfishly, wantonly.

I'm well aware, of course, that I wouldn't feel this way about it if I hadn't recently discovered Kierkegaard. It's really a very Kierkegaard-ian story. It has resemblances to "The Seducer's Diary", and resemblances to K's own relationship with Regine. Maureen – Regine: the names almost rhyme.

Regine put up more of a fight than Maureen, though. When K sent back her ring, she rushed straight round to his lodgings, and, finding him not at home, left a note begging him not to desert her, "in the name of Christ and by the memory of your deceased father." That was an inspired touch, the deceased father. Søren was convinced that, like so many of his siblings, he would die before his father – there seemed to be a curse on the family that way. So when the old man popped off first Søren thought he had in some mystical sense died *for* him. He dated his religious conversion from that time. So Regine's note really shook him. But he went on nevertheless pretending to be cold and cynical, breaking the girl's heart, perversely convinced that he "could be happier in unhappiness without her than with her." I just looked up his record of their last interview:

> I tried to talk her round. She asked me, Will you never marry? I replied, Well, in about ten years, when I have sowed my wild oats, I must have a pretty young miss to rejuvenate me. – A necessary cruelty. She said, Forgive me for what I have done to you. I replied, It is rather I that should pray for your forgiveness. She said, Kiss me. That I did, but without passion. Merciful God!

That "Kiss me" was Regine's last throw. When it didn't work, she gave up.

Reading that, I recalled again Maureen lifting her unhappy face to me, blue under the streetlamp's bleak light, and saying, "You can kiss me once," and my walking away. Did I ever embrace her after that, or did I continue to spurn the offer of a single chaste goodnight kiss? I didn't keep her last letter, and I can't remember what she said exactly, but the words were pretty banal, I'm sure. They always were. It wasn't anything she said, it was her presence that I remember: the swing of her hair, the shine in her eyes, the way she wrinkled up her nose when she smiled . . . I wish I had a photograph of her to hand. I used to carry a picture of her around in my wallet, a black-and-white holiday snap taken in Ireland when she was fifteen, leaning against a drystone wall, smiling and squinting into the sun, the breeze plastering her cotton skirt to her legs. The photo got creased and dog-eared from constant handling, and after we split up I threw it away. I remember how easily it tore in my fingers, the paper having lost all its gloss and spring, and seeing the scattered fragments of her image at the bottom of the wastepaper basket. The only other photographs I have of her are in a shoebox somewhere in the loft at home in Hollywell, along with other juvenile souvenirs. There aren't very many of them, because neither of us owned a camera in those days. There are a few snaps taken by other members of the youth club on rambles, and a group photo of the cast of the Nativity play. If I could be sure of picking a time when Sally is out, I've a good mind to drive up to Hollywell tomorrow and have a look for them.

6.30 p.m. Shortly after I had typed that last sentence, and switched off the computer, and as I was rolling up my sleeves preparatory to starting on the washing-up, I had an idea: instead of searching my attic for photographs of Maureen, why not try to find Maureen herself? The more I think about it, and I've thought of little else all afternoon, the more I'm taken with it. It's slightly scary, because I've no idea how she will react if I manage to trace her, but that's what makes it exciting. I've no idea where she is, or what's happened to her since we last met in the chemist's shop in Hatchford. She could be living abroad, for all I know. Well, that's no problem, I'd travel to New Zealand if necessary. She could be dead. I don't think I could bear that, but I have to admit it's possible. Cancer. A road accident. Any number of things. Somehow, though, I'm sure she's still alive. Married, probably. Well, certainly, a girl like Maureen, how could she not be married? She married a doctor, I expect, like most good-looking nurses, and stayed married to him, being a devout Catholic. Unless she stopped believing, of course. It does happen. Or she might be widowed.

Hey, I must be careful not to indulge in wishful fantasies here. She's probably a very respectable, rather dull, happily married woman, stout and grey-haired, living in a comfortable suburban house with curtains that match the loose covers on the three-piece suite, mainly interested in her grandchildren, and looking forward to getting her OAP railpass so she can visit them more often. She probably hasn't given me a thought for decades, and wouldn't know me from Adam if I turned up on her doorstep. Nevertheless that's what I'm going to do, turn up on her doorstep. If I can find it.

✳ ✳ ✳ ✳ ✳ ✳ ✳ ✳ ✳ ✳ ✳ ✳ ✳ ✳ ✳ ✳ ✳

Monday 7th June. 4.30 p.m. Whew! I'm exhausted, drained, and my knee aches. I've been back to Hatchford today. Hatchford Mon Amour.

I took the train from Charing Cross just after nine this morning. I was travelling against the rush hour, breasting waves of commuters with pallid Monday-morning faces who surged across the station concourse and swirled around the islanded Tie Rack, Knickerbox and Sockshop before being sucked down the plughole of the Underground. My train was almost empty for its return journey to the suburbs. Southern Electric the trains used to be called, Network Southeast they're called now, but nothing essential has changed on this line, except that the graffiti on the inside of the carriages are more abundant and colourful nowadays, due to the development of the felt-tip pen. *Vorsprung durch Technik*. I took my seat in the second coach from the front because that's the most convenient one for the exit at Hatchford, shuffled a clear space for my feet amid the litter on the floor, and inhaled the familiar smell of dust and hair-oil from the upholstery. A porter came down the platform, slamming the doors shut hard enough to make the teeth rattle in your head, and then the electric motor whined and ticked under the floor as the driver switched on the power. The train moved off with a jerk and rumbled over Hungerford Bridge, the Thames glittering in the sun through the trelliswork of girders; then lurched through the points between Waterloo East and London Bridge. From there the line is straight for miles, and the train rushed at rooftop level past workshops and warehouses and lock-up garages and scrap-merchants' yards and school playgrounds and streets of terraced houses, overlooked by the occasional tower block of council flats. It was never a scenic route.

It was years since I last travelled along this line, and decades since I alighted at Hatchford. In 1962 Dad had a bit of luck – the only bit of luck he had in his life, actually, apart from meeting Mum: £20,000 on the pools, Littlewoods' Three Draws. That was a lot of money in those days, enough for him to retire early from London Transport and buy a little bungalow at Middleton-on-Sea, near Bognor. After he and Mum moved there, I never had any need or inclination to return to Hatchford. It was eerie going back today, a dreamlike mixture of the familiar and the unfamiliar. At first I was struck by how little had changed around the Five Ways. There are different shopfronts and a new road layout – the florist's on the corner has turned into a video rental shop, the Co-op bakery is a DIY superstore, and the road is marked like a complicated board-game, with arrows and cross-hatching and mini-roundabouts – but the contours of the streets and buildings are essentially as I remember them. The sociology of the place has changed though. The little streets of terraced houses off the main road are now largely occupied by Caribbean and Asian families, as I discovered when I went to have a look at our old house in Albert Street.

The sash widows had been ripped out and replaced with sealed aluminium units, and a small glazed porch had been stuck over the front door, but otherwise it was the same house, greyish-yellowish brick, with a slate roof and a front garden a yard deep. There's still a big chip out of the stone window ledge at the front, where a piece of shrapnel hit it in the war. I knocked on the door and a grey-haired Caribbean man opened it a suspicious crack. I explained that I had once lived there and asked if I could come in and look around for a moment. He looked doubtful, as if he suspected me of being a snooper or a con-man, as well he might; but a young woman, who addressed him as Dad, appeared at his shoulder, wiping her hands on an apron, and kindly invited me to step in. What struck me first, apart from the spicy cooking smells lingering on the air, was the narrowness and darkness of the hall and staircase when the front door was closed: I'd forgotten the absence of light inside a terraced house. But the wall between the front and back parlours had been knocked down to make a bright and pleasantly proportioned living-room. Why hadn't we done that? We spent most of our lives crammed into the back room, where it was hardly possible to move without banging into each other or the furniture. The answer, of course, was the ingrained habit of always keeping something – whether it was a suit, a tea-service, or a room – "for best".

The extended living-room was cheerfully if gaudily decorated in yellows and purples and greens. The TV was on, and two small children, twin girls aged about three, were sitting on the floor in front of it, sucking their thumbs and watching a cartoon programme. The two fireplaces had been boarded up and the mantelpieces ripped out, and there were central-heating radiators under the front and rear windows. The room bore so little resemblance to what I remembered that I was unable to populate it with memories. I peered out at the small patch of ground we used to dignify with the name, "back garden". It had been largely paved over and partly covered by a lean-to extension of transparent fibreglass. There was a bright red barbecue on wheels, and a carousel for drying washing instead of the sagging rope that used to run diagonally from end to end, propped up by a cleft stick. The young woman told me her husband drove a Routemaster bus, and I seized gratefully on this thread of continuity with the past. "My Dad used to drive a tram," I told her. But I had to explain what a tram was. They didn't offer to show me the bedrooms, and I didn't ask. I pressed a pound coin into the hands of each twin, thanked their mother and grandfather, and left.

I walked back to the Five Ways and then began to climb Beecher's Road. It was quickly apparent that a certain amount of yuppification had taken place on the higher levels of Hatchford, probably in the property boom of the eighties. The big houses that had been divided up into rented flats in my childhood had in many cases reverted to single ownership, and been smartened up in the process, with brass fittings on the front doors, hanging flower-baskets in the porches, and potted shrubs in the basement areas. Through front windows I glimpsed the signs of AB lifestyles: ethnic rugs and modern prints on the walls, well-stocked black ash bookshelves, angular lampstands, state-of-the-art hi-fi systems. I wondered if the same fate would have overtaken 94 Treglowan Road, where Maureen's family used to live. First left at the top of Beecher's Road, then first right and right again. Was it the exertion of the climb or nervous expectation that made my heart beat faster as I approached the last corner? It was highly unlikely that Maureen's parents, even if they were alive, would still be living there; and even if they were it would be a chance in a million if she happened to be visiting them today. So I told myself, trying to calm my pulse. But I was not prepared for the shock I received when I turned the corner.

One side of the road, the side on which Maureen's house had stood, had been demolished and cleared, and in its place a small estate of new detached houses had been built. They were flimsy, meanly-proportioned brick boxes – so narrow they looked like sawn-off semis – with leaded windows and fake beams stuck on the facades, and they were laid out along a curving cul-de-sac called Treglowan Close. There was not a single visible trace of the monumental Victorian villa in which the Kavanaghs had lived, not a brick, not a stone, not a tree. I calculated that the entrance to the estate passed directly over the site of the house. The basement area where we had kissed, where I had touched Maureen's breasts, had been filled in, levelled off, and sealed under a coating of tarmac. I felt robbed, disoriented and quite irrationally angry.

The Church of the Immaculate Conception, on the other hand,

was still standing. Indeed, it had hardly changed at all. The statue of the Virgin Mary still stood on her pedestal in the forecourt signalling a wide. Inside there were the same dark stained pews, confessionals like massive wardrobes against the wall, votive candles dripping stalactites of wax. There was something new, though: up at what Philip Larkin called the holy end, in front of the carved and pinnacled altar that I remembered blazing with candlelight at Benediction, was a plain stone table, and there were no rails at the bottom of the altar steps. A middle-aged lady in an apron was hoovering the carpet on the altar. She switched off the machine and looked enquiringly at me as I hovered nearby. I asked if Father Jerome was still attached to the church. She had heard his name mentioned by some of the older parishioners, but thought he must have left long before she came to Hatchford herself. She had an idea that he had been sent to Africa by his order to work in the missions. And Father Malachi, I presumed, was dead. She nodded, and pointed to a plaque on the wall in his memory. She said the present parish priest was Father Dominic, and that I might find him in the presbytery. I remembered that presbytery meant the house where the priests lived, the first one around the corner from the church. A thirty-something man in a pullover and jeans opened the door when I rang the bell. I asked if Father Dominic was in. He said, "That's me, come in." He led me into a cluttered living-room, where a computer screen glowed green on a desk in the corner. "Do you understand spreadsheets?" he said. I confessed I didn't. "I'm trying to computerize the parish accounts," he said, "but really I need Windows to do it properly. How can I help you?"

When I said I was trying to trace someone who had lived in the parish forty years ago, he shook his head doubtfully. "The order who had the parish in those days were pretty hopeless at paperwork. If they had any files on parishioners, they must have taken them with them when they pulled out. All that's left by way of an archive are the registers of Baptisms, First Communions, Confirmations and Marriages."

I asked if I could see the marriage register, and he led me round to the back of the church, into a small room behind the altar that smelled of incense and furniture-polish, and took a large oblong leather-bound book out of a cupboard. I started with the year in which I last saw Maureen and worked forward. It didn't take me very long to find her name. On 16th May 1959 Maureen Teresa Kavanagh of 94 Treglowan Road married Bede Ignatius Harrington of 103 Hatchford Rise. "Bugger me!" I exclaimed thoughtlessly, and apologized for my unseemly language. Father Dominic didn't seem bothered. I asked him if the Harrington family still lived in the parish. "It doesn't ring a bell," he said. "I'd have to check my database." We returned to the presbytery and he searched for the name on his computer without success. There weren't any Kavanaghs in the parish either. "Annie Mahoney might know something," he said. "She used to be the housekeeper in the presbytery in those days. I look after myself – can't afford a housekeeper. She lives in the next house but one. You'll have to shout, she's pretty deaf." I thanked him and asked if I could make a contribution to the parish software fund, which he received gratefully.

Annie Mahoney was a bent, withered little old lady in a bright green tracksuit and Reebok trainers with Velcro fastenings. She explained to me that because of the arthritis in her fingers she couldn't manage buttons and laces any more. She lived alone and obviously welcomed company and the chance of a chat. At first she thought I was the man from the Town Hall come to review her entitlement to a Home Help, but when that misunderstanding was cleared up she brought her mind to bear on my enquiry about the Kavanagh family. It was a tantalizing interview. She remembered the family. "Such a giant of a man, Mr Kavanagh, you could never forget him if you saw him only once, and his wife was a nice woman and they had five beautiful children, especially the oldest, I forget her name now." "Maureen," I prompted. "That's it, Maureen," she said. She remembered Maureen's wedding, which had been a posh one by the standards of the parish, with the groom and best man in tail-coats, and two Rolls-Royces to ferry the guests to the reception. "I think Dr Harrington paid for the cars, he was always a man to do things properly," Annie reminisced. "He died about ten years ago, God rest his soul. Heart, they said." She didn't know anything about Bede's and Maureen's married life however, where they lived or what Bede did for a living. "Maureen became a teacher, I think," she hazarded. I said I thought she wanted to be a nurse. "Oh yes, a nurse, that was it," said Annie. "She would have made a lovely nurse. Such a sweet-natured girl. I remember her as Our Lady in a Nativity play the youth club put on one Christmas, with her hair spread out over her shoulders, beautiful she looked." I couldn't resist asking Annie if she remembered the Herod in the same production, but she didn't.

I checked out the Harringtons' former house, a large villa set back from the main road with, as I recalled, a rather impressive entrance – two gateposts with stone globes the size of footballs on top. It belongs to a dental practice now. The gateposts have been removed and the front garden tarmacked over to make a parking lot for the partners and their patients. I went inside and asked the receptionist if she had any information about the previous owners, but she was unable or unwilling to help. I was tired and hungry and not a little melancholy by this time, so I caught the next train back to Charing Cross.

So Bede Harrington is my Schlegel. Well, well. I always thought he had his eye on Maureen, but I'm a bit surprised that she chose to marry him. Could you *love* Bede Harrington? (Without *being* Bede Harrington, I mean.) I can't flatter myself that it was on the rebound from me, though. Judging by the date of the wedding, it took him several years to persuade her, or to pluck up the courage to pop the question – so he must have had some attraction for her. I can't deny that I feel absurdly, pointlessly jealous. And keener than ever to trace her. But where do I go from here?

7.06 p.m. After devising various ingenious plans (e.g., find out which local estate agent handled the sale of 103 Hatchford Rise to the dentists, and see if I could get an address for Mrs Harrington Snr. out of them) I thought of a simpler expedient to try first: if Bede and Maureen still lived in London, they would probably be in the phone book, and Harrington wasn't such a common name. Sure enough, there were only two B. I. Harringtons. One of them, with an address in SW19, had OBE after his name, which I thought was just the sort of thing Bede would show off about if he had the chance, so I tried that

269

number first. I recognized his voice instantly. Our conversation went more or less like this:

BEDE: Harrington.

ME: Is that the Bede Harrington who used to live in Hatchford?

BEDE: (*guardedly*) I did live there once, yes.

ME: You married Maureen Kavanagh?

BEDE: Yes. Who is this?

ME: Herod.

BEDE: I beg your pardon?

ME: Laurence Passmore.

BEDE: I'm sorry, I don't . . . Parsons, did you say?

ME: Passmore. You remember. The youth club. The Nativity play. I was Herod.
(*Pause*)

BEDE: Good God.

ME: How are you, then?

BEDE: All right.

ME: How's Maureen?

BEDE: She's all right, I think.

ME: Could I speak to her?

BEDE: She's not here.

ME: Ah. When will she be back?

BEDE: I don't precisely know. She's abroad.

ME: Oh – where?

BEDE: Spain, I should think, by now.

ME: I see . . . Is there any way I could get in touch with her?

BEDE: Not really, no.

ME: On holiday, is she?

BEDE: Not exactly. What is it you want?

ME: I'd just like to see her again . . . (*racking brains for a pretext*) . . . I'm writing something about those days.

BEDE: Are you a writer?

ME: Yes.

BEDE: What kind of writer?

ME: Television mostly. You may know a programme called *The People Next Door*?

BEDE: Never heard of it, I'm afraid.

ME: Oh.

BEDE: I don't watch much television. Look, I'm in the middle of cooking my dinner –

ME: Oh, sorry. I –
BEDE: If you leave me your number, I'll tell Maureen when she gets back.

I gave him my address and phone number. Before he rang off, I asked him what he got his OBE for. He said, "I presume for my work on the National Curriculum." It seems he's a fairly high-up civil servant in the Department of Education.

I'm very stirred up by this conversation, excited and at the same time frustrated. I'm amazed how much progress I've made in tracing Maureen in a single day, yet she's still tantalizingly out of reach. I wish now I'd pressed Bede for more details as to where she is and what she's doing. I don't like the idea of just waiting, indefinitely, for a phone call from her, not knowing how long it might be – days? weeks? months? – or whether Bede will even pass her my message when she gets back from wherever she is. "Spain by now . . . not exactly a holiday" – what the fuck does that mean? Is she on some kind of educational coach tour? Or a cruise?

9.35 p.m. I rang Bede again, apologized for disturbing him, and asked if we could meet. When he asked me what for, I elaborated my alibi about writing something set in Hatchford in the early fifties. He was less abrupt and suspicious than before – indeed his speech was slightly slurred, as if he'd had a bit too much to drink with his dinner. I said I lived quite near Whitehall, and asked if I could give him lunch one day this week. He said he retired at the end of last year, but I could visit him at home if I liked. SW19 turns out to be Wimbledon. Eagerly I suggested tomorrow morning, and much to my delight, he agreed. Before he rang off, I managed to slip in a question about Maureen: "On a sort of tour, is she?" "No," he said, "a pilgrimage."
   Still a devout Catholic, then. Oh well.

✻ ✻ ✻ ✻ ✻ ✻ ✻ ✻ ✻ ✻ ✻ ✻ ✻ ✻ ✻ ✻

Tuesday 8th June. 2.30 p.m. I travelled by Network Southeast again this morning, but this time from Waterloo, and in a cleaner, smarter train than yesterday, appropriate to my more upmarket destination.

Bede and Maureen live in one of the leafy residential streets near the All England Club. It's entirely typical of Bede that he has never watched a tennis match in all his years in Wimbledon, and regards the Championships as merely an annual traffic nuisance. I've been to Wimbledon myself a few times in recent years as a guest of Heartland, (they host parties in one of the hospitality marquees, with champagne and strawberries and free tickets to the Centre Court) and it gave me a funny feeling to realize that I must have passed within a hundred yards of Maureen on those occasions without knowing it. I might well have driven past her in the street.

The house is quite an ordinary large inter-war semi, with a long back garden. They moved there early in their married life, Bede said, and extended it, building on top of the garage, and out at the back, and converting the loft, to accommodate their growing family, instead of moving. They have four children, all grown-up and flown the nest now, it appeared. Bede was on his own in the house, which had an unnaturally clean and tidy look, as if most of the rooms hadn't been disturbed since the last visit of the cleaning-lady. I peeped into some of them when I went upstairs to use the loo. I noticed that there were twin beds in the master bedroom, which gave me a silly satisfaction. Aha, no sex any more, I said to myself. Not necessarily true, of course.

Bede hasn't changed much except that his coarse unruly hair has turned quite white, and his cheeks are sunken. He still wears horn-rimmed glasses with lenses like bottle ends. But apparently I've changed a lot. Although I arrived at the time appointed, he greeted me uncertainly when he opened the front door. "You've put on weight," he said, when I identified myself. "And lost most of my hair," I said. "Yes, you had rather a lot of hair, didn't you," he said. He led me into the sitting-room (where, I was amused to note, the curtains matched the loose covers) and invited me rather stiffly to sit down. He was dressed like a man who has spent most of his life in a suit and doesn't know quite what to wear in retirement. He was wearing a tweed sports jacket with leather patches, and a checked shirt with a woollen tie, grey worsted trousers and dark brown brogues – rather heavy clothes for the time of year, even though it was a cool, blustery day.

"I owe you an apology," he said, in his familiar pompous way. "I was speaking to my daughter on the telephone this morning and she informs me that your programme – what is it called? – is one of the most popular on television."

"*The People Next Door*. Does your daughter watch it?" I asked.

"She watches everything, indiscriminately," he said. "We didn't have a television when the children were growing up – I thought it would interfere with their homework. The effect on Teresa was that she became completely addicted as soon as she left home and was able to get a set for herself. I have come to the conclusion," he went on, "that all effort to control other people's lives is completely futile."

"Including government?" I asked.

"Especially government," he said. He seemed to regard his career in the civil service as a failure, in spite of the OBE. "The educational system of this country is in a much worse state now than when I joined the Department," he said. "That isn't my fault, but I was unable to prevent it. When I think of all the hours I spent on committees, working-parties, writing reports, writing memoranda . . . all completely futile. I envy you, Passmore. I wish I'd been a writer. Or at least a don. I could have done a postgraduate degree after I got my First, but I took the Civil Service exam instead. It seemed the safer bet at the time, and I wanted to get married, you know."

I suggested that now he was retired he would have plenty of leisure to write.

"Yes, I always used to think that is what I would do in my retirement. I used to write a lot when I was young – poems, essays . . ."

"Plays," I said.

"Quite so." Bede allowed himself a wintry reminiscent smile. "But the creative juices dry up if they're not kept in circulation. I tried to write something the other day, something rather personal about . . . bereavement. It came out like a White Paper."

He left me for a few minutes to make some coffee in the kitchen, and I prowled round the room in search of clues to Maureen's

273

existence. There were a number of fairly recent family photographs on display – graduations and weddings and one of Bede and Maureen together outside Buckingham Palace with Bede in morning dress – in which she appeared as a proud, smiling, matronly woman, her hair grey and cut short, but with the same sweet heart-shaped face I remembered. I stared greedily at these images, trying to reconstruct from them the missing years of her life (missing for me, I mean). Propped up on the mantelpiece was a brightly coloured picture postcard of St Jean Pied-de-Port in the French Pyrenees. On the other side was a brief message from Maureen to Bede: "Dear Bede: Am taking a rest here for a few days before tackling the mountains. All right except for blisters. Love, Maureen." I would have recognized the round, girlish hand anywhere, even though there were dots instead of bubbles over the *is*. The card was postmarked about three weeks ago. Hearing Bede in the hall, I hastily replaced the card and scuttled back to my seat.

"So, how's Maureen?" I said, as he came in with a tray. "What has she been doing with herself while you were climbing the ladder in the DES?"

"She was a qualified nurse when I married her," he said, pushing down the plunger in the cafetière with both hands, like a man detonating dynamite. "We started a family almost immediately, and she gave up work to look after the children. She went back to nursing when our youngest started junior school, and became a sister in charge of a ward, but it's frightfully hard work, you know. She gave it up when we no longer needed the money. She does a lot of voluntary work, for the Church and so on."

"You both still go to church, then?" I said.

"Yes," he said curtly. "Milk? Sugar?" The coffee was grey and insipid, the digestive biscuits damp. Bede asked me some technical questions about writing for television. After a while, I pulled the conversation back to Maureen. "What's this pilgrimage she's on then?"

He stirred restively in his seat, and looked out of the window, where a boisterous wind was blowing, shaking the trees and sending blossom through the air like snowflakes. "It's to Santiago de

Compostela," he said, "in north-west Spain. It's a very ancient pilgrimage, goes back to the Middle Ages. St James the Apostle is supposed to be buried there. 'Santiago' is Spanish for St James, of course. 'St Jacques' in French. Maureen read about the pilgrimage route somewhere, a library book I think. Decided she wanted to do it."

"On foot," I said.

"Yes, on foot." Bede looked at me. "How did you know?"

I confessed to having peeped at her card.

"It's absurd of course," he said. "A woman of her age. Quite absurd." He took off his spectacles and massaged his brow as if he had a headache. His eyes looked naked and vulnerable without the glasses.

"How far is it?" I asked.

"Depends on where you start." He replaced his spectacles. "There are several different starting-points, all in France. Maureen started from Le Puy, in the Auvergne. Santiago is about a thousand miles from there, I believe."

I whistled softly. "Is she an experienced walker?"

"Not in the least," Bede said. "A stroll across Wimbledon Common on Sunday afternoon was her idea of a long walk. The whole idea is completely mad. I'm surprised she got as far as the Pyrenees, to be honest, without injuring herself. Or being raped, or murdered."

He told me that when Maureen first proposed doing the pilgrimage he offered to accompany her if they went by car, but she insisted on doing it the hard way, on foot, like the mediaeval pilgrims. It was apparent that they'd had a major row about it. In the end she went off defiantly on her own, about two months ago, with a rucksack and a bedroll, and he's only had two cards from her since, the latest being the one I had just seen. Bede is obviously worried sick as well as angry, and feeling not a little foolish, but there's nothing he can do except sit tight and hope she gets to Santiago safely. I found the story fascinating and, I must admit, derived a certain amount of *Schadenfreude* from Bede's plight. Nevertheless it seemed a surprisingly quixotic adventure for Maureen to undertake. I said something to this effect.

"Yes, well, she's been under a lot of stress, lately. We both have," Bede said. "We lost our son Damien last November, you see."

I blurted out some words of commiseration, and asked about the circumstances. Bede went to a bureau and took a framed photograph from one of the drawers. It was a colour snap of a young man, healthy and handsome, dressed in T-shirt and shorts, smiling at the camera, leaning against the front mudguard of a Land Rover, with a background of blue sky and brownish scrub. "He was killed in Angola," Bede said. "You may have read about it in the newspapers. He was working for a Catholic aid organization there, distributing relief supplies to refugees. Nobody knows exactly what happened, but it seems that some maverick unit of rebel soldiers stopped the truck he was in, and demanded that he hand over the food and medicine to them. He refused, and they pulled him and his African driver out of the truck and shot them. Damien was only twenty-five."

"How awful," I said, inadequately.

"Not much sense to be made of it, is there?" said Bede, turning his head to gaze out of the window again. "He loved Africa, you know, loved his work, was totally dedicated . . . We had his body flown back. There was a Requiem Mass. Lots of people came, people we had never even met. People from the charity. Friends of his from university. He was very popular. The priest who gave the address, some sort of chaplain to the charity, said Damien was a modern martyr." He stopped, lost in thought, and I couldn't think of anything to say, so we were silent for a moment.

"You think your faith is going to be a consolation at times like these," he resumed. "But when it happens, you find it isn't. Nothing is. Our GP persuaded us to see some busybody he called a Grief Counsellor. Stupid woman said we mustn't feel guilty. I said, why should I feel guilty? She said, because you're alive and he isn't. I never heard such rubbish. I think Damien was a fool. He should have given those brutes the damned food and driven away and never stopped until he was out of the whole bloody continent."

His gills were white with anger as he remembered. I asked him how Maureen had taken the tragedy.

"Hard. Damien was her favourite child. She was devastated. That's why she's gone off on this absurd pilgrimage."

"You mean, as a kind of therapy?" I said.

"It's as good a word as any, I suppose," said Bede.

I said I thought I had better be going. He said, "But we haven't talked much about the old days at Hatchford." I said perhaps another time. He nodded. "All right. Give me a ring. You know," he went on, "I never much liked you, Passmore. I used to think you were up to no good with Maureen at the youth club."

"You were absolutely right," I said, and wrung another thin smile from him.

"But I'm glad you came this morning," he continued. "I'm a bit lonely, to tell you the truth."

"Does Maureen ever talk about me?" I asked.

"No," he said. "Never." He spoke without malice or satisfaction, merely as if stating a matter of fact. While we were waiting for my taxi to come, he asked me if I had any children. I said two, one married, the other living with a partner. "Ah yes, they do that nowadays, don't they?" he said. "Even ours do. Think nothing of it. Not like it was in our youth, eh?"

"No indeed," I said.

"And your wife, what does she do?"

"She's a lecturer in one of the new universities," I said. "In Education. As a matter of fact, she spends a lot of her time counselling teachers who are having nervous breakdowns over the National Curriculum."

"I'm not surprised," said Bede. "It's a total shambles. I'd like to meet your wife."

"I'm afraid she's just left me," I said.

"Has she? Then that makes two of us," said Bede, in a characteristically clumsy effort at humour. At which point the doorbell rang, and I was driven off to Wimbledon station by an annoyingly loquacious driver. I didn't want to make small talk about the weather or the prospects for the tennis. I wanted to think about the fascinating revelations of the morning.

A plan is forming in my mind, an idea so daft and exciting that I dare not even write it down yet.

Friday 11th June. Well, I've made up my mind. I'm going after Maureen. I'm going to try and track her down on the road to Santiago de Compostela. I've spent the last three days making the necessary arrangements – booking the car ferry, getting a green card, buying guidebooks, maps, travellers cheques, etc. I ripped through the backlog of mail and phone messages, and dealt with the most urgent ones. There was a series from Dennis Shorthouse reporting that Sally has made a court application for a maintenance order to meet the running costs of the house, and asking with mounting urgency for instructions. I phoned him and told him I wouldn't obstruct divorce proceedings any longer, and would agree to appropriate maintenance and a reasonable financial settlement. He asked me what I meant by reasonable. I said, let her keep the house and I'll keep the flat, and the rest of the assets can be divided fifty-fifty. He said, "That's not reasonable, that's generous. The house is worth considerably more than the flat." I said I just didn't want to be bothered with it any more. I told him I was going abroad for a few weeks. I don't know how long it will take me to track down Maureen, or what I will do if I find her. I just know I have to look for her. I can't stand the thought of spending the summer cooped up in this flat, taking calls from people I'm trying to avoid in case it's her.

I haven't told Bede about my plan, in case he gets the wrong idea, though what the right idea would be I've really no idea. I mean I don't really know what I want from Maureen. Not her love back, obviously – it's too late for a Repetition. (Though I can't stop myself from going over every bit of evidence that her marriage to Bede has grown cold – if it was ever warm – like the single beds, their row over her pilgrimage, the rather cool "Dear Bede" postcard, etc. etc.) But if not love, then what? Forgiveness, perhaps. Absolution. I want to know that she forgives me for betraying her all those years ago in front of the Nativity play cast. A trivial act in itself, but with enormous consequences. You could say that it determined the shape of the rest of my life. You could say it was the source of my middle-aged *Angst*. I made a choice without knowing it was a choice. Or rather (which is worse) I pretended that it was Maureen's choice, not mine, that we split up. It seems to me now that I never recovered from the effect of that bad faith. It explains why I can never make a decision without immediately regretting it.

I must try that on Alexandra next time I see her, though I'm not sure she'll be pleased. I seem to have abandoned cognitive therapy in favour of the old-fashioned analytical kind, finding the source of my troubles in a long-repressed memory. It would be a consolation, anyway, to share that memory with Maureen, to find out how she feels about it now. The fact that she is nursing a fresh grief of her own makes me all the more anxious to find her and make my peace with her.

Also in my mailjam was a draft script by Samantha filling out her idea for a kind of *The People Next Door*-meets-*Truly, Madly, Deeply*-meets-*Ghost* episode to end the present series. It wasn't at all bad, but I saw at once what needed doing to it. She had Priscilla's ghost appearing to Edward after the funeral. What must happen is that Priscilla appears to Edward immediately after her fatal accident, before anyone knows about it. He doesn't think she is a ghost at first, because she tries to break it to him gently. Then she walks through a wall – the party wall – into the Davises' house and back again, and the realization sinks in that she's dead. It's sad, but it isn't tragic, because Priscilla is still there, in a sense. There's even a kind of comedy in the scene. It's very thin ice, but I think it would work. Anyway, I did a quick rewrite and sent it back to Samantha with instructions to try it on Ollie.

Then I called Jake and listened meekly to ten minutes' bitter recrimination for not returning his calls before I was able to tell him about my work on Samantha's draft script. "It's too late, Tubby," he said flatly. "Clause fourteen applied weeks ago." "Have they hired another writer, then?" I asked, bracing myself for a positive reply.

279

"They must have," he said. "They need an agreed script for the last episode by the end of the month at the latest." I heard the creaking of his swivel chair as he rocked himself in it, thinking. "I suppose if they really went for this ghost idea, there might just be time," he said. "Where will you be the next two weeks?"

Then I had to break it to him that I was going abroad tomorrow for an indeterminate time and couldn't give any phone or fax numbers where he could contact me. I held the phone away from my ear like they do in old comedy films while he swore. "Why d'you have to take a holiday now, for fuck's sake?" I heard him exclaim. "It's not a holiday," I said, "it's a pilgrimage," and put the phone down quickly while he was still speechless.

It's extraordinary what a difference this quest for Maureen has made to my state of mind. I don't seem to have any difficulty in making decisions any more. I no longer feel like the unhappiest man. Perhaps I never was – I had a look at that essay again the other day and I don't think I got it quite right before. But I'm certainly present to myself when I'm remembering Maureen, or hoping to find her – never more so.

I'd just finished typing that sentence when I noticed a regularly blinking light reflected in my windows – it was dark, about ten o'clock, but I hadn't drawn the curtains. Squinting down into the street I saw the roof of a police car parked right outside the building with its blue revolving light flashing. I switched on the video monitor in the hall and there was Grahame, rolling up his sleeping-bag in the porch under the surveillance of a couple of policemen. I went downstairs. The more senior of the two policemen explained that they were moving Grahame on. "Were you the gentleman who made the complaint?" he asked. I said I wasn't. Grahame looked at me and said, "C'n I come up?" I said, "Alright. For a few minutes." The cops looked at me in astonishment. "I hope you know what you're doing, sir," said the senior one disapprovingly. "I wouldn't let this toerag into *my* house, I can tell you." "I ain't no toerag," said Grahame indignantly. The policeman eyeballed him fiercely. "Don't give me any of your lip, toerag," he hissed. "And don't let me catch you kipping in this doorway again. Understand?" He looked coldly at me. "I could have you for obstructing an officer in the performance of his duties," he said, "but I'll overlook it this time."

I took Grahame upstairs and gave him a cup of tea. "You're going to have to find another place, Grahame," I said. "I can't protect you any longer. I'm going abroad, probably for a few weeks."

He looked at me slyly from under his lank forelock. "Let me stay 'ere," he said. "I'll look after the place for you while you're away. Like a caretaker."

I laughed at his cheek. "It doesn't need a caretaker."

"You're wrong," he said. "There's all sorts of villains round 'ere. You might be burgled while you're away."

"I wasn't burgled before, when the flat was empty most of the time."

"I don't mean *live* 'ere," Grahame said, "just sleep. On the floor – not in your bed. I'd keep the place nice and clean." He looked around. "Sight cleaner 'n it is now."

"I expect you would, Grahame," I said. "Thanks, but no thanks."

He sighed and shook his head. "I just hope you don't regret it," he said.

"Well," I said, "if the worst comes to the worst – I'm insured."

I saw him out of the building. A light drizzle was falling. I felt a bit of a heel as he turned up his collar and shouldered his bedroll – but what could I do? I'd be crazy to give him the key to my flat. I might come back and find he'd turned it into a dosshouse for philosophical vagrants like himself. I thrust a couple of notes into his hand, and told him to get himself a room for the night. "Ta," he said, and sloped off into the warm wet night. I never met anybody who could accept favours with such nonchalance. I have a feeling I shan't see him again.

Thursday 17th June. I didn't get away as soon as I had planned. Shorthouse phoned me to say that he would feel happier if I waited a few days while he sorted out the details of a settlement with the other side. So I've hung about impatiently this week, filling in the time by reading everything I could find in the Charing Cross Road bookshops about the pilgrimage to Santiago. I went up to Rummidge this morning to sign the papers, and came back by the next train. This evening, as I was packing, I got an unexpected call from Sally. It was the first time we had spoken for weeks. "I just wanted to say," she said, in a carefully neutral tone of voice, "that I think you've been very generous." "That's alright," I said. "I'm sorry it's been such an unpleasant business," she said, "I'm afraid I was partly to blame." "Yes, well, these things are always painful," I said, "it doesn't bring out the best in people, divorce." "Well, I just wanted to say thankyou," said Sally, and rang off. I felt rather uneasy, speaking to her. Knowing my mind as I do, it wouldn't take much to make me start regretting my decision. I want to be out of here, away from it all, on the road. I'm off tomorrow morning. Santiago, here I come.

* * FOUR * *

SEPTEMBER 21st. I've come to the conclusion that the essential difference between book-writing and script-writing isn't that the latter is mostly dialogue – it's a question of tense. A script is all in the present tense. Not literally, but ontologically. (How about that, then? Comes of reading all those books about Kierkegaard.) What I mean is, in drama or film, everything is happening *now*. That's why stage directions are always in the present tense. Even when one character is telling another character about something that happened in the past, the *telling* is happening in the present, as far as the audience is concerned. Whereas, when you write something in a book, it all belongs to the past; even if you write, "*I am writing, I am writing*," over and over again, the act of writing is finished with, out of sight, by the time somebody reads the result.

A journal is halfway between the two forms. It's like talking silently to yourself. It's a mixture of monologue and autobiography. You can write a lot of stuff in the present tense, like: "*The plane trees outside my window are in leaf* . . ." But really that's just a fancier way of saying, "*I am writing, I am writing* . . .*" It's not getting you anywhere, it's not telling a story. As soon as you start to tell a story in writing, whether it's a fictional story or the story of your life, it's natural to use the past tense, because you're describing things that have already happened. The special thing about a journal is that the writer doesn't know where his story is going, he doesn't know how it ends; so it seems to exist in a kind of continuous present, even though the individual incidents may be described in the past tense. Novels are written after the fact, or they pretend to be. The novelist may not have known how his story would end when he began it, but it always *looks* as if he did to the reader. The past tense of the opening sentence implies that the story about to be told has already happened. I know that there are novels written entirely in the present tense, but there's something queer about them, they're experimental, the present tense doesn't seem natural to the medium. They read like scripts. A present-tense autobiography would be even queerer. Autobiography is always written after the fact. It's a past-tense form. Like my memoir of Maureen. Like this piece I've just finished writing.

I kept a journal of sorts on my travels, but my laptop packed up in the mountains of León, and I didn't have the time or opportunity to get it repaired, so I started keeping a handwritten diary. I've printed out my disks, and laboriously typed up the diary, but put together they made a very rough and rambling account of what happened to me. Conditions often weren't ideal for writing, and sometimes at the end of the day I was too tired or had imbibed too much *vino* to do more than make a few allusive notes. So I've written it out in a more coherent, cohesive narrative, knowing, so to speak, how the story ended. For I do feel I've reached the end of something. And, hopefully, a new beginning.

✳ ✳ ✳ ✳ ✳ ✳ ✳ ✳ ✳ ✳ ✳ ✳ ✳ ✳ ✳ ✳ ✳

I drove from London to St-Jean-Pied-de-Port in two days. No sweat. The only problem was holding the Richmobile under the speed limit on the autoroute. The cruise control came in handy. So did the air-conditioning – the road was shimmering in the heat on the flat marshlands south of Bordeaux. When I climbed into the foothills of the Pyrenees the weather turned cooler, and it was raining when I reached St Jean Pied-de-Port (St John at the Foot of the Pass). It's a pleasant little market-cum-resort town of red gabled roofs and rushing brooks, nestling in a lumpy patchwork quilt of fields in various shades of green. There's a hotel with a restaurant that has two Michelin rosettes where I was lucky enough to get a room. I was told that a little later in the season I wouldn't have stood a chance without a reservation. There were already lots of hairy-kneed walkers in the town, wandering about disconsolately in wet cagoules, or mellowing out in the cafés while they waited for the weather to improve. You could tell which ones were pilgrims on their way to Santiago because they had scallop shells attached to their rucksacks.

The scallop shell, or *coquille* (hence, *coquilles St Jaques*, which they did extremely well at my hotel) is the traditional symbol of the pilgrimage to Santiago, for reasons that, like most things associated with this saint, remain obscure. One legend has it that a man rescued from drowning by St James's intervention was dragged from the sea covered in scallop shells. More probably it was just a brilliant piece of mediaeval marketing: pilgrims returning from Santiago wanted souvenirs, and scallop shells were plentiful on the shores of Galicia. They were a nice little earner for the city, especially as the Archbishop of Santiago was empowered to excommunicate anybody who sold them to pilgrims outside it. Nowadays, though, pilgrims wear the *coquille* on their way to Santiago as well as on the way home.

I was surprised by how many of them there were, even in St Jean Pied-de-Port. I had imagined Maureen as a solitary eccentric, retracing an ancient trail forgotten by the modern world. Not so. The pilgrimage has enjoyed a big revival lately, encouraged by a powerful consortium of interests: the Catholic Church, the Spanish Tourist Board and the Council of Europe, which adopted the Camino de Santiago as a European Heritage Trail a few years ago. Tens of thousands hit the road every summer, following the blue and yellow *coquille* signs erected by the Council of Europe. I met a German couple in a bar one evening who had walked all the way from Arles, the most southerly of the four traditional routes. They had a sort of passport issued by some society of St James which they'd had stamped at various stopping-points along the route. When they got to Santiago, they told me, they would present their passports at the Cathedral and receive their "*compostelas*", certificates of completion like the pilgrims of old used to get. I wondered whether Maureen had obtained such a passport. If so, it might help me to trace her. The Germans directed me to the local passport-stamper, advising me not to arrive outside her house by car. Genuine pilgrims must walk, or cycle, or ride horseback.

I walked up the narrow cobbled hill to the house, but I didn't pretend to be a pilgrim. Instead I pretended (in a mixture of pidgin English, fractured French and sign-language) to be Bede Harrington, trying to trace his wife who was urgently required back at in England. A lady who was a dead ringer for Mary Whitehouse opened the door, frowning as if she was fit to kill another pilgrim knocking on her door late in the evening, but when I told my story she became interested and co-operative. To my delight she had stamped Maureen's passport and remembered her well: "*une femme très gentille*", but suffering from badly blistered feet. I asked her where she thought Maureen might have got to by now, and she frowned and shrugged, "*Ça dépend . . .*" It depended, obviously, on how many kilometres Maureen could walk per day. It's about 800 kilometres from St Jean Pied-de-Port to Santiago. A young and fit walker might average 30 kilometres a day, but Maureen would be lucky to do half as well as that. I got the map out in my hotel room and calculated that she might be anywhere between Logroño and Villafranca, a distance of 300 kilometres, and that was guessing in the dark. She might have rested somewhere for a week to let her blisters heal and be way behind schedule. She might have used public transport for part of the way, in which case she could have already arrived in Santiago – though knowing Maureen I doubted if she would bend the rules. I imagined her gritting her teeth and walking on through the pain barrier.

The next day I crossed the Pyrenees. I put the automatic shift in "Slow" to avoid excessive gear changes on the twisty road and breezed effortlessly to the top of the Val Carlos pass, overtaking several pilgrims slogging their way up the hill bowed under their backpacks. The weather had turned fine and the scenery was spectacular: mountains green to their peaks, valleys smiling in the sunshine, caramel-coloured cows with clinking bells, flocks of mountain sheep, vultures hang-gliding at eye level. Val Carlos, my guidebook informed me, means valley of Charles or Charlemagne, and on the Spanish side of the mountain is Roncesvalles, where there was a famous battle between Charlemagne's army and the Saracens, as recorded in the *Song of Roland*. Only they weren't Saracens at all, in reality, but Basques from Pamplona, narked because Charlemagne's boys had knocked their city about a bit. Nothing associated with the

Camino is quite what it claims to be. The shrine of Santiago itself seems to be a complete con, seeing there's no evidence the Apostle is actually buried there. The story goes that, after the death of Jesus, James went to Spain to convert the natives. He didn't seem to have much success because he returned to Palestine with only two disciples, and promptly had his head chopped off by Herod (I don't know which one). The two disciples were told in a dream to take the saint's remains back to Spain, which they did in a stone boat (yes, stone), which was miraculously wafted through the Mediterranean and the Straits of Gibraltar, up the west coast of the Iberian peninsula, and beached on the shores of Galicia. Some centuries later a local hermit saw a star twinkling above a hillock which, when excavated, revealed the remains of the saint and his disciples – or so it was claimed. They could have been anybody's bones, of course. But Christian Spain badly needed some relics and a shrine to boost its campaign to drive out the Moors. That's how St James became the patron saint of Spain, and "*Santiago!*" the Spanish battle-cry. According to another legend, he appeared in person at the crucial battle of Clavijo in 834 to rally the wilting Christian army, and personally slew seventy thousand Moors. The archdiocese of Santiago had the face to lay a special tax on the rest of Spain as a thankyou to St James, though in fact there is no evidence that the battle of Clavijo ever took place, with or without his intervention. In churches all along the Camino you see statues of "*Santiago Matamoros*", St James the Moorslayer, depicting him as a warrior on horseback, wielding his sword and trampling the corpses of swarthy, thick-lipped infidels. They could become an embarrassment if Political Correctness ever gets a hold on Spain.

I found it hard to understand why millions of people had walked halfway across Europe in times past, often under conditions of appalling discomfort and danger, to visit the dubious shrine of this dubious saint, and even harder to understand why they were still doing so, albeit in smaller numbers. I got a sort of answer to the latter question at the Augustinian abbey of Roncesvalles, which has been offering hospitality to pilgrims since the Middle Ages. It looks fantastic from a distance, a cluster of grey stone buildings tucked into a fold in the green foothills, with the sun gleaming on its roof – only when you get close do you see that the roof is made of corrugated zinc, and the buildings are mostly undistinguished. A man in black trousers and a red cardigan watched me get out of my car and, observing the GB plates, greeted me in English. He turned out to be the monk on pilgrim duty. I did my Bede Harrington act, and he asked me to follow him to a little office. He had no memory of Maureen, but he said that if she had presented her passport at the monastery she would have been asked to complete a questionnaire. Sure enough he found it in a filing cabinet, completed in Maureen's big round hand four weeks earlier. "*Name*: Maureen Harrington. *Age*: 57. *Nationality*: British. *Religion*: Catholic. *Motives for journey (tick one or more)*: *1. Religious   2. Spiritual   3. Recreational   4. Cultural   5. Sporting*." I noticed with interest that Maureen had only ticked one: "Spiritual."

The monk, who introduced himself to me as Don Andreas, showed me round the monastery. He said apologetically that I couldn't stay in the *refugio* because I was travelling by car, but when I saw the bleak, breeze-block dormitory, with its naked lightbulbs and rough wood-and-wire bunks, this seemed a deprivation I could bear. It was empty: the day's quota of pilgrims hadn't yet arrived. I found a little hotel in the nearby village with creaking floorboards and paper-thin walls, but it was clean and comfortable enough. I went back to the monastery because Don Andreas had invited me to attend the pilgrim mass which was held at six every evening. It seemed churlish to decline, and anyway I liked the idea of doing something Maureen would certainly have done a few weeks earlier. I thought it might help me to get inside her head, and track her down by some kind of telepathic radar.

I hadn't attended a Catholic service since we split up, and the pilgrim mass didn't bear much resemblance to anything I remembered from the repertory of the Immaculate Conception in the old days. There were several priests saying the mass at the same time and they stood in a semi-circle behind a plain table-style altar (like the one

I had noticed recently in the Hatchford church) facing the congregation in an island of light amid the general gloom of the huge chapel, so you could see all the business with the gold-plated goblets and plates quite clearly. The congregation were a motley crew of all ages, shapes and sizes, casually dressed in sweaters and shorts, sandals and trainers. It was obvious that most of them were not Catholics, and had even less of a clue about what was going on than I did. Perhaps they thought they had to attend the service if they were getting a free bed for the night, like dossers in a Sally Army hostel; or perhaps they got a genuine spiritual kick out of hearing the mutter of the liturgy echoing round the pillars and vaults of the ancient church, as it had for centuries. Only a handful went to communion, but at the end everyone was invited to go up to the altar steps to receive a blessing, pronounced in three languages – Spanish, French and English. To my surprise everybody in the pews stepped forward, and I rather sheepishly joined them. I even crossed myself at the blessing, a long-forgotten action I had copied from Maureen at Benediction years ago. I sent up a silent prayer To Whom It May Concern that I would find her.

I spent the next two weeks cruising up and down the roads of northern Spain, staring at every pilgrim I passed who remotely resembled Maureen, sometimes drifting dangerously into the middle of the road as I looked back over my shoulder to scrutinize the face of some walker with a likely-looking rear aspect. Pilgrims were always easy to identify – they invariably displayed the *coquille*, and usually carried a long staff or stick. But the further I went, the more of them there were on the roads, and I didn't have much to go on by way of distinctive features. Mme Whitehouse had recalled that Maureen was shouldering a backpack with a rolled polystyrene mat on top, but she couldn't remember the colours of either of these items. All the time I was tormented by the thought that I might be overtaking Maureen without knowing it – while she was resting her feet in some church or café, or while she was walking those parts of the Camino that veer off the modern road system and became a track or footpath impassable to four-wheeled traffic (certainly to my decadently low-slung vehicle). I stopped at every church I spotted – and there are an awful lot of them in this part of Spain, a legacy of the mediaeval pilgrimage. I checked out every *refugio* I could find – the hostels that offer free, very basic shelter to pilgrims all along the route. Most of them were so basic – stone-floored stables virtually – that I couldn't imagine Maureen would have slept in them; but I thought I might encounter in this way somebody who had met Maureen on the road.

I met all sorts of pilgrims. The most numerous were young Spaniards for whom the pilgrimage was obviously an impeccable excuse to get out of the parental home and meet other young Spaniards of the opposite sex. The *refugios* are unsegregated. I'm not suggesting any hanky-panky goes on (there's not enough privacy, anyway), but I sometimes seemed to catch in them of an evening a whiff of that puppyish flirtatiousness I remembered from the Immaculate Conception youth club. Then there were the more sophisticated young backpackers from other countries, bronzed and muscular, attracted by the buzz on the international grapevine that Santiago was a really cool trip, with great scenery, cheap wine and free space to spread your bedroll. There were cycling clubs from France and the Low Countries in matching T-shirts and bollock-hugging lycra shorts – a group much despised and resented by everybody else because they had back-up trucks to transport their luggage from stage to stage – and solo cyclists pedalling pannier-festooned mountain bikes at 78 r.p.m. There were couples and pairs of friends with a common interest in walking, or Spanish history, or Romanesque architecture, who were doing the Camino in easy instalments, year by year. For all these groups, it seemed to me, the pilgrimage was primarily an alternative and adventurous kind of holiday.

Then there were the pilgrims with more particular and personal motives: a young sponsored cyclist raising money for a cancer ward; a Dutch artist aiming to get to Santiago to mark his fortieth birthday; a sixty-year-old Belgian who was doing the pilgrimage as the first act of his retirement; a redundant factory worker from Nancy contemplating his future. People at turning-points in their lives – looking for peace, or enlightenment, or just an escape from the daily rat-race.

The pilgrims in this category were the ones who had travelled furthest, often walking all the way from their homes in northern Europe, camping on the way. Some had been on the road for months. Their faces were sunburned, their clothes weather-stained, and they had a kind of reserve or remoteness about them, as if they had acquired the habit of solitude on the long lonely miles, and found the sometimes boisterous and hearty company of other pilgrims unwelcome. Their eyes had a distant look, as though focused on Santiago. A few were Catholics, but most had no particular religious beliefs. Some had begun the pilgrimage in a light-hearted experimental mood and become deeply obsessed with it. Others were probably a little mad when they started. Heterogeneous as they were, it was this group of pilgrims who interested me most, because I thought they were most likely to have met Maureen on the road.

I described her as best I could, but drew a complete blank until I had got as far as Cebrero, a little village high up in the mountains of León, only a hundred and fifty kilometres from Santiago. It's a curious place, halfway between a folk village and a shrine. The dwellings are of antique design, circular stone-walled huts with conical thatched roofs, and peasants still live in them, probably subsidized by the Spanish government. The church contains relics of some gruesome mediaeval miracle, when the communion bread and wine turned into real flesh and blood, and the place is also said to be associated with the legend of the Holy Grail. It was certainly a crucial stage in my own quest. In the bar-cum-café next to the church, a homely place of bare boards and refectory tables, I got into conversation with an elderly Dutch cyclist who claimed he had met an English pilgrim called Maureen in a *refugio* near León a week before. She had a bad leg and had told him she was going to rest in León for a few days before continuing her journey. I had been in León recently, but I jumped into the Richmobile and headed back there, intending to check out every hotel in the city.

I was driving eastwards along the N120 between Astorga and Orbigo, a busy arterial road, when I saw her, walking towards me at the edge of the road – a plump, solitary woman in baggy cotton trousers and a

293

broadbrimmed straw hat. It was only a glimpse, and I was doing seventy miles an hour at the time. I trod on the brakes, provoking an enraged bellow from a huge petrol tanker on my tail. With heavy traffic in both directions on the two-lane road, it was impossible to stop until, after a kilometre or two, I came to a drive-in café with a dirt carpark. I did a three-point turn in a cloud of dust and raced back down the road, wondering if I had hallucinated the figure of Maureen. But no, there she was, plodding along ahead of me on the other side of the road – or there was somebody, largely concealed by a backpack, rolled bedmat and straw hat. I slowed down, provoking more indignant hooting from the cars behind me, and turned to look at the woman's face as I passed. It was Maureen alright. Hearing the noise of the car horns, she threw a casual glance in my direction, but I was concealed behind the Richmobile's dark-tinted glass, and unable to stop. A few hundred yards further on I pulled off the road where the verge was broad enough to park, got out of the car, and crossed the tarmac. There was an incline at this point, and Maureen was walking downhill towards me. She walked slowly, with a limp, grasping a staff which she plonked down on the road in front of her at every second step. Nevertheless her gait was unmistakable, even at a distance. It was as if forty years had been pinched out of my existence, and I was back in Hatchford, outside the florist's shop on the corner of the Five Ways, watching her walk down Beecher's Road towards me in her school uniform.

If I had scripted the meeting I would have chosen a more romantic setting – the interior of some cool dark old church, perhaps, or a country road with wildflowers blowing in the breeze along its margins, where the bleating of sheep was the loudest noise. There would certainly have been background music (perhaps an instrumental arrangement of "Too Young"). As it was, we met on the edge of an ugly main road in one of the least attractive bits of Castile, deafened by the noise of tyres and engines, choked by exhaust fumes, and buffeted by gusts of gritty air displaced by passing juggernauts. As she approached I began to walk towards her, and she took notice of me for the first time. She slowed, hesitated, and stopped, as if she feared my intentions. I laughed, smiled, and held out my arms in what was supposed to be a reassuring gesture. She looked at me with alarm, clearly thinking I was some kind of homicidal maniac or rapist, and drew back, lifting her staff as if prepared to use it for self-defence. I stopped, and spoke:

"Maureen! It's all right! It's me, Laurence."

She started. "What?" she said. "Laurence who?"

"Laurence Passmore. Don't you recognize me?"

I was disappointed that she obviously didn't – didn't seem even to remember my name. But as she reasonably explained later, she hadn't given me a thought for donkey's years, whereas I had been thinking of almost nothing else except her for weeks. While I had been scouring north-west Spain, hoping to run into her at every turn of the road, my sudden apparition on the N120 was to her as bizarre and surprising as if I had parachuted out of the sky, or popped up through a hole in the ground.

I shouted above the howl and whine of traffic, "We used to go around together, years ago. In Hatchford."

Maureen's expression changed and the fear went from her eyes. She squinted at me, as if she were short-sighted, or dazzled by the sun, and took a step forward. "Is it really you? *Laurence Passmore?* What on earth are you doing here?"

"I've been looking for you."

"Why?" she said, and a look of anxiety returned to her face. "There's nothing wrong at home, is there?"

"No, nothing wrong," I reassured her. "Bede's worried about you, but he's OK."

"Bede? When did you see Bede?"

"Just the other day. I was trying to trace you."

"What for?" she said. We were now face to face.

"It's a long story," I said. "Get in the car, and I'll tell you." I gestured to my sleek silver pet, crouched on the opposite verge. She gave it a momentary glance, and shook her head.

"I'm doing a pilgrimage," she said.

"I know."

"I don't go in cars."

"Make an exception today," I said. "You look as if you could do with a lift."

In truth she looked a wreck. As we parleyed, I was mentally coming to terms with the sad fact that Maureen was no longer the Maureen of my memories and fantasies. She had reached that point in a woman's life when her looks begin irretrievably to desert her. Sally hasn't quite reached it, and Amy is still several years on the right side of it. Both of them, anyway, are resisting the ageing process with everything short of plastic surgery, but Maureen seemed to have surrendered without putting up much of a fight. There were crowsfeet at the corners of her eyes, and bags under them. Her cheeks, once so plump and smooth, were slack jowls; her neck was creased like an old garment; and her figure had gone soft and shapeless, with no perceptible waistline between the cushiony mounds of her bosom and the broad beam of her hips. The general effect had not been improved by the weeks and months she had spent on the road: her nose was sunburnt and peeling, her hair lank and unkempt, her knuckles grubby and her nails broken. Her clothes were dusty and sweat-stained. I must admit that her appearance was a shock for which the posed and retouched photographs in Bede's living-room had not prepared me. I daresay the years have been even harder on me, but Maureen hadn't been nurturing any illusions to the contrary.

As she hesitated, leaning forward in her scuffed trainers to balance the weight of her backpack, I noticed that she had placed some lumps of sponge rubber under the shoulder straps to protect her collarbone from chafing. For some reason this seemed the most pathetic detail of all in her general appearance. I felt an overwhelming rush of tenderness towards her, a desire to look after her and rescue her from this daft, self-lacerating ordeal. "Just to the next village," I said, "Somewhere we can get a cold drink." The sun was basting my bald pate and I could feel sweat trickling down my torso inside my shirt. I added coaxingly, "The car's air-conditioned."

Maureen laughed, wrinkling her sunburned nose in the way I remembered so well. "It had better be," she said. "I'm sure I stink to high heaven."

She sighed and stretched out luxuriously in the front seat of the

Richmobile as we moved off down the highway with the silent speed of an electric train. "Well, this is very swish," she said, looking round the interior of the car. "What make is it?" I told her. "We have a Volvo, at home," she said. "Bede says they're very safe."

"Safety isn't everything," I said.

"No, it isn't," she said, with a little giggle.

"This is a dream come true, you, know," I said. "I've been fantasizing for months about driving you in this car."

"Have you?" She gave me a shy, puzzled smile. I didn't tell her that in my fantasies she was still in her teens.

A few kilometres further on we found a bar with some chairs and tables outside in the shade of an old oak, away from the jabber of television and the hiss of the coffee machine. Over a beer and a *citron pressé* we had the first of many conversations that slowly filled in the information gap of thirty-five years. The first thing Maureen wanted to know, naturally enough, was why I had sought her out. I gave her a condensed account of what I have already written in these pages: that my life was in a mess, personally and professionally, that I had been suddenly reminded of our relationship and how shabbily I had treated her at the end of it, and had become consumed with a desire to see her again. "To get absolution," I said.

Maureen blushed under her sunburn. "Goodness me, Laurence, you don't have to ask for that. It was nearly forty years ago. We were children, practically."

"But it must have hurt, at the time."

"Oh, yes, of course. I cried myself to sleep for ages –"

"There you are, then."

"But young girls are always doing that. You were the first boy I cried over, but not the last." She laughed. "You look surprised."

"You mean, Bede?" I said.

"Oh no, not *Bede*." She screwed up her face in a humorous grimace. "Can you imagine anybody crying over Bede? No, there were others, before him. A wildly handsome registrar I was hopelessly in love with, like every other student nurse at the hospital. I doubt if he even knew my name. And after I qualified there was a houseman I had an affair with."

"You mean . . . in the full sense of the word?" I stared incredu-lously.

"I slept with him, if that's what you mean. I don't know why I'm telling you all these intimate details, but somehow the older you get, the less you care what people know, don't you find? It's the same with your body. In hospital it's always the young patients who are most embarrassed about being washed and bedpanned and so on. The old ones couldn't give a damn."

"But what about your religion? When you had the affair."

"Oh, I knew I was committing a mortal sin. But I did it anyway, because I loved him. I thought he would marry me, you see. He said he would. But he changed his mind, or perhaps he was lying. So after I got over it I married Bede instead."

"Did you sleep with him first?" The question sounded crude as I formulated it, but curiosity overcame good manners.

Maureen rocked with laughter. "Good heavens, no! Bede would have been shocked at the very idea."

I pondered these surprising revelations in silence for a few moments. "So you haven't been bearing a grudge against me all this time?" I said at length.

"Of course not! Honestly, I haven't given you a thought for . . . I don't know how many years."

I think she was trying to reassure me, but I was hurt, I have to admit. "You haven't followed my career, then?" I said.

"No, should I have done? Are you terribly famous?"

"Not famous, exactly. But I've had some success as a TV writer. Do you ever watch *The People Next Door*?"

"Is that a comedy programme – the kind where you can hear a lot of people laughing but you can't see them?"

"It's a sitcom, yes."

"We tend to avoid those, I'm afraid. But now I know you write for it . . ."

"I write all of it. It was my idea. I'm known as Tubby Passmore," I said, desperate to strike some spark of recognition.

"Are you really?" Maureen laughed and wrinkled her nose. "Tubby!"

"But I'd rather you called me Laurence," I said, regretting the revelation. "It reminds me of the old days."

But from then on she called me Tubby. She seemed delighted with the name and said she couldn't get it out of her head. "I try to say 'Laurence', but 'Tubby' comes out of my mouth instead," she said.

The day we met, Maureen was aiming to get to Astorga. She refused to let me drive her there from the café, but, admitting that her leg was painful, agreed to let me take her backpack on ahead. She was planning to spend the night at the local *refugio*, uninvitingly described in the pilgrim's guidebook as an "unequipped sports hall". Maureen pulled a face. "That means no showers." I said I would be bitterly disappointed if she wouldn't be my guest for dinner on this red-letter day, and she could shower in my hotel room. She accepted the offer with good grace, and we arranged to meet in the porch of the Cathedral. I drove to Astorga and checked into a hotel, booking an extra room for Maureen in the hope of persuading her to take it. (She did.) While I waited for Maureen I did the tourist bit in Astorga. It has a cathedral which is Gothic inside and baroque outside (I was just about able to tell the difference by this time) and a Bishop's Palace like a fairy-tale castle built by Gaudí, who designed that weird unfinished cathedral-sized church in Barcelona with spires like enormous loofahs. Astorga also boasts a lot of relics, including a chip off the True Cross and a bit of a banner from the mythical battle of Clavijo.

Maureen turned up at the Cathedral about three hours after we had parted, smiling and saying that, without the weight of her backpack, the walk had been like a Sunday-afternoon stroll. I asked to see her leg and didn't much like what I saw under the grimy bandage. The calf was bruised and discoloured and the ankle joint swollen. "I think you should show that to a doctor," I said. Maureen said she had seen a doctor in León. He had diagnosed strained ligaments, recommended rest, and given her some ointment which had helped a little. She had rested the leg for four days, but it was still troubling her. "You need more like four months," I said. "I know a bit about this sort of injury. It won't go away unless you pack in the pilgrimage."

"I'm not going to give up now," she said. "Not after getting this far."

I knew her well enough not to waste breath trying to persuade her to drop out and go home. Instead I devised a plan to help her get to Santiago as comfortably as possible with honour. Each day I would drive with her pack to an agreed rendezvous, and book us into some modest inn or b. & b. Maureen had no principled objection to such accommodation. She had treated herself to it occasionally, and the *refugios* were, she said, becoming increasingly crowded and unpleasant the nearer she got to Santiago. But her funds were low, and she hadn't wanted to ring up Bede and ask him to send her more money. She agreed to let me pay for our rooms on the understanding that she would repay her share when we got back to England, and kept scrupulous note of our expenses.

We inched our way to Santiago in very short stages. Even without her backpack, Maureen wasn't capable of walking more than ten to twelve kilometres a day without discomfort, and it took her up to four hours to cover even that modest distance. Usually, after arranging our accommodation, I would walk back along the Camino eastwards to meet her, and keep her company on the home stretch. It pleased me that my knee stood up well to this exercise, even when the going was steep and rugged. In fact, I realized that I hadn't felt a single twinge in it since I got to St Jean Pied-de-Port. "It's St James," Maureen said, when I remarked on this. "It's a well-known phenomenon. He helps you. I'd never have got this far without him. I remember when I was climbing the pass through the Pyrenees, soaked to the skin and utterly exhausted, feeling I couldn't go any further and would just roll into a ditch and die, I felt a force like a hand in the small of the back pushing me on, and before I knew where I was, I found myself at the top."

I wasn't sure how serious she was. When I asked her if she believed St James was really buried in Santiago, she shrugged and said, "I don't know. We'll never know for sure, one way or the other." I said, "Doesn't it bother you that millions of people may have been coming here for centuries all because of a misprint?" I was showing off a bit of knowledge gleaned from one of my guidebooks: apparently the original association of St James with Spain all goes back to a scribe who wrote mistakenly that the Apostle's patch was "Hispaniam" instead of "Hierusalem" (i.e., Jerusalem.) "No," she said. "I think he's around the place somewhere. With so many people walking to Santiago to pay him homage, he could hardly stay away, could he?" But there was a twinkle in her eye as she spoke of these things, as if it were a private joke or tease, designed to scandalize Protestant sceptics like me.

There was nothing frivolous about her commitment to the pilgrimage, however. "*It's absurd, quite absurd,*" I remembered Bede saying, but the word had a Kierkegaardian resonance for me which he didn't intend. In the mediaeval town of Villafranca there's a church dedicated to St James with a porch known as the *Puerta del Perdón*, the Doorway of Pardon, and according to tradition if a pilgrim was ill and made it as far as this door, he could turn back and go home with all the graces and blessings of a fully completed pilgrimage. I pointed out this loophole to Maureen when we got to Villafranca, and pressed her to take advantage of it. She laughed at first, but became quite annoyed when I persisted. After that I never attempted to dissuade her from trying to get to Santiago.

To tell the truth, I would have been almost as disappointed as Maureen herself if she had failed to make it. The pilgrimage, even in the bastardized, motorized form in which I was doing it, had begun to lay its spell upon me. I sensed, if only fragmentarily, what Maureen had experienced more deeply and intensely in the course of her long march from Le Puy. "You seem to drop out of time. You pay no attention to the news. The images you see on television in bars and cafés, of politicians and car bombs and bicycle races, don't hold your attention for more than a few seconds. All that matters are the basics: feeding yourself, not getting dehydrated, healing your blisters, getting to the next stopping-place before it gets too hot, or too cold, or too wet. Surviving. At first you think you'll go mad with loneliness and fatigue, but after a while you resent the presence of other people, you would rather walk on your own, be alone with your own thoughts, and the pain in your feet."

"You wish I wasn't here, then?" I said.

"Oh no, I was almost at the end of my tether when you turned up, Tubby. I'd never have got this far without you."

I frowned, like Ryan Giggs when he's made a goal with a perfect cross. But Maureen wiped the frown off my face when she added, "It was like a miracle. St James again."

In due course she talked about the death of Damien, and how it had led to her making the pilgrimage. "It's a terrible thing when a child dies before its parents. It seems against nature. You can't help thinking of all the things he will never experience, like marriage, having children, grandchildren. Fortunately I think Damien knew love. That's a consolation. He had a girlfriend in Africa, she worked for the same organization. She looked very nice in photographs. She wrote us a beautiful letter after he was killed. I hope they had sex. I should think they would have done, wouldn't you?"

I said yes, undoubtedly.

"When he was a student at Cambridge he brought a girl home once, not the same one, and he asked if they could sleep together in his room. I said no, not in my house. But I would've let him, if I'd known how short his life was going to be."

I said she mustn't blame herself for actions that were perfectly reasonable at the time.

"Oh, I don't blame myself," she said. "It's Bede who does that, though he denies it. He thinks he should have tried harder to persuade Damien not to make his career in relief work. Damien did VSO, you see, after graduating. He was going to go back to Cambridge afterwards and do a PhD. But he decided to stay in Africa. He loved the people. He loved the work. He had a full life, a very intense life, though it was short. And he did a lot of good. I kept telling myself that, after he was killed. It didn't help Bede, though. He became terribly depressed. When he retired he just moped around the house all day, staring into space. I couldn't stand it. I decided I had to get away somewhere on my own. I read an article about the pilgrimage in a magazine, and it seemed just what I needed. Something quite challenging and clearly defined, something that would occupy your whole self, body and soul, for two or three months. I read a book about the history of it, and was completely fascinated. Literally millions of pilgrims went along this road, when the only way of doing it was on foot or on horseback. They must have got something tremendous out of it, I thought to myself, or people wouldn't have kept on going. I got myself a guide to the route from the Confraternity of St James, and a rucksack and sleeping-bag and the rest of the kit from the camping shop in Wimbledon High Street. The family thought I was mad, of course, and tried to talk me out of it. Other people presumed I was doing it as a sponsored walk for charity. I said, no, I've done things for others all my life, this is for me. I've been a nurse, I'm a Samaritan, I'm –"

"Are you really?" I interjected. "A Samaritan? Bede didn't mention it."

"Bede never really approved," said Maureen. "He thought all that misery would leak out of the phone and infect me."

"I bet you're good at it," I said.

"Well, I've only lost one client in six years," she said. "I mean, only one actually topped himself. Not a bad record. Mind you, I found I was less sympathetic after Damien was killed. I didn't have the same patience with some of the callers, their problems seemed so much more trivial than mine. Do you know what our busiest day of the year is?"

"Christmas Day?"

"No, Christmas is second. Number one is St Valentine's Day. Makes you think, doesn't it?"

In our slow, looping dawdle along the Camino we were frequently overtaken by younger, fitter, or fresher walkers. The nearer we got to Santiago, the more of them there were. The annual climax of the pilgrimage, the feast of St James on 25th July, was only a couple of weeks away, and everybody was anxious to get there in good time. Sometimes, from a high point on the road, you could look down on the Camino ribboning for miles ahead, with pilgrims in ones and twos and larger clusters strung out along it like beads as far as the horizon, just as it must have looked in the Middle Ages.

At Cebrero we ran into a British television unit making a

documentary about the pilgrimage. They were ambushing pilgrims outside the little church and asking them about their motives. Maureen refused point-blank to take part. The director, a big blond chap in shorts and tee-shirt, tried to persuade her to change her mind. "We desperately need an older woman who speaks English," he said. "We're up to here in young Spaniards and Belgian cyclists. You'd be perfect." "No thank you," Maureen said. "I don't want to be on television." The director looked hurt: people in the media can never understand that the rest of the world doesn't have the same priorities as themselves. He turned to me as a second-best alternative. "I'm not a true pilgrim," I said.

"Ah! Who is a true pilgrim?" he said, his eyes lighting up.

"Someone for whom it's an existential act of self-definition," I said. "A leap into the absurd, in Kierkegaard's sense. I mean, what could be –"

"Stop!" cried the director "Don't say any more. I want to film this. Go and get David, Linda," he added to a freckled, sandy-haired young woman clutching a clipboard. David, it appeared, was the writer-presenter of the programme, but he couldn't be found. "He's probably sulking because he had to actually *walk* a bit this morning," muttered the director, who was also confusingly called David. "I'll have to do the interview myself."

So they set up the camera, and after the usual delay while the director decided where to set up the shot, and the cameraman and his focus-puller fiddled about with lenses and filters and reflectors, and the sound man was satisfied about the level of background noise, and the production assistant had stopped people walking in and out of shot behind me, I delivered my existentialist interpretation of the pilgrimage to camera. (Maureen by this time had got bored and wandered off to look at the church.) I described the three stages in personal development according to Kierkegaard – the aesthetic, the ethical and the religious – and suggested that there were three corresponding types of pilgrim. (I had been thinking about this on the road.) The aesthetic type was mainly concerned with having a good time, enjoying the picturesque and cultural pleasures of the Camino. The ethical type saw the pilgrimage as essentially a test of stamina and self-discipline. He (or she) had a strict notion of what was correct pilgrim behaviour (no staying in hotels, for instance) and was very competitive with others on the road. The true pilgrim was the religious pilgrim, religious in the Kierkegaardian sense. To Kierkegaard, Christianity was "absurd": if it were entirely rational, there would be no merit in believing it. The whole point was that you chose to believe without rational compulsion – you made a leap into the void and in the process chose yourself. Walking a thousand miles to the shrine of Santiago without knowing whether there was anybody actually buried there was such a leap. The aesthetic pilgrim didn't pretend to be a true pilgrim. The ethical pilgrim was always worrying whether he *was* a true pilgrim. The true pilgrim just did it.

"Cut! Great. Thanks very much," said the director. "Get him to sign a release, Linda."

Linda smiled at me, with pen poised over her clip board. "You'll get twenty-five pounds if we use it," she said "What's your name, please?"

"Laurence Passmore," I said.

The sound man looked up sharply from his equipment. "Not Tubby Passmore?" I nodded, he slapped his thigh. "I knew I'd seen you somewhere before. It was in the Heartland canteen, a couple of years ago. Hey, David!" he called to the director, who was walking away in search of another victim, "Guess who this is – Tubby Passmore, the writer. *The People Next Door.*" He turned back to me: "Great show, I never miss it when I'm at home."

The director turned round slowly. "Oh no," he said, and mimed shooting himself in the head with his forefinger. "So you were just taking the piss?" He laughed ruefully. "We really fell for it."

"I wasn't taking the piss," I said. But I don't think he believed me.

The days passed in a slow, regular rhythm. We rose early, so that Maureen could set off in the cool of the early morning. She usually arrived at our rendezvous around noon. After a long, leisurely Spanish lunch we retired for a siesta and slept through the heat of the afternoon, coming to life again in the evening, when we would take the air with the natives, snacking in *tapas* bars and sampling the local *vino.* I can't describe how at ease I felt in Maureen's company, how quickly we seemed to resume our old familiarity. Although we talked a lot, we were often content to be together in a companionable silence, as if we were enjoying the sunset years of a long happy life together. Other people certainly assumed we were a married couple, or at least a couple; and the hotel staff always looked mildly surprised that we were occupying separate rooms.

One night, after she had been talking at some length about Damien, apparently in good spirits, even laughing as she recalled some childish misadventure he had had, I heard her weeping in the room next to mine, through the thin partition wall of the no-star hotel where we were staying. I tapped on her door and, finding it unlocked, went in. A street-lamp outside the window shed a dim illumination into the room through the curtains. Maureen was a humped shape that stirred and rearranged itself on the bed against one wall. "Is that you, Tubby?" she said.

"I thought I heard you crying," I said. I groped my way across the room, stumbled over a chair beside the bed, and sat down on it. "Are you alright?"

"It was talking about Damien," she said. "I keep thinking I've got over it, and then I find I haven't." She began to cry again. I felt for her hand and held it. She squeezed it gratefully.

"I could hug you, if that would help," I said.

"No, I'm alright," she said.

"I'd like to. I'd like to very much," I said.

"I don't think it would be a good idea, Tubby."

"I'm not suggesting we do anything else," I said. "Just a cuddle. It'll help you go to sleep."

I lay down beside her on the bed, outside the blanket and sheet, and put my arm round her waist. She turned over on to her side, with her back to me, and I curled myself around her soft ample bottom. She stopped crying, and her breathing became regular. We both fell asleep.

I woke, I didn't know how many hours later. The night air had grown cool, and my feet were chilled. I sat up and rubbed them. Maureen stirred. "What is it?" she said.

"Nothing. Just a bit cold. Can I come under the bedclothes?"

She didn't say no, so I lifted the sheet and blanket and snuggled up to her. She was wearing a thin, sleeveless cotton nightgown. A pleasant warm odour, like the smell of fresh-baked bread, rose from her body. Not surprisingly, I had an erection.

"I think perhaps you'd better go back to your own bed," Maureen said.

"Why?"

"You might get a nasty shock if you stay here," she said.

"What do you mean?" She was lying on her back and I was massaging her stomach very gently through her nightgown with my finger-tips – it was something Sally liked me to do when she was pregnant. My head was pillowed on one of Maureen's big round breasts. Very slowly, holding my breath, I moved my hand up to cup the other one, just as I had done all those years ago, in the damp dark basement area of 94 Treglowan Road.

But it wasn't there.

"I did warn you," Maureen said.

It was a shock, of course, like climbing the stairs in the dark and finding there is one step fewer than you expected. I pulled my hand away in a reflex action, but put it back again almost immediately on the plateau of skin and bone. I could trace the erratic line of a scar, like the diagram of a constellation, through the thin fabric of the nightgown.

"I don't mind," I said.

"Yes you do," she said.

"No I don't," I said, and I unbuttoned the front of her nightdress and kissed the puckered flesh where her breast had been.

"Oh Tubby," she said, "that's the nicest thing anybody ever did to me."

"Would you like to make love?" I said.

"No."

"Bede will never know." I seemed to hear the echo of another conversation from the past.

"It wouldn't be right," she said. "Not on a pilgrimage."

I said I took her point, kissed her, and got out of the bed. She sat up, put her arms round me and kissed me again, very warmly on the lips. "Thanks Tubby, you're a darling," she said.

I went back to my room and lay awake for some time. I won't say that the problems and disappointments of my life seemed trivial beside Maureen's, but they certainly seemed smaller. Not only had she lost a beloved son – she had lost a breast, the part of a woman's body which defines her sexual identity perhaps more obviously than any other. And although Maureen herself would certainly have said that the former loss was the greater, it was the latter which affected me more, perhaps because I had never known Damien, but I had known that breast, known it and loved it – and written about it. My memoir had turned into an elegy.

I walked the whole of the last stage of the pilgrimage with Maureen. I put a few overnight things in her rucksack, and we shared carrying it. I left the car in Labacolla, a hamlet about twelve kilometres outside Santiago, near the airport, where the pilgrims of old used to wash themselves in preparation for their arrival at the shrine. The name literally means, "wash your bottom", and the bottoms of the mediaeval pilgrims probably needed a good scrub by the time they got there.

It was a warm, sunny morning. The first part of the route was through a wood and across some fields with pleasant open country to our left and the grumble of traffic from the main road to our right. Then we came to a village, at the far end of which is the Monte del Gozo, the "Mount of Joy", where pilgrims get their first view of Santiago. In olden times there used to be a race to the top, amongst each group, to be the first to see the long-desired goal. It's a bit of an anticlimax nowdays, because the hill has been almost entirely covered with a huge amphitheatre, and from this distance Santiago looks like any other modern city, ringed by motorways, industrial estates and tower blocks. If you look very hard, or have very good eyes, you can just make out the spires of the Cathedral.

Nevertheless, I was very glad I walked into Santiago. I was able to share something of Maureen's excitement and elation as she reached the finishing line of her marathon; I even felt a modicum of excitement and elation myself. You notice much more on foot than you do in a car, and the slowness of walking itself creates a kind of dramatic tension, delaying the consummation of your journey. Trudging through the ugly modern outskirts of the city only heightens the pleasure and relief of reaching its beautiful old heart, with its crooked, shady streets, odd angles and irregular rooflines. You turn a corner and there, suddenly, you are, in the immense Plaza del Obradoiro, looking up at the twin spires of the great Cathedral.

We arrived on the 24th July, and Santiago was bursting at the seams. The four-day *fiiesta* was already in progress, with marching bands, huge walking effigies on stilts, and itinerant musicians roving through the streets and squares. The pukka pilgrims like Maureen were swamped by hundreds and thousands of visitors, both secular tourists and pious Catholics, who had arrived by plane or train or bus or car. We were told the crowds were particularly big because it was a Holy Year, when the feast of St James falls on a Sunday, and the blessings and indulgences attached to the shrine are especially potent. I suggested to Maureen that we ought to see about getting accommodation without delay, but she was impatient to visit the Cathedral. I indulged her. It seemed unlikely that we would find anywhere to stay in the old town anyway, and I was resigned to going back to Labacolla for the night.

The Cathedral is a bit of a dog's breakfast architecturally but, as we say in television, it works. The elaborately decorated façade is eighteenth-century baroque, with a grand staircase between the two towers and spires. Behind it is the portico of the earlier romanesque building, the Portico de la Gloria, carved by a mediaeval genius called Maestro Matteo. It depicts in amazing, often humorous, detail, some two hundred figures, including Jesus, Adam and Eve, Matthew, Mark, Luke and John, twenty-four old codgers with musical instruments from the Book of Revelations, and a selection of the saved and the damned at the Last Judgement. St James has pride of place, sitting on top of a pillar just under the feet of Jesus. It's the custom for visitors to the Cathedral to kneel at the foot of the pillar, and place their fingers in the hollow spaces, like the holes in a knuckleduster, that have been worn into the marble through centuries of homage. There was a long line of people, many of them local to judge by their clothes and complexions, waiting to perform this ritual. Clocking Maureen, with her staff and rucksack and sunfaded clothes, as a genuine pilgrim, the people at the front of the line fell back respectfully and gestured her forward. She blushed under her tan and shook her head. "Go on," I urged her. "This is your big scene. Go for it." So she stepped forward and fell onto her knees and, with one palm pressed against the pillar, fitted the fingers of the other hand into the holes, and prayed for a moment with her eyes closed.

On the other side of the pillar, at the foot, Maestro Matteo has carved a bust of himself, and it's the custom to knock your head against his to acquire something of his wisdom. This was more my kind of mumbo-jumbo, and I duly banged my forehead against the marble brow. I observed some confusion between the two rituals. Every now and again somebody would bang their head against the pillar under the statue of St James as they put their fingers in the holes, and then everybody in the line behind them would follow suit. I was tempted to try slapping my buttocks like a Bavarian folkdancer as I paid homage, just to see if it caught on, but I didn't have the nerve.

We joined another line of people taking their turn to embrace the statue of St James on the high altar. The holy end of the Cathedral is an over-the-top fantasy in marble and gold leaf and carved painted wood. St James Matamoros, dressed and mounted like a Renaissance cavalry officer, charges with sword drawn above the canopy, which is supported by four gigantic, trumpet-blowing angels. St James the Apostle, swathed in jewel-encrusted silver and gold plate, presides over the altar looking more like a pagan idol than a Christian saint, especially as, seen from the main body of the church, he seems to have grown an extra pair of arms. These belong to the people who, standing on a little platform behind the altar, embrace him and, if they are pilgrims, pray for those who helped them on their way – the traditional "hug for St James". Beneath the altar is a crypt with the small silver coffin containing the remains of the saint – or not, as the case may be.

"Wasn't it wonderful?" Maureen said, as we came out of the Cathedral, into the bright sunlight of the square with its milling crowds. I agreed that it was; but I couldn't help contrasting the pomp and circumstance of this shrine with the small, austerely furnished room in the Copenhagen Bymuseum, its half-dozen cabinets containing a few homely objects, books and pictures, and the modest monument in the Assistens Kirkegård. I wondered whether, if Kierkegaard had been a Catholic, they would have made him a saint by now, and built a basilica over his grave. He would make a good patron saint of neurotics.

"Now we really ought to see about finding somewhere to stay," I said.

"Don't worry about it," Maureen said. "First I must get my *compostela*." We were directed to a little office off a square at the back of the Cathedral. Outside, a group of bronzed, elated-looking young Germans in *Lederhosen* and boots were photographing each other, triumphantly waving their pieces of paper at the camera. Maureen lined up inside and submitted her creased, stained passport to a young priest in a black suit seated behind a desk. He admired the number of stamps she had collected, and shook her hand as he passed over her certificate.

"*Now* can we see about a hotel?" I said, as we came out of the office.

"Well, actually," Maureen said, with a slightly embarrassed laugh, "I've reserved a room at the Reyes Catolicos. I did it before I left England."

The Hostal de los Reyes Catolicos is a magnificent Renaissance building which flanks the Plaza del Obradoiro on the left-hand side as you face the Cathedral. Originally the *refugio* to end all *refugios*, founded by King Ferdinand and Queen Isabella for the reception and care of pilgrims, it's now a five-star *parador*, one of the grandest hotels in Spain or indeed anywhere else.

"Fantastic! Why didn't you tell me?" I exclaimed.

"Well, there's a little problem. It's just the one room, and I booked it in the name of Mr and Mrs Harrington. I thought Bede might fly over and join me. But he was so mean about the pilgrimage that I never told him."

"Well then," I said, "I'll just have to impersonate Bede. It won't be the first time."

"You don't mind sharing then?"

"Not a bit."

"I asked for twin beds, anyway," said Maureen. "Bede prefers them."

"Pity," I said, and enjoyed her blushes.

As we approached the hotel a gleaming limousine pattered over the cobbles to pick up a smartly dressed elderly couple standing outside the entrance. The liveried, white-gloved doorman pocketed a tip, shut the car door and waved the driver on. He eyed us disapprovingly.

"My *compostela* entitles me to a free meal here," Maureen murmured. "But I'm told they give you rather nasty food and make you eat it in a grotty little room off the kitchens."

The doorkeeper evidently thought that this must be our reason for approaching the hotel, for he said something rather dismissive in Spanish and gestured us towards the back of the building. It was an understandable presumption, I suppose, given our somewhat scruffy appearance, but we took some satisfaction in putting him in his place. "We have a reservation," said Maureen, sweeping regally past the man, and pushing through the swing doors. A porter ran after us into the lobby. I gave him the rucksack to hold, while I went up to the reception desk. "Mr and Mrs Harrington," I said boldly. The clerk was suavely courteous. Funnily enough, he looked rather like Bede, tall, stooped and scholarly, with white hair and thick glasses. He checked his computer, and gave me a registration card to fill in. Maureen had booked for three nights, and paid a substantial deposit.

"How could you be sure you would get here, at exactly the right time?" I marvelled, as we followed the porter, who was trying with some difficulty to carry our rucksack as if it were a suitcase, to the room.

"I had faith," she said simply.

The Hostal is laid out in four exquisite quadrangles, with cloisters, fllowerbeds and fountains, each dedicated to one of the evangelists. Our room was off Matthew. It was large and luxurious, the single beds the size of small doubles. Samantha would have loved it. There were sixteen fluffy white towels of different sizes in the marble-lined bathroom, and no nonsense about getting a red card if you wanted them changed. Maureen cooed with delight at the array of taps, nozzles, adjustable mirrors and built-in hair dryer, and announced her intention of taking a bath and washing her hair immediately. At the bottom of her rucksack, folded flat as a parachute inside a plastic bag, was a clean cotton dress which she had been saving for this moment. She gave it to the hotel's housekeeper to be ironed, and I took a cab back to Labacolla to pick up my car, which contained a linen suit I hadn't previously worn on the trip.

So we didn't disgrace the hotel's elegant dining-room that evening. The food was amazingly expensive, but very good. Afterwards we went out into the square and squeezed into the vast crowd waiting to watch the fireworks. This is easily the most popular event of the *fiesta*. Spaniards love noise, and with this display they seemed determined to make up for their exclusion from World War Two. The climactic setpiece resembled an air raid on the Cathedral, with the whole structure apparently on fire, statues and stonework silhouetted against the flames, and cannonades of rockets exploding deafeningly overhead. I couldn't see what it had to do with St James, but the crowd loved it. There was a huge collective sigh as the vast stage faded to black, and a burst of cheering and clapping when the street-lights came on. The crowd began to disperse. We went back to the Reyes Catolicos. The doorman greeted us with a smile.

"Goodnight Señor, Señora," he said, as he held open the door.

We took turns to use the bathroom. When I came out, Maureen was already in bed. I stooped to give her a goodnight kiss. She put her arms round my neck and drew me down beside her. "What a day," she said.

"It's a pity sex isn't allowed on pilgrimages," I said.

"I'm not on a pilgrimage any more," she said. "I've arrived."

We made love in the missionary position. I came – no problem. No problem with the knee, either. "I'll never knock St James again," I said, afterwards.

"What d'you mean?" Maureen murmured drowsily. She seemed to have had a good time too.

"Never mind." I said.

When I woke next morning, Maureen wasn't there. She had left a note to say that she'd gone to the Cathedral early, to bag a seat for the great High Mass of St James; but she came back while I was having breakfast to say the church was already crammed full, so we watched the mass on television instead. It's a state occasion, broadcast live on the national network. I don't think Maureen missed much by not being there. Most of the congregation looked stupefied by the heat and the tedium of waiting. The high point of the service is the swinging of the *botafumeiro*, a gigantic censer, about the size of a sputnik, which is swung high into the roof of the cathedral, trailing clouds of holy smoke, by a team of six burly men pulling on an elaborate tackle of ropes and pulleys. If it ever broke loose at this mass it could wipe out the Spanish Royal Family and a large number of the country's cardinals and bishops.

We took a stroll round the old town, had lunch, and retired to our room for a siesta. We made love before we napped, and again that night. Maureen was as eager as me. "It's like giving up sweets for Lent," she said. "When Easter comes, you make a bit of a pig of yourself."

In her case Lent had lasted for five years, ever since her mastectomy. She said Bede hadn't been able to adjust to it. "He didn't mean to be unkind. He was wonderfully supportive when the tumour was diagnosed, and while I was in hospital, but when I came home I made the mistake of showing him the scar. I'll never forget the expression on his face. He couldn't get the image out of his head, I'm afraid. I tried keeping my prosthetic bra on in bed, but it made no difference. About six months afterwards he suggested we changed our double bed for two singles. He pretended it was because he needed a special mattress for his back, but I knew he meant that our sexual life was over."

"But that's terrible!" I said. "Why don't you leave him and marry me?"

"Don't be ridiculous," she said.

"I'm perfectly serious," I said. And I was.

That conversation took place on the edge of a cliff overlooking the Atlantic ocean. It was our third evening since arriving in Santiago, and our last together in Spain. The next day Maureen was flying back to London, with a ticket purchased months ago; after seeing her off at the airport I would drive the Richmobile to Santander to catch the ferry to England.

We had driven out of Santiago that afternoon, after a particularly passionate siesta, in search of a little peace and quiet – even Maureen had had enough of the crowds and clamour of the streets by now. We found ourselves on a road signposted to Finisterre and just kept going. I must have heard the name a thousand times on the radio in shipping forecasts and gale warnings without knowing that it was in Spain or twigging that it means "end of the world" in Latin. It was a long way – further than it looked on the map. The rolling wooded hills of the country around Santiago gave way to a more rugged, heath-like terrain of windblown grass broken by great slabs of grey rock and the occasional stubborn, slanting tree. As we approached the tip of the peninsula the land seemed to tilt upwards like a ramp, beyond which we could see nothing but sky. You really felt as if you were coming to the end of the world; the end of something, anyway. We parked the car beside a lighthouse, followed a path round to the other side of the building, and there was the ocean spread out beneath us, calm and blue, shading almost imperceptibly into the sky at the hazy horizon. We sat down on a warm, flat rock, amid coarse grass and wildflowers, and watched the sun, like a huge communion wafer behind a thin veil of cloud, slowly decline towards the wrinkled surface of the sea.

"No," said Maureen, "I couldn't leave poor old Bede. What would he do without me? He'd crack up completely."

"But you have a right to happiness," I said. "Not to mention me."

"You'll be alright, Tubby," she smiled.

"I like your confidence. I'm a notorious neurotic."

315

"You seem very sane to me."

"That's because of being with you again."

"It's been wonderful," she said. "But it's like the whole pilgrimage, a kind of kink in time, when the ordinary rules of life don't apply. When I go home, I'll be married to Bede again."

"A loveless marriage!"

"Sexless, perhaps, but not loveless," she said. "And I did marry him, after all, for better or for worse."

"Haven't you ever thought of leaving him?"

"No, never. It's the way I was brought up, I suppose. Divorce just wasn't thinkable for Catholics. I know that it's caused a lot of misery for a lot of people, but it's worked for me. It simplifies things."

"One less decision to make."

"Exactly."

We were quiet for a while. Maureen plucked and chewed a stalk of grass. "Have you thought of trying to get back together with your wife?" she said.

"There's no point. Her mind is made up."

I had of course told Maureen all about the break-up with Sally, in the course of our conversations over the past few weeks, and she had listened with a keen and sympathetic interest, but without making any judgements.

"When did you last see her?" Maureen asked. I worked it out: it was about three months. "You may have changed in that time, more than you know," Maureen said. "You told me yourself you were a little bit off your head in the spring." I admitted that that was true. "And Sally may have changed too," Maureen went on. "She may be waiting for an approach by you."

"That hasn't been the tenor of her lawyer's letters," I said.

"You can't go by them," Maureen said. "Lawyers are paid to bluster."

"True," I conceded. I recalled Sally's rather surprising phone call, just before I left London. If I hadn't been in such a hurry to be off, I might have interpreted her tone as conciliatory.

We sat and talked until the sun set, and then we had supper at a restaurant on the beach that looked as if it had been built out of driftwood, where we chose our fish from a sea-water tank and they grilled it for us over charcoal. Nothing we had tasted at the Reyes Catolicos could touch it. We drove home in the dark, and somewhere in the middle of the heathland I stopped the car and doused the lights and we got out to look at the stars. There was not an artificial light for miles, and hardly any pollution in the atmosphere. The Milky Way stretched across the sky from east to west like a pale, glimmering canopy of light. I had never seen it so clearly. "Gosh!" Maureen exhaled. "How wonderful. I suppose it looked like this everywhere in the olden days."

"The ancient Greeks thought it was the way to heaven," I said.

"I'm not surprised."

"Some scholars think that there was a sort of pilgrimage here long before Christianity: people following the Milky Way as far as they could go."

"Goodness, how do you know all these things, Tubby?"

"I look them up. It's a habit."

We got back into the car and I drove back fast to Santiago, saying little, concentrating on the road unwinding in my headlights. Back in the Reyes Catolicos, we fell asleep quickly in each other's arms, too tired, or too sad, to make love.

I had plenty of time on the ferry to ponder Maureen's advice, and by the time we docked in Portsmouth I had determined to give it a shot. I phoned Sally just to check that she would be in, and drove straight to Hollywell without stopping. The crunch of my tyres on the gravel of the drive brought Sally to the front door. She offered me her cheek to kiss. "You look well," she said.

"I've been in Spain," I said, "Walking."

"Walking! What about the knee?"

"It seems to be better, at last," I said.

"Wonderful. Come in and tell me all about it. I'll make a cup of tea."

It felt good to be home – I still thought of it as home. I looked round the kitchen with pride and pleasure in its sleek lines and smart colour scheme. Sally looked in good shape too. She was wearing a red linen dress with a long slit skirt that showed an occasional flash of tanned leg as she moved about the kitchen. "You're looking well yourself," I said.

"Thank you, I am. Have you come to pick up some of your things?"

"No," I said, my throat suddenly dry. I coughed and cleared it. "I've come to have a talk, actually. I've been thinking, Sal, perhaps we should have a go at getting back together. What d'you say?"

Sally looked dismayed. That's the only word to describe her face: dismayed. "No, Tubby," she said.

"I don't mean straight away. We could go on with separate living arrangements in the house for a while. Separate bedrooms, anyway. See how it goes."

"I'm afraid it's impossible, Tubby."

"Why?" I said, though I knew the answer before she spoke.

"There's someone else."

"You said there wasn't."

"Well, there wasn't, then. But now there is."

"Who is he?"

"Somebody at work. You don't know him."

"So you've known him for some time, then?"

"Yes. But we didn't . . . we weren't . . ."

Sally for once seemed at a loss for words. "We haven't been lovers till – till quite recently," she said at last. "Before that it was just a friendship."

"You didn't tell me about it, though," I said.

"You didn't tell me about Amy," she said.

"How did you know about Amy?" I said. My head was spinning.

"Oh, Tubby, everybody knows about you and Amy!"

"It was platonic," I said. "At least it was until you walked out."

"I know," she said. "When I met her I knew it must be."

"This chap at work," I said. "Is he married?"

"Divorced."

"I see."

"We'll probably get married. I expect that will make a difference to

318

the divorce settlement. You probably won't have to give me so much money." She gave me a wan smile.

"Oh, fuck the money," I said, and walked out of the house for ever.

It was a nasty shock, of course – to have my carefully prepared offer of reconciliation brushed aside, rendered redundant, cut off at the knees, shoved back down my throat almost before I'd uttered it. But driving back down the M1 through dwarf forests of cones, I began to see a positive side to the reversal. It was obvious that Sally had begun to lean towards this other bloke years ago, whatever the exact nature of their relationship. It wasn't, as I had thought ever since Brett Sutton turned out to be innocent, that she'd left me simply because she would rather be lonely than married to me. I found that curiously reassuring. It restored my self-esteem.

The day's shocks weren't over though. When I got back to London and let myself into the flat, I found it completely empty. It had been stripped bare. There was nothing movable left in it, down to the light bulbs and the curtain rails. The chairs, tables, bed, carpets, crockery and cutlery, clothes and household linen – all gone. The only thing that was left, very neatly placed in the middle of the bare concrete floor, was my computer. It was a thoughtful touch on Grahame's part: I had explained to him once how precious the contents of my hard disk were, and he didn't know that I had deposited a box of back-up files with my bank before I left for Spain. I don't know how he and his friends got in, because they hadn't damaged the door and had carefully locked it behind them when they left. Perhaps Grahame had taken an impression of my keys one day when he was in the flat and I was in the loo – I used to keep a spare set hanging in the kitchen. Or perhaps he just borrowed them once without my noticing. Apparently they arrived one morning in a removal van and had the cheek to ask the police for special permission to park outside the building while they moved the contents of my flat to some spurious new address.

When I stepped into the flat and looked round, after half a minute of mouth-open astonishment, I laughed. I laughed till the tears rolled down my cheeks and I had to lean against the wall and finally sit down on the floor. The laughter was a touch hysterical, no doubt, but it was genuine.

If this was a television script, I would probably end it there, with the final credits scrolling over the empty flat, and yours truly sprawled in one corner, his back against the wall, weeping with laughter. But that happened several weeks ago, and I want to bring this story up to date, up to the moment of writing, so that I can carry on with my journal. I've been very busy working on *The People Next Door*. Ollie and Hal really loved my rewrite of Samantha's script for the final episode of the last series. It went down a treat with the studio audience too, apparently. (I wasn't there, it was recorded on 25th July, the feast of St James.) And Debbie was so taken with playing Priscilla as a ghost that she changed her mind and signed up for a whole new series based on the idea. I'm writing the scripts, but Samantha will get a prominent credit, which is only fair. She's become Heartland's number one script-doctor in a very short time. I had a bet with Jake at lunch today that she'll have Ollie's job before two years are out.

Jake wasn't very sympathetic about my burglary. He said I was insane to have ever trusted Grahame, and pointed out that if I'd let him use the flat as his love-nest while I was away, Grahame and his mates wouldn't have dared to loot it. But I was able to refurnish the flat quite quickly – the insurance company were very fair – and I never liked the original furnishings much anyway. Sally chose them. It's been like starting a new life from scratch, replacing everything in the flat. It's too small to live in permanently, though. I'm thinking of moving out to the suburbs, Wimbledon to be precise. I see quite a lot of Maureen and Bede these days. It would be nice to be near them, and I thought I might try to join the local tennis club – I always did fancy wearing that dark green blazer. I went up to Hollywell the other day to empty my locker at the old Club. A slightly melancholy occasion, brightened by the circumstance that I ran into Joe Wellington and challenged him to a game of singles for a tenner. I beat the shit out of him, 6–0, 6–0, rushing the net after every serve and scampering back to the baseline when he tried to lob me. "What about your knee?" he gasped afterwards. "Just pay up with a smile,

Joe," I said. "Reason not the knee." I don't think he recognized the quote.

I have my eye on a nice little house up the hill from the All England Club. I shan't give up the flat, though. It's useful for business to have a base in the West End; and every now and then Maureen and I have a siesta here. I don't ask her how she squares it with her conscience – I've got more sense. My own conscience is quite clear. The three of us are the best of friends. We're going off together for a little autumn break, actually. To Copenhagen. It was my idea. You could call it a pilgrimage.

MISSISSIPPI IN AFRICA

Alan Huffman

GOTHAM BOOKS

GOTHAM BOOKS
Published by Penguin Group (USA) Inc.,
375 Hudson Street, New York, New York 10014, U.S.A.
Penguin Books Ltd, Registered Offices: 80 Strand, London WC2R 0RL, England
Penguin Books Australia Ltd., 250 Camberwell Road, Camberwell, Victoria 3124, Australia
Penguin Books Canada Ltd, 10 Alcorn Avenue, Toronto, Ontario, Canada M4V 3B2
Penguin Books (N.Z.) Ltd, Cnr Rosedale and Airborne Roads, Albany, Auckland 1310,
    New Zealand

Published by Gotham Books, a division of Penguin Group (USA) Inc.

First printing, January 2004
10 9 8 7 6 5 4 3 2 1

Copyright © Alan Huffman, 2004
All rights reserved

Gotham Books and the skyscraper logo are trademarks of Penguin Group (USA) Inc.

LIBRARY OF CONGRESS CATALOGING-IN-PUBLICATION DATA

Huffman, Alan.
    Mississippi in Africa : the saga of the slaves of Prospect Hill Plantation and their legacy
in Liberia today / by Alan Huffman.
        p.   cm.
    ISBN 1-592-40044-2 (acid-free paper)
    1. Slave insurrections—Mississippi—Jefferson County—History—19th century.
2. Plantation life—Mississippi—Jefferson County—History—19th century.   3. Jefferson
County (Miss.)—Race relations.   4. Ross family.   5. Wills—Mississippi—Jefferson
County—History—19th century.   6. Plantation owners—Mississippi—Jefferson County—
Biography.   7. Slaves—Mississippi—Jefferson County—Biography.   8. Freedmen—
Mississippi—Jefferson County—Biography.   9. Jefferson County (Miss.)—Biography
10. Liberia—Biography.   I. Title.

F332.J4H835   2004
976.2'28300496073—dc21

                                                                    2003013458

Printed in the United States of America
Set in New Caledonia

This book is printed on acid-free paper. ❦

For my parents

MISSISSIPPI
IN AFRICA

INTRODUCTION

LONG SLATS OF MOONLIGHT fall through the shuttered window, across the floor, and up the legs of the massive old grand piano that commands a corner of my living room. It is the middle of the night and the room is still and quiet, which is odd, considering that a few moments before, I was awakened by the sound of random banging on the piano keys. I had pictured my dog Jack with his paws on the ivory, chasing a moth, but in the dim light I see that the piano's keyboard is closed, and that Jack is nowhere to be found. There is no moth fluttering dumbly against the windowpanes.

When I later recount the story to friends, their first reaction is to blame the noise on ghosts, but that is not what comes to mind as I stand scratching my head at three A M I think instead of the discord unleashed upon the world by one of the piano's former owners, Isaac Ross Wade, who has been consuming my thoughts lately and, from all appearances, is now entering my dreams.

I first saw the old square grand piano in my friend Gwen Shipp's home in Slate Springs, Mississippi, in the late 1070s, when her son, Tinker Miller, and I stopped by to visit during a duck-hunting trip. Gwen was particularly proud of the piano because it had originally belonged to a Revolutionary War veteran named Isaac Ross, who was Wade's grandfather and from whom Gwen is descended. It is a beautiful piece of furniture, crafted of rosewood and ebony, made for the sort of pleasant, restless melodies that once resonated through the hushed parlors of the Old South. But after too many long, hot summers in houses without air-conditioning, its soundboard is warped and most of its notes are false. It has not played music for a very long time.

The piano had previously occupied a prominent spot in the parlor of Gwen's old family home, Holly Grove, which is now my house, and prior to that it had narrowly missed destruction at two family homes that burned. The first fire, at Ross's plantation mansion, Prospect Hill, occurred in 1845, midway through a decade of litigation over his controversial will, allegedly as a result of a slave uprising. The uprising and fire, as well as their preamble and aftermath, were defining moments for many people in Jefferson County, Mississippi, at the time, and would remain so for certain of their descendants for the next century and a half. The piano was my portal into the story.

You hear a lot of interesting stories growing up in the South, and if you listen closely, you can't help wondering how much of what you're told is true. The story of Prospect Hill was the most intriguing I had come across, and had one of the widest margins for error, if only because so much was at stake and the cast of characters was so diverse. Before I knew what I was getting into, I was committed to finding out what really happened, and now, after devoting several years to researching and unraveling it, I am finally able to tell the story in full.

Holly Grove was an early kit house, manufactured in Cincinnati and brought down the Mississippi River and overland to Jefferson County, where it was assembled on the Killingsworth family's cotton plantation in 1832. When I first visited the house in 1971, it had been empty for decades and was used only for family reunions, but it still contained furnishings dating from the frontier era to the 1940s. It was isolated and had never been repainted, and had no electricity or running water. It felt frozen in time. When we were in high school, Tinker and I and a group of our friends sometimes camped in Holly Grove's musty parlor, in sleeping bags stretched out atop faded, tattered Oriental rugs. It was on one of those trips that Tinker first told me the story of Prospect Hill, which stood a few miles down the road. As we sat on the rotting gallery of Holly Grove, he told me about the vast cotton plantation that Ross had established, how he had planned to free his slaves after his death to emigrate to a new nation called Liberia, in West Africa, and how a dispute over his will instigated a legal conflict that spawned a slave uprising in which the house was burned. The idea of American slaves settling an African colony was particularly intriguing to us then, because there had recently been a fatal shootout in Jackson, Mississippi, near where we lived, between a group known as the Republic of New Africa and police and FBI agents at the group's heavily armed headquarters. The RNA had issued a manifesto demanding that the U.S. government cede to them the states of Mississippi, Louisiana, Alabama, Georgia, and South Carolina to form a black separatist nation, and pay $400 billion in slave reparations. Clearly, the conflict at the core of the story of Prospect Hill was far from over, and even in the 1970s it was far from dry, old history for us. For Tinker, it also had personal meaning.

Over the next few years, most of the original furnishings were stolen from Holly Grove, after which the house began an inexorable decline. Our camp-outs became fewer and farther between, until finally we stopped going, aside from rare day trips. Gwen had earlier moved Isaac Ross's piano to her home in Slate Springs, but with the family dispersed from Jefferson County and no one around to maintain it, Holly Grove's poignant, evocative decay began lurching toward certain doom. By the late 1980s it was going down fast.

I had grown to love the house and had been badgering Tinker for years to do something to preserve it, so when it became apparent that no one in the family would return to live there, Gwen decided to give it to me, if I would move it to my own property and restore it. It was not an easy matter to convince the elderly ladies who shared ownership, and lived mostly in other states, because they remembered the house the way it once had been, with no leaks in the roof and no rats or snakes roaming freely through its empty rooms. In their mind's eye it was filled with family members gathered around the long dining table or dancing with friends to tunes by minstrel groups at locally famous parties. To force the familial hand, I took a series of graphic photos—of walls that had given way from rot, sunlight visible through holes in the roof, gang graffiti on the doors, and the ground exposed through gaping cracks in the floor, and eventually they agreed to let it go. In 1990 my friends and I took the house apart, board by board, and hauled it sixty miles to my property, where we put it all back together again and replaced the rotten lumber.

Moving and restoring Holly Grove was not so different from the challenge that grew from it—reconstructing the story of Prospect Hill, which became increasingly important to me the more I learned about the Ross family and the slaves who "returned" to Africa before the

Civil War. Holly Grove today is restored, but it is my reconstruction, and though it has been saved, it now stands at a new location, facing a different way. It is, essentially, a new interpretation that I hope will last.

I had heard bits and pieces of the story of Prospect Hill over the years, but my interest grew after Gwen presented me with Ross's piano. No one knew how the piano had survived the fire that consumed the Prospect Hill mansion and took the life of a young girl, but Gwen knew that it had also been spared from a second conflagration, at another family home, Oak Hill, because it had been moved to Holly Grove. With Holly Grove now secure, she felt it was time for the piano to return. After she filled me in on the details of the alleged slave uprising at Prospect Hill and all that led up to it and came after, the sounds of the piano evoked for me less the echoes of sonatas than the cries of lynched slaves and of a doomed girl being burned alive. Eventually, it would also invoke an endless series of calls for help over the phone from Africa.

Ross was a slaveholder in the Wateree River region of South Carolina, and had the piano made in Philadelphia soon after the end of the Revolutionary War. Whether he played it himself has been lost in the telling, as has been a great deal more. But according to family accounts, in 1808 he hauled it with his other possessions, his family and his slaves to the Mississippi Territory, where he established Prospect Hill. Gwen, who is a member of the Isaac Ross chapter of the National Society of Colonial Dames of America, inherited the piano a century and a half later, after it had been passed down the family line.

At first the piano seemed a dubious gift to me. In addition to its uselessness as a musical instrument, it was extremely heavy. Gwen could not bear to watch as Tinker and I wrestled it down the stairs from her balcony, accompanied by alternately discordant and sonorous protests from the strings. We had trouble holding on to its smooth surfaces, and broke off a piece of the veneer as we awkwardly rounded the bend and collided with the wall. I would later discover that these were the least of the transgressions it had endured during its years of wandering.

The difficulty in moving the piano left me wondering how it could possibly have been rescued from a burning mansion. The odds seemed long that anyone could have gotten it out in a hurry, particularly when they were unable to save the girl. I wondered if something had been left out of the story of the uprising—and even if it was entirely true. As it turned out, I would begin to question a great deal more, for the fire was part of a larger maelstrom unleashed by Ross's will that would ultimately span two centuries and two continents—the unintended result of his effort to do what he believed was the right thing.

There were legions of wealthy planters in Jefferson County before the Civil War, but what set Ross apart was that he ordained, from his deathbed, the destruction of the very thing that he had spent his life building up—his prosperous, 5,000-acre plantation. Ross's will, which was probated in 1836, described a radical plan to ensure that his life did not end as might have been expected, its sum total reduced to an embarrassment of riches for his heirs, and a hopeless fate for the slaves on whose backs his fortune was made. Ross stipulated that at the time of his daughter Margaret Reed's death, Prospect Hill would be sold and the money used to pay the way for his slaves who wanted to emigrate to Liberia, where a colony of freed slaves had been established by a group called the American Colonization Society. There was already a community there called Mississippi in Africa, founded by a Mississippi chapter of the Colonization Society a decade before.

Margaret Reed would remain faithful to her father's wishes, but some of his heirs did not cotton to the idea of handing the bounty of his estate over to the slaves, and then setting them free. Those heirs filed a contest of the will with the Jefferson County probate court soon after Reed's death in 1838, and pursued the litigation to the state supreme court. They also attempted an end-run around the courts in the state legislature. They had many supporters, because some area planters and state elected officials were convinced that the colonization plan smacked of abolitionism. The fight dragged on for a decade, and during that contentious time, according to the family account, the slaves grew restless and set fire to the mansion, hoping to take out the offenders.

The heirs ultimately lost the contest of the will. By 1849 approximately 200 of the 225 slaves had been given their freedom and had emigrated to Mississippi in Africa, where they were joined by approximately 200 slaves freed by other, more sympathetic Ross family members. The rest of the Prospect Hill slaves chose to remain behind, enslaved. According to the provisions of the will, the remaining slaves were sold at public auction, in family units, so that close relations were not separated. Some of the freed slaves for a time wrote letters to their former masters at Prospect Hill, but when I began my research no one knew what had become of them.

Once I began reading about the colonization movement, I found that it stirred controversy far beyond Prospect Hill. Opponents, including many abolitionists, saw the effort as essentially a deportation of free blacks, while supporters—who also included abolitionists—were embarrassed by reports that some of the freed-slave immigrants had resorted to enslaving members of Liberia's indigenous tribes. Many of the new settlers, including some of the Prospect Hill immigrants, established large plantations and built grand mansions in the same Greek Revival style they had known back home, and some of the native tribes had a name for them, which is still occasionally used to refer to blacks of American ancestry: white. This may have been because they occupied the master's role in this African version of a Southern plantation society, or because they tended to have complexions that were considerably lighter than the native groups. The settlers were also referred to as "kwi," which means "western" or "civilized."

So it turns out that the story of Prospect Hill is more complicated than it first appeared, and covers a lot of ground. Over a span of 175 years or so, in fact, it has managed to touch just about every hot button in the histories of the American South and colonial Africa—slavery and exploitation, conflict and greed—while encompassing almost every imaginable human predicament. And as I probed deeper into the details, I detected what I believed were a few flaws in the narrative thread that had long been accepted by local tradition.

Old stories in the South tend to get a lot of grooming, often to within an inch of their lives, but inevitably they start mixing with other narrative lines. Sometimes the stories are ephemeral and, as a result, endlessly malleable. With no documentation to support or refute, the details blossom fantastically, in ways that are unlikely to be corroborated by any written record. Other times there is ample documentation, which helps if it says what you expect it to, but there is always the question of who did the documenting and why. For the most part, in the Southern storytelling tradition, big things happen, people talk about them, hone a few ideas, revise the story and delete here and there, add entertaining details from other sources, then take the finished product out for a test drive. This goes on for generations, and sometimes myth and reality are blended seamlessly into what passes for fact. This is how you end up with something like the minié ball pregnancy, which was the tale told by a Vicksburg, Mississippi, family whose daughter had hastily married a Yankee soldier during the Civil War, after which it was said that a sniper's bullet had passed through his testicles and into her womb. (If anyone needed proof, of course, there was the actual child.)

The story of Prospect Hill was a natural target for this honing instinct, and the more people I talked with, the less sure I was of the veracity of the official account, which until now had been firmly rooted in the slaveholders' vantage point, because they alone had the power to document history at the time. Yet even the versions told by otherwise attuned slaveholder descendants vary to some degree, depending largely upon whether the person traces his lineage to Isaac Ross or to his grandson, the contester of the will. As the piano stared back at me in my living room, I began to wonder about the circumstances of the infamous fire, including whether the uprising itself may have actually been a fabrication, designed to discredit the slaves. Notably, the threat of insubordination had been a key component of the opponents' legal argument against the will. I wondered if, upon closer scrutiny, the familiar parlor story of Prospect Hill would still play after so many decades, or if, like the piano, it was hopelessly warped. I also wanted to know what had become of everyone involved, from the divided slaveholding family to the slaves who chose to remain behind and those who emigrated to Africa. What might their descendants know about the story? And what revelations might come from a more thorough review of the written record?

Tinker Miller and I mulled over the possibilities one summer evening as we sat on the porch of the newly relocated Holly Grove. We had spent many hours deconstructing history there over the past twenty-five years, and none of the stories intrigued us more than how there came to be a place called Mississippi in Africa, and what the saga meant for all the key players on both sides of the Atlantic.

On this particular evening, fireflies drifted randomly across the lawn and the air was soft and sweet with the scent of Japanese honeysuckle. The songs of crickets, cicadas, and frogs rose to such loud crescendoes that now and then we had to raise our own voices to be heard.

We are of a generation and bent that once dissected Civil War battles as we might a football game, but when it came to the story of Prospect Hill our knowledge had until now been mostly hearsay. We knew what we had been told, and we have had no real reason to question it until now, when I had decided to try to piece the story together in detail. Tinker was to be my first official interview.

For Tinker, our conversation probed a very personal history, and I was gently challenging him to reconsider the comfortable, accepted truths that were told to him by people he loved and respected. He had no trepidation about digging deeper, because we know each other well and it was unlikely that either of us would go anywhere with the story that the other could not follow—or, if we did, there would be no acrimony in pointing it out. It was just that we were dragging the memory of people like his late Uncle Anon into the twilight, critiquing what he said when he was not there to answer.

We talked about Uncle Anon for a while, and when the conversation found its way back to Prospect Hill, Tinker glanced disapprovingly at my tape recorder. "That thing," as he called it, made him overly aware of his words, because he knew he could not retract any of them. There were a lot of long silences.

I said I had no pretenses about being able to uncover the all-encompassing, indisputable truth of Prospect Hill, mainly because I knew from reading Faulkner that with a story as complicated and sweeping as this one, where the characters are so diverse, the likelihood was that everyone claimed only a piece of the truth and the pieces did not necessarily jibe. I wanted only to isolate the narrative thread, find out what became of the people involved, and see what hand history had dealt their descendants.

He nodded, noncommittally.

What Tinker thinks matters a great deal to me, particularly because he first told me the tale one afternoon as we sat on this same porch with our friends, drinking beer and watching the sun set. It was still a favorite story of his because he loves history, it concerns his own family, the whole premise is so unexpected, so oversized and dramatic, and after 165 years its effects still reverberate in both Mississippi and in Liberia. He was also aware that my version had the potential to trump the others, and I had to admit that the family lore had already started to seem a bit stylized.

There is no question that Prospect Hill burned on April 15, 1845, and that a family member, Martha Richardson, died in the fire. But once I started to dig, I became increasingly dubious about the slave uprising, which so many descendants point to as the cause of the fire, because every account of the incident harks back to a single source— Thomas Wade, the son of the man who contested the will. Like many local histories, this one has been honed to a narrow focus over time, told by people with their own agendas, and there is a lot that the more recent narrators simply did not know.

As we talked about the alleged uprising, Tinker allowed that "It's possible that the whole thing was a fabrication, but why? What would anyone have to gain? My perception of the family tale was that these blacks were not mean; they were misguided or confused by the situation. There were no harsh feelings from the ancestors of my family toward the ancestors of the blacks. These families were close, have always been close, and this whole episode with Isaac Ross Wade trying to nullify the will is just contrary to everything they were about."

This disclaimer was not an effort to further distance himself from a man whose character had been called into question. He had told me many times before that his family falls squarely on the side that supported the will.

I watched the red dot of his cigarette dancing in the gathering darkness as he repeated the family lore—the story of the slaves growing restless prior to the uprising, the cook drugging the slaveholders' coffee, the slave at the door with the axe to kill the man who stood in their way of emigrating to Africa. "That's just the story," he said. "It was part of the family history. There was no variation of the story when I was growing up . . . it wasn't questioned."

Tinker is open-minded, and I knew that if he is not willing to budge from the family line, it was unlikely that other descendants of the slaveholding family would. That would leave only the slave descendants to test my theory that there was more at work than a simple conflict involving irrational slaves. Perhaps the descendants of the Prospect Hill slaves, if I could find any, would have something to add

to all of this. The same is true for the descendants of the emigrants to
Liberia, although the nation has been in turmoil since 1980, and at this
point I was not at all inclined to travel to a war zone to find out.

He shrugged when I suggested this.

"Growing up, you couldn't help but be proud of what Isaac Ross
did," he said. "Everybody in the family was proud that he freed his
slaves. The fact that the will was contested by his grandson . . . the family didn't really play that aspect of it up much. We didn't see Isaac Ross
Wade as representing our family. We were proud that our family wasn't
the malevolent, mean, make-a-dollar-off-the-slave-industry type people, that they had a history of compassion for people. They didn't voice
it like that, but that was the primary story. Then again, Isaac Ross was
still a slaveowner, and my family were still slaveowners and that's a horrible thing."

He said his own views have been influenced by contemporary history, which include his having lived through the Civil Rights era and
having attended racially integrated schools. "The Mississippi we grew
up in was a segregated place, but we saw that change," he said. "Our
parents grew up in a different world. You hear all this stuff, and it's
confusing. You know your ancestors owned people, you kind of have
this paternalistic moonlight-and-magnolias mentality, then you read
about people that you grew up admiring, like [Confederate General]
Nathan Bedford Forrest and his involvement with the Klan, and you
know it was a bad, bad thing. And deep down, no matter what gloss you
put on it, it was always a bad thing. It never got good. . . .

"I can't pass judgment on them because that was the culture, that's
the way life was. But the fact that some of the freed slaves or their
descendants, whatever, enslaved the indigenous people in Liberia—
that just shows what a terrible thing it is. . . .

"I guess it's just human nature to try to dominate other people.
Which is why you have to give someone like Isaac Ross credit for trying, even if it was late in the game, to basically do the right thing."

With that, he thumped his spent cigarette over the rail.

"Now turn that thing off," he said, motioning toward the tape
recorder.

But I have one more question: How did the piano make its way
from Prospect Hill to Oak Hill?

He shook his head and shrugged.

The piano is one of the few surviving items that was contested during the litigation, and one of the last heirlooms of the original Prospect Hill mansion. The irony is that had Wade not removed it from the house, however he did, it would have burned in the fire. But then, had he not contested the will, there would have been no fire.

In a region beset by racial divisions and economic disparities, sorting through numerous differing accounts can get complicated, with key roles reversed in different sources' tellings—heroes transformed into villains, and vice versa. This may be true all over, but it is especially so in the South, where major conflicts from the past are routinely distilled to very personal encounters today. The backdrop of history looms constantly, and sometimes its weight can be overwhelming, and you just have to let it go, and move on. Other times the story is too compelling and too provocative to ignore. That was the case with Prospect Hill, which is why I began digging through moldering records that had not seen the light of day for perhaps a hundred years, and eventually, found myself on my way to war-torn Liberia, where Mississippi means something altogether different, and where the conflicts of the old American South not only still matter, they are matters of life and death.

Part I

MISSISSIPPI

CHAPTER ONE

NEKISHA ELLIS WATCHES AS I hoist the massive old record book onto the Xerox machine, unable to prevent it from pulling apart at the seams. With each turn of a page, bits of parchment break away and rain down upon the floor. I look up at her and wince.

"Don't worry," she says, and smiles apologetically. "It's just old."

Nekisha is a deputy court clerk in Jefferson County, where the surviving documents chronicling the Prospect Hill litigation are housed. A smile comes naturally to her face. She watches brightly as one irreplaceable record after another crumbles in my hands.

This particular book, which contains county probate records for the 1840s, has been sheltered at the back of a dusty, unopened box for decades, and represents one of our first major finds. Nekisha is happy to have unearthed it, although this is more due to her desire to help than her interest in what the book contains. Irreplaceable though it may be, the book is just one more piece of moldering detritus in one of the poorest counties in the poorest state in America.

The lack of funds may partly explain why there seems to be almost no official interest in maintaining records from the time before the Civil War, but there also seems to be some deep-seated inertia at work—the kind that keeps things from being done, and the kind that ensures that what is already happening continues (which in this case is the steady decay of the county's oldest records). Day-to-day life here is harder in many ways than in most parts of the country, while the literal burden of history is heavier, which is why I did not expect much when I arrived. It turns out I am lucky.

When I explain to Nekisha why I am searching for the records, she tells me that she recalls hearing the name of Prospect Hill before, although there is little left of the community that the plantation once anchored. This is not unusual—in a county as historic as this one, many residents remember things for which there is little or nothing to show. I am hoping this communal memory will improve the chances of finding descendants, but it is a big haystack that I am probing for a handful of needles. Nekisha, in fact, was at first skeptical that any of the documentation existed, because the county's oldest records have been in serious disarray for years. I had been told that prior to the disastrous fire in the 1980s that consumed the former, Gothic-style courthouse, which had stood since around 1900, one local resident had taken to carting off historic records after finding that they were being ruined by leaks in the roof, and that no one seemed to care. So began a systematic, surreptitious looting in the name of preservation. I have also heard of less noble inroads. One woman recalled finding purloined pages torn from deed books and Spanish land grants for sale at a flea market in nearby Natchez, which she bought but did not return. Instead she donated them to the state Department of Archives and History, in Jackson, saying she had little hope for their preservation in Jefferson County. All of this was discouraging, because the corresponding records in Liberia were reportedly lost in the burning of that nation's archives at the height of the country's civil war in the 1990s— a conflict precipitated by long-running animosity between the descendants of the freed slaves and the indigenous tribes. So I was undertaking my research with a certain urgency. I needed to pull together what was left, or, in cases where nothing was left, glean the details from a diverse array of people.

Nekisha tells me that some of the county's older records were removed to an annex prior to the fire, and because she is energized by the discovery of the probate book in a rusty filing cabinet, she begins probing every decaying cardboard box she can find. Along the way she inspires others in the research room to join in, and before long discovers the mother lode of records relating to the litigation over Isaac Ross's will.

As we plunder cabinets and the dark recesses of closets, one man whom Nekisha has pressed into service, who is doing his own African-American genealogy, listens to my fledgling account of the story with a slightly bewildered look on his face, then repeats the words "Mississippi in Africa" aloud, nodding, with a furrowed brow. I have seen this response before, and will see it again many times before my research is over. He is not sure what to make of this. The story seems implausible, defies conventional wisdom, and lends itself to opposing stereotypes. Several people have asked, "How come I've never heard of this?"

From all appearances, Jefferson County is an unlikely launching pad for a saga of such bafflingly broad proportions. The county, which borders the Mississippi River between Vicksburg and Natchez, is barely even flyover country, and what's worse, it seems to be in the throes of an extraordinarily long death scene. Piles of bricks, a few old storm-battered trees and the occasional roadside display of daffodils in spring are all that remain of a hundred former plantation homes, while at isolated crossroads, junked cars surround clusters of small houses and trailers that look more like encampments than permanent settlements. Telltale slave quarters have quietly vanished from the landscape, abandoned roads have degenerated into unofficial dumps, historical markers have been stolen for scrap metal, and marble angels and filigreed cast-iron fences sprawl across forgotten cemeteries, toppled by vandals and falling trees. By the standards of twenty-first-century America, the county has, essentially, nothing—no factories, no significant retail business, no evidence of any real production or commerce. Even the cotton gins closed down years ago.

The county's population has been declining for years, and now stands at just under 10,000 people, most of whom are supported by government programs or commute to distant jobs. Some get by on interest on old money, the sale of timber, or income from hunting leases or the sale of discarded aluminum cans picked up from the side of the road. Others benefit from more unpredictable windfalls—drug deals or multimillion-dollar class-action legal verdicts. Jefferson County's poverty today has contributed to a national reputation as an attractive venue for personal-injury lawsuits—it is essentially a victim-based economy. In 2001, the Jackson *Clarion-Ledger* newspaper noted that asbestos manufacturer Owens-Corning had been slapped with a landmark $48 million judgment by a Jefferson County jury in June 1998, and that the company had subsequently filed its own suit in the county against tobacco companies that it claimed were partly responsible for the injuries cited. An attorney for R.J. Reynolds Tobacco told the newspaper that Jefferson County has a particularly bad reputation for corporate defendants.

Aside from legal cases, much that is important to the community happened long ago, and old stories still spark debate, but for the most part the physical evidence is fast fading away.

Jefferson County was the second county chartered in the Mississippi Territory, in 1799, and its history spans the frontier, the boom of the South's plantation economy, the bust that followed the Civil War, the tumult of Reconstruction, and the inevitable upheaval of the Civil Rights era. The region, which was originally known as the Natchez District, was first settled by the French and later occupied by Spain and Great Britain, but did not reach its full flower until it became part of the United States in 1798. By the outbreak of the Civil War in 1861, it stood at the forefront of the antebellum cotton empire, an aspect of local history that is often misconstrued as a sort of "white phase" by people of both races, although it was also the formative era of local black culture and political power. Back then, slaves far outnumbered slaveholders, and nearby Natchez boasted more millionaires per capita than any other city in the United States. Money transformed a remote wilderness into a region of wealthy fiefdoms anchored by Greek Revival, Federal, and Italianate mansions filled with imported furnishings, the most elaborate of which were surrounded by landscaped gardens, sometimes stepping down toward the river on terraces, while just out of sight were the rude dwellings of the slave quarters, with dirt yards. These were the sets upon which Jefferson County's high dramas were acted out, which is something no one seems to have forgotten.

Despite its contentious history and pervasive poverty, there is an odd romance about Jefferson County's decline, with its abandoned gardens overgrown with flowering vines, its silent churches redolent of incense and mildew, its scores of ruined houses with tattered curtains twisting on the breeze through broken windows. For sheer historical weight, none of the sites can compare with the cemetery at Prospect Hill, which lies a short distance from the second house on the site, built by Ross's grandson after the first was burned. The cemetery was wrecked a few years back by a falling cedar tree that narrowly missed a marble monument to Ross, which was erected by the Mississippi branch of the American Colonization Society and bears this hopeful inscription:

"His last will is graced with as magnificent provisions as any over
which philanthropy has ever rejoiced and by it will be erected
on the shores of Africa a monument more glorious than marble
and more enduring than Time."

That the inscription is written in stone does not mean that its conclusions are indisputable, yet there is no question that Ross was destined
to leave an enduring wake.

Although his family in South Carolina was at the time comparatively
wealthy, Ross must have found the availability of good, cheap cotton
land in the Mississippi Territory an irresistible lure. White settlers from
Europe and the eastern United States were pouring into the region in
wagon trains, on horseback, and aboard steamboats in search of opportunity. The boom is evident in the cemetery at the now abandoned river
town of Grand Gulf, which includes numerous graves of young men
from France, Scotland, and the eastern United States, some killed in duels
or by yellow fever, who were drawn to the area by the promise of the
new, and by stories of fortunes made from the fertile soil. To many people at the time, the burgeoning cotton empire meant very much the same
thing that the dot-com economy of California would mean to men and
women in the late twentieth century, and its crash would be equally sudden and profound. The slave-based boom ended in 1865, after passage
of the Emancipation Proclamation and the Confederacy's defeat in the
Civil War. For those who reaped the largess of the cotton empire, fewer
than thirty years separated the highest peak from the deepest valley.

During the war, army and naval battles swept across the region, and
the local economy and social order fractured. Jefferson County, like
much of the rural South, began losing population soon after, with the
first wave of emigration led by newly freed blacks and by whites who
had seen their way of life collapse. Simultaneously, the area's fertile
topsoil began to wash away, with erosion sending huge, hungry chasms
creeping into the hills. For the next 150 years the population and tax
base spiraled downward, taking with it much of the infrastructure that
had supported the one-crop economy—railroads, farms, ports, ferries,
bridges, roads, countless communities, and more than a few towns.
Since nothing came along to take cotton's place as an economic
engine, the county foundered. Today the county seat of Fayette is a

study in small-town desolation. Even the parking meters in front of the courthouse don't work, and in many cases the meter itself is gone—there's only the rusted pole.

The status of the black majority changed dramatically in the second half of the twentieth century, but they inherited a dying commonwealth. Jefferson County now has the highest percentage of African-American elected officials in the United States, but with a population that is largely undereducated and poor, and with few resources to exploit, it has increasingly come to rely upon the federal government for support. Less than half the residents have a high school education and only 10 percent have a college degree, while 20 percent are on Social Security and about a third live on income that is below the poverty level. The per capita annual income at the turn of the twenty-first century was around $10,000.

Because the county is poor and 90 percent black, stories of innovative slaveholders and the colossal homes they built with slave labor do not inspire the kind of ancestral pride that drives the narratives at mansion tours in nearby Natchez and Vicksburg. For the average resident of Jefferson County, those days are long gone, and many have bidden them good-bye and good riddance. It is not so surprising, though it is distressing, that the written record of the county's tumultuous history has been consigned to what amounts to a communal attic, the recesses of the courthouse. Yet Ross's story is not easily dismissed as a relic of a dead era. For one thing, none of the descendants—black or white—can claim exclusive ownership of the tale.

While Nekisha and company are busy plundering the record room, I notice a woman watching me curiously from another table. When she catches my eye, she rises and approaches my table. She does not introduce herself, but asks, rather officiously, "What are you here to do?"

I am a bit put off by her tone, and say, simply, "Research." It is not a satisfactory answer, but she backs off.

When she goes to lunch I ask Nekisha who she is.

"That's Ann Brown," she says. "You need to know her."

When she returns, Nekisha introduces us. It turns out that Ann Brown is actually quite friendly, and helpful. She is a transplanted Canadian whose husband was descended from a local slaveholding family, and who, in recent years, has undertaken a wholesale genealogical survey of Jefferson and Claiborne counties, including the lineages of African-American families, which are notoriously poorly documented. Ann is interested in everyone's family line, which is why she might be seen as a busybody were she not on an inspired public mission.

I tell Ann what I am looking for and why, and she fills me in on her own genealogical efforts with the explanation, "There's just no one else doing it." She asks a few questions about Isaac Ross and Prospect Hill, takes my name, number, and e-mail address, and says I will be hearing from her. With that, she returns to her own work.

I now have numerous boxes scattered before me on a massive, old wooden table. So far I have primarily scanned the probate and land records books, deciding it would be best to make copies and decipher the baroque handwriting of the other documents later. As soon as I open the first of the new boxes, though, the scanning ends. It becomes clear that the box's contents will encompass far more than simple legal arguments. All of the stories that I have so far heard refer primarily to the slaveholding Rosses, with few detailed references to the slaves themselves, but the first item I come to is a ledger, written in what will soon be a familiar style of florid, archaic hand, with a title that speaks volumes: "Births of the Negros on Prospect Hill Place." In it are the names of more than a hundred slaves born at Prospect Hill, beginning in the early 1800s, including many whose names I will come to recognize from the letters they wrote home to Prospect Hill from Mississippi in Africa.

CHAPTER TWO

ISAAC ROSS WAS BORN in Charlotte, North Carolina, in 1760, moved with his family as a child to near Camden, South Carolina, and then, as a young man, enlisted in the revolutionary army. By war's end he had been promoted to the rank of captain and commanded a company of South Carolina dragoons who fought in the battles of Kings Mountain, North Carolina, in 1780, and Cowpens, South Carolina, in 1781, both of which were patriot victories. In the latter battle, he lost his right eye. He wore a glass replacement for the rest of his life.

By his early forties, Ross no doubt had heard tales of Mississippi's productive climate from his brother, Arthur, who had immigrated to the territory a few years before. In 1808 he joined the exodus of planters from the East who were being crowded out by other heirs or whose comparatively old farmlands had declined in productivity.

The soil of Jefferson County was among the most fertile in North America, but for ambitious men like Ross it held little value without the addition of slaves. Cotton was a labor-intensive crop, and no one could have grown as wealthy as many of the region's planters did, as quickly as they did, through their own labor. The fertility, which carried southwest Mississippi's slave-based cotton economy to new heights, was the result of two ancient geologic forces—dust storms that had borne down continually across the plains of North America at the end of the last ice age, and scouring torrents from melting glaciers through what is today the basin of the Mississippi River. Over time, the channel of the river carved a chasm deep into a bed of limestone that was once the bottom of a sea, and the exposed cliff on the eastern bank caught deposits of wind-blown dust the way a beached log captures sand. The result was a series of undulating hills with fine, deep topsoil that in some places ran a hundred feet deep, bordered by broad bottom lands where fertile silt had been deposited by successive floods over thousands of years. Atop these rich foundations had been laid several feet of fecund humus from decaying trees and leaves, which left the soil so soft and malleable that in the early years, it was said, farmers could plant their crops without the need for plows. Until the richest organic matter was depleted (which took only a few decades), seeds were simply scattered on the surface and walked into the ground by the feet of men and women.

The combination of rich soil and subtropical climate proved both a boon and a bane to the early settlers. All vegetative growth was prolific—not just the crops selected for cultivation—and there were plagues of insects and other pests. French settlers who arrived in the early eighteenth century encountered dense jungles of towering beech and magnolia trees festooned with long falls of moss, great brakes of cane on the open ridge tops, and lakes brimming with fish that were cast in perpetual shadow by primeval cypress trees. Much of the terrain was impenetrable. From all appearances the French were wholly unprepared for the task they faced, and because they were never fully supported by their government, their attempts at colonial settlement failed. Their contributions to the history of the region were nonetheless profound: the annihilation of the Natchez Indians in retaliation for an attack at Fort Rosalie in 1729, and the introduction of African slaves to replace Native American slaves who had proved both susceptible to European diseases and adept at escape. The occupation of the new lands by transplanted Africans would be entwined with the region's history from that day forward.

The French reign ended with the conclusion of the French and Indian War in 1760, after which the district came under British rule. Britain's tenure was also short-lived, but it brought the first permanent settlements, in the 1780s, peopled by immigrants who had largely sided with the crown during the Revolution. Afterward, the region briefly fell into the hands of Spain, and the first serious attempts were made to clear the land for agriculture, mostly for tobacco and indigo. These efforts were only sporadically successful. It would take another change of regime, and the invention of the cotton gin, to transform the Natchez District into the venue for one of the most lucrative and controversial enterprises in the history of American agriculture. Nearly all of the great houses that tourists come to Mississippi to see today were built during that era, from roughly the 1820s to 1860.

It was just prior to the great boom, ten years after Spain had ceded the region to the United States, that Isaac Ross arrived. For white settlers like Ross and his brother, the region was just opening up, but for blacks and people of mixed race it was about to begin closing in. Under newly imposed U.S. laws, free mulattoes, who had previously inhabited a cultural and political gray area of society, were officially classified as black, which made them subject to more rigid legal restrictions that were also being imposed on free blacks. Greater prohibitions were also placed on slaves. Notably, Ross counted a large cadre of mulattoes among the slaves he brought with him from South Carolina, along with a core group of free blacks.

One of Ross's descendants, Thomas Wade, noted that during the Revolution Ross had fought alongside "several free negroes, who made good soldiers," and that "when he moved to Mississippi they followed him and settled near him on land he helped them to buy. Drew Harris, one of these old soldiers, who drew a pension from the government, was buried near the Drew Spring on Prospect Hill Plantation, the home of Captain Ross. Some of his descendants were living in Claiborne County a few years since and some of them may be there now."

Aside from the more restrictive laws, Ross and company arrived at a fortuitous time, when refinements to the cotton gin, which had been invented in 1793, were changing the economic landscape. Small subsistence farms of tobacco, indigo, and corn were being supplanted by large plantations devoted primarily to cotton, which greatly increased in value after Europe's most readily available supply was interrupted by a slave uprising on the Caribbean island of Saint-Domingue (now Haiti). With the Caribbean supply cut off, cotton prices skyrocketed, and after a Natchez slave fabricated an improved cotton gin based upon a description by his owner, who had seen Eli Whitney's invention, many planters began converting all of their fields to cotton. Some no longer grew corn to feed their horses, mules, cows, oxen, and slaves, but instead bought it from other markets so as to devote all of their acreage to the more valuable crop. With so much incentive, and the

only limitation the availability of labor, the value of slaves escalated.
Because the U.S. Constitution banned the importation of slaves after
1808—the year Ross arrived—most of the new slaves came from
established plantations back East.

A large part of the acreage that Ross bought upon his arrival in Jefferson County would have certainly been classified as "unimproved,"
meaning stands of timber would have to be cleared before it could be
converted to arable land. On the Mississippi frontier, this usually
involved deadening trees—girdling the trunks with an axe to cut off
the flow of nutrient-laden sap. Because deadened trees take a few
years to finally die, and even longer to fall, crops were routinely
planted in the soils of a ghost forest, nurtured by sunlight falling
through ominous snags. Most planters occupied crude log structures
until they made their fortune and a more lavish dwelling could be
built, but Ross appears to have made his splash upon arrival. The best
description of his house comes from Ross's great-grandson, Thomas
Wade, who described Prospect Hill as a monument to style and substance, built of poplar milled on the plantation, with wainscoting
throughout the downstairs, bookcases that rose to the ceiling of the
parlor, and a finely executed stair rail, all crafted of cherry wood.

"The book cases in the parlor were filled with the best books
obtainable at that time and among them was a complete file of the
National Intelligencer, a weekly paper, published at Philadelphia,"
Thomas Wade wrote. "On the walls of this parlor, along with other fine
pictures, there hung the picture of the sloop of war *Bonhomme
Richard*, and the frigate *Constitution* of the War of 1812. Captain Ross
prized those two pictures highly and often spoke of the daring exploits
of John Paul Jones."

According to Wade, Ross designed the house himself and supervised its construction by his slaves. The lumber was milled in a pit, with
one man below and one above operating a long ripsaw. "During wet or
excessively dry weather the poplar lumber expanded and contracted
and at night often worried those not accustomed to the noise," Wade
observed.

At the time Ross began work on Prospect Hill, the methods of
farming had changed little since the medieval era, but advancements
came quickly, in improved gins, plows, cotton presses, and strains of
seeds. The effects of these technological advances were far-reaching.

Slavery, which had been practiced throughout recorded time, was soon transformed from a comparatively small-scale system of feudal bondage to a rapidly expanding, fully institutionalized and widespread engine of economic growth. The advent of the steamboat, meanwhile, meant that commodities could be moved in volume over long distances, and shipped wherever they were needed in response to world markets, which was particularly important to the lower Mississippi Valley, where a network of rivers, lakes, and bayous meant that even remote plantations were seldom far from a navigable waterway.

The era brought unprecedented development to the Natchez District, though there were downturns. Historian John Hebron Moore noted that the price of ginned cotton dropped dramatically from a high of thirty-two cents per pound in 1801 to fourteen cents per pound in 1809, the result of a federal tariff on European trade. During the War of 1812, the price further dropped to twelve cents per pound, and continued to fluctuate for the next decade. In 1811 a particularly aggressive fungus began attacking the crop, which prompted local planters to experiment with new varieties of seed. One, a strain known as Petit Gulf developed by Dr. Rush Nutt, a Jefferson County planter and amateur scientist, proved a godsend. Petit Gulf was resistant to the fungus and more productive than previous strains, and as a result, by the 1820s field slaves were picking significantly larger volumes of cotton than they had in previous years. With the availability of abundant raw material, the textile industries in England and the northern United States also experienced unprecedented growth, which in turn increased the demand for cotton and yet again for slaves.

Ross's fortune and the number of his slaves grew significantly during the boom, but what should have been a happy time of flush finances and a growing family was marred by a succession of deaths. Some descendants say the series of tragedies caused Ross to diverge from the path of a typical Mississippi slaveholder and planter toward the role that he would become most famous for—as the man responsible for sending the largest group of freed-slave emigrants to the colony of Liberia, and in so doing, for dividing his family, his community, the courts, and the state legislature.

Ross and his wife, Jane, who was also from South Carolina, had two sons, Isaac Jr. and Arthur, and three daughters, Jane, Martha, and Margaret. The 1820 census for Jefferson County also includes two unnamed young men living in the house at Prospect Hill, along with 158 slaves on the plantation. Among his offspring, only Isaac Jr. and Jane would have children—he, a son, Isaac Allison Ross; and she, several by two husbands, including Isaac Ross Wade, who would later join her in the contest of her father's will.

From all appearances Ross's children ascended easily through local society and were poised to make their way in the world when the series of tragedies began unfolding. Descendant Annie Mims Wright wrote that the first was the death of the fiancé of Ross's daughter Martha, in a duel in 1813. According to family accounts, a messenger galloped up the drive to Prospect Hill on the day of the couple's intended marriage to deliver the news that the young man was preparing to fight a duel in nearby Rodney. The reason for the duel is unclear, and the timing is debatable, because there seems to be an inordinate number of tales circulating through Mississippi history of young belles whose intended grooms were killed on the day they were to be married. Still, having her fiancé killed at any time near the planned wedding would have been shock enough. As father and daughter raced to the scene to intervene, they reportedly encountered a second messenger who told them that her betrothed was already dead.

The next tragedy came five years later, in 1818, when Martha herself died of yellow fever, at age twenty-five. She had been helping care for her second fiancé, who preceded her in death, and who had contracted the disease while caring for his mother, another victim. Two years later, the husband of Ross's daughter Jane also succumbed to fever, and Ross became legal guardian of the couple's son, Isaac Ross Wade, his grandson and later the executor (and would-be nemesis) of his will. In 1829, at the age of sixty-four, Ross's wife died, and she was followed the next year by another son-in-law, U.S. senator Thomas Reed, who had married Margaret. In 1832, Isaac Jr. died, and two years after that, Ross's son Arthur died. All of these losses, in such close succession, must have taken a heavy toll, but, according to Wright, it was Martha's death that shook Ross to his foundation.

Wright contended that after Martha died, "Captain Ross was so overcome with grief, he left the familiar scenes and went with his nephew, John B. Conger, through the then wild Indian country to Mobile, where he took a boat for the North. He visited Princeton, where his son [Isaac Jr.] was at school, but not wishing to burden him with grief, did not even call on him. On his return, by way of the West, he was taken ill in the Indian country and was found by some hunters, who took care of him and sent word to his family." Members of his family traveled to the western frontier to escort Ross home.

There is no mention of where in the West (which at the time encompassed today's midwestern states) Ross's sojourn took him, and there is some disagreement over exactly when and why he went, but there seems no question that he returned a changed man. Thomas Wade noted that Ross's nephew had left him upon their arrival in Mobile, and that once up North, "Ross came in close contact with the people of wealth and culture as well as the masses, and talked with some of them interested in the American Colonization Society. From these men he learned of the growing sentiment in the North relative to the ultimate abolition of slavery in America. It was from this contact in the North that he learned that the institution of slavery could not last." When he returned home, Wade wrote, Ross had been gone for more than a year, "and this was the first word his family had that he was still alive. They feared that he had been killed by Indians or lost at sea."

Although Wright attributed Ross's wanderings to grief over Martha's death, historian Harnett Kane speculated in the 1940s that the sojourn followed the death of his wife, Jane Allison Ross. According to Kane, when Jane Ross died in the summer of 1829, Ross was so aggrieved that he could barely attend the funeral, and when he managed to rise to the occasion his slaves crowded around and cried with him. Kane believed it was daughter Margaret's idea for Ross to travel as an antidote to the depression that afterward gripped him.

Kane described Ross as "an individual of stringent honesty, proud that he had won his place in the world, who scorned pettifoggers, people who put on airs or tried to cut corners," and a man who shared the responsibility for operating the plantation with his wife. Jane Ross, he noted, "was modest, but talked over the plantation management with him, helped him in dealings with men and women in the fields," while Margaret, his favorite surviving child, inherited both her mother's reticence and her father's stubbornness.

Kane's account had Ross returning from his travels with an obsession about slavery, which had always been a favorite topic of conversation. He described Ross questioning his slaves about their ideas of freedom—what it would mean to them, and what they would do if they were freed. Ross reportedly had never allowed any of his slaves to be sold, had sequestered them away from slaves on other plantations, and had allowed many of them to be taught to read and write. It seems safe to assume that he was concerned not only about the future of slavery but that his carefully constructed slave world might not outlast his daughter Margaret, who shared his desire to keep the community intact and under the family's comparatively benign rule.

Either way, Kane wrote, after Ross returned from the wilderness and broached the subject of freedom, "In the flickering of the cabin lamps, excitement spread."

CHAPTER THREE

IT IS A HALCYON day, the sun high and warm but the ground still cool in the shadows, and in Jefferson County's remaining fields the last of its farmers are breaking ground. It is mostly the bottom lands that they plow now, for soybeans rather than cotton, using great John Deere tractors that belch diesel smoke as they groan against the earth. The plowing still brings the scent of fresh earth to the countryside, but the field cabins are mostly gone, and one man can do in a day what took weeks for more than a hundred men in 1825.

Before the Civil War these fields would have been crowded with men and horses, and on any given spring day, the ground would have been laid bare by a hundred plows, with earthworms clamoring in the raw sunlight, attracting great flocks of red-winged blackbirds to swoop down and feast. The birds would rise and fall above the already sweating brows of men for whom another year, another crop of cotton, had just begun. Now and then the breeze might carry a whiff of desire, of catfish and bream spawning in the ponds and creeks, or of wood smoke curling in thin tendrils from distant cabin chimneys from the remains of last night's fires, on which the morning's meals of biscuits with cane syrup and fatback were cooked and quickly consumed in darkness. Each day the ringing of the plantation's great cast-iron bells heralded the rising sun.

Then, as now, the crop year would begin as soon as the land dried out in spring, interrupted only when periodic rains fell in torrents upon the exposed ground, making it too wet to plow. Soon summer would roll inexorably over everything, and it would seem to last forever. It would be hot when the sun came up, hot in the fields all day, hot in the houses at night. There would be no relief—no air-conditioning, no electric fans, no screens on the windows, or insect repellant. Horses and plowmen would travel in their own personal clouds of dust, bucking and weaving between the narrow rows, cultivating the young crop up and down the sun-drenched hillsides.

By midsummer the fields would be filled with women, too, chopping the weeds from the cotton rows when the crop grew too tall and lush to plow through. Afterward, pink and white cotton blossoms would unfurl beneath the broad leaves, the bolls at their base slowly maturing before finally bursting open, making the fields beautiful, white with cotton. In the fall the awful, backbreaking, finger-slitting picking would commence, the world smelling of cotton, a smell like nothing else, the smallest children smelling of it from playing in the piles, lint in their hair. Cotton was everywhere, and for the people working in the fields, it was someone else's cotton.

The ritual was repeated, year after year. When slavery ended, sharecropping took its place, and then in the mid-twentieth century the tractors came, along with mechanical cotton pickers, and just when things were getting easier came the onslaught of full-scale erosion. As late as the 1970s, a few old men in Jefferson County were still working small patches of ground with horses, the jangle of trace chains and the whoosh of the plow an echo of the old world, but they—and eventually, cotton itself—slowly passed from the scene. Today only a few isolated fields remain. What is left is a careworn landscape, and fading memories.

Not surprisingly, descendants of slaveholders tend to harbor happier memories of the old days than the descendants of slaves. People like Laverne McPhate, a descendant of Isaac Ross who now lives across the river in Ferriday, Louisiana, can envision scenes from the old days with fondness.

"When you stood on the old galleries at Prospect Hill, you could see just beyond that old brick wall the fields of indigo and cotton, and I could just imagine sitting on the porch, watching them work," she says, over the phone. "They had a good relationship. To know how well they got along and then to look at the situation today, well . . . hostility is just rampant now. I'm sure there were many hotheads and rebellious ones in that day and time, but from all that I understand Isaac Ross helped all that he could."

A large percentage—some say more than half—of white Mississippians before the Civil War owned no slaves, and a handful of free blacks did, but the line of demarcation between slave owners and their descendants and slaves and their descendants is abundantly clear. The plantation and its cotton belonged to Isaac Ross, and when Laverne pictures the gangs of slaves toiling in the fields, it is with pride over the plantation legacy that encompasses the Rosses and another prominent local family, the Davenports.

"I remember my grandmother talking about a slave man who helped them when she was a child," she says. "He helped around the farm. He chose this woman to marry and he took the Davenport name. He always kept the property up. He farmed with them. They killed hogs together. There was no big deal, they were just happy. This girl that works for me now, my aunt named her. We just all grew up together.

"But then comes the change of times. If I had my druthers I would have rather lived in the 1800s, because it would've proved interesting. Jefferson County was one of the most prosperous counties around. To me it was just fascinating. We all had to get along, and everyone was provided for. Isaac Ross provided everything for his slaves."

Laverne's pride is not universally shared, but the fact that Ross freed his slaves makes the story of Prospect Hill more palatable in a racially charged place and time. She is buoyed by the belief that Ross was driven by a sense of noblesse oblige, that in the case of Prospect Hill, nothing was simply black and white. It is an attractive idea, but a hard sell.

Scant information about the daily lives of Prospect Hill slaves can be found today, aside from those birth records found in plantation ledgers, random entries in area planters' journals, court-ordered inventories associated with the contest of Ross's will, and family lore. Slaves were chattel, utterly subject to their owners' desires, and had no role in drafting the written record. The dearth of records to corroborate, clarify, or contradict hearsay has robbed their descendants of many of the details of their ancestors' world, but by the same token, it has given them, and their descendants, free rein to create an oral record of their own choosing.

From existing records, it seems clear that one of the Prospect Hill slaves, Grace Ross, held a place of some importance in the household, because for many years she cooked for the entire family and spent most of her waking hours in close proximity to them. Described in Isaac Ross's will as "my negro woman cook," she would also have lived close by, perhaps just across the yard. We have no way of knowing other details, though, and some of them are crucial. Grace seems to have been cast as a villain in many accounts of the alleged slave uprising at Prospect Hill, without ever actually being named. According to Ross and Wade family tradition, when the slaves revolted during the long period of litigation over Ross's will, they set fire to the house in an effort to kill Isaac Ross Wade. To ensure that no one escaped the fire, the story goes, the cook had laced the family's coffee with an herb that was supposed to induce deep sleep. Although she would likely have had help in the kitchen, Grace is the only slave who is specifically identified in the record as a cook, and while it is possible that Isaac Ross Wade replaced her when he took over the management of Prospect Hill during the litigation, there is no reference to his having done so. In the record, Grace is never given an opportunity to refute the charge.

We also know that Ross provided in his will that upon his daughter Margaret Reed's death, Grace and her children were to be inherited by his granddaughter Adelaide, unless Grace chose to emigrate to Liberia (she did, which also seems to indicate that she was not held accountable for the uprising). Grace's husband Jim appears to have been inherited by Ross's daughter Margaret Reed, because her estate is the provenance listed on his registration on the barque *Laura*, on which the couple and three of their four children set sail for Africa.

Grace is listed in the 1836 inventory of Ross's estate, age thirty-five, with a value of $1,000. Her children Paris, fifteen, Levy, thirteen, Julia, nine, Peggy, five, and Virginia, three, ranged in value from $200 to $700. Judging from the inventory, very young slaves were valued low, owing to their comparative lack of utility and the possibility that they would not reach a productive age, while older slaves declined in value simply because they could not do much and often required special care. As a result an infant and a sixty-year-old might both be valued at $100, while slaves in between often ran as high as $1,500. A few who had specialized skills or were for other reasons considered indispensable could go as high as $2,000. All of which means that, from a financial perspective, Grace was highly valued but not considered utterly irreplaceable.

Grace's kitchen would have occupied a structure separate from the big house to isolate the heat of cooking and the danger of fire, and would certainly have been well-stocked, because this was not a household where any expense was spared. From the receipts of the Ross estate, we know that the family was fond of peppermint and brandied cherries, fine china, and Irish linen, and that in addition to wild game and fish from the surrounding fields, forests, and streams and vegetable and herb gardens tended by the slaves, there was plenty of domestic meat on the table. Included in one inventory of the estate were 198 hogs, 193 sheep, 109 cows, and thirty young steers. The bulk of the meat would have been destined to feed the slaves, although certainly not as filets with Bernaise sauce, and in comparison with the big house, the cupboards of the slaves' cabins would have been spartan. Similarly, while the women in the big house were ordering up bolts of velvet, lace, and silk, the master of the plantation was buying calico and gingham in bulk to be fashioned into dresses for the female slaves— 483 yards total in one order, along with a dozen palm-leaf hats, scores of shoes, and 172 packages of tobacco.

Most of Ross's descendants, and published accounts by the American Colonization Society, stress that the Prospect Hill slaves fared better than most, and house servants such as Grace would have had it better still. Cooks typically consumed much the same food as their masters, became more intimate with them, and over time, perhaps, picked up some of their speech patterns and mannerisms. They were also more likely to be educated. This was true of house help on most plantations, and as a result, a dichotomy often developed between them and the field hands, which sometimes led to mistrust. Wash Ingram, a former slave in the Tidewater South who was quoted in a series of narratives compiled by the Federal Works Progress Administration in the 1930s, noted that house servants were envied because they "et at tables with plates," while field hands were "fed jus' like hosses at a big, long wooden trough."

Judging from the slave narratives, the relationship between slave and master was complicated for both, regardless of the strata of slave society one occupied. Some former slaves recalled feeling a kinship

with their masters, and many chose to remain on their home plantations after emancipation, though it is impossible to say whether this
was a result of affection, necessity, or simple inertia.

Among the narratives is an interview with Charlie Davenport of
Natchez, who was owned by Laverne McPhate's forebears. Davenport
was of mixed blood, part African-American and part Native American,
the result of a union between a slave and a member of the Choctaw
tribe, some of whom still lived in the area in the early nineteenth century. His memories were certainly mellowed by time, but it is telling
that much of what Davenport had to say concerned the status of his
former master, whom he described in the vernacular dialect tran-
scribed by the WPA interviewers as "one o'de riches' and highes' quality gent'men in de whole country. I'm tellin' you de trufe, us didn'
b'long to no white trash." Davenport could have fallen prey to a sort of
postbellum Stockholm syndrome, identifying with his captors, but he
may also have been using the memories at his disposal to elevate his
own status, a natural human urge.

The tone of the narratives was certainly influenced by the fact that
the subjects were reacting to white interviewers, but they provide
some of the only recorded personal recollections of the lives of slaves,
and it is evident that those lives were more variable than one might
expect, despite being framed by the inevitability of forced servitude.
Historian Christopher Morris wrote that one slave owner in the Mississippi Delta, Basil Kiger, enjoyed indulging his slaves now and then,
perhaps as much for his own entertainment as theirs. Kiger went so far
as to provide elaborate clothes for slave weddings in the big house at
his Buena Vista plantation, near Vicksburg. In describing the festivities
of one slave wedding in a letter to his wife (who was notably absent),
Kiger joked that the table was "quite bountifully supplied the variety
however was not very great consisting principally of Hog, Shoat, pork,
& Pig, with any quantity of cakes & whiskey." He recounted a slave
dance in the mansion's wide central hall, complete with a fiddle player,
and said he attended the party but fell asleep around two A.M., "leaving
them still at it in high glee."

"It does my heart good to see them so cheerful & happy," he wrote,
vowing that he would not sell his slaves "for 10000 dollars."

Other accounts mention slaveholders allowing their slaves small
stipends, which they spent on shopping sprees in nearby towns, and in

his will, Isaac Ross provided for some of his slaves to receive up to $1,000 should they not choose to emigrate to Liberia. But drawing from the WPA narratives, historian Paul Escott pointed out that this generosity, familiarity, and even intimacy was nonetheless based upon an immovable barrier: the fact, for the vast majority, of permanent enslavement.

Northerner Joseph Holt Ingraham recalled observing the raw deal at the famous Forks of the Road slave market on the outskirts of Natchez. "A line of negroes, commencing at the entrance with the tallest . . . down to a little fellow of about ten years of age, extended in a semicircle around the right side of the yard," Ingraham recalled. "Each was dressed in the usual uniform of slaves, when in market, consisting of a fashionably shaped, black fur hat, roundabout and trousers of coarse corduroy velvet . . . good vests, strong shoes, and white cotton shirts, completed their equipment. This dress they lay aside after they are sold, or wear out as soon as may be; for the negro dislikes to retain the indication of his having recently been in the market."

Ingraham described a transaction in which his companion bought a carriage driver for $975, which included having the slave show his teeth for inspection. "The entrance of a stranger into a mart is by no means an unimportant event to the slave," he wrote, "for every stranger may soon become his master and command his future destinies." How would one react to such a situation—by fading into the background, or by making eye contact with the most attractive prospective owner? And what kind of man would you want to own you?

In this case, the coachman, who was twenty-three, seemed eager to be sold, because he apparently had concluded that the man would be a fair master. When the transaction was complete, the slave "smiled upon his companions apparently quite pleased, then entreated his new owner to also buy his wife, which the man did, contingent upon the approval of his own wife, for $750. The poor girl was as much delighted as though already purchased," Ingraham wrote.

Slavery in the United States traced its origins to a small enterprise in the early colonies, when about twenty black indentured servants arrived in Jamestown, Virginia, in 1619. Many of the indentured who followed were white, and like their black counterparts, could buy their way out of servitude, but eventually nearly all blacks were subject to lifelong enslavement.

According to Escott, the consensus among former slaves was that a good owner was one "who did not whip you too much," while a bad owner "whipped you till he'd bloodied you and blistered you." Those who were fortunate enough to have good owners could expect to have most of their physical needs met but still faced a life of hard work with almost no hope of freedom. The less fortunate faced the potential for hunger, illness, separation from family members, and whatever abuse an angry, disturbed, or bad-tempered owner might inflict.

Escott quoted a Louisiana slave who said that when his masters lamented the departure of their two sons to fight in the Civil War, "It made us glad to see dem cry. Dey made us cry so much." Another slave, interviewed by researchers at Fisk University, told of her effort to get back at a particularly cruel mistress. When the elderly woman suffered a stroke, the young slave was assigned the task of fanning her and keeping the flies away. Taking advantage of the time when the two were alone, the slave would strike the woman across the face with the fan, knowing that she could not tell anyone. "I done that woman bad," the slave admitted. "She was so mean to me." After the mistress died, "all the slaves come in the house just a hollering and crying and holding their hands over their eyes, just hollering for all they could," she said. "Soon as they got outside of the house they would say, 'Old God damn son-of-a-bitch, she gone on down to hell.'"

Even slaves who were treated relatively well by their owners faced the threat of white "patrols" that roamed the countryside at night looking for slaves who were at large without a pass. A slave could, under Mississippi law, venture eight miles from his plantation and be gone for up to two days without being considered a runaway, but it is unlikely that such legal details mattered to some of the patrols. According to many accounts, capturing a lone slave was sometimes a source of entertainment for the men on the patrol, and often ended with whippings.

Among the other indignities of slave life was the appearance of the "breedin' nigger," as former slaves called him, who would be rented by the master to improve the genetic stock of his slaves. One slave said his master's interest in slave husbandry went so far as to include castration of what he called "little runty niggers . . . dey operate on dem lak dey does de male hog so's dat dey can't have no little runty chilluns." Sexual incursions by the master were also common, sometimes as a result of affection but at other times by force.

In an 1852 article in *The New York Times*, Frederick Law Olmstead wrote of a visit to an unnamed Mississippi plantation during which he observed that the slaves were predominately "thorough-bred Africans"—what his host labeled "real black niggers"—but that there were also numerous mulattoes, including one girl who was "pure white with straight, sandy-colored hair." It was not uncommon, Olmstead wrote, citing comments from his host, to find slaves "so white that they could not be easily distinguished from pure-blooded whites." His host, he wrote, "had never been on a plantation before, that had not more than one on it.

" 'Now,' said I, 'if that girl should dress herself well, and run away, would she be suspected of being a slave?' "

His host replied, "Oh yes; you might not know her if she got to the North, but any of us would know her."

"How?" Olmstead asked.

"By her language and manners."

"But if she had been brought up as a house-servant?"

"Perhaps not in that case."

Sexual intermingling was common enough both before and after the Civil War that the Mississippi legislature passed a law imposing stiff penalties on whites who engaged in the practice. In what was known as the Black Code, which was instituted after the war, the legislature ordained that white men who had sexual relations with freed slave women could be fined $200 plus up to six months in jail. The penalties were worse for whites than for the blacks involved.

According to Escott, some slave women acquiesced to sexual relations with their masters in order to improve their status. One former slave in the upper South recalled that one reason this was done was because "They had a horror of going to Mississippi and they would do anything to keep from it." Mississippi represented the most frightening aspects of slavery because so many of the plantations were isolated and large, which meant that slaves often had less personal identity to shield them from abuse. In addition, laboring in the vast, steamy fields, which had recently been carved from the hostile wilderness, was reportedly more brutal than having to work the older, smaller, and more established plantations back East. Escott wrote that there were "fabulously wealthy and tastefully cultured families who could afford to treat their slaves with the indulgence that comes from unquestioned security. But most planters were not of that stripe." The latter was particularly true in developing plantation regions, he wrote.

Some planters recognized the importance of keeping their slaves comparatively content, providing them with their own vegetable plots, access to smokehouses, and even opportunities for occasional parties and repasts. These relative indulgences and freedoms may have had their basis in humanitarianism, or they may have been simply a part of the proper maintenance of the human machinery that produced the crop. No doubt the horses, too, were well shod, got their vaccinations, and enjoyed an occasional treat of sweet feed. It is evident, though, that Isaac Ross was among the more progressive planters in the treatment of his slaves. Thomas Wade noted with obvious pride that the Prospect Hill slaves "were taught to be self reliant in many ways as he would give each family a certain number of corn fed hogs for their year's supply and each one had smokehouses and cared for their own meat. His large herd of fine cattle was used for the most part in supplying his slaves with fresh beef during the summer and fall as it was his custom to have two fine beeves slaughtered each week for their benefit." While it is tempting to think that Wade, as a proud descendant, may have embellished his portrait of antebellum Prospect Hill, the record shows that a large number of Ross's slaves were taught to read and write, in clear defiance of state law, that he never sold any of them or allowed families to be broken up, and that he provided them posthumously with the option of freedom, albeit with strings attached.

During Ross's years at Prospect Hill more than 100 slaves were born, and like many planters of the era, he often bestowed upon them lofty names that belied their status, such as Alexander the Great, and Plato. According to Wade, the slaves represented much more than interest on an investment. In Wade's view, Ross treated his slaves more like an extended family. An 1848 report by the New York Colonization Society seems to confirm Ross's paternalistic leanings, as well as his practice of keeping his slave community sequestered and intact. According to the report, "To render them happy appears to have been a principal object of their owner. He was an excellent planter; yet for many years, instead of endeavoring to increase his estate, he developed and applied its great resources to comforts of his people." Furthermore, the slaves "enjoyed almost parental care and kindness."

The possibility exists, of course, that some of the slaves were actually related to Ross. A researcher for a 1996 public television documentary on prominent mixed-race families in America claimed that Isaac Ross's mother was black or of mixed race. Family accounts and genealogical records cite Ross as the offspring of Isaac and Jean Brown Ross, but historian Mario Valdes disagreed in a memo to the producers of the Public Broadcasting Service's *Frontline* report, "Claiming Place: Bi-Racial American Portraits." Valdes wrote that Ross was a "prominent descendent of those Gibsons of colour" in South Carolina who later emigrated to Mississippi, adding that historical references that cite the elder Isaac Ross and Jane Brown as his parents have "conveniently glossed over the fact that Captain Isaac was in fact the son of a Gibson woman (Mary Gibson who was married to Isaac)."

Valdes is not alone in making that assertion. Ed Adams, a retired Chicago police detective who responded to one of my Internet postings about the family, said he believed that Ross was the son of the elder Isaac Ross and a woman of African descent named Mary Gibson. Ed wrote that Mary Gibson "was married to Isaac Ross (the elder) in a wedding performed by a Reverend Randall Gibson, who was believed to be of African descent," and added that he traces his own lineage to a mixture of slaves and slave owners, and calls himself an indirect descendant of Prospect Hill.

Thomas Wade noted that the marriage of Ross's daughter, Jane, to John I. W. Ross (her first cousin) was performed by Rev. Randle Gibson, and while it seems unlikely that Gibson was of obvious African descent—he served in the U.S. embassy in Madrid and later as a Confederate general, a U.S. congressman, and a U.S. senator, he was also among the prominent Americans mentioned in the Public Broadcasting Service report.

Laverne McPhate seems unperturbed when I throw out this provocative tidbit, and allows that history and family lore are notoriously inexact. It is sometimes difficult just to keep the branches of the family tree straight, she says, because so many names are repeated over time. Records of births and deaths in family Bibles and the tombstones at Prospect Hill seem fairly reliable, but even they must be closely scrutinized. In the cemetery are the graves of three Isaac Ross Wades, all brothers, grandsons of Isaac Ross. The first two died as toddlers, only a year apart, while the third grew up to become the executor and contestor of Ross's will.

As for Valdes' claim, Laverne says, "I haven't heard that, but it's highly possible. When they left the Carolinas and came down here, so many things changed. But that's the sort of thing . . . well, they always leave that part out."

CHAPTER FOUR

AS A SLAVEHOLDER IN 1830s Mississippi, Isaac Ross's motives for seeking to repatriate his slaves were no doubt questioned by his Northern peers in the American Colonization Society, and likewise his devotion to the Southern way of life was likely questioned by neighboring planters who considered him a closet abolitionist. One can't help wondering, too, if his slaves wondered whether he would ever make good on the deal.

Slaveholders who supported African colonization were caught in the crossfire of a burning issue of the era: how best to deal with free blacks, whether for humanitarian reasons or out of fear. Many in the colonization society saw free blacks as potential emissaries, who would use their freedom to help educate and Christianize native Africans, while others saw colonization simply as a mechanism for deporting free blacks from America. Free blacks were a source of great concern for the white power structure in the South because they had the potential to upset the status quo. As historian Mary Louise Clifford noted, "the free Negro posed a threat to the economic system of the American South, for he was an example to cause discontent and rebellion among the slave labor upon which the system rested."

At the time Ross drafted his will, the memory was comparatively fresh of the Nat Turner slave revolt in Virginia, in 1831, in which fifty to sixty whites had been killed. During the revolt, which effectively ended the fledgling abolitionist movement in the South, Turner's approximately seventy followers moved from farm to farm in Southampton County, murdering whites and taking on new followers among the slaves they freed. In the aftermath, new laws controlling the activities of slaves were passed across the South, and the Maryland general assembly joined in the colonization effort in Liberia, providing an annual appropriation to the Maryland Colonization Society. Maryland already had a statute forbidding free blacks from other states from settling there, but in 1831 the penalties were stiffened. The assembly also forbade free blacks from buying liquor, owning guns, selling food without a license, and even attending religious meetings if no whites were present. State law required that slaves who were freed following passage of the act be transported out of state.

Fear of the potential dangers posed by slaves and free blacks was not limited to the South. Indiana enacted restrictive laws in 1831, including a requirement that free blacks entering the state post a $500 personal bond, while the District of Columbia enforced a ten P.M. "colored curfew" which carried penalties of arrest, fine, and flogging. When slavery was eventually abolished in Washington by an act of Congress in 1862, $100,000 was set aside to pay the transportation costs of D.C. slaves who chose to emigrate to Haiti, Liberia, or any other country outside the United States.

The idea of removing free blacks had first been seriously considered in 1800, when whites managed to prevent a Virginia slave uprising and subsequently hanged thirty-five slaves. The Virginia house of delegates had called upon the governor to speak with President Thomas Jefferson "on the subject of purchasing lands without the limits of this state, where persons obnoxious to the laws or dangerous to the peace of society may be removed." The legislators considered removal to the "vacant western territory of the United States," but Jefferson subsequently began talks through the American ambassador in London for a joint effort with Great Britain, which was repatriating freed slaves in what would become the West African nation of Sierra Leone. The talks apparently went nowhere. Then, in 1810, slaves revolted in two Louisiana parishes, and following another uprising in Virginia in 1816, the American Colonization Society came into being.

Although Jefferson owned slaves and made no secret of his belief that blacks were inferior to whites, he was also on record as saying he considered slavery wrong. He was ambivalent—or hypocritical—in other ways, supporting colonization in part as a way of preventing the mixing of the races, while fathering children by his own slaves. If the president and author of the Declaration of Independence personally held conflicting views, however, he was forthright in his support for repatriation, arguing that "Deep rooted prejudices entertained by whites; ten thousand recollections, by the blacks, of injuries they have sustained . . . will divide us into two parties and produce convulsions which will probably never end but in the extermination of one or the other race."

In creating its Liberian colony in 1820, the American Colonization Society used as a template the colony of Sierra Leone, immediately to the west on the coast of West Africa. Freetown, the capital of Sierra Leone, had been founded thirty years earlier by English philanthropists as a home for freed British slaves, many of whom had originated in America but had won their freedom by fighting for the crown during the American Revolution. West Africa was chosen for the colonies for several reasons, but primarily because it was known as the "slave coast" and was the general area of origin of large numbers of slaves, including the majority of those who ended up in the Americas. Historians estimate that approximately sixty million Africans were captured as slaves in West Africa from the first recorded slave sale in 1503 to the end of the trade in the mid-nineteenth century. Of those, an estimated forty million died before arriving at their destinations.

Until the establishment of the two colonies, the territory that would become Liberia had been held by indigenous tribes, many of which were (and in some cases continued to be) active in the slave trade. In hindsight, it was a recipe for disaster.

The society claimed significant support on the national scene, including presidents Jefferson, Andrew Jackson, and James Monroe (for whom Liberia's capital, Monrovia, was named), as well as Henry Clay, Daniel Webster, Francis Scott Key, and Robert E. Lee. Its first president was George Washington's nephew, Supreme Court Justice Bushrod Washington.

Although most of the big names belonged to Southerners, the society's membership also included prominent Northern clergymen and abolitionists. All they agreed upon, apparently, was that "returning" freed slaves to Africa was a good idea. Henry Clay, to whom Isaac Ross's daughter Margaret Reed would leave some of her slaves for repatriation, based his argument on the premise that slaves would never be treated as equals in the United States, that because of "unconquerable prejudice resulting from their color, they never could amalgamate with the free whites of this country." Clay was among a group that reportedly included Monroe, Jackson, Key, and Webster that convened in the Davis Hotel in Washington, D.C., on December 21, 1816, to form the American Colonization Society.

The society's plans were clothed in a garment of philanthropy, and designed to encourage the repatriation of emancipated slaves, rather than only blacks who were already free. Another of its stated purposes was to enlighten the tribes of West Africa through Christian missions and leadership by comparatively educated freed-slave emigrants. For three years beginning in 1816, the society raised funds by selling memberships, and in 1819 the U.S. government granted $100,000 to aid the effort. Congress also authorized President Monroe to use U.S. Navy vessels to seize slaves from American ships at sea that were caught smuggling them to Cuba, Puerto Rico, and Brazil, the primary markets after the slave trade was abolished in the United States by constitutional provision. The slaves liberated from the ships were known as "recaptures," and ultimately, they added another variable to what would be an already volatile cultural mix in the Liberian colony.

In January 1820 the society's first chartered ship, the *Elizabeth*, set sail from New York for West Africa with three society agents and eighty-eight emigrants aboard. The ship first landed in Freetown, then made its way along the coast to the future Liberia, where the colonization effort got off to an inauspicious start. Within three weeks all of the society's agents and twenty-two of the immigrants had died of fever. The survivors were evacuated to Freetown. Undeterred, the society organized two more voyages and began buying additional land, sometimes under threat of force, from tribal chiefs along the coast. According to historian Clifford, U.S. officials struck a deal with indigenous tribes that allowed the emigrants to disembark in exchange for official tolerance of the tribes' active slave trade, which would have meant that as freed slaves were arriving to settle in Liberia, new slaves would have been setting sail. The colonization society board rejected the deal, however. A compromise that gave the coastal region only to the immigrants, and apparently made no mention of the slave trade, was accepted, but when the immigrants actually landed they met armed resistance and so moved farther down the coast, where they were again attacked. Some escaped to Freetown while others remained trapped within crude, hastily built fortifications. Only a small group persevered.

The colonization society received a significant public relations setback in November 1822, when a concerted attack was mounted by the tribes on those settlers who had remained. Although the immigrants were armed with cannons and guns, they were besieged until a British warship came to their aid. According to Clifford, one female emigrant, Matilda Newport, became a folk hero for her role in thwarting the attack. Upon seeing that all the cannoneers were dead or wounded, Newport reportedly lit the fuse of a cannon with the ember from her pipe and thereby repulsed the approaching tribesmen. Matilda Newport Day afterward became a national holiday in Liberia.

By the end of 1822 a tenuous peace was negotiated between the settlers and the tribes. Soon after, colonization society officials rebuked the immigrants for what they considered to be a poor effort at self-sufficiency. Clifford wrote that the settlers considered farming too closely akin to the slavery they had known in the United States, yet they had few other economic options aside from trade, which was dominated by the tribes.

To engender a sense of purpose, and because the colonization society was having difficulty finding leaders who would remain in place, the group named the colony Liberia and sought to regiment its government on the local level. The colonists began bartering for more coastal land and eventually took control of most of the valuable slave trading ports. By 1830 more than 2,500 immigrants had arrived in Liberia from the United States, and the next year the state of Maryland incorporated its colonization society, distinct from the American Colonization Society, and appropriated money for its own colony.

Even as the colonization effort was getting on its feet, opposition in the United States grew. The concept of colonization was challenged by both white abolitionists and free blacks who argued that African-Americans had earned a stake in the United States, and that repatriation was tantamount to deportation. Those concerns would still be echoed in 1851, when Frederick Douglass, in a speech to the Convention of Colored Citizens, attacked colonization, saying, "But we claim no affinity with Africa. This is our home . . . The land of our forefathers." African-Americans, he said, "do not trace our ancestry to Africa alone. We trace it to Englishmen, Irishmen, Scotchmen, to Frenchmen, to the German, to the Asiatic as well as to Africa. The best blood of Virginia courses through our veins." New York University linguist John Singler, who spent several years studying and teaching in Liberia, noted that "In general African-Americans viewed the ACS with profound mistrust."

The colonization effort was meanwhile denigrated in the South as a tool of abolitionists, despite protests from supporters that the potential for slave uprisings would be lessened by the removal of freedmen and slaves. The fact that the latter argument fell on so many deaf ears illustrates just how polarized the slaveholding and anti-slave camps had become. Yet there was support for the effort in Mississippi. In addition to Isaac Ross, state supporters included Stephen Duncan, a prominent Natchez planter who owned approximately 1,000 slaves; Jefferson County Judge James Green, who was among the first to send a group of his slaves to Liberia and for whom Greenville, Liberia, was named; and state Senator John Ker, who helped found the Mississippi Colonization Society, was a close friend of Ross's, and would successfully defend the legality of his will in the Mississippi legislature.

Ross's death came just two years after the founding of the colony Mississippi in Africa, which, like the Maryland settlement, was initially distinct from the greater colony of Liberia. According to a report published in 1848 by the New York Colonization Society (which included an appeal for funds to help repatriate the Prospect Hill slaves), "In 1834 the friends of colonization in Mississippi sent out two worthy and very reputable colored men by the names of Moore and Simpson to examine Liberia and return with their Report. They were highly gratified, and not only made a most favorable report, but actually emigrated the next year, and are still among the most honorable and prosperous citizens of Liberia.

"This gave such an impulse to the spirit of Colonization, that within a short time several large Estates were emancipated in the vicinity of Natchez, among these, the large Estate of Capt. Ross."

The first documented arrival of Mississippi settlers had been in 1835, when sixty-nine freed slaves, most of them emancipated by Judge Green, arrived aboard the *Rover*.

In 1838 the commonwealth of Liberia was founded under a constitution drawn up by the president of the Massachusetts Colonization Society, with the curious provision that citizenship was to be granted only to "persons of colour"—an effort, some say, to exclude white slave traders—and another that limited the right to vote to slave immigrants, excluding members of indigenous tribes. All government officials continued to be white agents of the American Colonization Society until 1842, when the first African-American was appointed governor. That year also saw the incorporation of Mississippi in Africa, at the mouth of the Sinoe River, into the greater colony of Liberia.

In 1846, in response to growing interest among the immigrants in self-government, the ACS officially severed its ties with the colony, and the next year Liberia declared itself an independent nation, the first in Africa, under the motto, "The Love of Liberty Brought Us Here." The U.S. government did not immediately recognize the new nation, however. Some say this was as a result of misgivings in Congress over the idea of black diplomats in Washington.

The colonization effort was the vehicle for the repatriation of one man who would become Mississippi's most famous slave—Prince Abdul Rahman Ibrahima, whose efforts to return to Africa became a cause célèbre during the nineteenth century. Ibrahima's story was chronicled in numerous newspaper accounts and books in the early nineteenth century, and in a later book by historian Terry Alford.

Ibrahima was a West African prince who had been sold into slavery at age twenty-six, in 1788, after his army was defeated in battle. He was subsequently transported to the United States, and eventually found himself at Foster Mound plantation, near Natchez, struggling to convince his owners and anyone else who would listen that he was a nobleman. He was said to have promised Thomas Foster, who had bought him, a ransom of gold in exchange for his freedom, but Foster had scoffed at the offer. Alford suggested that Foster had heard similar stories before. "Whites were suspicious of pretensions of royal birth," he wrote. "They caused dissension in the quarters and were an annoying source of extra-institutional authority."

Apparently most people recognized that Ibrahima was different. Part of a larger group of African prisoners of war brought to Natchez to be sold as slaves in 1788, he reportedly carried himself in a regal manner and at first refused to perform manual labor. He also tried to escape several times, but returned when it became evident that he had no place to go. Although the accounts of others eventually confirmed that his father was the king of a nation known as Timbo, which is now part of Guinea, Ibrahima had no choice but to settle into the life of a common slave, marrying a slave woman named Isabella, with whom he had nine children.

Ibrahima's story took its second major turn with a wildly coincidental meeting in 1807. An Irish ship surgeon, John Coates Cox, who had been rescued by Ibrahima's father in Africa many years before, recognized Ibrahima in Natchez, and confirmed what the prince had been saying all along. Cox had gone ashore on the West African coast in 1781 to hunt, and had become lost and eventually left behind. Ill with fever, ravaged by insect bites, with one leg lame from the bite of a poisonous worm, Cox was near death when Ibrahima's family found him and nursed him back to health. Cox later immigrated to Natchez and spotted Ibrahima in a market where Foster allowed him to sell vegetables from his personal garden, as well as Spanish moss, which he pulled from the trees and used as stuffing for mattresses. Cox offered to buy Ibrahima's freedom but Foster refused, saying he valued his services as an accountant. It is apparent that by then even Foster recognized Ibrahima's noble birth. In addition to his dignified bearing, education, and refined knowledge of Islam, Ibrahima was a master equestrian, and so also became a groom at Foster Mound. Thomas Foster was an avid horse racer and according to local lore once won a race against Andrew Jackson, who owned a trading post in the area, but when Jackson also offered to buy the groomsman, he again refused.

Andrew Marschalk, a local newspaperman, took an interest in Ibrahima and wrote numerous articles and pleas on his behalf, and eventually the story made its way to Secretary of State Henry Clay, who petitioned President Adams to intervene. Adams persuaded Foster to free Ibrahima twenty-five years after Cox had confirmed his identity and forty years after the prince had been enslaved.

Few people seemed clear on where Ibrahima's kingdom lay, a fact that Ibrahima used to his advantage. Marschalk was convinced that Ibrahima was a Moor from Morocco, and, according to Alford, Ibrahima wisely assumed the role, perhaps hoping that a North African identity would improve his chances of release. The ruse seems to have worked. On July 10, 1827, President Adams wrote in his diary that he had been approached about coming to Ibrahima's aid, describing him as "an African, who appears to be a subject of the Emperor of Morocco. . . ." Adams authorized the purchase of Ibrahima, if the price was right. The sale was negotiated with Foster's stipulation that Ibrahima's passage to Africa be guaranteed, and that his offspring remain behind as slaves. The mechanism for the emigration would be the American Colonization Society, which proposed sending Ibrahima to its colony in Liberia.

In a January 12, 1828, letter to the society, Clay cinched the deal, and in February Ibrahima was freed in Natchez. The question then presented itself: what to do about Ibrahima's wife, Isabella? Eventually Thomas agreed to sell her, too, and the necessary funds were raised among the local citizens. The couple then set out on a long tour that ended in Washington, D.C., during which they hoped to raise enough money to buy their children. Prior to the trip, Clay had authorized the expenditure of $200 to outfit Ibrahima in "handsome Moorish dress appropriate to his rank prior to his captivity."

Once he reached Washington, Ibrahima met with the president and told him that he would rather go to Liberia than Morocco. Then he asked that his five sons and eight grandchildren be allowed to accompany him. The latter request was denied.

Before his ship set sail, the colonization society had Ibrahima appear in public, in his Moorish costume, before a panoramic painting of Niagara Falls, and charged an admission of twenty-five cents per head, with half of the proceeds going to him. Ibrahima, whose health was by then declining, finally left for Africa in 1829. Upon his arrival in Liberia, he wrote back to family members at Foster Mound, saying he hoped to raise money for their emancipation and emigration. "I shall try to bring my country men to the Colony and try to open the trade," he wrote. He died five months later, before a caravan from Timbo bearing gold could reach him. Hearing of his death, the caravan turned back.

Ibrahima apparently had a bad feeling about Liberia. According to Alford, he "was appalled with the succession of funerals and asked a man who was fluent in English to draft a letter to a New York minister who had helped him immigrate and was considering joining him there. 'I beg you not mention to come to Africa,' Ibrahima wrote. 'You must stay where you are for the place is not fit for such people as you.'" By the time of Ibrahima's death, $3,500 had been raised in the United

States to pay for the purchase and emigration of his children, but the intractable Foster refused to sell. Among Ibrahima's five sons and four daughters, only three are now known by name: Simon, Prince, and Levi. When Foster died shortly after, his heirs received his slaves, and all except Prince and his wife and children were sold to sympathizers and departed Natchez for Liberia in 1830.

In the summer of 2000, while researching the story of Prospect Hill, I encounter two of Ibrahima's descendants following the same path I am on, but going the other way. They have arrived in Natchez from Liberia in hopes of finding their Mississippi kin, and their visit has created a minor stir in the local news media. Natchez is known for its lavish mansions, and not surprisingly, most visitors come with white antebellum culture on their minds. The city is a mecca for those interested in the romanticized lifestyles of the Old South—the grand balls, the Victorian empire furniture, the formal gardens of camellias, azaleas, jasmine, and wisteria. In recent years, however, tourism officials and historic preservation groups have begun to recognize the importance of African-American culture in the city's history, and among the relevant stories, Prince Ibrahima's is the most remarkable.

The descendants, Youjay Innis and Artemus Gaye, are descended from his son Simon. Growing up in Monrovia, Liberia, Innis tells me over the phone, he heard a lot about Mississippi—about the cotton fields in which his ancestors had toiled as slaves and about Ibrahima's efforts to win his freedom. Youjay, who is attending the University of Evansville, in Indiana, was curious about what Mississippi looked like, about the people who had owned Ibrahima, and about what had become of the family members who remained behind when the prince succeeded in emigrating to Liberia in 1829. He also wanted to see how his ancestors had lived here before they emigrated. So he set out for Natchez with Artemus, his cousin, to see what they could find. In Natchez they talked with anyone who was knowledgeable about Ibrahima's story or about Foster Mound, and when they met Ann Brown, she called me. The slaves of Foster Mound, she said, were distant relatives of the Rosses.

Innis told the *Natchez Democrat* that he had long wanted to return to Mississippi to get a greater understanding of Ibrahima's experience there, and their arrival in the city coincided with the anniversary of Ibrahima's sale as a slave on August 18, 1788. Gaye told the newspaper that they did not see the timing as a simple coincidence. "The spirits of our ancestors are guiding us," he said. "Everything was leading to Mississippi."

Innis and Gaye visited the site of Foster Mound and strolled nearby cotton fields, and Gaye said he was moved by the experience, and felt "no bit of anger. But a sense of healing and reconciling the past with the present." After meeting one of Foster's descendants in Natchez, they moved on.

Few of the immigrants to Liberia shared the sort of notoriety enjoyed by Ibrahima, but his emigration brought attention to the repatriation effort. During the height of colonization, between 1820 and 1870, the American Colonization Society sent an estimated 13,000 emigrants to the colony, the majority of whom were sponsored by societies in Georgia, Louisiana, Maryland, Massachusetts, Mississippi, New York, Pennsylvania, and Virginia. The largest group came from Prospect Hill.

How Ross decided to repatriate his slaves is still subject to debate, even among his descendants. Some attribute his interest to philanthropy, others to something close to a filial love for his slaves, and still others to fear—either of the fate that would befall his slaves after he died, or of what would become of the South once they and hundreds of thousands of others were inevitably freed.

That Ross shared the society's missionary zeal appears doubtful. Although descendant Annie Mims Wright described him as "of a deeply religious nature," Harnett Kane, citing testimony from the litigation of his will, concluded that "far from being minister-ridden, Ike Ross had a good natured tolerance toward all faiths." John Ker, who alone among them had firsthand knowledge, went a giant step further, arguing that Ross was not a religious man in the traditional sense at all.

"To those who enjoyed his acquaintance, it would be superfluous of me to say that no man could sustain a higher character for unsullied probity and honor; or for vigor, energy and independence," the senator wrote in a published defense of Ross's will. He added that he felt it necessary to stress those points "inasmuch as great pains have been taken to make the impression, that the Will was made in the immediate prospect of death, and under the influence of 'priests and fanatics.' The truth is, he counseled with no priest or clergyman, and no man was ever more free from the influence of that class of men, or of any description of fanaticism." On the contrary, Ross "was rather hostile, than otherwise, to religion, or at least to the creeds taught by any of the prevailing Christian denominations; and although kind and hospitable to clergymen, and all others, who visited his house, he was far from being influenced by any one. Even the Reverend Mr. Butler, who, from having been a classmate in college with a son of Captain Ross, had visited and become intimate in the family, had never been in any way consulted by him relative to the Will."

While Ker was unwavering in his fidelity to Ross's dying wish, his support for repatriation was rooted more in pragmatism than benevolence. In a July 25, 1831, letter to Isaac Thomas, a Louisiana planter who was trying to organize a colonization society in his own state, Ker wrote, "You avow your willingness 'to see every colored person moved from the United States' and I agree with you in thinking the first introduction of them the greatest curse that was or perhaps will be inflicted on the country. The free colored people are more injurious to society than the same number of slaves, and their removal would therefore confer a greater benefit.

"Already," he continued, "an extensive and fertile region in Africa the land of their forefathers but a few generations removed, holds out to the free men of color in the United States the tempting allurements, of a *Home and a country of their own, of freedom, and self government, of a rich reward of industry in plenty and even in wealth.* It certainly would not be contended that there are not inducements which ought to decide Him, to abandon the country where He has experienced only degradation, and the almost necessary consequences, *poverty, vice and misery."*

Regarding Ross's motivation, Ker argued that the will "was no death-bed alarm of conscience from the abolitionists' sin of slaveholding; on the contrary, if that had been the case, he would have required all of his slaves to immigrate rather than giving each of them a choice." As for a perceived link between colonization and abolition, he wrote that "the most *deadly hostility* exists, on the part of the abolitionists, to the Colonization Society."

Thomas Wade postulated that Ross's motives were rooted in concern over abolition and a desire to reward his slaves, "rather than a deep religious conviction concerning the moral issues of slavery. While he was religious, I am sure, he stated that it was his firm belief that the institution of slavery could not last more than twenty-five years. Subsequent momentous events confirm the fact that he visioned the future well."

Another descendant, Robert Wade, now a retired civil engineer in Port Gibson, says he was always told that Ross had "mixed emotions about slavery," and that "he realized they were going to be more of a liability than an asset in the long run.

"The intent of the Colonization Society was good," Robert says, then adds, rather sardonically, "like so many other intents over the years."

The closest to a consensus among the descendants is that Ross cared about his slaves and that he was both concerned about what would happen after he was gone and convinced that the eventual emancipation would spell trouble for everyone. Although the succession of deaths among his own family members had no doubt shown him that his ability to maintain the balance of life at Prospect Hill was fleeting, freeing his slaves outright was not a viable option. It would have required the approval of the state legislature, which was not likely to grant it. And even if it had been granted—then what? There were few opportunities available to the average free black in the United States at the time.

Ultimately, Ross wanted his slaves to have an opportunity to make their own way, and for whatever reasons, he decided that their best chance was in Africa.

CHAPTER FIVE

BY MID-JANUARY 1836, everyone would have known that Isaac Ross was dying—the family, the neighbors, and the slaves, including Enoch, his manservant, with whom Ross had had a close but tumultuous relationship during the last few years. Ross's dying meant very different things to his grandson, Isaac Ross Wade, who was to be the executor of his estate, and to his daughter Margaret Reed, who was about to lose her father and face the consequences of carrying out the directives outlined in his will.

The scene must have been awkward when Ross called his remaining family to his side, a few days before he died, to reiterate those plans. It is easy to imagine Wade and Reed exchanging a cool glance as the old man lay prostrate on a couch in his salon, finally succumbing to a long and painful illness.

The fallow winter fields of Prospect Hill would have been visible beyond the wavy glass of the windows, with row after row of bare cotton stalks marching away to the horizon, flecked with lint hanging from empty bolls. In earlier days, Ross might have been reading on this very couch, or sitting at his desk reckoning accounts, or hunting in the woods, or making sure there was enough firewood in store and enough food for his family and his slaves and his livestock. But the unnamed sickness had triumphed over everything. In four or five days he would be dead, and everything would be in Wade's and Reed's hands, until her death, which would be the true moment of reckoning.

Wade and Reed were the two people whom Ross had decided he could trust to carry out his plan. If she did not know it then, Reed would find out soon enough that her father had made a crucial, disastrous mistake.

The two would later recount the substance of Ross's words on the day he called them to his side, in an affidavit filed in Jefferson County Probate Court—a document that, it seems safe to assume, marked the last time they agreed upon anything pertaining to Prospect Hill. In the affidavit, Wade and Reed verified that Ross had restated his plans for the repatriation of the slaves, which was to take place after Reed herself had died. Soon, however, Wade reportedly told Reed that he had no intentions of abiding by his grandfather's wishes, which prompted her to draft her own will, mirroring her father's, and to spend the remaining two years of her life doing everything in her power to see that his plan was carried out. Wade would spend the next decade, and most of the funds of the estate, doing everything he could to prevent it.

As he lay dying, Ross apparently knew nothing about the rift. He had no reason to believe his plan would not prevail, for it must have seemed as well-laid and manageable as a fire burning in the hearth. He had succeeded at almost everything he had undertaken in life, sometimes at great peril. He was an honored veteran, respected in the community, and owned 5,000 acres of fertile land in the wealthiest cotton district in Mississippi, perhaps the world. In his house were portraits painted by skilled artists, cases of leather-bound books, carpets from the Orient, massive looking-glasses in gilded frames and other elaborate furnishings, including one of his prized possessions, the rosewood and ebony piano. In his stables were fine horses and expensive, well-sprung carriages. Scattered across his holdings were nearly 200 people whom he owned. All of it was his to do with as he saw fit. Still, even a fire in the hearth must be tended lest it burn itself out or rage out of control, so Ross left nothing to chance.

He had refined the will on several occasions, but the thrust was always the same regarding the repatriation plan. He also provided for contingencies. Should the slaves choose not to go to Liberia, they were to be sold along with the plantation, and the proceeds used to found an institution of learning in Liberia. If the colonization effort failed, the money was to be used to found a school in Mississippi. In any event, his own heirs would receive a comparatively small inheritance. Notably, Isaac Ross Wade was to receive only his secretary desk and a case of books.

Ross directed that the plantation be cultivated under the supervision of the executors for one year after Reed's death, with the profits from the sale of the crop applied to an account for the repatriation of the slaves. Another of his plantations, Rosswood, was to go to Jane B. Ross, the mother of Isaac Ross Wade. From the sale of Prospect Hill, prior to applying the funds to the repatriation, his granddaughter Adelaide Richardson was to receive a bequest of $10,000, along with several slaves—Grace and all of her children; Daphne, Dinah, and Rebecca (unless they chose to go to Liberia, which they did); and Hannabal, who was to receive an annual stipend of $1,000 during the remainder of his life (again, unless he chose to emigrate, which he did). The executors were to carefully explain the repatriation option to the slaves, who would decide whether to stay or go, ten days after the cotton crop was picked.

A few of the slaves were excluded, including those identified as Tom, William, Joe, Aleck, and Henrietta, whom Ross had bought in 1833 and 1834 and so were not part of the cohesive slave community, and another identified only as Jeffers, the son of Harry, whose reasons for being denied were not given. These six were to be sold at public auction. Ross also made it clear that if any of the slaves chose not to go to Liberia the families were not to be divided by their eventual sale.

Ross was apparently most concerned with the fate of Enoch, who seems to have disappointed him once and in retaliation had initially been denied the option of emigrating. According to a coda that Ross attached to his will, Enoch was to have been "absolutely sold" at public auction, to remain enslaved while the rest, including Enoch's wife and children, were given the option of freedom in Liberia. Ross later relented, instructing Reed and Wade while lying on his deathbed to restore to Enoch the option of freedom in Africa as well as to provide for another, unique alternative—emancipation, along with his family, with passage to a free state in the North, and 500 silver dollars to help him on his way. It was the most generous offer any of the slaves received, and Enoch took it.

During what would be their last years together, Ross and Reed had laid careful plans not only for Prospect Hill but for other family plantations, including her own, which was known as Ridges. In addition, although it is not mentioned in later court documents or in family accounts, Isaac Ross Jr. appears to have preceded them in leaving his slaves the option of repatriation. It is possible that Ross Jr.'s slaves were absorbed by his father's or sister's estates, or that his widow or son followed through with his plan, but the colonization society's 1848 report notes that he provided for the repatriation of slaves at his St. Albans plantation in his own will, drafted in 1830, two years before he died.

Reed's life must have taken a particularly difficult turn after Ross Sr. died on January 19, 1836. She faced overwhelming responsibility, declining health, and unsympathetic family members and neighbors. Reed had already endured more than her share of travails, losing her parents, one sister, both brothers, and two husbands. Her first husband had died soon after they were married, leaving her childless, at which point she had moved back into the house at Prospect Hill. Eventually, at a party, she had met Thomas Reed, who had moved down from Kentucky, and they began to court in her family home. They married and in 1818 bought an old house in the area and enlarged and modernized it, adding a columned front gallery nearly a hundred feet long, and named it Linden plantation. The honeymoon proved short-lived. Thomas Reed, who had served as Mississippi's attorney general and had recently become the state's first U.S. senator, was suddenly stricken with a "hopeless illness" and died. She sold Linden to John Ker, her father's close friend, and again moved back to Prospect Hill.

Once her father was gone, some of Reed's neighbors reportedly discouraged her from following through with his plan, saying that it was unladylike and foolhardy, and that the will would not hold up in court. She responded by hiring a lawyer, consulting with others whom she knew would be sympathetic to the cause, and drafting her own will stipulating that Ridges plantation and Prospect Hill be sold and that her own 123 slaves be given the same option of emigrating to Liberia under the direction of the American Colonization Society. She also added a coda in September 1838, a short time before she died: "Having information that an effort will be made to invalidate or annul the last will & testament of my late beloved, venerated father," and "in the event of said will and testament being legally pronounced null & void and his Christian and benevolent plan of colonizing his slaves in Liberia in Africa thereby be frustrated," she wrote, her property should go to Rev. Zebulon Butler and Stephen Duncan, both members of the colonization society.

According to Ker, Reed had initially planned to name one of her nephews as executor of her will, but changed her mind after learning that one of them, Wade, was hostile to the cause and planned to contest it. Ker wrote that, "the course of action taken with regard to his Will had changed that determination, and embittered her feelings towards her relations. She was still further exasperated, by declarations made to her, that a learned lawyer had given his opinion, that she could not make a will, to effect her known wishes, that he could not break." Ker wrote that Reed did not ask Butler or Duncan for permission to leave them her estate. Butler, in fact, "regretted, as he has done ever since, that his dying friend would not release him from the duty of serving her in that capacity," he wrote. More determined than ever, she simply drafted the will along the lines of her father's, and included a letter addressed to her slaves explaining what she had done.

Soon after adding the coda, Reed, whom the 1848 colonization society report described as "a lady of large fortune, cultivated intellect and a heart full of noble and elevated sentiments," died. Wade and his mother Jane Ross then filed his contest of her and Ross's wills.

To Wade and other like-minded family members, it all came down to property, and in particular, the Prospect Hill mansion, the 5,000 acres of prime cotton land, and the slaves, who, by the time of Reed's death, had grown in number to nearly 225. In Thomas Wade's view, which he outlined in an August 21, 1902, letter to the Port Gibson *Reveille*, "It was not expected that the heirs of Captain Ross would quietly permit this valuable estate to pass out of their possession."

After Reed's death, Isaac Ross Wade moved into his grandfather's mansion and set himself up as master of Prospect Hill. He was only twenty, but he was ambitious and determined. He saw himself as the heir apparent. His mother, Jane Ross, was his staunchest ally, and perhaps his inspiration. Working in tandem with her, he was clearly willing to do just about anything to hold on to Prospect Hill.

In the litigation over the wills, Wade initially deferred to his mother, who filed the first lawsuit in Jefferson County Probate Court in 1840, but before it was over, there could be no question that it was his fight. Both Jane Ross and the brother of her late husband, Walter Wade, eventually granted him the power to file appeal bonds in their names, of which there would be several. Isaac Ross Wade, meanwhile, assumed the reins of the plantation and the control of its slaves, earning a commission from the estate as its chief executor and submitting invoices to the probate court for his expenses, which the estate paid even as he sought to undermine the very will that had put him there.

His own legal argument was straightforward: Ross's and Reed's wills violated state law governing the manumission of slaves, which required legislative approval, and were designed "for the benefit of negro slaves and therefore void." But if he expected to sail smoothly through the judicial system, he was wrong.

Almost immediately, the co-executors of his grandfather's will came after him. Soon after the contest was filed, in September 1840, Ellett Payson, attorney for co-executors Daniel Vertner, James Parker, Elias Ogden, and John Coleman, filed a petition in Jefferson County Probate Court asking that Wade be removed as executor. In the petition, Payson explained that the four had agreed to pay Wade a $1,500 annual salary from the estate for operating the plantation, but that on June 13, 1840, he had been cited for "appropriating to his own use about twelve thousand dollars of the funds of the estate which he was unable to refund. . . ." The court prohibited the removal of the current crop of cotton from the plantation "except by the direction of the majority of the Executors," and suggested that after the crop was harvested, the executors "might dispense with the services of a superintendent and thereafter give their personal attention to the management of the Estate."

According to the order, Wade had, "in violation of the resolution, shipped some fifty or a hundred bales of cotton of the present crop . . . in his own name, and refused to obey the wishes of the majority of the Executors. . . ." The petition sought reimbursement from Wade and the authority to disburse $10,000 to Sargent S. Prentiss, a locally famous lawyer known as "the silver-tongued orator," no doubt to come after Wade in court. In addition, the co-executors asked for approximately $2,000 from the estate in balance due for a monument to be erected in tribute to Ross by the Mississippi Colonization Society in the Prospect Hill cemetery, a short distance from the house where Wade now lived, as well as for other outstanding debts that Wade had refused to pay. In the coming months the court would twice enjoin Wade from selling or removing the Prospect Hill cotton crop, under penalty of $1,000. Court records also reflect a February 1844 payment from Ross's estate to Wade's chief attorney, Henry Ellett, of $500 for

representation in his case against the American Colonization Society—
evidence that Wade was using the profits of the plantation to pay for
his legal fight to retain control of the estate.

Wade clearly saw Prospect Hill and everything it encompassed as
rightfully belonging to him, and must have been extremely frustrated
by having to share the management of the estate with his legal opponents, who were forever looking over his shoulder, second-guessing his
management, disputing his claims, and waiting for him to make a mistake for which they could drag him back into court. It must have
seemed a godsend to him when that impediment was suddenly elimi-
nated, through a technicality.

According to the New York Colonization Society's 1848 report,
three of the executors "by some omission were disqualified and
removed." In the words of the report, "the Estate fell into the entire
care of the only remaining Executor, of the name of Wade, who has,
with other heirs at law, left no plan unassayed to defeat the Will." The
fourth co-executor had already stepped down, for unexplained reasons, and the technicality is not described in existing court records.
Certainly a lot was going on. When the American Colonization Society
filed a complaint against Jane Ross in the Superior Chancery Court for
attempting to enjoin them from removing the slaves and for attempting to claim the estate in court, included among the defendants were
three of the co-executors, Parker, Ogden, and Coleman. The court
responded by enjoining Wade, under penalty of $5,000, from distrib-
uting the proceeds of the estate to his mother or anyone else. When
the colonization society won its case, Wade and company appealed.

Parker, Ogden, and Coleman may have been caught in the middle.
They were sued alongside Wade because they had allegedly shirked
their responsibility to see to the transfer of the slaves to the colonization society, yet they argued that they had been prevented from doing
so by Wade, and would have, had they been ordered to do so by the
court. Ultimately the state's High Court of Errors and Appeals upheld
the ruling in favor of the colonization society.

If it galled Wade that the courts continued to rule against him and
his mother, and to undermine his attempts at unilateral rule over
Prospect Hill, he appears to have been undaunted by these legal
episodes. Even had he lost the contest in court, its significance tran-
scended local politics, and if Wade managed to ultimately triumph,

none of the rest would matter. So when the probate court ruled against him, finding the wills valid, he sought relief in the chancery court, and when it ruled against him, he turned to the court of appeals. When that court also ruled against him, he filed follow-up suits. He had no intention of stopping until he won, or until he ran out of options.

Jane Ross's attempted end-run around the colonization society was multifaceted, but her primary interest in the suit she filed in Jefferson County Probate Court was to have the bulk of the estate awarded to her and her nephew, Isaac Allison Ross. It is not clear why she did not name her son, Isaac Ross Wade, but perhaps the separate suits were designed as a safety net for a group effort. It is also possible that she and her son did not trust each other. Her own familial status was complicated; after being widowed she had married her first cousin, which made her Jane Brown Ross Wade Ross, but as she explained to the court, she was the sole surviving offspring of Isaac Ross. Her nephew, as the son of Isaac Ross Jr., was her father's sole surviving direct male heir.

As with most lawsuits, hers was all about technicalities. Although she questioned her father's legal right to provide for the repatriation of his slaves, and indirectly, his prudence in doing so, her main contention was that the whole affair was moot, because during the two years that Reed had lived after her father, and the two years since her death, nothing had prevented the executors (which, of course, included her son, Isaac Ross Wade) from polling the slaves on their interest in emigrating, as stipulated by the will. Likewise, there had been no court order during the time to remove the slaves from the state. She argued that the provisions of her father's will had essentially lapsed. As she and her attorney interpreted the will, there was a deadline of ten days after Ross's death for polling the slaves about going to Africa, and no provisions for what to do with them if the deadline was not met. With the supposed deadline passed, and in the absence of further directive under the will, state law required that the estate pass to the nearest heirs, which meant her and her nephew. She asked the court to appoint a "disinterested commission" to divvy things up between the two of them, although she was willing to forego the $10,000 and the slaves (including Grace) who were earmarked in the will for her niece, Adelaide Wade Richardson, as well as "some small pecuniary legacies left to some of the slaves." Also exempt were "said slaves named Enoch and Marilla and her children who have been removed from this state." Otherwise, she asked the court to order her son to distribute the proceeds, which was obviously something he would have been happy to do.

As for Reed's will, Jane Ross contended that it had been more or less a product of conspiracy, of a "secret trust" among Reed, Butler, and Duncan. One of her attorneys, identified only as D. Mays, asked the court, "Is it not part of the policy of Mississippi, to protect her citizens against fanaticism in religion, and a morbid sensibility on the subject of slave holding?" He argued that emancipating slaves by will amounted to nothing less than disinheriting the next generation, and if it were allowed, the court would have "thrown open the doors to the abolitionists and invited them to . . . revel in the destruction of the slave property of the state."

Apparently the court was as unimpressed by these arguments as it had been by Wade's. On March 22, 1843, the Superior Chancery Court enjoined Jane Ross from filing further claims until the court had ruled on the matter at hand, which was the suit brought against her by the American Colonization Society. She must have been particularly bothersome to the court, for the injunction carried a penalty for violation of $5,000. She lost the suit the following year. On June 25, 1844, she, Walter Wade, and a man whose name is illegible in the court record turned to the High Court of Errors and Appeals in Jackson, posting a $500 bond payable to the colonization society in the event the courts again ruled against them. Clearly, they were also in it for the long haul.

Jane Ross and her son had some important allies in the state legislature, for as the lower courts were initially deliberating the case, lawmakers passed an act requiring that slaves freed by will be transported to their destination within one year. This forced the colonization society to file suit claiming that they had been prevented from removing the Prospect Hill slaves, although the court of appeals later ruled that the law did not apply to the case, because the ACS had attempted the removal and been thwarted by the heirs even after a ruling in their favor by the courts.

In arguing before the appellate court, Jane Ross's attorneys cast slavery as the paramount concern. "Slaves constitute a portion of the vested wealth and taxable property of the state," they noted in their legal argument. "Without them her lands are worthless. Would it not therefore be contrary to the policy of the state, to part with this vested wealth, this source of revenue, with that which alone renders her soil valuable . . . would it not be productive of mischief, and would it not be spreading a dangerous influence among the slave population of the country, for the slaves of the whole plantations to acquire their freedom, take leave of the country and make their departure, proclaiming liberty for themselves and their posterity? Would this not render the other slaves of the country dissatisfied, refractory, and rebellious? Would it not lead to insubordination and insurrection? And if so, would it not be contrary to the policy of the law? So certain as the heavens afford indications of a coming storm, so certain will scenes of blood be the concomitants of such testamentary dispositions in this state."

The suit questioned the credibility of the colonization society and its right, under its charter, to actually assume ownership of slaves, even temporarily. Ross's attorney referred to the opponents' conviction that "the colony of Liberia is an object worthy of all philanthropic encouragement," and with self-righteous disdain, responded, "What! That institution from which *reverend agents*, thrust themselves among the slave population of the country, and proclaim the advantages and blessings of Liberia: for it is charged in the bill, that some such persons visited Mrs. Reed. Such a colony may indeed be an object worthy of all commendation and encouragement to some persons, but it can never be so, to the peaceable citizens of a slave holding state."

In what proved to be a series of landmark cases, the high court concluded, among other things, that the state's manumission laws did not apply to slaves removed from the state. The justices cited Mississippi's constitutional prohibition, enacted in 1833, against the commercial importation of slaves (although slaves brought in for private use by their owners were allowed until 1845). There was disagreement over the purpose of the prohibition—some argued that it was designed to prevent the "dumping" of sometimes inferior slaves from eastern states where abolitionist sentiments were then taking hold, but the justices attributed the measure to a general need to reduce the state's population of slaves, a purpose the Ross and Reed wills served.

Regarding Jane Ross's suit against the co-executors, the high court upheld a Superior Chancery Court ruling that stated that "Mississippi has no concern with the question of manumitting slaves elsewhere than within her own limits."

Despite the early rulings against him, Wade refused to release the slaves or any other part of the estate. As a result, the colonization society filed its 1842 suit to force him to abide by the court's decree. The ACS won, Wade appealed, and the high court again ruled against him, noting that although the slaves "are not now free, they have an inchoate right to freedom." It is hard to imagine how such a proclamation, recognizing even an incomplete right to freedom by slaves, could go unnoticed, and it did not. According to the high court's Justice Harris, after the announcement of the opinion, and in express reference to it, the legislature passed a law making it illegal to free slaves by will for any purpose without state approval. But if the court upheld the right to free slaves in Africa, Harris also used the occasion to lament the practice of sending freed slaves to Ohio, a state that he described as beset by "negro-mania."

In upholding the ruling in favor of the American colonization society, Justice Clayton noted that the slaves—whom he described as "the bounty" of Ross's estate—"have been detained against the will, against the will of society, and that of all the executors except one. . . ." He called the suits "a fraud"—borrowing a term Wade had used in describing the American colonization society's effort. The heirs' attempts to thwart the will, Clayton wrote, were "a breach of trust and perversion of power," adding, "Rights acquired by fraud cannot be sustained . . . We need not determine the validity of the law. It has nothing to do with the case; the fraud of the party has placed him beyond the pale."

Those were remarkably strong words for an antebellum Mississippi judge to direct at a powerful slaveholder, which gives an indication of the degree of animosity that the Prospect Hill case had engendered.

During and after the Prospect Hill litigation, several other cases made their way to the high court involving the contests of wills that provided for the freeing of slaves through emigration, including one by the heirs of James Leech, of Wilkinson County, south of Natchez, who died the same year as Isaac Ross. His will stipulated that "his negro woman . . . and her four children" should be freed and sent to "Indiana or Liberia, whichever they might choose." In delivering the opinion that Leech's will was valid, Justice Clayton noted, "This will bears a strong resemblance to that of Isaac Ross, which has been the subject of so much controversy in the courts of this state." In that and every other case involving granting freedom to slaves for the purpose of emigration, the court upheld the wills.

During the long period of Prospect Hill litigation, it appears that nearly all of the slaves remained on the Ross and Reed plantations, including those who were to go to Richardson, because the assets were, ostensibly, frozen by the courts. Wade was under court order to keep detailed records of all transactions involving Prospect Hill, including property taxes paid, expenses, sales of cotton, and scheduled payments to Richardson. Perhaps because Richardson was his sister, he chose to honor the portion of the will affecting her bequest while vigorously repudiating the rest. The receipts and annual inventories covered everything from pantaloons and silver and candy to farm implements, livestock, carriages, wagons, stored cotton, tools, and hundreds of shoes. Most importantly, they listed all of the Prospect Hill slaves, together with their offspring, throughout the litigation.

News of the legal proceedings no doubt made its way to the Prospect Hill slaves, and although Wade and his allies were clearly losing every battle, nine years after Ross died their status had not changed. If the highest court in the state had granted them their freedom, why were they still enslaved? Why was Isaac Ross Wade still their master? Notably, Enoch and his family had at some point been freed, according to the stipulations of Ross's will. Enoch had appeared in the first inventory, twenty-five years old with a value of $1,200, along with his wife Marilla, twenty-six and valued at $900, and their children Anna, seven, and Mathilda, five, valued at $300 and $250, respectively. The family was missing from later inventories, with no reference as to where they had gone.

To forestall any effort to claim the slaves, Wade's attorney, Henry Ellett, sought an injunction in Jefferson County Probate Court in July 1844 against John Chambliss, who had been appointed as receiver for the society by the Superior Chancery Court, to prohibit him from seizing the slaves. After Ellett failed in that effort, he successfully sought an injunction in April 1845 against Jefferson County Sheriff Samuel Laughman to prevent him from seizing the slaves from Wade and delivering them to Chambliss, who had posted a $100,000 bond. The next month Ellett sought another injunction against Chambliss and an order to have Laughman arrested. "We have no desire to hold the Sheriff in close confinement if he will consider himself in custody and not at liberty to proceed further without additional authority . . ." Ellett wrote in his request to the court.

The Superior Chancery Court, meanwhile, authorized Chambliss to take control of the Prospect Hill slaves and plantation in the name of the American colonization society. According to the New York colonization society report, Chambliss, who was a neighbor and friend of Ross's, was undeterred by the possibility of 500 vigilantes united to oppose him, as was rumored, when he agreed to act as receiver for the slaves. Wade again responded by asking the probate court to restrain Sheriff Laughman from seizing the property and to place him under arrest. According to the report, "The Sheriff, evidently did not know how to act; in the double fear of offending the Chancellor on the one hand, or those on whose favor he and the Probate Judge depended for their offices on the other."

Ultimately Laughman chose to obey the Chancellor. He notified Chambliss to prepare to receive the slaves, then failed to show up on the appointed day. The court had issued the order Wade asked for and Laughman had been arrested by the county coroner. Clearly, the rule of law was teetering under the weight of Wade's political influence.

With the sheriff out of commission, there was no one to force Wade to turn over the slaves to Chambliss, and as late as June 7, 1848, Ellett wrote Wade to say that he had no objection to Sheriff Laughman being discharged from his duties through habeas corpus, with the warning that, "if he becomes rebellious afterward we can attach him again."

Some of the slaves had managed to get out before that point. Notably, a large group had been secretly seized by sympathetic whites and marched at night to a steamboat waiting on the Mississippi River, which transported them to New Orleans, and from which they sailed to Liberia. Those who remained at Prospect Hill still had a long row to hoe, however. With lawmakers who had never known Ross having entered the fray, pounding their fists on the podium at the capitol in Jackson and railing against his will, Wade and his mother had other avenues to explore. Before the conflict was over, Ross's Prospect Hill mansion would become his belated funeral pyre, lighting the sky with its flames and taking with it the life of a young girl, and before the ashes were cold, men whom Ross had owned, and for whom he'd laid careful plans, would be hanging from the nearby trees.

CHAPTER SIX

TURNER ASHBY ROSS is a glib man with a deep, gravelly voice who speaks slowly, as if he has all the time in the world. He lives in Vicksburg, Mississippi, and is the brother of Laverne McPhate. Like her, he is proud of his ancestry—proud both that Isaac Ross voluntarily freed his slaves, and that one of his grandfathers fought for the Confederacy in the Civil War.

"My name come from the general he fought under in the war—Turner Ashby," he says. Ashby was an icon of the lost cause, known as the Black Knight of the Confederacy, because of his dark complexion and eyes, black hair and beard, and what most accounts describe as his regal bearing while mounted on a horse. He was killed in a skirmish in Virginia early in the war, in 1862.

Proud as he is of his Confederate heritage, Turner is not a stereotypical, unreconstructed Southerner. He clearly sympathizes with the freed slaves of Prospect Hill when it comes to the trials they faced after emigrating to Liberia. "You think of what they went through," he says. "Some of 'em was writin' back wantin' more money, 'cause I'm sure they got a little money and a little education, and then they found out right quick there was always gonna be somebody waitin' by the side of the road to blink 'em out of it."

Still, if he can empathize with them as individuals, he views the collective slaves of Prospect Hill in the oldest sense, as chattel. The way he sees it, if Isaac Ross wanted to free his slaves, it was nobody else's business. He doesn't like the idea of neighboring planters voicing objections, much less forming vigilante squads to prevent the will's provisions from being carried out.

"They say all the plantation owners figured this would start a new trend," he says. "This was way before the Civil War, but there was already a lot of talk about antislavery. But what Isaac Ross did was his business. That was his money he paid for those slaves, and he had every right in the world to set 'em free or to do whatever he wanted with 'em."

Offensive as the concept may be to modern sensibilities, the right to ownership did, in fact, drive the contest of the will, and was at issue during the remarkably vitriolic debate in the state legislature, which was later recounted in Ker's published account. Although Ker was a biased participant, he seems to have had a high regard for facts and made no secret of his opinions. He drafted his narrative in response to a December 10, 1841, letter from eleven men who supported Ross's will and wrote to express their gratitude for his efforts to defeat a bill that would have made emancipation and repatriation by will retroactively illegal. Ker, they wrote, had precluded "a gross and dangerous violation of private rights," and he owed the public an unflinching account of what had happened.

Ker's notice, a copy of which lay buried in the haphazard records of the Jefferson County courthouse, seems to have anticipated an attack upon the character of the slaves, if not their potential for violence. Its chief interest lay in the debate over three key issues: fears and allegations that the Prospect Hill slaves were verging on insubordination; the supposition that Ross had written his will under the influence of "terrors of death and judgment, inspired by 'priests and fanatics'" and abolitionists; and the claim that Ross's slaves were by law rightfully the property of his family. Although he addressed each issue, Ker obviously considered property the only one worthy of lengthy debate. Like Turner Ross, he believed in the sanctity of the slaves as property, which meant that only Isaac Ross could, within obvious limits, determine their fate.

Ker began his account with this disclaimer: "Whilst I feel conscious that I am influenced by no intention of injuring any fellow man, either in character or fortune, a solemn sense of duty forbids that I should suppress or disguise the truth, whatever may be the consequence to myself.

"That said, during the last session of our Legislature measures were introduced into the House of Representatives, and passed by that body, which were evidently intended to annul the provisions of the last Will and Testaments of the late Captain Isaac Ross, and his daughter, Mrs. M. A. Reed, both of Jefferson County. Those measures were defeated in the Senate, but, I regret to say, not without difficulty, arising, as I believe, from misrepresentations by interested and prejudiced persons; and I have reason to believe that the purpose is not yet abandoned, but will be renewed." He portrayed the bill as "an attempt to legislate away one of the rights most dear to men and hitherto held sacred, the right to dispose of property, by will or otherwise, at pleasure. . . ."

Isaac Ross could not have had a more able or dedicated champion in the legislature, which convened at what is now the Old Capitol State Historical Museum, but was then a gleaming Greek Revival edifice built just two years before, in 1839. The building was actually the fourth devoted to the purpose, the first having been located in Washington, Mississippi, the territorial capital, and the second in nearby Natchez, which was the epicenter of political power throughout much of the nineteenth century. The third was a temporary assembly hall in the new city of Jackson, which had been selected for the capital in 1817 precisely because it was outside the controlling interests of the Natchez District. Relative isolation from the plantation stronghold may have reduced the influence of vested interests in the contest of Ross's and Reed's wills, but the subject of slavery was overarching. In one way or another, it mattered to everyone, in all parts of the state.

Jackson at the time was an inconsequential town, unimportant as either an agricultural or industrial center, but during each legislative session it became a political battleground, hosting a seasonal mélange of lawmakers from places as diverse as wealthy Natchez, the largely undeveloped Delta, the yeoman-farm country in the northeast hills, and the no-man's-land of the piney woods toward the coast, which included one region that would unofficially secede from the Confederacy during the war. It was a town where lawmakers could spend their free time playing chess or backgammon under the portico of a grand hotel, watching a horse race on the street running before the statehouse, or swilling ale in a basement saloon. One observer, Thomas Wharton, who visited the city in 1837, recalled a bar directly across from the capitol "crowded with a gay and festive party, making night hideous with their bacchanalian revels." Wharton wrote of his disappointment in finding that "Instead of the flourishing young city my imagination promised I should see, the population did not exceed, I would suppose, 900."

The capitol, and the nearby governor's mansion and city hall, represented significant departures from the typical buildings, which Wharton described as "wholly devoid of architectural taste and design." The House of Representatives met in an ornate and spacious chamber at the opposite end of the building from the more restrained Senate chamber, which was embellished with columns modeled after a monument in Athens, Greece. Immediately behind the building was the labyrinthine Pearl River swamp, while the front lawn served an array of public purposes, including occasional slave auctions. There was an odd mixture of pretense and recklessness about the place that provided fertile ground for the pitched battle over the slaves of Prospect Hill.

Ker's turf was the Senate chamber, and it was there that he led the defeat of the offending bill on the last day of the 1841 legislative session. The bill, which originated in the House, proposed to make it illegal to free slaves by will for any purpose, including emigration, without legislative authorization, and sparked heated debate over the "dangerous example the emancipation of the estimated 300 slaves of the Ross and Reed estates would set." In its original version the measure was retroactive, which meant that it would stifle the American colonization society's plan for the Prospect Hill slaves. After the Senate refused to concur, the bill returned to the House, where it was revised and returned. Sensing the danger of compromise, Ker successfully introduced a motion to table the bill until the following Monday, which would be after the close of the session. Tabling was equivalent to rejection.

"By joint resolution of the two Houses, the session was to close on Saturday evening, the 6th of February, at 7 o'clock," he wrote. "Long after 7 o'clock, perhaps 9 or 10, on the evening of the 6th, whilst I was for a moment absent from the Senate Chamber, an attempt was made to call up the bill." When Ker returned and realized the bill had been resurrected, he appealed to his peers in the Senate to abandon the effort, and prevailed on a parliamentary technicality. "Thus ended, for that session, this extraordinary attempt to legislate away the solemn decisions of the highest judicial tribunals of the State," he wrote.

Afterward, when he approached a member of the House with

whom he had been friendly and expressed his surprise that the representative had supported the retroactive measure, he recalled being told that "if the Wills should not be defeated by the Legislature, they would be by violence, and that every man in Jefferson County was opposed to the Wills, and that 200 men were ready to oppose their execution by force of arms, and that he wished to save that county from the odium or disgrace of such a procedure." Ker recalled telling the man that he could not fathom how a legislative act that superceded legal wills affirmed by the highest court "could exert any *moral* influence. Nothing that I can conceive of could be more *demoralizing* in its effects."

As for some lawmakers' claims that the wills were the product of a cartel of abolitionists and religious fanatics, Ker wrote that, on the contrary, the proponents were "emphatically men without reproach. One of them, it is true, is a clergyman; but this, I trust, can only be a subject of reproach, even among those who make no profession of religion, when the life and conduct is inconsistent with the profession." He posed the question: what was the accusation against Rev. Butler, who was one of the men Margaret Reed had named to receive the slaves on behalf of the American colonization society? The answer: "Attempting or desiring to remove, to Liberia, in Africa, *his own slaves*.

"Who will deny that Mrs. Reed had the right to make these gentlemen her heirs?" he asked. Who could question their motives, when they could not benefit from the bequest? Ker recalled being told that Stephen Duncan, another of the recipients, had "actually obtained his portion of the slaves by having them run away from the plantation, and secreted on the banks of the Mississippi until a steamboat was hailed to take them on to Louisiana, whence he sent them to Liberia."

Considering that so many controversial court cases today are tried, at least in part, in the media, it is interesting to note that opponents of the will undertook their own newspaper blitz. "Publication was made in the newspapers of the briefs of the lawyers, and other exparte views of the case, for no other obvious purpose than that of operating, through popular prejudice, upon the Courts," Ker wrote. "There was nothing in this case to justify or even to apologize for such attempts to create popular excitement."

For Ker, the issue extended beyond his support for colonization. "If we quietly fold our arms and passively acquiesce to such proceedings, what security, I ask, have any of us for the protection of law to our property, or lives, or our liberty? Has it indeed come to this, that the laws of the land are to be annulled by one man, or even 500 men, because certain testators did not happen to make their Wills in accordance with their views, or with public sentiment? Let us not deceive ourselves. Passive acquiescence in such doctrines or in such measures is criminal. 'The poisoned chalice may soon be returned to our own lips.' *We may be the next victim of the ruthless hand of lawless usurpation and violence."*

The defeat of the retroactive provision was a major coup for Ker and other defenders of the will, despite contemporary accounts cited in the New York colonization society's 1848 report "that 500 men 'are pledged and ready to prevent' the full administration of the laws of the land." The report added, "Truly, the spirit of anarchy is stalking with a bold front in our land, when 'people have been called upon to rise up and put the laws at defiance'; when calls have been made upon the Legislature to usurp power not granted to them by the people in the Constitution, to annul the solemn decrees of the Courts—to wrest from the hands of the citizens, property which has been devised to them under the laws of the State."

As for the sentiment that the potential for freedom would undermine the ability of slave owners to control their slaves, Ker was dismissive—perhaps overly so. "It was alleged," he wrote, "that insubordination existed among the slaves of these two estates, to such an extent as to produce great and general alarm in the neighborhood, and even lively apprehensions of an insurrection, &c. I cannot do justice to the eloquence which was called into exercise in the description of the dangers and the horrors which impended over this ill-fated neighborhood. But, like many other splendid passages of poets and orators, this eloquent description had much more of fiction than fact for its foundation. Subsequent investigation has enabled me to say, that on the estate of Capt. Ross there never had been the slightest insubordination; and on that of Mrs. Reed, none more formidable than frequently occurs from the change of overseer; and none that was not promptly quelled by the energy and resolution of a single citizen. But for the sake of argument, suppose it had been true, that the negroes were a vicious, insubordinate and dangerous set. What would have been the danger to the neighborhood, or to the State, of sending them off to Africa?"

The slaves, he added, were first and foremost the possessions of Isaac Ross, who "ardently desired to provide for their welfare and happiness after his death. It is not for others to determine whether the plan he adopted was wise or unwise."

As Ker predicted, the affair was far from over when the legislature failed to circumvent the first round of judicial rulings. Although the courts ultimately ruled that the law that was later passed, without the retroactive clause, did not apply to the Ross and Reed wills, there was still the matter of forcing Isaac Ross Wade to relinquish his claim and allow the transfer of those slaves who had not already been spirited away. The majority of the slaves were still marooned at Prospect Hill, despite the courts' rulings, and were growing increasingly restive, according to the traditional family account, which attributes the burning of Ross's house in 1845 to an uprising of those slaves who had lost patience with the delays.

The threat of slave rebellion was at the forefront of the debate over Ross's and Reed's wills, so it seems remarkable that there is no documentation of the alleged uprising or the burning of the Prospect Hill mansion in April 1845. Every reference I initially found could be traced only to Thomas Wade, who cited the recollection of his father, Isaac Ross Wade, who clearly had his own spin.

Wade's version, chronicled in his emphatic letter to the Port Gibson newspaper in 1902, is accepted as gospel by most of the heirs of the slaveholding family, although others I would find—particularly from the descendants of slaves—are not convinced of its veracity. There is no doubt that the house burned and that Martha Richardson died. The date is on her tombstone in the family cemetery a short distance away. It also seems plausible, despite the lack of documentation, that the lynchings took place. Beyond that, I found no record of the uprising.

For Thomas Wade, setting the record straight appears to have been a lifelong mission. In his letter to the Port Gibson *Reveille*, he referred to the doomed Prospect Hill house as "Judge Wade's residence," despite the fact that his father (who, indeed, later became a judge) did not have legal title to the property at the time the estate was being contested. According to his account, "this commodious and most substantial old plantation home with all the handsome furniture, valuable books, and beautiful pictures, the accumulation of a lifetime by wealthy, educated and refined people, was burned on April 15, 1845, at 1 A.M., by Captain Ross' slaves more than nine years after his death."

This was to be the nexus of every account that came after.

Among the occupants of the house at the time of the fire, Thomas Wade wrote, were his parents and the three small children they had at the time; his mother's niece, Mary Girault, of Grenada, Mississippi; his father's sister, Adelaide Wade Richardson and her three small children, including Martha, who was about six years old; and Dr. Wade and his business partner, a man named Bailey. Thomas Wade also offered the first written account of the cook spiking the coffee with a drug or herb, and carefully noted that Girault and Dr. Wade, Isaac Ross Wade's uncle, were the only adults who chose not to partake.

"The house was a large, two-story house, and Dr. Wade, Mr. Bailey, Mrs. Richardson and children and Miss Girault occupied the rooms in the second story," he wrote. "Dr. Wade was the first occupant to discover the fire, and immediately set to work to arouse the family." The doctor apparently had difficulty waking the others and "probably would not have succeeded, owing to the size of the house, had it not been for the assistance of one of my father's own slaves and body servant Major, who was faithful, and rendered every assistance in his power."

Richardson, the mother of the fated girl, "was dazed and stupefied," while Girault, who was staying in the same room with her, took charge of the youngest children, Cabell and Addie, and instructed her to take care of Martha. "She did not discover that Mrs. Richardson, in her dazed condition, had left the child in bed until they all met in the yard," Wade wrote. "When this was discovered, Mrs. Richardson, terror-stricken, frantically appealed for assistance and volunteers to go with her to the second floor to save her child. To this appeal, a brave and faithful slave, Thomas, responded, and started with her up the steps to the second story, but before ascending far the steps sank under them into the fire. They were both rescued from the flames, but badly burnt. Mrs. Richardson was pulled out by her hair. The next morning the child's heart was found and buried in the family graveyard, only a few paces from the spot where she met her tragic death."

Thomas Wade credited his father with throwing open the doors of the house to enable the others to escape, but said the front door at first appeared to have been jammed. Once he managed to swing it free, he waited before escaping himself, which Wade believed saved his life. When Girault ran through the door, he wrote, "to her horror there stood Esau, one of the estate's slaves, with a drawn axe, evidently for the purpose of killing my father, whom he expected to pass out the door, as it was nearest his room. Miss Girault bounded out unexpectedly, and seeing Esau with a drawn axe, quickly remarked, 'Uncle Esau, are you here to help us by cutting away the door?'" According to Thomas Wade, Esau replied, "'Yessum, Mistus,' and walked away. My father afterward learned that Esau had been standing at the front door for some time, and did not make any effort to arouse them or knock the door in, and that he had gone there for the purpose of killing my father should he escape from the flames," Wade wrote. "Esau, with six or seven other leaders, were burnt or hung. This was all done by the neighbors without my father's knowledge, as he was then with his mother, Mrs. Ross, at Oak Hill, two miles away."

It is hard to imagine how the scene could have been more horrible: the house quickly engulfed in flames, the frenzied occupants struggling to escape, the trapped girl screaming, the terrifying and disastrous rescue attempt. Thomas Wade noted that the house was completely destroyed in a very short time, and under the circumstances it seems remarkable that anything was saved, yet somehow, someone managed to rescue the portraits of Isaac Ross, his wife, and her sister. Also saved was the piano—unless, of course, Wade had made off with it prior to the fire. The fire was no doubt so intense that the crowd of distraught family members and slaves was forced to move farther and farther away as the flames lit the sky, accompanied by a fusillade of containers exploding inside. The aftermath, too, must have been particularly devastating for the survivors, who knew that Martha Richardson had died a terrible death, even as the family was saving themselves and their portraits. For days after, the lawn would have been littered with debris while the stench of the fire and perhaps even of the corpses of the lynched slaves hung in the air.

Thomas Wade wrote that the family members sought refuge at Oak Hill, and it seems safe to assume that they spent the following days sifting through the ashes, even after finding the remains of the girl. Such

a fire would have smoldered for a long time, and the ruins would have
been riddled with dangerous, hidden hot spots for days, although some
remnants would have survived—cast-iron hinges, clumps of melted
silver and gold, even fragile items like a glass saltshaker or a piece of
fine china, protected, perhaps, by a metal trunk or left unscathed when
the collapse of a wall sent unburned debris tumbling into the yard.
Even the story of finding the girl's heart does not seem too far-fetched
to anyone who has probed the ruins of a house fire.

But in the absence of evidence or documentation, many questions
come to mind. Why would Girault have chosen such a tumultuous
moment to question Esau about his reason for being at the door, and
frame it in such carefully scripted language? Would a man who was
part of a murderous, secret plot simply walk away from a house on fire,
with people shouting and screaming, inside and out? How could the
slaves have expected to get away with such a bold murder, in front of so
many witnesses? And again, how could the cook—whether it was
Grace or someone else—have betrayed the family she was no doubt
close to, including the children? At the same time, how could Richardson have forgotten her daughter in a burning house unless she was
drugged?

Thomas Wade's account does not provide answers to those questions, but he claimed that the family account was corroborated by
some of the slaves, two of whom "ran off when the leaders were executed, but were caught in the woods . . . and were hung on the spot
and left there." His father, he wrote, "found their bodies afterwards by
the buzzards hovering over them." Wade claimed that the slaves had
been encouraged by certain whites to kill his father. "Ross Wade never
knew positively, up to the time of his passing, that this statement was
correct, but his descendants have the satisfaction of knowing that
those slaves told the truth, as will be shown in the ex-parte statement,
through letters over their signatures, from members and sympathizers
of the American colonization society, in [the] Mississippi Historical
Society's *Publications IX*. These letters, as reported, confirm without a
question of doubt that the advice given these slaves was responsible
for the burning of the old Prospect Hill dwelling and the attempted
murder of Ross Wade and his entire family and friends then in the
house, and the actual burning to death of his niece Martha Richardson. Some time after the fact some of the more intelligent slaves

admitted this fact to my father, and told him that they had been told by some white people that if they could get rid of my father the provisions of the will would be carried out; that they would be sent to Liberia at an early date. My father was charitable enough to believe that, if any white person had told these things, they did not mean it in the literal sense, but to get rid of him by the process of law as acting executor."

Armed with Wade's pronouncement, I read the letters in the Mississippi Historical Society's *Vol. IX*, but found no reference to the fire or any attempted murder. Perhaps it is necessary to read between the lines, or to be fervently looking for validation.

The letters from the Prospect Hill slaves who later emigrated to Liberia further muddy the waters. The immigrants corresponded with their former masters for years afterward, repeatedly expressing their affection and in one case entreating the recipient to "give my love to Master Isaac [Wade]." Tinker Miller cites this as evidence that there were "good and bad people on both sides—some of the white Rosses were for the will, some were against it, some of the slaves may have been in favor of an uprising, and some of them against it."

For Thomas Wade, the immigrants' letters represented a clear exoneration of his father's efforts to defeat the will. He wrote that his father received letters from the Liberian immigrants "as late as 1861, on the eve of the great civil war, but we have never heard of them since. The last letters received discussed their pitiable condition; they applied for help, and begged to have him send them some farming and mechanical instruments and clothing, especially calico dresses. Their colonization in Liberia, judging from their letters, was an absolute failure." He sounds a bit smug when he adds, "In fact they reported they were destitute and great sufferers. From these letters it was most natural to conclude that their condition was much worse there than it was in slavery, as they had always had kind and considerate masters."

Regarding the uprising, Wade wrote that for his father, "This great tragedy in his life was a favorite theme, when we were gathered around the fireside, especially in the declining years of his life." No doubt the story and the subsequent trials of the immigrants seemed to validate both the contest of the will and the fear gripping the surrounding countryside that should the Prospect Hill slaves go free, insurrections on neighboring plantations would follow. All of which makes it even more curious that the event did not garner so much as a footnote in the official written record.

Robert Wade, who is a descendant of both Isaac Ross and Isaac Ross Wade, says he does not doubt the story of the uprising. The slaves, he contends, "were waiting for their freedom and things like that took time because you had to go all the way to the Supreme Court. There was a Presbyterian preacher here in Port Gibson named Zebulon Butler who was an avid abolitionist. He came from Wilkes-Barre, Pennsylvania. He incited the slaves, told them there was no way they would get their freedom as long as Isaac Ross Wade and his family were living.

"So the night the house was burned the cooks drugged the coffee—or whatever it was—at supper, they set the house on fire, and one little girl burned to death. One or two escaped, but they hung the rest. There was a big old white oak tree back of Prospect Hill that I remember as a boy, and I was told that was where they hung them. A vigilante committee hanged eleven slaves. So this pastor, Zebulon Butler, was responsible for twelve deaths, and he is revered in my church. And that is a bitter pill to swallow."

Robert Wade's version diverges from Thomas Wade's account on one important point. In his version Isaac Ross Wade was either at his family's Oak Hill home or visiting at Rosswood, home of his uncle, Dr. Walter Wade, on the night of the fire. "A storm came up that night and he did not get back home and that's the reason he was not killed," he says.

CHAPTER SEVEN

FROM CORRESPONDENCE BETWEEN Isaac Ross Wade and his chief attorney, Henry Ellett, it is apparent that the restraints issued by the lower courts were making it increasingly difficult for Wade to foot the bill for the ultimately futile litigation. In July 1847 Ellett wrote to say that "the whole case in which I was originally employed—to resist the right of the colonization society to the negroes—has been settled against us by the High Court and the remaining controversy must relate entirely to the adjustment of your private interests with the Estate and the Society. It is now a question of the settlement of your accounts in the Probate Court." The letter referred to another legal tack that Wade was considering as a means of recovering some of his financial losses, and that Ellett agreed to pursue, with the caveat, "you cannot expect me to embark in this new litigation without some prospect of reward." For that, he required a contingency fee of 5 percent of the final proceeds to be awarded to Wade by the court.

Ellett initially had expressed confidence that they would win the suit against the American Colonization Society, which he referred to as "the Africanists." Later his tone soured. In March 1847 he admonished Wade: "In the settlement of your accounts as executor it will be well not to forget that you owe me $100 for going to Fayette in Sept. 1845 to attend to the settlement of your case." In May 1847 he wrote, "I observe a condition that you are to pay me $250. It is proper I should say that the account has been due since Jan. 1, 1841 and I shall expect to be paid 8% interest on it from that time."

In 1848, Wade had run out of avenues of appeal and could no longer prevent the colonization society from executing the will. But by then, fees paid to Ellett and other attorneys, along with the $28,699.50 salary paid to Wade as executor, and losses resulting from the alleged mismanagement of the plantation, had greatly depleted the funds of the estate. Further diminishing its value was the erection of the monument in the cemetery at Prospect Hill in tribute to Ross, which had been commissioned by the Mississippi Colonization Society in 1838 for an astronomical cost—reputedly, $25,000.

Annie Mims Wright, Ross's great-granddaughter, speculated that Ker had insisted on the erection of the grand monument, adding, "I have often heard my father say his grandfather had told him repeatedly that he wanted a plain box tomb, like others he had erected in the graveyard. I can't imagine why his wishes were not carried out, as some of the slaves had to be sold to help pay for the splendid monument, that being one of the unexpected drains on the estate along with the lawyers' fees."

To undertake the final repatriation, the American Colonization Society would be forced to resort to private fund-raising. In its 1848 appeal for donations, the New York Colonization Society noted that the Prospect Hill immigrants represented one of the greatest challenges of the colonization effort. The ACS had sent only 480 emigrants to Liberia over the past four years, while the number of applications for emigration exceeded 1,000 for 1848 alone. Among the recent immigrants were 129 aboard the *Nehemiah Rich* who set sail on January 7, 1848, many of whom were Ross and Reed slaves. The New York report observed that the slaves "are represented to have no superiors among their caste in good morals, industry and intelligence. The estimated 200 slaves for whom additional funds were needed would be the last from Prospect Hill to go." The long wait, the report lamented, had "deferred the hopes of these poor slaves until their hearts are sad with waiting."

The ACS noted at the time that the next crop year was looming, "and unless they can leave before arrangements are made for it, they will certainly be delayed another year, in slavery, and risk a final disappointment in their hopes for freedom." Banking on the belief that there would be no delay, the ACS reported, "a vessel is authorized to sail from New Orleans on the 1st of January with about 300 immigrants, among whom are two hundred slaves on one plantation in Mississippi, emancipated by Capt. Ross, whose peculiar condition makes a most urgent appeal upon our sympathies."

Apparently the society got the desired financial response. Although there were no funds to found the institution of learning that Ross had envisioned in Liberia, enough money was raised to pay the way of the last group of slaves to emigrate, and with their departure, Ross's house was finally, completely, and literally divided.

After more than a decade of legal wrangling, the seemingly endless rounds of political chicanery, the fire, the lynchings, and the threat of vigilante violence—followed by a midnight march for some of the slaves to a steamboat waiting on the Mississippi River, and finally, weeks spent in squalid New Orleans refugee camps, during which scores died of cholera—setting sail for Africa must have seemed like a dream for the newly freed slaves of Prospect Hill. Slowly but surely, small groups had been released, and on January 22, 1849, almost twelve years after Isaac Ross died, the largest group—142—departed for Liberia aboard the barque *Laura*. On board were the cook, Grace, her husband, Jim, and three of their four children, but not their son Levy, who appears to have either died or been among those who chose to stay behind.

After they were gone, the indefatigable Wade continued making ineffective court claims against the ACS, right up to the eve of the Civil War, in 1861. By that time all that remained of the estate was the land, the piano, the portraits, an array of farm implements and livestock, and whatever else Wade and his family may have secreted away. The "bounty of Ross's estate," including the coveted house, almost all its furnishings, and the majority of the slaves, was gone. That was not to say that Wade was destitute. In fact, he managed quite well. The court battles had cost him dearly, yet he was able to buy back Prospect Hill when it was sold at public auction, along with many of the slaves who chose not to emigrate, and in 1854 built an imposing new house on the site of the old one. According to the New York Colonization Society's 1848 report, he had also by then "reputedly become the possessor and owner of a large plantation, well stocked with slaves, in Louisiana."

Remarkably, Isaac Ross Wade continued to busy himself with trying to find some new mechanism for recouping his losses, even as the rest of the country turned its attention to the looming civil war. His attorney, Henry Ellett, however, had no time for litigation now—on January 7, 1861, he was participating in the Mississippi Secession Convention in Jackson.

Soon after war broke out and Mississippi voted to secede from the Union, companies of Rebel soldiers began forming under the Confederate banner across Jefferson and Claiborne counties. Among the family members who joined the cause were Earl Van Dorn, the father of Arthur Ross's widow, who became a Confederate general, and Arthur Ross's son, Isaac Allison Ross, who served as a private in a Confederate cavalry unit based in Natchez. Although Wade would have been in his mid-forties at the time, he apparently stayed behind at Prospect Hill.

Most of the local soldiers were shipped up the Mississippi River to Memphis and from there by rail to the eastern theater of the war, which is where nearly all the fighting initially took place. In 1862, when the Union navy captured New Orleans, the war moved closer to home. Soon after, President Lincoln issued the Emancipation Proclamation, freeing slaves held in rebelling states as of January 1, 1863, and Union forces fanned out across the Mississippi Delta and attacked Vicksburg, Jackson, and Port Gibson. Natchez, where many residents had opposed both the American Revolution and secession from the United States, surrendered without a fight, but smaller river ports such as Rodney, in Jefferson County, and Grand Gulf, in adjacent Claiborne County, were repeatedly caught in the line of fire.

The main focus of the Union effort in Mississippi was Vicksburg, about forty miles north of Jefferson County, which was a heavily fortified city commanding a horseshoe bend in the river from a series of steep bluffs. Union General Ulysses S. Grant attacked the city from the swamps of the Delta—only to see his troops become hopelessly mired in the gumbo mud—and from the river, where gunboats and transports proved easy targets for the lofty Confederate guns. Frustrated, he pressed freed slaves into service to dig a canal across a Louisiana peninsula in hopes of diverting the Mississippi away from Vicksburg, to no avail. Finally, with few other options to explore, Grant marched his troops around the city on the Louisiana side, crossed the river at Bruinsburg, Mississippi, a few miles southwest of Port Gibson, and fought his way into the interior. It was a bold maneuver to sever an entire army from its lines of supply in enemy territory, and it marked the first time the citizens of inland Jefferson and Claiborne counties felt the war's heat. Because Grant found that he could feed and supply his soldiers from the pillage of plantations, local slaveholding families now had more to worry about than just the safety of their loved ones on distant battlefields, or the fate of their new nation—they had to contend with the prospects of widespread looting, the torching of houses and barns, food shortages, the confiscation of their cotton stores, and most importantly, the liberation of their slaves.

It soon became clear that no place was safe. First Port Gibson fell, next Raymond, and then Jackson. After subsequent Union victories at Champion Hill and the Big Black River, the Rebels beat a hasty retreat into Vicksburg, where frenzied residents watched in dismay as the troops entered the city at a full run, driving cattle and hogs before them. Surrounded on all sides, Vicksburg was besieged for forty-seven days, until Confederate General John Pemberton surrendered on July 4, 1863. With the surrender, the Mississippi River and most of central and southwest Mississippi fell into Union hands. The only remaining line of defense for area planters came from Confederate guerillas who roamed the countryside for the next two years, engaging Union cavalry in random skirmishes.

Many landowners chose to evacuate with their slaves and livestock, or to hide food, cotton, silver, and other valuables from the invaders. Today there are tales from seemingly every antebellum home in the area, including Rosswood, that involve the burial of silver by family members and their "faithful" slaves, which for inexplicable reasons was never found.

Confederate troops also hid what could not be hauled away. In a July 24, 1863, dispatch from Natchez, Union officer T. E. G. Ransom reported finding a stash of Rebel ammunition hidden in a nearby ravine along with 750 bales of Confederate cotton. Ransom noted that his scout "reports large quantities of private cotton everywhere in the country," adding that the Rebels had driven 2,000 cattle ahead of them as they retreated.

"The people of the country back of here have been running their negroes and horses into Alabama," Ransom wrote. "Very few good horses were found. . . . The people through the country are reported by Major Worsen to be discouraged and hopeless of the rebellion, and ready to do almost anything that will keep their negroes in the fields. There was a large public meeting at Hamburg on the 22d, to consider the question of abandoning the Confederacy. I have not heard the result of it."

There are surprisingly few references to the Civil War in the Ross and Wade family histories, but Robert Wade recalls hearing about a skirmish that took place in the nearby community of Red Lick, during which a Union soldier was badly wounded and taken for treatment to Prospect Hill. He does not know if Isaac Ross Wade was home at the time, nor who won the conflict.

"The occupants of the house at Prospect Hill were just young people, old people and slaves, and anyway they took him in," he says. "Of course there was no real medicine or doctors or anything, and they did what they could, but he died, and they buried him in the family cemetery. The family got his family's address from his personal effects and wrote them in Indiana and said they'd given him a Christian burial, and after the hostilities were over the family came down and removed the remains. His rifle is on display at the Grand Gulf museum. My mother and I gave it to the museum."

He says he heard the story often as a boy growing up in the second Prospect Hill house—much to his dismay, because it frightened him. "I slept in one of the old tester beds, and there was a jar with an old tarnished spoon in it on the mantle," he recalls. "It was always there on the mantle. And if I acted up, they'd say, 'You better watch out, because you're sleeping in the room where the Yankee soldier died.' They told me that jar and spoon were from his last dose of medicine before he died, and that the spoon was tarnished because he was a Yankee."

It is not clear if the fighting at Red Lick was related to a skirmish known variously as the Battle at Coleman's Plantation or the Battle of the Cotton Bales, which was fought in the vicinity on July 4, 1864, during which the family's Rosswood plantation home served as a field hospital. Both sides claimed victory in that one. According to a later account by another descendant, B. D. Wade, Rosswood was looted during the war and its owner, Walter Wade, was captured and briefly held by the Union army in nearby Rodney. After a brief confrontation between soldiers of the occupying force and Walter Wade's son, who B. D. Wade wrote was unable to serve in the Confederate army, the Yankee soldiers appropriated Rosswood's prized thoroughbreds.

No one with whom I spoke knew how many of the remaining Prospect Hill slaves left during the war, but there is no question that some departed when Union troops arrived, or simply fled on their own. According to Laverne McPhate, among those who remained behind were a few who lived out their lives in the same cabins they had previously occupied as slaves.

Keeping the slaves on the plantation was a major priority for all of the area's planters, even if, as things were headed, it appeared that they would have to pay rudimentary wages or allow farming on shares. A large workforce would be necessary to plant another crop, regardless of the outcome of the war. Some area planters tried to keep their newly freed slaves from leaving by playing upon their insecurity in a world with which they were wholly unfamiliar. In testimony before the U.S. Southern Claims Commission, which was deliberating whether to award remuneration to former slaveholder Kate Minor of Natchez, former slave Lee Scott described her mistress gathering the slaves around her and telling them that they were, in fact, free to leave. According to Scott's account, Minor then warned the slaves that the Yankees "were coming to take and work us to death and put us to work harder than they did, and take us to Liberia or some other country, and work us to death . . . I believed it . . . she said they were cruel and would take all of us colored understrappers and carry us off to Liberia, that they were tight, but we would find the Yankees a little tighter." Minor's overseer, Thomas Spain, also recalled her telling the slaves, "You can leave . . . but you will repent it & I will treat you well. They will make out they are going to treat you well for a little while & then they will turn you loose & you will be treated like dogs. . . ."

Despite Minor's admonitions, the majority of the slaves left, although some would indeed return after the war. During the post-war deliberations the Southern Claims commissioners asked Minor why, if she was so concerned about the welfare of her hundreds of slaves, she had not prepared and then freed them before the occupation. She explained that she was "an abolitionist at heart, but I am not a philanthropist. I did not know how to set them free without wretchedness to them and utter ruin to myself. . . . We were very much attached to each other, and they begged me to continue my watchfulness over them."

In hindsight, Minor's comments seem laughable—and may have seemed so at the time to the commissioners, but in his interview with the WPA, former slave Charlie Davenport recalled feeling an affinity with his owners, and remembered the war itself in unexpected terms. Although he was glad to be freed, Davenport said, he remembered the war less for the emancipation it brought than as a time of tumult and waste. When his owners made the painful decision to burn their stores of cotton to prevent them from falling into Union hands, the destruction was equally distressing to the slaves who had labored to plant, cultivate, harvest, and gin the crop, he said. He also lamented the death of his master's son in battle, saying that he had been a favorite of the slaves.

Some of the freed slaves who left their plantations made their way into the Union army and fought in the Vicksburg campaign, including James Lucas of Natchez, who conceded that freedom proved to be a mixed blessing. "Slaves didn' know what to 'spec from freedom, but a lot of 'em hoped dey would be fed an' kep' by de gov'ment," Lucas explained to a WPA interviewer. "Dey all had diff'nt ways o' thinkin' 'bout it. Mos'ly though dey was jus lak me, dey did't know jus' zackly what it meant. It was jus' somp'n dat de white folks an' slaves all de time talk 'bout. Dat's all. Folks dat ain' never been free don' rightly know de *feel* o' bein' free . . . When de sojers come dey turnt us loos lak animals wid nothin'."

Among the freed slaves who joined the invading armies were several in Mississippi named Ross, but it is unclear if any of them hailed from Prospect Hill or other Ross plantations. Two Ross veterans are listed in the records of the U.S. Colored Cavalry rolls for Vicksburg, with the space for birthplace left blank, and another, Jackson Ross, a member of the U.S. Colored Infantry, is buried in the nearby Grand Gulf cemetery (Jackson Ross's body was exhumed and reburied by the Sons of Confederate Veterans in February 2003, along with another black Union soldier, after erosion threatened their graves).

Historian Paul Escott noted that some former slaves recalled troubling encounters with Union soldiers to whom they had looked for salvation. "When the Yankees arrived they brought theft, destruction, and even mistreatment of slaves with them," he wrote. "Instead of acting as friends, the soldiers caused suffering and hardship for many bondsmen. In the context of the war between North and South, destruction of southern foodstuffs and property served to bring Union victory and emancipation nearer. But for the individual bondsmen, Yankee depredations only made a burdensome life more trying still. How was one to eat when the soldiers had gone?" In addition, he wrote, "There was considerable racism in the northern armies that found an outlet around the slaves."

Although there are numerous accounts of Union troops coming to the aid of freed slaves, giving them food and money, the uncertainty of how the freedmen would be treated is evident in the account of Hester Hunter, a freed slave in Marion, South Carolina, who was cited by historian Belinda Humence. "Remember the first time the Yankees come," Hunter recalled. "I was sitting down in the chimney corner and my mammy was giving me my breakfast. Remember I been sitting there with my milk and my bowl of hominy, and I hear my old grandmammy come a-running in from out the yard and say all the sky was blue as indigo with the Yankees coming right over the hill. Say she see more Yankees than could ever cover up all the premises about there.

"Then, I hear my missus scream and come a-running with a lapful of silver and tell my grandmammy to bury and sew that up in the feather bed, 'cause them Yankees was mighty apt to destroy all they valuables. Old Missus tell all the colored people to get away, get away and take care of themselves, and tell we children to get back to they corner, 'cause she couldn't protect us noways, no longer."

Hunter's account seems to indicate that her plantation mistress was concerned not only with her personal valuables, but with the well-being of her slaves, but in many cases such care vanished with the abolition of slavery. Another former slave quoted by Humence recalled his father saying, "the War wasn't going to last forever, but that forever was going to be spent living among the Southerners, after they got licked."

As it turned out, the cataclysm that was visited upon the South during and after the Civil War was not the exclusive burden of whites. The majority of the freed slaves could neither read nor write, and had comparatively little knowledge of finances and few means to support themselves, which is why so many returned to plowing the very fields in which they had been enslaved. The fact that some freedmen turned to looting made it more difficult for the law-abiding among them to coexist with whites who no longer had even a tangential vested interest in their well-being.

The war and Confederate defeat also brought hardship to Union loyalists such as Stephen Duncan, one of the Natchez area's largest slaveholders, who had been instrumental in helping the Ross and Reed slaves emigrate. Duncan, who had once been held in high esteem as president of the Bank of Mississippi, found himself ostracized in Natchez both during and after the war for his pro-Union stance. A Pennsylvania native who had arrived in the Natchez District the same year as Isaac Ross, Duncan reportedly grew disenchanted with the South and moved to New York, where he died in 1867. His mansion, Auburn, is now part of a Natchez city park.

Henry Ellett, meanwhile, suffered the indignity of being ejected from his home by black and white Union troops. The prominent lawyer, a New Jersey native who was also a state senator and a former U.S. senator (he had been appointed to fill the remainder of Jefferson Davis's term in 1847) was at home with his wife in Port Gibson when a skirmish broke out between Union and Confederate forces in September 1864. Following the Union victory, the troops arrived and put the family out in the street. After the war, Ellett managed to adapt to his new situation. In what must have been a gratifying turn of events for him, after having been rebuffed by the courts during the Wade litigation, Ellett was elected to the Mississippi High Court of Errors and Appeals, where he served from 1865 to 1868. Afterward he moved to Memphis, where he died in 1887 while delivering a welcome address for the visiting President Grover Cleveland.

Although the Wades and Rosses had landed on their feet following the long crucible of the litigation, after the war they experienced the same reversal of fortune that broke slaveholders across the South. At the outbreak of hostilities they had been among the more prominent planters in the Natchez District, but afterward, with slavery abolished, they saw their considerable fortunes evaporate, and found themselves struggling simply to maintain their properties.

They were able to put many of the former slaves back to work in the fields, utilizing a system that involved their cultivating and harvesting the crop in exchange for a share of the profits. It was a system ripe for abuse, because the sharecroppers depended upon the plantation commissary for their seeds and supplies, and typically, once the ledger was tallied at the end of the year, their debts exceeded the profits from the sale of the crop. No one with whom I spoke knew how Isaac Ross Wade treated his sharecroppers, and no doubt many planters were fair, but for decades those who were cheated had no choice but to stay put.

Isaac Ross Wade stayed put himself, in a diminished yet comparatively powerful role, until his death at Prospect Hill in 1891.

Laverne McPhate describes the Civil War as a time when "everybody got their heart broke," but it seems likely that "everybody" did not include the remaining slaves of Prospect Hill. Despite the uncertainty of their future and continuing restraints, they were now free, and some of them surely felt relieved that they had chosen to remain behind when the majority had left for Africa.

CHAPTER EIGHT

"IT'S A HELL OF a lot of Rosses in this town that aren't related to us, that we know," Delores Ross says, over the phone. "They're a darker complexion, the ones I'm talkin' about."

She is referring to the descendants of the Prospect Hill slaves who did not take the one-way trip to Liberia, whether by choice or because they were not given the option. Delores, is descended from slaves from other plantations, but, surprisingly, also traces her ancestry to the slaveowning Rosses, which means she is no blood relation to the Rosses whose slave ancestors remained at Prospect Hill.

The Rosses have made and sometimes written history in both Mississippis, American and African, but the descendants of the slaves who stayed behind—presumably, the least mobile among them— have managed to slip through the historical record largely unnoticed. Part of the problem is that slaves were poorly documented, having been listed in census records by first name only, if at all. Surnames do not appear in the census records for African-Americans until 1870, and often the names were selected at whim. Sometimes freed slaves chose the name of their most recent master, while in other cases they chose a former owner, or a name they simply liked. As a result, the direct lineage of their descendants can be extremely difficult to determine.

From talking with Ann Brown, I have reached the bewildering conclusion that I will have to descend into the genealogical maw to find descendants of the Prospect Hill slaves who stayed behind. This is not something I really want to do. I have seen the family historians sitting bleary-eyed before the microfilm readers in the research room of the

state archives, and I am not eager to join their ranks. It is as if the
world can only be validated by reconciling certain significant names
and numbers from the past, by proving that someone from whom you
are descended lived and died in a way that is more important than
someone else. My thoughts inevitably wander as the genealogists in
the research room reel off these beatitudes with the zeal of rabid
sports fans reciting players' stats. Perhaps the safely completed record
of an ancestor's life can give context to one's own, but the process
seems mind-numbing and looks a lot like math. Still, as Ann pointed
out, it will be hard to make sense of things without knowing who is
who. Genealogical records often contain pertinent information that
can be found nowhere else, and could lead to other descendants.

Ann is all about connecting the dots. I have received stacks of records that she has collected from old censuses and from tombstones in
abandoned African-American cemeteries, which I compare with listings in Jefferson County phone books. I have noticed that some of the
genealogical records contain errors, and not just differences in the
spellings of names, but actual dates of births and deaths, which means
that I will have to subjectively judge their veracity just as I have the
Ross family lore. It is daunting. Yet there are also some interesting
genealogical side-trails to explore, such as the fact that Isaac Ross
Wade and his branch of the family did not share the Ross family's
predilection for slaves of mixed race, according to the slave census of
1860. Isaac Allison Ross owned 115 slaves, including nineteen mulattoes, while John Ross owned sixty-one slaves, only one of whom was of
mixed race. The various branches of the Wade family owned approximately 170 slaves, all of whom were listed as black.

The probate court's inventory of slaves in Isaac Ross's estate and
the immigrant ship registries are even more telling. Comparing the
two, it appears that about twenty-five of the Prospect Hill slaves did
not embark—four were freed outright, and the remainder chose to
stay behind, were not given the option, and were sold. It appears that
at least twenty-five also remained from the Reed estate.

Unfortunately, Ann has had no luck helping me find the missing
Rosses. Delores, whom she had expected to be descended from the
black Rosses, was her best bet. "There aren't many records for black
people, and the ones I've checked don't show many Rosses at all, surprisingly," she says. It is possible that the slaves who remained did not

take the Ross name, which would make it nearly impossible to track down their descendants now.

Tracing a black family tree beyond the limits of personal memories often involves scouting abandoned cemeteries and undertaking tedious searches of white genealogical and legal records for passing references and clues. The effort is complicated by the fact that slavery carries an enduring stigma, which is doubtless why so many Rosses I contact who are likely slave descendants decline to be interviewed. Slavery is a perennial source of political debate in Mississippi, and is sometimes a source of a sort of adverse power, but for a great many it remains a very personal and sensitive subject. And why wouldn't it be? Slavery was demeaning, and even freed slaves had to contend with second-class status among often embittered former slaveholders who steadfastly sought to maintain their own superiority. One freed slave recalled asking if slaves would still have to say "Master" after freedom, and being told by his fellows "Naw." But, the slave added, "They said it all the same. They said it for a long time."

Although there were certainly instances of bravery, courage, wit, and compassion among slaves, little of it was written down. According to historian Paul Escott, the WPA slave narratives prove "that if men have a body of culture on which to rely, they can endure conditions that are very unfavorable indeed," but in most cases, how they went about enduring those conditions has been lost. Old memories may not be the most reliable source of information, and it is certainly hard to find solace in the record of one's family's enslavement when the scant documentation that exists was compiled by people whose interests tended to be diametrically opposed. Typically, it was only the "faithful" slaves, or, at the opposite end of the scale, the violent or thieving ones whose actions were recorded. Beyond that, there is not much information to consider. There are no written accounts of the bittersweet day at Prospect Hill when the last of the emigrants departed. Those who remained behind would have had plenty of time to reflect on their decision to stay, particularly after they were sold at public auction, but the only reference I found in the historical record was a December 29, 1848, letter from David Ker to Isaac Ross Wade, informing him that his father would attend the Prospect Hill sale. The dearth of written records poses a significant obstacle to fully understanding the story of Prospect Hill, and to accounting for each of the key groups.

Some of the names of the slaves who remained behind are mentioned in the emigrants' letters, but always without an identifying surname. The same is true for slave births in the Prospect Hill plantation
ledger for the years after the emigrants departed. There is a notation
for a Daphney giving birth, for instance, but Daphney who? A female
slave named Linder was listed as being sold after having given birth to
a boy who lived only a week in 1853, with a notation by Catherine
Wade that, "Richardson and Little Susan given to come in her place."
Where did Linder go? Who were Richardson and Little Susan? Even
as Catherine Ross recorded the births of Little Susan's three children,
she noted, "I guess at their ages."

The task is further complicated by the mass dispersal of freed
slaves after the war. According to the 1850 census there were fifty-four
free people of color in Jefferson County, up from seventeen in 1830
and thirty-three in 1820. That number swelled into the thousands in
1865. The majority of the births recorded at Prospect Hill occurred
after the transfer of the estate, from the 1840s to around 1870, and
among them, thirty-two were born during the Civil War, and six more
in the years after, which indicates that their families were among the
most stalwart, or perhaps recalcitrant, of the slaves. Those slaves had
foregone the opportunity to leave Prospect Hill twice, yet I found no
record of who they were. Where are their descendants today? What, if
anything, might they know?

It seems likely that many of those who stayed did not take the surname Ross. For one thing, the Rosses did not own them at the time
they were freed, and hadn't for nearly thirty years. The list of freedmen's taxes for 1869, which is incomplete, includes only four Rosses in
Jefferson County: David, Boswell, John, and Rankins. Others may have
owned land, but their surnames were apparently different. Likewise
the 1900 Jefferson County Enumeration of Children of black families
lists only Henry Ross and his children Sam, Ann, Katie, Leota, and
Mary. The U.S. Colored Cavalry rolls for Vicksburg in 1864 list two
Rosses: Peter, age thirty-five, and John, twenty-two, both of whom also
appear in the Freedmen's Bureau Register of Marriages in Mississippi.
John Ross is again listed in the Freedman's Bank records in Vicksburg.
It is a short list, but the names are common, spouses do not always
share the same surname, and there is no way to definitively link them
to Prospect Hill. Ultimately the records lead nowhere.

❁   ❁   ❁

At no time is the dearth of information more evident than when I sit down, hopefully, with Susie Ross, who is among the few slave descendants I meet who is inclined to talk. Susie (to whom I was referred, again, by Ann Brown), greets me at the screen door of her Port Gibson home, hastily tying a scarf around her head, still in her housedress and slippers because she is recuperating from a recent illness. She is a quiet, unassuming woman, whose expression rarely changes. Though elderly, her face is remarkably unlined. Her home is small and nondescript, and stands on a knoll behind the county jail.

"The place don't look too good right now," she says, glancing doubtfully at her yard, which is devoid of landscaping and dominated by a rusty swing set. Her husband always kept the place neat, she says, but nine months ago he was run over and killed by a drunken driver at age eighty-four, and she hasn't mustered the energy to hire any help. Her dream is to have the place painted and burglar bars and an alarm system installed.

"My husband was a good man," she says, and motions for me to sit down in an overstuffed chair in her living room. "I had a good husband. He was raised to keep everything up. He kept things intact. He was a dutiful man. Now I don't have anybody much to depend on but the Lord and myself."

Before we are far into our conversation, it becomes apparent that the past is a vast network of gaping holes for her. Both her and her husband's family histories are discouragingly attenuated. She is a Ross by marriage, and her husband came from the vicinity of Prospect Hill. She knows little beyond that. She is related to another family, the Greens, some of whom emigrated to Liberia in the 1840s, but she was unaware of the connection until I showed her the records. She has little hard data to work with.

Her husband, Adel Crezet Ross, was from the community of Pattison. She hands me a framed photograph of him and points across to what she says was his favorite chair, which sits empty. "It's so much memory here," she says. His visage stares out from photographs on the coffee table and atop the TV alongside photos of other family members. His naval commendation hangs on the wall. "President Clinton mailed that to me after the death of him," she says.

The room is as crowded as a tiny Victorian-era parlor, with a mix of older furniture, electric fans, stuffed animals, books, a piggy bank, vases filled with plastic flowers and a large, framed print of Jesus. There is an antique buffet, which matches the dining room table, whose chairs, she tells me, are in a shed out back. "They need to be made over," she says of the chairs. She doesn't know the origin of the antiques other than that they belonged to her husband.

Adel Ross seldom talked about his family history, "but he had this picture," she says, and rises from her recliner to probe the dusty recesses behind the sofa. She first pulls out a .22 rifle, which her husband used to chase off stray dogs, then a very large, elaborately framed, late-nineteenth-century photograph of a dignified man with a neat goatee, dressed in a dark suit and vest and a starched white collar. She wipes off the cobwebs. The man in the picture is handsome, his expression is confident, and the portrait clearly did not come cheap. "My husband was a handsome man, too," she says. "I meant to clean this up before you came. I had it on the back porch for a long time, until one of the supervisors said it was important and I should take it inside." The gilding is flaking off and the plaster ornamentation is broken in places, but the photo is in good condition.

She leans the portrait against the sofa and returns to her recliner. "His father had that picture," she says. "That was his granddaddy on the Ross side. I don't even know his name. There's a lot I don't know."

She knows that her husband was born to George and Flora Patterson Ross and worked at a paper-tube plant alongside his father and brother until he was disabled. One of his uncles, Matt Ross, was a Claiborne County supervisor. The county administration building is named for him. "Most of his family is passed away," she says. Among her husband's family, she says she recently spoke with a brother-in-law, but he's not interested in talking to me, and he's the last one in the line. I tell her I have found a scattering of records relative to the black Rosses, and that perhaps the man in the gilded frame is Henry, because he alone was listed in the freedman's tax records, but her own family documentation doesn't go back that far, and it would be a stretch to say that it matters that much to her.

She shows polite interest when I tell her that the ship registry of emigrants from Mississippi to Liberia provides a link between her and the Greens of Liberia, that the slaveholding Greens were friends of

Isaac Ross's. Then she brings the story back to its more immediate focus: the family she has known. "My brother, Lesley Green, was a good man," she says. "My grandfather lived to be a hundred and seven. He was like a slave man." She says the Greens, together with her mother's relations, the Hills and the Fields, still hold reunions, most recently in 1999 at nearby Alcorn State University. "We all get together and they have barbeque and beer," she says. "I enjoy that." The distant past is not often a topic of conversation, she says. There is really no tradition for looking too far back. Yet this is a family that steadfastly holds together, which places great importance on reunions at a time when most American families are becoming increasingly fragmented. That is the irony of Susie Ross's family history—that its members so value their continuity yet know so little about their past.

As she thinks back on the reunions, she excuses herself to go into her bedroom and retrieve several T-shirts emblazoned with silk-screened photos and graphics commemorating the events. "These shirts mean a lot to me," she says, and holds up one with the image of an elderly woman's face. "This is my favorite one. That's the only aunt I have left. I try not to wear it too much, because I want it to last."

She says she wishes she knew more, but that she's hesitant to refer me to other family members who might be knowledgeable because they may not want to talk. She does give me one name, and wishes me luck. When I later call him and ask if he knows anything about his family's ties to Prospect Hill, he says, simply, "No," and then, "Good-bye."

When I ask Robert Wade what he knows about the slave descendants associated with Prospect Hill, he recalls a few whose family had remained. "They were old Negroes, as we called them, part of the family," he says. "They helped my daddy. He raised a big garden and let them come and get food out of it. They killed hogs together. You know, the old stories. I don't know if there's any of the families left out there now."

He confirms that the black families at Prospect Hill were not all named Ross. "The ones I knew of, in my time, their surnames were Bruce, Foster, Davis, Odom. These were families that were sharecropping on the place with my daddy. Then Daddy got tired of fighting Bermuda grass, and we moved to town. I can't say I really know what became of them all."

CHAPTER NINE

THE SIGN, SET AGAINST a backdrop of used car lots, convenience stores, and nondescript houses along U.S. 61, offers a curious introduction: WELCOME TO PORT GIBSON, TOO BEAUTIFUL TO BURN. Even without the incongruous setting, it seems a dubious boast.

The quote is attributed to General Grant, whose army passed through after defeating the Confederate forces in the area during the Civil War, and who, it is said, spared the town the torch for aesthetic reasons. At first it is easy to imagine that Grant, at war behind enemy lines and preoccupied with chasing the Rebels back into Vicksburg, literally had no time to burn, but after you cross the bridge over Bayou Pierre, the idea that a hostile general could be smitten by the place seems strangely plausible. Church Street, the main boulevard, presents a rich tableau, which is what tourists now come to see. The sunlight glints off the steeple of the old Presbyterian church, with its giant golden hand on top, one finger pointing skyward, and a wide boulevard opens up, lined with immaculate, painstakingly restored churches, gracefully arching live oak trees, and block after block of columned mansions that float serenely in clouds of pink and white azaleas in the spring.

Port Gibson bills itself as a quintessential antebellum town and in many ways it is, but the unlikely context of the welcome sign tells you that there is more to the place than meets the eye. This is clearly no set piece for the Old South, unless it was for a movie directed by Spike Lee. During the Spring Pilgrimage tour of antebellum homes, low-slung Delta 88s cruise Church Street, rattling the old window panes with music from far distant streets, while on the galleries of the

mansions girls dressed in crinoline and lace smile and greet paying visitors at the door. There is the requisite statue of a Confederate soldier
standing guard before the restored courthouse, but nearly all the
elected officials who work inside are black, and the building was said to
have been riddled with gunfire during the 1980s, when the county was
beset by bitter intraracial political fighting. History is a palpable presence in a place like this, and it encompasses far more than tourist sites
and events dutifully commemorated on historical markers.

No one knows that better than Delores Ross, whose family has
lived in the area longer than she knows, and who has occupied the
same house, a weathered, Queen Anne–style cottage just off the road
leading from the courthouse to the Mississippi River, for nearly forty
years. Delores knows all about the racial tumult that has characterized
so much of the history of Port Gibson and surrounding areas in Claiborne and Jefferson counties—the oppression, resentment, conde-
scension, the efforts at reconciliation, the unlikely alliances, the
awkward shifts in power. She knows all about the struggle for dominance by both blacks and whites, but manages to straddle the lines of
racial demarcation because she was born there, right on the line, the
product of an interracial union. In a town where so much seems to
come down to black and white, she is an anomaly.

At first glance, Delores's lineage is difficult to discern. Before now
we have spoken only on the phone, after I was given her number by her
niece, Laura "Butch" Ross. During my research into the story of
Prospect Hill, I have often conducted first interviews on the phone
rather than in person, and sometimes have found myself deliberating
whether the person I am speaking with is descended from slave or
slave owner, because many have similar accents and frames of reference. I wait for their perspective to reveal itself through some telltale
sign—a verbal marker such as the use of "aks" in place of "ask" by
blacks, or a reference to "faithful slaves" by whites. Sometimes the clue
lies in what is left out of their account. The prevailing white version of
the story of Prospect Hill always includes the slave uprising, but the
prevailing black version never does. In many cases my assumptions
have turned out to be entirely wrong, and I might be deep into a conversation before I know for sure.

In Delores's case, neither her speech nor her perspective gave her away on the phone. Finally she said, "I'll just be frank with you, it was kinda hard growing up in the South with a black mother and a white father."

After greeting me at the door and inviting me in, Delores launches into one of the more curious genealogies that I have come across.

"I tell you, *Roots*, the best movie ever made, don't have nothin' on the Ross family," she says. "We're all over the place. Go way back, all over the place. Here some of 'em started out in Africa, come to Mississippi, then end up back in Africa. And a whole lot of 'em—black, white, you name it, been right here all along—and I'm talkin' a long, long time."

Delores's hair is long, wavy, and black, carefully molded with pomade, her skin midway between black and white. Her house is a catchall sort of place, with furniture from the 1960s and 1970s, potted plants and vases of plastic flowers, and every available surface crowded with memorabilia and framed photos of people, both black and white. Many area residents have a tendency to reduce key figures in local history to archetypes and stereotypes—good guys and bad guys, everything black and white, but not Delores. She listens patiently to a summary of the history of Prospect Hill, then leans back on her sofa and takes a long drag off her cigarette. She is unpretentious and self-possessed, and has no qualms about entertaining my questions about her family history—in fact, she relishes the opportunity.

"One thing it ain't, is black and white," she says, and blows cigarette smoke toward the ceiling. She glances toward the front door as it swings open.

Her niece walks in, smiling broadly, and extends her hand to me. "I'm Butch," she says.

"Sit down, Butch," Delores says. "We just gettin' started."

"You're gonna hear a different version of the story now," Butch says, and smiles at Delores as she pulls up a chair.

"Here, pass me that picture there, Butch," Delores says, and Butch hands her a framed photograph from among the group clustered on the coffee table. "That's Thad Ross, my daddy," Delores says, and passes the photo to me. "He was a descendant of Isaac Ross." The photo looks to have been taken in the 1930s. A white man is seated on a sofa beside a dark-skinned girl with a black woman seated in a chair nearby. There is no mistaking that they are a family. "It was taken down in Jefferson County," she says. "That's my father there. The girl is Jimmie, my sister, Butch's mother. The lady's Queen Esther Polk, Jimmie's mother."

The photo would be right at home in many family albums across the South but for the mix of skin colors. There are many people of mixed race in this part of the country, but they are usually the result of clandestine encounters. Racial mixing is rarely documented for posterity, particularly by members of prominent white families like the Rosses.

Delores awaits my response, but all I think to say is that the average Mississippian would not know what to make of the picture.

"Mm-hmm," she says, agreeing with me.

"Probably think Queen's the maid," Butch says, and laughs.

Delores points to a group of framed photos on the mantel, and adds, "That's all my family up there." She goes down the line, naming names. Most of the faces are black, but some are white, and others are in between. She pulls out her albums and shows me snapshots of blacks and whites intermingling unself-consciously—fishing on a lake, visiting in someone's living room, gathering for a graduation. She points to a painting above the TV set of one of the local white community's beloved landmarks, the Presbyterian church with the gilded hand atop its steeple. "My uncle painted that," she proclaims.

Butch hands me another photo of her mother as an adult. She is beautiful, and Butch favors her. When I mention this Delores says, "She was pretty from a baby on up. All the way through."

It is tempting, studying the photo, to see the beauty of these women as the heart of this particular outcropping of the Prospect Hill story, yet there is no discounting the exceptional circumstances that gave rise to the love affair, particularly on the Ross side.

The family of Isaac Ross is best known for his controversial will. The saga of his descendants, and particularly that of Thad Ross, has not been so widely circulated. Thad Ross's family, it turns out, had a reputation for being mavericks, and in many cases for being randy and high-strung. More independent than most, and prone to grand gestures, the family exhibited a strong penchant for sometimes wildly contradictory behavior, the one constant being their apparent distaste for being told what to do. Thad Ross did his part to maintain the family's reputation, fathering children by three black mistresses, including Delores's mother, Consuelo Conti, as well as Queen Polk and Rosie Lee Jordan, the latter of whom lived in Natchez before moving to Illinois, where she died. By the time Thad Ross was born, the once wealthy family was landed but poor, with little to call their own other than acreage and a scattering of old houses and barns that had been handed down through the generations. He resorted to logging to make ends meet and became acquainted with Conti at a logging camp near Harriston, Mississippi. She had drifted up the river from New Orleans to Natchez and lived with him at the camp for a while. They never married.

"She was of mixed nationality," Delores says. "She knew all about my father's family, but she died in 1987."

"There was just something about those Ross men," Butch observes. "They liked black women. And nobody said anything about it. Back in the sixties people were ready to kill over a black and white living together, and here they were doing it back in the thirties, and they didn't hide it. Of course, all the Ross men carried guns."

"Sure did," Delores says, and nods.

"My grandfather was the great-great-grandson or whatever of Isaac Ross," Butch says. "He was a fool. She [Queen] was, too. That's probably why nobody bothered them—they were both crazy. My mother told me very little, but I heard a little bit—how Isaac Ross freed his slaves and offered them land and money. I just know what I grew up hearing through the years."

Delores sits up, a fire suddenly rekindled in her eyes. "Thad wasn't the only one," she says. "Uncle Frank, he had two black girls. They're well-educated. One lives up in Virginia. She's on TV."

"She's my namesake," Butch says, proudly.

"Robert Ross—he's on the white side of us, too," Delores says.

"He's got a black history, too, though," Butch points out.

"It's just all mixed up," Delores says.

I ask how they reconcile their family history in a place like this, where everything, on the surface at least, seems so divided.

"I guess it's just different for us," Butch says. "Us and the Harrises, we're the only ones I know that are on both sides. I guess we just all been around each other too long." She glances over at Delores and they throw their heads back and laugh. I ask if the Harrises are descended from Drew Harris, who accompanied Isaac Ross to the Mississippi Territory from South Carolina, but neither of them knows.

My expression must betray my surprise at this new twist in the story, because Butch and Delores are clearly amused. They are aware that such intermingling does not sit well with everyone, and is rarely mentioned in most portrayals of the Ross family. This is the Deep South, after all, known worldwide for its troubled racial politics. On the morning we talk, there is another round of vitriolic letters to the editor in the Jackson *Clarion-Ledger* about the Mississippi state flag, which incorporates the Confederate battle emblem, and in my interviews so far the subject of race has been a constant undercurrent. One slave descendant asked me over the phone, not suspiciously, but pointedly, "Are you a white person?" At the Claiborne-Jefferson County Genealogical Society, where I would later speak about my research, I received a few blank stares when I mentioned that some of the area's black Rosses were actually descended from the slaveholding family. One woman asked, politely but with obvious skepticism, "Can they prove it?"

At this point the question presents itself: aside from those cases where it is obvious, what determines whether a person is black or white? What if, as Frederick Law Olmstead proposed following his Mississippi plantation visit in 1852, the light-colored slave had been a house servant, had been given finer clothes, and had moved to the North—if she had "passed," would she in fact have been white? In antebellum Mississippi a person's "blackness" was defined by law: anyone who had ⅛ black blood was black. It did not matter if the person was ⅞ white. That is why a slave on an antebellum plantation could have light skin and straight, blond hair and still be a slave. But what of the people who came after—people who, like Delores, are of mixed race?

In the census of 1870, which was the first to include surnames for African-Americans, there were three choices in the guidelines given to census-takers: black, white, and colored (in addition to four other racial types). In 1880, "mulatto" was added, but with no clear criteria for making a distinction. The guidelines for 1890 were more explicit, delineating anyone with ¾ black blood as black; ¼ black blood as quadroon; and ⅛ black blood as octoroon. In the final analysis, all were black. By 1920 the definition had again changed, defining any "full-blooded Negro" as black and anyone with some white blood as mulatto. The 1930 census narrowed the focus considerably: "A person of mixed white and Negro blood should be returned as a Negro, no matter how small the percentage of Negro blood. Both black and mulatto persons should be returned as Negroes, without distinction. In cases where an assessment was difficult, the race was to correspond to the non-white parent." Not surprisingly, the term "mulatto" eventually lost its official meaning, and although the wording of the instructions slowly became less "white," for lack of a better term, for the next sixty years the census limited the options to a determination by the census-taker of "black" or "white."

The census of 1990 for the first time allowed those being counted to make their own racial determination, selecting from sixteen categories. For those at issue here, the choices were simply black and white. It was not until 2000 that the racial designation itself began to lose its importance. That year, respondents were allowed to check more than one racial category, meaning there need not be an official racial designation. If that sounds like welcome news in a country that has at times seemed overly concerned with race, not everyone thought so. Because black voting power is dependent upon racial divisions—i.e., in districts where blacks are in the majority, some black leaders were concerned that the new system would dilute their constituency. The NAACP, notably, urged "blacks, regardless of the racial percentages in their blood, to mark only one race on the census form," which would return the method of census recording to the concept of "some black is all black."

Why would it follow that any amount of black blood makes a person black, while the converse would not be true—that any amount of white blood makes a person white? I have found no clear answer.

For whatever reasons, most people of mixed race consider themselves black. Delores Ross considers herself something altogether different, a free agent, but she lives in a predominantly black neighborhood and socializes, for the most part, with blacks. Usually the answer is determined by the racial makeup of the majority of the family. If a person grows up in a black family, they tend to think of themselves as black, regardless of the shade of their skin. The same is true for whites of similar circumstances. As a result, the actual skin color may belie a person's race. Black is not always black, and white is not always white. A "white" person can be darker than a "black" person, and vice versa.

The dilemma, of course, is how to prevent social and governmental systems from using race as a criterion and still maintain racial integrity when it seems sensible or useful to do so. How is one to ignore race and yet account for it?

Race is only one factor influencing people's views, but it can be a bewilderingly potent one. During the 1980s, when Claiborne County was beset by bitter political fighting, federal election observers and state officials (most of whom were white) were reluctant to intervene. Both of the feuding factions were black, and although one side actively sought outside government help, cries of racism followed even minor overtures by such officials to enter the fray. The legislature eventually passed a law that divided the lucrative taxes from the county's Grand Gulf nuclear plant, reducing the largesse and with it some of the political incentive, and the situation quieted down. A residue of mistrust remained, however. It still seemed to be about race, because the law did not divide the revenue from power plants elsewhere in the state among the counties they served.

The county prosecutor at the time, Bob Connor, told me that the area's divisive racial history was clouding what would otherwise have been a routine case of political corruption. In Connor's opinion, a small group of unscrupulous, corrupt elected officials were subjecting black voters to "the same tactics that they were subjected to by whites a hundred years ago." It did not matter that the officials were black, he argued; the effect was the same.

Claiborne County School Board President Jimmy Smith gave an opposing view: "The problem here is that whites don't want to see blacks controlling any money, and money is totally the problem in Claiborne County. There are a few decent whites, but most of them are rednecks."

Of the approximately 11,500 people who live in Claiborne County, 9,500 are listed in the census as black and 2,000 as white; of the 9,750 people in neighboring Jefferson County, 8,650 are black and 1,100 white, the highest percentage of African-Americans of any county in the United States. Together the counties also have the highest percentage of black elected officials in the United States, and because blacks control most of the politics while whites control most of the money, the region has found itself at the forefront of a contemporary power struggle that is as complicated and unpredictable as any in Mississippi, where the stakes of racial politics are always notoriously high. As much as it is an Old South town, Port Gibson is today a proving ground for those politics.

For all these reasons, the descendants of the various Rosses of Prospect Hill share a history that is even more complicated and conflicted than it appears on the surface. For an outsider accustomed to typical American neighborhoods, which are segregated both economically and racially, it is surprising to find that blacks and whites of different economic backgrounds live in close proximity to one another here. They see each other every day, they share meals at local restaurants, visit on street corners, chat on the phone. They know a good bit about each other's family trees. In many ways theirs is a remarkably integrated society. Yet there is always a rarefied space between the races. Talk with enough people and you encounter racial polarization and outright prejudice—whites who blame blacks for the area's surprisingly high rural crime rate, blacks who see discrimination enduring in subtle yet pernicious forms.

The 1980s were a racially contentious time, but only the most recent in a series of tumultuous periods that have gripped the area for more than 200 years. None of the more famous stories much concern themselves with what blacks experienced during the Civil War era, but this much is known: once they were freed and given the right to vote, they quickly assumed the reins of political power. It took a decade for the whites to wrest that power back, after Reconstruction, and another century before the majority ruled again.

Of all the upheavals that have beset the region, the Civil Rights era of the 1960s and 1970s is the one most people personally remember. With whites struggling to maintain political power, blacks encountered intimidation and the threat of violence when they sought to exercise their right to vote and to enter cafés and stores that had traditionally been off-limits to them. They faced incredible odds because the local white power structure was bolstered by a state government that often worked hand in hand with paralegal organizations such as the Ku Klux

Klan, which targeted, threatened, investigated, and sometimes attacked people who posed a threat to the status quo. The period brought less outright violence to Claiborne and Jefferson counties than erupted in other parts of the state, but injustices fueled boycotts of white-owned businesses, public protests, and voter drives that ultimately succeeded in ending a century of officially sanctioned racial segregation.

Those and other past injustices linger over the region today, but not all the tumultuous stories cast whites as villains. Butch cites as an example the lynchings that followed the murders of several white men by black men in the nearby community of Harriston in the early 1900s.

"I remember people pointing out the hanging tree," she says. "From what I understand, it started during a gambling game at the [cotton] gin. Somebody found somebody cheating and the next thing the streets of Harriston was running red with blood. Every white person they saw, they killed." Butch's family ran the Ross Café in Harriston and she was raised near the site of the mayhem, she says. "I'm still right there on the Ross place," she adds. "I had a trailer there and then I re-did the trailer. Now I've got a brick home."

Delores has a flare for drama and takes over the story, at points assuming the voices of the different characters. "The Bell brothers were gambling and they took a black boy's money and wouldn't give it back," she says. "He said, 'Why won't you give me back my money? I worked hard for that money.' And they said, 'We ain't gonna give it back.' He thought they had cheated him. So he went home and got his brother, his horse, and his gun, and they killed every goddamn one of 'em. My daddy, Thad Ross, stuck his head out the door and they said, 'Get back in there or we'll get you, too.' Apparently they was close to Thad. Probably saved his life."

I nod, unsure how to respond.

I ask Delores how other people view her family's mixed lineage. She shrugs.

"People think what they wanna think," she says.

I ask if she is close to the Rosses who are descended from Prospect Hill slaves, and she quickly shakes her head.

"But I tell you who you should talk to," she says. "Pet." She turns to Butch. "Pet could probably tell him some shit."

Butch agrees. Pet Houston, she says, is part of an old black family.

"They know all about the Rosses. We'll drive out to her house. I'll go with you, that way she'll talk."

Delores gives us directions to the place, and soon Butch and I are driving out into the rolling Claiborne County countryside. The area is surprisingly sparsely populated, with only the occasional cluster of mobile homes and modest houses punctuating long stretches of quiet road. Here and there old crepe myrtle trees and solitary chimneys mark old house sites, hinting at the population that has left. When we get to Pet Houston's small, 1970s ranch house, she is in the kitchen serving an early supper to her elderly mother, who does not seem to notice us as she eats at the small table. Butch explains what I am there for. "He's all right," she says. "He's doing a story of the Rosses. He wants the black version. He's already heard the white version."

Pet considers this. "Well, when Mama get through chewin', she may know somethin'," she says.

We sit down in the living room, where a young woman is working on a quilt in front of a football game on TV, above which hangs the ubiquitous framed portrait of Jesus. Butch and Pet make small talk and presently the old woman, Ruth O'Neal, inches her way into the room with the help of a walker. She is nearly blind and deaf but her eyes are bright. Her hair is braided into tiny pigtails.

"Careful how you get in that chair," Pet says. "There's a man in the room."

Ruth slowly lowers herself into the chair. "Do I know the man?" she asks in a tremulous voice.

"No," Pet says. "But he won't bite."

Butch makes Ruth guess who she is, hugs her, then repeats her endorsement of my purpose. She prompts Ruth to talk about the Rosses.

Ruth's mind is a triumph over her failing senses. She is ninety-eight years old but her recall is total. She has lived in the area all her life. She trains her eyes on empty space, as if peering into the past.

"I know Thad Ross and his daddy, Bob Ross," she says, summoning the players from the wings. "His mama named Kate. There was Willie Ross. Frank. Little Kate. Little Bob got killed in World War I. There was a Ross they called Sonny. Ollie. It's a Ross had a store on Russum Road—Robert, Delores's first cousin. I ain't no kin to 'em, just raised close to 'em."

"Which ones had black children?" Butch asks.

"Louis had two black children," she says. "One of 'em left the country, went to California. Thad had two girls."

"That's right," Butch says.

Pet, who has been silently listening as the parade of Rosses goes by, interjects, "Katie Bell ain't no half-white. She ain't bright—she's darker than me. The children have a beautiful complexion."

"Mm-hmm," Ruth says, staring wide-eyed into space.

"Did the Ross sisters have any black children?" Butch asks, and shoots me a glance. On the way here, she had told me that one of her family members raised a child borne of such a union.

Ruth says only, "Mmm."

I ask her where she grew up.

"I was raised back in the country close to the Rosses. My people farmed near Stonington. After my husband passed I moved to Fayette, in the projects. I was an O'Quinn before I married." She says her husband originally lived on Holly Grove plantation, and for a moment I feel a commonality, since Holly Grove is now my home. But I do not mention this because I am mindful of widening the gap between us, and perhaps putting her on guard, by pointing out that I own one of the inaccessible big houses of her youth.

She continues. "Bob Ross, that's the furthest back I know about," she says. "And Thad Ross. They was good people. We used to have revival meetings at Shady Grove church and he'd come. Way back yonder, eighty years ago. He's the only white person that come. He'd come around to Mama's house and sit down at the table and eat. He was a farmer. All the colored folk liked him. Some of the white folks'd take up with colored people. That's the way them Rosses were."

She pauses. The football game blares from the TV. I try to think of a polite way to ask if she knows any Rosses whose family were slaves. I have noticed that when I bring up the subject of slavery with whites they talk about it easily, as if they are discussing a war fought long ago, full of victories and defeats, and familiar names. When I bring up the subject in conversations with blacks, particularly older people, I sense a distance, as if I have mentioned a dread disease. Knowing that so many are reluctant to talk about the subject, it seems rude to confront this elderly woman, who has been reminiscing about old times in the quiet refuge of her daughter's home, with the specter of her people's enslavement, but it is a crucial point.

When I do, she says nothing for a moment, then shakes her head.

"I sure don't know," she says. The subject falls flat.

"Well, I wish I could remember things as good as you," Butch says. "I can't remember near about as much as you." She and Ruth resume their small talk, and a few moments later say their good-byes.

As Butch and I drive back through the countryside toward Port Gibson, she seems satisfied that her account has been verified by an unassailable source. "Didn't I tell you?" she asks. "Miss Ruth knows all about it, the whole story. And it's a very complicated story, too—whole lot more complicated than most people think."

CHAPTER TEN

LAVERNE MCPHATE DID NOT think of it as trespassing, though it sounds a lot like it. The land was posted and the gate locked, so she slipped through the woods to approach the stranger's house with her video camera. She wasn't there to film the decaying manse, which is hidden far down a dirt road that is almost impassable when it rains. It was the cemetery she was after, because Isaac Ross is buried there. Although Laverne never lived at Prospect Hill, and she is aware that the current owner jealously guards his privacy, she felt she had every right to be there, as a descendant.

"It's quite an impressive thing," she says of Ross's monument, which she shot from every angle before hightailing it back to her car. The monument is an icon for descendants because it is all that is left to show for Ross's legacy, and any cemetery is sacrosanct in Laverne's mind. She was once appalled to find that someone had stolen tombstones from another of the Ross family burial grounds, most likely, she believes, to use for a sidewalk. She pauses to let the gravity of the affront sink in. "People's tombstones," she repeats. "For sidewalks."

Such remnants have become increasingly important to Laverne as her family has dispersed from the area. Most of the family members have not moved far—she and her husband, who operate a logging business in Jefferson County, live just across the river in Ferriday, Louisiana, and her brother Turner Ross lives in Vicksburg, but over the years all of the old home places have slipped from their grasp. What remains of their family's long occupation is now largely unattended. Their sense of ownership is derived from ghosts. They are holdouts, in absentia.

The family's regime is slow to fade because it lasted so long—nearly 170 years, from the arrival of Isaac Ross in the Mississippi Territory to the sale of Prospect Hill in 1973. When Isaac Ross Wade died in 1891, Prospect Hill passed to his brother, B. H. Wade, who lived out his life there. Family members also occupied several neighboring plantations, including Oak Hill, the original Rosswood, which was just down the road, and the second Rosswood, built nearby by Walter Wade for his second wife in 1857.

The Rosses' and Wades' continued occupation was more or less by default, because the properties were handed down through the generations. Until the 1940s brought the biggest wave of mobility, most of the old houses throughout the region were owned by their original families, but by then they were nearly all in disrepair, and there were few avenues available for making a decent living in the area, much less for maintaining houses built by wealthy men with large forces of free labor. Such families, according to Edna Regan, an elderly woman I spoke with at Vernalia plantation, just across the line in Claiborne County, were often "too poor to paint, too proud to whitewash." In the case of Vernalia, Edna and her husband had been reduced to setting up house in one of the dilapidated slave quarters, even as her mother-in-law continued to receive company in her threadbare brocade dresses, and forbade her son to take a job because she said it would ruin his hands.

This loss of financial stature did not exert a leveling influence on local society. Whites struggled to maintain a tenuous hold on the economic, political, and social status quo. When the WPA Writer's Project visited the area in the 1930s, its report noted that although many of the mansions were falling into ruin, "enough of them remain to stamp the scene with their character." Port Gibson, the largest town in the immediate area, was described in similar terms as "purely ante-bellum in tone."

Robert Wade, who is among the last surviving family members who actually lived at Prospect Hill, remembers when most everything was intact there—the main house, the separate kitchen, the slave quarters, a smokehouse, and several barns. All but the big house are gone now, rotted down. There are only a few reminders of Prospect Hill in Robert's Port Gibson home, including a scattering of photos and a parlor table. There are no oversized, gilt-framed portraits of his ancestors, no massive armoires, no shelves loaded with cracked leather books. When I ask why, he says, "It just all kind of got away through the years."

Robert is a tall, upright man in his sixties with a flat-top haircut, who looks more conservative than he is. He chooses his words carefully, and for someone who has lived his life in the quintessential Deep South town, has no noticeable drawl. He describes himself as "something like the fifth great-grandson of Isaac Ross," and is proud of his family legacy despite his belief that slavery was wrong. He and his family lived at Prospect Hill until 1956, when everyone except his mother moved to a more modern house in town. His mother stayed at the old place until her health began to fail, after which she moved into a trailer behind his house. That was in 1968, and afterward the family did not return to Prospect Hill, even for reunions. With the old house now weathered and empty, "People broke in and stole things out of it," he says. "They stole the stained glass windows, stuff like that. We cleaned it all out except an old upright piano, and they stole that, too."

The plantation acreage had over the years been divided among the heirs, leaving Robert's family with only the portion on which his father farmed. His father had inherited the place from his own father, and left it to Robert, who plans to leave the remaining 173 acres to his son. In the 1970s he made the difficult decision to sell the house and three acres to a Natchez man who planned to restore it but never did. "I realized it was a bad deal afterward but it was too late to get out of it," he says. The house was later sold to its current owner, John McCarter.

Most of the area's old houses were eventually abandoned or sold, Robert says, because they were isolated, expensive to maintain, and uncomfortable by twentieth-century standards. Prospect Hill, he recalls, was "cool in the summer and cold in the winter," and until the late 1940s was heated by fireplaces and lit by candles and kerosene lamps. As an only child, Robert spent a lot of time roaming the woods, playing Confederate soldier with an old rifle that he would sneak from behind an armoire in the hall—the same hiding place where the family kept the Union army gun left by the soldier who had died in Robert's boyhood room. Most of Robert's playmates were descendants of Prospect Hill slaves, although he sometimes stole away on his horse and rode for miles to play with white children whose families his parents did not approve of. He recalls being chastised by his family's housekeeper, who was herself a descendant of Prospect Hill slaves, for visiting families she called "poor white trash," and who threatened to tell his parents if he did not stop.

At this point Robert pulls a small album from a drawer beside his sofa and turns to a photo of a second housekeeper standing on the lawn before Prospect Hill, beside his mother. "Her family—those families, all of them had been on the place all along," he says. This housekeeper, whom he called Nonnie, moved with his mother to Port Gibson in 1968 and lived with her until she died.

Robert has visited the Prospect Hill house only a few times in the last thirty-five years, once when the Daughters of the American Revolution erected a marker near Ross's grave, and again when John McCarter had the family out to lunch and to install a second marker commissioned by the Isaac Ross chapter of the Colonial Dames. Robert retains the right of access to the cemetery, but he says it pains him to see the old house in its current condition. Likewise, "I haven't been through downtown Fayette since the courthouse burned. It made me sick when I drove through."

The sorry state of Fayette and Jefferson County in general is a common theme in conversations with Ross descendants, but Robert, who is more circumspect than most, is reluctant to criticize government officials who are responsible for an infrastructure that in many ways mirrors the old house at Prospect Hill. Still, he can't help but mention the poor quality of the county schools, the deterioration and later the burning of the courthouse, and certain black elected officials whose motivations he believes are as racist as some of their white predecessors. Because Robert had earlier suggested that Ross may have repatriated his slaves because he was concerned that emancipation would lead to problems, I ask how he thinks Ross would view the area today. He seems chastened by the question, and does not answer immediately.

"Well," he says, finally, "I wonder what my *grandfather* would think."

Considering the changes that have taken place since the antebellum era, he adds, "I'm glad I didn't live back in that time, myself. I do not believe in involuntary servitude in any way, shape, or form. I think it's wrong. Isaac Ross was antislavery and his belief was they would be more trouble than they were worth in the long run. He created a lot of enemies among his neighbors because they thought he was an abolitionist."

Growing up at Prospect Hill, as a descendant of slave owners, he says his racial views have at times been mixed. "Being raised like I was down here, I can't help but admit that sometimes I was a little prejudiced. But I would never knowingly mistreat one at all. I have some good friends that are black, that I would do anything in the world for, and they would do anything for me. There are some white people that . . . Anyway, in their case, I'd rather associate with the blacks."

Laverne McPhate's views on the state of Jefferson County are similarly mixed. She laments the hostility she says is increasingly common today, but says she has had no racial problems herself. She realizes her family history sets her apart in many ways, but not that far apart. Their history, which she recorded her grandmother recounting on tape, is more inclusive than one might expect. When I mention the racial mixing that Delores and Butch brought up, she says, simply, "As it came down through the twenties and thirties, it was not uncommon for the Ross men to have black mistresses. I just spoke with one yesterday, and they're just as white as I am. We all knew that. They're proud of it and I have nothing against it myself. They're well-educated people."

Her brother, Turner Ross, who runs a welding shop in Vicksburg, actually seems to relish the idea of so many black Rosses and white Rosses hailing from the same place, the same piece of ground. "Some of 'em are actual kinfolk," he says, over the phone. "Some of the Rosses had something to do with the blacks—I know that for a fact. Years ago. And when they set 'em free, the federal government allowed 'em to take the name of their last master, and ninety-nine percent of 'em did. So it's all kind of Rosses, black and white."

Turner mentions an elderly man who picks up cans along the roads around Vicksburg. "Black fella," he says, from Arkansas, which is where his own grandfather, Thomas Alonzo Davenport, moved after the Civil War. "And I'm here to tell you, that man that picks up tin cans on the side of the road is named Thomas Alonzo Davenport—same damn name as my grandfather. Whenever he comes around my shop, he always says the same thing—he's glad to be around kinfolk again."

✿   ✿   ✿

If such unconventional kinships are common in the history of Prospect Hill, the contest of Ross's will illustrates that kinship does not always imply affinity, much less harmony. While Isaac Ross and Prospect Hill occupy an odd middle ground, the region's history is beset by turbulent cross currents, and their pull is often influenced by race. Aside from comparative free agents such as Delores Smith, the line of demarcation is usually obvious, and despite concerted efforts to minimize the difference politically, economically, and socially, race still matters in a variety of ways. Not all whites are descended from slave owners, and not all blacks are descended from slaves, but how a person views Jefferson County today has everything to do with their own circumstances and the circumstances of their ancestors, and historically, those circumstances have been very different for blacks and whites.

The differences may manifest themselves in trivial ways, or may be extremely consequential, as during the Civil Rights era. But they present themselves again and again, sometimes as the context of a story that is otherwise generally agreed upon, as when Turner Ross mentions a long-ago mass murder in Harriston—the same story, it turns out, that Delores had mentioned.

While Delores couched the tale in terms of a misguided man who became enraged and sought vengeance over a perceived injustice, Turner calls it "the time the blacks went on a rampage." His version also begins at a poker game at the cotton gin, mentions the wounding of Thad Ross, and cites several victims, all white. Beyond that, it diverges.

As he remembers it, "There was seven or eight of 'em got killed. White men. Two of my uncles on the Ross side got wounded, one in the hand and one in the back of the leg." The sheriff, his deputies, and a group of other men eventually cornered the gunmen, who were hiding under the gin, and afterward, "They hung 'em, then shot 'em all night long." He summons the last, harrowing image with no apparent emotion—no satisfaction, dismay, or judgment in his voice.

The only documented account of the incident, which ran in the Fayette newspaper in 1913, tells still another version, under the headline CARNAGE AT HARRISTON; 8 DEAD AND 14 WOUNDED—SHERIFF HAMMETT KILLED AND CIRCUIT CLERK GILLIS WOUNDED; TWO NEGRO MURDERERS HANGED. Several black victims were also listed, which is something even Delores left out. The reporter took pains to discount the notion that the incident was "anything resembling a 'race war.'" According to his account, the main gunman was an eighteen-year-old mulatto man who began shooting "at a Negro house, where Willie Jones had some trouble with two other Negroes, whom he shot, at the same time shooting a woman. From there he proceeded to the village proper and shot everyone he saw, indiscriminately, with the exception of Shaw Millsaps, a Harriston merchant, whom he called to the door and asked for a drink of water, and whom he warned to stay inside."

Jones allegedly continued through town, shooting several men, including the sheriff, before being wounded himself. Eventually, he and his two alleged accomplices gave themselves up. By then a special train from Natchez had arrived with more men and arms and a supply of dynamite. The newspaper concluded: "Immediately following the orderly execution of the two murderers the crowd began to disperse, and before the noon hour the village of Harriston had resumed its normal appearance, except for the congregation of two small groups of citizens who discussed the affair."

In fact, people would be discussing it almost a century later.

Despite the newspaper's disclaimer, the incident clearly represented the white community's worst nightmare—a "black rampage"—and ended with the black community's worst nightmare—a lynching. It is not surprising that it is remembered in different ways today.

When I mention the melee to Robert Wade, he shakes his head but offers no comment. I ask how anyone can know what actually happened, when everyone, including the reporter who was responsible for the only documentation, seemed to have an agenda. He again shakes his head.

It seems a crucial point. But only when I offer as a similar example the different accounts of the alleged slave uprising at Prospect Hill does he sit up straight. "I have a copy of the original version of the burning of the house," he says. I ask if it is the account written by Thomas Wade. "Yes," he says. "That's the original account. I was shown the white oak tree where the perpetrators were hanged. That's basically true. Now, just exactly what the facts were, well, that's hard to come by."

As someone who was born in Jefferson County, yet who saw something of the world during World War II and later as a college student in Washington State and in the Naval Reserve, Robert is at once self-assured and cautious. He respects his ancestor's account but is aware that there is a lot he does not know. The same is true for many of his peers. Although Laverne McPhate might warmly embrace tales of happy slaves, she has no storehouse of information about what life was actually like in the quarters. It is one of the reasons so many black residents disregard local history: it was written by whites, whose agendas and personal knowledge were sometimes very different than their own.

Aside from a brief flurry of activity during Reconstruction, the first real opportunity blacks had to write local history came in the 1960s, and by and large they have been writing it ever since.

In the 1870s, during Reconstruction, parts of Mississippi were occupied by federal troops, which provided a measure of protection for newly franchised blacks. Soon blacks held elected office throughout the Natchez District and other parts of the state where they represented the majority of the population. After the troops left, though, whites found methods for regaining control. Literacy tests at the polls, harassment of potential voters and violence against black leaders soon vanquished black voting strength. Dissatisfaction with the return of white power brought about the first wave of emigration by black residents, and the trend continued, with a few intermissions, for the next hundred years.

During the Depression and after World War II, more whites joined in the exodus, mostly in search of jobs. The loss of population proved nearly fatal to many communities, particularly places such as Rodney, which was already grappling with survival after being abandoned by the wandering Mississippi River. Although Rodney once had its own newspaper and opera house, fewer than fifty people call the place home today, and the remaining historic buildings are slowly succumbing to fires, floods, and preservationists bent on relocating them to more viable locales. Rodney's most notable structure—the Presbyterian church, where Confederate guerillas captured Union officers attending services during the war, and which still has a cannonball lodged in its front wall—is an empty shell. Rodney resident Laura Piazza, who lived across from the empty church, once recalled a carload of intrepid tourists asking her if they'd found the "ghost town." She replied, indignantly, "Do I look like a ghost?"

The departure of whites from Jefferson and Claiborne counties escalated when black residents reasserted their political power. The Civil Rights era reached its stride in 1964 and 1965, and activists began to fan out across the state during what was known as Freedom Summer. The pivotal event in Jefferson County came when state police fired on demonstrators at Alcorn State University with rubber bullets, which energized the fledgling movement in the area. A year later black boycotts were imposed on white-owned businesses in Fayette and Natchez, which led the Ku Klux Klan, the Louisiana Citizens' Council, and a group called Americans for the Preservation of the White Race to stage "buy-ins" in support of the store owners. In 1966, a similar boycott was brought in Port Gibson to try to force store owners to address black customers with courtesy titles such as "Mr." and "Mrs." and to wait on them in turn, which led to a successful lawsuit by eighteen stores against the NAACP and other supporters—a ruling that was later overturned by the U.S. Supreme Court.

In 1968, Fayette Civil Rights activist Charles Evers defeated six white candidates in the Democratic primary for the district's congressional seat before losing in the general election. He garnered 43,000 votes, the majority of them cast by newly registered black voters. Later that year, Evers helped overthrow the state's whites-only delegation to the Democratic National Convention in Chicago, and in 1969 he was elected mayor of Fayette, the first black to hold such a post in a racially mixed Mississippi town since Reconstruction. Two years later, during his unsuccessful gubernatorial campaign, Evers stood on the old courthouse steps in Fayette and lambasted Theodore Bilbo, a former governor whom he had heard speak as a boy, recalling how he "spit that ol' racist fire." Evers then proclaimed, "But look out Bilbo, we comin' at you!"

By 1980, when about 200 white residents organized another "buy-in" in response to a boycott of a Fayette business that had fired its black employees, the majority of elected offices in both the town and the county were held by blacks, and in Fayette, at least, both white stores and white shoppers were clearly on their way out.

Hobbs Freeman, a descendant of Isaac Ross who was born in Fayette and lived there until the mid-1990s, says there were only about ten whites in town when he sold his store and moved to the community of Yokena, on the outskirts of Vicksburg.

"I had just wasted enough of my life thinking it would get better, and it never did," he says, explaining his painful decision to move. "It seems like nobody cares about anything. And the crime. My store was robbed—burgled, rather—twice in one week. They tore the door off, and it was right next door to the sheriff's office. But I really do miss the people. I know a lot of good people there."

Hobbs, whose earliest ancestors arrived in Jefferson County in 1780, still owns a parcel of land granted to the family by Spain. The original house on the property, which was known as Indigo plantation, was abandoned and decaying when a black family bought it and renovated it. "I was glad to see that," he says.

"The white people in Jefferson County for the last fifty years have encouraged their young people to get out—to get out and start a new life," he says. "And after the Civil Rights movement, a lot of blacks who had gone to Chicago and Detroit, they moved back, so there are more of them, and less and less whites."

Hobbs's mother is among those who have stayed, and he returns often to visit. He says most of the county's residents, black and white, try to get along. They have different ways of viewing local history, just like there are different versions of the story of Prospect Hill.

"It's kind of like a car wreck," he says. "Everybody sees something different, but you know that there was definitely a wreck."

Robert Wade says that he, too, is optimistic that area residents will eventually come to terms with their differences. In fact, he believes most of them already have. But he has experienced his share of racism, he says. In the 1980s he was among several whites who crossed swords with Claiborne County tax assessor Evan Doss, the first black elected to the position in Mississippi, after Doss allegedly refused to sell them license tags because they opposed him politically. Robert felt vindicated when Doss later went to prison on embezzlement charges.

The biggest stumbling block to the region's progress, Robert says, is the local economy, particularly in Jefferson County. "When they took the tax money from Grand Gulf away from Claiborne County, that was wrong," he says. "But why is there nothing in Jefferson County?" He mentions the Mississippi Band of Choctaw Indians, who have grown wealthy from casinos and industrial development in east Mississippi, and says, "When you look at what the Choctaws have been able to accomplish, and you consider how they've been treated, you wonder why something can't be done in Jefferson County."

The lack of jobs is just one reason so many young people leave the area, he says. Because the area has such a small tax base, anyone who owns anything of high value "is just taxed to death. In Jefferson County they have no other way to produce revenue. But the main reason for young people with children is the schools. It's so expensive to send them to private schools, and they can't go to public schools, they just can't. It's not possible."

Of Robert's five children, only one has stayed in Port Gibson. The others are scattered from Jackson to the Gulf Coast. Of his grandchildren and great-grandchildren, all who are of age have left. He says that when he sold the house at Prospect Hill it was already clear that none of the family members would ever return there to live. Because four of his children were born while the family was still at Prospect Hill, and they were the last generation of the family to live there, I ask if the story matters to them, if they ever go back to visit, to see the monument over Isaac Ross's grave.

"Not really," he says, sounding more empathetic than sad. "They all have their own lives now."

The same is true for Turner Ross's children. Although his sister Laverne would surely beg to differ, he says, "None of 'em was ever interested in all this but me and my mama."

CHAPTER ELEVEN

THE ROAD TO PROSPECT HILL is narrow and rutted now, threading its way through the depopulated Jefferson County countryside, past abandoned houses and barns, and old cotton fields long since grown up in trees. Great mats of purple wisteria bloom over entire groves, marking the sites of forgotten houses with a psychedelic display each spring. Here and there fallen trees funnel the road down to one lane, which poses no real problem, because we pass only two trucks and a handful of houses over the last ten miles or so.

Aside from a couple of posted signs, there is no evidence of Prospect Hill from the road, just an unremarkable metal gate, a seemingly random and obscure portal through the green. Today the gate is open, which is unusual because John McCarter, who owns the place, does not welcome uninvited guests. He has agreed to let me visit the family cemetery because he recognizes that its importance transcends his ownership of the surrounding area, but he has told me that the house itself, his personal domain, is off-limits.

I met John when I was dismantling Holly Grove, which originally stood in the vicinity, in 1990, and during a subsequent visit to Prospect Hill was amazed by the house's contradictions. The structure itself is near ruin, the ground visible through the rotten floor of the elevated porch, slivers of sky peeking through the rotten lath of the crumbling plaster ceiling. The late Tom Perrin, with whom John owned the house, let me go inside on that first visit. The interior was a showplace of antiques and nineteenth-century Southern decorative design—great tester beds draped in mosquito netting, Victorian-era sofas, side chairs and marble-topped parlor tables, and freshly painted walls.

Passing from one plane of existence to the other—from the external ruin to the exquisitely preserved time capsule within—was surreal.

The approach to the house ends in a quagmire a few hundred feet before the structure itself, and when my friend Scottie Harmon and I roll to a stop this day, we see John standing on the lawn amid his chickens and his English shepherd and two Great Pyrenees. Beyond him the house looks like a grand, weathered barn with six monumental chimneys. Attached to the fence is the Colonial Dames' brass plaque, which reads PROSPECT HILL PLANTATION HOME AND GRAVE SITE OF ISAAC ROSS PATRIOT-HUMANITARIAN-PHILANTHROPIST.

John greets us on the lawn. Beyond him, the setting of Prospect Hill is as tragically beautiful as I remembered it. The house is surrounded by ancient, storm-damaged cedar trees from which Spanish moss hangs to the ground. Architectural remnants are crammed beneath the gallery and flow into the yard. The fine facade of cypress siding, scored to resemble stone, stands exposed to the elements by a massive hole in the gallery roof. The roof has been leaking for years but the hole is large enough to have been made by a bomb blast. John says one of the old cedars fell on the house during a tornado a few years back. The gallery is elevated perhaps ten feet off the ground, and the ceiling rises to fourteen feet or more, and with its scattering of antique chairs and faded bunting over the door, it has the appearance of a ruined stage set floating in the air.

The once purple fabric draped over the elaborate doorway with a wreath of blackened magnolia leaves at the center are the remains of a funerary display for Perrin, who died in a car wreck several years back. John says he has had no real interest in working on the house since then. Everything about the place—the storm damage, the decay, the funeral bunting—brings to mind a gaping, long-untreated wound. Although the house has a haunting beauty that seems apropos for the Prospect Hill story, John notices the camera slung over my shoulder and asks that I take no photographs of the structure itself, because he does not want it to be remembered this way.

The grounds are a lush, overgrown garden of traditional Southern landscape plants—camellias, jasmine, irises, dogwoods, azaleas, blue phlox, and wisteria. The cemetery stands in a field of blue and white flowers. Two old cedars also fell onto the cemetery during the tornado, toppling several tombstones and narrowly missing Isaac Ross's monument, which is a towering, cupola-like marble structure ringed with columns. It is as impressive as everyone has said. The whole family is here: Ross, his wife, his sons and daughters, their husbands, children and wives, and little Martha Richardson, who died in the fire. Curiously, Isaac Ross Wade's tombstone faces away from the others. All of the tombstones except his are oriented toward Ross's monument, and, like most I've seen, are read from the side facing the grave. Wade's faces away from Ross's monument, and away from his own grave. It seems backward.

When I mention this, John says, "Yes, it's unusual. A lot of people have different ideas of what it means, but what's the point in speculating? There's no way to know about that sort of thing." Of the massive, toppled tombstones he says, "I don't like seeing them like that, and if I had a gang of slaves, I'd get them to stand them back up, but it's not a priority for me right now."

John appears dubious about the history that frames his life at Prospect Hill. He appreciates its physical evidence but seems weary of long-running disputes and efforts by certain "old families" to stake their claim to fame. The cemetery at Prospect Hill is one of many historical crosses that he has to bear. It is a demanding remnant of an overwhelmingly significant history, right in his own backyard, but none of the interested parties seem inclined to help him keep it up.

The majority of the graves belong to Wades, several of whom fought for the Confederacy, with the most recent dating from 1908. There are three Isaac Ross Wades. The first two died as boys, one in 1846 at age five, the other in 1847 at age one, and the third, the one who contested the will, in 1891 at seventy-six. Isaac Ross's monument is the centerpiece. John says he hopes to resume work on both the cemetery and the house eventually, but he has no firm plans right now.

Few people would take on a project like this, sinking incalculable time, energy, and funds into a huge, crumbling house in a remote corner of Jefferson County, Mississippi. Red Lick, the community nearest to Prospect Hill, is now largely the domain of a Muslim group that operates a small school known as Mohammed's University of the New Islam, which shares the neighborhood with a perfectly preserved antebellum estate and the Good Ole Boys hunting club. Nearby Church Hill was for a time the site of a Hare Krishna compound, based at an old plantation known as The Cedars, which had previously been owned by actor George Hamilton. The roads between are scenic tunnels through overhanging trees, but the pavement is pocked and the shoulders are uniformly littered. Here and there are empty mobile homes, overgrown with vines, the windows broken out. It is hard to imagine anything more forlorn-looking, or more telling, than an abandoned mobile home—something designed specifically to be mobile, which has been left behind. The nearest town of any size, Fayette, is dominated by federal housing projects and empty storefronts.

There are a few prominent holdouts of the Old South scattered around the region, and many people showcase their homes during the annual pilgrimage tour in Port Gibson. Most of them, with poetic names like Disharoon, Idlewild, and Collina, are repositories for a vanished way of life. On our way to Prospect Hill, Scottie and I stopped by a few of the tour homes in Port Gibson, which had all been spruced up for the pilgrimage, their lawns neatly mowed and tables set up on galleries to dispense tea cakes and punch. The first, Tremont, was filled with antiques, family memorabilia, and decorative arrangements of artifacts that serve as tiny Civil War shrines, mostly for local Confederate General Earl Van Dorn. A pretty young woman in a lavender and blue floral hoopskirt guided us through several rooms, reading from index cards. The furnishings were a hodgepodge from the 1830s to the 1960s, and unlike tour homes that faithfully mimic a specific historical period, this one had clearly been occupied by a single family for a very long time. The tour's treatment of antebellum history was equally venerable, which is to say that it was not politically correct. At one point a second, incongruous-looking guide with tattooed cleavage pointed to an old tea cart and said, cheerfully, "Back in the days of slavery, your little maid would roll this out to serve you!"

A few blocks away, amid a hundred acres of lush woodlands, was Collina. The home, built in 1834, is now owned by Dr. David Fagan, a native of Portland, Oregon, who bought it more than a decade ago and carefully restored it. The house is grandly appointed and could easily be the subject of an article in *Architectural Digest*. It is a tour de force of interior design, yet the doors at either end of the wide hall stood open on this day, filling the rooms with the scent of wisteria and wild azalea, and enabling the family dog to roam through at will.

"The house has great karma. This place is like a sanctuary," said a friend of David's, Donna Smith, who was helping to greet visitors. "Mississippi is just such a wild place."

Donna is originally from Cleveland, Ohio, and said that when she moved south she was surprised to find that in addition to the familiar sources of conflict, Rankin County, near Jackson, where she works in forensic psychology, is overrun with drugs. "It's the crystal meth capital of the country," she said.

The world, in fact, seemed noticeably uncontrolled and unkempt after we departed the landscaped grounds of Collina. Out in the countryside the roadsides were again littered and the landscape had a lush, abused look.

Most of what passes for an economy in the rural areas is a sort of picking over bones. As we depart Prospect Hill we pass a man with a metal detector probing for artifacts at an old house site, of which there are seemingly hundreds to choose from. The most famous of the area's old sites is Windsor, the state's grandest antebellum home before it burned during a party in 1891. The ruins of Windsor are evocative, dominated by twenty-three towering columns topped by massive, cast-iron capitals embellished with acanthus leaves, and here and there linked by surviving sections of elaborate iron railing. Built in 1860, the house was new when the Civil War came, and was used as a Union army field hospital while the family was sequestered in its upper stories. Its ruins were later used as a set for a romanticized movie about the Old South starring Elizabeth Taylor and Montgomery Clift called *Raintree County*. Today it is owned by the state, and is a popular spot for picnics. The surrounding fields have been planted in pines, and the family cemetery is caving into a ravine. It is possible that it is even more impressive now, as a monumental ruin, than it was during its heyday.

Just beyond Windsor, the road leading to the old Mississippi River ferry has also caved into a ravine, and the ferry no longer runs. The remaining roads are occasionally closed for long periods by bridge failures and landslides.

Nothing epitomizes the region's decline more than the house at Prospect Hill, and nothing embodies the hypersensitive desire to hold on more than Rosswood, the only other Ross family house still standing in the area. Thinking it might be interesting to see Rosswood, I had phoned ahead, explained my research, and asked if I might visit. Jean

Hylander, who owns the house with her husband Walt, replied, "Yes, you may, for seven dollars and fifty cents." The admission fee is more than twice what other tour homes in the area charge, perhaps because the massive house is so expensive to maintain, but it seems a small price to pay to see the only surviving Ross home that retains its ante-bellum splendor.

After driving roads lined with substandard houses, many of which have burglar bars on the windows, and where refrigerators and sofas have been dumped into every eroding ravine, the approach to Ross-wood is certainly impressive. The massive, gleaming white Greek Revival edifice surmounts a hill in the distance, surrounded by old trees draped with moss. It beckons visitors down the long, oak-lined drive, although signs clustered at the gate send a different signal, informing you more than once and in no uncertain terms that anyone who proceeds further will be charged admission. There is also a sign for a security service displayed prominently on the front wall, and when Hylander opens the front door the first thing that comes into view is a cash register.

The Hylanders operate Rosswood as a business, and have spared no expense in re-creating the sort of ostentatious display they think would have greeted guests during the antebellum years. An eclectic array of period sofas, china cabinets, and bookshelves brim with cut glass, china, and silver, and crystal chandeliers hang from elegant plaster medallions. Hylander is obviously proud of the history of the house, but it is clear that her own furnishings are her real passion. There is something overproduced about the whole affair, which was probably true in the antebellum era as well.

The Hylanders had no connection to Rosswood, or to the area, before they bought the mansion in 1975, but for personal credentials she points out that she is a fifth-generation Mississippian. "Walt's grandparents," she adds, "couldn't even speak English." I assume this to mean that her family has its Mississippi bona fides, while her hus-band's ancestors are comparatively recent arrivals.

As she goes through the litany of tour-home highlights, she offers an unexpected aside, noting that the house "has a lot of black history." For evidence she points out that the plantation was originally owned by Isaac Ross, whom she claims was "the first person to free his slaves before the Civil War." Ross's slaves, she says, "worked this land. As for my own part, I had black crews do all the work on the house." The restoration work included installing a new roof and applying 220 gallons of white paint. She goes through the cast of housekeepers and handymen she has employed over the years, some of whom she says she occasionally still talks with on the phone. She mentions one housekeeper who was "the best help I've ever had. There's no way I could make up all those beds myself."

We talk about Ross family history and I explain why I am here.

"It's too bad you can't go out to Prospect Hill," she says.

When I tell her that we have just been to Prospect Hill, she is incredulous.

"You've been to Prospect Hill? No one gets in there! You're the first person I know who's ever been allowed in. He has the fence electrified so you'll get shocked if you try to climb over!"

I am torn between defending John, who was unfailingly polite, and going along with the notion of the electric fence to aid in his effort to keep the tourists at bay. I say I don't know about the fence, but am aware that John values his privacy.

Hylander thinks this over for a moment, then says she has a book about Prospect Hill. She points to a group of folding chairs that seem out of place amid the fancy sofas and armchairs, and says, "I invite you to sit down here while I go find it."

It turns out I have seen the book, so she reverts to tour mode, pointing out the Mallard case where her collection of cut glass, Dresden china, and jade is on display, along with a fragment of a cannonball she says was fired at the house during the Civil War skirmish in July 1864 that involved the Second Mississippi Infantry, part of the U.S. Colored Troops, some of whom had previously been slaves in the area. "We found it when we put the pool in," she says. "The Rebels won that one."

Hylander says that Walter Wade, the builder of the house, was living in an earlier house by the same name at the time of the controversy over Ross's will, but that he happened to be spending the night at Prospect Hill the night of the disastrous fire. "He's the one who didn't drink the coffee, which had been drugged," she says, offering her own version of the night's events. "He was the one who woke everybody up. When they came out the front door there was a man with a sword or an axe or something, and the mistress of the house said, 'Did you come to rescue us?'"

She shows us a copy of Wade's plantation diary, which chronicles life at Rosswood between 1855 and 1862. One entry reads: "Go to Conrad's shopping for Negroes." Another reads: "Sat by the fire all day—dull—Negroes no fun."

Hylander recalls that Rosswood was in disrepair when she and her husband bought it and she began fulfilling her lifelong dream of owning an antebellum mansion. Then she turns toward the door and says, "I invite you to come into our parlor, our most beautiful room."

The parlor and the dining room adjacent to it are undeniably rich, with elaborate, gilded mirrors, a rosewood square grand piano, heavy drapes, and a gloomy, oversized dining room set embellished with carved boars and dogs. The china cabinet is loaded with more silver, cut glass, and china. "While we were living in different places all over the world, I was always collecting," Hylander says. A mirror in the hall "was collected in Berlin. It always reminds me of my life in Berlin." The dining room set "is from the Jacobean period."

The doorbell rings and Hylander excuses herself, leaving us in the dining room. We stroll into the hall, and beneath the stairway see a door with a sign that reads TO BASEMENT GIFT SHOP AND SLAVE QUARTERS. I have been hauling my camera around during the tour, and when Scottie suggests I snap a photo, I do. Hylander, who is rushing through a tour of the preceding rooms with a man from Kentucky—trying to catch up with where we left off—hears the shutter and hurries into the hall. "No photographs are allowed in this house!" she says, with surprising rancor. "Did you not see the sign?" She points to the corner where the cash register sits. I still do not see the sign.

"No, I didn't," I say. "But I won't take any more."

"I can't get insurance if you take pictures," she says. "That's why I have that sign." She glares at me from behind her darkly tinted glasses, then adds, "I'm going to have to ask you not to have that film developed."

I nod. The Kentuckian looks at the floor, bewildered. I am hoping that that's the end of it, but it isn't.

"Did you take other pictures when I wasn't looking?" she asks.

"No, I did not," I answer.

"Do you have some kind of card with your name on it that says what you're doing here?" she asks.

I do not.

It is apparent that her anger is building. I glance over at Scottie and say, "Maybe we should just go."

He nods. We head for the door.

Hylander leaves the Kentuckian in the hallway and hurries after us, protesting that we have not seen the entire house.

"We've seen enough," I say, continuing out the door.

"Did you take pictures of my *furniture*?"

As we pull out onto the highway, and I notice there are signs along the road, flanking the Rosswood estate, delineating the boundaries of a neighborhood-watch crime prevention program. There are no other homes within those boundaries, which makes it clear that the estate is a neighborhood unto itself.

CHAPTER TWELVE

THE MINIVAN PULLS TO a stop before a nondescript building in Stone Mountain, Georgia, and a woman gets out, wearing a striking West African dress of vivid purple with golden sunbursts and red embroidery along the hem. She bears an armload of bulging plastic bags, and eyes me curiously.

"Is this where the . . ." I begin to ask.

"Yes!" she says, and offers a wry smile. "You must be the man who's working on the book on Ross."

I nod.

"Well, you come to the right place. Everybody knows the Rosses." She pronounces the name with a strong Liberian inflection, so it sounds like "th' RUH sez."

Soon other cars pull into the parking lot and people begin to gather in front of the building. Among them is Sandy Yancy, a Georgian who is chair of the Sinoe County Association of America, which was formed by expatriates from the Sinoe County region of Liberia that included Mississippi in Africa. There are association chapters in several states, owing to a mass exodus of Liberians during the nation's two decades of unrest and civil war, which began in 1980.

Yancy left Liberia in 1982 and hopes one day to take his children to see their native land, but only for a visit, and certainly not now, when the country is still in the throes of something very close to anarchy. When things get better he would like to hold an association meeting in Sinoe County. "You know, ease back in, clean up the neighborhoods, not just send supplies," he says. "I want to help the people who remained behind."

Over the last year, as I have been trying to piece together the threads of the story of Prospect Hill, I have come to the unavoidable—and daunting—conclusion that I will have to travel to Liberia to fill in the most important blank—the fate of the freed-slave immigrants and their descendants. I have come to Stone Mountain hoping that some of the association's members will be able to offer leads in my search for the Liberian descendants of Prospect Hill. I have also posted notices on countless Internet bulletin boards, explaining my project, saying that I am planning on traveling to Liberia to do research, and asking in general about the Rosses, but the responses have been discouraging. Although many cite famous Rosses in Liberian history, none have provided names of descendants who live in Liberia today.

Ironically, most of the people I meet in Stone Mountain are searching for relatives in the United States, a sort of *Roots* in reverse. None knows of a Mississippi connection in their family, although Janice Sherman, whose mother's maiden name was Duncan, suspects she has one. I suggest that her ancestors may have been freed by Stephen Duncan, Ross's friend in Natchez, but that is as far as it goes. The meeting is primarily a social event, a time for the expatriates to eat traditional West African foods, hear news from home, and lament the current state of their native country. It begins more than three hours late because, as Yancy explains, the party the night before lasted until four A.M.

At the start of the meeting the association members sing the Liberian national anthem, which sounds like a mournful hymn, with one person counting time:

"We will o'er all prevail.

"We'll shout the freedom of a race benighted.

"Long live Liberia, happy land,

"A home of glorious liberty by God's command. . . ."

Then everyone holds hands and prays.

Wilfred Harris, chair of the Minnesota chapter, recalls celebrations in Sinoe County to which men wore tuxedos and top hats, and reminisces about people he once knew. I pick out the names David Ross, Hampton Ross Mosely, and Simon Ross.

"Gone are the days," he says. "Those were the days when so many people looked at Sinoe with so much conviction . . . there was so much pride. But it has changed. Brothers and sisters, things have changed.

We are scattered around the world, looking for things we do not have. But our being here is not a mistake. Just like Joseph in the Bible was sold as a slave, to prepare for the hunger, we were brought here for a reason." The reason, he says, is to help the people back home. He expresses gratitude for the opportunity America has offered, and suggests, "If you're in America and cannot advance yourself, then you go to Liberia."

During a break in the meeting, Evans Yancy, Sandy's brother, says that when he was growing up in Liberia, people heard his name and told him his family was originally from Georgia. "So when I came to the States, I came to Georgia," he says. He visited the state archives and found several Yancys in old phone books near Augusta, Georgia. "I found Isaac Yancy," he says. "Isaac Yancy was a common name in my family. I didn't know if he was black or white, but I figured, either way." He drove to the town where Isaac Yancy was listed as a minister, but found that he had recently died. As he inquired around town, he was shocked when one man recognized his relation to the Yancys. "He said, 'I knew you were related to Reverend Yancy—you have his eyes.'" Eventually Yancy organized a reunion of the two families—the Sinoe-expatriate Yancys and the native Georgian Yancys. He says he met a man there who looked more like his brother Sandy than he did, after 165 years of family separation.

Yancy says most of the expatriates do not expect to go back to Liberia to live. Why would they, when everyone else is clamoring to get out? They are only too happy to dream of Africa. Several other members suggest names of people in Liberia who may be related to Prospect Hill: Rosses, Reeds, Woodsons, but no one knows how to reach any of them. There are few phones in Liberia, and because the country is in turmoil, people tend to move frequently. Janice Sherman offers what proves to be the best lead I could hope for in the United States, a man named Nathan Ross who was in the Liberian congress and fled the country following the 1980 coup. But for now, as I am preparing to embark for Liberia, I have little to go on aside from warnings. Everyone is unanimous: this not a good time to go to Liberia. I heard much the same thing following my Internet postings, which prompted an array of responses ranging from concern to hostility.

✿　　✿　　✿

The Liberian conflict erupted from a variety of causes, but a major factor was the long-running conflict between the descendants of the freed slaves and those of the indigenous tribes. Most of the Sinoe association members are the former, who were once referred to as Americo-Liberians. Before the coup the Americos represented about 5 percent of the population, yet they controlled most of the nation's money and all of the elected offices. Their legacy included the re-creation of something like the society of the Old South, where the slave-master system was all the immigrants had ever known.

The coup followed an incident in 1979 in which police in Monrovia, the capital, fired upon demonstrators who were protesting the government's intention to raise the price of imported rice. Looting followed. The police and the army were divided in their loyalty for Americo President William Tolbert Jr. and the demonstrators. The following year Samuel Doe, a military legend who was of native ethnic descent, overthrew Tolbert and the long period of Americo rule ended. The later civil war, which broke out during the Christmas season of 1989 and lasted until 1997, included fighting among rival ethnic groups and the Americos, but by then the lines had blurred considerably. By many people's reckoning, the civil war has never really ended, and in fact, more intense fighting will break out in 2003.

Because most Liberians now in the United States fled their homes in Liberia following the coup or during the civil war of the 1990s, nearly all of the expatriates I meet at the Sinoe meeting are fearful of going back. One association member offers to act as my guide and protector in Liberia if I will pay his way, but this proves unnecessary after I hear from John Singler, the linguist at New York University who responded to one of my postings. John says that he can make arrangements for a guide who is already there.

John proves invaluable to my search, not only because he has lived and taught in Liberia, including Sinoe County, but because he is intimately familiar with both the country's history and its current situation. He manages to keep in touch with old friends through haphazard phone calls and letters, and offers much-needed advice on the logistics of getting to Liberia and what I can expect once I am there. He knows of no Ross descendants himself but is confident that his contacts will be able to help.

Everyone at the Sinoe meeting correctly predicts that the biggest hurdle will simply be getting there. Acquiring a visa from the Liberian embassy in Washington, D.C., proves a formidable task. The embassy is understaffed and I get nowhere on the phone. When I visit the embassy in person, it is closed. On my third try the door is open, and I present my papers and the visa is granted. I notice that the wall of the waiting area, where framed photos of Liberian dignitaries hang, has been stripped almost bare. Where once there were perhaps thirty photos, there are now only a handful interspersed with the shadows of those that have been removed.

As I plan my trip to Liberia, I keep in touch with several of the Sinoe Association members, who each time sadly report that the situation is not improving. Although my trip is delayed numerous times by outbreaks of fighting, eventually I decide that it is simply time to go. If I am going to find the descendants of the immigrants from Prospect Hill, I do not have the luxury of waiting for the right moment in Liberia, because who knows when—or if—that will come. Also, my visa has an expiration date.

The logistics of the trip are complicated. Because flights to Monrovia are often canceled without notice, John advises me to fly direct from Europe to Abidjan, in the Ivory Coast, which is the most stable country in the region. Just before my departure, however, an attempted coup in Abidjan forces me to change my plans. I will now fly to London and from there to Brussels, then to Conakry, Guinea, and finally to Monrovia. I will have two weeks on the ground. The date of my departure, by coincidence, comes 165 years to the day after Isaac Ross died.

Just before my departure, the ubiquitous Ann Brown phones to say that even if I find the people I am looking for in Liberia, she is not satisfied that I have found everyone I need in Mississippi to tell the story. She is still searching for descendants of the Prospect Hill slaves who chose to remain behind, and is determined to find someone among that group who knows the history.

The same goes for Delores Smith, who says, over the phone, "Give me a call when you get back, baby. We gonna find who you're lookin' for."

The next day I am on an early morning flight to begin my search, in earnest, for whatever might remain of Mississippi in Africa, and for the Prospect Hill emigrants, who long ago disappeared from the local radar screen, but whose story in Liberia was just beginning.

Part II

LIBERIA

CHAPTER THIRTEEN

A RIVER GLIMMERS DIMLY in the gathering dusk as the jet banks for its approach to the Monrovia airfield. Fires burn in clearings of the jungle nearby, sending smoke through the ruins of the Roberts Field Hotel and the roofless hangars and aircraft graveyard edging the runway of the bombed-out airport. Aside from a scattering of lights within the reclaimed terminal and tower, the airport is dark. Passengers clamor to get out when the plane rolls to a stop before the terminal: doe-eyed missionary volunteers from Minnesota; furtive businessmen from Libya, Germany, and France; ebullient young athletes on the Liberian Lone Star soccer team; women resplendent in traditional African dress toting large, ersatz Louis Vuitton bags filled with supplies from abroad.

Inside the terminal the atmosphere grows chaotic. The windows and doors are open to the tropical night as everyone jockeys for position in the queues for Immigration, for the baggage carousel, and finally, for the baggage search. Carts crash into one another at bottlenecks. Surly inspectors struggle to maintain order. Slowly the crowd pours through the turnstile into the night.

The shadows of soldiers with automatic weapons hover near the terminal. Across the darkened street a hundred or so people wait, cordoned off. Somewhere among them is Peter Roberts Toe, a friend of John Singler's who has come to meet me, to take me to Greenville, Liberia, the former center of Mississippi in Africa, where I hope to find the descendants of Prospect Hill.

I have been unnerved by Liberia before I even arrived. I have read harrowing news accounts of its wars and related atrocities, including stories of militia forces and rebels who tortured and mutilated women and children and drugged young boys and forced them to take up arms, and of the starvation and disease that have accompanied them over the last two decades. The U.S. State Department has issued repeated warnings against traveling to the West African nation, and while the warnings might fall upon deaf ears among seasoned foreign correspondents and rogue businessmen, I am a novice. My greatest fear was that there would be no one waiting for me at the airport, which lies an hour outside of Monrovia, a city that is itself hardly a safe refuge. And it is night. I have been told that it is too dangerous to travel in Liberia after sundown, although, like so much of what I have heard before coming here, this proves debatable.

My trepidation must be evident, even in the darkness, because a policeman standing alone in the wide street sees me and asks if there is someone to meet me. He seems relieved when I say yes. "Welcome," he says, and smiles.

I am elated to find Peter and his friends waiting for me, and they are relieved as well, because a rendezvous is a chancy thing in Liberia. It is not uncommon to make the expensive and time-consuming trip to the airport only to find that a flight has been canceled or, even if the plane does arrive, to discover that the person you are looking for is not aboard. There is no phone at the airport, and the few phones found elsewhere in the country are unreliable. Peter has driven ten hours on a notoriously bad road from Greenville, where he lives. After quick introductions he happily grabs one of my bags and leads us to the car he has hired, an old Nissan Sentra painted bright yellow, with a decal of an American flag stuck to the windshield.

Peter is a nurse who functions as a doctor in a place where there are almost no health care workers, and has brought with him Edward Railey, a young man originally from Louisiana, Liberia, who is to act as my guide in Monrovia, along with a student activist from Monrovia, who is to be my fixer, and a driver, whom he introduces simply as John.

We set out from the airport in high spirits and make it about a mile before the car breaks down. The engine sputters to a stop in front of a cluster of mud and thatch huts in which oil lamps glow dimly. John gets out and opens the hood, his face silhouetted by the headlights as he pries the gas line free and blows through it. He replaces the line and slams the hood. We lurch forward through the curious crowd that has emerged from the huts, but continue only a few hundred yards before the engine cuts out again.

This time everyone gets out. I have a flashlight in my bag. We try again, the engine fails again, and we coast to the shoulder of the road, scattering women with loads of firewood and fruit and other burdens on their heads. Again the young men emerge from the huts to check us out while the shiny Land Rovers bearing the soccer players, the businessmen, and the missionaries fly past.

I tell myself that had I known I would end up broken down on the side of the road, in the middle of the night, I would not have come. But I am here and everything is fine. After two more breakdowns, John manages to solve the problem, sucking and blowing on the gas line until whatever is blocking it comes free. We make our way toward the first checkpoint, where a gate blocks the road to Monrovia.

I have heard about the checkpoints, and have dreaded them. They are common all over Africa but have a particularly bad reputation in Liberia, where they are usually manned by former combatants in Liberia's civil war, many of whom had been pressed into military service as part of warlord (and now president) Charles Taylor's "Small Boys Unit," where they were given drugs and beer and AK-47s, then unleashed upon the terror-stricken countryside. There are many horror stories, of drunken soldiers at a checkpoint who slashed open the womb of a pregnant woman to settle a bet over the sex of the fetus, of travelers robbed, tortured, and shot. Most of the stories originated during the wars of the 1990s, and although the worst ended in 1997, there is still fighting along Liberia's borders, which increases the likelihood of encountering trouble, or at least facing its uncomfortable and sometimes dangerous aftermath.

There are fifteen or twenty men at the first checkpoint, mostly in their teens or early twenties, many of whom appear to be drunk or stoned and most of whom are armed with old automatic weapons. One of the soldiers, dressed in a T-shirt and dark khaki pants with his gun slung across his shoulder, approaches the driver's window and peers into the car. The interior light is on out of necessity, because cars with unknown occupants are sometimes fired upon. John, the driver, exchanges a few words with the soldier, delivered rapid-fire in a strange patois that sounds like southern American English with African inflections and is hard for the untrained ear to understand. Most Liberians speak English, the national language, but the influence of numerous ethnic languages complicates things. The word "flashlight," for example, becomes "flah-lah."

I gather that there is a demand for money or beer, and that John will have none of it. The exchange becomes more heated until finally the man with the gun gives up, the makeshift gate swings open, and we zoom away.

A few miles down the road we reach a second checkpoint. The scene is repeated. This time the demand by the man at the window for money or beer is echoed by men lurking beyond the light of the car. Again the exchange becomes heated. Finally the man with the gun says, very distinctly, "I'm speaking to the white man."

Until this point I have tried to stare straight ahead, at the gate illuminated by the dim headlights of the taxi, where a group of men are waiting for directions. Now I turn toward the rheumy eyes of the man with the gun.

He stares at me for a long moment before saying, simply, "Hello."

"Hello," I say, with all the enthusiasm I can muster.

We stare at one another. Finally he says, "Welcome."

It sounds like an ultimatum but the word is *welcome*.

"Thank you," I say.

He stares a moment longer, then signals toward the gate, which swings open. We speed through.

Soon we are passing the Land Rovers that earlier passed us, careening around blind curves, scattering dark figures on foot, barreling toward Monrovia.

"Could someone explain what just happened?" I ask. Everyone in the car bursts out laughing.

"They want money or beer," Peter says. "Next time, maybe you don't say anything."

CHAPTER FOURTEEN

THERE IS A LONG historical backdrop to the unrest that has gripped Liberia in recent decades. Beginning as early as the 1500s, the coastal region, which was crucial to trade with Europeans, had been contested, first by competing indigenous tribes and later by freed-slave immigrants, including those who arrived from Prospect Hill in the 1840s. Wars, revolts, and blockades have repeatedly swept the coastline, often spilling over into the interior. Although there have been periods of calm and prosperity, sometimes for decades at a time, the area's settlement history—even before colonization—has been hard fought.

The region that was to become Mississippi in Africa, on the southeast coast of Liberia, was first occupied by a complex amalgam of ethnic groups who were later lumped together by Europeans under the name Kru. They occupied autonomous villages and began trading with the Dutch and English in the sixteenth century, exchanging first rice, pepper, and slaves, and later coffee, cocoa, palm oil, ivory, and wood, for products such as cloth, iron, tobacco, and liquor. Beginning in the late eighteenth century, European vessels also began recruiting Kru members as shipboard workers.

As many as forty separate social, political, and dialect divisions were identified within Kru culture by the 1970s, when historian Mary Jo Sullivan conducted a definitive oral history project in Sinoe County, the site of Mississippi in Africa. The groups traditionally competed with one another for the most productive land, for other natural resources, and for trade, which often led to bloodshed and forced migrations, Sullivan wrote. Only after the arrival of the freed-slave

settlers, who provided the tribes with a common foe, was there anything resembling unity among them, and even then, some of the
groups broke away.

Although the Kru farmed and fished, trade was their most lucrative
enterprise. Those groups who were accustomed to plying the rough
coastal waters in canoes were able to control the landing, loading, and
unloading of European ships, which would give them an edge and be a
source of controversy for settlers and their descendants well into the
twentieth century.

Historically, Kru villages were formed when family groups from
the interior splintered and some of the members gravitated toward the
coast. Within their villages, political power was wielded by councils
comprised of the eldest members of each family in consultation with
religious oracles. The elders were responsible for appointing a governor, who presided over meetings, and a mayor, or chief, who was
responsible for ensuring order and maintaining trails and bridges.

Another important position was that of the *bodio*, who was charged
with keeping the community's idols, consulting the oracle, and making
sacrifices, to ensure successful trade, crops, and female fertility. Essentially, the *bodio* got the blame if things went wrong in a big way. His
house was considered a sacred place, but he was never allowed to leave
the village, and, according to Sullivan, "the office was not popular and
new *bodios* had to be conscripted against their will. . . ." Negotiations
between rival groups were usually left to women, including the *bodio*'s
wife, who could settle disputes.

Alliances between villages were rare, and always temporary. This
aspect of Kru culture would pose a significant impediment to good
relations with the freed-slave settlers, because the indigenous groups
did not consider their grants of land to the settlers permanent.
Another source of conflict would be the slave trade, in which the Kru
had been active for centuries.

When settlers began arriving in the 1820s, they attempted to interrupt the slave trade, and were aided in the effort by the U.S. Navy,
which was charged with seizing and freeing the human cargo of slave
ships. The subsequent addition of so-called "recaptured slaves"—people
who were neither indigenous to the area nor among the freed-slave
elite—only added to the colony's volatile cultural mix.

The settlers also competed with tribes for other types of trade—in such products as coffee, cocoa, palm oil, and ivory—that had become ever more integral to Kru society during the fifty years preceding the emigrants' arrival. In addition to selling goods to European traders and working on their ships, Krus acted as guides and interpreters and handled cargo. There was a highly developed trade hierarchy. It was not simply a matter of the settlers interfering or competing with those activities, although they did. It was also a matter of the Kru being in a comparatively strong position to defend their livelihood.

The settlers typically viewed the Kru culture condescendingly, as primitive and pagan, although they themselves had arrived, in many cases, with few possessions, no knowledge of the area, few trade contacts, and no land to call their own. As Sullivan noted, access to capital and contacts with Europeans gave the Kru a certain advantage. "This edge not only prevented the settlers from becoming established commercially, but also enabled the Kru to resist settler control for almost 100 years," she wrote.

Among the first emissaries of the American colonization society was Jehudi Ashmun, who arrived in what would become Liberia in 1822 to lead the colony, but who died of fever in 1828. Ashmun had envisioned an American empire in Africa, and from 1825 to 1826 arranged leases, annexations, and purchases of tribal lands on the coast and along the rivers leading inland. The first treaty with native leaders conveyed rights to land in exchange for tobacco, barrels of rum, powder, five umbrellas, iron posts, and ten pairs of shoes.

A few Mississippi immigrants arrived on their own in the 1820s, but it would be 1835 before the first sixty-nine sponsored by the Mississippi colonization society arrived in Monrovia. Of the latter group, two had been born free, eighteen had bought their freedom, and the others had been emancipated by Judge James Green and Mary Bullock from their plantations near Natchez. Three years later, thirty-seven more immigrants arrived in the new colony established by the society, Mississippi in Africa, which encompassed the land near the mouth of the Sinoe River. At the time, the Mississippi colony was distinct from the greater colony of Liberia, with its own administration and funding.

The Prospect Hill group was among thousands who made the crossing. Between 1821 and 1867 the American colonization society sent an estimated 13,000 immigrants to Liberia, but because the Mississippi colonization society reportedly did not feel that the American colonization society was placing enough emphasis on the Mississippi settlers—and, according to some accounts, due to their perception that the ACS was abolitionist in sentiment—the group eventually bought its own land down the coast from the other Liberian settlements. The immigrants were first sent to a settlement on the St. Paul River near Monrovia, but in 1837 the colony was shifted to the mouth of the Sinoe River and christened Mississippi in Africa. The Mississippi society members pledged $14,000 annually to establish and maintain the colony.

"The slaves of the Ross/Reed estate had been working in Mississippi since Mrs. Reed's death with the understanding that their labor would produce money which would be used to give them a start in Africa," John Ker wrote, in an account cited by New York University linguist John Singler.

"However," John Singler added, "when they arrived, they found out that this aid was not forthcoming."

Letters from the Prospect Hill immigrants include only passing references to the arduous journey to what was to be their promised land, but the accounts of others included recollections of strong gales that tossed their ships for days, resulting in broken windows, toppled masts, swamped holds, and widespread seasickness. Former Prince Ibrahima, who would die in Monrovia soon after his journey, recalled the "unforgettable motions and smells" and "creaking masts and thumping hull on the trip over," and described his first sight of land, Cape Mesurado, as "a majestic promontory covered with a rich mantle of green." Behind the beach was a solid wall of foliage rising up the cliffs, beyond which spread Monrovia, protected by cannons and companies of richly uniformed volunteers.

Many arriving immigrants described the scene as beautiful, although at least one lamented the sight of so many naked and "uncouth" people who came out in canoes to meet them. Immigrant Thomas Johnson recalled encountering native huts decorated with the skulls of enemies killed in battle, and hearing nightly communication by drums from village to village, indicating that "white men"—which is how the indigenous tribes referred to the African-American immigrants—had arrived.

❊   ❊   ❊

The immigrants faced an uphill battle from the start, particularly those who settled in Mississippi in Africa. In addition to epidemics of various African fevers, and conflicts with indigenous tribes, the Mississippi colony was underfunded and did not enjoy good relations with the Liberian government in Monrovia, partly due to disagreements between the Mississippi colonization society and the American colonization society. The Mississippi society was active only from 1831 to 1840, after which the colony was incorporated into Liberia, but by then its government was essentially bankrupt and its residents were isolated and reeling from depredations by tribes that had also been responsible for the murder of the governor, Josiah Finley, in 1838. The colony would have no official leader again until 1844.

"Difficulties plagued the settlement," Sullivan wrote. "Its small size, lack of communication with other settlements, little support from the American colonization society and the Mississippi Society, lack of knowledge of the human and physical environment, and sporadic hostility from African neighbors hampered progress."

The majority of the immigrants were unskilled laborers, and most were illiterate. "Those who were literate and educated went into international trade and commerce," according to Joseph Guannu, who teaches at the University of Liberia in Monrovia and is a former ambassador to the United States. "Those who became affluent because their slave masters put something in their pockets—gave them money—took to trading with the states from which they came," he says. "Those who were illiterate and came with little or nothing, most of them took to agriculture—field Negroes, as Malcolm X referred to them." Their primary crops included cocoa, coffee, rice, cotton, sweet potatoes, cassava, collard greens, cabbage, eggplant, and okra.

The passengers aboard the ships that brought the Prospect Hill immigrants were a mixed lot. Some were literate, some were not, and some were farmers while others were trained in more specialized tasks. Hilpah Ross, at sixty, was the oldest aboard the *Laura*, while the youngest was an infant born on the voyage over. Among those who died while waiting to board the *Laura* in New Orleans were Frederick and Sillah Ross, whose five children made the passage without them. Mechia Ross, sixty-five, was the oldest passenger aboard the barque *Nehemiah Rich* when it set sail from New Orleans in early spring 1848 on a voyage that took sixty-four days. Accompanying her was her husband, Hannibal, sixty-two, and daughter Lucy, twenty-five, who died the following summer in Liberia, according to an ACS representative, Dr. J. W. Lugenbeel, who attended to the medical needs of the Mississippi colony. Among those who never saw Liberia was Grace Ross, who died aboard the *Laura* en route from New Orleans at age thirty-eight. Her husband and children safely completed the passage.

A few years after the *Nehemiah Rich* and the *Laura* arrived, the *Renown* brought seventy-three more immigrants from Mississippi, sixty-seven of whom were slaves emancipated by the Ross and Reed estates. The *Renown* actually did not make it all the way to Liberia, but wrecked off the coast of the Cape Verde Islands. All of the passengers survived and completed the voyage on another ship, but they lost their possessions. The next year, sixty-nine more of the Ross and Reed groups followed on the *Lime Rock*.

The majority of the Mississippi immigrants hailed from the Natchez District, which had the state's largest concentration of slaves. Although blacks were the majority in southwest Mississippi in the 1820 census, only about 450 of 33,000 were free, and in 1830 the district had thirty-four percent of the state's white population but 65 percent of its slaves. In 1840, the average percentage of enslaved people among the total population of the six Mississippi counties that sent emigrants to what would become Sinoe County was 76 percent.

The freed slaves from Prospect Hill were the largest group to emigrate, and from the surviving letters they mailed home it is evident that they remained cohesive despite dispersing to various sites throughout Mississippi in Africa.

In a February 16, 1853, letter to Catherine Wade, the wife of Isaac Ross Wade, one of the Prospect Hill immigrants, Granville Woodson, recalled setting sail from New Orleans on January 7, 1848, and landing at Monrovia on March 19, 1848. During a long delay in New Orleans, the group had been held in open quarters with no sanitation facilities, and among those waiting to board the *Nehemiah Rich*, sixteen had died of cholera there and three had succumbed to the disease en route to Liberia. There was a particularly deadly outbreak of cholera, a type of dysentery, in New Orleans the following year, which took an estimated 3,000 lives, including about twenty-five would-be emigrants from Prospect Hill waiting to board the *Laura*.

In May 1848, Sarah Jane Woodson, Granville Woodson's sister, wrote Catherine Wade from Greenville "to inform you of our safe arrival to our destination in Africa and to let you know that we had a long and tedious passage to Africa of some sixty some odd days and I can assure you that we experience a very severe gale wind in the passage." Echoing a sentiment expressed in most of the letters, Woodson wrote that the colonists needed many basic necessities that were not available in the new land.

"To your children remember my love to them and to all the Prospect Hill people and to all the Oak Hill people," she wrote. "I expect something from them when our people comes and tell our people to bring all their things when they comes out. The children is all going to school every day. Bring some seed of all kind with you and everything you possible can. Bring with you of your things, bring them for you will stand in need of them in this country." In particular, she advised the next immigrants to bring feather beds and not to spend their money on the way. "I am very sorry that I left my Bed," she wrote, "and there is no way to get another in this country." In closing, she wrote, "Daphne sends her love to her mother and all of her children. Jefferson Bolton's children say that they are not able to bring him but hopes that the exectors will open their hearts and send him out." Then, in a postscript she added, "Bring out some castor oil."

Another Prospect Hill immigrant, York Walker, wrote Isaac Ross Wade in April 1852 to say, "This is indeed a fine country for the coloured man but we have to live by the sweat of the brow for every thing is scarce and high, such as provisions, clothing, etc., and I stand in need of many things. . . . You would therefore Sir confer a great favor on your humble servant by sending a few articles. If you can make it convenient please to send me a Whip Saw and some clothes and a pair or two of shoes and any other things that you may think proper to send will be thankfully received by your Humble Servant."

Granville Woodson also wrote to request schoolbooks, and noted that his sister had written to "Mrs. C. Wade and have not received no answer yet. You must excuse my handwriting. I was in a hurry as the Liberia boat had just return from Cape Palmas on her way back to Monrovia and had about two miles to go down the river."

The letters offer ample evidence of the physical challenges that faced the settlers. By all accounts, as many as half of the settlers succumbed to fever and disease, often within the first year or two after they arrived.

In one letter, Sarah Woodson wrote, "The last people of our State who came out are a great many of them dead, they came here so worn down with hard usage, and disease, that almost the one half of them were carried off in the acclimating fever. Tell Rufus that Rachel send her love to him and says will please to tell him her father is dead, and all the family except three, that is Rachel, Linthy and Garth. Rachel says she is doing tolerable well, as well as she could expect, but is quite lowspirited."

Joseph Tellewoyan, who maintains a website on Liberian history, noted that there were extremely high mortality rates among all of the immigrants from the outset. Of eighty-six immigrants who arrived on one ship in 1820, only eight were still living in 1843; of thirty-three who arrived in 1822, only five; of 655 who arrived in 1832, only 229; and of 639 who arrived in 1833, only 171. "Visitors who arrived in Liberia during this period were astounded by the number of fresh graves they saw," Tellewoyan wrote.

Many of the immigrants remained in Monrovia only long enough to acclimatize, or to die. According to immigrant Augustus Washington, all of the settlers had to endure the raw ordeal of acclimatization while living in small huts crowded with people, many of whom had fever. In Liberia, he wrote, "Where one succeeds with nothing, twenty suffer and die, leaving no mark of their existence."

Problems with the management of the Mississippi colony only made matters worse. In an undated letter to the American colonization society, which Sullivan cited, an immigrant from South Carolina observed the travails suffered by recent arrivals, including his family and a group of Rosses, due to mismanagement and corruption among local officials: "I am writing to tell you of our bad accommodations," he began. "When we landed, we were put into a small house with a very sick man in it. Raining and it took a long time to get out the dirt. The roof leaked. I have 7 children and they only gave me one quarter of an acre of land and near a swamp . . . Judge Murray [a local representative of the ACS] only had 18 rooms for 180 people. It is a shame that the Ross people are made to suffer. Provisions are sold for cash and poor people suffer. And now Murray have sold out all our pork and butter we have not received any but twice since we been here and he also sell our flour to a Dutch Capt and a English Captain my wife was very sick and I sent to Murray wife to buy some butter and she sent me word that they don't sell but would give me a spoonful. He had butter but we could not get any at all."

The accounts of Liberian immigrants often stressed the crudity of native culture, which is typical of many colonial efforts, including America's, but in Liberia both the settlers and the indigenous groups were of the same race, which complicated matters. Despite the claims of its chief proponents, the colonization of Liberia was not about going "back" to Africa, because "home" for the slaves had been America. Some had been educated by their masters and brought with them a devout missionary zeal, and although the native tribes held many advantages, the settlers' trump card was their knowledge of American capitalism and the occasional backing of American military power.

Guannu says the history of the Mississippi colony and of Liberia as a whole is both a transplanted African-American story and an African experiment with Western culture. "Since they came from the Deep South they brought with them the dominant culture of that region," he says of the settlers. "And that culture very much influenced their relationships with the indigenous tribes. The settlers, who called themselves Americo-Liberians, sought to build a society that melded certain African traditions with aspects of the culture they had known as slaves."

Historian Mary Louise Clifford contended that neither side had a monopoly on hostility. "The Free Negroes who came from America did not regard the Africans as their brothers," she wrote. "They were not returning to their homeland, but rather had left their homeland across the Atlantic because it denied them opportunity . . . few of the American Negroes even knew from which part of Africa their ancestors had been taken. Most of their memories and associations drew upon the agrarian society of the young United States. In their eyes, everything attractive and desirable had belonged to the wealthy masters of the plantations on which they had labored.

"Now, suddenly, they were in the incredible position of having not only escaped their degradation—and it had taken enormous courage for them to leave all that was familiar behind in America—but of assuming for themselves the mantle of command and aristocracy in their new Republic."

The settlers, Clifford wrote, adopted the eighteenth-century puritanism of the American colonies and "cultivated an elaborate facade of formal clothing (frock coats and top hats), stilted language, and porticoed mansions—everything they associated with elegance and gentility—in order to emphasize the social difference between themselves and the African heathens."

The Kru, for their part, seem to have recognized the vulnerabilities of the Mississippi colony, and although some subgroups were friendly with the settlers, most sought to exploit those weaknesses. Kru dominance of trade also hindered the colony's commerce, Sullivan wrote, because the Krus preferred to interact directly with British traders, who often undercut the settlers. Liberian government efforts to blockade ports against British vessels were only partially successful, and some local ethnic groups responded with their own blockades between 1846 and 1850, aimed at thwarting trade between interior groups and the settlers, which led to three years of outright war. Only two years after the fighting ended, in 1855, other tribes began warring with the settlers of the Mississippi colony.

"Resentment over trade and the expansion of the settlers led to surprise attacks on the Sinoe River settlements," Sullivan wrote. "Settlers and Kru were killed, houses burned, and crops destroyed on both sides. With the aid of European ship captains, the Monrovia government intervened to defeat the attackers."

The destruction of the tribes' crops led to years of famine, which further embittered them. And, as Sullivan noted, "The attack reinforced a siege mentality of a small group of immigrants in a foreign environment. Their presence, expansion, and interference in trade had brought about a reaction which many would have expected and feared from their African neighbors. With the size of the settlements reduced to earlier numbers, the small band who remained became even more determined to survive and more committed to resist than to cooperate with their Kru neighbors."

Even with these setbacks, the struggling settlement continued to receive new immigrants, and over time some of its residents prospered. From 1838 to 1847, Sullivan wrote, "the Sinoe settlement grew in numbers, began agriculture for consumption and export, traded with African neighbors and European traders, and began to expand geographically."

By 1845, the population of Greenville, the capital of Mississippi in Africa, had grown from seventy-nine in 1843 to 240, and new settlements had sprung up in the surrounding countryside. The greatest growth would follow the establishment of Liberia as an independent republic—Africa's first—in 1847. During the next seven years, 1,402 settlers arrived in what was then known as Sinoe County, including the last of the Ross and Reed groups, although immigration would taper off after word reached the United States in 1854 about settlers being killed, houses burned, and crops destroyed during fighting with the tribes.

As the immigrants settled in, the tone of the letters to Prospect Hill became more upbeat. In April 1851, Granville Woodson wrote to say that although the immigrants had experienced "a little difficulty since the attack of the African fever I have enjoy good health so have father. Mother had several severe attack of defness complaints but now enjoying good health both of them send there love to you both hoping that your latter days may be more prosperous than your former has been." His mother, he noted, "says she hope that the children are good and smart active children as they were when she left them."

Sarah Woodson wrote Catherine Wade in April 1852 to express her concern that in her last letter she may have sounded disappointed in her new country. "But it is improving so fast, that I am becoming quite satisfied, and especially since I have got my health as well as I have, my health has improved very much lately, so much so, that if I only had a little more means to start with I should like Liberia very well." She marveled at the prolific growth of crops in Liberia, explaining there was no winter and that, "we have all got our own land and the most of us are living in our own houses." That in itself may have made the effort seem worthwhile. It seems likely, too, that the settlers wanted to put a positive spin on the colonial endeavor—to proclaim success.

On June 17, 1848, ACS correspondent R. E. Murray wrote from Greenville to give his report on the fledgling Mississippi colony and described the immigrants who had arrived aboard the *Nehemiah Rich* as "clearing off the land quite fast." He said he had received word from the Louisiana colonization society asking that immigrants from that state be settled on the opposite bank of the Sinoe River from the Mississippi settlement, which mimicked the geography of their home states in the United States, in reverse.

The land at that location, known as Blue Barre, had not yet been bought, however. This would have facilitated the removal of the area's unruly inhabitants, according to a subsequent report by Luganbeel, in which he lamented "the uncommon treachery, barbarity, and thievish propensity of the Blue Barre natives, who are pretty numerous, and who I know are generally a cruel, roguish set of unprincipalled desperadoes— much more so than the natives in the vicinity of any of the other settlements in Liberia." The Louisiana colony was eventually located a short distance upriver instead.

On July 18, 1848, Luganbeel reported from Greenville that most of the Mississippians had become "quite reconciled to the place; and some of them express themselves as not only perfectly satisfied with their new place of residence, but much pleased with the appearance of things in and about this little settlement. Since the date of my last letter to you, none of the immigrants by the *Nehemiah Rich* have died. Most of them have got pretty nearly through the acclimating process. Those of them who have pretty good constitutions have required very little medical attention, during the last two months. A few of them, whose systems had become considerably impaired, in one way or another, before they left the United States, are rather feeble; and I fear that I shall lose one or two more of the company, especially one of the men, who, as his relations inform me, had long been accustomed to the too free use of ardent spirits."

Among the Prospect Hill slaves who died, Lugenbeel wrote, one was "a poor skeleton of humanity; who had been a helpless idiot from infancy, the daughter of Hannibal Ross. Another was a delicate girl named Catherine Witherspoon, and another, a youth, named Riley Ross, both of whom, according to the statement of their parents, had always been sickly. The other four were small children, the oldest of whom was less than seven years. None of the adults have died, except the idiot woman."

The ever prudent Luganbeel stressed the immigrants' enthusiasm for the colony. "Indeed, I have sometimes been obliged to interpose my authority to prevent some of the men from exposing themselves so much by laboring in the rain, and some of them have suffered considerably in consequence of being exposed," he reported. Of one group of Mississippi settlers, he added, "Nearly all of these people have drawn land a little back from the Sinou river, about two miles from this place. The tract which the Ross people have, being separated from that of the Patterson and the Witherspoon people, by a small creek, the former tract being sufficiently commodious to accommodate all the remaining people. . . . The location of these people is decidedly preferable to Readsville; the land being perhaps equally arable, more elevated, and farther from the river, and not being liable to overflows."

By then some of the settlers had taken to planting cotton, and although the plant survived from year to year in the tropical climate without replanting, the crop never really caught on. The plantation system did, however, and once the settlers became established, many built massive houses reminiscent of plantations back home, staffed with servants from the native tribes.

Architecture was perhaps the most striking aspect of Liberian settler culture. The many grand houses lining Greenville's Mississippi Avenue were impressive monoliths in a land of mud and thatch huts, graced by stately colonnades, spacious rooms, and breezy verandas. As late as the 1980s, the mansions remained in the hands of the Americo aristocracy, and although most had by then been faced with zinc siding, their lineage was unmistakable. The fighting during the 1990s doomed most of these structures. The rebels, seeing in them the physical manifestation of more than a century of Americo rule, would set many afire, while others would be damaged beyond repair by rockets and mortars.

The replication of Greek Revival architecture was not the only aspect of Southern culture that the immigrants imposed on the colony. They also subjugated the underclass of native tribes whenever they had the opportunity, creating a dynamic reminiscent of their former master-slave roles. Traditionally, the descendants of Isaac Ross have claimed that many of the Prospect Hill immigrants enslaved the native tribes of Liberia, and put them to work on their plantations and in their homes. Although slavery had been practiced in Liberia even before the settlers arrived, and continued to crop up as late as the 1930s (some say it continues in isolated pockets today), Guannu argues that there is no evidence that "classical" slavery was ever commonly practiced in the colony. Instead, most settlers relied for labor upon apprentices or wards who were financially dependent upon them, he says.

According to Sullivan, many settlers had difficulty making ends meet after paying wages to indigenous workers. "African labor was available," she wrote, "but few could afford even the low wages necessary." Still, in 1846, one immigrant, Washington McDonough, reported that his father had "twenty-four or five bound boys" working on his farm, some of whom had been taken from a slave trader.

Letters compiled by historian Wilson Jeremiah Moses paint a complicated picture of the relationship that resulted between the settlers and indigenous tribes. In one, dated 1855, John H. Harris wrote, "I have seen barbarous cruelties inflicted upon the aborigines by the Americans; whether the crime justifies the act, I am not able to say; but there is the same relation existing with many, as there is in the South among master and slave. . . ." Harris recounted occasional humanitarian acts by the settlers, but conceded that a kind of forced servitude "that strongly resembles slavery was also practiced by native traders. . . . An interior head man, or petty king, will come to them for a trade; he may have some three or four boys with him, that he has either stolen on the path (for there are no roads), or else captured in war; these he leaves as security with them for the return of produce for the goods; the probability is he will never come back; therefore, they become theirs, to work, feed and clothe, as they see proper. This the law does not recognize as valid, yet it is tolerated, and hard is sometimes their lot; and with many of the colonists here, they think they are naturally and morally superior; as superior to the native as the master thinks he is to his slave in the States."

By law the Americos were required to apply to the courts before binding their apprentices, who were free to go upon reaching adulthood, but in practice the system often skirted the law and was ripe for abuse.

There was little agreement about the extent of Liberian slavery, or its nature, among opponents and supporters of colonization. In his treatise *Four Months in Liberia: Or, American Colonization Exposed*, published in 1855, William Nesbit asserted that slave ownership was almost universal among the colonists. Nesbit, who immigrated to Liberia from Pennsylvania only to return, disenchanted, wrote that among the colonists, "There is not one who does not own more or less slaves." He added, "The great majority of the present colonists are from the South, and have adopted southern habits, the state of society being more southern than anything else. For instance, all love to have a servant to wait upon them, both gentlemen and ladies. If it is but to carry a lantern, or to carry a fish, it must be done by a servant."

Nesbit went so far as to argue that conditions for slaves in Liberia were worse than in the United States, partly because everyone in the country suffered from deprivations, and the shortage of beasts of burden meant that slaves had to do all of the work on the plantations, including the plowing of fields and the hauling of crops. According to Nesbit, the slaves were always members of indigenous tribes who had been sold by their families, and as in the American South, occupied "small buildings near to their masters' residence, known as the 'negro quarters'."

Nesbit took great pains to paint a bleak picture of every aspect of life in Liberia, and was accused by his detractors of exaggerating and in some cases outright lying. There is evidence to support some of the accusations, as when Nesbit wrote that the entire colony was inundated by floods almost daily. He also struck a nerve when he contended that the colonists were doing the tribes a disservice by seeking to interrupt the foreign slave trade, writing that, "I would a thousand times rather be a slave in the United States than in Liberia."

Among letters from other visitors to Liberia that Nesbit cites to support his contentions, one correspondent noted that all work on the plantations was indeed done by natives, but differed with Nesbit by pointing out that the laborers earned twenty-five cents per day. This was corroborated by other observers cited by Harris, one of whom noted that settlers who performed the same labor were paid seventy-five cents per day. Nesbit also included in his book a rebuttal written by Samuel Williams, who lived (and remained) in Liberia. Regarding the prevalence of slavery, Williams wrote that "Nesbit lied in making this assertion. Upon the contrary, our laws make it a criminal act for any Liberian to receive a native in any way that he might be held as a slave. The Liberians cannot receive them as apprentices unless they take them before the proper court and have them bound as such, and every one, as soon as he or she is of man's or woman's age, can leave at will and go where they please."

There seems no question that the labor on the plantations was rigorous, and that growing enough food to eat was often more critical than raising crops for export. Although cotton was grown in the colony, Harris cites sources who indicate that the primary crops on the plantations were more likely to be food for personal consumption (especially rice) and coffee or sugarcane for sale. Fields were typically twenty acres or less, rotated annually because impenetrable bush vegetation rapidly reclaimed the land. In most cases, male workers cleared the brush and trees with homemade knives, machetes, and axes, then burned the debris before turning over the prepared land to women for planting and cultivation.

The letters from the Mississippi immigrants make no mention of slavery. Aside from occasional observations about life in Liberia, they are more often chatty, and are invariably familiar and friendly in tone, which seems to belie the reported enmity between the Prospect Hill slaves and Isaac Ross Wade, who had fought to block their emigration. Was it possible that the immigrants had maintained a sort of friendship with Wade under the circumstances? If Woodson could hope for "more prosperous days ahead" for Wade, it appears that not all of the Prospect Hill immigrants begrudged the heirs for attempting to thwart their freedom. Under the circumstances, it may have simply made good sense to maintain amiable relations with their former masters, who occasionally sent them supplies, and who alone could keep the lines of communication open between them and the slaves who remained behind.

For all his acrimony, it also appears that Wade felt some sense of responsibility toward the former slaves. He and his wife continued to correspond with them until the outbreak of the American Civil War, when mail service was interrupted by a Union blockade of Southern ports. Perhaps Wade did not hold them personally accountable for the alleged uprising, but the correspondence seems to support Tinker Miller's contention that there were mixed motivations on both sides of the story of Prospect Hill.

As letters between the two Mississippis began tapering off, immigrant Peter Ross resorted to writing to an ACS representative, Reverend R. R. Gurley, to ask what had become of the bequests that the slaves had been promised in Ross's will, and the money they had supposedly earned while they were technically free yet still being held at Prospect Hill.

After Gurley apparently replied that the money had been spent on court costs, Ross sounded disheartened, and betrayed.

"Consider one thing, My Dear Bro," he wrote. ". . . old Captain Ross Leaves one hundred thousand Dollers for his People Be Said Land, stocks, &tc., &tc. and then we can not Get Twenty five Dollars. We ear Glad for all the advize you Can Giv us but while we speak to you we feild that Africa, yea Liberia, is our home and we will not Give up. . . . Please Do not Denigh me. Please send me one of those Dubble Boil Gun. Please be so kind. . . ."

Following Peter Ross's death as a result of sunstroke, his son, George Jones, wrote Gurley on January 7, 1860, offering to send him coffee or limes, and to point out, notably, that his father had not actually been the son of Isaac Ross.

"I would hav say or said Sum thing to you befor now," he wrote, "but the old man he thought it was best not. The old man or my father Claim the name of Mr. Ross So that you may know that he was one of his people. Old Captain Ross was my father master and were not his father. . . . My father's father name was Mr. Jones. We are all Ross people but have our father title."

In one of her last letters, Sarah Woodson asked Catherine Wade to give her love "to all who enquire after me, and to all the children," and passed along greetings from Paschall, her husband, to "Master Isaac" and others, along with his request that Wade "will please send him a cane or something to help him along. . . . Give my love also to old Mistress, and her daughter Jane, and say to Jude and Sissy, that I thought they would have sent me something as I do have come to a new hard country."

Woodson expressed gratitude for the supplies Catherine Ross had sent her and regretted that she had been unable to return the favor with a shipment of oranges, because she had found none growing in the woods and was unable to come up with the money to buy any.

"I suppose I shall never see you all again in this life, but I hope to meet you all in the pleasant house of deliverance," she wrote. "Do please answer my letter."

The correspondence between the Prospect Hill immigrants and the Wades apparently did not resume after the Civil War, perhaps because the Wades were by then occupied with their own travails.

Liberian settlement also began to trail off during the Civil War in America, but immediately after, "worry among African Americans as to their physical safety in the south induced a new wave of immigration that extended from 1866 to 1872," according to John Singler's paper. During the period, 281 more immigrants arrived in Sinoe. The last large group, including thirty-eight people, arrived in 1888—coincidentally, the year Brazil outlawed slavery and began its own repatriation program in nearby Benin.

Maps of Liberia during the period offer ample evidence of the original settlers' places of origin. In addition to Mississippi and Louisiana, there were communities called Georgia, Virginia, Kentucky, and Maryland, some of which still exist today. All of the settlements were clustered along the coast, with the interior still the uncontested domain of the various ethnic groups.

The freed-slave immigrants who rose to power to rule over the culturally divided nation were generally lighter-skinned or mulattoes, and that continued to be the case well into the twentieth century. Guannu cautions not to put too fine a point on this fact where the descendants are concerned, however. The settlers were often at odds, or at war, with the native ethnic groups, but that did not stop them from intermarrying, he says.

"There was seldom marriage between a settler woman and an indigenous man. More of the reverse. But in that case all traces of the woman's former culture were obliterated. She was baptized and given rudimentary education. She lost all of her tribal identification and was completely assimilated into the Americo-Liberian value system."

Guannu says the settlers, who have been reviled and even tormented at various times in Liberia's more recent history, "were really, really courageous, which is why the conflict with the indigenous people went on for so long. They shared nothing in common but color. Here were people who came to live among people who had sold them, essentially. That was a big source of conflict." Until the coup of 1980, many Liberians took pride in being Americos, he says. "They identified with this because it was the elite class. Were you a Ross, a Roberts, you had ready access to education and very few restrictions. There was envy because of this, but only after 1980 did it become very pronounced. What it comes down to is access to power."

CHAPTER FIFTEEN

AN AMERICAN IN THE bar of Monrovia's Mamba Point Hotel is giving Monica Morris a hard time. The selection of take-out pizzas doesn't suit him, his order takes too long, the beer is not cold. He glares at Monica, who listens politely as she leans against the bar, but appears unperturbed. Then he adds, "You've got something on your lip."

"It's my lipstick," she says, in a dulcet voice.

I glance over and see that her lipstick is flecked with silver sparkles. She is not looking at him. She gazes out the window at the long boats sliding past, on their way to the harbor from distant fishing grounds, loaded to the water line with people and fish, flags flying.

The American grabs his pizza box and swaggers out the door. I am amazed by a lot that I see here, but this exchange is particularly surprising—this example of pettiness and arrogance in a world that is so profoundly distressed. There is a lot of pettiness and arrogance and distress going around, everywhere, really, but in a place like this it stands out in bold relief.

"Jerk," I say, after the man is gone.

Monica smiles serenely, and says, "So tell me why you come to Liberia."

It is not a question I expect people to ask at the Mamba Point Hotel, although it seems natural to want to know. Sitting in the lobby bar, watching the curious mix of people talking intently at individual tables or on sofas clustered in the corners, I find myself wanting to go from group to group asking the same question, partly because everyone seems intent on concealing their purpose for being here. The place

is exactly as Associated Press reporter Alex Zavis, who covers West
Africa from the Ivory Coast, had described it: something like Rick's
Bar in *Casablanca*, peopled by an odd mix of curious allies and potential enemies—European and North African businessmen, some of
whom are doubtless trading illicit diamonds or guns; a few foreign correspondents; the odd missionary; and a handful of well-heeled locals. I
do a quick survey of the room. Table 1: two young Frenchmen talking
to an African man. Table 2: two Arabs. Table 3: a dark, bearded man
with two women, one of whom is wearing a fanny pack and looks like
she is from the American Midwest. Table 4: two French businessmen.
Table 5: a woman in high-style African dress.

A lot of the men smoke cigars. A parrot on a perch on the balcony
squawks. Pink geckos sun themselves on the rail. An Indian family
passes through, then an Asian guy with a shaved head. I hear singing
from the ruined mansion next door—haunting songs that sound part
tribal, part gospel.

The decor is unintentional kitsch, with bad paintings, cheap African
crafts, an obnoxious Big Mouth Billy Bass, a sign pointing toward Ireland, 3,000 miles away and the homeland of the owner's wife. Zavis
said the Mamba Point serves as a rendezvous point for much of what
matters in Liberia today, yet it is almost surreal in its disengagement
from the rest of the country. There is no African food on the menu
because the hotel caters mostly to people who want to forget that they
are in Liberia. There are guards at the gate and the rooms are unimaginably expensive by Liberian standards, about $120 U.S. per night.
Still, it is an interesting retreat from the raucous, battle-weary streets
of Monrovia, and proves to be a good opportunity for networking. I
spend many evenings in the bar trying to figure out what is going on.

I tell Monica that I am searching for descendants of people who
came to Greenville, in Sinoe County, Liberia, from Mississippi, in the
United States.

"I'm from there," she says. "That's where my family comes from."

I realize that her last name is on my list of Mississippi families who
preceded the Prospect Hill immigrants to the colony. She smiles when
I mention it. "My mother knows all about it. My brother, too," she says,
but before I can ask more she sashays off to wait on a Frenchman who
has snapped his fingers for another beer.

Earlier, in the lobby, I had met a young artist selling watercolors of village scenes, whose name was Michael Mitchell. His surname was also on my list. When I asked about his family he said, "I'm from Sinoe." He knew little about their history other than that they came from a place called Mississippi.

Charlie Kollie, the bartender, laughs when I tell him that everyone who works at the hotel seems to be from Sinoe. "Not me," he says. "But I know the place well. Most of them, they were driven here by the war."

Charlie is of native descent. He grew up at Harbel, where Firestone operated the largest rubber plantation in the world from the 1920s until the war reached the area in the 1990s. The plantation became the scene of intense fighting and numerous detainments, executions, and atrocities, and was later used as a refugee camp. Charlie says he occasionally works at a hunting lodge run by California-based West African Safaris, which hosted big-game hunts near Sinoe's Sapo National Park until recently, when the tours were suspended. The safari company's owner, Tom Banks, told me over the phone before I traveled to Liberia that he was canceling the hunts due to the threat of economic sanctions by the United Nations. He then offered to make my reservations at the Mamba Point.

The debate over the sanctions, which were proposed as a way of forcing Liberian president Charles Taylor to end his involvement in neighboring Sierra Leone's civil war, contributes to my own feeling of uncertainty in Monrovia. In recent weeks the government has sponsored two protests against the sanctions proposal, and the U.S. State Department has warned of the potential for anti-American backlash should the measures be imposed. Charlie scoffs when I mention this.

"I don't know why Tom wants to scare Americans," he says, and laughs. He says he expects no trouble.

Charlie says the wildlife at Sapo actually flourished during the war because it drove people, including poachers, from the region. He has seen his share of wildlife, he says, including forest elephants, pygmy hippos, leopards, monkeys, tigers, duiker, parrots, and crocodiles— icons of Africa that I, for one, will not be seeing on this trip. It was in Sinoe, he recalls, that he learned one of the laws of the jungle: "If you see a tiger, you don't trouble him, he won't trouble you. But if you shoot at him and fail to kill him, he eat you up."

Charlie is interested in my story because he loves history, which he says is the subject he would have studied had he been able to go to college. He asks me the name of the family I am looking for and brightens when I answer.

"There is a Ross staying here in the hotel," he says. "An American. Nathan Ross." He picks up the phone and dials Ross's room, speaks to him for a moment, then hands me the phone. By a strange coincidence, it turns out that I have spoken with Nathan Ross before, by phone, in the United States, although at the time he did not seem inclined to talk. Now he agrees to meet me on the hotel terrace in the morning.

When I hang up, Charlie beams and says, "So, you're off to a good start." Charlie is the kind of person who makes you feel good about the world—any world, really, even this one.

I stroll onto the terrace to watch the sun set over the Atlantic. Boys are playing soccer on the beach with a ball fashioned from a tightly stuffed canvas bag. Children climb atop two statues of lions surmounting the grand staircase of the ruined mansion next door, where perhaps a score of families are encamped.

The mansion is one more indication that there is no such thing as an abandoned building in Monrovia. All over town, families squat in roofless buildings with blown-out windows and doors, the most dramatic being the marble ruins of the Masonic temple, situated on the heights overlooking the city, not far from Mamba Point. Gunfire, mortars, and scavengers have stripped away most of the temple's architectural adornments, which makes the massive, Greek Revival building even more darkly imposing. Children balancing five-gallon jugs of water on their heads scurry in and out while mothers prepare meals of rice and whatever else they can find on coal stoves, crouching under the shelter of tarps stretched between nails in the walls.

Meanwhile, in the bar at Mamba Point, CNN reports on Laura Bush's decision not to wear a hat to her husband's inauguration.

I hear someone ask, "Having any luck with your story?" and turn to see an Englishman whom I had met on the flight to Monrovia, who invites me to have dinner with him. He says he has come to Monrovia to set up "physical security" at a new bank, something he does in trouble spots all over the world—Lagos, Nigeria, most recently, and before that in Pakistan, Colombia, Tanzania, and Yemen. I ask how Liberia compares.

"It's dangerous if you go to the wrong place," he observes, "but then again, the same could be said of Plymouth." The problem, he says, is that in Liberia it is often hard to know if you're in the wrong place. There may be no clear answer to the question, "Is this dangerous?"

Before coming to Liberia I talked with everyone I could think of who might give me useful advice on dealing with the unstable regime, and pretty much everything I had heard was bad. In the newspaper, in magazines, and on the Internet were accounts of torture, cannibalism, and random violence committed by juveniles dressed in outrageous costumes—Batman masks, life preservers, or women's wigs—and armed with automatic weapons, often drunk, high, or drugged. Some observers reported that during the war packs of dogs fed on human corpses on the streets of Monrovia and were in turn killed and eaten by hungry refugees. I read that it is possible to buy, on the streets of Monrovia, a home video showing warlord Prince Johnson drinking Budweiser and singing gospel songs as he cut off the ears of President Doe, who was slowly executed. The accounts were too numerous to be discounted as inflammatory journalism.

Bewildered by what I had read, I had tracked down Alex Zavis, who told me that despite all the guns, she found the place surprisingly hospitable. "The people are incredibly warm, and as a woman traveling in Africa I actually feel less threat there than anywhere else," she said. Another journalist, Sebastian Junger, who has faced his share of danger in places like Afghanistan, Bosnia, and Sierra Leone, told me that the government in Liberia should be my main concern, because it is corrupt, violent, and ridden with factionalism.

Otherwise, much of what I had been told about Liberia before coming here has proved irrelevant, overstated, or simply off the mark. Liberia is not a country where you can easily assess the dangers and act accordingly. There is no going forth from and returning to a secure point. When you ride down streets teeming with former combatants, it doesn't matter if your fellow passengers in the cab are happily singing along to Celine Dion on the radio. Something virulent is in the air. You are in potential danger, and so are they, and everyone knows it. The potential for trouble can appear out of nowhere and dissipate just as mysteriously, like the gently rolling sea rising up, at the last instant, in a huge wave that thunders down upon the beach. Only in a place like Monrovia, where trucks loaded with soldiers are constantly speeding past, the streets are defiled by sewage, and the air is filled with the sounds of children singing, transistors blaring, horns honking, and men chanting angrily from within the prison walls, could the unexpected booming of a wave send a chill down your spine.

The government of Liberia, the very foundation of the society, is notoriously unpredictable, and although in general the people are remarkably genial, they live in the ruins of a nation where anything can happen, any time. Liberians have lived with social conflict and contradictions off and on for 160 years—and with the ever-present threat of danger and deprivation for the last two decades—but they are not used to it. They face threats from ethnic factions, the government, disease, starvation, former combatants, thieves, and overloaded, speeding log trucks. Yet, the Englishman points out, it is in many ways a safer place for visitors than hot spots elsewhere. Pointing to the white skin of his arm he says, "Sometimes this comes in handy."

I have to concede that this seems to be the case. Whatever unwelcome attention might be focused upon me, it will not likely be because I am white. Back in Mississippi, either despite or because of the high level of racial integration, resentment and hostility between the races are common, but I never sense it here. On the contrary, no matter how much I protest, I am repeatedly ushered to the front of lines. Children greet me politely on the street. The taxi driver calls me "sir." Edward Railey, my local guide, says this is partly because people interpret the appearance of a white person on the street as a positive sign. When things start looking bad, the white people vanish, so when they start trickling back in the assumption is that things are looking up.

Using that barometer, I reckon that the situation remains precarious. I will walk the streets for a week without passing another white person, although I find many inside walled compounds protected by razor wire, with guards stationed every hundred feet or so, and inside a few surprisingly well-stocked neighborhood grocery stores where few locals can afford to shop. These stores, almost all of which are owned and operated by Lebanese, are the exception to all the rules in Liberia, which include rigid physical boundaries between the wealthy and the impoverished. The Lebanese have been in Liberia for a long time, and constitute the closest thing the nation has to a middle class. They first came during their own diaspora in the late nineteenth century, which also took them up the Mississippi River in the United States, where they founded grocery stores in cities like Vicksburg and Natchez. The grocery stores of Monrovia are spotless, in stark contrast to the streets outside, and stocked with American food. In one, the cashier was a friendly young man wearing a Texas A&M T-shirt. Strolling the aisles of the store, it is almost possible to forget that you are in Liberia. There is an armed guard, but mostly he just holds the door for customers. No doubt the stores are vulnerable at night to thieves who are actually hungry, but I hear no reports of burglaries during the time I am here.

I occasionally see a few white faces staring balefully from behind the windows of air-conditioned Land Rovers. When I ask whites whom I meet why they don't venture into the streets, most say it is because their skin color readily identifies them as someone carrying a lot of cash. Credit cards are accepted nowhere, and simply by traveling to Liberia a visitor has clearly demonstrated his comparative wealth. Unemployment in Liberia hovers around 85 percent, and money changers on the street, many of whom are college graduates, will trade a grocery-size bag full of Liberian dollars for $100 U.S.

Sad stories, I find, are the real hard currency of Liberia. While there is less outright begging and hustling than a visitor encounters in most Third World countries, friendliness has its cost. Everyone seems intent on meeting you, and sooner or later, you will have an opportunity to help. They say hello, how are you doing, what's your name, where are you from, and slowly weave the details of their troubles into the conversation: the brother who is dangerously ill with malaria, with no money for medication and no public hospital to go to since the only one in the country closed a few weeks ago; the dead mother whose bereaved have no money to pay for her burial, who lies waiting, embalmed, in a funeral home where the air-conditioning is as erratic as the power supply; the boy helping his blind, half-crippled mother hobble down the street, who can't afford his next meal, much less a cane to prop her up on; the children selling candy or peanuts on the street to try to pay their way through elementary school. The list goes on and on. The presumption is that after you have heard the sad tale you will feel compelled to offer cash, and you often do. Each time I find myself mentally affixing a price tag to the story—$1, $5, $20. I have an over-whelming urge to save the world one Liberian at a time, because so lit-tle money can have such a profound effect, but by the time I realize that even selected needs are too great for one person, it is too late to turn back. Everyone, it seems, now knows my name and where I stay.

At one point a man shows up at my door at the Mamba Point saying he has traveled seventy-five miles through the bush "to meet the white man who loves to sponsor students to study in the States." I am mind-ful of my diminishing cash. I tell him that he has unfortunately received some bad information, give him $5, and send him on his way. I wonder how he managed to get past the guards.

The common apology offered by visitors for the poverty is that the people have never really known better, but Liberians actually have. As recently as the 1970s the economy was robust, partly because the country was relatively stable and partly due to a massive influx of U.S. aid.

The current lack of money has made it impossible for most Liberi-ans to rebuild their lives after two decades of devastating war and eco-nomic hardship, and there seems little hope for change on the horizon. What passes for an economy is really a type of large-scale, international looting. Malaysia's Oriental Timber Company is rapidly clear-cutting some of West Africa's last remaining virgin rain forests in Sinoe County; illicit brokers are moving tons of diamonds mined with slave labor in neighboring Sierra Leone to trade for East European arms; and someone—I could never determine who—is exporting shiploads of rubber from the former Firestone plantation, while Liberians travel in ramshackle taxis on dangerously bald tires. Schools have no books, pharmacies have no medicine, and the National Museum, which was looted three times during the fighting, has only a dozen or so items left from a collection that once numbered nearly 6,000. The commemora-tive park on Providence Island, where the first settlers arrived in the 1820s and where the Prospect Hill immigrants landed, lies in ruins.

Even businessmen who manage to get by reasonably well from legitimate income are aware that the situation in Liberia can deterio-rate further. At the American embassy, where I stop by to register, I wait to talk with the consul, Abbie Wheeler, as she is emphatically rejecting yet another request for a visa by a Liberian woman. An African-American businessman named James Roberts, who is staying in Monrovia, walks in, nervous. "Things are getting a little hairy now," he tells me. "The sanctions, and other things as well. I need to get on a list in case things change." When she finishes with the hapless visa applicant, Abbie Wheeler tells him that the embassy has "wardens" in each part of the city whose job it is to notify U.S. citizens if there is trouble. The last time the embassy had to evacuate American citizens, by helicopter, was in 1996. Satisfied, the businessman asks me what I am doing in Liberia. When I tell him, he offers a few contacts. "I live in Virginia, in the States," he says. "My ancestors came to Virginia, Liberia."

The embassy is a tantalizing piece of America dangling right before Liberia's eyes. It is not just a building, it is an entire, enclosed section of Monrovia, and the scenery there is by far the most striking in the city. The grounds, high above the ocean, are meticulously landscaped and make a dizzying, dreamlike descent through palms toward the crashing surf, compromised only by a white-painted wall topped with razor wire, which means that you can't get to the beach, and more importantly, that anyone on the beach can't get to you.

Most everyone I meet at the embassy lives and works there. Their children go to school there. Aside from intelligence about the political situation, few have much firsthand knowledge about Liberia. No one, not even an American citizen, is allowed to loiter on the street outside the compound, where guards are stationed every hundred feet or so, all of them comparatively lucky Liberians. If there is trouble in Monrovia, anyone who has half a chance of gaining entry will rush to the embassy compound, and the guards won't likely be among those left outside. The American embassy's reputation is such that several British citizens tell me they go there when they feel threatened rather than to their own embassy.

On designated days there is always a line of people waiting at the consulate gate to apply for visas. For them the embassy represents a kind of earthly pearly gates, and playing the role of St. Peter is the officious, highly skeptical consul, Abbie Wheeler. During each of my visits to the consulate, I observe her emphatically denying visas to a steady stream of unhappy Liberians at the window. It seems the whole country wants to go to the United States, and judging from the handful of exchanges I overhear, some will do anything to reach their goal. I listen to the consul chastise a woman for apparently falsifying documents, because there are notable discrepancies between some of her forms.

In such an environment a man like Nathan Ross, who managed to emigrate in the 1980s to the United States and develop a successful business there, is considered very lucky. Nathan's father, a member of the Liberian Congress when Samuel Doe ascended to power in 1980, escaped the resulting mass executions of Americo leaders by seeking political asylum in the United States, and he now lives in a suburb of Washington, D.C.

I am watching the long boats of the Krus depart from the harbor for another long day of fishing when Nathan appears at my table on the terrace at the Mamba Point. He is dressed in a tailored suit, open collared shirt, and black fedora. He looks splendid. He is in Liberia doing telecommunications work, he says, but before I can ask what the work entails, his satellite phone, the first I have seen in Liberia, rings. He talks for a few minutes, then stands up, clicks off the phone, and returns it to his pocket. "I'm on my way to Abidjan," he says. "Have you talked with my brother Benjamin Ross?"

I tell him that I have talked with no Rosses yet, and in fact have no names of Ross family members in Liberia.

"Perhaps you can talk with Benjamin," he says. "He works at Central Bank, here in Monrovia. A lot of the people you're looking for are here in Monrovia."

He says he is expecting a vote on the UN sanctions any day now, and apologizes for not having longer to chat. With that, he picks up his briefcase, says, "Have a safe trip, and good luck," and hurries on his way.

CHAPTER SIXTEEN

OUT OF A POPULATION of just over 3 million, only about 5 percent trace their ancestry to the United States, yet from all appearances in Monrovia, this is a nation of America-philes. On the streets I see "USA" T-shirts, American flag decals on cars, even a "Proud to Be an American" bumper sticker on the back of a pickup truck. On the radio I hear an ad for Showbiz Ladies Boutique announcing a new shipment of "American fashions." Despite its uneven record in supporting Liberia during its moments of crisis, America represents the promise of a better life. Everyone knows someone who has emigrated or otherwise benefited from knowing someone there.

Sometimes the associations border on the bizarre. The Liberian government, while making claims that America is conspiring against President Charles Taylor, markets coins on U.S. TV, minted in Liberia, commemorating U.S. president John F. Kennedy and Confederate General Robert E. Lee. Kennedy is popular for his support of civil rights, while Lee is revered because he freed most of his slaves before the Civil War and paid the expenses of those who wanted to emigrate. (There is a catch to the coins, however: the $10 Lee coins are sold for $10 U.S. but are valued at $10 Liberian, which equals about twenty-five cents U.S.)

Whatever affinity the average Liberian may feel with the United States, it is not generally shared on the other side of the Atlantic. News of Liberia's seemingly endless travails rarely garners more than brief mention in the American media. Americans may have founded Liberia, but according to John Singler, the colonial effort was essentially "an American solution to an American problem," and subsequent

American policy toward the nation has never been cohesive or pre-dictable. Instead, that policy has been characterized by long periods of disinterest and then sudden and significant intervention.

After the colonial era, and prior to 1980, the most vulnerable period in Liberia's history was between the 1870s and the 1920s, when renewed hostilities between the settlers and the tribes coincided with disputes with Great Britain, which had claimed Liberian territory to the west for Sierra Leone, and France, which had claimed Liberian territory to the east for the Ivory Coast. At the time, Liberia was in many ways teetering as a nation. There was even talk in Britain of mak-ing it a British protectorate, to ensure reliable trade. The Kru revolts were ultimately defeated in 1920 with the help of the U.S. military and U.S. economic aid, and the boundary disputes were eventually settled, but by then Liberia's national debt had become unmanageable and its economy had stagnated. In response, the Firestone Rubber Company moved in to take over the nation's rubber production in 1926, and two years later, the Firestone Plantations Company negotiated a ninety-nine-year lease on up to one million acres of Liberian land at six cents per acre.

The 1920s ushered in a period of reassessment of Liberia's cultural and political identity, bringing the first tentative efforts to assimilate the indigenous tribes into the political system. The Liberian govern-ment also found itself for the first time coming down on the opposite side of the debate over repatriation of African-Americans. According to Joseph Guannu, the historian at the University of Liberia, the gov-ernment chose to distance itself from what was known as the "Back to Africa" movement, sponsored by the Harlem-based Universal Negro Improvement Association. The movement, led by Jamaican immigrant Marcus Garvey and lauded by certain conservative whites in the Amer-ican South, posed a potential embarrassment to the U.S. government, according to the Liberian government's reasoning at the time, and the country could ill afford to alienate its largest potential benefactor. More importantly, Guannu says, "The feeling was, it was time to forget the plantation, to recognize that you are an African. Then came the crisis of Fernando Po, when it came to light that the government was using indigenous tribes for forced labor, and the whole world began to criticize Liberia, saying, essentially, 'Coming from slavery, and you enslaved your own.' So people began to identify more with the indigenous people."

The crisis stemmed from a 1930 League of Nations report that alleged that the Liberian government was involved in the sale of gangs of tribesmen to work on coffee plantations on the small, Spanish-held island of Fernando Po. The *Report of the International Commission of Enquiry into the Existence of Slavery and Forced Labour in the Republic of Liberia* claimed that high government officials who were primarily Americo profited from the trade and allowed the pawning of tribal family members as security for personal debts. It concluded that "although classical slavery carrying the idea of slave-markets and slave-dealers no longer exists as such in the Republic of Liberia, there are cases of inter- and intratribal domestic slavery and cases of the pawn system. . . . In one region unhappy wretches are forced to swim from the harbour to a vessel anchored in the open sea, carrying hundredweights of goods of heavy luggage on their backs." Estimates of the number of people in forced servitude in Liberia at the time went as high as 400,000. Forced servitude was used primarily to provide contract labor for road-building, the cultivation of private plantations, and work in Fernando Po.

Among the key figures in the labor controversy was Samuel Ross of Greenville, who is said to have been a native of Georgia, in the United States, and not, apparently, among the Rosses who immigrated from Prospect Hill. "Forcible recruiting and shipment of native labour to Fernando Po from the County of Sinoe, with the aid of Frontier Force soldiers, armed messengers and certain Liberian government officials proceeded under Samuel Ross of Greenville as late as 1928, when he was appointed Postmaster General of Liberia," the League of Nations report noted, adding that even after Ross was transferred to Monrovia he continued to recruit forced labor in Montserrado County. The report alleged that between August 1 and September 21, 1927, soldiers aided in the capture of "a large number of natives to deliver to Ross in Greenville," who were carried across the Sinoe River to a special compound in Louisiana and shipped off to Fernando Po aboard the SS *San Carlos.* "The impression current was that Ross had powerful influences behind him in Monrovia, and any influence would be politically unwise. David Ross, adopted son of Sam Ross, testified that he and another young man carried gin, tobacco, and rice to Firestone Plantation Number 7 'to attract boys for Mr. Ross. . . . For the 4 shillings given, one native policeman sent his brother to Mr. Ross.'"

A town chief testified, "We must give twenty labourers. If you do not agree, they fine you. My two children, I pawned them."

Although there were discussions of indictments, including of Samuel Ross, none were handed down. The League of Nations' follow-up 1931 report described Liberia as "a Republic of 12,000 citizens with 1,000,000 subjects" and included a letter to a Liberian financial advisor from American Lester Walton, who had been appointed to what was then known as the "Negro post" at the American embassy, in which he wrote, "Forced labor, vicious exploitation of the natives by the Frontier Force, unjust and excessive fines are some of the contributory factors to occasion resentment and dissatisfaction, impelling many natives to reluctantly settle in Sierra Leone."

Following the release of the second report, Liberia's president and vice president resigned.

Slavery has existed throughout Africa's recorded history, and still has not entirely passed from the scene. The nation of Mauritania only outlawed slavery in 1980, and some say the law only moved slave sales from public markets to private homes. In an August 2000 article in *Vanity Fair*, Sebastian Junger noted allegations of widespread forced labor in the diamond mines of neighboring Sierra Leone, and a March 1999 lawsuit filed by the governments of four Liberian counties sought damages against the Catholic Justice and Peace Commission and another human rights group, called Focus, for alleging that slavery still exists in southeastern Liberia, including what was once Mississippi in Africa. The suits, filed by the governments of Sinoe, Maryland, Grand Kru, and Bong counties, charged that the allegations "gave a wrong impression to the international community and made it difficult for the counties to obtain international aid."

Many Liberian households today have "foster nieces" and "foster nephews," sometimes known as "wards," who are basically indentured servants working for room and board. Although critics say the system is an extension of slavery, its defenders claim it is motivated by charity and enables people who are comparatively well-off to improve the quality of life of people who have, essentially, nothing. At one home I visit outside of Monrovia, I notice a teenaged boy and girl who had been left out of the family's introductions, and when I later ask who they are, the family members exchange a curious glance.

"Are they part of the family?" I ask.

"Yes," one of them replies, then adds, "We got them far into the bush. They're like a part of the family."

Such wards are free to go once they reach adulthood, but their willingness to depart is sometimes governed by their financial status, and the oft-repeated refrain "they're better off this way"—sounds dangerously close to some white Southerners' apology for slavery. One need look no further than the sharecropping system of the Jim Crow American South after the Civil War to see that poverty can suffice where a method of coercion does not exist. And there is no guarantee that the wards will be educated in every household, as are the two in this particular family.

Still, the boy, who washes clothes in tubs while my host family and I have lunch, and later eats the scraps from our plates, seems as healthy, well-adjusted, and independent as any sixteen-year-old when he runs off to play soccer with his friends. The girl behaves more like a best friend to the daughter of the family, and cheerfully presents both cheeks for a kiss as we say our good-byes.

Before traveling to Liberia, I had met a woman who once worked in the Peace Corps in Africa, who said she had chosen to say nothing when she visited a friend's home and found children "who were a lot like slaves working there. It's the way things are done there, and who was I to say it was wrong?" she asked.

Such conundrums and disquieting scenes appear at every turn in Liberia, and it is often hard to know how to interpret or react to them. Watching the wards playing in the yard, it occurs to me that some of the myths I attribute to the traditional apologies for slavery may have been based upon truths that were misinterpreted for the slaveholders' gain. One of the more pervasive of those myths is the happy slave singing in the field, which is easy enough to dismiss as a racist idea. Yet, seeing so many hopeful—even joyful—people on the streets of Monrovia, where most lack basic necessities, I find myself wondering if it is simply human nature to maintain hope under unimaginably adverse conditions. I have never heard so much singing, whether in church, at school, in the cab, or on the street, anywhere else that I have traveled.

Liberia's ethnic and cultural mix was forever altered by the arrival of the U.S. military during World War II, which began what was arguably the most intense period of American involvement in the nation's affairs since the days of colonization.

Liberia initially remained neutral during World War II, but after German U-boats began sinking British ships in the nearby coastal waters, the government granted the United States a seaplane base and space for an airport near Monrovia, which later became Roberts Field. U.S. Secretary of State Cordell Hull wrote in a memo to President Roosevelt on September 14, 1943: "Our relations with Liberia from a strategic point of view have never been of more importance . . . as a result of the war, Liberian economy has been oriented almost entirely to the United States." Thousands of indigenous people flocked from the interior bush to the Americo-dominated coast to seek work with the military's massive construction projects. These included the airport, which was also used to support the Allies' North Africa campaign, as well as a network of roads and bridges and a new harbor in Monrovia, the latter of which was the base for a new trading concern known as the Mississippi Shipping Company. Most of those who left the bush never went back, which set the stage for lasting demographic change. No longer was Liberia as clearly divided, geographically, into different domains.

"Beginning in the 1950s, there was a struggle for African independence, and new interest in African identity," Guannu says. "There was a feeling in Liberia that it was time to reduce the cultural association with America. But in Liberia, even now, those who have settler blood in their veins still take pride in being described as settlers, while in America, only ten percent will accept that their ancestors were slaves. To some extent it's still a privileged class here, but not in America."

After World War II and throughout the Cold War, the United States continued to provide economic aid while using Liberia as a base for its covert intelligence operations in Africa. Among the recipients of the largesse was brutal, anti-Americo president Samuel Doe.

The U.S. government's stance toward Doe exemplifies its schizophrenic policy in Liberia. The old True Whig party government had been founded by a mulatto Americo elite and had ruled the nation since 1870 on behalf of the freed slaves and their descendants, who represented a small minority, at the expense of the descendants of indigenous tribes. Doe's overthrow of President Tolbert and the old-guard True Whig government in 1980 signaled the end of Americo power. Tolbert, who had served as vice president for nineteen years alongside President William Tubman before being elected president himself, had proved unable to find a middle ground between the Americo oligarchy and the increasingly dissatisfied indigenous tribes, who had seen colonial powers elsewhere in Africa overthrown in recent decades. Tolbert's effort to maintain Americo support and placate various ethnic groups led him to seek educational and economic assistance from nations such as Cuba and the Soviet Union, which did not sit well with the U.S. government. Although Doe was the enemy of the descendants of freed American slaves, the Reagan administration rewarded the new government with $400 million in economic aid, including $50 million for the military, which in many cases was used against the Americos. The U.S. government initially supported Doe due to concerns that communism would otherwise gain a foothold in Liberia, as was threatening to happen in other African nations such as Namibia and Angola.

The coup came as a surprise to many in the West, because Liberia had long been seen as a source of stability in West Africa, but in hindsight, the nation was a powder keg waiting to go off. Simmering unrest over the second-class status of indigenous ethnic groups for 150 years finally boiled over when the government proposed raising the price of rice during a particularly trying time for the poor.

"When the explosion came, it was violent, and it revealed the almost uncontrollable rage felt by the country's majority," journalist Sanford Ungar wrote in *The Atlantic* magazine. "The angry band of soldiers broke into the executive mansion, rushed upstairs, and surprised Tolbert in his luxurious quarters. They shot and killed the President, disemboweled him, stuck a bayonet through his head, and tossed his body into a mass grave.

"Ten days later, in a ceremony recorded by television and still cameras, the army took thirteen of the wealthy Americo-Liberian officials who had been arrested . . . marched them nearly naked through the streets of Monrovia, to ensure that they lost their dignity, tied them to seaside posts at the Barclay Training Centre, and executed them at point-blank range. A crowd of thousands cheered, and by all accounts there was jubilation throughout the country."

Other accounts described a frenzy of rapes, floggings, imprisonments without trial, castrations, dismemberments, executions, and mutilations of corpses following Doe's takeover. The victims were at first primarily Americos, but grew to encompass others who were simply weak or who posed potential opposition. During the ensuing crucible, *The New York Times* reported that Doe's militia arrived in the picturesque fishing village of Marshall, Liberia, and "quickly rounded up all of the Ghanian refugees they could find, marching them off together with Liberian friends and sympathizers for execution. In the massacre that ensued, perhaps 1,000 people were shot to death. Survivors say that children were swung by their feet by laughing soldiers as their heads were smashed against palm trees. Many say they can still hear the screams of the countless others who drowned as they attempted to swim across a river for the safety of a nearby island."

Alton Johnson, who later immigrated to America's Mississippi, where he teaches at Alcorn State University, was a college sophomore in Monrovia when Tolbert was executed, and remembers the night well. He was on the campus of the University of Liberia when shots rang out in the nearby executive mansion and a wounded man came running onto the campus.

"He was a Caucasian fellow," Alton recalled during a phone conversation back in America's Mississippi. "I personally helped him into a vehicle to go to the hospital. He was shot in the stomach." There would be much debate after that night about what had happened at the executive mansion, but the consensus, Alton said, is that the American embassy was directing the coup. "When you look at the executive mansion, there was something mysterious about it," he said. "To go into that building to kill the president—no Liberian could have done that on his own. The U.S.A. is not clean on that one."

Why would the United States assist in the overthrow of the Americo regime? Alton takes a cynical view, arguing that, "The United States has never supported highly educated people in Africa because they feel these educated people will not be puppets for them." He believes the United States was operating on its own agenda in allowing

Tolbert's overthrow, and later the overthrow of his successor, Doe, by Charles Taylor. In his view, the relationships of the various leaders toward the descendants of the freed slaves who colonized Liberia proved incidental to U.S. policy, and the U.S. government's current anti-Liberia stance is rooted in the same self-interest. "America founded Liberia, but they have been very much hypocritical toward the sons and daughters of the freed slaves who went over there," he said.

Until the September 11 attacks exposed the terrifyingly high stakes of foreign policy, diplomatic dallying by the U.S. government rarely registered on the radar of most Americans, but it has had profound effects in Liberia. As Alton sees it, when Tolbert sought to overcome a legacy of poverty by improving Liberians' access to foreign education, he found himself largely shut out of American colleges and universities. In response, he turned to nations with whom the United States was unfriendly at the time.

"Tolbert was looking for schools to send Liberians to get an education—in veterinary medicine, in medicine, in engineering—and he found that the United States does not take people from just any country," he said. "So what Tolbert did was to find Eastern European countries like the Soviet Union, Romania, Bulgaria, to send a lot of Liberians on scholarship. That did not go over well with the U.S. government. It was not that he was a Communist or a Marxist, but Liberia needed help. Those countries had something to offer. China opened their hands to us for development. The U.S. didn't like that at all."

Today, long after Tolbert's fall, there is still evidence of international aid for Liberia. The parking lot of the war-ravaged University of Liberia is filled with vehicles donated by the United Nations, Japan, and the People's Republic of China, but none from the United States. A Libyan firm, meanwhile, has announced a $20 million renovation of the empty Hotel Ducor Intercontinental in Monrovia.

It is hard to know how much credence to place in allegations of U.S. involvement in the 1980 coup, particularly because there is a lot of wild speculation about the time and about the civil wars of the 1990s. Many Liberians, after all, believed that the warlord known as General Butt Naked could fire bullets from his anus. Still, it is impossible to entirely discount the role of the U.S. government, because it is well-known that the CIA was very active in Africa at the time. For

Alton, seeing the wounded American fleeing the mansion that night told him all he needed to know. Five years later some of his family members were executed by the Doe regime and, he claimed, "all were betrayed by the U.S. government."

Alton believes that the United States concluded that Doe was unmanageable and so shifted its support to Taylor. When Taylor turned out to be intractable—he has since been accused of fomenting wars with and within neighboring nations and of his own human rights abuses within Liberia—he, too, fell from grace.

Taylor is unique among Liberia's leaders in that he is a descendant of both slave immigrants and indigenous groups, and that, from all appearances, he has been both attracted to and repulsed by the United States. Born in Arthington, Liberia, near Monrovia, to an Americo father and a mother of the Gola tribe, he enjoyed a comparatively privileged upbringing due to the family's Americo ties. He was sent to private preparatory schools (although he was ultimately expelled), and in 1972, at age twenty-four, received a student visa to the United States. He moved to Rhode Island and Massachusetts, ostensibly because he was interested in the region that had been the point of departure for so many of Liberia's immigrants, and enrolled at Chamberlayne Junior College. He eventually transferred to Bentley College, where he received a degree in economics in 1977. Whether he felt antipathy toward the ruling regime in Liberia before moving to the United States is unclear, but after graduating from college he remained in Boston and became an outspoken opponent of Liberia's President Tolbert. He was elected chair of an opposition group called the Union of Liberian Associations, which staged a protest outside the Liberian mission in New York City when Tolbert visited in 1979. Tolbert responded by challenging Taylor to a debate, after which Taylor declared himself the winner and announced that he was taking over the mission. Although he was arrested, Tolbert refused to press charges. Instead, Tolbert invited Taylor and a group of his compatriots to Liberia, with all expenses paid, in the spring of 1980, hoping to win them over. As it turned out, the timing of the trip was fateful. In April 1980, soon after Taylor's group arrived, Tolbert was overthrown and murdered by the forces of Samuel Doe. Sensing an opportunity, Taylor worked his way into Doe's confidence and was appointed head of the nation's purchasing agency, serving in that capacity for three years, until he was accused of approving the transfer of $900,000 to an apparently bogus company based in New Jersey.

After investigators in Liberia found that the money had actually been deposited in Taylor's own U.S. bank account, he was removed from his post and he fled back to Boston. The Liberian government then issued a warrant for his arrest on embezzlement charges, and in May 1984 federal agents arrested Taylor. He spent sixteen months in a Massachusetts prison before escaping with four other inmates, all of whom, except him, were eventually recaptured. Rumors later flew that the U.S. government had been less than zealous in its effort to track Taylor down, and he vanished. By most accounts he fled to Libya, where he was given sanctuary by Muammar Qaddafi, and where he set about planning his own Liberian coup. On Christmas Eve 1989, he resurfaced in Liberia with a force of several hundred men who called themselves the National Patriotic Front of Liberia. He had cultivated a rogue's gallery of allies, and joined forces with warlord Prince Johnson to attack Doe's army. The fighting, which swept the country before closing in on Monrovia, resulted in a bloodbath. In one of the most horrific acts, in July 1990, Doe forces shot and killed 600 and wounded 150 refugees being fed in a Lutheran church in Monrovia. Later that year Prince Johnson executed Doe, and in 1992, Taylor launched his own offensive to take Monrovia, which pitted him against his former ally. Johnson surrendered his command to peacekeepers a few months later and was exiled to Nigeria as the United Nations sought to reimpose order on Liberia. The shaky disarmament process that followed broke down after other factional militias began to proliferate.

The U.S. State Department responded to the increasingly unstable circumstances by advising Americans to depart Liberia immediately, and in the early morning hours of October 29, 1992, forces of the National Patriotic Front of Liberia fired three artillery or mortar rounds that struck or passed close to the U.S. embassy compound on Mamba Point, according to a U.S. State Department dispatch. The following June, 600 civilians were massacred at the former Firestone plantation in one of many such atrocities committed by rival warlords. Later that year, hundreds of civilians were allegedly beheaded. By then, hundreds of thousands of Liberians had been killed or had fled the country.

By 1994, *The New York Times* reported, Liberia had "come to bear little resemblance to a modern state, becoming instead a tribal caldron governed less by commonly understood rules than at any time since it became Africa's first republic in 1847 under freed American slaves." The newspaper quoted Amos Sawyer, Liberia's interim president from 1990 to 1994, saying, "'If we don't arrest the situation quickly, we will soon be back to where we were at the end of the nineteenth century, when this country was a stage for roving tribal gangs that fought back and forth for territory.' Others say the country has already deteriorated to that point."

In April 1996, Liberian forces again fired upon the American embassy, and a flotilla of five U.S. ships manned by 1,800 marines soon arrived off the coast of Monrovia. Navy Seals and Green Berets were sent to the embassy to evacuate hundreds of Americans and more fortunate Liberians and other foreign nationals by helicopter to Sierra Leone. The evacuees dodged bullets to reach the helicopters while the stench of rotting bodies filled the air. Some Americans remained trapped outside the embassy compound. One Liberian who was left behind recounted watching Taylor's security forces murder his brother, cut out his heart, fry it in a pan in palm oil, and eat it. Most of the refugees watched helplessly as the U.S. helicopters flew off overhead.

After the civil war subsided, in 1997, Taylor was elected president by a landslide, some say due to fears that if he were defeated he would make the country ungovernable. Such was the fear of a return to fighting that the common refrain prior to Taylor's election was, "You killed my Ma, you killed my Pa. I will vote for you."

By all accounts, Taylor has since grown extremely wealthy through the exploitation of Liberia's gold, diamonds, oil, iron ore, timber, and rubber resources, even as the quality of life of the average citizen has spiraled downward. Because his overthrow of Doe coincided with the collapse of the Soviet Union, Liberia no longer held much strategic importance for the United States. When American aid was subsequently cut off, Taylor's looting of Liberia's natural resources in exchange for East European arms began—an effort that is now part of the focus of the UN sanctions debate.

Not surprisingly, Taylor has been unable to generate diplomatic support in Washington, and instead has cultivated some very dangerous allies elsewhere, including, by numerous accounts, the terrorist network al Qaeda. He also has allegedly sought to destabilize his neighbors, arming rebels in neighboring Sierra Leone, engaging in border clashes with Guinea, and supporting a failed coup in the Ivory Coast which later erupted into civil war. By March 2003 the war in the Ivory Coast had resulted in the deaths of more than 3,000 and displaced more than one million people, and it was happening simultaneously with a new outbreak of fighting by rebels in adjacent regions of Liberia.

Journalist Tom Kamara, writing in the Liberian expat journal *The Perspective*, published in Smyrna, Georgia, attributed Liberia's current turmoil to its "culture of crime," and what he saw as a related trend, that the "centuries old tradition of accepting authority and wisdom of an elder's verdict, has been replaced with the 'wisdom' and authority of armed and drugged rebels. . . ."

"The worst disaster for Sierra Leone came when the neighboring state of Liberia was transformed from a symbolic one-party state into an essentially criminal polity," Kamara wrote. The diamond trade brought "a world of shadowy South African, Israeli, and Ukrainian businessmen" and "eastern European weapons bought with the proceeds from the sale of illicit gems." Taylor's associates, Kamara alleged, ferried out suitcases full of rough Sierra Leonean gems on presidential trips overseas, aboard jets loaned by Libya's Muammar Qaddafi. "Middlemen deliver the stones to the traditional diamond capital of Antwerp in Belgium, and increasingly to Tel Aviv where they are cut, polished and sold," he claimed. Kamara also accused Taylor of "brutal tactics of using drugged children as soldiers, terrorizing civilians, financing the war by exploiting diamonds and kidnaping peacekeepers."

There is evidence to support some of Kamara's allegations. In 1999, Liberia exported $300 million worth of diamonds, although the country is said to have a maximum mining capacity of about $10 million per year. The bulk of the diamonds were believed to be coming from Sierra Leone, whose "blood diamond" exports had been banned by international merchants due to charges that the gems were mined with slave labor, and the revenues used to fund military groups responsible for the upheaval in the region.

Since December 1999, the Association of Liberian Journalists in the Americas has sought a UN war crimes tribunal for Liberia, citing similar tribunals following revelations of war crimes in Nazi Germany, in the former Yugoslavia, and in Rwanda. Lamenting what it character- ized as international complacency, the association has sought to bring international scrutiny to such crimes as the execution of leading oppo- sition leader Samuel Dokie along with his family and bodyguard unit; the attack upon the Monrovia church in which hundreds of people, including women and children, were killed; the disappearances of dissidents and the murders of ordinary citizens, some for affronts as simple as overtaking or passing official vehicles; and the continuing harassment of both foreign and domestic journalists by the Taylor regime.

The media has been a particular target of Taylor's in recent years. In March 2000, the U.S. government officially protested the Liberian government's closure of two independent news radio stations, Star and Veritas, supposedly because they posed a security threat. Star was run by a Switzerland-based, nongovernmental organization that estab- lishes radio stations in post-conflict countries, and although its short- wave radio frequency had been withdrawn in 1998, and the Veritas headquarters had been burned during clashes in Monrovia in 1996, both stations had continued to transmit until the government shut- down.

By summer 2000, when I began making plans to travel to Liberia, the situation seemed to have stabilized, and although a travel advisory remained in effect for U.S. citizens, the American embassy was again at full staff. Then, in August, a British film crew was arrested and charged with spying. The crew had been working on a documentary about Liberia for Britain's Channel Four network, and had briefed Liberian government officials on the nature of the documentary before being given permission to conduct filmed interviews. Their tim- ing turned out to be particularly bad, as Liberia was under increasing international pressure for its involvement in the diamonds-for-arms trade. The members of the film crew, Britons Davie Barrie and Zimbabwean-born Timothy Lambon, South African Guglakhe Radebe and Sierra Leonean Samoura Sorious, were held in solitary confine- ment in Monrovia, where they faced the prospects of prolonged imprisonment and possible execution. The elder South African states- man Nelson Mandela and America's Jesse Jackson successfully lobbied Taylor for the journalists' release, but not before the crew was repeatedly threatened with mutilation and death. *The Perspective* reported that Taylor had publicly stated that the film crew had planned to poison him with a camera that he said would have caused him to develop cancer within weeks of the crew's departure. He also claimed Americans were involved in plots to assassinate him.

The next month, former U.S. president Jimmy Carter shut down his Carter Center in Monrovia, saying that "prevailing conditions and the actions of the government have made it increasingly difficult for the Center . . . to be effective in supporting democracy, human rights and the rule of law." In a letter to President Taylor, Carter cited human rights abuses and intimidation of journalists as part of the reason for the closure.

During all of this, refugees continued to stream out of Liberia, and many have ended up, ironically enough, in the United States. An estimated 150,000 Liberians died during the civil war of the 1990s, and an estimated one million fled to refugee camps in neighboring countries. Few of the refugees return to Liberia for more than brief, uncomfortable visits, often to care for less fortunate relatives, which poses a conundrum for U.S. Immigration officials. When about 10,000 Liberian refugees in the United States faced the loss of their protected immigration status in the fall of 2000, which would have required that they be sent home, Attorney General Janet Reno vowed not to extend the protection. President Clinton overruled Reno, citing Liberia's shortages of food, electricity, hospitals, and schools, the crackdown on the Liberian media by the government, the disappearance of political dissidents, and the fact that the U.S. State Department still considered Liberia too dangerous for Americans to visit.

Soon after, the U.S. State Department again advised U.S. citizens in Liberia to maintain contact with the embassy and to "carefully consider whether to remain in the country." In November 2000 the State Department issued a new travel warning, and prohibited family members from accompanying U.S. government employees to Liberia, noting that, "the ability of the embassy to provide direct assistance to U.S. citizens outside of Monrovia is severely limited. Many ill-trained and armed government security personnel continue to constitute a potential danger."

That same November, more than a hundred disgruntled former combatants severely beat two Taylor critics, former interim president

Sawyer and Commeny Wasseh, director of the Centre for Democratic Empowerment. Both men were hospitalized. Some alleged that the attack was made with Taylor's backing to divert attention from the diamonds-for-arms trade and the related UN sanctions debate.

"Under the current political climate in Liberia, no one is capable of organizing over 100 hoodlums without the President's blessings," *The Perspective* editorialized. "It is not possible."

As it turned out, the sanctions debate would loom over my entire stay, with the threat of flight cancellations, political unrest, and retaliation by the government against the United States for its efforts to push the punitive measures through. Although there is widespread dread of the potential sanctions, which were expected to worsen the plight of the average Liberian, most of the people I meet in Monrovia express growing resentment over Taylor's policies and hope that he can somehow be reined in. While the old economy favored the Americos, few people, whatever their family background, have ever felt as financially hopeless as so many feel now.

As one young man in Monrovia whose family was dispersed by the fighting tells me, the current situation is debilitating and unnerving for the average Liberian. His family, he says, is both fearful of a return to war and concerned about where their next meal will come from.

"My mother isn't working, my uncle who I live with isn't working, I'm not working," he says. "We are just making it because of God."

CHAPTER SEVENTEEN

THE CAB BARRELS TOWARD a bomb crater so large that there is only room for one car to pass. A Mercedes approaches from the opposite direction, lights flashing, which prompts our driver to step on the gas. Suddenly we pass into a different zone—from manageable disorder to chaos, just like that.

We careen toward a young, one-legged man who hobbles on crutches near the curb, blocking our only escape route should we lose the contest with the Mercedes. The passengers in the backseat begin shouting at the driver as we head toward the crippled man, who watches us bear down upon him but makes no move to get out of the way. At the last moment the Mercedes shoots past, and we skid to a stop beside the crippled man. The passengers go wild, berating the driver, growing so angry that I expect someone to reach over the seat and begin hitting him. I watch the crippled man's stoic face drift slowly past my window.

The driver shouts back, and the cab lurches onto the sidewalk, causing a young girl to spill an impossibly massive load of clothes that had been balanced on her head. She falls to the ground and disappears beneath the mound of clothes. I cannot understand much of what anyone is saying but hear the word "dead." As the angry passengers pile out of the cab, the driver shouts, "Why you say I be dead? Why you say such a negative thing? You be dead!"

The passengers continue shouting as they walk away in search of another cab. The driver drives on. Edward Railey and I say nothing.

It is the first sign of overt hostility I encounter in Liberia, though the evidence of turmoil is painfully obvious—in the buildings, in the

faces of people, in the large number of cripples on the street. Everywhere we go, we see injured people, mostly young men in wheelchairs,
on crutches, some missing one or both legs. They mark the line
between the planes of existence we crossed just moments before. Few
of them ask for money, although one man, hobbling on crutches with a
broken leg, approached me earlier in the day on crowded Broad Street
and introduced himself. I had noticed him before because his leg is
excruciatingly swollen and badly bent. It is painful to look at, yet
impossible to ignore. I imagine he is among the patients who were literally put out on the street when the John F. Kennedy hospital closed a
few weeks before, due to lack of funds and because frequent power
outages made it impossible to properly operate the morgue. The man
said his name is Sheriff, and offered the local handshake, a combination of seemingly every handshake in the world, with a twist—the traditional grasp, then something like a soul-shake with a finger snap off
of the other man's index finger at the end (I'm not sure where the
handshake originated, but it became popular in some parts of the
United States in the 1990s, usually without quite the same finesse as I
observe here). I reached into my pocket and gave Sheriff a few dollars.
He smiled, said, "Thank God," then turned to Edward and his brothers, Kaiser and Augustus, and said, "Thank you for your friend." Again
we shook hands, and when I failed to get it right the first time he made
me practice until I did.

It is hard to reconcile such friendliness, which you encounter
everywhere in Monrovia, with the pervasive scent of violence in the
air, and with the accounts of depravity that characterize the recent
war. There is no question that Liberia and neighboring Sierra Leone
have both dissolved into terrifying anarchy on numerous occasions,
with armed young men fighting, in some cases, because they have little
else to do. Many of the young rebels are orphans who have known little besides war. Some claim the youths are excited by the smell of
blood, which seems possible when you consider that they were weaned
on it. But walking the streets of Monrovia, I wonder how it can come
to this, particularly in a place where everyone's emotional default setting seems to be friendliness and warmth. How can a society based
upon such lofty ideals, where people say "good morning" to everyone
in every cab they enter, descend into such absolute chaos?

Although I rarely see its evidence in the interaction of people on the streets of Monrovia, I had heard a good bit about the historic enmity between the descendants of freed slaves and indigenous tribes in my Internet research. Typical of the articles was one in *The Perspective*, in which editorialist Tarty Teh cited a comment by Jesse Jackson that the Taylor government has failed to deliver Liberia from its nightmare. That nightmare, Teh wrote, "began for us when the free American slaves hit the shores of West Africa. We only got a respite in 1980 when the first African, who packed a gun, ended the 130-year rule over native Africans by the self-proclaimed Americos who had fled slavery in America and founded Liberia in the name of democracy."

I was amazed to find that so much of the vitriol harked back to the arrival of those intrepid freed slaves, among them the Rosses of Prospect Hill. Even the American Civil War, which in the South has turned out to have the half-life of plutonium, no longer holds the power to induce mass violence.

"What more do the African-Americans and Americo-Liberians want from us?" Tey demanded to know. "We surrendered a century and a half of our lives to absorb the anger of the returnees on behalf of any African who had anything to do with selling our brothers and sisters abroad. . . . If these returnees still don't like us after 150 years, then they have returned to the wrong part of Africa."

Such bitterness pervades Liberian chat rooms and message boards on the Internet. In Ciata's Chat Room, a website where Liberians post messages, exchange information, and argue about the history and current state of the country, the discourse frequently becomes vengeful, despite repeated warnings from the webmaster and entreaties from other visitors. When I posted a query about the descendants of the Rosses of Prospect Hill, I received many helpful replies. Then came the following:

"Seek yee first IN-BRED, BREAD FRUIT EADING, BOLLD SUCKING EX-SLAVE BASTARDS, FREE LIBERIA AND EVERY-THING WILL BE ADDED UNTO IT. I hope you know that blacks in America are a minority so total payback for what white DID to them is impossible. You ELITIST BASTARDS ARE in the minority. Just wait we will 'SKIN' your ELITIST ASSES AND USE THE SKIN FOR SHOES. If there is any thing to get over I suggest you get over your 'NO MORE WAR' crap . . . Take Heed asshole you better start filling more INS forms to bring over your sole-foot great grand and grand mother from up river or else when the shit hit the fan they will become part of a sad history."

Subsequent postings tapped a deep reservoir of remembered atrocities and resulting hatred. One person recalled a group of rebels cornering a woman named Esther Paygar and forcing a sharpened bayonet into her jittering hands to kill her own children. " 'Noo! I can't do that' the despairing woman cried. 'I can't kill my own children. You can kill me if you want.' They didn't kill her, but one by one, while the defenseless children cried 'Mama, Mama' to their wailing mother for help, Charles Taylor's wicked 'freedom fighters' got to work [and] the helpless children were beheaded right in front of their mother. Then with laughter, the rebels attempted to give the bloody heads to the children's mother, but Esther Paygar fainted before they could reach that stage."

New York University linguist John Singler had told me that the Liberian conflict is not solely about the long-running division between descendants of freed slaves and indigenous ethnic groups. "The war was about greed, not about ethnicity, not about ideology," he said. "It was the armed against the unarmed."

The Internet discussions, however, inevitably find their way to the subjects of slavery, oppression, and prejudice, and the lasting horror of slavery is glaringly apparent in the unremitting, personal, contemporary hatred that spews forth from every chat room and message board.

One person wrote: "Natives vs. Congo, slave vs. master, light skinned black vs. dark skinned black . . . white vs. black, Hutus vs. Tutsi, apartheid, slavery, segregation, nazism, facism and neo-nazis, and the list goes on. If you really think about it, all they are trying to do is survive at the expense of the next man. . . . Think about it. How can a person who was a slave in one land be a master in another?"

In response, another wrote: "The war in Liberia is a result of ongoing hostility and conflict between repatriated slaves and the indigenous people of Liberia. Today's war torn Liberia is not the result of the modern day politics and internal strife, but result of over 133 years of animosity between the 'haves' and the 'have nots.' "

"What I can't understand," came the next reply, "is why a people that were practically driven out of a nation that hated and brutalized them continue to cling to such a nation. And why would an African sell another African? . . . The truth of the matter is that we should be a shame of ourselves. We are a disgrace to all people of color. The first independent republic in Africa. Independent for over 153 years. What do we have to show for that? Not a damn thing. A bunch of American educated fools, a group of displaced people who practiced apartheid against their own, a group of citizens who murder their own people because they are Congo, a group of arrogant bastards who feel good by putting others down, leaders who murder, maim and raped for the sake of power."

The Internet discussions were bewildering, and yet I had devoured every detail. Because the fighting had ceased by the time I began planning my trip to Liberia, neither they nor the other warnings I received were enough of a deterrent. From conversations with foreign correspondents, I was aware that aside from the British film crew, journalists were continuing to travel to and from Liberia without incident, and overall, the situation seemed more stable than it had been in years. Sebastian Junger correctly pointed out that the government would pose the greatest threat, but he and other journalists offered practical advice that bolstered my confidence to go. Most importantly, Sebastian said, I was not to discuss the diamond trade with anyone.

Once I arrived, I had resolved to approach the Liberian government directly. It seemed crucial for me to establish my credentials because I had more than one mission during my stay. In addition to finding the descendants of the Mississippi immigrants, I needed to build a case for my own defense should the government focus unwelcome attention on me. So before proceeding any further in my quest for Mississippi descendants, Edward Railey and I stop by the Liberian Ministry of Information office, so that I can register as a journalist. We meet with J. Paye Legay, a gregarious, reassuringly friendly guy who is deputy director of research and planning.

As we sit in his office, he seems interested in the story I have come to research and offers suggestions for people to interview. He hopes the book will prove beneficial to Liberia by sparking American interest in the country's plight.

"It's a mystery why America doesn't care about Liberia, considering this is the only country America ever colonized," he says. "When there was trouble in Haiti, they got involved. You see the names of places here, just like in America, and if I name my son for you, I expect something in return." He runs through the list of American investments in the country—the airport, the Firestone plantation, then points out that, "Half of the population of Liberia is in America now."

"Liberia should be resting in the bosom of America," he says. "They created this country. But it's like they put a bowl of rice before a hungry man, then tie his hands. That's what America do to the free slaves."

I am encouraged by his straightforward approach but refrain from offering any meaningful response, particularly after he begins talking about diamonds and the election of President George W. Bush. He tells a story about an American or Dutch firm—I can't remember which, because by this point I have purposefully stopped taking notes—that extracted diamonds from its iron ore mines without the knowledge of the Liberian government. Finally I say, "It's an interesting story, but I made a rule for myself not to discuss politics or diamonds with anyone in Liberia. I hope you can understand."

He laughs. "Well, maybe you can help us develop tourism in Liberia," he says. "That is what I would like for you to do." He takes my $50 fee for journalists' accreditation, along with copies of my photograph, my itinerary, and the outline of my book, then stands and offers his hand. "Come back this afternoon and you can pick up your papers to do your interviews," he says. He laughs again when I am unable to manage the handshake and makes me try again and again until I get it right. This is becoming the routine of every adieu in Liberia.

After a pleasant lunch of jollof rice—a sort of jambalaya dish of rice, peppers, and chicken—at a nearby restaurant, with Donna Summer singing the disco hit "Don't Leave Me This Way" on a raspy speaker, Edward and I return to the Ministry of Information. This time I am referred to a different man, whose demeanor is a marked departure from J. Paye Legay's. He is overtly hostile. He does not introduce himself. "If you go to Sinoe," he says, pausing to give me a belligerent stare, "sometimes journalists pass this way and see things that embarrass us." I am unsure if this is a lament or a reproach. "If you photograph the executive mansion," he adds, "you will be arrested."

"I have no interest in the executive mansion," I say.

He glares at me for a moment, then passes me my papers and asks for the $50 fee. He is visibly angry when I say I have already paid.

I am a bit chastened by the exchange, but feel better now that I have my papers and return to the café to find that Peter Roberts Toe has arrived with a car. Next stop: Mississippi in Africa. There is only the matter of the summons to the U.S. embassy.

When I had earlier stopped by the embassy to register as an American citizen, the consul, Abbie Wheeler, had taken a noticeably greater interest when she found that I was a journalist. After hearing of my plans, she had stressed that it would be important for me to maintain contact with the embassy while I was in Sinoe County, which I already knew would be impossible, and said she was concerned that the situation in Liberia could suddenly change as a result of the UN sanctions debate stemming from the country's involvement in the diamonds-for-arms trade. Then, this morning, I had received a message from her at the hotel, calling me back to the embassy to meet with the ambassador.

Edward is both impressed and bewildered when I tell him that I am to meet with the ambassador. He stares at the broken pavement as we walk, mulling things over, occasionally wondering aloud what this new development may mean. He waits out the meeting across the street from the embassy gate.

As it turns out, when I arrive at the consulate Abbie Wheeler greets me and tells me that I will not meet with the ambassador, but with the directors of security and politics for the embassy. She also mentions that she is processing papers to ship home the body of an American missionary who was killed on the road to Greenville the previous week. The missionary's car was overrun by a log truck operated by the Oriental Timber Company, and although the Liberian government officially blamed the accident on the woman's driver, the embassy has questions about that, she says. She adds that the embassy has some information particular to my own travel, then ushers me in to meet with Lon Fairchild, the director of security.

Lon Fairchild looks completely out of place in Monrovia. He is all-American, with gym-muscles bulging beneath a bright red polo shirt. His air-conditioned office is an oasis of comfort and control in a country where both are in short supply. I outline my travel plans for him. He is friendly but direct.

"I advise you not to go," he says. "If you worked for the government I wouldn't let you go. The Liberian government may turn you back. There's no security outside Monrovia. Our radios won't reach there. Supposedly there are dissidents in that area, dropping off caches of weapons—fighting, basically. We cannot help you there."

I have prepared myself for this lecture. By anyone's standards, traveling to Greenville is risky, but I have been told that once I get there I will find the place peaceful. It is the ten-hour drive through the bush, through countless unsupervised checkpoints, that worries me, although I have the utmost trust in Peter Toe, and on the flight down I had met a group of elderly Minnesotans who were traveling to Greenville to build a playground at a Methodist school. I told myself that if a group of elderly Minnesotans could go to Sinoe, so could I.

I thank Lon for his advice, then throw the Minnesotans on the table.

His response is, "The rules are different for you. Missionaries are accepted. They're here to spread the word of God. Journalists are perceived in a completely different light. Even though your interest is innocuous, you're here to gather information. That changes everything. The last ones to attempt what you're talking about doing was the British film crew, and you know what happened to them."

He then broaches the subject of the UN sanctions debate. "They are poised to impose the sanctions, and there's a very strong likelihood that they believe you're part of that effort," he says, and pauses, meaningfully. "I'm concerned for your safety. The biggest threat we face are the people who are supposed to protect us. They fly choppers sixty feet high over the embassy—that's what we deal with every day. It's aggression. Charles Taylor is paranoid, and in his mind the UN equals the United States. You're gonna be out there with a bunch of crack addicts with AK-forty-sevens who blame America for their troubles, and when the sanctions come down Taylor's gonna flip out. Anything can happen when he's in a cocaine-based rage, and you—you'll be out there someplace where our radios won't reach, where we can't help."

I have known all along that the sanctions debate could pose a problem. The UN discussions tapped into my two main fears about traveling to Liberia: the country's recent history of horrific violence, and its notoriously unpredictable, paranoid, and sometimes violent government. I have told myself that as long as the sanctions debate continued Taylor would have no incentive to implicate a foreign journalist in an alleged international conspiracy, as he had the British film crew, but that if they were imposed while I was in Liberia, he would have nothing to lose. It might not matter that I am a bit player in the grand scheme of things, because the government could confer upon me a starring role if it served its purposes.

Lon then raises the possibility that the government of Liberia does not believe that I have come here to research the Rosses of Prospect Hill—that, instead, they believe I am here for a more sinister purpose. It is an absurd notion, but, "What we deal with here is not reality," he says. "It doesn't matter if you're not here to gather information for the UN sanctions debate. What matters is what Liberia perceives as reality, which is skewed."

I concede that I was a bit unnerved by the guy at the Ministry of Information warning me that I might see things that would embarrass the government.

"That's not really a warning," he says. "It's a veiled threat."

This is clearly a battle of wits for him, and the ball is now back in my court. I tell him I understand that it is his job to keep people like me from causing trouble for themselves and for others. "I appreciate what you're saying, but I'm still going to go," I say. "I have to."

He doesn't miss a beat. "If you go, do whatever they tell you to do," he says. "Give them whatever they want. Comply with every order. Be very nice. Have two or three hundred dollars Liberian for each checkpoint because those guys haven't been paid in months. And if you do decide to go, call me." Then he adds, "If you stay in Monrovia, where they can keep an eye on you, you probably won't have any problem."

I thank him and move on to my next meeting, with Anthony Newton, who heads the embassy's political division. Newton is a spare, unassuming man who looks like he might just as easily be a high school principal, and his office offers no clue to the turmoil that has boiled over only a few hundred yards away. He speaks with quiet authority as he goes over the UN sanctions, the diamonds-for-arms trade, the possibility of a worldwide travel ban for Liberian government officials. I tell him I am aware of these things. "It's not just about diamonds," he says. "What also matters, in your case, is timber. The Oriental Timber Company is clearing old forests on the way to Greenville. It's very controversial, and you will see that. The government is frantic over the possibility of an embargo because it would cut them off from their source of income. The government says the sanctions debate is part of

an international conspiracy, and there's a chance they are going to portray you as part of an effort to besmirch Liberia's image. That's the
context in which you've arrived."

This information seems more specific, and I am beginning to wonder if he and Lon Fairchild may actually work for the CIA, so I ask if
he has reason to believe that my presence has been discussed at the
executive mansion—if Charles Taylor actually knows that I am here.

"Yes," he says.

It is the one piece of information that I cannot disregard.

"Here's how it looks to them," he says. "They're looking for some
nefarious American plot, and it could not possibly be a coincidence
that you would arrive at this time, trying to go to Greenville. Maybe
you could go to Greenville and nothing will happen. Maybe some
moderates in the government will prevail and actually help you if the
situation gets bad. But I would suggest you go back to the Ministry of
Information and reiterate what you're here to do, say you recognize the
dispute, you're sensitive to the government's concerns. Then see how
that's received."

My second meeting with J. Paye Legay is markedly different from the
first. He now seems detached, impervious. He tells me a parable
involving African animals of equal intelligence, one of whom is clever
and manages to deceive the other. It is a long, cryptic story. I am
unsure if he is warning me, testing me, or . . . what? I explain that I am
now wary of going to Sinoe and wary of the government, which
prompts him to launch into another parable.

"If you go into a certain area and a snake bites you," he says, "the
next time you see a small tail, you think it is a snake. But we also have a
saying in Liberia: 'If you climb a tree and you fall, it shortens your
journey to the ground.'"

So much for getting a straight answer from him.

Leaving the meeting, I am bewildered. I think of something Sebastian Junger told me: "It's very easy to get accused of being a spy even
when they know you're not. It gives these types of governments a little
bit of bargaining power without getting branded a criminal state."

The question is whether to stay or go. I do not want to turn back,
having come so far, but neither do I want to embark upon a dangerous

folly that could result in my having my notes confiscated, or worse. In a place like this, it is hard to know if your fears are proportional. Unsure of what to do, I backtrack to the U.S. Information Service, a branch of the embassy, and talk with the media liaison, Sarah Morrison.

"If you stay in Monrovia, they probably will not bother you," she says. "Don't be alarmed if you're followed, because you will be, most likely, but the chances are you won't be bothered. It's possible there would be no trouble going to Sinoe. Anything is possible in Liberia—that's the problem, really." She says she visited Greenville a year ago. "It was beautiful. The people were delightful, the food was great. But then, I flew in and out in a helicopter."

My greatest concern is my notes, since the British film crew was relieved of all their footage, yet I am dubious about the embassy's advice, because the staff is paid to minimize dangers for people like me and no doubt errs on the side of caution. Still unable to make up my mind, I decide to put the question to Peter Toe, who is to take me to Greenville and host me while I am there.

Peter Toe is someone I would trust my life with. He is a caregiver, a provider, a brave and intelligent man, and is willing to lead. He has been hunted by rebels and twice has led groups of refugees through the dangerous bush, beginning when he set off on foot for the Ivory Coast with his wife and six children, aged three to twenty, on Christmas Eve, 1989.

During lunch at a Monrovia café, he recounts the ordeal. "I had to leave," he says. "I was being hunted. The fighting come, all the people rush into town. If you have money they want to kill you."

He and his family arrived safely in the Ivory Coast after an exhausting, frenzied journey through Liberia's coastal jungles and swamps, and remained there until 1992, after which the family returned briefly to Liberia, then fled again.

"We heard the gunfire in church," he says. "We left again. We walked to the Ivory Coast. It took us one month. The children were sick. I had fifteen in our house, and another group joined us, then another, and by the time we got to Ivory Coast we were more than a hundred and fifty. The rebels see us, they are beating us, but they left me because I am a doctor."

As Peter talks, I notice through the open window of the café one of the ubiquitous groups of destitute women sweeping the street with worn-out brooms. One of them glances through the window at us, her eyes alighting on Peter's. He reaches into his pocket and gives her a small Liberian bill. Next a group of soldiers stops by. Two enter the café while another guards the jeep, gun ready. Peter pays no attention to them, but Edward whispers, "These are the president's personal security. They are looking for someone."

The soldier standing guard glances at me through the window. I give him a nod. He nods back, and looks away.

Peter says that when the fighting ended in 1998, he returned from the Ivory Coast with no money and no way to start his life over again. John Singler, he says, gave him the money he needed. "Now I operate a drug store and a clinic," he says. "There is no doctor in the whole county. People give me chicken, rice, in payment. I have a lot of chicken." As a result, he is one of the few Liberians I talk with who has no interest in moving again.

I tell him what Lon Fairchild and Anthony Newton said about my traveling to Greenville, and his response is unequivocal. "I wouldn't go," he says. Peter is not one to overestimate danger. Although I have only known him for a few days, he inspires confidence, and I trust him. I would go anywhere that he was willing to go. But even if I were intent on taking the risk myself, it seems unfair to put him in jeopardy as well. If he does not think I should go, I cannot ask him to take me.

There is little else to consider. "Well, at least tell me what I'm going to miss," I say.

"You'll be missing my wife's cooking!" he says, the smile returning to his face. "She going to be very disappointed. She preparing for you. But really, two-thirds of the people in Greenville have left. Most of the old people who could have told you things—the ones it mattered about Georgia, Mississippi—they starve during the war. All of them are dead. The hunger kill all of them. There are only young people there now. Many people from Sinoe come here, to Monrovia, during the fighting. You can talk to them. I know you want to see Mississippi Street in Greenville, but most of it has washed into the sea. Most of the big houses, the houses with the pillars, were burned, destroyed in the fighting. All of the Southern houses are gone—the ones that did not burn, the rust eat off the roof."

I accept this, grudgingly. It is the people I am looking for, after all, more than the buildings. But if I stay in Monrovia, I will not be able to remain at the Mamba Point. All transactions in Liberia are cash, and I don't have enough on hand to be comfortable spending fourteen days there at $120 per night. The last thing I want to do in Liberia is run out of money.

Security, or at least the feeling of security, is a major consideration, and it is something that other, more affordable hotels in Monrovia cannot always provide. I ask Peter's advice, and he says that he needs to pick up some supplies to carry with him to Greenville and will try to come up with an idea while he is gone. In the meantime, Edward Railey and I will head back to Mamba Point.

I am disappointed that I won't make it to Greenville, that I may not get what I came for, that I may be chickening out. But walking back to the Mamba Point, Edward and I discuss the possibilities. He is an optimist, and is convinced that the change of plans will be a blessing in disguise. Plus, he seems upbeat about the fact that I won't be leaving him tomorrow.

We pass the imposing ruins of the old Masonic temple, its statues and balustrades damaged by mortars, toppled here and there, and I stop to take what I hope is an officially sanctioned photograph. I make a point of leaving out the antiquated artillery cannons on a bluff overlooking the building, aimed at the city below, which are rusting and partly overgrown with vines. The city lies in ruins, hazy with pollution, yet pulsates with life. A toddler is standing before the building when I take my photo. A woman who is washing clothes in buckets, out of sight behind a monument, hears my shutter click and hurries forth, talking excitedly. She is barefoot, pretty, wearing a bright red dress and bandana. I can't understand her accent but assume she is upset because her child was in the picture. Edward talks to her and she begins to smile. He gives her a few Liberian dollars.

Afterward he says she was concerned that I would get in trouble. She said guards sometimes patrol the building and that if they saw me taking pictures they might arrest me. She was relieved when Edward told her that I had my accreditation papers. Still, it makes him a little nervous, my taking photographs there. "Just take the picture," he snaps as I peer through a window opening at the ruined lobby, with its grand staircase partially stripped of its elaborate cast-iron rail. Clothes hang to dry in all the openings because the temple is full of squatters.

Edward says his parents taught him to be suspicious of the place because a secret society, the Masons, once met there.

"It's funny," I say, as we walk away. "That the woman was concerned for me."

"The Liberian people are mostly good people," Edward says. "They are warm. It is only when the heat is on that things can get very bad."

"I don't understand why the people put up with the government," I say. "They're doing nothing to fix the country, yet Taylor and his friends are riding around in brand-new Mercedes and Lexuses and building mansions outside of town. They're looting the country, and the average Liberian has nothing, not even the basic essentials of life. It seems like it would be in Taylor's best interest to keep people pacified."

He nods. "The Liberian . . . don't do nothing," he says of his countrymen's acquiescence. "And the reason is because no one wants the war to come back."

I ask him about the underlying conflict of Liberia's civil war. Although I have read much about the dispute between the descendants of the freed slaves and the indigenous tribes, in the short time that I have been here, I have sensed more unifying despair than ethnic animosity. Taylor traces his lineage to both sides, and with everyone so uniformly polite, how could the country erupt into such unimaginable violence?

"Everybody want to be the boss," Edward says. "I know what you are saying—people so warm, so friendly. I've thought about it a lot. Liberians killing one another. It all comes down to one thing: everybody want to be the boss."

CHAPTER EIGHTEEN

REVEREND CHARLESTON BAILEY LIVES in a small, cinder-block house behind St. Teresa's convent, where Peter Toe has arranged for me to take a room. The house is almost devoid of furniture, but is otherwise comparatively comfortable. It stands in an area that feels more like a neighborhood than a war zone, though no place in Monrovia, aside from walled compounds, feels in any way protected.

Edward has known Reverend Bailey, who is originally from Sinoe County, for years, and had hoped that he might be able to supply me with contacts in Greenville. Now that I won't be going to Greenville, he hopes for the same here in Monrovia.

At the front of the house is a swept dirt yard and a breezy porch. A large, horned lizard stalks insects atop the painted cinder-block wall as Edward and I wait for the reverend to amble out from the recesses of the darkened house. When he does, he shakes our hands and eases down into a chair on the porch. A younger man sits on the rail listening to world news on a boom box.

I explain myself. The reverend runs his tongue across his lips, thinking back. He is eighty-six years old, his eyes appear bewilderingly large behind Coke-bottle lenses, and most of his teeth are gone. He has a few teeth on the top on one side, and a few on the bottom on the other, which seems the worst possible combination. His memory, though, is sharp. He says he has ten living children, including two daughters in the United States. He says he remembers the soldiers torching the columned mansions of Mississippi during the civil war, remembers eating crawfish in Louisiana, and collard greens and okra. He remembers crossing the languorous river that flows between

Mississippi and Louisiana in a canoe. There is a strobe effect to these images from old Liberia, juxtaposed with images from eponymous places in the United States. Listening to him talk induces a sort of mental vertigo. He switches back and forth often enough that sometimes I have to listen closely to know if he is talking about Liberia or America.

The Baileys, he says, were originally from Georgia, in the United States, and after being freed by their owner in the early nineteenth century, immigrated to Monrovia and then sailed to Sinoe County aboard a ship named the *Mayflower*. There they settled alongside earlier immigrants from Mississippi and Louisiana, who had built the Mississippi colony's first ocean-going vessel, which they christened the *Natchez*. Soon after, the groups began to splinter.

"They had different ideas. Some of the settlers—the Baileys, the Raileys, the Walkers, the Murrays—went to Louisiana," he says. "The Reeds went to Readsville, the Rosses to Rossville. The Witherspoons and Burches went to Lexington. They wanted to establish their own place."

Establishing their own place was everyone's raison d'être, but some of those places had already been taken by the tribes.

"My grandfather was killed in a war with the tribes," he says. "He was shot in the stomach. The tribes wanted the settlers to go back to America, but after all the settlers conquer them and they surrender."

The Bailey family fled Louisiana during the fighting of the 1990s, as did most of their peers. "The war ran me from there," he says. "It ran many people from there." With Sinoe in ruins and the nation's economy in shambles, few had reason to return home when the fighting ceased. "Some came here, to Monrovia, some went to Ghana, some to Nigeria," he says. "There are not many old people left in Sinoe." The possibility exists, he adds, that I might actually find the people I am looking for here in Monrovia. "Most of the people in Sinoe now, they came there, they not born there. The majority of the Sinoe people now are in Monrovia. There are no Rosses in Rossville. The old, old people—they knew about Mississippi, but no one now."

Ever the optimist, Edward points out that had I been able to travel to Greenville I might actually have missed the people I am looking for—because they had fled to Monrovia.

There is little left of the Sinoe County that Reverend Bailey knew before 1994, he says. I ask him about the buildings, which I had wanted to see because they are said to resemble antebellum architecture in the American South. He confirms that most of the mansions were destroyed by rebels who saw in them the manifestation of the ancien régime. There are a few examples of settler architecture on the streets of Monrovia, he says, perhaps as many as survive in Greenville.

The buildings were apparently seen by many as an affront after the 1980 coup and during the civil wars of the 1990s. Monuments were bulldozed, historic buildings were looted and burned, and written and photographic archives were scattered to the winds. The destruction was wholesale, and devastating beyond Americo culture. Today there is no public library in Monrovia, and with so little surviving documentation within Liberia, and so few elderly people who can help fill in the blanks, the best sources of the nation's history are housed in libraries in the United States.

Later in the day, when Edward and I visit his mother, Abbie Jones, at her home in a rural community called Duport Road, she reiterates the reverend's assessment of the situation. Abbie, who is in her fifties, also left Louisiana during the fighting and settled outside Monrovia. She leans back in a chair beneath the shade of a massive plum tree, shakes her head and says, "I tell you! My people! Je–SUS! All of the old people, gone."

Edward explains: "Most of the old people, they starve during the war. In the early eighties Rossville, Louisiana, Lexington, Blountsville were all places to see. The old people were there. Now you have mostly the youth, born since the early seventies. They don't know. We did not have time to sit and talk to the old people, and now they are mostly gone."

The loss of the elders is much lamented, but for most people, making it through the day and maintaining some sense of normalcy are more pressing concerns. Neither Abbie, nor Edward, nor any of their family members can find jobs, and when I ask her about the bare utility poles leading past her house that have been shorn of their lines, she says that the electricity was cut during the war and never restored.

"They only have lights in parts of Monrovia and parts of Greenville," she says. "There is none in Louisiana."

She entertains no illusions about ever returning to her native Louisiana, but remembers the place fondly.

"It's just a small farming community, with wooden houses," she says. "No jobs. The women mostly just sit on the porches and enjoy the breeze. Sunday, go to church. All the men go deer hunting on Saturday."

"Deer hunting?" I ask.

She nods.

Suddenly we are back to strange juxtapositions. I tell her that deer hunting is popular in the American South, too, where hunters often mount the antlers of the biggest bucks on the wall.

"It's the same here," she says. "They hang the horns on the wall, something like a decoration."

Edward says that when he was young, he and his brothers often went on deer hunts, to help control the dogs.

"Most of the time they hunt around Rossville," he says. "It's up the river from where we live."

I ask if they know of any Rosses who still call Rossville home, but both shake their heads.

"There is not much there now," Edward says.

I ask if they still have family in Louisiana.

"Just a few," Abbie says. "Most of them are here. My family came from Louisiana, to Louisiana, but they leave during the fighting. One of my sisters went to the U.S. She is in Louisiana."

"Louisiana, in the U.S.?" I ask.

She nods. "I don't really know the name of the place. All I know is Louisiana."

Beyond her, a flock of white cattle egrets probes for insects in an open field. Edward notices me studying the birds and volunteers the name—"cow birds."

I tell him we have the same birds in Mississippi. I've been told they flew in from Africa in the eye of a hurricane, years ago.

"The same birds," he says, and smiles.

Beyond fading memories and crumbling facades, many cultural links remain between Liberia and the American South. The most pronounced, literally, is Liberian English, which has an antiquated sound and mixes pronunciations and expressions from the antebellum South with the cadence of traditional West African speech.

John Singler, who spent years studying this hybrid dialect in Sinoe

County, wrote that the language of Greenville reflects the greater contact of the original settlers with what he called "speakers of White
Southern Vernacular." Greenville was settled primarily by more educated slaves, while upriver settlements such as Readsville were settled
primarily by illiterate field workers. Paradoxically, Greenville's greater
exposure to outside influences caused the city's residents to become
more African in speech, while the upriver settlements "remain funda-
mentally North American," he wrote.

The slow erosion of homogenous Americo culture began, as most
such disintegrations do, when the old people—in this case, the original
settlers—began dying off. Some of the original settlers had continued
to communicate with family members in the United States until the
turn of the twentieth century, but in their wake the personal attachment began to fade. Incrementally, their culture became more mixed,
and more African.

As Edward and I stroll through an outdoor market and pass a vendor
selling dirt for human consumption, I mention that some African-
Americans in the rural South have eaten dirt habitually for generations—not just any dirt, but dirt dug from favored sites—and that there
has been speculation that the habit was brought to America from Africa.

"Sometimes it's hard to say where something comes from," he says.
"You look to America and you see some things you recognize, but really
it's hard to say: did the African take it from here to there, or did the
settler bring it from there to here?" Or from here to there and back—
and perhaps from here, back to there again?

Most Liberians of immigrant descent identify with African-
Americans in the United States but consider themselves the reverse—
American-Africans, he says. This is certainly true of Reverend Bailey,
who was born and raised and has lived his entire life in Liberia, but is
quick to point out that he's "originally from America" on both sides of
his family.

"If you are an American-African, what happens if you emigrate
to the U.S.?" I ask. "Are you an African-American-African, or an
American-African-American?"

Edward laughs. "I guess in the U.S. I would just be African-
American."

Having a connection with America is still considered an important
edge, and it remains a source of pride for many despite the civil war,

Fernando Po, and the seeds of cultural integration that were planted in the 1950s and 1960s, when other African nations began overthrowing the rule of colonial powers. Although the 1980 coup was the crowning blow to Americo cultural dominance, neither side has presented a united cultural front in the years since. On the contrary, Liberia's contemporary elite consists of Taylor, his family, and a small group of friends and associates, while the average Liberian's lot is poor regardless of ancestral descent.

Still, old times here are not forgotten. One Liberian with whom I spoke, who is of indigenous descent, lashed out at the nation's flag, which vaguely resembles the American flag, with broad red and white stripes and a blue canton bearing a single star, saying it is a symbol of old Americo dominance. His offense mirrors the feelings of many black Mississippians over the state's official flag, which incorporates the banner of the Confederacy in its canton corner. One is a reminder of slavery, the other of the empowerment of freed slaves in Africa. Both are divisive.

Later in the day I meet with a teacher at the University of Liberia, Sleweon Nepe, who is originally from Sinoe County. Like so many others, he fled to Monrovia during the fighting. In Greenville, he says, memories of American culture once colored every aspect of life, and before the war the city held an Arrival Day celebration on Mississippi Street each July 9–10.

"There was a big dance, a formal ball," he says of the celebrations. "People give candy to the children. They cook food, drink beer. There was always a special program to tell friends about how the pioneers came, how they landed, how they were received by the local tribes. They wore the suits with the top hat and long tail coats. The women wore the long dress, white, like a hoop skirt. Some of them kept these clothes during the war, put them in plastic and buried them. The local people, they wore their local dress. Everyone participated. They allowed the militia to turn out in khaki for a big drill.

"In the 1920s and 1930s there was tension, but when Tubman took over in 1944 he brought all of these people together," he continues. "We all went to the same schools. There is the feeling that we are all Liberian. But even today the people look to America. The settler people, they know what state their ancestors immigrated from, and the indigenous people, they see that a connection with America is important. The Liberians showed other people in Africa that you could be independent—even South Africa. We showed you do not have to be a slave. We have a commonality, despite our differences. It all goes back to America, because America established this country, which is why America cannot allow everything to be in vain."

CHAPTER NINETEEN

EVERY NIGHT THE YOUNG men who work at St. Teresa's convent gather in the TV room to watch movies on the VCR. It is a real luxury for them, and they will watch anything that is available. When I return to the room I've taken at the convent, after a day spent trudging the streets in search of Rosses while trying to sort out real and perceived threats from the government, I see them gathered before the TV watching old American movies like *The Sound of Music*. Tonight, as I pass through the room, Abraham Johnny, who does the laundry, stands and greets me with the Liberian handshake. Abraham is a supremely happy man with a ready smile that makes his eyes squint. It is almost as if the structure of his face makes it difficult for him not to smile.

"Alan, you must come watch the movie with us," he says, and plops down in a round rattan chair.

"What's showing tonight?" I ask.

"It's called *Mississippi Burning*," he answers.

"Huh," I say, unsure what to think of this rather bizarre twist. "Well, you know, I'm from Mississippi," I remind him, and he beams and leaps to his feet to give me a high five.

All the other guys in the room do the same, and we go through the whole round of handshakes. This is a personal milestone: never before have I gotten high fives from a group of black guys after telling them I'm from Mississippi. They are amazed at their good fortune, to be watching a movie about America's Mississippi with someone who is from there. It is one of the perks of working at St. Teresa's convent that the staff occasionally has the opportunity to meet people from beyond Liberia, because in addition to operating a Catholic school, the convent has a dormitory used by visiting Catholic officials, international groups and—as is the case with me, who was brought here by Peter Toe—people who simply come with a recommendation and need a place to stay. So here is an opportunity for the workers gathered in the TV room to talk with someone who is actually from the place that the movie is about.

"It's actually a terrible movie," I say, which deflates things a bit. "The good people and the bad people are all white. The black people are portrayed just as victims." They wait for more. I sit down.

"Is the movie true?" asks Gargard Menyongar, the convent's resident artist and librarian.

"The story is true," I say. "It was bad in Mississippi at one time. But it's much more complicated than this movie makes it seem."

"Are these men actors or is this really happening?" Abraham asks, glancing back at the screen, where a Klansman is setting fire to a poor black man's barn.

"They're actors," I say. "But it's based on a true story."

Scenes flicker by, mostly of black people reacting helplessly to the assaults of bad whites while the good whites, actors Willem Dafoe and Gene Hackman, argue over how to save them. Abraham and Gargard are impressed when I tell them that the FBI car in which Dafoe and Hackman tool around town belonged to my sister, and was rented to the movie company.

"You have ridden in this car?" Gargard asks, motioning toward the old black Impala in which Dafoe and Hackman are now dramatically arguing.

I nod. My having ridden in the car in the movie delights them, but further confuses the issue of what is real and what is not.

When the movie again descends into violence, Abraham asks, "Alan, do I really want to watch this?"

"It's very violent," I say. "It's painful to watch. It was pretty rough in Mississippi back then."

They nod. I think: my God, you guys have seen a lot worse. Still, it is embarrassing to see whites attacking blacks on the screen, to hear them saying "nigger" this and "nigger" that.

I explain that the men were never convicted for the killings, in the 1960s, of the three civil rights workers who are the subject of the story, whose names were Goodman, Cheney, and Schwerner, but that the state is now preparing a case against the surviving suspects.

"Really? *Now?*" Gargard asks, pointing to the floor.

I nod.

He grins, gives me two thumbs up. "I love America," he says.

As it turns out, *Mississippi Burning* proves to be more or less a lame action movie for them. They show no reaction to any of the scenes except for those in which blacks gather in church to sing spirituals, at which point they all sing along. Eventually they get bored and one by one get up and leave. I head back to my room. The TV plays to the end of the movie, for no one.

Later a group staying at the convent as part of a UK-based human rights workshop takes over the sitting room, and I hear them laughing hysterically at *The Brady Bunch.* There is something unsettling about this, their laughing at a silly American sitcom from the 1970s as I sit on the edge of my bed before the oscillating fan, listening to the sound beyond my window of men chanting angrily within the walls of Monrovia Central Prison a block away, where the British film crew was held.

Each night I hear the chanting, the sound intermingling with African hymns being sung to the beat of a drum in a nearby church and the laughter and squeals of children playing in the darkness below. Sometimes I am unsure what I am hearing, how to interpret the sound. One morning I awake before dawn to hear a man singing and calling out in the distance, which sets the neighborhood dogs to howling. He sounds as if he is in the grips of an insane outburst, or perhaps he is preaching. It is pitch-black outside. Perhaps it is a call to prayer—I know that there is a mosque nearby.

Other times I hear a bell ringing in the wee hours, like a church bell. It rings and rings and rings—for what? Is it an alarm clock for people with no electricity? But it is too early, five A.M. I ask several people but no one knows. I ask a missionary volunteer from Massachusetts, Lucy McGovern, who is also staying at the convent, but she doesn't know.

"In the village where I live I often hear drums early in the morning, from village to village, and I wonder what message they're sending," she says. "But then I drift back to sleep and I always forget to ask anyone their meaning."

One night I hear a soccer game playing on boom boxes and transis-tor radios scattered through the darkness. Liberia is playing Ghana. A cheer erupts in the neighborhood, telling me that Liberia has scored. The sound is both joyful and unnerving.

As a white American, I bring my own prejudices. I often think, as I walk around Monrovia, that I would never be caught on a street like this in the United States. This night, hearing the cheering and the chanting of crowds gathering in the streets after the Lone Star victory, I think of the riots in Chicago after the Bulls won, and of fights at British soccer matches. But there is only joy. Cars honk, drums beat, people cheer. There is something indiscernible about all this, the cacophony of familiar and unfamiliar sounds, these messages that I do not understand, this overlay of joy upon an undercurrent of violence that seems pervasive yet does not crop up when you expect it. I am reminded of another law of the jungle: that when you're on a hunt, what you're looking for often appears from where you aren't looking.

Most nights at the convent I go down to the gate to hang out with the guards, two middle-aged men who invariably want to talk about the war that broke out on April 6, 1996. During the war, six of one of the guards' eight children starved to death. As I jot down notes, he asks, "You put our names in your book?"

"Do you want me to?" I ask.

"Noooo," he says.

"We have nothing to gain from that," the other guard says. The gov-ernment does not like it when Liberians talk about the war, he adds.

This is not surprising, yet few of my conversations fail to touch upon the subject.

During the war, fighting between the forces of Doe, Johnson, and Taylor raged back and forth across the city from Capitol Hill to Mamba Point to Bushrod Island.

"They see you on the street, they quick, they cut you and eat you," one of the guards says. "They eat human beings. Terrible war. But it is not the fighting that kills the most people, it is the hunger. People eat the leaves on the trees, the flowers. One cup of rice costs one hundred and fifty dollars." I do the math: it amounts to less than $4 U.S. "A woman will sleep for a rebel for rice," he adds.

They recount the daring wartime exploits of Sister Barbara Bril-liant, who once ran the convent and still works here. I had met Sister

Barbara, who is from Maine, when I arrived, and she had not been glad to make my acquaintance. She had listened as I explained the purpose of my trip, then said, "You are here at a very dangerous time for a journalist, particularly an American journalist. You know that. You came here knowing there is a U.S. travel advisory. You should not be here." That pretty much ended the conversation. I wanted to say, *Hey, even the drunk guy with the AK-47 at the checkpoint said, "Welcome."*

The guards laugh when I tell them how Sister Barbara received me.

"You have to know about Sister Barbara," one says, then launches into a series of Sister Barbara stories that sound apocryphal, yet plausible.

According to his version, one morning during the war a hundred of General Butt Naked's troops arrived at the convent, naked, of course, and demanded that the archbishop be turned over to them. They were going to take him to the barracks, site of many recent executions.

"Sister Barbara comes out," he says, "and she have her gun. She tell them no one is going to the barracks, they will have to kill her first. So she have that gun, and she turn them away. She spend the rest of the day in her jacket, driving everybody from the archbishop on down to the embassy. She drive them to the embassy while the guns are shooting. That woman is a fighter. She is very brave. No one mess with her. When the Sisters are in Gardnersville, she want to go and rescue them. They don't want to leave, they think they are safe in Gardnersville. You cross the bridge you are killed. So the ambassador find out that Sister Barbara is going, and he park a vehicle across the convent gate, so she cannot go. He know she would never get there. She would be killed."

By then the nuns—among whom were five Americans from an order in Illinois—had already been murdered by the rebels.

"General Butt Naked is now a street preacher," he adds. "Someone told me he is in the States."

At this point, two pretty young girls who belong to staff members emerge from the convent door and sashay out to the gate, singing "Tomorrow" from the musical *Annie*. They are all dressed up, slowly waving their long scarves. When they reach us, they stop singing. They listen silently as we talk.

I ask the guard what happened at the convent during the fighting. He points to bullet holes in the convent wall, which is topped with shards of broken glass.

"The rebels are coming over the walls," he says. "The nuns have gone to the embassy. I am at my house. They take what they want and destroy everything else." UN Drive, he says, which leads from the convent to the American embassy, was littered with bodies.

I glance down at the two girls, who seem uninterested. They soon sashay off into the darkness.

During another of our meetings at the gate a guard's wife arrives, hoping to sell me a coconut. The tub of coconuts she balances on her head is very heavy but she walks confidently and purposefully, even gracefully, under the burden. The guards have to help lift the tub off her head to set it on the ground. She wears traditional African dress, which looks truly traditional—not superimposed, as it so often appears on more affluent women, who wear makeup, jewelry, fashionable handbags, and decorous, carefully coiffed dreadlocks. Her dress and bandana are shades of bright aqua and lime.

I buy one of the coconuts and she pulls out her machete and chops the skin away until there is a hole to the center, which is filled with milk. She hands me the coconut, motioning for me to drink. "Make small, small lips," she says.

The milk is sweet. She makes me drink it all, then smiles with satisfaction. She is a beautiful woman, her skin smooth and very dark, her cheekbones high. She and her husband have seven children, aged six to twenty-five.

Her husband tells me, "My gift to you will also be a gift for me. I will give you one of my seven children to take home with you as a servant!" He laughs.

I laugh, but it ends in a rather awkward *ha-ha*.

He later tells me that each morning his wife goes to the dock to buy coconuts for $2 Liberian apiece (which equals about five cents U.S.), then roams the streets selling them for $5 Liberian apiece (or about twelve or thirteen cents U.S.). She works as long as twelve hours a day, sometimes returning to the dock for more coconuts. If she sells her entire load, she may make a profit of $2.50 U.S.

Such small exchanges are what keep Liberians going. Monrovia is a city of a million people, give or take 100,000, depending upon the flow of refugees, and the whole place is a frenzied market with people rushing down crowded streets with wheelbarrow-loads of batteries and used shoes and dried fish and towels for sale, serenaded by the constant honking of cabs. At one point I see a woman dart across the street with a small refrigerator balanced on her head. I wonder where everyone is going. With unemployment so high and even those who have jobs often going months between paychecks, it seems that everyone has places to go and people to meet. Even more amazingly, they are almost all immaculately dressed. I stop by a laundry and find people making starch from scratch, from vegetable matter, and pressing clothes with coal-fired irons that are heated by a chamber filled with embers. Shoe-shine men do a brisk business along Broad Street, alongside the money changers and people selling used clothing, counterfeit watches, peanuts, transistor radios, and flashlights.

Most Liberians, I notice, are careful about their appearance, and are sticklers for shiny shoes—even tennis shoes are slathered with white polish. One Sunday morning, before I attend church with Edward Railey and his brothers, they take one look at my shoes and haul me down to Broad Street to have them shined. Somehow just keeping clean and pressed is enough to keep people getting up each day to wander the squalid streets, hoping something good will come along.

When I mention this obsession with neatness to a British woman I meet, she scoffs. "It's absurd the way they spend money on shoe shines and cheap jewelry that's just in bad taste to us, when they can't afford lunch," she says. "What's that about?"

"Self-esteem?" I suggest. "Pride?"

She rolls her eyes.

I am reminded of whites back home who joke about the stereotype of the shiny Cadillac parked before a dilapidated shack. From the vantage point of Monrovia, the stereotype looks different. I think: isn't that what land-poor white women did in the American South after the Civil War, when they dressed in their best clothes to receive company on the galleries of dilapidated mansions that they could no longer afford to maintain?

Lucy McGovern, who is visiting at the convent but lives at the Catholic mission in Maryland County, is not entirely enamored of Liberia, but says she is impressed by the resiliency and decorum she has observed here. She repeats the familiar horror stories—torturings, murders, robberies—but adds, "I'm amazed that the people can still laugh and talk like normal people at all, considering what they've been through."

I am also amazed by their knowledge of American politics. One night, the guards talk about the American presidential election, which they know all about, down to the cabinet appointees. When they pause to listen to the news of the sanctions debate on a transistor radio, I glance down at the pristine white tennis shoes one is wearing, and think: here is a man laughing and talking earnestly about politics, who keeps his shoes white while strolling through the muck of the streets of Monrovia, who watched six of his children starve to death five years ago. This resiliency, gentility, and unflagging joyfulness was never mentioned in anything I read about Liberia before coming here.

Most mornings I awake to the relentlessly cheerful sound of children in the courtyard of the convent assembling for school. They sing songs, including the Liberian National Anthem, say "The Lord's Prayer" and the Liberian Pledge of Allegiance, then shout, very loudly, when the headmaster arrives, "Good morning, how are you!"

"I'm well, thank you! How are you!" the headmaster calls out.

"Well! Thank you!" the children shout.

When I mention the Liberians' perfect manners to Brother Dennis Hever, who teaches at the convent, he smiles, then quickly brings me back to the opposing reality. He lives in the compound where the American nuns were murdered in 1992, and, "a few months ago the children were in our yard laughing and playing and suddenly gunfire erupted," he says. "Everything was perfectly normal and suddenly there was gunfire, and the children started screaming. Even when things are normal you're aware that anything can happen. So there was panic. It was a small incident between different security forces, but it set off this panic. Things can change very quickly."

Each morning when I emerge from the convent gate I am met by a group of men who spend the day there, first sitting in the morning shade of the convent wall, then moving to the shade of the wall on the opposite side of the street. I see groups like them gathered on street corners all over Monrovia, listening to the radio. It is a familiar urban scene, but for one important detail: they're not listening to rap or hip-hop music, as is so common in the United States, but to the world news.

This group calls me over each time I exit the gate and again when I return. They want to talk about anything, but particularly the contested American presidential election. One points out that America would condemn such a questionable election if it had been held in an

African nation. I can't argue with that, I say. They are also interested in my story and tell me they know a descendant of one the families I name who came from Prospect Hill. He lives nearby, in an empty walled compound. They promise to take me there.

The men always ask for cigarettes, never money, but one eventually asks, "Why is it America sends no money? No medication, no books, no food, no clothes? We look to America. Why they not help? Liberia is covered with the blood of Jesus!"

Another offers an answer. "They not help because if they send money, you just see the big car, and the big car run over the foot of a man like me."

I nod. I have seen the big cars, the air-conditioned Lexus and Mercedes SUVs speeding down the streets of Monrovia.

"Do you know what happens to a poor man if he gets sick?" another asks. "The hospital have close. So if you are a poor man, you get sick, you die."

At this point I see Edward approaching. He does not condone my being friendly with the malingerers outside the convent gate, because he knows they have an agenda and he is not sure what it is. I trust them, but I trust Edward more.

"Gotta go," I say. "I'll see you this evening."

Today Edward is taking me to J. J. Ross High School, whose director, Maurice M. G. V. Pelham, is a descendant of the man for whom the school was named.

When we arrive at the school I ask Maurice about J. J. Ross and he says, "He came from a place, a state, called Mississippi." I ask if he was not among the Georgian Rosses, because I have read that some of the Rosses from Sinoe County originated there, but he says, no, that J. J. Ross was from Mississippi, and that he settled in Mississippi in Africa and later in Greenville. Eventually he moved to Monrovia. The school is in Ross's former home, a sprawling, three-story structure hard by the sidewalk on Ashmun Street, with a large courtyard out back that is now home to several families of squatters. The school was founded by Ross's granddaughter, Louise Rogers, to educate orphans, says Maurice's sister, Kema Langama.

"For the needy and the less fortunate in society," adds another brother, Aaron Pelham. "But right now, nothing is doing. We used to have a family in France that gave money, but now, because of the war, we have nothing. So the school is private, which is to say that a small, but for many, unaffordable, tuition is charged."

J. J. Ross illustrates that not all of the slave immigrants sought to exploit the indigenous people. He served as a senator from Sinoe County and was later vice president of Liberia. Maurice does not know much about the family history, but when I show him a copy of an immigrant ship registry he points to a line identifying the passengers as slaves freed by the estate of Captain Ross and says, "I have heard this name mentioned."

Maurice allows that some Rosses "were not related at all," and that others among Sinoe's original immigrants were Africans recaptured from slave ships, who, he says, "did not make it to the plantation." Some of the latter also took the Ross name, perhaps as wards. J. J. Ross, he says, was primarily a trader and farmer of cocoa and coffee. The family was once prominent in Sinoe, but Maurice knows of no Rosses who still call the place home. He has visited Greenville only once, he says. "I went to bury. I remember the port there is named for Alfred Ross, who was also a vice president."

There are about 400 students at J. J. Ross High School, he says. The students wear uniforms of blue-and-white striped tops with navy pants or skirts. Their mascot is a type of raccoon, which is similar to the North American species except that it has spots. The school's motto is "Docility." Because Isaac Ross included in his will plans for the funding of an institution of learning in Liberia—an effort that was thwarted when the legal contest consumed much of the money in his estate, I tell Maurice that it seems appropriate that one of the Ross immigrants managed to do so. He agrees, but says the future is in doubt. He has entreated the government to provide some financial help, "but they say people don't have clothing or shelter, and they have to wait for education," he says. Charles Taylor's niece graduated from the school in 1999, and the president made a commencement speech, he adds.

"A lot of our students are self-supporting," says his sister Kema, the school's business manager. "They sell in the market to make money to go to school. Come, let me show you our library."

Down the hall we enter a dark, musty room where dust motes drift through sunlight falling from a single window. A few ruined books litter the floor, with perhaps a dozen more, all with broken spines, tilting on broken shelves. "This is all there is," she says, and waits for a reaction. "So you see, we need books."

Books, I have found, are in short supply all over. I met one man who was preparing a speech to a Baptist Bible seminar on the separation of church and state in the United States, using as his source a book published in 1950. The only accessible books I have come across are used Barbara Cartland romance novels for sale on the sidewalk.

Further down the hall, we peek into classrooms that resemble scenes from Walker Evans photos during the Depression. The rooms are starkly beautiful but almost devoid of teaching tools, with bare wooden floors, unfinished wooden desks, and old-fashioned blackboards.

"What we would most like to see happen is for the school to grow and reestablish the family's full might," Aaron says.

Kema nods. "We have been waiting for you to come along," she adds, with a wry smile. She says she has long held out hope that the school would receive some outside attention that would result in a charitable gift or sponsorship. It is a common kind of hope in Liberia. Before I leave she goes out onto the street to hire one of the itinerant photographers who always seem to be lurking about Monrovia, so that they might document my visit for posterity. She gives me a copy of a videotape of the 1999 graduation, when Taylor spoke, and says, "I beg you to remember us."

Later in the day I meet Maurice at the National Museum, a nearly empty, decaying husk of a building that once housed a massive collection chronicling one of the more interesting histories in Africa. After three separate lootings during the wars, the collection is down to only a few items, including the boot of warlord Roosevelt Johnson, which hangs from a nail in the wall. There are a few photos and letters, an American flag, and what the curator describes as "a traditional journalist's hat and vest"—an elaborate woven helmet decorated with seashells and a similar vest, which were worn by runners who delivered news between villages, chief to chief.

"The building was damaged by bullets and rocket fire," the curator tells me. "People come in and take things. Display bows were used for firewood. More than ninety-five percent of the collection was looted in 1980, 1990, 1996. We need donations of items, but people are slow to give."

"Not surprisingly," I say.

He looks at me curiously, nods, then introduces me to the museum director, Robert Cassell, who says he has heard about me from the Information Ministry. The two show me through an exhibit depicting UN efforts to repatriate Liberian refugees, who at one time represented about a third of the country's population. I say it's interesting that "repatriation" was also the term used for the American colonization effort in the nineteenth century, but they offer no reply.

The museum has a small collection of historic photographs that Maurice wants to help me go through, but the curator is not happy to hear this. Like so many people in positions of responsibility in Monrovia, the curator's demeanor can change abruptly from friendly to officious without warning, and Maurice's request to see the pictures, which does sound more like a demand, gets a decidedly cool reaction. The curator would rather have had more time to get the photos in order, he says, though in the end he agrees. He charges me $5 U.S. to look at the pictures, another $5 to photograph them.

Maurice goes through the photos, pointing out now-vanished mansions built by the freed slaves, which look like the antebellum homes of Mississippi—imposing frame buildings, most of Greek Revival architecture, with broad, columned verandas and shutters on the windows. Although many are sheathed in metal siding in a vain effort to forestall tropical rot, the houses are not the naive approximations I had expected. Most are finely executed. I don't know why this should come as a surprise, because even without access to architects, some of the immigrants were no doubt among the artisans who built the houses that have been so lovingly restored in Natchez, New Orleans, and Savannah. Maurice only comes across two photos of people whom he recognizes, both Rosses, one of whom poses demurely before a painted backdrop in a long, black hoopskirt.

After going through the photos, we stroll the nearly empty museum. Maurice turns to the curator and asks, "Why do you have the boot of Roosevelt Johnson?" Clearly, he is not a fan of Johnson's.

The curator bristles, and glares at him.

"It's a part of history," I offer.

The curator looks at me. "Exactly," he says, then turns his back to us.

Maurice and I head off to lunch. Walking down Broad Street we pass a garbage barrel emblazoned with the words KEEP OUR CITY CLEAN, which is overflowing with refuse. It seems such a futile effort, with litter everywhere, sewage flowing in the gutters, the air hazy around the clock with the pungent smoke from burning garbage dumps. A maddeningly loud electric generator belches black smoke from the Ministry of Finance building directly into the faces of passersby.

Men urinate on the streets, keeping their backs to the crowd, and here and there are signs painted on the walls of buildings admonishing PLEASE DON'T PEE PEE HERE or DON'T PEE HERE IF I CUT YOU. What is a person to do? I think. There are few bathrooms in Monrovia. There is no garbage pickup. Maurice has been drinking from a bottle of water, and when he finishes, throws the empty container to the ground.

We pass the ubiquitous shoe-shine men under their umbrellas, working away. We enter a walled compound at a corner where there is a small, air-conditioned restaurant, where Maurice's younger brother, Oso J. J. Ross Pelham, joins us. The younger Pelham has a brooding face that immediately erupts into a broad grin when the conversation touches upon the subject of America.

"You know," Maurice says, "the settlers, they had goals in life, and they worked. Joseph Ross made his mark. We're still trying to keep on."

"We are proud, but it is on our sleeves," Oso says. "Our pride will not be lifted until we regain our citizenship. We're American. We're not really Liberian. We're proud that J. J. Ross was vice president, proud of the school, but for us it is kind of hard to be proud. I don't want to move to the United States to stay. I would like to go there to complete my college education, because here I have no tools to work with. If the U.S. would grant me a visa, and I could complete my education, I could be everything my grandparents wanted. I want to study computer engineering. I want to gain knowledge. But for now I'm out of high school and can't go to college. I won't stay in America because I have to come back and make my country proud."

He says the farthest back his family can see is Mississippi. They do not know where their ancestors originated in Africa. "All we know is we went to America and we came here," Oso says. "When I was in high school, studying history, one day I realize: my great-grandfather is not from Africa! I wonder if that was where my vernacular, my dialect comes from. I wonder about Mississippi."

"Sometime we get sick of being here, ourselves," Maurice says. "The war. But we feel we have an obligation. A responsibility."

"The love of liberty brought us here," Oso says, quoting the Liberian national motto. "We fought for independence to prove we aren't outcasts. We can make something. That's why we're the oldest African nation.

"It's a funny thing, since the war we socialize more than before. We can play basketball at night. Play soccer. During the war the only place that was jammed was the club, the disco. A lot of people were scattered by the war. Liberians in Ghana, in our refugee camps. Our refugee camps make us proud—they say the camps don't look like refugees live there. So you know, whites are not the only creature of God. You guys mechanize things. . . ."

"And you have the facilities," Maurice interjects. "I feel I owe a loyalty to my family and to society," he adds. " 'What you're left, leave after you,' is the saying. I live for my family and society. I don't live for selfish gain. I live for the people. I can assist in life. People come and ask me to put their child in school, they can't pay, they come and ask and I accept. When it comes to hospitality, the Liberian people are good. We know how to treat people who come here. We make them feel they are a part of us. Ninety percent of what we are came from America. Someone like a Ross is always in a better position to help. Louise Ross worked at Firestone, reared a lot of orphan children, became a reverend mother. She founded King Peter's Orphanage Elementary School. In 1974 she founded J. J. Ross High School, so you could go on from there. They always felt we left America as a slave, we need to do something with ourselves in Africa. They had to do something on their own. We still consider ourselves Liberians, but we know where we come from."

Oso says he has a favor to ask, and already I know what it will be. He wants help getting a visa, and perhaps a scholarship to an American school. He is one of many bright, motivated young men, including Edward Railey and his brothers, whom I have met in Liberia who deserve a chance. I tell him I will see what I can do.

After lunch I return to the museum, where I meet Edward, who has been sitting with a relative who has malaria. On the way back to the convent, we pass a group of children on Broad Street flying a kite fashioned from a newspaper. We pass a food vending van parked on the street advertising "Jumbo is the ultamost good taste until you lick the plate!" Every cab we see has a motto or name painted on the side: "Even Jesus Wept," "Baby Dog," "Mother Knows Best," "No. 1 Gentleman," "Only God Knows," "Why Now?" and "No Situation Is Permanent."

We pass three children selling Cokes and candy bars from a makeshift stand on the curb. The oldest child, a boy of seven or eight, is playing a board game with his sister, who looks to be around six, while a toddler sleeps on a towel nearby, protected from the sun by an umbrella and from the pandemonium of the street by an ice-chest barricade. There are no adults around. Across the street, painted on a wall, is the only graffiti I have seen in Monrovia. It reads, "Bad Boyz of Mechlin St. Merry Christmas and Happy New Year 2001."

We pass a vendor selling cassettes, and, as always, it seems, Celine Dion is blaring from a raspy speaker. I understand the affinity with America, but the love of schmaltzy, hyperwhite pop music baffles me.

"What's the deal with Celine Dion?" I ask Edward. "We hear her everywhere we go."

"You don't like her?" he asks.

"No," I answer, emphatically.

"What about Michael Bolton?" he asks.

"Actually, no," I say.

"I like them very much!" he says.

As we approach the convent, we come upon a friend of Edward's whose name is Elvis Crusoe. We chat for a moment and then move on. I tell Edward I feel the circle is complete.

"I've watched *Mississippi Burning* in Liberia, I've found descendants of the Rosses of Prospect Hill, and now I've met Elvis on the street in Monrovia."

"And you have many days left!" he says, quite happily.

CHAPTER TWENTY

AN INCUBUS OF SMOKE from burning garbage slowly drifts over the wall of St. Teresa's, enveloping the garden where Benjamin Ross and I sit beneath a tree filled with pale pinkish orchids. I have asked several people what kind of tree this is but surprisingly, no one knows. It is something like a magnolia, very old, with roots that sprawl over the surface of the ground.

This garden is the closest thing to a sanctuary I have found in Monrovia, aside from the carefully manicured, fortified compound of the American embassy. It provides a welcome respite from the din of the streets, although there is no escaping the miasma that drifts and hovers over the city day and night. There is no garbage collection in Monrovia, so refuse piles up in every green space, including the cemeteries, until someone sets it on fire. The postcard view of the Atlantic from the city's highest hill, at Mamba Point, is spoiled by the sad specter of children picking through smoldering garbage beneath the swaying palms. Real estate like Mamba Point would be worth a fortune elsewhere, but its value has been subverted here, like so much of the country's real and potential wealth. Most of Mamba Point is a scenic dump, a wasteland with palms.

It is hard now to imagine Liberia as a promised land, yet that is how Benjamin Ross's ancestors saw it in 1849. Benjamin is the brother of the entrepreneur Nathan Ross Jr., whom I met at the Mamba Point Hotel, and we have come to this garden to talk about those ancestors, about his family history, which for all practical purposes began with their departure from Mississippi for Liberia, where crops grow year-round and the hills and streams are riddled with diamonds and gold.

One of Benjamin's ancestors, William Nathaniel Ross, left Prospect Hill with his family when he was a boy. The name of the plantation has been lost in the family's telling over the years, and likewise there is no account of the decade of litigation that preceded their immigration, but the link is there in the ship registry of immigrants from Prospect Hill. All anyone in his family knows is that a Mississippi slave owner named Isaac Ross paved the way for them to come to Liberia, and that, after an arduous ship passage from New Orleans, they arrived in 1849.

From that point the story becomes more real for Benjamin: the trials the family faced on the Liberian frontier, their rise to prominence over the decades, their political alliances and feuds, the outbreak of civil war, which occurred during his own lifetime and which, although it has officially ended, never seems to end. Somewhere along the way he happens upon an enchanted night, the most important moment in his personal history, when he meets the woman who is now his wife.

It is a tale of love in the ruins. It was during the war, early on, and Benjamin had bought an old taxi to shuttle people around Monrovia. "I was driving that evening and she hailed the taxi," he says. "She was the only passenger."

I know from experience what a rarity that is in Monrovia.

They were two strangers, alone, wending their way through the darkened streets of the war-torn city, through the throngs of people, serenaded by the incessant horns. Benjamin made small talk as he drove, sizing things up, getting up his nerve. She was very attractive.

"Finally I ask her if she is obligated to anyone," he recalls. "She said no. I ask for an invitation to visit her. She said no." When Benjamin put her out at her house, he made a mental note of the address.

"After a few months, I went to the house where I had left her," he says. "I thought maybe the big brother would give me a hard time, because she is younger than me, but he didn't."

Her name was Georgia Ezeagu, and she was then a student at Monrovia Business School. She had no money for the tuition to enroll in the University of Liberia, so Benjamin decided to help out.

"I sent her to the university," he says.

He pauses to brush a few ants from his shoulder that have dropped from the tree. People in Liberia are constantly brushing ants off their shoulders, and off mine, when we sit or stand beneath trees.

"So that is how it started," he says. "Now I am hoping to go to

America, where she is." Georgia Ross, who now lives in Philadelphia with the hope that her husband and children will soon join her, will laugh when I tell her, over the phone, after I return to the United States, how her husband recalls their meeting.

In her version, "It started as a friendship. It was 1987. The war had not started. We met through a friend of mine. He must have told me he wanted a friendship, but I really didn't take to the relationship in the beginning. Then I saw the way he was treating me. He was chasing me wherever I go! I would be at my school activities and he would show up. So in the end I give in. He became a part of me."

The remembered cab ride? "Oh, so many nights he picked me up in the cab," she will say, with a sigh that is audible even over the phone.

The irony escapes neither Benjamin nor me, that his ancestors risked their lives to emigrate from America to Liberia, and now he is struggling to get back. But it is not about failure, he says. He is simply responding to the situation at hand, just as they were. Liberia is his home, but like most descendants of freed slaves here, he feels a very real tie to America. If he is allowed to leave he hopes one day to return, but for now he must do what is best for his family.

The couple's marriage, in 1993, took place during a break in the fighting between factional groups in and around Monrovia. The year before, Charles Taylor had launched his successful offensive to take the city, and proclaimed himself Liberia's leader. When Interim President Amos Sawyer, representing the political party with which Georgia Ross was aligned, resigned, no one could be said to have control of the country. Reports by international refugee organizations and the United Nations estimated that during the worst fighting more than 150,000 people had been killed and more than 700,000 forced to seek refuge in the Ivory Coast, Guinea, Sierra Leone, Ghana, Gambia, and Mali.

Through it all, Benjamin and Georgia Ross remained in Monrovia, where he worked as an administrator in a bank, and she worked for the interim government, and later, the National Investment Commission.

"We went through a lot of things," Benjamin says. "Just in '99 my wife and I decided that one person should go to the States. She's a lady, so I said she should go ahead. It's faster for women to attain [immigrant] status. She left in September 1999 and she was granted citizenship. Now she has filed for me and the children. We sent all the children to Ghana, to the resettlement. Everything is at a standstill. If things work out well in Ghana, they'll leave and I will follow. Then after four or five years I will come back to see how the country is."

The couple's five children, aged fourteen to nineteen, are being supervised in a refugee camp by an aunt. "They went in 1999," Benjamin says. "The war was over," he adds, but they were in danger due to Georgia's association with Amos Sawyer's Unity Party. "In 1993 the country was divided, with Taylor controlling one portion, Sawyer another. Our side was relatively calm because of the ECOMOG intervention forces. It was right after a bad time. There was mass destruction during Octopus, in 1992. Then, we could move about. ECOMOG had things pretty calm." ECOMOG stands for the Economic Community of West African States Cease-fire Monitoring Group, which briefly maintained the peace in the region. Octopus is the name Liberians give to the particularly intense fighting that swept across Monrovia when the forces of Taylor and Johnson converged in October 1992, their tentacles reaching out from the various strongholds in and around Monrovia.

"I have not seen her since she left," he adds. "We talk twice a month over the phone and we have had three letters carried by people."

I had expected Benjamin Ross to be something of a maverick—an influential banker who had chosen to stick it out in Liberia. But he seems chastened, subdued, diffident, as if he has been forced to repress his self-assuredness. He chooses his words carefully. His clothes are nondescript, designed to say nothing: a short-sleeved white shirt, dark pants, dark shoes.

Yet his status is evident in subtle ways. On the day we first met and arranged for our talk in the convent garden, I had arrived at the Central Bank to find a boisterous crowd in the vestibule, calling out entreaties to two armed guards sitting at a desk with telephones. It was clear that no one was allowed to enter the bank without the permission of the guards, who grant it only upon the confirmation of someone inside. The crowd was excited because the Central Bank is where the money is. They sensed access. As soon as I walked through the door, one of the guards summoned me to the front of the line. Everyone noticed, of course, but no one seemed to mind. They were more curious than anything, as were the guards, who exchanged a glance when I asked for Benjamin Ross.

The guard made a phone call, spoke to someone, and soon Benjamin appeared and we retreated to a side room to talk. He seemed interested, if slightly mystified, by my explanation for why I had come to Liberia. He seemed aware of the guards' attention, and said he could not talk at the moment but suggested we meet a few days later, at the bank, and then move to the quiet courtyard at St. Teresa's convent. We shook hands—the more traditional handshake, I noticed, without the snap, and agreed on a time for me to come back.

Today, when I returned, Benjamin and I left the bank in his battered old Volvo, which is a luxury car by the standards of the average Liberian. As we pulled away, a wild-eyed beggar with a long beard approached the driver's window, talking excitedly. Benjamin gave him five Liberian dollars and the man responded with a crazy diatribe that I could not understand, but that made Benjamin smile. A policeman who observed the exchange laughed and waved, and I told myself that any Liberian who is able to give money to beggars is relatively fortunate, and recognizes it.

As we sit on a bench in the convent garden, he wants to hear what I know about the story of Prospect Hill. I give a thumbnail account, then ask if it is the same story he has heard. "Similar to what you told me. . . ." he says. "I believe there were three brothers, and one settled in Sinoe, one in Montserrado and one in Maryland. I came from the one in Montserrado."

He has not heard about the painful crucible that preceded their arrival. Perhaps the details were lost in the overpowering memory of the mayhem the family encountered once they arrived in Liberia.

Benjamin was born in Paynesville in 1944. His father, James Monroe Ross, was named after the American president from the time the colonization began. After his father died, he was reared and educated by his uncle, Nathan Ross Sr. The elder Ross, who was in the Liberian Congress, sought political asylum in the United States following the coup in 1980. "Our grandfather was William Nathaniel Ross," he says. "He was born in Caldwell, Montserrado County. Our great-grandfather, also William Nathaniel Ross, came over at age four. Our grandfather was a cousin of the late President William Tubman. He was a Methodist preacher and was in the Liberian army. Later he worked with the maritime bureau. I think he was the first Commander of Maritime Affairs in Liberia. Our grandfather used to fight with Tubman. He ran against the late Frank Tolbert, brother of the late president, in an election to be senator from Montserrado County. It was a close election, but because of the relationship they gave the position to Frank Tolbert. Our grandfather was outspoken, so the president was afraid of him. After that, the president found a job for him, the maritime job."

During his career as a Methodist minister, his grandfather erected three churches in Liberia, in Johnsonville, Paynesville, and New Georgia. "The Sinoe brother was John Ross," Benjamin says. "He lived on Mississippi Street. My grandfather's brother. The family was original to Sinoe. Some were traders, some were farmers. Our grandfather here farmed cattle and rubber. He established cocoa farms. The one in Maryland, he had a rubber plantation. It was large—if I'm not mistaken, about one thousand acres. Joshua was his name." Along with the plantations the family owned large, antebellum-style houses.

"Being from Mississippi meant something to them," he says. "Even the natives wished to be a part of that because they were privileged. Having an education helped a lot. They educated the natives, they shared what they had. Some of the natives took the Ross name. They took them into their house. It still happens, but not like before where you carry the children and they take your name."

It occurs to me, listening to him, that the Ross name has a strange currency, a strange fluidity. The white Ross clan originated in Scotland but emigrated to Ireland and then to the United States. From Isaac Ross the name was passed on to his slaves, who in turn passed it on to their wards in Liberia.

"I would be curious about the Rosses in the U.S., to get the family tree," he says. "Most of those who had traced the family tree here are gone. Most of the old people die." I offer to mail him copies of the records I have, but he points out that the postal system in Liberia is unreliable. "Maybe you will be able to mail it to me in the U.S.," he says, and smiles. "If my wife's request to bring the family is approved this year, I leave this year."

In the meantime, there is only the waiting. "Some days it's very difficult," he says. "Some days you can't afford a meal. We are working, I'm an administrator; I've been at the bank fourteen years, but some days you can't afford a meal." He is not complaining—he is simply describing the lay of the land.

*   *   *

When Benjamin suggests that I talk with his uncle, Nathan Ross Sr., I tell him that we have already spoken, on the phone, before I came to Liberia. I had been referred to him by a woman I met at the meeting of Sinoe County expatriates in Atlanta. Nathan Ross Sr.'s account of the family history differs from Benjamin Ross's, possibly due to the replication of names, because there were at least two William Nathaniel Rosses, as there are two Nathan Cicero Rosses. During my research I also found a 1984 article in the Jackson, Mississippi, *Clarion-Ledger* about the immigrants from Prospect Hill, which noted that General William Nathaniel Ross, who died in 1969, was aide-de-camp to the president of Liberia and the son of William Nathaniel and Caroline Rebecca Hannah Ross of Cape Palmas, in Maryland County. He had moved to Monrovia with an uncle, Reverend W. N. Ross, in 1912, returning to Cape Palmas in 1929, where he worked at one of the Firestone plantations. This was apparently the man Benjamin Ross referred to as his grandfather, because he later became a Methodist minister. The article noted that he also rose to the rank of captain in the state militia, and in 1950 was commissioned an aide-de-camp to President Tubman. It seems possible that the Reverend W. N. Ross also had the same name.

Nathan Ross Sr. had said that the boy, William Nathaniel Ross, who immigrated from Mississippi, was his father. At the beginning of the call he had very politely told me that it was not a good time for him to talk because, "One of my sisters' sons is dead in Liberia," yet just as I was about to offer my condolences and say good-bye he added, "My father was a Ross. He was William. He was from Mississippi. He came in the 1800s. He was a freed slave." William Ross was four when the family immigrated in 1849 and fathered children into his old age, including Nathan Ross Sr. in 1916, he said. The odds seem impossibly long—that I should happen upon anyone today who is the son of a slave, much less one who immigrated from Prospect Hill to Liberia, but the math adds up.

Nathan Sr. said his father married his mother in 1913, when he was fairly old, "and I'm the offspring of them." Most of the Rosses, he said, settled in Rossville, north of Greenville, but many later left that part of Liberia in search of jobs. "Monrovia is more central. Some went to Cape Palmas in Maryland County. They landed in Sinoe and from Sinoe they found themselves in different places," he said.

Nathan Sr.'s immediate family moved to Monrovia, where he was elected to the Liberian Congress, which is patterned after the United States Congress. He was a member of Congress in 1980 when the coup took place, and, "After that, my children, who were in school here [in the United States], suggested my wife and I come over." This sounded like something of an understatement, and in fact his wife, Alice, later told me that following the coup he likely would have been executed.

When the 1980 coup came, his wife said, the couple was attending an international meeting of parliamentarians in Norway. "That's where we were when they killed the president, Tolbert," she said. Because her husband was in Congress and considered part of the Tolbert regime, it was unsafe to return. Some of his fellow congressional representatives did return and were killed.

"So we left all our things there. We left to go to a meeting and then we could not go back. They raided our house and took everything in the house. The house is still there. They shot at it and shot at it but they couldn't knock it down," she said, with some satisfaction. "My mother died during that tumult," she added, her voice growing quiet. "She was living in the house there with us. Some of our children were there and they had to run for their life. Luckily, my daughter was working for the American Cooperative School and they helped her to get to the United States, to Colorado, where she was given a job as a teacher. But my mother was wounded. She was paralyzed and they pushed her wheelchair down the steps. She died from the injuries. Our children took her to the hospital but she died, and they buried her before they left.

"It's difficult," she said, describing their inability to attend their nephew's funeral in Monrovia. "We're here, we're not working, we can't go there." The couple has been back only once since the coup, she said. "We left to go back and live and then decided they are fighting again and we have to get out again."

Nathan Sr. told me that he knows very little about his family's Mississippi connections in the United States. "One of the young men in World War II stopped at Roberts Field and he came to Monrovia and said he was a Ross from Mississippi, but we lost his address," he said, ruefully.

With the loss of the Mississippian's address, he added, the possibility of reestablishing an American connection dimmed. But when he emigrated to the United States he found that there were "quite a lot of Rosses, white and black. Once I met a man named Nathan Ross, who was white." He said he is still surprised by the number of American Rosses. "I look on the TV and there are Rosses. In Hollywood there are Rosses. Diana Ross—I've met her. Ross seems to be a very popular name on this side."

Alice told me the family still considers Liberia home, but that for her and her husband the prospects of returning are slim. She said her last visit to Liberia was in 1986. She went alone. "I told him, 'You stay. You were in the government. I can go.'"

She still has cousins in Liberia, and they are apparently among the more fortunate, since they have a telephone. "It's difficult to talk to them sometimes, though," she said. "Just recently we heard they were fighting again. It's a civil war. . . ." Her voice trailed off. Then she regrouped. "Both sides of our children are in the U.S. They are all married and have children. Our oldest boy, Nathan Jr., travels all the time. He goes to Liberia." This will turn out to be the same man whom I meet at the Mamba Point Hotel.

After talking with Nathan and Alice Ross, I checked the list of immigrants aboard the barque *Laura*, which sailed from New Orleans on January 29, 1849, for Liberia, and found William Ross, age four, the child of Frances Ross, who was also listed in the inventory of Ross's estate, age twelve in 1836 and valued at $500. William Ross was number sixty-nine among 141 Mississippi immigrants on board who had been emancipated by Isaac Ross's will. Also listed were William's siblings, Epsey, age nine, Sarah, age one, and their mother, Frances, whose age was listed, perhaps erroneously, as twenty-eight at the time.

Benjamin says he is mindful of the sacrifices made by so many to establish his family in Liberia, and of the irony of his attempting to reverse the course, as he now seeks to emigrate to the United States.

"I don't know what that makes me," he says. "I guess when I get to the U.S. I will be an African-American, but one day I hope to come back. This is my home. We in Liberia always like to identify with the black American. It's a prestige. It seems as though you are above the other Liberians just to be connected with America. I think the reason is poverty—it gives you hope of getting out of poverty. When your name is linked with some family in America, it gives you privilege. It gives you hope."

That hope, which once buoyed the family in Liberia, now beckons him to the United States.

Benjamin's family separation is only the most recent episode in a drama that is filled with bittersweet longing. Like their ancestors before them, he and Georgia faced significant obstacles from the start. There was the matter of their age difference—twenty-two years. There was the noteworthy difference in their ancestry—she is half Nigerian, half descendant of the Kpelle tribe, from near the Liberian border with Guinea, while his ancestors were among the ruling class of freed slaves. There was the war, which often pitted descendants of native tribes against the descendants of freed slaves. Now there is the aftermath of political instability and economic devastation, which has scattered the family to three countries.

Today, he says, the Ross family's numerous homes are mostly gone.

"In Sinoe the family house was frame, with plank floors and pillars, two-story," he recalls. "In Paynesville the house was three stories. They're both gone now. All of them are gone. The war, in 1990, took them down. The soldiers sprinkled gasoline inside them and burned them." The monument erected to the freed slaves on Mississippi Street in Greenville was razed by rebels who believed there were diamonds and gold in the foundation.

"Only the vaults in the cemetery, they don't bother," he says. "There is nothing left, really. Just vast land. Nothing."

CHAPTER TWENTY-ONE

EDWARD RAILEY WAS A small boy in 1990 when his family's Louisiana home was nearly destroyed by the war. The family repaired the house only to see the fighting return, and this time they were forced to scatter, which was a serious trauma for him at such a young age. He fled Louisiana on foot with a local Methodist official and two other boys, walking for two days.

"We walked by the beach from Sinoe to the Cesta River so the soldiers, the fighters—who were mostly sixteen- or seventeen-year-old kids—would not find us," he says. "If they found us they would make us fight. They make everyone fight, boys and girls."

His group managed to elude the rebels, then crossed the Cesta River on a bridge the soldiers had built and found a man to drive them to Monrovia, where Edward had heard that his mother had taken refuge. As it turned out, many had fled the city as well, trying to escape the fighting that was sweeping the country. No place was safe.

"No one was hardly living in Monrovia then, we were hearing," he recalls. "We did not know what we would find. But I found most of my relatives, and then I went to find my mom."

He found her living on the outskirts of Monrovia, in Duport Road. He found his brothers, Kaiser and Augustus, and his sister Princess. There was a joyful, if tenuous, reunion. Duport Road became their adopted home. Then the fighting came to Duport Road.

"This area was very heated during the war," he says as we walk the path to his mother's house. "Many die." The community is not far from the highway he followed from Sinoe to Monrovia in 1992. "The war introduced the road," he points out. "They made the way easier." The soldiers and rebels had needed better routes to maneuver through the bush, and once they were built, such roads offered the refugees more and quicker avenues of escape.

Despite the fragmentation of his family's life in Liberia, Edward says his life is not all bad. He has known worse, just as he has known much better. As we talk about his family history, I picture the sort of dotted lines that might be used to trace an explorer's voyage around the globe. But the point of origin, like the final destination, is unclear. In Atlantic, to the United States, where he wants to go to school to study theology. From that point it would backtrack to Monrovia, where his dream is to return and help resurrect his country from its ongoing despair.

The aftermath of the war is what compels him to try to leave. He spends his days honing dreams of escape, which are as pervasive in Liberia as the stories of dispersal that brought the original immigrants here. Dreams are contemplated during quiet times, and despite all of their troubles and the threat of violence, that is how most Liberians view the current period. Many, including Edward, recall walking a hundred miles or more to flee the fighting, thinking only of survival.

Duport Road is a half-hour drive from Monrovia, but the trip requires three changes of cabs, which makes for an adventure since the old yellow Nissans often break down and no cab driver in Liberia considers his car full until there are seven passengers aboard. Many of the cabs have cracked and even shattered windshields, which provide a disquieting vantage point from which to view the passing scenery. On the way to Duport Road, we pass an old, tidewater-style house, long unpainted, with a swept dirt yard, which looks as if it has been lifted from a scene in the Carolinas in the 1930s. We pass a monument inscribed with the words, EVEN WARS HAVE LIMITS. Scattered along the road are the bare chassis of cars, stripped of everything that can be removed. We dodge gaping holes in the pavement where sewer grates have been scavenged for cooking grills. We stop to pick up a bewildered-looking old woman in a country dress who approaches the cab and scans the door, trying to figure out how to open it. When she gets in, she slams the door on her foot, and Kaiser Railey leans over to tell me, "The car is a new thing for her. The war force many people from their homes in the bush and they have no way to get back." The old woman watches the road ahead tentatively.

When we get to Duport Road, we take a red-dirt footpath to Abbie Jones's home, past a crudely built open-air market, a soccer field, and a scattering of houses in groves of palms surrounded by fallow fields. There are no vegetable gardens behind the country houses here, as there are in the American South, which seems odd. When I mention this, Edward says that people buy produce from farmers who live farther out in the countryside.

Abbie lives in a small duplex with no electricity or running water, both of which it had before the war. When we arrive she is busy preparing a ceremonial meal for me, the out-of-town guest. Most everyone is here—Edward, Kaiser, their brothers Augustus and Prince, their sister, Princess, and two wards named Amie and Samtoinette, who everyone tells me are like a brother and sister to them. Another sister, Joetta Railey, and several uncles and aunts live in Monrovia. The "Old Ma," as they call their grandmother, Nora Jones, lives in nearby Barnersville in her son Boy Jones's home. The father and grandfathers are dead. Edward is the one who helps care for his niece who has malaria and helps arrange the funerals of two aunts who die during my stay in Monrovia.

Seeing them gathered together, I am amazed at how upbeat everyone appears. They are a happy family despite their circumstances, and glad to be together. We sit for hours outside, greeting passersby who follow the footpath that crosses Jones's yard. There is a cool breeze under the palms, but step into the sun, and it is like moving close to a fire. The wards and Princess wash and starch clothes in buckets as we listen to news of the sanctions debate on the radio, and later, to a soccer game, which is the passion of seemingly every boy and man in Liberia. Sitting here, watching the chickens search for bugs beneath the palms, listening to the soccer game, it is easy to forget what the family has been through, and what they are still going through. Stories of unimaginable sadness and horror come up in conversation, sometimes at strategic points, but they only accentuate the joy and determination that people like the Raileys and the Joneses project. It is important to everyone, even strangers, for visitors to have a positive experience in Liberia, particularly because so many come, as I came, expecting the worst. Princess Railey had earlier questioned me about my opinions of various Liberian foods and today, as she goes into her mother's house to help prepare the meal, says, "I have not forget the plantains," and smiles.

Jones has prepared a dish called foo-foo, which is a patty of ground cassava root eaten with a stew of meat and greens. Foo-foo takes days to prepare. First you grind the cassava root, then mix it with water and place it in a container to sit for a day or longer. Finally, it is cooked in something like a Dutch oven over a fire. Preparing comparatively elaborate meals is the done thing when visitors are in town, and it is not negotiable.

When we later visit Joetta Railey's house in Monrovia, she insists that I sit down at a tiny, rickety table and eat the meal that she has prepared. She sends her daughter out onto the street to buy Cokes.

Joetta lives in a crude shelter perched at the end of an alley strewn with rubble overlooking Providence Island, where the freed slaves landed in the nineteenth century. Hers is a community of hapless souls, with low expectations, where street vendors' racks lean against the walls of their dark houses. She has two tiny rooms, no water or electricity, and a single, shuttered window without glass. She has a thin foam pad for a bed. Her clothes hang from nails in the wall. There is an old dresser with a broken mirror.

Joetta looks as if she might once have been attractive but she is worn down now. Her eyes are watery. She has a cold, and smokes. Still, what she has she will share.

"You will always be welcome here," she says. "If you ever need a place to go, you can come here. If there is trouble, you can come here. If you find yourself on the street at night with no place to go, you can stay here." Then she adds, "I am over the family, and I have nothing. Anything would help."

I realize then that her meal has a hidden cost, which is the exception to the rule. She wants money, which will anger her brothers when they later find out. Joetta takes me outside to ask, and I never mention it to the brothers, but somehow they figure it out on their own. The brothers are, if nothing else, aware. They want to know how much she asked for, and it becomes apparent that a family meeting will soon follow.

"This makes me very angry," Edward tells me after he finds out. "You are our guest, she should not ask for money. We have seen how you volunteer money, without being asked."

There is so little that someone in Edward's position can control. Like anyone would, he clings to what he can.

Joetta's ragtag house in Monrovia is a stark departure from the home Nora Jones shares with her son in Barnersville, on the outskirts of the city. Nora is the true matriarch of the family, and her home is immaculate. Flowers bloom in beds scattered throughout the swept-dirt yard. She greets us at the door, resplendent in a purple and green plaid dress, green beads, a silver bracelet, and tinted glasses. Inside, the walls are painted vivid pastel green and the floor is gleaming, faux-marble tile. White ladder-back chairs are perfectly arranged around a coffee table, and sunlight filters through a skylight above.

Nora is a quilter from Louisiana, although, she says, "People don't buy the quilts now." When I ask why, she replies, "No money, my dear."

"I was born in Lexington," she says. "My mother was from Louisiana. Her grandfather was a Walker." When I tell her that the Walkers were among the group who immigrated from Prospect Hill, she nods. "These are the people you are looking for?" she asks.

Some of them, I say. I have a list of the Walkers who immigrated, and it seems likely that her ancestors were among them, but there are no written records and she does not have names of her own.

"I don't know much about where they came from," she says. "Most of the people have left Sinoe. Sometimes people talk about going back, but not many do because they don't know what the future holds. Still, you know, there's no place like home."

She pulls out her only remaining quilt, which has an appliqué of a basket overflowing with red and green flowers, surrounded by borders of yellow, green, and red interspersed with flowering vines. There are two large, red patches where she has repaired tears in the fabric

She lost most of her quilts during the fighting, she says. "They put a rocket on my house during the war—I was in the Ivory Coast at the time—and the roof fell. This is the only quilt I could find."

She says she remembers when people grew cotton in Louisiana because she used it in her quilts. The practice of quilting, too, was brought to Liberia by the immigrants from America.

Such remnants are among the few that people have managed to preserve during their forced wanderings. The disruption of family life and everything it encompasses has been total for many. I notice a very beautiful little girl, Joyce, who lives with Nora, and when I ask whose child she is, she answers, "My son, he found her." The family will rear her as one of their own, christen her, and see that she is educated. Wherever Jones's family lives will be her home.

For people like the Joneses, the Raileys, and the Rosses, home is literally where the heart is, and seldom more. Physical buildings collapse or are destroyed and are left behind. People take with them the familiar customs and whatever else they can, but their history is a series of encampments of varying duration—the slave cabins of the American South, the frame houses of Sinoe County, whatever accommodations they may find in Monrovia now, perhaps an apartment in America somewhere down the line. The quest for home started when the first of their family members were dragged from their huts somewhere in Africa and shipped off to America as slaves.

This is not to say that they do not firmly identify with their communities. Nora's family, after all, lived in Sinoe County for 150 years. The only constants now, though, are their family ties and certain aspects of their culture, the most lasting of which has proved to be the church.

For slaves in the old American South, religion provided the greatest source of hope and the only outlet for their longing for freedom that was generally sanctioned by their masters. The colony of Liberia was seen as an opportunity to spread Christianity to Africa. As a result, churches are found everywhere in Liberia, and aside from the single, aberrant massacre of hundreds of refugees in a Lutheran church in Monrovia in 1992, most have been immune to the fighting. The predominant religions are Methodist, Episcopalian, and Catholic, although there are also places of worship for the Muslim, Lutheran, and Baptist denominations, as well as for native faiths. Revival meetings are popular, often held under tents at night. Along one rural road I saw a sign pointing to the mission of a group that called itself the Explosive Messengers of Christ. When I asked my student-activist friend the most important legacy of colonization, he said, without hesitation, "The church."

The Joneses and Raileys are active in the Methodist church, and on my first Sunday in Liberia, the brothers took me to services at S.T. Nagbe United Methodist Church in Monrovia. The service was familiar but with an occasional exotic twist. There was a lot of music, the songs ranging from soft, reverent lullabies to a rousing "Holy, holy, holy" with drums, to what sounded like slave spirituals, to something like trance music that went on and on with an off-tempo clap. I noticed that there were holes in the stained-glass windows, which Kaiser Railey later told me came from stray bullets. Ceiling fans stirred the muggy air as the preacher, who once lived in America, delivered a poignant, inspiring sermon. At one point the visitors were asked to speak into a portable microphone and tell where they were from, and each announcement drew thunderous applause. The response I got was similar to those given to the other visitors, but I felt the spotlight when the minister made the requisite plea for money and mentioned—pointedly, it seemed to me—that because America is unimaginably rich, Americans with money could do a lot for a church in Liberia. Afterward the plate was passed, twice.

The service was long, and after a couple of hours Kaiser Railey and I took our leave during a prayer. As we slipped out, a man leaned into the aisle and quietly asked for my address and phone number.

Kaiser often accompanies Edward and me on our forays around Monrovia, and we have developed a rapport. I ask how he spends an average day, because he is unemployed, has no job prospects, and cannot afford to go to college now. He has a room in a relative's house but does not spend much time there, he says.

"I can't work, I can't go to school," he says. "The time is wasting out. I don't stay in my room because I think about this. So I walk."

Kaiser's abiding passion is for soccer. Aside from the church, it is his greatest source of joy, and it is uncompromised. Although church is important to him, he refuses to take communion because, he says, "I see people taking communion and then they go back to living their life just like before. I do not take communion until my life is right."

Soccer is another story. I have come at a fortuitous time, during the playoffs leading up to the Africa Cup. After several languorous hours in Duport Road, the brothers and I head back to Monrovia to watch the Nigeria-Ghana soccer match on television, which is particularly important because Liberia will play Nigeria next, and both teams are in the running for the cup. The beauty of soccer is that you can play it anywhere—I see boys playing on the beach, in empty lots, in the streets. When the country's team is elevated in international status, it puts every Liberian on the map. Everyone feels a rare national pride.

On the main dirt route through Duport Road, we catch a cab to the highway, where we board another cab back to Monrovia. As we pass

the president's second home, which is known as the Number Two executive mansion, a band is playing on the road shoulder with a sign wishing the president a happy birthday. Tomorrow Charles Taylor will be
fifty-three. There are sandbag bunkers on the roof of the mansion, as
there are on the roofs of the buildings at the American embassy. In
Monrovia, we take another cab to a neighborhood that looks rundown
even by Liberian standards, where a house similar to Jefferson Davis's
Brierfield plantation home, but smaller, stands at the end of the street.
Inside a small building, through a curtained door, men are watching
the soccer match for $25 Liberian, about sixty cents U.S.

Kaiser looks inside, tells me to check it out. Behind the curtain,
perhaps thirty men are crowded into a tiny room, sitting in straight-
back chairs, watching the fuzzy picture on an old black-and-white TV.
It is stiflingly hot and stuffy.

"It's very crowded," I say, doubtfully.

Kaiser looks at Edward.

"Why don't y'all watch it, and I'll go find something to eat?" I say.

They think about this. They would forgo the match if that was what
I wanted, but I insist that they watch the game, so Kaiser walks me
back to the junction to catch a cab to the convent, where I follow the
action by the sound of cheering in the neighborhood outside my window each time Liberia scores. The scene is repeated a few days later
when Liberia beats Nigeria and the cheering erupts again, accompanied by a serenade of horns in the streets.

The next day the Railey brothers and I discuss the match at a bar called
the Rivoli, which is their favorite place to stop because it is normally
beyond their reach—a place right on Broad Street that sells Guinness
beer, which is expensive to them but remarkably cheap to me. Whenever there is a break in my appointed rounds—which normally drag us
along the streets of Monrovia all day long—the brothers sense an
opening and I know that the path will soon lead us back to the Rivoli.
The bar is above a rundown theater that shows Indian movies, Rambo-
style action flicks, and films that were never released in the United
States, and each time we come Augustus makes a point of saying that
his birthday is approaching and that the best gift he can imagine would

be to have enough money to spend an entire day at the movies. I take the hint.

From the balcony of the Rivoli we watch the man with the badly broken leg, whose name is Sheriff, as he attempts to navigate the traffic on one crutch. I feel bad when I find that I ignored him as we were coming up the stairs. "Hey, chief," he had said, and I pretended not to hear even though he was only a few feet away. I had not recognized him.

When we get to our table Edward says, "Did you know that was your friend who you gave the money to?"

I shake my head. I had seen someone out of the corner of my eye, but had heard what sounded like a sales pitch in his voice, and so ignored him. It was an American moment for me. I was at a low ebb, one of many during my stay in Monrovia, when I grow weary of the constant attention of people on the street. It is something no one in Liberia apparently feels, or if they do, it does not show. Sometimes I can't endure any more heartfelt attention, any more plaintive calls from strangers, any more solicitous, hopeful stares from people wanting to meet me, to get my name, my phone number, my address, thinking maybe I can get them out of this mess. How can I help everyone find a home? The push and pull of conflicting forces that characterizes everything about life in Liberia affects me, too. I vacillate between wanting to help and wanting to be left alone. There is so much need. Unable to escape their notice, I am often overcome with a desire to go home.

My interaction with people on the street occasionally draws unwelcome attention to the Raileys, as when Kaiser and I are walking to their sister's house and speak to a man in passing, and he responds by berating Kaiser. "Why does the white man speak to me and you don't?" he shouts as we head down the street.

When I ask the brothers what most people think when they see us walking down the street together, Augustus Railey says, "They think you are from the U.S. . . ."

"And they think we are trying to get money from you," Kaiser adds.

On another occasion, when Kaiser and Edward are waiting for me outside the American embassy, they overhear one of the guards say to another, "I've been seeing these guys going up and down the street with that white man."

At times I tire of all this recognition and seek refuge at the convent, but it is only a matter of time before the attention follows me there. People find out where I am staying and a few convince the guards to let them through the gate, find my room, knock on the door, and introduce themselves to me and tell me their lament. Eventually people within the convent begin to fill me in on their travails. Someone knocks on my door. I don't answer. I hear someone say, "Mr. Alan, Mr. Alan." Then I hear him say to someone, "I am looking for the white man, Mr. Alan." I go to the door. He wants to give me his résumé. He wants me to give it to someone, anyone, maybe a member of Congress, maybe they will hire him as a security guard at the embassy. When I realize I can no longer even retreat to my room, I am briefly overcome with a need to escape. I want out.

Then I realize: this is how many Liberians feel every day—trapped. How could they leave me alone?

Lucy McGovern, the missionary volunteer from Massachusetts, told me that she reaches this point of saturation now and then. "Sometimes I hear the knock on the door and I don't answer," she said. "I never thought it could feel so good not to answer a knock at the door. I ask myself, What would Jesus do? He wouldn't hide. But he's God, and I'm a human being. I have limits. And I know that Jesus came empty-handed. He didn't come to bring them money. I have come empty-handed, but they don't believe that. I have given them my life but they want money. Even the UN has gotten tired of Liberia not being able to help itself."

Lucy is here to help but feels frustrated, taken advantage of, and seems to grow more so during the time I am here, in part because her closest friend, another American missionary volunteer, has given up and headed home. There is also the matter of a severe and inexplicable breakout on her face, a rash that people have been telling her often besets visitors to Liberia and will go away, but which is, in fact, getting worse. It is not just her soul that is reeling right now. Her face is changing.

I can relate to Lucy's confusion. Sheriff, the man with the swollen, broken leg, experiences the full range of my waffling. Yesterday I chatted amiably with him on the street and gave him money, and today I act like I don't know him.

"You know, I feel bad that I snubbed Sheriff," I tell the Raileys. "I feel like the guy in the Bible who crosses the street to avoid the beggar."

"It's okay," Edward says. "You made him happy that you gave him some money. He thinks maybe you don't hear him this time."

Edward is perennially upbeat. His face seems always to be verging on a smile, though sometimes, in between smiles, his brow is noticeably, deeply furrowed.

The friendliness of everyone around me can be infectious, and I welcome the overtures of strangers, which bewilders Edward because he knows that once I start handing out money there will be no end to it. Every introduction wends its way hopefully toward a transaction, and once someone finds out that you have given away money, they naturally want in on the action. I forget that I am often the lone, comparatively wealthy American on the streets of Monrovia, a city of a million people. As I waited for Edward on the street in front of the National Museum, I was actually surprised that he managed to spot me and wave from two blocks away—forgetting the obvious, that mine was the only white face in a very large crowd. I was reminded when I glanced back toward the street and noticed that the cabs were slowing down and people were staring at me as they passed, as if I was a traveling exhibit at the museum. In a city where cab drivers have been known to go out of their way to pass through the one functioning traffic light, it is impossible to discount the novelty of a white man loitering on the street, particularly because I have more money in my belt than most people here will see in a lifetime. I am a flash of hope in their world that will fly away in a few brief days.

Among the Liberians who have jobs, few make more than $20 to $25 U.S. per month, if they get paid at all. Most are hopelessly uncmployed and have been for some time. People need money for everything: amputees need crutches and wheelchairs, students need tuition, schools need books, sick people need medication, almost everyone needs food, and hundreds of thousands need simple protection from the elements. Homelessness is not a condition of people on the fringes here—it affects a significant part of the population. The one need that cuts through every sector of Liberian society is for help in leaving the country. For all their resiliency, and despite long-standing disputes between the descendants of freed slaves and indigenous tribes, the majority of Liberians need what America has to offer. They are not alone, of course. The world is full of people who share that need. The biggest difference is that Liberia and the United States have significant family ties.

Before I came to Liberia, I read an article in the Baltimore *Sun* concerning the possible deportation of approximately 10,000 Liberian refugees in the United States whose special political refugee status was about to expire. The article quoted Danlette Norris, president of the Liberian Community Association of Rhode Island, who said of her homeland, "The whole region is in chaos. Sending us back is like sending us back to a death trap. We consider America our mother country." This view of Liberia, as a satellite of America, is not limited to refugees or to people who want to emigrate.

J. Paye Legay, at the Ministry of Information, said he has no desire to emigrate, but still believes that America should have a greater role in supporting the country. It is a recurring theme in all our conversations. I ran into him on the street outside the convent after he had dropped his car off at a garage, and as we talked a large slab of concrete broke from one of the ruined buildings across the street and crashed to the ground. Luckily, no one was standing nearby. Watching the dust billow into the street, he said, "You see? You see how much needs to be done?"

In his mind, Liberia is the Liberian's rightful home, not America. This is true whether your family once lived in America or has been in Africa all along. But he asserts that America has influenced Liberia's history in profound ways, and has a responsibility to ensure that the country survives.

It is hard to argue with him. The expectation pervades Liberian culture, which is why I—as an American—attract so many entreaties. Faced with such an onslaught of need, sooner or later I have to tune it out, until someone comes along and says, with a broad smile, "Hello! How are you today?" and I get pulled back in. Sometimes these encounters reinforce my feeling of separateness, but more often they obliterate it. The approach is almost always gentle, which is why I have no qualms about walking streets that I would not venture down in the United States. For whatever reason, and despite the transience, the overwhelming need, and the constant undercurrent of fear, I feel strangely at home here. If nothing else, everyone I meet is intent on making me feel at home. As we walked through a crowded market one morning, Edward and I came upon a friend of his who asked if anyone had bothered me on the street. "Has anyone humiliated you? Anyone?" he asked. I shook my head. "See?" he said, smiling. "Liberians are not all bad."

Later, one of the guards at the convent told me that I could move freely through Monrovia because no one wanted to see harm come to me. "Liberia is not a bad place, not completely bad," the guard said. "You, a white man, could walk all the way across Monrovia at night and no one bother you. Only when the heat is on, then you have trouble."

Edward says much the same thing, although he does not agree with the notion that I would be safe alone at night. He says that making sure I am comfortable is everyone's concern, and although the cynic in me thinks that there is often a thinly veiled agenda—that there is some benign duplicity at work—most of the time the interest I encounter seems genuine. If anyone were to bother me on the street, Edward says, others would rush to my defense, but he makes clear that I am not to be out after 9:30 P.M., because there are no lights and thieves and prostitutes take over the streets. He is alarmed when I tell him that the men who hang out by the convent wall in the morning have asked me to meet them there one night.

"No," he says, flatly. "They may be okay, but maybe later this month they be talking about armed robbery, because they hungry. So promise me you will not go out the gate alone at night."

I acquiesce, thinking that before I came here I could not have imagined needing such advice. I had expected the worst. I had envisioned Liberia as a place where nothing is sacred, where people roam the countryside and the battle-scarred city streets without regard to laws, where only a few stalwart souls, including the residents of old Mississippi in Africa, struggle to remain rooted and civil in a world that is disintegrating around them. I had imagined that Mississippi in Africa, Sinoe County, would be my refuge. My idea of Liberia was carefully researched and constructed, and all wrong. There is no safe harbor, but there is the kindness of strangers. You may be uprooted, but if you can survive the tumult there will always be someone to take you in.

I read nothing of this aspect of Liberian life before coming here. Instead I came across endless accounts of the war's atrocities and its aftermath of despair, and numerous bold-faced warnings for anyone crazy enough to consider traveling to a place that epitomizes chaos and the dark end of the civilized world. Even seemingly objective accounts were unwavering: according to the most recent U.S. State Department travel advisory, "Monrovia's crime rate is high. Theft and assault are major problems and occur more frequently after dark. Foreigners, including U.S. citizens, have been targets of street crime and robbery. Residential armed break-ins are common. The police are ill-equipped and largely incapable of providing effective protection. Hospital and medical facilities are poorly equipped and incapable of providing basic services."

Reading this, I had pictured a place that was like a sprawling, crime-ridden housing project in America, where there is little regard for life, where even crossing the street poses a considerable risk. What I found instead is a place where soldiers sometimes commit acts of unspeakable violence, where the government is astoundingly corrupt, where atrocities are a part of the backdrop of daily life, but where most people are remarkably friendly and crime is typically the petty kind. Coming from a place where people are held up at gunpoint before scores of witnesses in broad daylight, where drive-by shootings are common, where robbers follow elderly people home from grocery stores and pistol-whip them or shoot them in their driveways for their money, the pickpockets and prostitutes of Monrovia seem almost quaint. It is the monster lurking beneath—the threat of renewed civil war, and the menace of the government—that makes you wonder how useful warmth and generosity will be in the end. No doubt that is why so many want to leave.

I try to remain mindful of my safety on the streets. I heed Edward's advice because I have a lot to lose. I let the Raileys make all of my transactions for me, including changing money. They are my go-betweens. I let Edward order another round of Guinness at the Rivoli.

When we first met, Edward and I knew nothing of each other. We had only John Singler, who had taught his mother in school, in common. John's name comes up in conversation often because Edward and his family have all benefited from his kindness and consider him family. John taught in Sinoe County in 1969 and 1970, lived there again in the 1980s, and considers Liberia his home away from home.

Edward is shocked when I tell him that John and I have at this

point never met, that we communicate over the Internet and have spoken only by phone. This sort of friendship is unimaginable in Liberia,
where despite the dispersals, relationships are almost always built upon
physical presence. Our visits to the homes of Edward's family members, which are scattered around Monrovia and in communities in the
nearby countryside, are rarely scheduled. We just show up and are welcomed. If someone is not home, we come back later. Although there
are always long lines at the handful of Internet cafés that first opened
here in October 2000, the average Liberian's daily life is a world away
from virtual friendships, cell phones, and e-mail. This is not to say that
finding someone is always easy. You just head out and hope for the
best. From what I can tell, no one ever gives up on finding someone.
Liberians, of necessity, are tenacious.

As we have traipsed around Monrovia and the surrounding countryside, Edward and I have become friends. He has let me into his life,
and has probed every resource at his disposal to help find leads for me
in my research, while keeping my personal safety a paramount concern. My search for the descendants of Prospect Hill intrigues him in
part because he knows little about his own family history other than
that they lived in Louisiana. Beyond that, the past is as hazy as the
future. But as we sit at the Rivoli bar, it dawns on me: I know where his
family is originally from. In my zeal to find the Rosses, it had slipped
my mind that before I had left the United States, John had told me that
the Raileys were emancipated from the same region of Mississippi as
Prospect Hill.

"Railey is an old Mississippi name," he said, referring to Mississippi
in Africa. "They were there by the 1843 census. They were freed by
James Railey, who was the brother-in-law of James Green." Green was
the Mississippi planter for whom Greenville, Liberia, was named.
James Railey was also a member of the Mississippi colonization society,
and his home, Oakland Plantation, is now a bed-and-breakfast on the
Natchez African-American historical tour.

Railey beams when I tell him the news.

"So!" he says. "When I come to America, the first place I go is
Mississippi!"

Kaiser and Augustus raise their bottles of Guinness. Everyone clinks.

"Well, I'd love that," I say. "I'd love to take you there." But I offer
a disclaimer, that Mississippi is very poor—the poorest state in the

United States, and that Jefferson County is among the poorest counties.

Their smiles fade. They look incredulous. Sudden dreams dissipate into the filthy air.

"But why?" Kaiser asks.

For a moment I am stumped. Poverty is such a given in Mississippi today, I have never been asked to account for it. "I guess because most poor people in the U.S. are black," I say (although I later realize this is not actually the case), "and Jefferson County is the blackest county in the country." It is an insufficient answer, and the brothers aren't satisfied. "Maybe because the whole economy was built on slavery, and it never really recovered," I add, realizing that this, too, is an incomplete explanation.

Edward stares at me. Kaiser glances down toward Broad Street, thinking it over. Augustus picks at the label on his bottle of Guinness. Mariah Carey whines, loudly, over the tattered speakers.

Then Edward grins. "Well," he says, "when we come to Mississippi, we go to a similar place like this and have a beer. We will do that!" He has no intentions of letting history, politics, or poverty—here or there—bridle his hopes.

Kaiser is circumspect. "When people we know go to the U.S., they are working within three or four months," he says, flatly. "So if they are not working they must be lazy." In other words, we are not talking about people like him.

I shrug.

"Well, Alan, now that we know about our family, you should find out about your own family here," Edward says. "You should find out about Huffman Station."

A friend of his whom we had met on the street had told us that there is a community called Huffman Station in Cape Palmas, in Maryland County. "There is also a Huffman River," he said. "There are many Huffmans right here in Monrovia."

My first thought, upon hearing this, was to check the phone book, until I realized that I have seen no phone books in Monrovia. I don't know much about the Huffman history, other than that they were mostly small farmers and not, as far as I know, slave owners. My mother's family, the Ainsworths, had slaves, but I have not come across their name here.

"Are you sure it isn't Hoffman Station?" I ask. "I've read about an Episcopal missionary from the U.S. who came to Liberia whose name was Hoffman."

"No, it is Huffman. H-U," Edward says, and laughs. "It's funny that you come to Liberia, you are doing this other family, these other families, and now you find out your family is here also."

"Well, it would be funny," I say, "but I don't really know if they're family."

"But, they are here!" he says. "The Huffmans are here, in Maryland County! Before it's over, we find out that we ourselves are related." He smiles at the idea of Liberian Huffmans and Raileys intermingling, then glances at his watch. "But now we should go."

It is time to head down to Broad Street to join the crowds for the Lone Stars' triumphant return, which is scheduled for today. Although it was also scheduled for yesterday, Edward is confident that the team will arrive this time, so we pay our tab and head out. We go only a short distance before we hear the roar of a crowd at the far end of Broad Street, coming down the hill toward us. For a moment I revert to American mode, and mindful of an escape route, steer us to the side of the street toward the convent. The roar of the crowd is unnerving. It grows louder. We hear people cheering and chanting. I see thousands of people running toward us.

"The team is coming!" Edward cries.

We take a position in the median, then climb atop a monument painted red, white, and blue, along with a group of other men. People are rushing toward Broad Street along all the side streets. The crowd quickly fills the street, jostling the women peddlers, who reach up with one hand to steady the loads on their heads. Suddenly the thronging mass pushes through, in front of, around, and behind an open car bearing several jubilant athletes who stand up in the back. One, Salinsa Debbah, stands above the rest, shirtless, his muscled arms pumping the air victoriously. A few people grab my sleeve and exclaim, "He's the star of our national team!"

Everyone cheers as the team speeds past, and the crowd surges after the car down Broad Street. Some people disappear down the side streets hoping to catch the team on their return, the next street over. As we climb down from the monument I realize how absurd it was for me to have been worried. Did I really think that anyone would concern themselves with me when Salinsa Debbah was coming through? It was a beautiful, awesome spectacle, and it felt good to see this outburst of joy along such godforsaken streets.

The memory lingers for several days after, so when I move from the convent back to the Mamba Point for my last three nights in Monrovia, I invite the Raileys to my room to watch soccer on TV. They are giddy with excitement: soccer games on a color TV in a private, air-conditioned room! Kaiser, in particular, frequently bursts into hysterical laughter for no apparent reason. They forget everything else—their troubles in Liberia, their fractured home, their yearning for America. They chatter away, paying me no mind. Kaiser ends up spending the night, watching one soccer game after another until he falls asleep atop the sheets with the remote control in his hand.

CHAPTER TWENTY-TWO

ONE OF THE GUARDS stops me as I am leaving the convent to tell me
he has a message for me from the American embassy. Someone had
attempted to deliver the message to my room, but I did not answer the
knock at the door, he says. The message is from Sarah Morrison at the
U.S. Information Service, asking me to come to her office.

It has been more than a week since I have been called to the
embassy compound, but I have been half-expecting to hear from them
each day, because the UN sanctions vote seems imminent. I ask the
guard to tell Edward, when he arrives, to meet me at the embassy compound, then hurry off down UN Drive, wondering what news Sarah
has for me.

As the date of my departure from Liberia approaches, I have
grown increasingly apprehensive about the government. When I
stopped by the Liberian Ministry of Information one afternoon for an
unplanned meeting, hoping simply to gauge J. Paye Legay's attitude, he
had told me a few more parables, then described a particular landscape
scene along the beach near Roberts Field. The scene was inconsequential but what struck me was his comment, "You will see what I am
describing, assuming you are on that plane when it leaves on Monday."

"Assuming?" The word bounced around my head as I lay in bed
that night. When I asked Edward what he thought the comment
meant, he said it was a standard disclaimer, that he might as easily have
said, "God willing." But I am not so sure. It did not help that as I was
leaving the Ministry, J. Paye had said, "I'll see you on Monday,"
although we had not planned to meet.

Throughout my time in Liberia, I have been concerned that the government would detain me. I have made many friends in Monrovia—history professors, school officials, student activists, ministers, even a human rights worker from the United Kingdom. I would like to think that they would rush to my defense if I were accused of spying, though I am unsure whether it would matter in the short run. My greatest concern is that my notes, which I carry in my money belt, will be confiscated.

As I walk toward the embassy, I am startled by a truck loaded with soldiers in fatigues and red berets that screeches to a halt beside me. The soldiers, all carrying automatic weapons, leap from the truck, blocking my path. It is the moment I have been dreading. As I stand frozen in the middle of the street, I watch the driver back the truck onto a lot where people are washing cars. They have stopped to have their truck washed. I realize then that the Taylor government's paranoia is infectious, and it has infected me.

When I arrive at the embassy compound, it turns out that Sarah just wants to show me photos of Greenville that she took a year before, because I will not be able to go there myself. I look through the photos, which are mostly crowd scenes against a backdrop of plain buildings. I thank her, then return to the gate to wait for Edward. I am growing weary of wondering, of not knowing if my imagination is running away with me or if the threats are real.

A cluster of shops in an alley near the embassy represents the closest thing Monrovia has to a tourist market, and I decide to browse their wares for a few souvenirs. I cannot imagine what sort of souvenirs would be appropriate reminders of this trip, but it seems I should buy something. I had noticed one shop selling old tribal masks, which struck me as curious because there were no such masks in the National Museum. I decided that I might buy a few of them and perhaps donate one to the museum. The lack of tribal masks at the museum is an obvious shortfall, and I decide that if a tourist can take home such relics of Liberian history as souvenirs, the museum collection should have at least one of its own.

When Edward arrives, we enter the shops, which causes quite a commotion, because tourists are so rare. The shops sell mostly paintings, carvings, and fabric. Some of it is pretty nice, but the hawkers are relentless. There are probably twenty vendors and I am the only customer, and no doubt the first in many days. I don't have room to carry much of anything in my bags, and the truth is, I feel guilty spending money on any sort of indulgence in a place where there is so much deprivation, particularly in front of Edward. Still, I have to get something for the folks back home. All that really catches my eye are the masks.

I have seen a few African dance masks in shops in the United States, all reproductions with exaggerated features, carved in ebony. These are the real thing. They are very old and worn. Coming from a variety of tribes—there are sixteen or seventeen distinct ethnic groups in Liberia—the masks are remarkably varied. Some are stylized and unadorned, others have beards fashioned of burnt reeds and long mustaches of black animal hair. Some depict a hybrid creature, part human, part bird. The going rate is $50 U.S., an exorbitant amount of money here, but as the only customer, I know I am in a good position to bargain. I don't have to have a mask. I offer $50 for two and the guy immediately says yes, which means I have overbid. I pick out two, then make the same transaction in another shop. I now have four masks— one for myself, one each for friends back home, and one for the museum.

It occurs to me that the masks may actually have been housed in the museum at one time, before the lootings, but my decision to donate is not entirely philanthropic. It seems prudent, and in any event I will need a letter from the museum authorizing me to take antiquities from the country. A donation would dovetail nicely into my personal PR campaign and no doubt make friends in the museum. I decide the largest and most elaborate mask will go to the museum.

Robert Cassell, the museum director, who was so somber when we first met, is clearly stunned when I tell him what I propose to do. "I must go and get someone from LCN," he says, referring to the Liberian Communications Network, the government-run print and radio media.

"That's not really necessary," I say.

"No," he says, already on his way out the door. "*It is necessary.*" He says this very sternly, almost as a reprimand.

In a few moments he returns with a slightly confused reporter carrying a tape recorder. I realize, listening to the director explain what I am doing, that he has in mind to showcase the mask as a gift from an American benefactor—for that is how I am to be portrayed, which points out the need for funding for the museum. His spin is that my gift of the mask proves that the museum has international importance, which strikes me as a bit pathetic, though if my casual donation draws attention to the museum's needs, I am happy to accommodate him.

The reporter asks how I embarked upon "this cultural exchange program," and I tell him it would be overstating the case to call it that, because I simply wanted a mask for myself and decided it would be appropriate to give one to the museum. I recount the sad story of the museum lootings and point out that it will be a monumental effort to rebuild the collections, but that you have to start somewhere. Then he asks me about my book, which the director has mentioned. Although I had started out my trip trying to maintain a low profile as a journalist, I soon realized that this was going to be futile. At this point, I figure, I have nothing to lose. If people all over Monrovia hear of my book in the context of my donation, I will have greatly expanded my retinue of protective friends. I tell him the story of the slave immigrants from Prospect Hill.

He nods. "It is an interesting story," he says.

And it's true! I want to proclaim, from every boom box and transistor radio in town. But I merely agree.

The reporter turns to the museum director, who reiterates the importance of the museum's collections in chronicling the history of Liberia. He then gives me my letter, and we say our good-byes.

I miss the interview on the radio, and never manage to find the newspaper in which it runs, but a few days later when I stop by the Information Ministry on my way out of town, it is obvious that J. Paye Legay has heard about it. He is full of warmth and praise. He smiles, gives me the Liberian handshake, and is pleased to see that I have finally mastered it.

He chats amiably about relations between our countries and says he has decided that there are two reasons why the United States does not support Liberia: "The United States helped Taylor remove Doe so he could do their bidding, and then he refused. Also, Liberians in the U.S. try to paint the country in a bad light, so they will be allowed to stay in the U.S." Then the smile returns to his face. "I hope you got the information you came for," he says.

It seems that if he did not before, he now believes that I came to Liberia for the reasons I gave him. The irony, of course, is that I could probably travel to Sinoe County with the government's blessings now, when it is too late. Then again, maybe not—and it's a moot point any-way, because I found descendants of Prospect Hill here in Monrovia.

After the meeting at the Ministry, I stop by to see Sarah Morrison, who says she has been asking around and has found that the story of the masks has tipped the scales in my favor. The Liberian journalists and others with whom she has spoken have told her that the government accepts my reasons for being here.

"There's no reason to expect a problem at the airport," she says, but just in case, she gives me the name of a man who works for the embassy as an expediter there. "If there's a problem, he will see you," she says. "Just tell him that you are here as my guest."

As the day of my departure approaches, I begin to feel a sort of vicarious desperation regarding the Railey brothers. The one unifying factor among the majority of Liberians I meet, of whatever ethnic or economic background, is their desire to emigrate. U.S. visas are extremely hard to come by, even with a recommendation from an American citizen, because so few Liberians who leave want to return home. Single young men like the Railey brothers have it the hardest, because they have no vested interest in going back.

The only way they can reach the United States, even as students, would be to find someone who will sign an affidavit stating their will-ingness to support them financially while they are in college, and to have a college that is willing to take them. This is a challenge for many reasons, not the least of which is the difficulty communicating with people in the United States. I certainly am in no position to do so. Without the ability to communicate with others, how can they find such a school? How can they find a benefactor? How can they effect the paperwork? How can they get inside the embassy compound, and once there, manage more than a terse dismissal from Abbie Wheeler or one of her employees?

None of this seems to diminish anyone's hope. Whether they want to emigrate or are resigned to stay, hope is all that most Liberians have, and they nurture it. When I mention to one of the guards at St. Teresa's that almost everyone I meet wants to emigrate to the United States, he nods, then says, in a tone that sounds as if he is trying to con-vince himself, "In some ways it is better here. If I'm American, I walk down the street I get arrested or a gangster take my money and kill me. So I hope things will get better for us here."

"Maybe I can't go," says a second guard. "But I have hope, because God is here."

Sister Scholastica Swen, an administrator and cook at St. Teresa's, tells me that she has high hopes for just about everything—for the convent school, for the souls of Liberia, for the future of her country, and for a better life in the United States. Swen spreads hope in her wake as she shuffles from the kitchen to the dining room to the offices of the convent. She is self-confident, pragmatic, and kindhearted, and can turn a couple of fish into a feast. On one of many nights when I am at the gate talking with the guards, she comes strolling through the compound singing in a beautiful voice, and lingers with us for a while. She tells me that her father is from Sinoe, her mother from Maryland.

Then she puts the question to me: "So tell me, how do you find Liberia?"

Many people have asked me this, and I always give the same answer. "I love Liberia," I say.

She smiles, but it is an ironic smile. "You love Liberia, and we're all fighting to get out," she says, and laughs.

"Well, let me qualify that," I say. "I love the people of Liberia."

She nods.

"I love their warmth, and their resilience," I add.

She nods again, claps her hands, then strolls off into the darkness, singing. Clearly love of Liberia is one thing, staying there another.

The student activist who met me at the airport when I arrived, and again a few times at St. Teresa's convent, tells me he also intends to leave Liberia if he can, at least for a while. He wants to better himself, to expand his network of connections. It is not that he cannot endure Liberia, because endurance is his countrymen's strong suit, he says, and he, if anyone, should know. Although he never volunteers the information to me, John Singler had told me the young man's painful story, while cautioning me not to name him for fear of government reprisal.

The young man has long been involved in politics as a student at the University of Liberia. During the Doe regime, he was suspected of being involved in an explosion on campus, and so fled to Freetown, Sierra Leone. While in Freetown, he was imprisoned with a group of other Liberian students and, as John said, "The government forgot about them, literally. And of forty-seven LU students, only six lived.

He was one of them. He came back to Liberia and was hospitalized. It was '92, Octopus was going on, they were fighting in Monrovia. One day he was napping and a stray bullet hit him. Knowing all that, it's hard to believe how sweet he is."

I have to agree, yet as sweet as he is, the student activist shows no fear. When I tell him that I was concerned that the government might arrest me, perhaps even as I am attempting to depart the airport, he says, "Not in my Liberia."

The student activist is now a member of an international student organization and has participated in several conferences outside Liberia. In June 2000 he was invited to a UN conference in New York, but the U.S. government would not grant him a visa due to the supposition that he would not return home after the event was over. He has since been invited to an international student conference in Norway, based on an essay he submitted, but is having trouble raising the money to go. He is a brilliant, controlled, and determined man, and wants to help improve Liberia, and so would never leave without planning to come back. He represents the potential for Liberia, waiting in the wings, and not all that quietly, either.

When I broach the subject of Liberian emigration with Brother Dennis Hever, who lives in the Catholic compound in Gardnersville and teaches at St. Teresa's, he says the Marist brothers in the United States recently asked him to come home. "There is a feeling that something is going to happen," he says. At the Gardnersville compound, he reminds me that five American nuns were murdered there by rebels during the worst of the fighting, but says that he had decided to stay because he has a group of young men who depend on him.

Brother Dennis invites me to the compound for Sunday lunch, and later to a nearby beach controlled by another American religious group. We are accompanied by several young men who work at the compound. Because the undertow is so fierce along Liberia's coast, we spend most of the afternoon sitting in chest-deep water in a tidal pool, tilting to and fro with the shifting currents, watching guys playing soccer on the beach, and, at one point, a bare-breasted woman running through the surf with a monkey on her shoulder. Two bright, motivated, and frustrated guys sit with me for a while in the tidal pool and tell me their stories. One had a promising career as a soccer player and even had a chance to go to the United States to play, before the war.

He had a friend, Mike Burkely, from Boston, who was with the Peace Corps, who was trying to work it all out. "Then the war came. I had to flee from village to village," he says. "I would have been forced to fight. They force everyone to fight. I lost all my documents, all my addresses, all my contacts, my sources. Everything. It was 1996. Now, nothing is doing."

Both young men reiterate the difficulty of getting visas and say that what they most need right now is a radio so they can hear news from the world outside. "I once had my own radio but it spoiled," the soccer player says. "I think, maybe if we listen to the radio long enough we will hear about a scholarship." He asks if I would try to find his Boston friend, and when I agree he hugs me twice, then shakes my hand four times.

Another young man tells me that if he manages to get to the United States he will eventually return to Liberia, although he knows that most who emigrate never do. He knows a woman who studied abroad to be an obstetrician gynecologist, but just as she was making plans to return, the John F. Kennedy hospital in Monrovia—the only public hospital in the country—closed, leaving her plans in limbo. Many people go to the United States and get an education with the intention of coming back to make a contribution to Liberia, but, "What do you do?" he asks. "There is nothing to do. You're making fifty-thousand dollars a year in the U.S., and there is no job for you here. Those people you see on the street changing money, a lot of them have a B.A. There's nothing. Liberia has so much—iron ore, diamond, they have just discover oil! We have the largest rubber plantation in the world and people are driving around on worn-out tires, and the tires are imported. Why?"

These are very personal problems for everyone, including Edward Railey and his brothers, all of whom are in their early twenties, motivated and frustrated. Their lives are ahead of them, they are ready to begin living them, but they have nothing to do, and there is no sign that things will change for them in Liberia. The Raileys have family in America, but there is not much they can do to help. Augustus Railey wants to go to study business management. Kaiser Railey wants to study computer science. Edward is interested in theology. We go through all of this again in the hours leading up to my departure. I will find out if there is any possibility that they can get an invitation to go to school, if there are scholarships, what must be done to acquire the necessary visas. I am not optimistic, but they are. They are determined to go to Mississippi, in America.

On my last day in Liberia, the brothers leave me at the Mamba Point for a while as I pack my bags, then return with a parting gift, an African shirt they want me to wear. We stroll the streets of Monrovia, me in my incongruous shirt, imagining a future meeting in Mississippi, and then suddenly it is time to go. We return to the Mamba Point, get my bags, and wait for the car that Edward has arranged for the drive. There is some confusion because he has impressed a cousin to provide her car, and she and two friends, as well as Princess Railey, want to join us. It becomes clear that someone is going to be left behind. The brothers decide that it will be Augustus, the youngest, and he watches sadly as we drive away. Augustus, more than his brothers, has a look of almost desperate hunger on his face, and it is excruciating to leave him behind. He will follow us in a cab, Edward says, but I do not see him again.

There are eight of us in the car, wending our way through the streets of Monrovia, past the comparatively modern sports complex, past Sky High Jewelry—not the best advertising, I think—past the military barracks where so many executions occurred after the 1980 coups, and the two executive mansions, through the gates to the city. Outside Monrovia is a landscape of old Africa—mud and thatch huts, palm groves in broad, swampy fields, women carrying firewood in stacks on their heads. I take photos freely along the way, because no one is around. I am still not convinced that I won't be hassled at the airport, but I tell myself that I have built my case.

When we arrive at the airport, I get out of the car and the student activist puts his hand on my shoulder and says, rather urgently, "Put the camera in the bag." Then I hear him say, "He is not taking photos of the airport. It's all right. He has not taken photos of the airport."

I do not look up. I stuff the camera in the bag. From the corner of my eye, I see a guard walking away.

We wait for a while in the parking lot of the ruined Roberts Field Hotel, making small talk. No one likes good-byes. Then the time comes and I head out, promising to do what I can. As I walk toward the airport, I am more curious than nervous about whether I will be hassled inside.

As it turns out, there is only one small problem. One of the men at the baggage search is concerned about my tribal masks—not because he cares about them, apparently, but because they represent an abnormality, which means: an opportunity. I show him the letter from the museum, but he is unimpressed. He must show the letter to his superior. This takes a long time. He returns, still skeptical. I suspect that he wants a bribe, that he expects me to get impatient, to take the hint, and slip him some money to expedite things. He tells me to step out of line while the issue is resolved, because I am causing a bottleneck, but I hold my ground. Before coming to Liberia I had been told repeatedly that I would have to bribe everyone, yet I have bribed no one and I don't intend to start now. I have the letter.

People are getting restless behind me, waiting to have their luggage searched, and eventually the guy gets irritated, stuffs the masks into my bag, and tells me to move along. The airline check-in comes off without a hitch, as does the payment of the special airport tax, which leaves only Immigration. The same man who checked me through Immigration upon arrival checks me through for departure, and he is extremely friendly. He remembers me. Things are going well. Then, as I am waiting in line to board the plane, convinced that I am home free, that no one is going to confiscate my notes, I hear a man's voice call my name.

I turn to see a uniformed man. Everyone else who is in line or waiting in the departure lounge turns to watch. Then I recognize the man from Immigration. He is smiling, and beckons me to step out of line. He wants my name and address, a contact in the United States, and asks if I will mail a letter for him when I get home. He is grateful for whatever help I can provide, and says that if I or anyone I know needs assurance that they will be allowed to pass through Liberian Immigration in the future without a hassle, I should let him know. I take the letter, we shake hands—a truncated version of the Liberian handshake—and I follow my fellow passengers out onto the tarmac.

The jet's cabin lights glimmer in the darkness. I smell the smoke of fires in the bush. I follow the missionaries, the women in African dress toting empty bags, the Eastern European businessmen talking conspiratorially among themselves, onto the plane. I take my seat next to a

British woman who has lived in Monrovia for three years, and it soon becomes evident that the experience has embittered her.

When I tell her that I will miss my friends in Liberia, she says, "You think you have friends here, but no one is your friend. They just want your money. If they find out they aren't going to get money they're no longer your friend. The white person always gets better treatment and always pays more."

She is particularly angry, she says, because someone in Immigration told her that when she returns, she must bring him a basketball if she does not want to be hassled.

She goes on like this until I say, "You must really hate the place."

"I do," she says.

"Then why do you stay?"

"I fell in love," she says, "and my boyfriend won't leave. He's in mining. But really, the place is hopeless, and you can't blame them all for wanting out. If I could, I'd leave and never look back."

I think of Kaiser Railey telling me that if he were able to emigrate, he would not be one of those Liberians who decide not to come back. He said he does not understand why his relatives in the United States can't or won't help him. "I want to go to the U.S. for a lot of reasons," he said. "But one of them is, I want to see if I will go there and then forget. I want to see if I am the kind of person who will forget the people back home."

As the plane takes off I glance back at the darkened airport and think of the Railey brothers turning back toward Monrovia. When I set out for Liberia, the last thing I expected was to try to help people like them, descendants of Mississippi immigrants, to essentially reverse the last 165 years. Although Liberia is the only home they have ever known, I feel like I am abandoning them.

Part III

COMMON GROUND

CHAPTER TWENTY-THREE

IT IS A BRIGHT spring morning in McComb, Mississippi, when I arrive at James Belton's house to find him sorting through stacks of papers at his kitchen table, piecing together the riddle of his family's tumultuous past.

James represents an unexpected windfall—a crucial source who appeared after I thought my research was finished. He is an inquisitive man with a quietly keen mind. A retired schoolteacher who now works as a federal housing inspector in McComb, he has spent the past several years researching his family history, which stretches back to South Carolina and encompasses the saga of Prospect Hill. Like Youjay Innis and Artemus Gaye, the two Liberians who were tracing the lineage of their ancestor, Prince Ibrahima, James is on the same path I am on—but he and I are going in the same direction.

Earlier in the week, before Ann Brown called to forward me James's name and number, I had pretty much resigned myself to the fact that some of the blanks in the story of Prospect Hill would never be filled. I still did not know for sure what Isaac Ross's motives were for seeking to repatriate his slaves, I had found no corroboration of the slave uprising, and I had not spoken with anyone who was knowledgeable about the slaves who chose to remain behind. But when I phoned James to arrange a meeting, I felt renewed hope that I would find some answers.

As we begin our conversation, James explains that he has no particular genealogical mission other than documenting what he has been told. He has done his homework, has thought things through, and before our meeting is over, the story of Prospect Hill presents itself in an entirely new light.

"I just know what I was told by my father, what was passed on by my grandfather and great-grandfather from my great-great-grandmother, Mariah Belton," he begins, then drops the first of many bombshells: "My father told me I had two great-uncles who were part of the uprising at Prospect Hill—Wade and Edmond Belton."

Just like that, a major line of demarcation between the black and white versions of the story vanishes.

In fact, James says, his father believed that Edmond Belton was one of the masterminds of the uprising. "Dad said he was a high-tempered fella," he explains.

The back story begins in Camden, South Carolina, where his ancestors were originally enslaved. There, before emigrating to Mississippi, Isaac Ross came into possession of the Belton slaves from relatives who, in some ways, set a precedent for the terms of his own will. According to James, the chief directive of those slaveholding relations was that the slaves be kept together because they were kin to each other as well as to them, the slaveholders. The slaveholders sought to remove them from the Camden area, he says, because the influential families found the combination of geographic and familial proximity discomfiting. He shows me copies of some of the Belton slaveholders' wills, which, as he puts it, "indicate that these people were not to be sold, in no uncertain terms, and that they were to receive the best of care."

After receiving the Belton slaves, Isaac Ross, whose sister-in-law was Mary Allison Belton (who is also buried at the cemetery at Prospect Hill), took them with his own slaves to the Mississippi Territory. "Most of the slaves he brought with him to Mississippi were mulattoes," James says. Among them was Mariah Belton, who lived first at Prospect Hill, and then at Rosswood, where she remained enslaved after choosing not to emigrate to Liberia. She was listed in the Rosswood Plantation inventory in the 1850s, valued at $400. "She got her freedom after the Civil War, and ended up in the community of Union Church, when the government gave them the 'forty acres and a mule,'" he says.

The core of the Belton family account of the uprising is almost identical to the slaveholders' version, although its prologue and denouement are very different. "The house was burned by the slaves in retaliation against Isaac Ross Wade, who contested the will," James says. "Eventually the courts ruled in favor of the will. But before that happened, there was the uprising. During the uprising, the white family's after-dinner coffee was drugged and the house set afire, but without the intended result—eliminating Isaac Ross Wade. I wish it could have been resolved in a better way. When you have to resort to—I guess you could call it violence, to burning the house that the slaves themselves had built, when the little girl lost her life, that's sad. I don't like that page of the story. Everything else, though, I'm proud of it. I don't think it was their intent to get the children. Why would anyone let the children drink the coffee? They thought if they could just get rid of Isaac Wade, they could go to Liberia and have a better life."

Edmond and Wade Belton, he says, subsequently fled Prospect Hill to avoid the lynchings. "Obviously, they didn't want their identity known," he says. "From what I was told, Edmond was last seen crossing the Mississippi River on a ferry from Rodney."

No one knew what became of Edmond or Wade Belton until the early 1990s, when James became intrigued with the story and traveled to Converse, Louisiana, across the river from Rodney, and found the descendants of Edmond Belton. "Then, I found out that Wade had gone to It, Mississippi, in Copiah County," which is east of Prospect Hill. There, again, he found Belton descendants, he says.

How did Edmond and Wade escape, and avoid recapture as fugitive slaves? Did they manage to pass for white, or were they simply assimilated into another community of slaves? Belton considers the questions.

"Them being mulattoes, they might have just blended in," he says. "But I am almost positive that they got help in escaping. I don't think they could've done it alone. It had to have been more or less people who were connected with the colonization movement, but I have to admit that I was small when my daddy was telling me all of this. He was proud of the story, and he loved to tell it to us children at night. He was a sharecropper and we didn't have a radio."

James says that as an adult, he noticed in his travels that there were enclaves of Beltons in other Southern states, and wondered what their connection might be. He suspected that they were all related to the South Carolina Beltons, but when he found the connection with the

Beltons in Louisiana and in Copiah County, he knew he was onto something. That was what set the genealogical hook.

I have no doubt now about the veracity of the story of the uprising, but it still seems incredible that so many slaves would agree to embark upon an endeavor that was clearly doomed to fail. Even had they killed Wade, how could they have expected to get out alive?

"From all indications," Belton says, "from listening to what my father told me, the slaves were coached by members of the American colonization society to get rid of Isaac Ross Wade." Such encouragement may have instilled more confidence, he says. More importantly, the slaves were desperate. They believed they had an opportunity for a better life, and this was their last shot at claiming it. If they had lost the fight to emigrate, they would have become common slaves, which was something they had heretofore never been.

"Isaac Ross was a unique fella during that time," James says, in typical understatement. "He went along with slavery but his slaves were not slaves in the traditional sense. I doubt seriously if you would find anything written about the slaves before 1870, when blacks were first included in the census. But from word-of-mouth, folklore, what was passed down from generation to generation, it is apparent they were not like other slaves. I was told, you know, that some of those Beltons actually attended Oakland College. They were not free, per se, but they were educated."

Before the Civil War, Oakland College was a private school for planters' sons, and Isaac Ross sat on its board. Today it is Alcorn State University, which was founded in 1871 as the first land-grant college for blacks in the United States.

Most historical accounts note that many Prospect Hill slaves were taught to read and write, and that they all enjoyed relative freedom within the confines of the plantation. Ross never sold any slaves, and it appears that he kept them sequestered from the slaves on neighboring plantations. When Isaac Ross Wade took over as master of the plantation, however, they were treated like any other group of slaves, James says. "By the time of the burning of the house, from what I gather, all of the slaves but a few were extremely bitter. Isaac Ross had treated them like relatives, and the truth is, a lot of them were relatives. The Belton ladies who worked around Prospect Hill were very light—you couldn't hardly tell 'em from white ladies, my father said. But after

Isaac Wade contested the will, they weren't getting the treatment they had gotten during Ross's lifetime, and resentment just built up. That was how they came to set fire to the house."

Why did any of the slaves choose to remain behind when the majority emigrated to Liberia? James has a ready answer. A few were not given the option of being repatriated, he says, "most likely because they were just bad apples, like you have in any community."

The others, he says, may have been wary of traveling to a distant, unknown land. But Mariah was different. Belton believes she chose to remain behind because her two sons, Wade and Edmond, had fled Prospect Hill to escape being lynched in the aftermath of the uprising, and she perhaps knew their whereabouts.

"It may have been the grief she was keeping within over what had happened," he says. "She knew her sons did not go to Liberia, and perhaps she thought, 'For me to ever see my sons again, I have to stay in the area.' So she was sold to Walter Wade and transferred to Rosswood with her son, William. He was my great-grandfather." He digs through the stack of papers on his kitchen table and pulls out a photo of the young man, which looks to have been taken around the 1850s, with an inscription that identifies him as a carriage driver.

Given the bitterness that led to the uprising, why did the letters from the Liberian immigrants express such affection for Isaac Ross Wade and his wife? "It's possible that was in their best interest, to do that," he says. In other words, they had nothing to gain from distancing themselves from Wade once they had immigrated to Liberia. It is also likely, he says, that many of the slaves did not support the violence.

James still has a lot of questions, but most of them concern the genealogical riddle. He has organized the documents pertaining to his family and Prospect Hill on a CD-ROM, complete with images of the portraits of Isaac Ross and his wife, and of tombstones in the grave-yard, and he plans to give a presentation on the subject at the next Belton family reunion. Since 1984 the Beltons have held reunions, often several times a year, at various locations. Last year the event drew more than 4,000 people, he says. "I had to get my facts in order," he says of his Prospect Hill presentation. "I don't like to lose history, and the first time I mentioned all this at the Belton reunion, the whole place went quiet. People's mouths dropped. They said, 'A white man did that before the Civil War—in Mississippi?' They didn't believe me.

One fella who did believe the story said, 'Man, you need to get in touch with Spike Lee. It'd make a great movie.'

"There's a lot about our history people don't realize," he says. "Like that a lot of blacks in the South owned slaves." In his view, the story is complicated, and it is shared. "Some of the white Rosses have helped me put a lot of information together, and the white Beltons, too," he adds.

When I mention what so many have said about the story not being simply black and white, he smiles. He says there are a lot of gradations between any two extremes, and cites as an example the quasi-ward system that he remembers as a child, which was similar to that which exists in Liberia today.

"It was basically the same way here," he says. "It wasn't like slavery, but I grew up with a stepbrother and -sister, who Dad took in and raised 'em, and they worked for the family. They were like family, and they were less fortunate, and they worked for us. I see a lot of that—people who are less fortunate, maybe because they're darker skinned, and they weren't given the same opportunity.

"It's a funny thing, I was playing gin rummy with my daughter not long ago, and I don't know why she asked me this but she said, 'Dad, what do you like about yourself?' I thought about it and I said, 'Well . . . everything!' And she said, 'There's nothing you don't like about yourself?' and I said, 'There is one thing: my complexion.' My wife looked up and said, 'What're you talking about?' I said, 'It's always kinda bothered me that sometimes there might be several of us applying for a job or something, and maybe some of them were more qualified than me, but I got it because I'm lighter skinned.' That's happened a lot in my life. I feel I'd have been a stronger person if I was darker and had to work harder. I feel bad that I was given preference over darker people—even by blacks—because of my complexion. If we look at ourselves and get a true picture—you can see, even back in slavery, people just . . . how did you put it? They use the tools at their disposal to make the best of the situation. And sometimes they just go too far."

CHAPTER TWENTY-FOUR

ENOCH ROSS IS A high school basketball player in Walla Walla, Washington. He was a founder of an African-American church in Connecticut. He participated in Iowa's constitutional convention in 1844. An Internet search for "Enoch Ross" produces nearly one hundred hits, but none of the incarnations fits the parameters of the story of Prospect Hill. It is still unclear what became of the remaining key player in the story—Isaac Ross's mysteriously treated manservant.

Court documents show that Enoch and his family were freed two decades before the Civil War and allowed to emigrate to a free state in the North. Beyond that the trail is cold. It is not even certain that his surname was Ross, though I work under that assumption because I have nothing else to go on.

Some of the Enoch Rosses I find are white and some are black. In another time and place, which is where Enoch eventually found himself, he could have been either. Perhaps he passed for white, or he might just as easily have been among the African-Americans who fled white mobs in Cincinnati to Canada in the 1840s. His descendants could be writing letters to the editor of a local newspaper arguing for slave reparations, or they could be living in a midwestern suburb with a black-faced lawn jockey by the front door. They could be anywhere in between.

Thinking about Enoch as a white man *and* as a black man is a reassuring exercise. It would be simpler for blacks if all their problems could be blamed on white people, and for whites if all their problems could be blamed on blacks, just as it would be simpler for those of settler descent in Liberia if they could blame the tribes for all their troubles, and vice versa. But there are always people with whom one has a kinship among the other groups. There are always connections. The trouble starts when people choose to ignore their affinities, to see others as intrinsically different—as more prone to exploit the weak, perhaps, or to resort to violence. For whatever reasons, people all over the world expend a lot of energy searching for, and then fighting over, common ground. All of this clamoring has taken its toll on Mississippi, but the effects are far more pronounced in Liberia, a place the South begot.

It is the failed connections that my friend Scottie Harmon mentions when he tries to summarize the legacy of Prospect Hill and Mississippi in Africa. "So, they brought them over here from Africa, then they went back to Africa, and now they're trying to come back here," Scottie says. "It sounds like, whatever it is they're looking for, they keep just barely missing it." Another friend reached an even more disheartening conclusion: "So, basically," he said, "the whole colonization experiment was a failure."

For some reason these observations surprised me. I know that many who hear the story will inevitably draw similar conclusions because they seem to be pure and simple truths. Liberia is undeniably a mess. My friend Paul de Pasquale even suggested, half tongue-in-cheek, that the title of this book should be *Mississippi: Role Model for Disaster*. Yet the truth, as Oscar Wilde noted, is rarely pure, and never simple. No one I spoke with who is knowledgeable about Liberia sees the country as a failure. They are saddened or even embarrassed by events of the last two decades, but see the turmoil as similar to periods of unrest in other nations' histories. When I asked John Singler if he considers the colonization a failure, he said, America "basically dumped people there without the tools they needed, so how could it succeed? Yet some of them did succeed. The war really devastated Liberia's self-esteem. They ask, 'What have we done to bring this onto ourselves?' Nora Jones asked me, in 1994, 'What did we do to God?' The U.S. government made a mockery of democracy when they certified Doe's election, knowing it was fraudulent. Reagan sent five-hundred million dollars to the Doe regime. Now the U.S. is looking for reasons to turn their back."

With so many Liberians trying to use their American connections to make their way to the United States, it is tempting to think that the descendants of the slaves who remained at Prospect Hill are better off today than those whose ancestors remained in or emigrated to Liberia. The unintended benefits of American slavery were the subject of an essay written by Booker T. Washington back in 1932, in his book *Selected Speeches*. "Think about it," Washington wrote, "we went into slavery pagans, we came out Christians. We went into slavery pieces of property; we came out American citizens. We went into slavery with chains clanking about our wrists; we came out with the American ballot in our hands. . . . Notwithstanding the cruelty and moral wrong of slavery, we are in a stronger and more hopeful condition, materially, intellectually, morally and religiously, than is true of an equal number of black people in any other portion of the globe."

The idea is contentious, to say the least—particularly in the context of the debate over slave reparations. It is also countered by the desires of people such as Georgia Ross to return to Liberia if the current problems can be solved. Georgia, whose husband Benjamin waits in Monrovia while she works to bring him and their children to Philadelphia, does not believe Liberia is a failure. "It's a temporary situation," she says. "Most would go back if the situation improves." She hopes that her family will eventually be able to return to a Liberia at peace. "As I speak to you on this phone, I would go home," she says. "Nothing is like a home. Things get better in Liberia, I'd be the first to go. People who have been here twenty years, they have a small apartment, they are not able to pay their bills."

She misses the Liberia that existed before the turmoil, and prays that it will return. "I miss the way you always have some help in everything you do, unlike here where you do everything for yourself," she says. "People help each other in Liberia, they care about each other. Generally, it's love. We still have some good things that we cherish. The little we have we try to share. Liberia was formed on Christian principles, and the concern, the care, the love—that is what I miss. Here, you can't afford to call people sometimes. They say they are busy, they can't talk. That never happens in Liberia."

Still, she adds, "I do love America. There is equality here. You can't really be cheated. It's not the same in Liberia. You never get anything if you're not part of the government there, now. Education won't get that for you. If you go to the university in America you are able to get a job. It's not the same in Liberia."

Talking about the current situation is difficult, she says. "I just spoke to my children in Ghana. I talk to them every other week. The situation there is deplorable. I try not to discuss it because it brings depression on me. I just ask God to take care of them."

Before the war, Georgia says, "Liberia had been a peaceful country. It's hard to predict trouble, to predict war. We didn't think about it. The people are now suffering. The tribe-settler problem is still there, but you don't see it as much because we have a recognized government on the ground. When the war struck they used that opportunity to get even, to pay back."

Alton Johnson, who immigrated from Liberia to the United States in 1985 and now teaches at Mississippi's Alcorn State University, sees connections between the respective places everywhere he goes, but they're mostly academic for him now, because he sees himself as an American. Alton lives in Natchez, a city known for its elaborate, columned mansions—emblems of the culture and power of slaveholders. When he first arrived, he says, "I was impressed that there were so many skilled woodworkers and carpenters. I was told it was because of slavery, that the masters had their slaves trained to build the mansions." The architecture was also familiar to him. "Every time I pass these houses," he says, "I think they look like the houses back home."

Though he is descended from Liberia's indigenous groups, Alton's father was a ward of a family of slave descendants and ultimately took their name, which gave him access to both cultures. Returning to the source of one of those cultures has further broadened his view.

"Folks who were descendants of slaves, their forefathers, they help the master in the house, they cook for him, they wash his clothes, they take out the chamber bucket," he says, describing the lives of house slaves in antebellum Mississippi. "This is the same lifestyle back home [in Liberia]. They learn that way of life, so they treated the indigenous people that way. So there was a rift. It was the same arrangement like here in slavery days, but not with bad intentions. That was the only way of life they knew here. The indigenous sons and daughters were interested in getting an education, so people like my father lived with the people like the Johnsons, took their name and went to school."

He notes that Mississippi and Liberia have gotten their share of bad publicity, much of it deserved, but says he does not believe Liberians are more violent than people elsewhere, or that Mississippians are more racist. On the contrary, he says, "Liberians are very hospitable. You're riding a bus, you give a lady your seat. You don't do that here. People in the South are generally hospitable compared to people in the North—here in the South everybody speaks. Maybe it's just a little shake of the head, but they do it. They say 'sir' and 'ma'am.' You don't do that a lot in the North. In Liberia it's a different type of hospitality. People take you into their home, they give you something to eat. They share what they have."

Likewise, he says, he has never personally encountered racism in Mississippi "as such." The reason, he says, is "if it occurs, I ignore it. I think Mississippi gets a bad rap a lot. I've encountered that in Alabama, you see it in Arkansas. If you go to Maryland you see a lot more. I have not heard about the Ku Klux Klan marching in Mississippi, but I've seen them march in Arkansas. Their headquarters is in Missouri. Louisiana to me is scarier than Mississippi, but because Mississippi was the last state in the union to undo the racism it has a bad rap.

"The racism that I see here is different, it's more subtle. My son and your daughter go to the same school as the white kids, and every little village you go to in Mississippi you see one white house, one black house, all in the same place, which you don't see everywhere in America. We can go to the same school, we can have a fish fry together, but we can't go dancing together. Racism is not blunt like it used to be. It gets into academia—we will do work together as professionals, you praise me, but if I want a job in your department you don't want me. I don't let it bother me because I know people want their kind. It's human nature. Once you get an education nobody can take that away from you, you don't have to prove anything to anybody, and one day people will forget. I've had people who apologize to me. They're old, they realize what happened here was bad. So I just live my life."

Though he is now a U.S. citizen, Alton says he does not encourage Liberians to try to immigrate to the United States, particularly if they have no means of support. Neither does he plan to return to Liberia. For him that connection has been broken.

"If a person like me went back they'd say I was taking their job," he says. "When I was leaving Liberia fifteen years ago, the guys carrying weapons of destruction were boys of five or ten; now they are older and I'm a threat to their society. I don't really think a lot about that country now. I don't go to places I'm not invited. I may go there in the long run, but I will have to work for an international organization—the USDA [U.S. Department of Agriculture] or something. I'm not going to go there as a Liberian."

As we discuss the historical ties between Liberia and the American South, he mentions the Mississippi state flag, which has brought so many old prejudices to the fore, and I tell him about the similar controversy brewing in Liberia over its national flag, which some of ethnic descent want to change. Even Liberia's motto, "The love of liberty brought us here" is considered an affront by some of native descent.

"I don't see any problem with the flag over there," he says. "That's how it was, how the country was established, period. I've heard about the motto, and some people say it would be better if they changed it to, 'The love of liberty brought us together.' I have no problem with that. But changing the flag itself—are we going to go back and redo independence? There are eleven stripes for the eleven signers of the Declaration of Independence, there is the lone star on a dark background representing the only republic, the first republic, in the dark continent of Africa. If you look at what's happening here, one of the things that made the Mississippi flag look bad is people using it for something different, using it for a sign of hate. That's what they've been doing with the rebel flag. People have abused the flag, using it to show hatred. It is heritage, and people should keep that. It should be remembered and put in a very good place. Life goes on. It's time to start improving relationships."

Many hoped the vote on changing the state flag would present an opportunity to put Mississippi's divisive history behind, but the prospects of that happening looked slim even before the votes were tallied. Prior to the special election, every other editorial in *The Clarion-Ledger*, it seemed, was written by a sixth-generation Mississippian descended from someone who fought in the Civil War. Surprisingly, many supported changing the flag, as a gesture of reconciliation, but more expressed their conviction that it was time to stop giving in to the demands of blacks.

On the other end of the spectrum was Kenneth Stokes, a Jackson city council member who was vehement in his opposition to the existing flag, and publicly vented his anger after other council members proposed an ordinance regulating the naming of streets and bridges in Jackson. Stokes said the ordinance effort was racist, since he had earlier named three bridges for black ministers, and warned that if the regulation was put in place he would research every street name in the capital and, "If any end up after slave owners, we might have to change those names." Notably, the city of Jackson was itself named after a slave owner, President Andrew Jackson, who was in office when the state joined the Union. In fact, the vast majority of American presidents prior to the Civil War owned slaves.

There is certainly no shortage of wedges to drive between people. Some of the pro-flag editorialists fretted that if the flag was changed there would be no end to the cleansing—that place names would indeed be changed and that the ubiquitous statues of Confederate soldiers on the state's courthouse squares would inevitably be removed. In one letter to *The Clarion-Ledger*, a man wrote, "How far do you go to appease a group that suddenly decided that our heritage offends them? You think destroying the flag will stop their ruthless attack on us?"

For supporters of the flag, the effort to change it was rooted in expediency or a desire for retribution. But for those who fought tooth and nail for racial equality, the flag represented a blatant reminder that in some people's minds black Mississippians are still to be treated, essentially, as uninvited guests in their own home.

On April 17, 2001, statewide voters opted to keep the existing banner, Confederate emblem and all. Jefferson and Claiborne counties were among only four which voted overwhelmingly to replace it. The day of the vote the national media swarmed over Jackson in search of sound bites representing the extremes, and in one curious aside, a group of reporters and cameramen crowded around a black man who sat on a bench at a bus stop, draped with a rebel flag. Meanwhile, white children waved from the backs of pickups decorated with state and Confederate flags as they rolled past the capitol. I found myself wishing that blacks would start waving the Confederate flag themselves, so that they could co-opt the symbol and make the whole thing just go away. But that would be a bold maneuver, and in truth I am not sure that everyone wants this issue to go away.

If there were not ample evidence in the historical record, Mississippi's contemporary life is filled with reminders that slavery and its aftermath were devastating, and that the wounds have been slow to heal. The toxic residue includes widespread poverty, political divisiveness, and crime. Mississippi is today the poorest state in the nation, and Jackson, the capital, with a population of less than 200,000, was listed in the top ten highest-crime cities in the United States in 2002. In such an unstable environment, it is possible to forget about race, but not for long. The same is true for the settler-tribe division in Liberia. Both places are struggling to extricate themselves from the legacy of conflict that drove the story of Prospect Hill, and unfortunately nothing can ameliorate the evil of slavery and oppression, which started all the trouble in both places. Such longstanding conflicts are rarely resolved. Both historical and contemporary news accounts make clear that even if the source of trouble goes away on its own, memory lingers and by nature tends to preserve and even magnify the thing that gave it life.

Two weeks after I left Monrovia, the situation in Liberia began to deteriorate. First, four Liberian journalists were arrested and charged with espionage. Their crime: publishing an article critical of the Taylor regime's spending policies.

The Liberian government simultaneously shut down Monrovia's four independent newspapers, allegedly for delinquent taxes. *The Perspective*, the Liberian expatriate periodical, reported that the arrests followed the publication of an article in *The News*, a Monrovia newspaper, titled "U.S. $50,000 Spent on Helicopters," which challenged government spending on repairs to helicopters and an additional $23,000 U.S. on Christmas cards and souvenirs. The article noted that the expenditures were made at a time when the John F. Kennedy hospital had been forced to close due to lack of funds, and alleged that the arrests and shutdowns were designed to repress the independent media in Liberia.

"The prevalent view expressed is that in the midst of the discussion of sanctions and scrutiny, the Liberian Government is paranoid about views emanating out of the country that could challenge its propaganda campaign," *The Perspective* asserted.

The arrests disproved my theory that journalists would likely be immune from government harassment while the sanctions were pending. To make matters worse, the journalists faced the possibility of execution under Liberian law.

Two weeks later, the United Nations imposed partial economic sanctions on Liberia. The UN Security Council voted unanimously for a resolution which reimposed an arms embargo first used during Liberia's civil war. In May 2001 the council also imposed a diamond embargo and travel ban on top Liberian officials after concluding that the government was still backing the rebels of Sierra Leone's Revolutionary United Front, who had violated a peace deal and reignited that country's nine-year conflict in May 2000 by taking 500 UN peacekeepers hostage. Liberian timber exports, the subject of increasing concern by international environmental groups, which were also linked with the arms trade, were exempted from the trade ban at the insistence of France, a major importer of the commodity.

The Washington Post foreign service reported that Taylor had expanded his timber harvests into the virgin forests of Sapo National Park, and had received several million dollars from the Oriental Timber Company, based in Hong Kong, which, according to UN reports, he had used to buy weapons. "Sources with direct knowledge of Taylor's arms shipments, whose information was confirmed by intelligence sources in West Africa, said most weapons were coming to Liberia by sea, primarily in logging ships, because such shipments are much more difficult to monitor and detect than air shipments," the newspaper reported. According to internal OTC documents obtained by the newspaper, ships chartered by the company had on three occasions in the fall of 2001 delivered weapons to Taylor at the Liberian port of Buchanan, including 7,000 boxes of ammunition for AK-47 assault rifles, 5,000 rocket-propelled grenades, 300 howitzer shells, and tons of other equipment. An additional thirty tons of weapons reportedly arrived in mid-January 2002.

When I e-mailed Sarah Morrison at the U.S. Information Service to ask about the sanctions and the journalists' arrests, she wrote back to say that the guards at the Monrovia prison "call me by name these days, I've been there so often." Reactions to the sanctions were mixed, she wrote, but most people considered them fairly tame and assumed Taylor would manage to work around them. "The arrest of the journalists as the vote was imminent shows he really doesn't care," she wrote. "There are many angry people out there, and the numbers are growing. . . ."

Several international Liberian groups, including the West African Journalists Association, the Writers in Prison Committee of International PEN, and Reporters Sans Frontieres, called for the journalists' release, but there seemed to be less international outrage than there had been over the arrest of the British film crew in August 2000. The American media paid scant notice to the story.

The journalists' arrests prompted students and faculty at the University of Liberia to organize a rally to raise money for their legal fees, and the government responded by storming the campus with police on March 21, 2001. The police allegedly flogged numerous participants and arrested others, and some students claimed that several female students had been raped by security forces after the rally. The University Student Union reported that fifteen students were detained at the executive mansion and feared dead, according to an article by the Panafrican News Agency, though *The Perspective* later reported the students had fled to a refugee camp in Ohana. The Panafrican agency reported that James Verdier, director of the Monrovia-based Catholic Justice and Peace Commission, claimed to have had his life threatened for offering free legal services to the jailed journalists. The article noted that Verdier's predecessor had fled Liberia following a similar death threat.

In late March 2001 the journalists were finally released, after issuing apologies for the offending story, but a few days later, Milton Teahjay, former deputy information minister and Taylor's personal media consultant, disappeared. Teahjay had been outspoken in his opposition to the logging of old growth forests in Sinoe County, and was presumed to have been executed, according to *The Perspective*, which noted that he had been "sacked for 'acts inimical to the security of the State,' and arrested while trying to leave the country." The Liberian government originally confirmed Teahjay's arrest, then changed its story and denied that he was being held. The pro-government newspaper the *Monrovia Guardian* claimed that Teahjay was actually in hiding at the U.S. embassy, although Sarah Morrison told the newspaper the claim was "unfortunate and certainly not true."

Subsequent developments underscored the deteriorating situation that summer. On June 17, a U.S. diplomat, Sgt. James Michael Newton, was shot after refusing to stop at a checkpoint on the outskirts of Monrovia. Newton, the assistant military attaché at the U.S. embassy, was evacuated to the Ivory Coast for treatment of his wounds. During the same period, a ship of Liberian refugees was reported to be wandering the coast of West Africa while its captain searched for a country that would allow him to dock. The ship, with about 170 passengers, most of whom were children, had been turned away from numerous ports due to rumors that it was a slave transport. As with so much of the news out of Liberia, the details of the situation were difficult to discern.

In June 2002 another Liberian journalist, Hassan Bility, editor of Monrovia's *The Analyst* newspaper, was arrested and charged with collaborating with the rebel group Liberians United for Reconciliation and Democracy (LURD). Taylor claimed that Bility was an illegal combatant, and said he would not turn him over to the country's civil courts but would try him before a military tribunal. According to the international Committee to Protect Journalists, Taylor's government had ransacked the offices of *The Analyst* in April 2002 and closed it down on two occasions.

Meanwhile, the BBC News reported that fighting in northern Liberia had sent tens of thousands of civilians fleeing from the area, and that the conflict had moved to within 200 kilometers of Monrovia. Foreign aid workers, according to the article, "said Liberia was now facing a new and highly volatile situation."

The Liberian government responded to the bad news by imposing new restrictions on foreign journalists and diplomats, prohibiting them from traveling outside the city limits of Monrovia and from moving about the city after 8:30 P.M. Journalists were also required to give seventy-two-hour notice before arriving in the country, and a twenty-four-hour waiting period was imposed before accreditation could be granted. According to a Ministry of Information news release, "These guidelines are intended to minimize the impact of anti-government propaganda that is currently being orchestrated by a select number of foreign journalists and news organizations." The release referred to a recent *Newsweek* magazine article which portrayed President Taylor in a negative light.

I became increasingly anxious as I read of these developments, wondering if any of my Liberian friends had been caught up in them. I realized that I had managed to slip in and out of Liberia during a brief period of relative calm, and my own good fortune only emphasized the need to help the Railey brothers get out.

✿　　✿　　✿

Soon after the government takeover of the university campus, I get a
phone call from Edward. His voice sounds urgent. He wants to know if
I've had any luck finding a way for him and his brothers to immigrate
to the United States.

Unfortunately, I have not. U.S. Immigration officials are clearly not
inclined to grant visas to young men who have no obvious reason to go
home, and none of the universities I check with offer scholarships for
anyone other than U.S. citizens. The Methodist church offers a small
stipend for international theology students, but the cap of $1,000 per
year is far too little to satisfy Immigration's demands for proof of financial support. I have sent letters of invitation to Edward through the
U.S. consulate in Monrovia, and have asked my congressional delegation to intervene, to no avail. An aide to U.S. senator Thad Cochran
seemed sympathetic, but said it was not possible for the senator to
influence the visa process, and insisted that the denial of Edward's visa
had had nothing to do with his being African. My congressional representative, U.S. representative Bennie Thompson, did not return my
phone calls. So I do not have good news for Edward. But I am glad to
know he and his family are safe. I also get a call from John Singler, who
tells me that he has heard from the student activist who acted as my
fixer in Liberia and that he is safe as well.

Around the same time, I start getting numerous poignant letters
and collect phone calls from other people whom I had met in Liberia,
asking for money or help in immigrating to the United States. I now
understand why I was warned not to give out my phone number in
Liberia. I refuse the calls.

The Railey brothers call now and then to check on my progress
with the immigration effort, and I am torn between wanting to give
them hope and not wanting to set them up for disappointment. Like
millions of refugees across the world, they yearn for what America has,
and while it is easy to become enervated by so much global suffering,
and to turn away, it is not so easy when you know the sufferers, their
history, and their faces. I find myself wondering how their lives might
have been had their ancestors not been freed, had they not chosen the
dangerous path to freedom when it was first made available to them.
But all I can really do for them is wire money for emergencies, which
always seem to be developing.

Their calls become more frequent as the situation in Liberia worsens. On September 11, 2001, they call to see if I have lost anyone in the terrorist attacks, and Edward, for the first time, sounds despondent. He knows that his chances of getting a visa have evaporated for now, particularly after the allegations surface that the Liberian gold trade—in which American televangelist Pat Robertson is involved—and the illicit diamond trade are helping fund the al Qaeda terrorist network.

More driven than ever to raise the money which alone might improve his chances of escape, or, at least, of enduring increasingly unstable circumstances, Edward calls to ask me to wire him money so that he might travel into the bush to buy gold at the mines near the border with Guinea, to resell at a profit in Monrovia.

"It is very bad now," he says, not knowing that it will soon get much worse.

The gold idea proves worse than fruitless. On his trip to the mines Edward is caught in the fighting and forced to flee into the bush and hide for three weeks, during which he contracts malaria. The next call I get is from Kaiser, asking for money to pay for Edward's hospitalization and recovery. Edward has been lucky to be admitted to the Catholic clinic, but he still has to pay before receiving treatment.

The brothers call a few times after that, to tell me that Edward is recovering, to wish me Happy New Year, to send greetings from their mother, "the Old Ma," and their sister, Princess. But the next time Kaiser calls, I hear only muffled voices speaking in the background. I say hello several times, get no reply, and hang up. He does not call back.

A few days later comes bad news over the wire about the fighting between LURD and the president's security forces. Taylor has declared a state of emergency and begun forcibly rounding up young men and boys from churches and the few still-functioning schools, taking them to detention centers to prepare them to fight. There is a terrifying precedent for the practice: the roundups during the civil war of Taylor's notorious "small boys unit"—some as young as elementary school age, whose parents had been killed by the fighting, who were drugged and armed with automatic weapons to fight for the rebels.

When LURD fighters come to within twenty-five miles of Monrovia, the United Nations begins evacuating nonessential personnel, and people begin fleeing into and out of the capital. Some observers claim Taylor is staging the fight to draw international sympathy—raising alarums

and excursions, in effect, to prompt the United Nations to lift the sanctions imposed upon Liberia. Whether Taylor is posturing is immaterial
to the Raileys. What matters is that the atmosphere is again turning
lethal.

"The Old Ma wants us to leave and go to Ghana, to the refugee
camp," Kaiser says during his next call. "They are hunting people here
left and right, especially young boys. We are mostly staying indoors.
The Old Ma wants us to go, but it is costly. We've been thinking of you
a whole lot."

I have no doubt about that. I realize that from the Raileys' perspective, I am no longer just reporting on the story, I am a part of it.

The brothers are now determined to flee, to become refugees. I
wire them money for passports, but they also need money to make the
overland trek to the refugee camps in Ghana, to buy food, bribe soldiers, pay for rides, do whatever is necessary to increase a refugee's
odds. It is endless. A few days later, as they are preparing to go, Augustus calls to again express his hope that by becoming refugees they will
be admitted to the United States. "We pray to be there for the launching of your book," he says, echoing the brothers' familiar refrain.

I imagine many reasons for their anticipation over the publication
of this book—that it might bring them attention, good or bad, or that I
might grow richer than they imagined me to already be, and feel
inclined to share the wealth.

After Augustus calls I do not hear from the brothers for several
days. All I know is that they are planning to strike out for Ghana. I e-mail
their aunt, Annie Demen, who has a job at the United Nations in Monrovia, but she replies, "I have not heard from my nephews for some
time now. Yes, it is true that young men are being picked up to fight,
and some times relatives have to pay large sum of money before they
are released. I will try to find them over the week end by God's grace as
we are living on a day by day basis in Liberia now." In the next e-mail,
she says she has still not located them.

A week passes, and finally the brothers reach me on an Internet
phone. All I can hear are a few syllables now and then, but they manage to give me a number at a nearby house before the line goes dead.
When I phone the house they are all there, and take turns talking.
There is good and bad news: On the way to Ghana, Edward came
down with typhoid, which he had also likely contracted while hiding in

the bush. He became extremely ill, and his brothers had taken him to a Liberian National Red Cross clinic, where he was treated. By the time he was well enough to travel again, the fighting between LURD and Taylor's security forces had ended.

On the phone, Edward sounds like a very tired, old man.

"It's unfortunate the sickness will not leave me alone," he says, but adds that the medication seems to be working. Referring to the fighting, he says, "Things have subsided. It's some, but small. So we shall see. We are walking freely now in Monrovia."

I ask what he plans to do next. He thinks for a moment. "For most people leaving now, they are going to a church conference," he says. "They get an invitation from a church in America. I hope to get such an invitation, because everybody at the clinic is dying of typhoid. We pray that we will be together like we were before, in Liberia."

Sounding winded, he puts Kaiser on the line, who again asks when the book will be published. "We pray one of us will be there," he says.

The now-familiar ritual becomes more frequent in the coming months: the phone ringing at three A.M., the operator asking if I will accept a collect call from Kaiser in Liberia, his voice saying, "So, Alan, how is life? We pray that you are keeping well." No matter how much I remind them, the Raileys almost never take into account the six-hour time difference between Liberia and Mississippi, because if they find themselves near a phone they feel compelled to call. Sometimes when they reach me they come close to reproaching me for not being home to receive earlier calls. At my urging they eventually set up a free e-mail account, and although Monrovia's few Internet cafés are crowded and plagued by technical problems, this at least proves a more reliable method of communication, for a while. Usually their messages include further requests for money. Sometimes I hold back, as when Princess asks for money for a new dress to wear at her coronation as queen of her Methodist church conference. I do not have the means to fulfill every need of an extended family living in a destitute country. But my resolve never lasts long. In a subsequent e-mail Edward informs me that the consulate at the American embassy has been closed, and weary Liberians seeking visas to the United States now have to travel to Abidjan, in the Ivory Coast, to apply and, in all likelihood, be rejected.

In August, Edward writes, "Please be inform that things are not fine with us." Because of the recent serious illnesses of his mother and

Prince, the family has used up their cash reserves and without another infusion, will in a matter of days be evicted from the house that provided their final sanctuary during the war.

Meanwhile, the Ivory Coast, where he had been directed to apply again for his visa, is erupting in civil war.

There seems to be no real hope of improvement in the coming months, and for whatever reason the Raileys cease using their e-mail account. Their calls become more frequent, and more persistent. When the phone rings in the wee hours I know it is them. If I do not answer, they call again a few minutes later. Sometimes I am curt, asking why they do not e-mail me instead. They do not know what to make of my behavior. Once, when Edward calls, collect, and wakes me, he says he's been robbed, and has a number for me to avoid the high collect call charge. I say, "No, Edward, you must e-mail me. The money can be put to better use than long-distance charges. There's only so much of it, anyway. I'll wire some money, but e-mail me."

"Okay, I do that when I leave here," he says. "Good-bye."

I feel sorry immediately, because he sounds chastened by my impatience. I get no e-mail from him.

In April 2003 Artemus Gaye—one of the descendants of Prince Ibrahima—organized a small "freedom festival" in Natchez to commemorate the 175th anniversary of Ibrahima's release from slavery and emigration to Liberia. The Associated Press reported that a group of academics, together with descendants of Ibrahima, his master, and his liberators, gathered in Natchez to reenact the tale. The city government embraced the occasion by placing a portrait of the prince on the cover of a tourist brochure promoting African-American heritage sites.

Barry Boubacan, a Guinea native and visiting professor of African Studies at New York University, told the AP that hearing Ibrahima's story strengthened the connection in his own mind between American slavery and African history. "It's always been considered a separate history," Boubacan said. "It's one history."

This was a comparatively minor news event in the context of all that has happened and continues to happen in the interwoven histories of Mississippi and Liberia, yet it seemed to hint at a telling shift in public perception. There is a lot of give-and-take in those histories, a lot of back and forth, just as there are innumerable crosscurrents and conflicting personal and political views and motivations. But there is no denying that they are connected.

But as Artemus was staging his festival in Natchez, Liberia once again began degenerating into civil war. Complicating matters this time were reports that al Qaeda has capitalized upon the nation's economic anarchy to fund its global terrorist efforts—a detail often overlooked in media editorials that cautioned against any U.S. intervention in Liberia's strife.

As early as November 2001, *The Washington Post*'s Douglas Farah reported on a European military intelligence investigation which claimed that the Taylor government had recently hosted senior al Qaeda operatives who oversaw a $20 million Liberian diamond-buying spree and briefly cornered the market on the precious stones. The proceeds of the diamond sale were said to have been earmarked to buy assault rifles, ammunition, rocket-propelled grenades, and missiles from the Nicaraguan army for use by Liberian forces. Then, in December 2002, Farah reported that Taylor, who denies any involvement with al Qaeda, allegedly received one million U.S. dollars for assisting the operatives, some of whom had hidden out at a Liberian military camp for two months following the September 11 attacks in New York City and Washington, D.C.

The diamond-buying operation was said to have been a response to U.S. efforts to freeze al Qaeda assets after the attacks, and the *Post* reported that three of the senior operatives who were said to have supervised the deal—Abdullah Ahmed Abdullah, Ahmed Khalfan Ghailani, and Fazul Abdullah Mohammed—were on the FBI's most-wanted list for their role in al Qaeda attacks on U.S. embassies in Tanzania and Kenya. Abdullah was also believed to be al Qaeda's chief financial officer. The article noted that in the months following the September 11 attacks, the Pentagon had prepared a Special Forces team in neighboring Guinea to catch two of the men while they were in Liberia, but that logistical problems had prevented the mission from being carried out.

Equally alarming was a revelation in another *Post* article that U.S. intelligence sources were concerned that al Qaeda might be planning to undertake terrorist attacks at sea using mother ships flying so-called "flags of convenience," which offer registration under hidden ownership. Notably, Liberia is one of the leading suppliers of flags of convenience in the world.

Taylor has become an international pariah for his role in Liberia's turmoil and for the destabilization of West Africa, but as the *Post* reports indicate, there is an even broader context to the threat his government poses. Al Qaeda's involvement illustrates the danger of allowing the kind of turmoil that has gripped Liberia to go unchecked. In the absence of a workable connection with the United States, Taylor has begun forging dangerous alliances elsewhere.

Among the people who were allegedly involved in the al Qaeda scheme were Lebanese diamond merchants, Israeli and Russian arms dealers, Libyan security forces, and Senegalese and South African mercenaries. Their activities reportedly have included visits or communications with contacts in Afghanistan, Bulgaria, Belgium, Burkina Faso, Iran, Iraq, the Ivory Coast, Nicaragua, Panama, Pakistan, and Sierra Leone. David Crane, the American prosecutor for the special court, told Farah in June 2002 that Taylor "is not just a regional troublemaker; he is a player in the world of terror and what he does affects lives in the United States and Europe."

Following an expansion of the United Nation's economic sanctions against Liberia, in May 2003, Taylor was said to be increasingly desperate for money and arms to fight rebel insurgencies near the country's borders with Guinea and the Ivory Coast. The head of Sierra Leone's international war crimes tribunal meanwhile hinted that Taylor might be indicted for his role in that country's civil war in the 1990s, and specifically for his alleged involvement in the assassination of a fugitive from the UN-backed court. In an article in the Monrovia *News*, Liberian senator Thomas Nah Nimely responded by saying that any effort to arrest Taylor by the special court would result in a "full scale regional war." On May 22 the U.S. State Department advised Americans in Liberia to leave.

Farah wrote that the situation within Liberia had become so dire that it was unclear if Taylor's ouster would even help. According to intelligence sources Farah cited, the rebel force Liberians United for Reconciliation and Democracy, fighting near the Guinean border, were "a motley assortment of some of the worst elements who fought in Liberia's civil war both for and against Taylor." The rebels, he added, "have offered no program for governance, no ideology and no political vision beyond getting rid of Taylor," and were said to be "as likely to prey on the civilian population as Taylor's notorious government forces."

After another front broke out in eastern Liberia in April, relief organizations designated eleven of the nation's fifteen counties war zones. In May, attacks upon aid workers halted the delivery of food and other humanitarian assistance to hundreds of thousands of refugees, according to an article in *The New York Times*. "Over the last two months, armed groups have attacked these camps at the most opportune times—the very days on which the United Nations and private groups deliver aid," the newspaper reported. On such days, armed groups looted sacks of rice, flour, and other essentials, stole cell phones and trucks, forced aid workers to act as beasts of burden, and set fire to refugee huts—sometimes with people inside. "You falling down, you keep going, you hear bullets raining," one aid worker was quoted saying, after he had been forced to carry sacks of supplies on his head during a six-day journey through the bush. "They talk about killing you like it was nothing."

By then more than 300,000 Liberians had fled the country and 2.7 million had been displaced.

In May the worst of the fighting was centered around Greenville, the seat of old Mississippi in Africa, which had also been ravaged during the civil war of the 1990s. A group called the Movement for Democracy in Liberia had seized the city and its port, and all shipping had ceased after a Liberian navy gunboat began shelling the rebel positions. About fifty of Taylor's troops had fled the MODEL rebels by reportedly commandeering a Croatian ship in nearby Harper, which they had sailed to Monrovia with an estimated 1,000 refugees aboard. At a May 16 press conference in New York, a UN official told reporters that unless the situation stabilized, the fighting would soon engulf Monrovia, where an estimated 500,000 refugees were squatting in shantytowns on the outskirts of the city.

These were certainly alarming developments, with the potential to grow much worse, and I found myself wondering about Peter Roberts Toe, who had met me at the Monrovia airport, had looked after me for several days in the city, and was to have hosted me at his home in Greenville. Among the people I met while researching this story, none was more generous or determined than Peter. If he sought to dominate anything, it was adversity—the seemingly endless series of events which had threatened to undo not just him but his family and a widening circle of dependent friends. He was one of the few Liberians I met who never mentioned a desire to emigrate to the United States, and I felt a strong personal connection. He gave the continuing story of Mississippi in Africa a clear and personal focus.

In late May I received word from Peter via a mutual friend's e-mail account.

"The ongoing rebel war in Liberia has forced us to escape from Greenville for safety," he wrote. "My family and I are presently squatting in Monrovia—the only relatively safe place in Liberia. News reaching us from Greenville indicates that my house is burnt down to ashes.

"I am presently efforting to erect a structure to accommodate my family, which includes my wife and a dozen children (my natural children and others I have adopted). I am desperately in need of assistance presently. I would very highly appreciate any assistance you could render in this respect."

He signed the message, "Hopefully, Peter Robert Toe."

I got no immediate response to my e-mail reply, which was not unusual considering Peter's circumstances. Though he was clearly desperate for money, getting to an Internet café would be a challenge, and no doubt responding to e-mails is far down the list of priorities for someone who has a dozen people dependent upon them for survival.

After a few days I call our mutual friend John Singler and ask if he knows how to get in touch with Peter. He says Peter now has a cell phone, surprisingly, though the service is unreliable, and that he seems to be holding up well, even if his continuing travails are beginning to take their toll. He gives me Peter's number, and after several tries, I get him on the phone. He sounds more cheerful than I expect, and far more than I would, were I in his shoes.

"Hello, Alan, how are you?" he says. "I pray you're keeping well."

"Everything's fine here," I say. "I'm glad to hear you're safe."

"Yes, yes," he says.

The connection is bad, and it is difficult to understand some of what he says, but he manages to tell me that the Raileys and our friend the student activist are okay. I then ask about the situation in Greenville.

"The rebels are just killing people, burning down the houses," he says. "But I made it here with all my children. Everybody's here." The family is squatting in an area known as New Kru Town, he says, and he needs money for materials to erect a temporary shelter.

Then the phone goes dead. It takes several tries to get through again, so we cut to the chase. We make arrangements for a money transfer through Western Union. He promises to keep in touch, and then he's gone.

I phone Western Union. The operator takes the necessary information, then says I am required to give Peter a security code, and to pose a question for him to answer in order to claim the cash. These are safeguards, she says, to ensure that he is the rightful recipient.

For some reason I am stumped. What sort of question? It is a simple task, but so many questions are bouncing around in my head that I can't think of a logical one to pose. *Why is this happening? When will it end?*

"I'm thinking," I tell the operator. "For some reason I can't think of a good question."

"It just needs to be a simple question," she says, "like, 'Where is the sender from?'"

"Okay," I say. "'Where is the sender from?'"

I call Peter back, give him the code and the question. When I say, "The answer is—" he starts to laugh.

"The answer," he says, "is '*Mississippi*'!"

"Right," I say. We both laugh this time. It is obvious, of course. Mississippi is where I am from. It is where Peter is from. If there could be only one word for us to communicate between our respective worlds, to link us together, we both know what it would be. It would be "Mississippi."

It is the word that links our parallel universes, that connects a maverick veteran of the American Revolution to thousands of nameless refugees now fleeing their homes in Liberia. It forms the common ground between a retired schoolteacher in McComb and one very determined Monrovia banker who yearns for a better life, half a world away.

AFTERWORD

IN JUNE 2003 the fighting between LURD rebels and Charles Taylor's forces swept into Monrovia, killing hundreds of civilians and endangering an estimated 97,000 refugees huddled around the city, including 18,000 living in one high school without electricity or running water.

French military helicopters and a French warship had earlier evacuated about 500 trapped foreign nationals, including many Americans and Red Cross and UN staff. Soon England, France, UN Secretary-General Kofi Annan, and several African heads of state called on President Bush to deploy American troops as part of a proposed peacekeeping force in Liberia. Cameroon's UN ambassador, Martin Chungong Ayafor, said America should intervene in Liberia because, "It's their baby, and they have a responsibility there."

During the worst of the fighting, U.S. embassy officials opened the gates to a residential compound to allow thousands of Liberians to reach shelter from the shells, bullets, and rockets that were crisscrossing the city. Hours later, artillery rounds fell within the compound, killing at least nine and injuring eighty.

Journalist Sebastian Junger, who was in Monrovia researching an article for *Vanity Fair*, was at the compound when the refugees flooded in and the artillery rounds began to fall, and later said he believed the rounds came from Taylor's forces and were aimed at the refugees. He and photographer Teun Voeten soon found themselves helping carry the injured to a clinic operated by the international group Doctors Without Borders.

Sebastian also encountered a shootout between police and Taylor's forces over "looting rights" to one sector of town. He said that because the forces have not been paid in two years, looting was considered an acceptable form of reimbursement for their services. Even the refugees' shantytowns were looted, though there was next to nothing there to steal. I received word from John Singler that the National Museum had not been looted this time around, although the building supplies Peter Toe had bought to build his shelter were.

Pro-American sentiment was evident in the streets of the city, from civilians who begged for U.S. intervention and from soldiers who wore do-rags fashioned out of American flags or who dressed in a style reminiscent of U.S. Marines. But Sebastian reported encountering anti-American feelings as well, both from crowds angry that the United States had not come to Liberia's aid and from pro-Taylor forces. After being accused of spying, Sebastian and Teun left Monrovia for the airport aboard an armed diplomatic convoy escorted by local militia that had been hired by the American embassy, but which still was harassed at numerous armed checkpoints along the way. At one point, he said, soldiers thrust bayonets through the open windows of the vehicles and demanded to know if anyone inside was American. He wisely kept his mouth shut.

By that point, with the capital surrounded by rebel forces, and with a war crimes indictment hanging over his head, Taylor found himself backed into a corner. He began making offers in order to save himself, most of which he reneged upon. He agreed to a cease-fire, then backtracked; he offered to step down, then said he would do so only if the UN war crimes indictment was scrapped.

On July 4, 2003, President Bush acknowledged that America has a "unique history" with Liberia, and national security advisor Condoleezza Rice noted the terrorist attacks of September 11, 2001, had shown that "failed states" can spawn "so much instability that you start to see greater sources of terrorism." But Bush insisted that U.S. forces would enter the fray only if Charles Taylor resigned, and Taylor insisted that he would resign only after U.S. peacekeeping forces were in place. Cholera and starvation meanwhile spread through the refugee quarters.

Bush subsequently embarked on a visit to several African nations (not including Liberia) that was originally planned as a feel-good media event, but which was dominated by international calls for U.S. intervention in Liberia. When a small contingent of U.S. military experts arrived in Monrovia on July 8 to determine the lay of the land, thousands of starving refugees who were packed into the city's soccer stadium began singing hymns, waving American flags, and chanting "USA, USA." Within a month, Taylor had accepted an offer of sanctuary in Nigeria and was gone. The next chapter in Liberia's history had begun.

AUTHOR'S NOTE

DURING MY RESEARCH INTO the story of the two Mississippis, I worked under the assumption that if I read everything I could find, listened to what everyone had to say, and saw as much as possible with my own eyes, the true story of Prospect Hill and Mississppi in Africa would eventually make itself known. Each time I thought it had, someone new sprang forth with new information that cast much of what I had previously heard into doubt. In some cases, firm conclusions proved elusive, because history is malleable, and it is still unfolding. But more information is better than less. The fact that there are conflicting versions does not alone make the story less true or whole.

Considering that the story of Prospect Hill and Mississippi in Africa unfolds against a backdrop that includes slavery, oppression, and war, it is not surprising that accounts and perspectives differ. What is surprising is how much goodwill can be found amid all the suffering—often, from unexpected sources. Isaac Ross was the most obvious benefactor, yet there is no discounting the monetary aid that Isaac Ross Wade sent to Liberia for a time, even after having fought tooth and nail against the freedom of the Prospect Hill emigrants, nor of the freed slaves and their descendants taking in less fortunate tribal family members out of a desire to help rather than exploit, such as J. J. Ross, who founded the school in Monrovia. Sometimes the generosity comes from people who might not seem to have much to share, such as Nathan Ross Sr., whose own life story begins with his father's enslavement, and who saw his power evaporate after the Liberian coups in 1980, yet managed to create a better life for his children in

the United States while continuing to provide financial support to
needy relatives back home.

Other connections are more difficult to reconcile, because even
generosity can be rooted in self-interest, and this is also a story about
the desire for control, and the quest for dominance—whether as a
means of survival or exploitation or out of necessity. Sometimes, it may
be a combination of all three. The desire to dominate was there among
slaveholders, among soldiers in both countries' civil wars, and among
slaves in the two Mississippis. It is there today among people in both
places who struggle against overwhelming odds. Dominance may
sometimes be the only alternative to being dominated, but it is dominance just the same.

The most dominant figure of the story was Isaac Ross, who helped
defeat the British as a captain in the revolutionary army, ruled over a
fiefdom of his own creation, controlled the fates of hundreds of slaves,
then triumphed, from the grave, over a legal and judicial system in
antebellum Mississippi that was at times overtly hostile to his aims.
Ross's success placed him at the forefront of those who contributed to
a broader legacy that still reverberates, in both Mississippis, and likely
will for years to come.

History is written according to the perspectives in vogue at a given
time, and during my research I found that even official documents
were sometimes erroneous or misleading. I figure my own account is
just the latest iteration, but I have tried my best to be objective and
fair, and to clearly frame my own subjectivity when I suspected it was
coming into play. A bona fide historian would have approached this
story differently than I have, partly because I was interested not only in
historical facts but in how the story was transformed by different narrators. As a result, when the record conflicted with or seemed irrelevant to the people I interviewed, I gave them leeway.

Those people included anyone I could find who knew about
Liberia or Prospect Hill or who was related to the Ross family, but
because African-American genealogy is so poorly documented, I
sometimes had to take leaps of faith—assuming, for instance, that a
black family with the surname Ross from the Prospect Hill area was
related to the story. My rationale was that a person who was descended
from slaves from the Prospect Hill area and who was related to the
Rosses could shed light on the story even if their own family line was

not clearly documented. Likewise, I did not question the provenance of certain Rosses who figured prominently in Liberian history, some of whom originated from Prospect Hill and others of whom immigrated from Georgia. There are only a handful of historians to document the nation's history, and while I drew much from them, in cases where family accounts and their research were in conflict, I let the families have their say.

In some cases the subjectivity of people I interviewed is not plainly evident, and there are no doubt mistakes that might need to be corrected—if only the information were available to correct them or to even prove that they are mistakes. I have been tolerant, perhaps to a fault, of variant spellings, genealogical hiccups, grammatical errors, and other irregularities from my sources, and I have preserved these variations. Even simple spelling errors can have a profound effect upon such a long, contentious and unevenly documented story as this one, but I have not attempted to correct them except when they were significant and obvious. I have let stand, undisturbed, certain disparities in the written record as well, such as the interchangeable use of the names Russ and Ross, and Read and Reed. Who can say, from this distance, in a world where a person might be documented just once in their entire lifetime in a single newspaper, and have their name misspelled, that one name might not be meant to represent another? In my account of the marriages of certain Ross relations who were said to be of mixed racial ancestry, it would have been useful to know whether "Randall" is interchangeable with "Randell" or "Randle," but I could not clarify these variations with any certainty.

I have quoted at length from the written record that I uncovered because in some cases this book may be the only publication of these facts. Whatever the outcome of Liberia's current tumult, history will be deprived of many of the details of how it all came to be, because the majority of the nation's historical records have been destroyed during the course of its conflicts. The outlook is only slightly better for many of the historical records in Jefferson County. A great many documents from Prospect Hill and the antebellum era are preserved at the Mississippi Department of Archives and History and in other public and private collections, but those that have managed to survive at the county courthouse are far from secure. County officials across the state have asked the Mississippi legislature for permission to destroy records that are taking up precious room, and regardless of whether they are granted their request, many irreplaceable documents that shed light on Prospect Hill and other stories that have yet to be told are moldering in tattered boxes and in some cases being surreptitiously hauled away. Those records are not always infallible, but they were crucial to the telling of this story, because they are often the most reliable source amid so many conflicting accounts. As an anonymous Liberian immigrant quoted on Joseph Tellewoyan's website said, when offering advice to others seeking to immigrate to the United States, "Remember: In America, if it is not written, it was never done." The written record is paramount—it was both the reason the Liberian journalists were arrested and the reason they were later released, because otherwise the government faced no accountability for its actions against them.

Finally, I have chosen not to provide the reader with certain tools typically offered in historical accounts—photographs, footnotes, indices, genealogical tables, and the obtrusive *sic*. I wanted the story to speak for itself as much as possible. I have mentioned the locations of unpublished manuscripts only when it seems germane, or when it is a prerequisite for their use (as with Thomas Johnson's memoir, *Twenty-Eight Years a Slave*, which is housed at the University of North Carolina at Chapel Hill). Again, my rationale is that this book is not a history, per se. It is an account of a story that gallops unpredictably and sometimes unaccountably across history, which is never cut-and-dried.

When Thomas Wade, the son of Isaac Ross Wade, was telling the story of Prospect Hill in the early twentieth century, he simplified it. When descendants repeat it today, they choose their own focus. I have sought to fill in the blanks, to point out significant discrepancies, to suggest other possibilities, to advance the story and draw from more varied stories, but it is still a process of winnowing. There is no doubt that I have left things out, misunderstood others, and imposed my own vantage point.

The history of the American South did not once have much room for details that we find particularly interesting today, such as intimate relationships between slave owners and slaves, the fact that Confederate soldiers deserted the cause by the thousands toward the end of the Civil War, that immigrants rioted over being drafted into the Union army in New York, that some African-Americans owned slaves, or that a traveler through the antebellum South might encounter "white" slaves, slaves on shopping sprees, or slaves along the road, at large without permission. Likewise, in revising history, we may steer away from essential truths that have been subverted in the past, in reaction to them. In the end we have only the story's pieces, and we pick among them.

We still have much to learn about the story of Isaac Ross, the slaves of Prospect Hill, and their legacies in Mississippi and Liberia today. As the story continues to unfold on both sides of the Atlantic, I hope that its essential truth will become clearer, and not lost to the vagaries of time.

SOURCES

The paper trail that forms the basis for this book ran from the haphazard files of the Jefferson County courthouse to a variety of state and national archives and Internet sites. Some of those sources are easily reviewed, such as those in the Library of Congress and the Mississippi Department of Archives and History, where a great deal of information is available in relevant subject files. Unfortunately, some are not so easily reviewed, if they can be reviewed at all. The Liberian national archives has been destroyed, and the most crucial documents relating to the litigation of Isaac Ross's will languish in the Jefferson County courthouse, where a prospective researcher must sort through boxes of incomplete documents in no particular order without the benefit of indexes. The following are among the more easily accessible sources:

Mississippi and the United States

Becoming Southern: The Evolution of a Way of Life, Warren County and Vicksburg, Mississippi, 1770–1860, by Christopher Morris, Oxford University Press, 1995.

Before Freedom, When I Just Can Remember, edited by Belinda Hurmence, John F. Blair Publishing, 1989.

"Claiming Place: Bi-Racial American Portraits," *Frontline* report memo, 1996.

Clarion-Ledger, The, November 18, 1984; February 1, March 17, 2001.

"Dear Master": Letters from a Slave Family, edited by Randall M. Miller, University of Georgia Press, 1978.

Emergence of the Cotton Kingdom in the Old Southwest, The, by John Hebron Moore, Louisiana State University Press, 1988.

Fayette Chronicle, The, October 3, 1913.

Journal of Mississippi History, Vol. IX, 1947, publication of Mississippi Historical Society, article by Thomas Wade.

Journal of Mississippi History, fall 2002, publication of Mississippi Historical Society, article by Rebecca Dresser.

Judicial Cases Concerning American Slavery, by Helen T. Catterall, Washington, 1926–37, William S. Hein & Co., 1998.

Library of Congress, WPA slave narratives and African-American Mosaic Exhibit.

Natchez Democrat, The, March 29, April 6, 2003.

Natchez on the Mississippi, by Harnett Kane, Random House, 1947; 1998.

Prince Among Slaves: The True Story of an African Sold into Slavery in the American South, by Terry Alford, Oxford University Press, 1977.

Record of the Descendants of Isaac Ross and Jean Brown, A, by Annie Mims Wright, Press of Consumers Stationery & Printing Co., 1921.

Reveille, The, August 21, 1902.

Selected Speeches, by Booker T. Washington, Doubleday, Doran & Co., 1932.

Slavery in Mississippi, by Charles Sydnor, Peter Smith Publishing, 1933.

Slavery Remembered, by Paul Escott, University of North Carolina Press, 1979.

Slaves of Liberty: Freedom in Amite County, Mississippi, 1820–1868, The, by Dale Edwyna Smith, Garland Publishing, 1999.

South-West by a Yankee, The, by Joseph Holt Ingraham, Harper, 1835.

Twenty-Eight Years a Slave, by Thomas Johnson, housed at the University of North Carolina at Chapel Hill.

Liberia

Abolitionists Abroad: American Blacks and the Making of Modern West Africa, by Lamin Sanneh, Harvard University Press, 1999.

African-American Diaspora: Who Were the Dispersed? The, by John Singler, unpublished.

Africana.com (undated).

Africanpubs.com (undated).

allAfrica.com, May 7, May 12, May 13, 2003.

American Colonization Society publications, including *Emigration to Liberia*, New York Colonization Society report, 1848, and *The African Repository and Colonial Journal*, February 1848.

Guardian, The, December 30, 2002.

Land and People of Liberia, The, by Mary Louise Clifford, Lippincott, 1971.

Liberian Dreams: Back-to-Africa Narratives from the 1850s, by William Jeremiah Moses, Pennsylvania State University Press, 1998.

New York Times, The, 1852, day unknown; October 22, 1992; February 4, 1998; May 15, 2003.

Panafrican News Agency, March 27, 2001, report.

Perspective, The, online periodical, spring 2000; fall 2000; spring 2001.

Roll of Emigrants to the Colony of Liberia Sent by the American colonization society from 1820 to 1843, The, housed at the University of Wisconsin.

Settlers in Sinoe County, Liberia, by Jo Mary Sullivan, Boston University Graduate School, 1978.

Washington Post, The, June 4, December 29, December 30, December 31, 2002; May 15, 2003.

ACKNOWLEDGMENTS

When I showed up at the Jefferson County Chancery Clerk's office in 2000, searching for records of the Prospect Hill litigation, I was blissfully ignorant of what I was getting into. It did not take long to realize that even the most rudimentary research was going to be difficult, and that I would need the help of others—a lot of others. Nekisha Ellis, in the clerk's office, quickly rose to the occasion, and introduced me to Ann Brown, the local genealogist who proved indispensable in helping locate people who could shed light on the story.

From there the list of people who were willing and able to help continued to grow. Among the more important were the two people who first told me the story, Tinker Miller and his mother, Gwen Shipp. When it became apparent that the most dramatic consequences of what happened at Prospect Hill were still unfolding in Liberia, my friends Lee and Dick Harding and Libby and Paul Hartfield overcame their reservations about my personal safety to give me the encouragement I needed to go. John Singler responded to one of my Internet postings and set about making the trip possible and ultimately productive, and helped me with contacts and background on Liberia. Sebastian Junger, who has covered more than his share of stories in dangerous places, offered valuable nuts-and-bolts advice that for all practical purposes enabled me to go, and later helped make this book possible by introducing me to my literary agents, Stuart Krichevsky, who saw merit in the book, and point person Patty Moosbrugger, who hit the ground running once the manuscript was in her hands, coached me on how to make it better, and sold my editor, Brendan Cahill, on the idea. I am indebted to Brendan, in turn, for making the book much better than it would have been without his involvement, which is everything you can hope for from an editor, and to his boss, my publisher, William Shinker, for sharing our enthusiasm. I met all of them through Sebastian, though at the time I first contacted him, we had never met. Sebastian has been highly successful as a journalist, but he has never forgotten why he became one or how important this kind of help can be.

Countless other sources helped me along the way, beginning with reporter Butch John, who referred me to Maureen Sieh, a Liberian living in the United States, who in turn led me to journalist Kenneth Best, who made his own recommendations. Ray Wright led me to Turner Ross, Nekisha led me to Butch Nichols, who introduced me to her aunt, Delores Ross Smith, who sent me to see Ruth O'Neal. The list goes on and on. The book benefited from the help of so many who responded to my Internet postings or recommended useful websites, including Ed Adams and Tewroh-Wehtoe Sungbeh, the latter of whom told me about the meeting of the Sinoe County Association of the Americas, where I met Evans Yancy and several other members who suggested people to talk with, including Janice Sherman and Jameille Nelson Ross, who then referred me to Nathan Ross Sr. At the U.S. State Department's Liberia Desk, John Olson put me in touch with people at the embassy in Monrovia and kept me abreast of breaking news as I prepared for my trip, while Associated Press correspondent Alex Zavis offered much-needed advice on travel there.

I am grateful to those who encouraged me and/or fretted over me while I was gone: my parents, A. D. and Inez Huffman, and the rest of my family, Judy and John Seymour, Pam and Buzz Shoemaker, Michelle and Devin Basham, and Erin and Bryan Anderson, as well as my friends the Hardings (and Lee, especially, for saving my eyesight by helping to transcribe nineteenth-century documents), the Hartfields, Andy and Jimmye Sweat, Josh Zimmer, Paul de Pasquale, Scottie Harmon, Neil and Catherine Payne, Robbyn Footlick and Robert Drury, Michael Rejebian and Cyrille Robic, who put me up in London and baby-sat me in the days before I left for Liberia.

I am indebted to countless Liberians, including those who not only ensured that my trip was safe but that it was productive and otherwise rewarding: the Raileys, my fixer in Monrovia (who, alas, must remain unnamed), the Joneses, Peter Toe, Charlie Kollie (to whom I was referred by Thomas Banks, owner of West African Safaris, who also helped with the logistics of the trip), the staff of St. Teresa's convent (especially Sister Scholastica Swen and Brother Dennis Hever), Drs. Joseph Guannu and Sleweon Nepe at the University of Liberia, and the staffs of J. J. Ross High School and the American embassy (especially Sarah Morrison).

I am equally grateful to everyone who was willing to sit down and talk with me about their lives and family history: the Raileys, the Joneses, the people at J. J. Ross, Rev. Charleston Bailey, Youjay Innis, Alton Johnson, Laverne McPhate, Tinker Miller, Hobbs Freeman, Butch Nichols, Benjamin and Georgia Ross, Nathan Sr. and Alice Ross, Nathan Ross Jr., Susie

Ross, Turner Ross, Delores Ross, and Robert Wade. Those toward the end of that list are the reason I chose to identify people in the book by their given name, rather than their surname, because in a story that follows several families so closely for so many generations, it was just too confusing otherwise.

I am also grateful to John McCarter for his efforts to preserve Prospect Hill and for indulging my interest in the cemetery and grounds, to Paul V. Ott for helping me track down and interpret old legal documents (which makes him *solely* responsible if there are errors), and to Judy Long, who tried.

Finally, I am thankful to James Belton, a very important and generous man, in my book, for bringing it all together in the end.

INDEX

SIERRA
LEONE

Lofa

Gbeya

Grand
Cape
Mount

Meno

Lofa

Saint Paul

Bong

Lake Piso

Bomi

Margibi

Montserrado

MONROVIA ⭐● ●Gardnersville

Grand
Bassa

Paynesville ●

North Atlantic

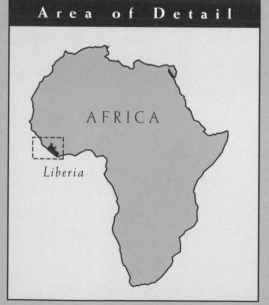

Area of Detail

AFRICA

Liberia